Jenny Colga[illegible]
After Edinbu[illegible]
years in the health service, moonlighting as a cartoonist and a stand-up comic. Film rights in her bestselling first novel, *Amanda's Wedding*, have been sold to Warner Bros. Jenny now lives in the City of London and is working on her third novel.

Talking to Addison

Amanda's Wedding

Jenny Colgan

HarperCollins*Publishers*

HarperCollins*Publishers*
77-85 Fulham Palace Road,
Hammersmith, London W6 8JB

This omnibus edition published in 2006 by HarperCollins*Publishers*

ISBN 000777771X

Typeset in Garamond 3 by Palimpsest Book Production Limited, Polmont, Stirlingshire

Printed and bound in Great Britain by Bookmarque Ltd, Croydon, Surrey

Talking to Addison

Acknowledgements

Thanks to: Ali 'the golden' Gunn, Rachel Hore and Fiona McIntosh: all, for everything. Nick Marston, Carol Jackson, Lorna McDonald, Jonathan Lloyd and all at Curtis Brown, and Nick Sayers, Anne O'Brien, Jennifer Parr, Yvette Cowles, Claire Round, David North, Martin Palmer, Adrian Bourne and all the reps at HarperCollins. Plus: Katie Stone for her unfailing support, Ben Moor for the science as well as being Ben Moor; Salty Sandra McKay, originator of McKay BMS; Susan Hoyer; Jason Foxwell-Moss for the chess and one or two other things; James Crawford for his kitchen; Shappi Khorsandi; Karen Murphy MRCS (!!! swot-tastic!), official medical adviser to TTA (although all inaccuracies and exaggerations are of course mine); Katrina McCormack, Lisa Jewell, and Robin and Dominic, my brilliant brothers.

This book is dedicated with love
to my truly fantastic and long-suffering
parents – Mum, sorry I didn't take
my accountancy exams,
Dad, sorry about all the swearing.

Part I

One

A famous arctic explorer once said that polar expeditions were the most successful form of having a bad time humans had ever devised. Of course, he'd probably never answered an ad for a flatshare with a bunch of complete strangers. Although if it hadn't been for them I would never have met Addison. Hmm. Which, when I think of it, is kind of like saying, OK, I lost all my fingers and toes to frostbite, but I met some very sweet penguins along the way . . .

Thirty-six hours after I moved in to 12a Wendle Close, Harlesden, I realized I'd made a terrible mistake. Tiptoeing around someone else's home is weird enough, particularly if it's just after a late night and you can't remember their name or where they keep the Sugar Puffs or, say, you're a cat burglar. Tiptoeing around your own is discomfiting to say the least. But here I was, creeping into my own house and closing my bedroom door extremely quietly, heart pounding, after only my very first quick jaunt to the shops, to try and make friends with my newsagent and see what flavours of Skips he had.

If I pressed my head against the thin wood veneer of the door I could just about hear my new best friends in the nearby ghastly open-plan Formica kitchenette.

'Well, I think we need a special *long-term* rota too. For cleaning the shower curtain and the drawers. And washing the skirting boards.'

'That's a great idea, Carol,' came another voice, deep with awe. 'Maybe we could do one big job every Saturday night and make an event of it. We could even get takeaway pizza!'

'And don't forget the nets!' screeched the unfortunately named Farah, who was about two foot tall and was always being mistaken for a monkey, or Martin Amis. 'I'll get my coloured pencils out and start drawing it up. This is going to be *such fun*!'

They all mewed.

'Didn't I just hear Holly coming in?' asked Laura, who was stolid and sat down a lot. 'That sounded like her bedroom door . . .'

Damn.

'No!' I attempted to telepathically send to them. 'It must have been the wind. That . . . mysterious bedroom wind.'

'. . . Why don't we go and ask her what she'd like to do?'

I inhaled sharply.

'Yes, let's!' yelled Farah. And there was a pounding at my door.

'Holly? Holly, are you there?'

Carol, official leader of Scary Clean Freaks Incorporated, put her head round the door assertively. Was it only a week ago I had checked out her ankle chain and pondered whether we'd ever get on? She looked at me sneerily. I sensed that she secretly knew of the scientifically proven inverse relationship between me and housework (the more messy things were, the less inclined I was to do anything about them), even though I'd attempted to be pristine for my first few days.

'We were just wondering . . .' she hissed.

Laura sniffed, noisily, behind her. Laura sniffed *all the time.* I always wanted to tell her that it was OK; no one was about to make her do double PE any more. Carol shot an evil sideways glance like a viper.

'Ahem. We were just *wondering*, given that we're – ha – divvying up the rota, if there was anything you particularly liked doing.'

I eyed her steadily, not about to be intimidated by someone who ringed their lips with dark lipstick pencil on their skin.

'How about I take lightbulb-dusting and big spider removal?'

'Ooh, that sounds good,' screeched Farah from somewhere beside my knee. Carol dispensed another one of those Robert de Niro-to-doomed-gangster stares.

'We thought you might prefer loos, sinks and floors,' she said pointedly.

'Oh . . .' I said. 'You mean, *all* of it.'

'Ha,' she smiled. 'Don't get around to much cooking, do we?'

I realized I'd been outmanoeuvred. Blast.

I counterattacked. 'What are you going to do?'

'I'm going to co-ordinate,' she said. Laura nodded happily.

'Oh, *tough* one.'

'. . . that means I buy all the cleaning materials, arrange the rota, organize the external cleaning contractors, e.g. the carpet shampooers I've got coming in, arrange everyone's telephone hours and oversee everyone's painting choices. So we've all got *quite* enough to be getting on with, don't you think?'

I wanted to try one last stance – perhaps suggesting that Farah take the floors, after all, she was closer – but all I could say was, '*Telephone* hours?'

'I know, I thought of it,' Carol said proudly.

'It's a *great* idea,' said Farah, standing between Carol's legs.

'Basically, it means you can only use the phone or get phone calls at your set time each night. Then, when we get the bill in, you pay for all the calls in your time, and nobody lies about the expensive numbers.'

I stared at her.

'Well, that's going to cut down on my sex-line income.'

Laura's eyes widened with shock. Carol laughed

politely, to show me that if I felt like fighting her, she was up to it.

'What's to stop me making phone calls on other people's time?'

'We're going to have a phone-lock that can only be opened by me. You come to me when you want to use the phone and I'll see if it's your hour or not. Really,' she said, shaking her head, 'your chores are *much* easier than mine, believe me.'

'Oh goodness me, I think I just heard my *mobile* go off,' I announced in a flurry.

'Excuse me,' I said, when they showed no sign of backing away from my door, 'I just have to, ehrm, excuse me . . .' Fortunately, the henchmen stuck next to Carol and backed away when she gave the signal, as my next move would have been to scream 'Fuck off! Fuck off! Fuck off!' whilst shoving them out of the door and pulling a hose on them.

I slammed the door behind them and sat on the bed. My mobile wasn't going off, naturally, but I took it out anyway and thanked this little machine. How could I ever have thought they were only of use to wankers on buses who thought that someone not on a bus might want to know when they were on a bus? Oh – and how the fuck was I going to get out of here?

Some people pick the wrong men all the time. I pick the wrong places to live. Well, OK, I pick the wrong men too, but anyway. So it was that after finally getting totally creeped out by my last landlord, in Hackney, who smelled of piss and used to turn up at random hours of the night to 'inspect' things (my knicker drawer included) – which followed the three girls in Dulwich who had all joined a beardy-weirdy religious cult and refused to allow men over the threshold, except for the cult leader, with whom they all slept whenever he wanted them to – I had ended up here, in a new house-share with three banana brains who all worked in the local hospital as phlebotomists. Apparently this meant they took blood samples from people. I assumed in Carol's case she simply bit them.

Anyway, they'd advertised in *Loot* for a fourth member to join a new household in tasty Harlesden, and, amazingly, I got it. Perhaps I was the only one who didn't blanch at the interview, when Laura came in and reported obediently to Carol that she had just bleached the teacups.

'And how often do *you* boil-wash the crockery?' Carol had asked me.

'Ehm . . . I find about every half-hour just about does it,' I'd gone for, and noticed her put a big tick on my application form, which had been broken down into sixteen handy sections. The relief of going from the dissipated seediness of Hackney – where they wanted extra rent if you got an inside loo – to a brand new 'executive' flat in the famous industrial waste area of North West London made it seem like a good deal at the time, but had blinded me to the obvious: i.e., all these people were mad, but because they outnumbered me in the house I was beginning to think that they were right.

I began to inspect my mobile for germs, and was getting really close up when it rang in my face.

I shrieked, did a comedy clown fumble, and dropped the phone under the bed.

'Are you all right?' said Carol's voice from just outside the door. She was obviously listening to everything. I shrieked again, swallowed some air, choked, coughed, and managed to wheeze, 'Fine, thank you.'

'It must be pretty dusty under your bed.'

'Yes, yes it is, thanks,' I said, sitting upright with the phone. Then I jumped – how the hell did she know where I was? I felt a cold hand of fear.

'Hello?' I finally choked into the phone.

'Do you know, I haven't made a woman scream like that for years,' drawled the well-modulated voice.

I relaxed slightly.

'Josh, you have never made a woman scream like that. In fact, have you ever made a woman?'

'Oh ho ho. Yes, of course.'

'In your country of origin?'

He paused.

'Not precisely.'

I'd been teasing Josh about this for as long as I'd known him, which was a l-o-o-ong time. Because he was attractive and also nice to girls, most people assumed he was gay. For someone with a posh background, a good job, and a nice haircut, he did horrendously badly with the opposite sex, which I couldn't understand – not that I'd ever wanted to shag him myself; he was so *nice*.

Anyway, thank God he'd rung me back. Worriedly searching the ceiling for CCTV, I sat back on the bed.

'Josh, you know when you moved into Pimlico and I said I didn't want to move there because it was snooty London and you were moving in with Kate who hates me?'

'Um, yes.'

'Well, you know, how's it . . . how's the whole flatshare *thing* going?'

'It's going fine.'

'Right – GREAT! Right. How's that other guy you got in to fill the space doing?'

'Addison? He's just great . . . Well, quiet, and undemanding.'

That didn't sound much like me.

'Uh huh. So, no one's moving out or anything, then?'

Josh sighed. 'Don't tell me. Not another Turkish Lesbian Women's Collective?'

That had been Hoxteth, two years ago. I'd been kicked out for not liking chickpeas and buying that symbol of male forced dominance, sanitary protection.

'No. Worse.'

'The cat lady?'

'Christ. No, not worse than her. But still, pretty bad.'

I heard Carol's voice:

'Holly! Would you like some tea? Because it's your turn to make it!'

I ignored her.

'Josh, this is absolutely desperate. Listen, you know that little boxroom you were going to turn into a study?'

'The one you described as a coffin?'

'Yup, yup, that's the one. Ehm, have you . . . ?'

'Turned it into a study? Not since you were last here. I've leased it out as a bedroom, though.'

'NOOO!'

He laughed.

'You bastard! Josh, I know this is a huge favour – and please say no if you don't want to – but please, please, please can I come and live in your coffin? I mean, boxroom?'

'You've asked me this before, Holl,' he said with a sigh.

'I know.'

'Then you always dash off and the next thing I hear from you you're on the run from a postgraduate mathematics badminton team.'

'I *know*. I'm crazy.'

'You are crazy. Why didn't you just move in when I bought the place?'

'Because you're rich and Kate makes me miserable.'

'I am not rich, and Kate can't help being . . . Kate. Anyway, if that's how you feel . . .'

'No, no! I'm sorry! Please. Please. Please.'

There was a loud knocking at my door.

'Tea, please, Holly! It's in the lease!'

'It's the Gestapo!' I whispered. 'How soon can you come and get me?'

'I'll have to check with Kate and Addison.'

'Josh!' I screeched, near to tears. '*Please.*'

'OK,' he relented. 'I'll pick you up at about seven. Have you got much stuff?'

'Just a coffinful.'

'And no diving off again, do you hear me?'

'Yes, sir,' I mumbled meekly.

I could have snogged Josh, I was so pleased to see him. I wanted to grab hold of his legs round the ankles and sob with gratitude and pour unguents over his feet. Or is that glue?

Carol had not taken the news well, particularly when I retrieved my deposit cheque from the shiny silver box to which only she had a key (I distracted her by upending her coupons box all over the kitchen floor then making a dive for the key when she bent over). In fact, she had advanced on me until her face was only a few inches from mine – well, her make-up was. Her face was probably about a foot away.

'Think you can just do what you like round here?' she asked menacingly.

'Yes, I do, actually. That's why I don't live with my parents any more.'

'So, who's going to take your room? You've got to sort that out.'

'Ah. Yes, well . . . I'm afraid you're going to have to sue me for my friends and acquaintances. Here, I've written down my forwarding address on this piece of paper –' I waved it reassuringly. It said: 1 Holly

Lane, Hollywood, 020 8555 5555 – 'and don't forget to send those bills on to me!'

'We won't,' said Carol grimly. Laura opened and shut her mouth like a fish.

'Well, I think it's disgraceful the way you're leaving Carol in the lurch like this,' she announced, quivering. 'All the trouble she's been to.'

'And me!' piped up Farah from somewhere around my ankles. 'I did the rotas!'

'I'm sorry,' I said. 'My best friend's got cancer. I'm nursing him till he dies.'

Laura backed away, crestfallen.

'I'm *so sorry*,' she muttered.

'Oh really?' said Carol. 'What kind?'

I couldn't think. 'Ehm, nose cancer?'

'You're sick,' she said, turning to march out of the room.

'So are you!' I yelled after her.

She turned once more, her brutally permed hair a weapon.

'Well, at least I'm *clean* and sick.'

Fortunately, Josh's sporty little spitfire had turned up, and he was honking enthusiastically. Josh did *everything* enthusiastically.

I tore out of the house.

'Where the hell am I going to *put* anything?' I wailed, after hugging him over-affectionately then examining his two-seater.

'I'm so sorry, darling. I meant to trade Bessie in

for a Volvo but, you know, I just couldn't find the time.'

'Ha ha ha. Listen, would you mind sitting on my duvet?'

He gave me a look.

'Well, it's not like real sex, is it?'

It took us an hour and a half to crawl back into town. Even though it was only April, Josh insisted on having the roof off, so I had to hang on to everything I owned, like an earthquake refugee.

'Freedom!' I yelled into the air. 'I am never going to move into a crappy flat again.'

'Except for the one you're about to move into.'

'Josh, it could be a shed at the bottom of the garden, I don't care! I'm FREEE!'

'OK, steady on,' said Josh, obviously worried I was about to start leaning dangerously far over the bonnet and singing 'My Heart Will Go On'.

There are two schools of thought concerning the children of parents who divorce nastily just as you're approaching puberty. One school says, Well, life is like that – chin up, and maybe the seething atmosphere at home will spur you into staying late at the library and moving on to better and brilliant things in an attempt to pull yourself out of the flotsam. Lots of famous people have divorced parents. They over-achieve for attention. That wasn't exactly my school.

The *other* school says you should instantly become

über-truculent and demanding, and put everything you do your entire life down to your bad upbringing. I tended to this school, it being rather easier and low maintenance, plus it tended to mean better Christmas presents, if dodgier exam results. It had worked reasonably well during my teens, but when your friends no longer *have* to see you every day in class and are too busy off doing horrid careers and stuff – well, so, now I was twenty-eight, and it was definitely becoming less fun by the day, especially when everyone I used to know had suddenly become fascinated by MORTGAGES, for fuck's sake. I just didn't get it. Boys and pop music – fascinating. Mortgages are what you get when you look up the dictionary definition of 'not fascinating'. Hence my precipitative flat-hopping.

To make matters even worse, I was starting to realize that my anti-establishment tendencies were beginning to marginalize me – not as a free spirit, as I'd always thought, but instead along with the old hippies and socialist workers and people who talked about smashing the state but couldn't actually get it together to wash their trousers – ever. It was extremely depressing. I mean, nobody likes washing their trousers, but I didn't want it to define my entire existence. To make matters worse, my father, who took up bringing home blonde women full time after he left my mum, had recently brought home one my age. Who also had a mortgage. And a sports car. Sigh.

Josh had a mortgage, but he was also a complete sweetie pie who could be endlessly relied upon in a crisis, as I knew and had shamefully abused in the past.

We finally pulled up in front of his dilapidated Victorian pile in Pimlico.

'I see you've still not got the builders in.'

'No, I couldn't afford them,' said Josh, hopping out of the car without opening the door and pulling up two bin-liners of my stuff. 'Until now,' he smiled sweetly in my direction.

'Ah yes, about that . . .' I followed him in, clutching my socks and pants bag, my cheese plant and Frank Sinatra the bear. One of the reasons that I'd wound up in Harlesden in the first place was that being a freelance florist and general under-achieving free spirit didn't exactly pay very much, and Pimlico was basically posh these days.

He told me, and I breathed a sigh of relief. The going rate for coffins wasn't so bad after all.

The flat was quiet inside. It was big and tatty and comfortable, and I'd always liked it. Josh had bought right at the top of the market and paid a stupid amount of money for it – apart from being infested with dry rot and woodworm and all sorts of other nasty moving things, it needed a new roof – but it was a good homey home. The kitchen was large, with nasty old units, a rickety table and four chairs in the middle, cracked floor tiles, and a huge window at the back which opened on to a rusty excuse for a fire escape. I pottered about in my tiny new room, mostly leaning against cupboards to get them to shut and stuffing things under the bed.

'Umm, sorry about the mess,' hummed Joshua when I went back into the kitchen for a cup of tea. 'It's not usually . . . Well, in fact, it is.'

'Great!' I said.

He smiled weakly at me. I leaned across the table.

'Josh, thank you. I'm sorry I forced you into this. I promise I'll be a good tenant. You'll see. I promise.'

He grinned back at me.

'Good. And I could do with the company, to be honest – Kate works all the time and Addison is, well . . .'

'Yikes!' I pounced immediately. 'Tell me the gossip about Kate.'

'Oh, she's a complete bitch, as ever,' said Kate, striding into the kitchen and dumping a Marks and Spencer's bag, an enormous briefcase, a Nicole Farhi raincoat and an expensive leather handbag on to one of the rickety chairs.

'Hello, Holly. Josh left me a message on my voicemail. Which I got about ten minutes ago. But never mind, eh? Welcome anyway.'

I went to give her a hug or something, but she was already en route to the bottle opener. Josh touched her lightly on the arm.

'How was your day, Skates?'

'Great. Great. As usual. Two sexist comments, four reports to do this week, one irregular forecasting, and I have to be in Dublin for 8 a.m. tomorrow morning, to give a presentation on a report I haven't even *read* yet. Then back in the office by noon to account for myself, two more meetings and a 4 p.m. deadline for the Kinley account. Oh, and then a client dinner with a bunch of ghastly old bores who'll try and feel me up in the Met bar.'

Josh nodded sagely. Kate pulled the cork with a savage 'pop' and poured out three humongous glasses of wine.

'So, Holly, what are you up to these days?'

Kate had always intimidated me. We'd only really met because the three of us were on the same corridor of student halls. We'd both stayed friends with Josh – most people did – but never really got on with each other. She was rather more of a pull-yourself-up-by-the-bootstraps-type person – she didn't actually say 'lickspittle', but you could tell when she was thinking it.

She'd done business studies and got some hugely well-paid and prestigious job in the City, which hadn't helped relations between us particularly. I always felt she was just about to offer to buy a *Big Issue* off me.

Actually, that wasn't quite why we didn't get on. Specifically, well, you know in Freshers' Week, one is often, er, tacitly encouraged to get . . . Well, anyway. Originally, there were the three of us in a row on one of those grotty endless corridors that are completely not the Brideshead University model I'd always hoped for, even in Coventry. Students were still sharing showers, a good life lesson for future flatshares in how much YEUCH people are actually made of, and how, just when you think you've seen everything, there's always a new variety of repulsiveness.

Josh had opened his door on the very first day and sat there crudely beaming at everyone who walked past, a technique which probably wouldn't have worked so well if he hadn't been so blond and pretty. I wandered in there by accident, already worried by how keen my dad and Blondie had been to leave me, but faintly reassured by the seemingly enormous cheque now burning a hole in my pocket. It worked out to a lot of Caramac bars, although, as I found out four weeks later, not that many beers and taxis.

'Hello,' said Josh. 'This place is nice, isn't it?'

'It's a shit hole!' I said, looking around at the regulation stained walls, stained carpet and dodgy pinboard.

'Oh yes . . .' He took in the room. 'So it is. Oh well – only three years to go.'

'And a week,' I said.

'Of course. Hmm. What do you think the cooking facilities are like?'

'I don't know – what's a cooking facility?'

Through the paper-thin walls we could hear loud, fairly dramatic sobbing. We raised our eyebrows at each other.

'What is this, primary school?' I said, a tad callously.

'Maybe she misses her mother,' said Josh.

I sniffed derisorily, something I'd been practising throughout my teens to great effect.

'Come on,' he said, 'let's go cheer her up.'

'Ah, the beginning of my crazy university years,' I said, but I followed him dutifully outside.

Next door, perched on the narrow bed, with the door open, sat Kate, thin and a little pinched-looking, and dressed head to toe in immaculately ironed Benetton separates. Even though she appeared distraught with grief, she still had been composed enough to hang up lots of perfect shirts, I noticed.

'Hello there,' said Josh. 'I'm sure it won't be as bad as all that. When I went to boarding school I cried for my mother for four days. Mind you, I was six years old at the time.'

'My *mother*?' said Kate, spluttering. 'I don't miss my *mother*! I just can't believe I didn't do better in my A-levels than to end up in this shitty place!'

'Didn't you work hard?' I asked her. That was my excuse.

'Of *course* I worked hard!' she said, looking up. 'I had a fucking place at Magdalene.'

'Oh, I see. They only want really tall girls, don't they?' I said sympathetically.

'What the fuck's nervous anxiety, anyway?' Kate went on, ignoring me. 'I'll tell you what it is: it isn't enough to get your exam marks upgraded. I wish I'd had a fucking full-on nervous breakdown. Then they'd have *had* to let me in.'

'Have one now,' I suggested. I knew she wasn't actually shouting at me, but she was certainly shouting in my direction.

'Don't worry,' said Josh kindly, touching her on the

shoulder. 'Would you like to come out with me? I'm going ice skating at the Christian Union.'

'You're not Christian are you?' I said, disappointed. I'd liked him.

'No! But I sure can SKAAAAAATE!'

So the three of us ended up in one of those forced friendships that come together extremely quickly out of necessity in early college. Kate quickly decided that Josh was her own personal property, which annoyed me. OK, so both of them had flat stomachs and good posture, but I didn't like the assumption that as Kate was prettier than me I should butt out, especially as I didn't even fancy Josh and in fact assumed pretty much from the start that he was gay, rather than, as I later found out, completely and utterly confused.

Kate hadn't cottoned on to this, however, and insisted on treating me as an annoying kid sister hanging round with the grown-ups, her repertoire including: 'You again, Holly?' 'You don't mind, do you, but I've only got two cups?' and 'Sorry, Holl, but it's only a plus-one.' Soon their status as monied and classy students at a poor and common college became clear, and I started going out with a greasy sports science student who once tried to teach me kung fu and chipped my collarbone, so I pretty much left them to it – which doesn't mean to say that she didn't really fuck me off, Kate being the accepted sucking pig to Josh's sow and my runt. An analogy bordering on the disgusting, but that's how it was.

In time, of course, Kate realized that simply because her and Josh went to a lot of places JUST THE

TWO OF THEM, it didn't actually mean they were a couple. But not before I got my revenge . . .

In a misguided attempt at collegiate unity, two socially inadequate but horrifically bouncy 'ents officers' – to be involved in 'ents' of course meaning you are anything but – arranged a 'Corridor Convulsion' early on in our first term. There was a good and complicated reason for it at the time, but what it meant in effect was an excuse to haul in lots of weepingly cheap alcohol and stuff it down the faces of naïve but nubile eighteen-year-olds in the hope that they might accidentally strip their tops off and run down the corridor. Actually, maybe that was the official reason and it just sounded all right in those days.

Josh of course would do anything of a community nature enthusiastically and Kate was still in the 'gamely joining in' stage, before she realized that she could dress up as a giant antelope and it still wasn't going to make her sexually attractive to Josh, so we all trawled into the hallway to figure out what was happening.

What was happening was what happens anywhere with horribly diverse sects of shy and socially inept people away from home for the first time and unsure of their very identities: groups of twos and threes stood in small corners grunting nervously at each other and downing obscure former communist bloc spirits as fast as they possibly could. A group of rugby- or aspirant rugby-playing lads started getting rowdy in the corner, and the ents officers gibbered around, excited yet again at the possibility of not being one of the 29 per cent of students who *leave* Coventry certified virgins. What they didn't yet know was that 100 per cent of ents officers leave 100 per cent of all institutions certified virgins.

A petite, very pretty blonde girl who wore enormous fleeces and was clearly out to score with a rugby boy – Why? being the only unanswered question – became the first person, at around 10.30 p.m. and after a lot of goading, to take off her top and flee down the corridor, bouncing merrily, to massive applause. After that, about fifteen of the men immediately tried to do it with their cocks out – what *is* it about British men and being completely naked for no good reason? I've seen someone play the piano with his.

Anthropologists would have had a field day with all this, given, truly, how few of us that year had yet seen another buck-naked human being they weren't blood related to.

Finally, and it all starts to get a bit hazy around this point, pretty much everyone had done a quick streak and been accepted into the gang. Mine would have been sexier had I not stumbled over somebody's outstretched foot and made a noise which sounded like a fart (but *wasn't*) on my way down. Josh skipped along his, to yells of 'faggot', but generally good-natured ones.

And at last there was only one more person to go. Kate would clearly rather have died than take part in anything so vulgar. She had that faraway look in her eyes she got whenever she dwelt on what romantic and glistening evenings she could be having at Oxford *right now.* I started egging her on, and pointing out to people that she was the only one who hadn't done it, just in case she got away with it.

'Shut *up*, Holl,' Kate hissed.

'Kate hasn't gone! Kate hasn't gone!' I shouted loudly to the rugby players.

'KATE! KATE! KATE! KATE!' they started chanting.

Kate flushed redder than ever.

'Everyone else has,' I said petulantly.

'Go on, Skatie,' said Josh, who, due to his upbringing, was completely unable to understand why someone wouldn't want to take part in group-enforced humiliation in the name of fun. The rugby boys name-calling had failed to abate and formed an increasingly ferocious background.

'Oh, for fuck's sake!' said Kate, furious.

'KATE! KATE! KATE!'

Kate pulled up her top extremely quickly and made a sprint down the corridor. Immediately, silence fell. Quite simply, Kate had the flattest chest anyone had ever seen.

Of course, nowadays, that doesn't matter. Kate Moss resembles a boy who's been stung by two bees and nobody bats an eyelid. But when you're nineteen and desperate to find yourself attractive . . .

To cut a long story short, that was never a moment when anybody needed me to inadvertently expostulate:

'Christ, they look like two Pop-Tarts!' loudly enough for everyone to hear.

Kate handed me one of the glasses of wine.

'Sorry, I didn't hear that . . . what did you say you were up to again?'

'Ehm, I'm . . . I'm a florist.'

'Still! My goodness. Is it . . . fulfilling?'

'Huh?'

Fulfilling? I couldn't even conceive of what that might mean, and was standing with a confused expression on my face until I remembered that when Kate asked a question, she required a logical answer *quickly* – time being money, etc.

'Yes, it is,' I said. 'The pay is shit and the hours are crap and your hands are wet all day, but apart from that it's fantastic.'

She smiled thinly. 'Never mind, eh? You'd probably hate a career job anyway.'

'This *is* a . . .'

'Where do you work?'

'Actually, I'm freelance at the moment . . .'

Well, I couldn't commute to Hackney Flowerarama any more, but I did have a chum at New Covent Garden who was going to let me help out.

'Oh, so you're like a *temp* florist? How funny!'

I didn't know what to say to that, so I went and helped Josh, who was chopping onions for spaghetti bolognese. I could see Kate reflected in the kitchen window. She did look fantastic – tired, but fantastic.

Her dark hair was glossy and tied back in a chignon, and she was wearing an expensive fawn suit. I wiped my hands on my pinafore and sighed.

'Tell me about your mystery flatmate. Is he away?' I asked Josh.

Josh and Kate looked at each other and smiled.

'Away?' echoed Kate. 'Addison doesn't *do* away.'

'What – you mean, he's in the house?'

I felt nervous suddenly. I'd been stomping about merrily for two hours, singing and making loud noises in the toilet, and all along there had been an additional presence. Spooky.

'Oh yes,' said Josh. 'I'll probably leave some food out for him later on. He forgets to eat until he faints, so I put it by his door.'

Curioser and curioser.

'Can I meet him?'

They exchanged glances again.

'Ehm, best not.'

'Well, I'll have to meet him sometime,' I argued. 'What if he just pops up in the bathroom one day? I'll scream the place down.'

'You might do that anyway,' said Kate.

'Addison is very . . . well, sensitive. He's a computer buff, you see.'

Only Josh still used words like 'buff'.

'You mean, what – an anorak? A geek? Dork? Nerd?'

'Ahem.'

Josh gave a polite cough as a shadow flitted across the open kitchen door.

'Is that him?' I hissed. 'I'm going to see.'

Kate stepped in front of me and shut the door.

'What *is* going on?' I asked. 'Is he hideously deformed, like the Elephant Man?'

Josh patted me on the shoulder.

'Sorry, Holls. We're not doing this on purpose. Addison does a lot of highly technical, top-level computer work, and he hates being disturbed when he's working.'

'But he's in the flat.'

'He works from home.'

'And for about twenty-three hours a day,' muttered Kate. 'It's really easy to forget a hard day's work when you've got beeps and tapping going on all night next door to you.'

'Better than some things . . .' I started to say, then remembered that Josh's bedroom was next door to mine, and didn't.

'So, I mean, what's he *like?*' I started again. A man of mystery? Sounded good to me.

'Oh, you tell her, Josh. I'm absolutely exhausted,' said Kate. She took out her Psion and started stabbing at it, making me feel like a complete idiot. Then Josh and I shared our 'it's Kate' glance, and I felt a bit better.

'Well . . .' started Josh, stirring the sauce. I went and leaned on the cabinet next to him.

'He's quiet. Very quiet. In fact, I think he'd rather not speak at all. He was amazed when we didn't have e-mail in every room in the house so we could just communicate that way.'

I raised my eyebrows. At the table, Kate let out

a long 'How can I be so busy and successful when there are people in my kitchen making spaghetti bolognese?' type sigh.

'Whenever he bumps into one of us in the hallway he acts like a startled rabbit, like he genuinely wasn't expecting anyone to be there. And he refuses to answer the phone or the doorbell. And he never eats.'

'Hence the food drops.'

'Hmm? Yes.' Josh artfully splashed a measure of red wine into the sauce, crying out 'Whoops!' flamboyantly when he got a bit on his professional apron. I really could understand why women had a hard time taking him seriously.

He caught me watching him.

'Am I being gay again?'

I smiled at him, colouring slightly. When we were at college, I used to tease him on a semi-continual basis when he'd bring his girl stories to me, but now I was his tenant, and it felt a bit uncomfortable.

'That was a very masculine dash of wine. But I am definitely fascinated by my new invisible flatmate.'

'Try taking the room next to his – it'll wear off soon enough,' growled Kate from the table, where she continued to do Very Hard Sums.

'Oh, can I?!' I yelped, before realizing the faux pas.

'Sorry, darling,' said Josh, 'but you're not – aha! – *coffin* up enough rent for that!'

Kate and I stared at him in disgust until he apologized.

* * *

Dinner was good. Josh liked to cook, and was good at it. He had a sinecure at his family's ancient law firm near Chancery Lane, which required him to turn up at about ten thirty looking well groomed, take long lunches and impress foreign clients with his Englishness and hand-made shoes, before retiring to the senior partners' offices at four thirty to partake of an early gin and tonic before heading home. Which was just as well, as he wasn't the most academic of characters: you wouldn't want him defending you in a murder trial whilst simultaneously admiring the court cornicing. The only thing preventing the absolute outbreak of class war was that he didn't get paid *that* much for it. It just stunned me that such things still existed outside of the kind of stuff Rupert Graves does in all his films.

Kate ate about three bites, wiped her lips ostentatiously with a napkin then declared she had mounds to do and retreated to her room with the remainder of the wine. Her good night to me was curt, to say the least.

I looked at Josh.

'*What* is with her?' I asked. I mean, she'd always been uptight, but this was real carrot-up-the-bum stuff.

Josh toyed with his spaghetti.

'Oh, it's that stupid job of hers,' he said. 'She works fourteen-hour days, then comes home like a bear.'

'What, pooing in the woods?'

'Grizzly.'

'Oh. Good spag bol.'

'Thank you.' Josh coloured prettily. 'So, anyway, I keep saying she should change it, do something less stressful, but she just bares her teeth at me and hisses something about me being privileged and how I would never understand what it means to fight for something.'

'Her dad's a GP, isn't he?'

'Uh huh.'

'Hmm. But she must make an absolute fortune. Why does she live here?'

Josh looked faintly amused.

'Charmingly direct as ever, darling.'

'Oh, you *know* what I mean.'

'I know. I'm not sure, really. She does make a stinking amount of money, though. Something like more in her bonus than I do in a year.'

Than I will in a decade, I thought to myself mournfully.

'We moved in together when I came down,' Josh went on, 'and she's been here ever since, so I suppose she likes it. It's only four stops on the tube, and pretty cheap.'

I remembered a rather better reason though. Well well well, after all this time. But then, even if she didn't still fancy him, I suppose if I was feeling stressed out, I wouldn't mind coming back to a nice warm flat and spaghetti bolognese and someone nice like Josh you could be rude to. Well, she certainly wouldn't get away with being rude to me.

* * *

'Would you *mind* getting out of that shower!' screeched Kate, banging her Clarins bottles on the door at five o'clock one morning (I was doing nights at the market). She carried them daily in and out of the bathroom, presumably in case I stole them.

'I don't know what can be keeping you in there *that* long. You can only smell of flowers, surely.'

She banged again.

'OK, *OK*, I'm *coming*,' I yelled back, frantically drying myself and wondering if I could stab her with a cotton bud.

'I have got a plane to catch, Holly,' she said. Because I have a career and you don't, she might as well have added.

'Oh no! The Euro will fall!' I opened the bathroom door dishevelled, wrapped in two threadbare towels which almost but didn't quite cover all my bits.

'Will it?' she said, instantly alert, then relaxed as her brain realized the context. She gave a tight smile, said, 'Excuse me,' and slipped past me, unbelting her Liberty robe.

Bitch, I thought to myself – one of my litany of dreaded 'thought retorts' – and headed for bed.

Over the next week or so I started to settle in. I was working part-time shifts at the New Covent Garden market, day and night, and as Kate went to work at 6.30 a.m. and returned at 9 p.m., I normally missed her, and steered well clear of the shower in the morning.

The house, though always untidy, was clean – for me, a perfect state of affairs. Kate paid someone to come in and 'do' once a week, which I disagreed with in principle but thoroughly enjoyed the benefits of. It began to feel like home, despite the coffin, which was nine foot by seven. Not the kind of place you'd let a cat visit, in case its brains got bashed to bits in a nasty swinging incident.

I was used to creeping in at odd times of night, and was always amazed to hear the faint tapping of fingers on a keyboard, random beeps and small buzzing noises from Addison's room.

I never saw him, but fantasized wildly about him. A monster? Kate and Josh's deformed lovechild, half man half robocop? Perhaps he was blind! That was why he crept around in the dark and didn't go outside. I had a brief romantic reverie of my being his life partner, caring for him, being his lover and his guide; 'Holly,' he would say, 'you, *you* are my eyes.' And, plus it would be a double bonus when I got to forty and wouldn't have to bother about how I looked.

Then, ping, I realized that the Internet is in fact an almost purely visual medium, and apologized in my head to all the blind people in the world.

Finally, after about a fortnight, I cracked.

It was about 3 a.m., and the house was completely still. I'd been unpacking tulips from 11 p.m., but the work had thinned out and Johnny, my gaffer, had sent me home. It took about ten minutes on Josh's bicycle – in the very dead of night I would glide down hills, hands free, and have to restrain myself from shouting out loud to fill up the rare London silence.

I had crept into the house, exhilarated and pink-cheeked from the spring wind. My hair was tangled, and I didn't feel sleepy. My hours were so topsy-turvy, I didn't know when I slept. The television, however, was in the sitting room, which backed on to Kate's room – so, no Channel 5 soft porn for me. I was about to head through to the chilly kitchen to make some tea when I saw the omnipresent blue glow underneath the door, the familiar tap tap tap.

Well, sod it, I thought to myself. Two weeks living in the same house as someone and not seeing them is simply freaky and unnatural. There could be nothing wrong with just popping in and introducing myself, for fuck's sake. It was only . . . well, ten past three in the morning. I felt strangely excited, like playing ring-the-bell-and-run-away. If I got yelled at, I could always hide and say it was Kate.

I crept across the hall, instead of walking across it like I normally did when I came in late at night so everyone would know it was me and not a burglar; steeled myself and rapped gently on the door.

The typing noise stopped. Encouraged, I tapped again. 'Hello?'

There was no response.

Feeling like an idiot, I repeated, 'Hello?' leaning slightly on the door.

Clearly it wasn't locked.

Half horrified at what I was doing, I pushed open the door.

The large room was dark, but light streamed in from the moon and the streetlights. The place was also lit up with an unearthly green glow, which I realized, once my eyes adjusted, came from a huge VDU. The room was so filled with banks of electronic equipment it was like the flight deck of the Starship *Enterprise*. LEDs lit up and monitors bleeped quietly.

Sitting with his back to me was a very tall man, who resembled a normal man who'd been put on a rack and stretched out. His black spiky hair stuck up straight from his head, and I couldn't see his face.

He didn't turn round, although he must have heard me, because his back stiffened.

'Hello?' I whispered. 'Sorry to disturb you, but I saw you were still working and, well, I moved in here a couple of weeks ago and my name's Holly and I thought that, you know, since we lived together, we should perhaps lay eyes on one another.'

I swallowed. My voice seemed to echo in the empty room, and I felt like a complete dork. Then, when he didn't reply, I started to get annoyed. It wasn't like I was demanding anything unreasonable. This was only basic human contact, for fuck's sake! The way Kate and Josh tiptoed around him was ridiculous. He needed shaking up, if you asked me. He still hadn't even bothered turning round! That was bloody rude.

'Oh, I'm sorry,' I said. 'I didn't realize you were so rude. I won't bother you again. *Excuse* me.'

I turned to go. Slowly, I heard the revolving chair creep round behind me. I looked back.

A huge pair of dark brown eyes, blinking rapidly, regarded me with a mixture of curiosity and fear. I almost gasped aloud. He was . . . well, just spectacularly beautiful. Just, like, *Oh my GAWD*! Not in a pretty, boyband poofy kind of way, but that chiselled, sensitive look that cries out, 'I may have been staring at this computer screen for fifteen hours, but as my physiognomy suggests, I have the soul of a poet. And not one of those ones with hair in their noses that you see in the Sunday supplements.' Even from behind his glasses you could see that his eyelashes cast long shadows on his ludicrously high cheekbones and a frown seemed to pass over his exquisitely high forehead.

I managed to quell my first urge, which was to lie at his feet and present my stomach to him to be tickled, when I noticed he was wearing a *Star Trek* T-shirt. How original of someone who played with computers all day long to like *Star Trek*, I thought.

'Excuse me,' he said. His voice was quiet and soft, with no discernible accent – not like mine. I got very London, selling flowers every day.

He looked at his hands. His fingers were incredibly long – practically prehensile. I actually sighed.

'I was a bit caught up in what I was doing.'

He sounded apologetic, and I was in one of those brain-twisting moods whereby if you meet someone who is clearly your soul mate you feel an overwhelming urge to be rude to them.

'So you don't listen to people when they come to say "hello"? What were you doing?'

He stared at his hands again and didn't say anything. I thought for a bit.

'OK, shall we start again?' I announced. 'I'm Holly, and you're Mr Addison, I presume.'

'Not mister, just Addison,' he said quietly.

'Ooh, what a great name!' I said, reaching out to shake his hand. He didn't take mine, and regarded it with some alarm. 'Addison Madison?'

What? What magic potion had I just taken to turn me into the Moron of the Western World? I cringed.

He blinked. His eyelashes practically bounced off his sweetly pouted lips. 'Ehm, no . . . Addison Farthing.'

'*Farthing*, *Farthing* – *right*, of course, how *silly* of me,' I gushed, like I was interviewing him on a breakfast show. 'Of *course*.'

I was backing away and backing down big time.

'So, anyway, I thought, you know, time to say hello, pop in, have a chat . . .'

Addison continued to regard me impassively.

'So, here we are, having a chat . . . and it's been *lovely* chatting to you. Really. We must do it again some time.'

He continued staring at me as I backed out of the room.

'Great! Nice to meet you! Nice Starship *Enterprise*, by the way!' I said as I got to the door, but he was already turning back to his enormous screen and had clearly forgotten my very existence. Huge cables twisted round the table legs, heading off God knows where. The tapping started up again and I closed the door gently. Outside in the hall I leaned on the wall and let my jaw drop in wonder. Oh my God. No wonder Kate liked him locked away.

'*I* spoke to Addison last night,' I announced to Josh the next day. He was eating dinner and I was eating breakfast and trying to avoid his dinner – the smell of pork chops half an hour after I'd woken up made me feel a bit sick, I had discovered.

Josh looked up at me from an article he was reading in *Homes & Gardens*. I'd suggested *Loaded* as a slightly more useful manual for pulling, but it didn't quite suit him, somehow.

'And?'

'And?? *AND*?? Excuse me, but as landlord of this establishment, I do believe it is your duty to let me know when you're hoarding Johnny Depp in geek form on your property!'

'You never asked.'

'*Why* did I never think to ask?' I asked, slapping myself on the forehead. 'So many gorgeous computer geeks in the world, so little time. *Josh*! If it hadn't been for my extreme bravery last night I might never have met my future life partner! Ooh –' a thought occurred to me – 'and our kids get to be brainy, too!'

'He is very pretty, I suppose,' said Josh, a tad dreamily. I narrowed my eyes at him.

'Only in an objectively aesthetic way! Not in a romantic way! Not that there would be anything wrong with that! But I don't! Not that it's bad!'

'Stop, stop! You've got caught in the Richard Gere "I'm not gay/but it's OK" cycle of eternal justification. The only way to break free is to remove that plate of pork chops from my vicinity before I vomit on it.'

'Thank goodness for your magic spell-breaking powers,' said Josh, picking up his plate and moving over to the sink.

'You know, I must have him,' I went on. 'He will be mine.'

'But he doesn't *talk*.'

'That's OK. I can talk to you, or my mother. Addison is for *kissing* and *worshipping*.'

'So, like, there's no difference between me and your mother?' asked Josh gloomily, rinsing his plate off.

'Well, you haven't ordered me to help with the washing-up yet, so, perhaps there is.'

'Don't you have work to go to?' he asked, a tad crossly.

'Ah, *that's* more like it.'

'Fine. See you later. I'll just continue here on my lifelong mission of female identification.'

I popped my head back round the door.

'You know, if you meant that sarcastically, you should really take that pinny off.'

He gave me the V's.

'Bye, Addison!' I called out cheerily as I passed his door. There was a small break in tapping in response. I took it as a good sign.

Two

It was getting dark when I hopped on the bike and headed up to the market. Going out in the chilly nights was the worst; I knew I had several hours of rushing about with my hands wet to come, and all around me the nine-to-fivers were heading for home, fresh pasta and *The Bill*. And they all made twice as much as me. It didn't seem fair. Working in the market wasn't anything like working in a shop. Then, you got to choose things yourself and put them together, and if someone had been rude to you on the phone you could put a bug in their gladioli. Here, I had to check ten thousand tulips and try to work out which ones were the best.

I worked for Johnny, who was wizened and had

been on the flower markets for four hundred and seventy years, as he never stopped reminding me.

'Aye, you never saw colours like that in my day,' he'd snort derisively at one of the more over-the-top hybrids.

'That's because everything was in black and white, then,' I'd point out to him. 'It was the olden days.'

'People used to eat flowers during the war, you know.' He was quite one for reminiscing. In fact, he was absolutely, bar none, the best person I'd ever met at making up things about the war.

'Hey, Johnny,' I waved to him as I whizzed round the corner. The lorries hadn't started to unload yet, so people were standing around, smoking roll-ups and gossiping about magnolias. The flower people despised the fruit people in the next set of bays, and they in turn thought the flower people were a bunch of big pansies who couldn't lift a box of melons if their lives depended on it.

'Hey there, lass.' He regarded me critically. 'You know, when I was your age, I was selling out the back of my own van.'

'Johnny, you have no idea how old I am. In fact, I'm nine years old. And I have my own van. I do this for fun.'

'I never met a lassie who knew when to shut up,' he observed mournfully, and threw me over a pair of heavy gloves.

I'd only been there a couple of weeks, and already I hated it. It was exactly like school. The girls all wore inappropriate clothing, smoked behind the sheds and picked on me. Either that or they were so stupid they had to be reminded every day how to pick up a box of flowers without drooling on it.

So I tended to slog away on my own, pausing only to hurl abuse at Johnny or to point out things to the drooling girls along the lines of 'Box – there! . . . You see box? Pick up box?'

The smoking girls teased me because I'd been to college, particularly Tash, their queen, this scrawny girl with thick black eyeliner who had a real mother-smoked-in-pregnancy look about her. Tonight she sidled up alongside me, observed my work closely for several minutes, and then said:

'Hmm, yes, I see now why that needed a degree – getting all those tulip heads in a line can't be easy.'

The rough boys all guffawed and I tried to laugh but couldn't. I hated her, and I hated being bullied, and however rude I could be to Johnny it wouldn't translate to this lot. They were rough as badgers' arses.

'Could you pass the sign-in sheet?' I hated it but sometimes I just had to talk to her.

'Sorry, love, I've only got a GCSE in general studies.'

All the boys laughed again, and one of them shouted, 'Oi, watch out, Tash, she'll trip on the chip falling off your shoulder.'

I grimaced and pretended to join in, boiling inside, but really I felt like when I was taken by some older girls to see *The Rocky Horror Picture Show* when I was eleven – it was all too trashy and I just didn't get it, but I was laughing along anyway. They were mean, mean kids. Because I didn't blow cigarette smoke out of my nose they called me TinBits.

'Please,' begged one of the lads, bending on one knee before me, 'your exquisite virginal majesty, might I just for one second peek up your skirt?'

'She's got her knickers welded to her bottom,' yelled Tash.

I very nearly flashed my tits at him just to piss him off, but instead made a hasty vow to myself to apply for every florist's job in a five thousand-mile radius.

For the rest of the night, Tash contrived to make fourteen derogatory remarks, upset my flowers four times and spend at least an hour talking about me (I suspected) on prolonged fag breaks with the lads. I was being bullied! I couldn't believe it! This wasn't fair.

My shift finished at 4 a.m. and I freewheeled home as usual, down the hill back to the big house. I crept in and saw the light on under Addison's door. The urge to see him again was overwhelmingly strong so I wandered into the kitchen and made two cups of tea. I didn't know how he liked it, so I put three sugars in for luck as I'd never seen him eat – he probably needed the nutrition. Then I ferreted around for a couple of biscuits to add to it, but the only thing going was a very lonely Penguin – Kate allowed herself one every fortnight. I took it anyway, planning to replace it, pronto.

I knocked on the door softly.

'Addison, it's me.'

The soft clicking noises stopped for a second. I could imagine him desperately trying to wrack his brains for a single person he could be expected to identify from a 'me'.

I pushed the door again and popped in.

'I made tea!' I announced, like a fifties housewife.

His short-sighted – oh, but beautiful – eyes swivelled round to focus on me. His glasses were sitting on top of the mother-ship console.

'Tea!' I indicated by holding the cups up and motioning like a lunatic.

He focused on the cup and followed its path as I went to place it beside him whilst I wondered if he was mentally subnormal.

'Not there!' he barked.

'OK, OK, put the gun down. How about I hand it to you?'

Slowly he extended his arm. I placed the cup in his hand, handle facing outwards – which meant burning a hole in my hand, but I didn't mind because when he took it, the tips of our fingers touched, and I swear I felt a bolt of electricity shoot through me.

I waggled the Penguin at him.

'Penguin?'

He stared at it for a bit then shook his head, so I ate it. After all, as he'd taken the tea, that implied a contract that allowed me to stay for a little bit.

I leaned over. His computer screen was covered in bizarre symbols, just like in James Bond films.

'What are you working on?'

He tried to cover up the screen, but as his arms were

like matchsticks, it didn't have much effect. However, as the symbols meant as much to me as EC policy directives, it was a pointless exercise anyway.

'Ehm, nothing. Thanks for the tea . . .'

He sipped it, then tried to disguise his gagging reflex.

'That's all right. How was your day? Mine was shitty.'

And so I told him all about the nasty boys at the flower yard. Mainly for conversation really, because I knew the second I stopped talking there would be complete silence.

Much to my surprise he appeared to be listening – well, not doing anything else, which had to pass for it.

When I'd finished, I took another sip at my tea and said:

'So, what do you think I should do?'

He looked at me for a second, then cracked an absolutely heartbreaking smile.

'Not talk to anyone?'

A sentence! Almost. I grinned back at him, then decided to leave on a high note. I nodded with my mouth closed, mouthed 'good night' to him, and retreated, leaving him sniffing suspiciously at his tea.

'Success!' I crowed to Josh the following evening. 'He *talked* to me.'

'What did he say?'

'Well, he told me not to talk to anyone. But apart

from that I consider it an outright success.'

'Oh, speaking of outright success, did you steal Kate's Penguin?'

Shit; I'd forgotten all about it.

'Mmmm . . . maybe.' I surreptitiously checked round the outside of my mouth in case there was any chocolate left there from last night.

'You're in trouble.'

'OK, OK, I'll just go out and get her one.'

'It's too late. Plus, she knows it's a blue one. I'd make myself scarce, if I were you.'

Unfortunately I wasn't working that night and, annoyingly, felt that cold thing you get in the pit of your stomach when you know you're going to get into trouble later.

'Argh! I am not in trouble! I am going to go out now and buy her fifteen Penguin biscuits and . . . and make her eat herself to death like in *Seven*. I am NOT going to let her intimidate me like this. She is so damn ANAL about everything.'

'Which is why she's one of the best corporate raiders under thirty in London –'

'*Just* under thirty.'

'I know what she's like. Be nice to her. She has it hard enough at work. Everyone is really mean to her.'

'Ooh, gossip? 'Fess up.'

Josh was an indefatigable gossip, although he wouldn't thank you for pointing out this particular trait.

'Well, she just has an overwhelming inability to spot married guys. I mean, they can have a bloody suntan ring round their fourth finger and Kate believes them when they say it's impetigo. And she's seeing this guy now who only phones her in two-minute bursts from call boxes at eleven thirty at night, and they do a lot of their dating in their lunch hours . . . Any day now she's going to find out he's another louse. Deep down, I think she realizes they are and it's all a big psychological mishmash.'

'Wow,' I said, nodding thoughtfully. 'That whole big psychological mishmash thing.'

And we each thought about our own for a second or two.

'So,' I resumed, 'she's grouchy all the time and it's not my fault.'

'I don't think she's that happy at having another woman around the flat.'

'I'm not exactly a threat,' I said, looking down at where the button should have been on my pyjamas. Fortunately, I'd known Josh a long time.

'It's not that. It's a territorial thing.'

I grunted. 'What, like dogs have? I thought there was a funny smell in my room. Maybe she's pissed in it.'

'Ssh,' said Josh, as we heard the door open.

'Shit! I've forgotten to go out and get the Penguins!'

He winced at me as Kate did her normal arrival routine: an enormous sigh, an elaborate dumping of her expensive accoutrements, and a full-body lunge for the bottle opener.

Josh winked at me, and I smiled manfully.

'Hey, Kate, how's it going?'

'Shit! Holly, did you eat my Penguin?'

I cringed, which *wasn't* what was supposed to happen. I was supposed to say something along the lines of, 'Yeah – do ya wanna make somethin' of it?' and spit on the floor. Instead of which I said, 'Yes. Look, Kate, I'm really sorry, I'll buy you some more.'

'No, it's fine,' she sniffed, LYING. 'I've only been out working for twelve hours, slaving over a huge offshore investment, which is almost entirely my responsibility, something unheard of for someone under thirty . . .'

'Just . . .' I said, under my breath.

'. . . why on earth should I want or deserve a little bit of relaxation, which I've already bought and paid for, when I come home exhausted? I'm silly, really. I should just give it up and mess about with flowers and eat other people's Penguins all day long.'

She picked up the wine bottle and retreated from the room, continuing, 'Really, I must just be *so, so selfish*.'

Once she'd gone I beckoned to Josh.

'Hand me that bread knife.'

'Now, you remember what I said . . .'

'I heard what you said, and now I am going to kill her with a knife. GIVE it to me.'

'No.'

'I'm sorry. I don't think you understand the situation: I am going to have to kill Kate with a knife, and I'm asking you to pass it to me.'

'Sit down,' he said, handing me a plate of couscous.

'Ignore it. What else was Addison saying?'

'Nothing.'

'Don't sulk.'

'No, I mean it. Actually, nothing. Has he ever spoken to you?'

'Not really. He just turned up when we put the ad in, and he'd brought so much computer equipment we didn't have the heart to send him away again. Plus, Kate thought he was cute.'

'He's better than cute. Oh, did she try and pull him and fail?' I asked eagerly.

'No, she tried talking to him for ten minutes then ran out of attention span. Plus, also, he didn't show any of the normal signs of bastardy.'

'Ah, ooh, she is just SUCH a cow!' I exclaimed again.

'She's fine. Now, go out and buy the biscuits.'

'What! After all that – you must be joking.'

'Unless you want "all that" every night for the rest of your life, I would go and buy the biscuits.'

'Fine, fine, fine. I will go and buy the biscuits. Then, I will *pee* on the biscuits.'

I ended up heading to the gigantic supermarket which is open all night, all the time. I think they keep the staff caged there, like animals. They all have rickets from being out of natural light for so long.

I hate supermarkets. I can stand for hours in the shampoo section, stymied. Should I be putting fruit in my hair? What will happen if I don't? What *is* shampoo, anyway? Are there any more foods just out there waiting to be discovered? Etc, etc. As usual, it took me three hours to collect a more or less random selection of products, plus fourteen packets of Penguins. I'd wanted Josh to come with me or, ideally, volunteer to do it himself, but he'd started to get a bit shifty and got out work files to do stern lawyer stuff with – like, as if.

Finally I wandered home, feeling a bit mournful and stopping to put my bags down every five minutes.

When I walked in, the house was very quiet. Josh was locked away in his room – I hoped it was with his Playstation – and Addison had disappeared. I had never even seen him go to the toilet. I liked that. He was too unearthly for bodily functions. Men, or at least the ones I've always known, think that it's endearing to you if they fart a lot. Addison wouldn't be like that. And then, they'd smell of angel dew.

Feeling mildly nauseated, I backed my way into the kitchen with my sixteen bags, swung them round to dump them on the table and accidentally clobbered Kate on the side of the head. With the one with the tin cans in.

'Ow!' she growled at me.

'I'm sorry,' I cringed, though I wasn't really. But I didn't want her to think I'd done it on purpose.

'I didn't do it on purpose!'

'Oh, forget it,' she said.

I did a mental double take. That didn't sound like Kate. Surely she should be demanding my first-born child and threatening to take me to court.

'Really, I am sorry,' I said again, putting the rest of the bags down. I saw her properly for the first time. Her eyes were all red, and she was doing the giveaway, back-of-the-mouth sniff. As a world-class crier myself, I knew what had been going on.

'Are you OK?' I asked, as sincerely as I could, which of course meant it came out sounding like I was a confessional TV host.

'I'm fine, really.' She sniffed properly, and patted down her immaculately glossy hair. Now, there was someone who knew a bit about shampoo.

I started to unpack the shopping.

'What's the matter?' I asked, casually, as if I was a trained counsellor and did this kind of thing all the time.

'Nothing . . . nothing. Oh GOD.' Her face completely collapsed into tears. 'I HATE him. I really, really, really, really HATE him! And he doesn't even CARE!'

I put down the tin of Heinz spaghetti (where had that come from? Had I let a four-year-old do the shopping?) and sat down beside her.

'There you go,' I said, patting her lightly on the arm and saying the things you're supposed to. 'Don't worry. Don't worry. Absolutely, he's a bastard.'

'You don't even know him!' she snivelled.

'OK, is he a bastard?'

'YEESSS!'

I patted her harder. 'OK. Tell me, what happened?'

Her sobbing slowed down a little bit.

'I was seeing this guy, and I really liked him and I thought . . . well, stupid bloody me, eh, how dare I think that I could ever go out with someone who wasn't MARRIED?'

'Oh no!' I thought of what Josh had said. 'I'm really sorry. Didn't he tell you?'

'He said he thought I knew. I asked him to come out for my birthday and he said he couldn't, he had to take Saffy to the dentist . . .'

'Who's Saffy?'

'That's what *I* said. Then he coughed and said, ehm, it was his dog.'

'A dog dentist.'

'Uh huh.'

'So you guessed from that?'

'Ehm, no. I believed him.'

'Ooh, nasty.'

She hiccuped. 'Then I went in to give him a surprise birthday present a day early . . .'

'But it's *your* birthday.'

She ignored me and sniffed even harder. 'And he'd left his wallet open on the desk . . . and I saw a picture of Saffy.'

'Not a dog?'

'A five-year-old girl!'

'Well, kind of a bit like a dog then . . .'

'No!'

'He could be divorced, couldn't he?'

'He isn't. I asked him. And now it's all over.' She started sobbing again.

'Why did no one else in the office *tell* you this?'

'I don't know! I don't really . . . talk to the girls in the office.'

I bet you don't, I thought. In fact, they probably set you up.

'Would you like some Heinz spaghetti?'

She thought about it for a moment.

'Yes, please.'

We sat and ate spaghetti in silence. I wanted to broach the topic of Josh, but I couldn't bring myself to. Also, whenever I'm in Kate's presence and trying to think of something to say, I always have a horrible compulsion that I'm about to accidentally mention Pop-Tarts, like Basil Fawlty and the Germans.

Kate appeared slightly coy and lifted up her fork.

'Ummm . . . would you like to come out for my birthday?'

'Sure!' I said. I was so relieved she wasn't giving me trouble, I'd agreed before I realized what I'd just committed myself to.

Josh wasn't coming to Kate's birthday do. He was on parental duty. His parents were officially now genteel poor, living in a huge house they could no longer afford to run. They'd been cleaned out by that, Josh's education, and the education of his three sisters, who were all beautiful, and all completely stupid. Despite these extremely positive attributes, none of the girls had ever got married, which meant no new influx of old money into the fforbes' family coffers. The family, though, were holding up very well, marching on with some good stories and a lot of dogs and gin and tonics.

Which left, as far as I could make out, all of Kate's City friends and, ahem, me. Actually, I wanted to go. Young, rich, probably good-looking men . . . I liked the sound of it. Obviously, I was going to marry Addison, but that didn't mean I couldn't get taken to nice restaurants in the meantime.

Unfortunately, everything I had to wear was grubby – the market was going to make you dirty anyway, so it scarcely mattered – apart from my pyjamas, and I didn't think they would cut it. Finally, I dug up an old black summer dress which was so faded it could pass as grey, the colour *du jour*, apparently. It was too chilly, even in April, to wear it, and as I didn't have a tan it gave me an air of being clinically dead, but it really was all I had, which depressed me more than I wanted to think about.

I teamed it with my favourite daisy necklace and twirled in the mirror. I looked nine.

I was meeting Kate and her gang at some posh pub over an ice rink near Liverpool Street station. It was mobbed and full of braying, identical young men, who had rather better skin than the young men I'd grown up with but were just the same old wankers – with money.

'You've got to take it to the EXTREME!' one rather red-faced young man was hollering to his chum, two feet away.

'Quite!' the other, equally stolid, chap bawled back.

'That's why I'm chartering a helicopter in the Canadian Rockies next season!'

'Uh . . . yars! Me too!'

The women were all eerily like Kate: their hair was shiny, and their lips were pursed. In fact, it was quite difficult to track Kate down in the thicket of size-eight Nicole Farhi, but I spotted her eventually. She didn't exactly appear overjoyed to see me, which pissed me off – I was feeling a bit off-the-beam as it was.

'Thanks for coming,' she said a little stiffly – reminding me that we were only forty-eight hours from wanting to murder each other. I nodded stiffly back, handed her a parcel and looked around. There were about eight guys in various stages of hee-hawing: my kinds of odds, I thought to myself. All around were champagne bottles and buckets.

'Great!' shouted one of the men. 'More champagne!'

I realized they were talking to me, and I panicked. Meanwhile, Kate had opened my present – a furry penguin. I'd thought it would be funny, but everyone stared at it in disdain.

'Oh, how *charmante*,' said one of the blokes, before the company stared at me one more time, cottoned on to the fact that I probably wasn't going to be buying them any champagne, then turned back to each other.

Kate gave me a half smile, and handed me a glass of champagne, then prodded the man to her right.

'*James*, this is Holly.'

James grunted at me. Kate leaned over to the person he was talking to, and nudged him as well.

'And this is James B.'

'James B.' I nodded.

'And over there are Jamie Egbert, Jim, and, ehm, Finn.'

Only Finn heard and tilted up his head. At first sight he looked a little odd, and I couldn't work out what it was. Then I realized that his tie was loosened, and he appeared to be wearing dirty spectacles. This reassured me, and I gave him a rather gushy grin, which clearly terrified him, as he instantly returned to staring at his glass.

'So!' said Kate brightly. 'This is all very nice.'

'Who are all these Jameses?' I asked her.

'Work colleagues, mostly,' she said.

'All of them?'

'Err, yes.'

'Birthdays can be horrid, can't they?' I said sympathetically.

'What do you mean?' she snapped.

'Nothing! Lovely champagne.'

I played with the glass for a second, then tried to lean into the two Jameses' conversation. They were talking ferociously about tax liability and the nastiness of the government for trying to extract money from their enormous pay-cheques to finance boring old services, and they managed to avoid looking me in the eye for ages whilst I tried to think of a ploy to enter the conversation.

'I hate tax too,' I announced when one of them paused for breath. 'Mind you, I don't pay more than ten pee in the pound.'

They raised their eyebrows at me. 'Really? What do you do with it? Is it offshore?' asked James 1.

'God, I wish I could figure it out,' said James 2. 'Did you form a limited company? What's your secret?'

'Ehmm . . . actually, most years I, just, ehm, fall below the threshold,' I mumbled.

Their faces registered shock, then instant embarrassment at registering shock – after all, they were terribly well brought up boys.

'Oh, lucky you,' said one of them, then clearly wished he hadn't. I felt an absolute pariah; you really shouldn't go drinking in the City unless you have at least one toe made of gold or something.

'What do you do?' asked James 2, regretting he'd ever bothered to focus on me.

'Ehm . . .' I thought frantically. This conversation, however demeaning, was the only thing I had going on, and it was about to finish two seconds after I said 'florist'. And they may all have been wankers, but they were handsome, rich wankers, so a girl has got to try. Now, let me see: Astronaut? Philosopher? Nurse? Ooh, they loved that.

'I'm a nurse,' I said. It was worth it just to see their little faces light up.

'Way-hey!' shouted one of them. 'What kind of nurse?'

I took another slurp of champagne. 'I work in

the . . . waterworks department.'

James 2 turned white.

'Don't worry, I've washed my hands.'

'Oi! Jimmy! Egbert! Finn! Come and meet Kate's flatmate – she's a nurse!'

I hate boys.

Kate shot me a deadly look. I cringed at her. I'd only meant it as a laugh, but if she blew me out, I'd have to basically destroy myself with humbleness.

The other lads came over. They were a bit pissed, and up for ribbing someone they appeared to think was somewhat akin to a prostitute, but with an even kinder heart.

'Do you have to, like, you know, rub ointment in, like Joanne Whalley-Kilmer in *The Singing Detective*?' asked one of them, breathless.

'Sometimes.' I nodded sagely. 'Usually when I'm on night shift.'

There was a collective groan.

'Do, ahem, nurses still wear uniforms these days . . . ?' asked one of them, under the pretence of historical analysis.

'Oh yes. At St Mungo's our uniforms are white: it's like a hangover from the days when it used to be run by' – my *pièce de résistance* – 'nuns.'

'Ooh.'

'What do you find most interesting in your field? I mean, aren't you working a lot on prostate disease? Do you find this is becoming more of an environmental syndrome, or does it retain its genetic antecedence?'

Shite! This came from Finn, the one I'd noticed

earlier, with the smeared glasses. Smart aleck bastard. A collective groan went up from the other boys. I wondered what a prostate was. I knew it was something to do with willies, but I didn't know what.

'Ehm . . . really, with the greenhouse effect it's all getting pretty environmental,' I stammered.

'*Really*? Is that true? How fascinating! Where else do you see this type of phenomenon . . . ?'

Annoyingly, the other boys were starting to turn their backs on me. They were obviously used to whoever this mega-nerd was, and sexy nurse was being replaced with scientist nurse. Boo. Kate was still throwing visual daggers in my direction.

'Oh, all over the place,' I said carelessly.

'Really . . . oh, I know you're off duty now, and I hate to bother you, but medicine is a real interest of mine and . . .' He flushed. 'Ahem . . . would you like to get together to discuss it sometime?'

'Sure,' I said. You really have to be a troll for me not to agree to go on a date with you. I've always figured it's a law of averages. Of course, that probably explains a lot about my life.

'OK! OK, brilliant,' he said, clearly surprised and a bit overwhelmed. 'Ehm . . . I know, what about the Natural History Museum?'

What? But you're a rich City person. I mean, surely I deserved the Oxo Tower at least?

'Next Saturday? Are you on duty?'

I reluctantly said no, I wasn't on duty, which at least was the truth.

'Great! I'll meet you there at two! OK! Fantastic! Brilliant!' Unable to stop thanking me, he retreated back to his group of Jameses, where I was disgusted to see him being slapped on the back by his friends. And I wasn't too proud of myself, either.

Kate came over. 'Well, you've certainly made an impression. Do they know you actually run a daisy hospital?'

'I'm sorry, Kate. No one would have spoken to me otherwise. AND, hey, it worked! I got a date!'

'Finn is not a date. He's a walking CD-ROM.'

'That doesn't sound too bad to me. What does he do?'

'He's developing string theory for stock markets.'

'Wow, I don't know what that is, but it sounds like he must be RICH.'

'No – wow, he must be DULL. Just a friendly warning . . . Oh, and he actually works for the University of London, doing a research project, so he's not even rich.'

'I'm going to the Natural History Museum with a *student*?'

'And he's going with a nurse.'

The 'party' didn't last too long after that. Bizarrely, the pub shut at nine – it was probably run by the banks, making sure their bonus-slaves didn't stay up too late enjoying their youth. So we found ourselves back round the kitchen table, slightly drunk, by ten o'clock, opening another bottle of wine. Kate was talking about how much shit she put up with at work, but I kept getting confused with all those Jameses, so I just nodded along generally.

Josh finally returned, a bit wobbly on his gin and tonics.

'I got a date!' I hollered, as soon as he walked in the room.

'No!' he said, clearly amazed.

'Yeah, a full-on *nerd* date,' said Kate, leaning into her glass of wine.

Josh sat down, his eyes shining.

'Tell me,' he said, 'how did he ask you?'

'Well, he just said, "Would you like to go to the Natural History Museum . . . ?"'

'Under false pretences,' said Kate.

'And you said yes,' said Josh, breathless with admiration.

'Yup!'

'He just said, "Would you like to go to the Natural History Museum"?'

'Apparently they let you in half-price if you don't know anything about science,' added Kate.

'And that's all it takes to ask a girl out.'

'That's all it takes to ask me out,' I said, before Kate pointed it out.

'Wow,' said Josh. 'It's that simple.'

'It's that simple.'

We all stared at our drinks.

'Kate,' said Josh, 'would you like to go to the Natural History Museum?'

Kate's head snapped up and she looked perturbed.

'Are you asking me out on a date, or are you just testing?' she said crisply.

'Don't be daft, this is practice. Do you think I can pull it off?'

'Oh,' said Kate. 'No, that would never work.'

'Right. OK. Fine,' said Josh.

'It's not a universal chat-up line,' I said consolingly.

'No, Holly is what's technically known as *easy*,' explained Kate.

'OK,' I said, rising somewhat unsteadily to my feet. 'If you're going to be horrible, I'm going to talk to my *other* friend around here, Addison.'

I lurched out of the kitchen, a tad unsteadily, and wandered across the landing, to the fast becoming familiar under-door blue glow.

I pushed the door ajar.

'Addison!' I said loudly, for the benefit of my ex-friends sitting in the kitchen. He did that gorgeous rigid back thing. God, I love that.

'What are you doing?'

I leaned forward, peering over his shoulder. To my amazement, instead of indecipherable computer babble, on his monitor was a picture of a hugely breasted fat lady.

He coloured and immediately dived for the escape button, but it was too late.

'Addison!' I said again, shocked. In my slightly drunk frame of mind, I felt deeply insulted. After all, here I was, and he still felt the need to . . . well.

'Addison,' I said a third time. He still wasn't meeting my eyes. 'Do you know lots of women?'

His beautiful dark gaze was focused solely on his computer keyboard.

'Because, you know, you might find . . . what you're looking for . . . closer than you think.'

I couldn't believe I was being such a tart. On the other hand, tart tactics were required when dealing with someone as shy as this. Plus of course I was pissed – that wonderful moral leveller.

I took his hand.

'You know,' I said, 'you're very attractive.' Really, I like to take all my chat-up lines from *Dynasty*, *circa* 1986.

His hand lay in mine like a piece of wet melon. Not noticing, I leaned over and kissed his forehead. He smelled of that wonderful Banda paper you used to get in schools: fresh and dry and inky.

He wasn't kissing back though. I realized this after say, thirty, maybe forty seconds. No reaction. Nada. Nothing. I kissed his head again. He didn't even move.

'So,' I said tartily, 'ehm, you know where I sleep . . .'

Sheesh. This was it. This was the pits. Robocop or the Natural History Museum. Even I hadn't plumbed my own depths before.

Amazingly, he simply took my hand off his forehead and squeezed it. Less amazingly (given he was a sober person who'd just been come on to by a mad harpy), he then handed it back to me and returned to his keyboard. I stood there for about ten seconds more

– just to prolong the humiliation, I suppose – then retreated backwards slowly, whilst he busied himself with some computer stuff which, as far as I could see, had nothing more to do with big-breasted Betty.

'Oh God.'

'You'll get over it! You've got over worse stuff!'

'Like what, exactly?'

'What about that time you taught yourself to snowboard to impress big Eric and broke your ankle?'

Josh was failing to comfort me at the breakfast table. Not only this, but I had an interview today for a real live flower shop, which I had to do after the utter humiliation of basically prostrating myself in front of my flatmate. I wasn't sure that counted as extenuating circumstances.

'Anyway, I've done much worse things.'

'Like what?'

'I don't know . . . what about that time I got bitten by a dog?'

'Ehm, you know what, Josh? I don't think that really embarrassed the dog. So it does NOT compare.'

Kate of course had already gone to work, presumably clear-headed and 'motivated'.

'Yes, but I cried when I got my tetanus shot.'

'You must have been about eight years old.'

'Still embarrassing, though.'

'*And* they gave you a cream cake at the end of it,

which really means that it does not compare. Now, ask me a question about flowers.'

'Ehm . . . what colour are tulips?'

'OK, ask me a question about a flower you've actually met.'

'I'll have you know I took the church prize in our village for flower arranging three times in a row!'

'You surprise me.'

'They were very . . . manly arrangements. OK, how do you grow a sunflower?'

'Stick it in any old shit and ignore it for months.'

We both paused for a minute.

'That's my life,' we both said simultaneously.

I couldn't believe a flower-shop interview could be so intense. There were three people in the tiny office at the back of the shop: an old bloke who might conceivably have been dead; a woman with very high hair, a monobosom and an imperious expression; and a sullen Indian girl with either a very large bogey or a bolt through her nose – it was hard to tell in the gloomy room.

'Now, here at That Special Someone, we take our customer care *extremely* seriously,' announced the big woman (I'd known she'd start the talking). 'Can you give us a particular example of good customer care you've been involved with in your previous jobs?'

I fucking hate job interviews. They are crap. They ask you all these bloody questions, whereas really they only want to know what you smell like, and how much you're prepared to say you agree with their bizarre views on racial hygiene.

'Well,' I began, modestly, 'once, these schoolkids came into the shop; one of their little chums had been knocked down by a car – on the school-run, ironically enough – and they'd clubbed all their pocket money together to buy him a princess bouquet, but they didn't have enough for the delivery charge. So, I took them to little Tommy myself.'

They were buying this. I couldn't believe it! The big woman was practically wetting herself.

'Yes?' she said. 'Go on.'

'Well, it turned out that Tommy's dad owned a major chain of conferencing suites, and we got the contract to do all of them after that.'

The bolt/bogey girl smirked worryingly, but the big lady was overwhelmed. Well, it wasn't exactly a lie – I mean, if charitable situations like that ever presented themselves, I'd like to think I'd rise to the challenge. None had, that was all.

'Well, that's just wonderful. Perhaps you can bring a little bit of that magic to That Special Someone, don't you think, Mr Haffillton?'

Mr Haffillton declined the chance to appear any less dead.

'I thought so. So, Holly, what about your horticultural qualifications?'

What about them? They didn't test you on telephone manner and Cellophane wrapping, the only two genuine skills required.

'Yes . . . obviously, I've been gaining experience out of London' – I took the bet they wouldn't know where Harlesden was, and I was right – 'but I'll be back down the Chelsea Physic Garden right away, you bet!'

'Not on our time, of course!'

'Ha ha ha! Of *course* not.'

God, I wish I didn't need this job, but Tash had given me a wedgie the other day and I'd had to hide and have a cry.

'Chalitha! Wouldn't you like to ask a question?'

Chalitha shrugged her black-clad shoulders petulantly.

'Come on now, Chalitha! We're all just one happy family here!' Big Lady grimaced at me as if Chalitha had just made some enormous joke.

'I dunno . . . What's your favourite band?'

I judged the situation carefully.

'The Sex Pistols.'

'Cool.' She nodded her head and turned to the old dead man. 'She'll be all right, uncle,' she announced. Aha. She turned back to me.

'The last girl liked Mariah Carey.'

Actually, the question clearly wasn't any more or less stupid than any other job interview question, and certainly got to the heart of the matter.

'I couldn't have worked with her,' I said confidently.

'No, can you imagine? She'd have worn little miniskirts and warbled emotionally all day.'

'I just spit,' I said reassuringly, then burst into a

fake laugh when I realized Big Lady was staring at me with raised eyebrows.

'Ha! ha! Only kidding. Ehm, I think a happy work place is essential to provide the very premium in customer service, don't you?'

She nodded sternly. 'Yes. But this is a very efficient business. Naturally, we don't put up with any hanky-panky.'

'No, ma'am,' I said.

She loved the 'ma'am' thing, I noted instantly.

'Well, we'll be letting you know,' she said, rising imperiously to her feet.

'Thank you very much, ma'am.'

I practically walked out backwards.

I hung around that night, desperate for the phone to ring before I had to head up the hill – possibly for the last time.

'. . . Then I thought I'd say, "Tash, I'm sorry you didn't get better womb nutrition and have no prospects, but just LEAVE ME ALONE!"' I announced for Josh's benefit.

'And, for the boys, I thought I'd pity them too. Kind of like, "Isn't it a shame you're just so deeply ignorant?"'

Josh was chopping vegetables, but he stopped to look up at me. 'You don't think that's a little . . . well, you know, deeply deeply fascist?'

'I think it's only fair after what they've put me through. Really, I'm very humanitarian.'

'Ah yes, Mr Gandhi.'

'Exactly. I mean, it's not as if I'd ever have the balls to say any of it.'

'You could try, if you feel that strongly about it.'

Kate wandered in, and waved approximately, too exhausted to talk.

'Yes, and die in the attempt.'

I thought for a bit.

'Josh, you know, I lie all day long and think horrid things about people. Do you think I'm morally bad?'

Josh turned on the food processor for a minute to think about it.

'Don't turn on the food processor to give yourself time to think about it! You should know immediately!'

'I don't think you are.' This was from Kate. That was unexpected. 'I think you're normal. Lying all day long and secretly wanting to kill people is human nature.'

'Hmm, I don't know if I want to *kill* them, as such.'

'I don't . . .' Josh's forehead creased up in concentration. 'I don't think bad things about people. Or at least I don't think I do.'

Kate and I glanced at each other and Kate rolled her eyes. It was true actually. Josh was really quite 'good', in a primary school sense. The only reason we didn't hate him too was that he was a very easy tease and he cooked.

'Yes, but you're sickeningly nice,' said Kate. 'You're different and weird.'

There was a moment's pause.

'No, actually, I am thinking nasty thoughts about somebody now,' said Josh, turning the food processor back on. Kate and I shared a rare moment of bonding and grinned at each other when, thank God, the phone rang.

'JOSH! TURN THE FOOD PROCESSOR OFF!' I yelled, flapping my hands up and down.

'Oh yes, just boss around sweet old, pushed around "he's too nice" Josh,' he grumbled.

'SHUT IT!' I yelled, just as Kate picked up the phone.

'Holly Livingstone's office,' she said sweetly as I winced and lunged for the receiver. She held it at arm's length.

'Yes, she's here . . . May I ask who's calling?'

I jumped up and down on the lino in frustration and made clawing motions with my hands.

'I'll just see if she's free.'

Finally she handed the phone over.

'Hellayer!' I said in my best posh telephone voice. 'This is Holly Livingstone.'

'Hellayer!' said the voice back, so I instantly knew it was Big Lady.

'This is Mrs Bigelow' – oh, *that's* why I hadn't been able to remember her name – 'of That Special Someone. We've decided to offer you the post of Floral Executive. Nine to six, five days a week, alternate Saturdays off.'

Then she named the salary, which although more than I was getting for shift work down at NCG was still, I could practically guarantee, lower than that of every single person I went to college with, even that enormous girl with egg down her front and her glasses stuck together who treated English as if it wasn't her first language, even though it was, *and* the Art Historians.

'Great! That's great!' I stuttered, then remembered I was supposed to be the kind of person who would be fielding job offers constantly. 'I mean, I think that will be suitable. When would you wish me to start?'

'Saturday?'

Oh no. Saturday was my Natural History Museum date.

'Will Monday be all right? I wouldn't like to leave my former employers in the lurch.'

'Oh, yes,' she said, flustered. 'Of course, I absolutely agree. Employee loyalty is *extremely* important here at That Special Someone.'

So it was settled. Kate nearly slapped me for not renegotiating my salary offer when it would clearly be all such a high-ranking employee would deserve.

I debated with myself briefly whether to just blow off New Covent Garden completely, but couldn't quite bring myself to do so, and pedalled in an insouciant three-quarters of an hour late.

'You wouldn't have got away with those kinds of hours during the war, you know,' muttered Johnny as I swung into the forecourt.

'Actually, I'm sorry – I got bombed on the way here and had to stop and rescue some orphans from the rubble. Is that OK? Also, I quit.'

'Well, just get in there and get started.'

'Johnny, didn't you hear me? I just quit. I'll work tonight, then you can pay me and I'll be off.'

He stared at me, surprised.

'So, you're off then.'

'That would be my definition of "to quit", yes.'

He nodded his head slowly.

'What are you going to do?'

I decided to brighten up his evening.

'I'm going to join the army.'

'Are you really?'

'Absolutely. Going to continue with your valiant efforts to protect this country through the twin poles of duty and flowers.'

'Ah, get away with you, you liar.'

'I'll miss you,' I said.

He shrugged at me. 'No, you won't. In you go. Go clean up the daffodil line.'

I parked the bike and tiptoed into the vast shed.

'TinBits!' yelled one of the boys. 'Where have you been? Wanking behind the melons just hasn't been the same without you.'

It gave me a grim satisfaction to realize how little I was going to miss this place.

About halfway into the shift, the moment I'd been dreading arrived. Tash sidled up to me, her yellow teeth glinting.

'Bit late tonight, weren't we? Didn't learn to tell the time at college then?

I didn't say anything.

'Forgotten how to talk as well?'

Oh God, I was too *old* for this.

'Piss off, Tash,' I said quietly. 'I'm leaving.'

'WHAT did you say?' she said. 'Hey, lads, did you hear this?'

I pretended to ignore her, and picked up my first box. Inside, I started trembling.

'Miss Degree here just told me to piss off. Didn't you?' she said, pointing at me.

'Tash, I really don't want any trouble. It's my last night, so you can go and find someone else to pick on, OK?'

'Oh, diddums. Don't want any trouble?' She pushed her hand up under my box, so the flowers scattered all over the floor.

'You think you're just a bit too good for us here, don't you?' she said.

'No,' I said, meaning: 'Yes, I hope so.'

'Catfight!' shouted one of the lads.

'You think you're just a little bit special; a bit above all this.'

'Fight! Fight! Fight!' the lads picked up.

'No, I don't,' I said, but caught my breath in surprise when she pushed me. The blood started to rush in my ears, but I certainly didn't know how to fight. I leaned down to pick up the box, and she kicked me in the shoulder.

After that, everything seemed to rush. Immediately the boys and the other drooling girls formed a circle round us, and I was trapped. I got to my feet, wondering what on earth to do. Tash was looking at me, laughing.

'Not quite so up on the smart remarks now, are we?'

'Oh, for God's sake, leave it, Tash.' I was trying to be reasonable, but my voice came out all shaky. Then, suddenly, like one of those flying vampires in the movies, she launched herself at me. I was falling backwards, and someone was clawing at my face and hair. A jumble of thoughts rushed through my head, not the least of which was: How embarrassing; my first fight at the age of twenty-eight.

My focus swam back in, and I realized she was sitting on top of me, getting ready to punch me. The boys were yelling, and I thought what a turn-on this must be for them. I tried to twist her off, but she slapped me hard on the side of the head. Oh God. My heart was beating a million miles an hour.

'JUST FUCK OFF!' I screamed. 'FUCK OFF!' She slapped me again, hard, then made her hand into a fist and drew it back to punch me.

She crunched into me with such force that my head rattled off the concrete. I was stunned by the violation and thought I was going to pass out; I wanted to. I couldn't see anything, but suddenly she seemed to float off me; the weight was lifted and I wondered if I'd died and was having an out-of-body experience.

The next thing I knew, Johnny was pulling me up, brushing me down and exclaiming, 'Girls fighting! I don't know.'

'I told you I was going to the wars,' I snivelled, then realized I was crying, and there was snot and blood and tears all down my face. Tash was being held back by two of the lads, who were killing themselves laughing.

'BITCH!' she shrieked at me. 'PATHETIC BITCH.'

I certainly wasn't going to respond in any way that was going to antagonize her. In fact, I wasn't going to stay another second.

'I'm going home,' I sniffed to Johnny.

'We'll have to get you cleaned up a bit, don't you think? Could be quite a nasty shiner.'

'NO!' I said. 'I'm going home NOW!'

'Do you want me to phone someone to come and pick you up?'

'No . . . I've got my bike and I just want to go HOME.'

'All right then . . .'

He walked me to the bike, clearly concerned. Then he asked me to hang on a minute, nipped into his office and came out again with an envelope, which he handed to me.

'Take care of yourself,' he said. 'You're not as tough as you think you are.'

'I think I'm as tough as a small mouse,' I said. 'And I'm *still* not as tough as I think I am.'

He clapped me avuncularly on the shoulder. 'Don't cycle too fast.'

I didn't cycle at all, but wheeled my bike down the hill, crying and feeling very sorry for myself indeed. The road was quiet at that time of night, with only the occasional car flashing past me. I was glad. I didn't want to be seen.

The house was cold and still, as usual. And after last week's débâcle, I certainly wouldn't be popping in to chat to Addison. Sniffing, I went off to the bathroom to clean myself up. I could feel my left eye very sore and swollen, and there were scratches over my eyebrow and down my cheek.

As I crept past Addison's room, I spotted an amazing thing. Usually his door was tightly shut, a warning against any interruption. Tonight, however, it was *open* – just a tiny, tiny crack, barely noticeable, but definitely open. Was he out? No, it was just that my ears had become so inured to the tapping I didn't hear it unless I was listening for it. Plus, of course, he never went out. And given that he did everything on purpose . . . he must have left it open for a reason. Could it be . . . could it be possible that he wanted to talk to me?

Desperate for some human sympathy, even of the completely mute kind, I pushed the door a little more. He was there, as ever, transfixed by the computer screen. As I walked in, though, he moved his swivel chair a little, turning away from the screen and towards me.

'Addison . . .' I said in a very small voice, and immediately burst into noisy sobs. 'Addison!'

His face registered shock as he saw me, and he stood up. For the first time I noticed how tall he was, how long his legs were. I gazed at him, my lower lip wobbling uncontrollably.

'Look at you,' he said softly.

'It wasn't my fault!' I snorted.

'Did you get mugged?'

'Ehm, no, I was in a fight . . . but it wasn't my *fault*.'

He nodded, as if it didn't surprise him for a second that I'd been in a fight.

'Come on,' he said, and I followed him into the bathroom. Completely helpless, I let him sit me down on the side of the bath and dab my wounds with TCP. Although my insides were still churning and I was very upset, nonetheless there was definitely something thrilling about Addison touching my face. This was practically a date. Then I caught sight of my face in the mirror.

'Oh my GOD,' I moaned. My eye was twice its normal size, and as pink and purple as a prize fighter's.

'Don't worry,' said Addison comfortingly. 'Sit still.'

'I can't . . . I mean, I've got a date and a job and – oh *GOD*. Ouch! Where did you go to medical school?'

'If it stings, that means it's doing you good.'

'Yeah, a bee said that to me once.'

'Ssh,' he said, uncoiling an Elastoplast on to my right cheek. 'It'll be a lot better in the morning.'

'Will it be gone in the morning?'

'Ehm . . . no, but it will be better.'

'Thanks,' I said, still gazing at him, my eyes still wet. For the first time ever, he smiled at me. I felt faint.

'Get some sleep.'

'OK.' I toyed with the idea of feigning a few internal injuries so that he'd have to undress me, but remembered the other night and wisely decided against it.

I slept for ten hours, all the adrenaline flushing its way through my system. When I woke up the next afternoon, I rediscovered the envelope Johnny had given me. Inside were practically two weeks' wages.

Josh couldn't believe I'd been in a fight. He was unbelievably jealous. We'd decided that beer was really the only response to my ordeal – or white wine spritzer, if you were Kate – and the three of us had repaired to a new pub round the corner which, ideally for my benefit, mistook having the place in practically complete darkness for atmosphere.

I had pondered long and hard about whether to try and smother my eye – now vicious shades of yellow and green – in foundation, but this had only made me appear even more like a startled panda bear than I normally did, so I'd nitched that and gone the other way entirely, making up my right eye with dramatic eyeliner and green shadow. From a distance, it wasn't too bad; I just looked like I'd escaped from a glam rock band, and sufficiently tarty and hard that you wouldn't want to get any nearer. Close up, I was terrifying.

Kate, once she'd established that I hadn't been raped or anything, could barely stop laughing. And

Josh kept asking me stupid questions about whether or not the blood had rushed to my head. I pointed out that it had, and that it kept on rushing, straight out of my nose, and could he possibly be a bit more sensitive about it?

'Yes, these playground warriors can get a bit uptight about their traditional fighting techniques,' chided Kate. 'Watch out, or she'll give you a killer Chinese burn.'

'Ha ha ha,' I said, but stopped with my mouth hanging open as this unbelievably gorgeous guy loomed out of the darkness right in front of me.

Forgetting for a moment that I was tarted up like Marilyn Manson, I immediately tilted my profile up towards him, so that I could feel even more stupid when he swept right past me and went up and introduced himself to Kate.

Josh shot me a look of utter horror – how could this chap simply walk up to a group and introduce himself to a complete stranger? Then he sat back and waited for Kate to give the guy a good rude brush off. Josh really doesn't know much about women.

I mused for a moment that, if it weren't for my black eye, Mr Deeply, Deeply Suave – who was wearing a grey cashmere top and a Burberry trench coat which matched Kate's exactly – would have been after me first, but I couldn't even kid myself: I got the nerdy scientist guys, Kate got the rich ones. He even seemed familiar, in an American way.

Sure enough, he was American, and soon Kate

was giggling away – *not* one of nature's gigglers, but she was giving it her best shot – and chatting happily to him, and the very next moment a bottle of champagne had miraculously arrived out of nowhere and he was pouring her some. Not us, only her. I assumed she would remedy this deeply unfair state of events immediately, but when I looked at her I noticed she had subtly adjusted her body language so it seemed as if she hadn't even come in with us. And their heads were bent very close together. I was sure, still, that I'd seen him before.

Josh scuttled his chair round to me, muttering crossly.

'I'm sorry, but we appear to have been barred from the international Burberry convention,' I said to him, and he grunted. Then his face lit up.

'I know, why don't *we* have champagne? We can have fun, right?'

Kate and big beautiful thingy suddenly let out a pealing laugh.

'Josh, their definition of fun is probably comparing international money markets. But I would very much like another Becks, if you're buying. And some salt-and-vinegar crisps, which are essential medicine in the treatment of black eyes.'

Ridiculously, as the bar was trying to be trendy, it sold those cute teeny bottles of Moët & Chandon, and Josh returned laden with my beer, the crisps between his teeth, and a quarter bottle of champagne to himself, which he sipped morosely through a straw. I couldn't help laughing and had to restrain myself from rubbing him on the head with my knuckles.

'Don't worry!'

'How can I not worry? I'm twenty-eight years old and I haven't had a girlfriend for three years!'

'Or a boyfriend.'

'Would you *stop* with that already.' He pouted. 'Some of us just . . . take a bit longer to get round to things than other people.'

'What, like puberty?'

'Do you *want* to be homeless again?'

'No!' I said emphatically.

'And anyway, I've got a right to complain – you've got a date and Kate's obviously met her soul mate, and you'll all move out and have a squillion babies and I will die all alone.'

'I know!' I said brightly. 'When I marry Addison, we'll stay in the house and you can babysit our beautiful and brainy children.'

'Oh, right. And I'm the sad fantasist.'

'Not at all. He put this Elastoplast on my cheek. I'm going to keep it forever as a symbol of the first time we touched.'

Josh looked appalled.

'I think I'm going to be sick. Holly, *please* don't go all gooey over Addison . . .'

'Too late!' I exclaimed triumphantly.

'. . . I really think there's something a bit wrong with him. You know, like that weird form of train-spottery autism thing that boys are meant to get?'

He thought for a minute.

'I wonder if I could get it.'

'You could count things, I suppose. Then memorize them.'

'Ah yes. I can see the appeal.'

'Josh,' I said, 'don't worry about me and Addison.'

Kate, unsurprisingly – well, a little bit surprisingly, I'd have assumed she was a 'Rules' girl as it had the kind of anal, personality-smashing techniques she tends to like – chatted to the beautiful thing all night then swanned off with it to dinner somewhere. Le Caprice, I assumed. I had no idea what Le Caprice might be like, but it sounded the kind of place that people who wore designer underwear (I knew Kate did, because I stole a pair of her pants out of the drier once, but I couldn't get both legs in them) might go.

Josh and I hadn't stayed long. He'd decided he had to get back to gen up on some football scores.

I hung around the next morning, Saturday, to see if she'd come in or not and was disappointed to find that she had and therefore clearly hadn't gotten into something drunken and debauched, which would have been enjoyable for me. She swanned into the kitchen at around ten, carrying the *Financial Times* and looking composed and well rested. I busied around, pretending to be making coffee, and bursting to ask her what had gone on, however she calmly sat down and opened her newspaper. I tried to contain my frustration.

'Coffee?'

'Decaf, thanks, if you're making it. Black, no sugar.'

I looked over at her.

'That's a very pointless cup of coffee.'

She raised her eyebrows at me.

'Actually, it consumes more calories than it contains, like celery.'

'Aha.' I poured the water out. 'So *that's* what coffee is for.'

She smiled primly at me and went back to her paper. I tried again.

'It's *my* big date today. You know, at the Natural History Museum.'

'How nice for you.'

'Hey, maybe we could double date some time – Finn and I and you and . . .'

Kate put her paper down.

'Do you really think so?'

I tried to imagine the situation and couldn't.

'Oh, I'm sorry, aren't you seeing him again?'

She immediately bristled.

'Of course I am. I expect John and I will be seeing each other on a regular basis.'

'John? John what?'

She affected disdain.

'Oh, I don't recall.'

'Sounds made up to me.'

'What sounds made up?' mumbled Josh, wobbling in unsteadily like a new-born kitten.

'John Nobody – Kate's new love.'

'Oh God – another one,' said Josh, spooning sugar into his coffee.

'WHAT do you mean by that?' said Kate ferociously.

'I don't know – how many suave pretty-boy married men have chatted you up this year and not given you their last name in case you dig them up out of the phone book?'

'John is *not* married. I could tell.'

Josh and I glanced at each other.

Suddenly the phone rang, and we all jumped three feet. Kate hopped up, then, when she realized we were watching her, feigned a leisurely gait.

'Ehm . . . I'll get that . . . probably the office.'

'Probably Relate,' I said, 'calling you in as a witness.'

Josh and I peered round the kitchen door as she furiously motioned us away. Her expression quickly revealed her disappointment, however. She covered the mouthpiece with her hand.

'It's Addison's mother.'

'I'll get him,' I said quickly, and rapped on his door.

'Hrh?'

'Addison, it's your mum.'

'Can you tell her I'm out?'

'I don't think that's going to work.'

'He's in,' said Kate down the phone.

'Can you tell her . . . I'm . . . busy.'

'He's busy,' said Kate. 'Yes, he's eating. No, much the same. No, no sleep, no. OK, I'll tell him.'

She hung up.

'When's the last time you spoke to your mother, Addison?' I asked him.

There was silence from behind the door.

'Not since he's been here,' whispered Josh.

'I normally speak to her,' said Kate. 'She sounds all right most of the time.'

'Right.'

Kate bent down to pick up the post. As she did so, something slid out from the pocket of her exquisitely fresh Meg Ryanesque pyjamas.

'What's that?'

'Nothing,' she said, grabbing it, but it was clearly her little mobile phone.

'That pesky office, eh?' said Josh.

'Erm, right.'

I thought it would take me three minutes to get ready, but of course I had forgotten about my black eye, now puce and vermilion, and found myself in a desperate, excited rush whereby no matter how I tried I couldn't seem to get it together to leave the house. I'd forgone the Alice Cooper style for a prolonged attempt to whiten it out, which was now making me look like one of those eyebrowless sci-fi entities. I toyed with buying an eye-patch and pretending I was starting an early eighties revival, but it would take too much explaining, and, given that I'd only met this bloke for two minutes, I wanted to appear as non-mad as possible.

I still hadn't decided what to do about the nurse thing. After all, I had kind of got this date under false pretences, and it also meant he was a bit of a perv. I hummed and hawed and stomped around a bit, which was clearly annoying Kate. Normally on Saturdays she was up at eight, dashing to gyms and swimming pools and popping into the office and Joseph and the Fifth Floor at Harvey Nicks and going to exhibitions whilst Josh and I lay on the two squashy old sofas in the living room, watched black-and-white films, and ate Jaffa Cakes, but it was eleven thirty and she wasn't dressed yet. As well as the mobile, her pager was placed on the kitchen table and she seemed to have been reading the same page of the paper for some time.

'Holly, for God's sake, go. Otherwise he'll be hanging round the museum by himself all afternoon . . .'

'Nerds *love* that, though,' I argued.

'Just tell him. Tell him you were completely drunk . . .'

'Hmm, that's attractive.'

'. . . or temporarily insane. But please, stop hopping around the kitchen trying to make your mind up about it, because it's driving me crazy.'

'OK, fine. I'll go. Oh no, but what if he dumps me in the middle of the museum and I get lost amongst the brontosauri?'

'What if you don't go and you pass up the best thing you ever had?' said Kate in a surprisingly dreamy voice.

'What if he can only get off on the idea of people in uniforms? Yeugh.'

'Josh will lend you his old wetsuit. Now, just go.'

'In the wetsuit or not?'

'Out! Get out! Out! Good luck, it'll be fine. Now GET OUT!'

'Good luck to you too,' I yelled back.

'Oh God, I am ALL ALONE,' I could just hear Josh moan as I left the house.

Three

By the time I'd reached the museum in Kensington, I had decided, completely and utterly, that this was the worst idea I had ever followed through in my entire life, worse than the time I thought that that guy's motorbike would substitute for him not having a personality, and it took a wrist fracture to convince me otherwise. I tried to remember one single boyfriend I'd ever had who hadn't accidentally made me break a bone, and gave up in disgust. Great. Even if he was nice I was still going to wind up in hospital somehow.

I wasn't even sure I'd recognize Finn. And he even had a stupid fish name. God, what was I doing? It was a nice, warm spring day, and I could be lying indoors on the sofa watching TV. But no, here I was, tarted up even though I looked like a road accident victim, going off to meet some spawny pervy speccy git who thought I was porno-nurse.

This is always the way with me. Plus, I have Teenage Daughter of Nastily Divorced Parents Syndrome, which means, as people like to tell me late at night when I make only the *teensiest* complaint about my love life, that everyone I ever date will be:

- The exact opposite of my father, as I hate him so much
- Exactly like my father, as I hate him so much
- Some sort of freaky revenge on *both* my parents
- Doomed to disaster right from the start as a way of trying to get my parents' attention
- Doomed to disaster right from the start as I have never learned how good relationships worked
- Doomed to disaster right from the start as some sort of genetic fate
- Doomed to disaster right from the start as I am a Bad Person

That last one is my guess – plus, whose relationship has ever *not* ended in disaster? The best way out you can ever hope for is death . . . But this is why I'm not in therapy, although I wished I was on my way there – or anywhere – the second I saw Finn, standing awkwardly outside the entrance. He seemed as unhappy to be there as I was. God, why do we put ourselves through crap like this?

'Hi!' I said over-enthusiastically. 'Hi! Er . . . it's Holly . . .'

He looked at me confusedly for a second. For God's sake, he'd asked me.

'Hi! Oh, sorry, ha ha. My God, what happened to your eye?'

'Ehm . . . a mental patient hit me.' *Almost* true.

'Oh my God, you poor thing. What were you doing on the psychiatric wing?'

'Ehmm . . . just tidying up,' I said vaguely. Oh God, I couldn't put up with this for an hour and a half. When he went to pay for me, and I saw it was thirteen pounds for us to get in, I realized I had to act.

'FINN!' I screeched, as he handed over his Visa. 'Don't hand over that card.'

'No, really, I'll pay,' he said.

The swotty girl assistant held on to the card enquiringly.

'No, it's not that. Ehm, Finn, I think we're going to the Natural History Museum under false pretences,' I gabbled. 'Ehm, I'm not a nurse.'

He looked at me, confused.

'Sorry . . . are you a nursing student?'

'No, I mean, I'm nothing to do with nursing at all.'

'I think it's illegal to impersonate a nurse,' said the assistant helpfully. I shot her a hard stare.

'It was a . . . silly joke I was playing with . . . err, Kate,' I hastily improvised. 'She bet me I couldn't pretend to be a nurse all evening and . . . well, here we are!'

'Kate playing jokes,' said Finn meditatively. 'Never seen that happen.'

Neither had I.

'I'm so sorry that I dragged you all the way here . . . It was stupid. I'm really sorry. I'd better go.'

'Oh, great,' he said. 'You actually turn up to tell me you're going.'

'I'll go round with you,' said the swotty assistant eagerly. Finn must give off swotty scientist love vibes.

'Haven't you seen it?' I asked her rudely.

Then there was a silence.

'Well, bye then,' said Finn.

I looked at him again. He was wearing baggy old cords and a short-sleeved shirt with a pen sticking out of the top pocket, as well as a tweed coat, but – no leather patches. He seemed sweet, confused and not entirely unlike a grown-up Harry Potter. The assistant was already beckoning over her supervisor to tell her she was going on her break.

'I get in for nothing,' she whispered confidingly to Finn. Hang on, girlfriend! This was my date!

'Well, better make that one, please,' said Finn. 'Can you do a student concession?'

'For you, I'm sure,' said the girl, simpering greasily.

'Don't you want me to come then?' I said sulkily.

He turned round.

'I'm sorry, I thought you'd gone.'

'Well, you know, I'm here now.'

The assistant clucked her tongue against her teeth. Finn thought about it.

'Is your name actually Holly?' he asked.

'Yes. I promise.'

'What do you do, Holly?'

'Ehmm . . . astronaut?'

He smiled for the first time.

'Sounds good enough to me. Two please,' he said to the girl, who looked like she wanted to decapitate me with one of the velociraptor teeth they sold in the gift shop.

'So . . . who are you?' he asked, as we went up the rather sad lava-themed escalator.

'Really, nobody,' I said in shame.

'Nobody *at all*?'

'I'm Kate's flatmate.'

'Well, there you go,' he said. 'That makes you brave, for a start.'

'And I work as a florist.'

'Really?' His face lit up. 'I'm much more interested in botany than medicine, although of course one feeds so much into the other . . .'

'I don't know anything about botany either.'

'Really? Oh, you should. Did you know there's a kind of orchid that fills itself up with sticky stuff, like a pool. Then, when wasps come by, they go in and get so wet they can't fly out again. The only way out is through a tunnel at the bottom, where the wasp gets stuck and covered in pollen before he's let out. It's like a car wash.'

I was impressed despite myself, and more so when

he led me to the case holding it, and pointed it out to me.

'See? There you go – do you see? *Orchidae Coryanthus*. It's kind of like a theme park for bugs.'

'So do you just know everything about science then? Is that what you do?'

'Good gracious, no,' he said, laughing at the very thought, as if knowing the properties of *Orchidae Coryanthus* off the top of his head could possibly be conceived as knowing quite a lot about science.

'No, really, I just dabble in some things. I am a kind of physicist.'

'A kind of physicist? I didn't know they had different kinds.'

'A few, yes. I'm into string theory.'

'You look at pieces of string to see what they do? Are snakes involved?' I asked, glancing anxiously at a particularly long and malevolent one stretched out in front of us, thankfully in a case.

'Well, on a very small level. You see, particle physics only works when we pretend gravity doesn't exist, but if you want to use quantum and not just classical theory, then string theory can help close the gap.'

'Oh, I see. No, hang on, that makes no sense to me at all.'

'OK, ehm . . . just think of the world as a kind of resonating guitar string.'

'Really?'

'It's a very beautiful theory,' he said. 'It means the world plays like music.'

'What, even the person who punched me?'

'Did they soar like a butterfly and sting like a bee?'

'No, she hit me like a cow.'

'Did you tell her you were a nurse too?'

'*Noo*! I'm sorry about that.' But he was laughing. 'I got bullied at my last job. So I decided to leave and someone was obviously going to miss me.'

'You poor thing. You should just tell people you walked into a bus shelter. That's what I usually do.'

'Why, do you get beaten up a lot?'

'No, but I do walk into bus shelters.'

We were standing in front of an enormous grizzly bear, and I took the opportunity of Finn studying it closely to study *him* closely. Well, it was all natural history, after all.

He was tall, and had extremely curly brown hair sticking out in every direction. He wasn't skinny and elegant like Addison, but well built and solid. Round dark eyes peered out of what were obviously bottle-thick glasses. I thought longingly for a moment of Addison's long lashes and dark pools, then snapped myself back to the present.

'Why are you called Finn?' I said, as he examined the grizzly's paw prints and I made little growly motions to myself. 'Are your parents famous shark people or something?'

'Ha! Good variation. Well, it beats the fish-finger theory. Actually, it's Feynman. My father was desperate to have a physicist in the family. Richard

Feynman was a physicist,' he added, seeing my blank face.

'Why didn't he just call you Richard?'

'That would have been too obvious.'

'Wow. What's your middle name?'

'Lavoisier. Just in case the physics didn't work out.' He sighed, and I declined to question him any further.

We stood pondering the great blue whale for a long time, until I realized it wasn't actually real and got a bit pissed off with it. I was so full of relief, though, that the date wasn't turning into an unmitigated disaster that I managed to hide it.

'So why do you work at that wankerpit then?' I asked him.

'Where?'

'The City.'

'Oh, yes. I'm doing research there. It isn't very interesting.'

'It's interesting to me.'

'Really? Do you want to hear the advanced mathematics?'

'Ooh, is that the time?'

'See?' He regarded the whale glumly. 'Actually, I hate it. I'm trying to formulate whether the stock market works along roughly the same lines as other living systems, and all people seem to be interested in pointing out is that they have "considerably more money than you".'

'That must piss you off,' I said. 'If it helps, I'm probably poorer than anyone you know.'

'It's not really the money that bothers me,' he said grumpily. 'Want to go halfers on an ice cream?'

I'd started to feel that Finn and I were getting on surprisingly well. OK, his nose was a little pudgy, and he talked a lot about science, but here we were, doing a nice, adult, educational thing on a Saturday afternoon, and sitting out on the grass, eating ice cream and watching the duty tourists going crazy with boredom round South Kensington. He didn't seem like a perv, though. Which begged the question . . .

'Why', I asked, biting into my Magnum, 'did you ask me out?'

He looked at me, blinking in the mild sunshine, his eyes slightly enlarged behind the thick spectacles.

'Sorry?'

'Ehm . . . you know, why did you ask me on a date? If it isn't a nurse fixation, ha ha!'

'I'm sorry, I don't understand what you mean.'

However, he suddenly began to flush, and clearly did understand. I also began to understand something, and started to give him a run for his money in the flush department.

'Ermm, I didn't mean . . . I mean, sorry, but I just wanted someone to go to the museum with; I normally go alone . . . I didn't mean for you to think . . .'

'What else would I have thought?'

'I don't know. I'm terribly, terribly sorry,' he stuttered. 'Really, it wasn't that at all.'

'Why not? What's wrong with me?'

'Nothing, no, nothing . . . but I would never just ask someone out like that. I mean . . . I'm so sorry.'

'Yes, you said that,' I said sulkily, standing up whilst trying to keep my ice cream upright – not the most elegant of procedures. Finn stared at me in disbelief.

'I mean . . . can't we be friends?'

'Finn, that's what you say when two people have actually *had* a relationship and it's been deeply passionate and then it all goes wrong. Which, despite the big fish, has *not* happened this afternoon.'

'Fine.' He shrugged. 'Well, once again I apologize for the misunderstanding, and it was nice to have met you. Oh, and the "fish" was a "mammal".' And he held out his hand.

I *hate* it when somebody does that. Some people just have no sense of the appropriate drama. I didn't take his hand but muttered 'bye' and stomped off, cheeks high with humiliation. And, naturally, I had to stand that way, waiting for the lights to change, two feet in front of him, whilst he watched me in amazement. Shite.

'I HATE bloody scientists and I HATE bloody dates which are the bloody Schroedinger's Cat of dates/non-dates!' I hollered, as I slammed through the door three bloody quarters of an hour later, after being thrust up against tourists' armpits as the Circle Line attempted to take the scenic route.

'Where are the bloody Jaffa Cakes?'

Josh was prostrate on one of the sofas watching Bette Davis with his usual devotion.

'It's Penguins, sweetheart – don't you remember? We still have a hundred and sixty-six to get through since you went to the supermarket. Date not go too well?'

'You *could* bloody well say that.'

I stomped into the kitchen. Amazingly, Kate was still there, and still in her dressing gown. This was unheard of. She had hooked up an extension line to the phone in the hall, and her mobile was now connected up to her laptop computer, and she appeared to be continually switching between the two. The pager lay to one side, discarded, as did two cold pieces of toast, and there was a fax buzzing away in the corner which I'd never noticed before.

'Hey there,' I said, but she made no sign to show she'd heard me. 'Can I eat this bloody toast?'

She shrugged her shoulders, so I ate it anyway.

'Any luck?'

She noticed me at last and looked up, her face drawn.

'Kate, it's only the first day. You know, no self-respecting bloke would phone you on the first day after you'd met. Especially one as cool and pretty as John . . . Thingy. You'd think he was pathetic and needy and you'd probably turn him down.'

Kate nodded like an idiot.

'But he said he would.'

'Yes, but he's also a bloke. Those two things cancel each other out.'

She regarded me with narrowed eyes.

'How did your date go?'

'Fine. Oh, and also, why didn't you tell me he was a prick?'

'Finn?' This startled her out of her reverie, although she still kept half an eye on the phones. 'What happened?'

'You were there at your birthday, weren't you?'

'Ehm, yes, I would have thought so.'

'You heard him ask me out, didn't you?'

'Well, I heard him ask if you wanted to go to the Natural History Museum.'

'That's a date, right?'

'Ehm . . . why? What else did he say? Dinner? A drink afterwards?'

'He didn't have to say anything! You don't ask someone somewhere just because you want to go there.'

Kate raised her eyebrows.

'Anyway, that's not the point. The point is that I reckon when he found out I wasn't a nurse, he changed his mind and made out that it was just a *friendly* thing all the time.'

'Really? Well, maybe it was. To be honest, though, Holly, it didn't seem very like Finn to just start chatting a girl up out of the blue. He got some ribbing for it the next day, and seemed a bit surprised when the Jameses started ripping the piss. Certainly, I'm not used to seeing him being that forward – quiet as a mouse, normally.'

'What? You *knew* about this?'

'Of course not. I'm just saying, maybe he didn't mean to ask you out, and you made an honest mistake.'

'Well, of course, you're being incredibly reasonable about it, because it's not you who had to listen to stupid theories of FLOWERS for two hours by that annoying, geeky IDIOT.'

'Oh well, it won't bother you that he doesn't want to go out with you, then.'

'It DOESN'T.'

We both sighed. Kate picked up the pager and checked to see if it was on.

'God, Kate,' I said, counting it out on my fingers, 'let's see: you gave him your home number, your office number, your mobile, your car phone, your pager your e-mail and your fax number . . . ?'

She nodded miserably.

'I think we're just going to have to wait for the law of averages to kick in,' I observed, 'whereby he misdials another number, and gets you.'

Josh called a house meeting the next morning. Or rather, he ran up and down the corridor at 8 a.m. banging a ladle on a saucepan and yelling, 'Fire! Fire! Everyone out!' Then, when people put their heads round their bedroom doors blearily, he grabbed them and pulled them round the kitchen table.

When I got in there I couldn't tell if Kate had even gone to bed or not; she was still sitting in the same spot, walled in by electronic communication devices. Amazingly, Addison was there too, blinking in the daylight. He seemed extremely uncomfortable.

I'd never seen him during the day before. Properly lit, he was even more beautiful: the strong curve of his upper lip, and the fathomless depths of his heavy-lidded black eyes making me rush back out of the room to put some lipstick on – until Josh caught me, and forced me back down.

'OK, everyone,' he announced, 'this has got to stop.'

I trembled for a moment as I remembered cutting my toenails in the bath, however he didn't point directly at me but continued:

'I want this to be a nice happy home for my friends, not some sort of love harpy madhouse,' he said, as sternly as he could, which wasn't very. We all stared at him uncomprehendingly.

'Just look at the situation,' he said. 'We're all obviously deeply bad at running our own love lives.'

'I'm doing OK,' I said, untruthfully and petulantly.

'Holly, you can't tell the difference between a love life and a school trip, OK? Addison, you just seem completely uninterested . . .'

Addison was tapping something into a computer about the size of a pea, and didn't even look up.

'. . . and Kate, I'm worried about your mental health.'

'Huh?' she said listlessly.

'What about you?' I said.

'Hum,' he said. 'And, yes, perhaps I could improve on my own love life.'

'Michael Jackson', I said, 'has a better love life than you.'

'So, we're just going to have to do something about it.'

'Like what?'

'I think we should have a house-warming. We've never had one. And, I think we should all have to ask one member of the opposite sex.'

'. . . or the same sex, if you felt that way inclined,' I pointed out.

'Thank you, Holl, interjection accepted . . . We should all ask one member of the opposite sex who is definitely single and whom we think would be suitable for someone else who's coming – and then they ask someone too!' he finished triumphantly.

'What??'

Even Addison stopped tapping, looking up with a hunted animal expression on his face.

'It's called a singles party. I read it in *Vogue*. You invite a single person, and they bring along a single friend, who brings along a single friend, etcetera etcetera etcetera. It's a "fabulous and frivolous way to find a mate," says *Vogue*.'

He was clearly completely over-excited about his idea.

'Hang on a minute,' said Kate, still slumped into her chair. 'You realize that if we do that, within about five minutes you'll have invited every single single person in the entire world?'

'It's exponential,' mumbled Addison. 'But, if you got them all to stand close enough together, I think they could fit on the Isle of Wight.'

'What if some of them are burglars?' I asked.

'Guys! Have you no excitement?! No imagination?!'

'Addison,' I said gravely, 'can I ask you as my single friend?'

'Yes,' he replied. 'Ehm, can I ask you then, as my follow-up?'

'Yes! Ooh, that means I'll have to ask you again now.'

'No! No! Come on, guys! It'll be fun! Please! I'll hire the caterers!'

Josh believed *everything* he read in *Vogue*. As, of course, you should.

'You'll get caterers?' I asked, fatally. Well, I'd never been to a party before where catering didn't mean half a bowl of peanuts with a cigarette stubbed out in it.

'Oh yes – if it's going to be a proper party.'

'I doubt I'll be able to make it,' said Kate. 'John and I will probably be out that night.'

'Uh huh,' said Josh carefully. 'But say he's working abroad that night – you would come, wouldn't you?'

Kate shrugged her shoulders. 'I don't care. Sure.'

'But don't ask that Finny bastard,' I said. 'He'll make the punch explode or something.'

'Excellent!' said Josh. 'I'll get the invitations printed.' *Printed*? 'Shall we say . . . three weeks on Saturday?'

'Why are you doing this?' Kate asked him.

'This is our year,' said Josh. 'This is our summer.

People always get it together in the summer. And we should all do it together this year, seeing as we're all here together, all single, all still young, all supportive of each other . . .'

I snorted under my breath.

'. . . I mean, by this time next year you'll be thirty.'

Kate didn't say anything but got up to leave the room, her face like thunder. As she reached the door, however, she accidentally on purpose dropped one of Josh's Wedgwood teacups – the family-heirloom ones he wouldn't let me use, only Kate because she was so careful – on the floor. It smashed everywhere.

'Jeepers!' said Josh.

'Oh, did I break something of yours?' said Kate. 'So sorry.'

I couldn't say that Josh's party idea didn't excite me. Here, finally, was a chance to get Addison on his own, without me being drunk, in a proper copping-off situation. I had started to dream about him, with the two of us managing to use his computer chair in a variety of surprisingly inventive ways. And he was my fantasy too; it normally went something like this: Kate and Josh decide to run away to sea to be sailors, leaving Addison and me to run the house by ourselves. After some delightfully romantic faffing around – he inadvertently sees me through a gauze curtain over the bath, we go to outdoor markets and laugh loudly, we somehow find ourselves having a glorious night at the opera, that kind of thing – we sit one night in front of the roaring fireplace (currently choked up with bird nests and also illegal, but never mind) and he rests his head on my shoulder and says, 'Holly, I have never experienced human companionship before, and now I cannot remember why, as I am clearly not weird or anything. But thank God I have found you. Please, never leave me.' And I say, 'OK,' and then we have Olympic-standard rumpy-pumpy. I ignored my worries in that area – e.g. the fact that Addison flinched if one so much as brushed past him – by telling myself that he would be a natural.

I could tell by a footfall where he was; by the gentlest tapping, how engrossed he was in his work; but somehow I couldn't go into his room during the day – it took the wee small hours and that quiet sense of magic you sometimes feel then. I wanted Addison and I to be special, and that meant not accidentally seeing his dirty underpants. I had it bad.

Kate did not get up from that damn table the whole day. Josh, who was humming about merrily planning party doilies, tried his best to be sympathetic.

'Skates, do you know what I think?'

'Hn?'

'I think there's a reason he didn't give you his full name.'

'Hn.'

'It was dark in that bar, wasn't it?'

'Thank God,' I added. I was trying to iron a shirt

to wear for my first day at work, and making a crappy job of it.

'Was it dark in the restaurant you went to?'

'We went to Momo – it's pitch-dark in there. Proper Moroccan, you see. No electricity.'

'Not Le Caprice?' I said, disappointed. They both stared at me.

'*No one* goes there,' Kate said. She can't have been that depressed if she was still up to sneering.

'No, me neither,' I said, and tried to make the sleeves stay in the same place long enough for me to flatten them – unsuccessfully.

'*Well*,' went on Josh, 'I thought he looked a bit famous. Maybe he was someone famous and was trying to hide it.'

Suddenly it struck me who John Thingy looked like – that guy from all those awful films where he had long hair and the whole world had been destroyed except him and he had to drink his own piss.

'Oh-my-God,' said Kate.

'You mean . . .' I said.

'Yes,' said Josh, shaking his head portentously.

'It's impossible,' I said. 'Although he did have an American accent.' I turned to Josh.

'You would have *noticed*,' I added. '*Somebody* would have noticed.'

'Oh my God,' said Kate again.

'Not necessarily,' said Josh. 'I mean, you don't usually expect to see major international film stars in South London. He must have been travelling incognito. Trying to see if you liked him for himself.'

'Oh my God,' said Kate again.

'I've heard they do this kind of thing all the time – haven't you seen *Notting Hill*?'

'He talked about Los Angeles quite a lot!'

'There you go then – proof.'

'Oh my God. I had a date with *Kevin Costner*!' Kate rushed off to the bathroom.

'*What* are you up to?' I asked Josh.

'Come on, what would you rather do: get dumped by some ferrety-faced married schmuckmeister or some ferrety-faced international superstar?'

'You're a good man.'

'Too good,' he said soberly, following Kate out into the hall, yelling, 'He probably got called away the next morning to give out an Oscar or something. Don't blame yourself! He'll probably make a film about you!'

'Yeah, and that one can be shit as well,' I thought, but I kept it to myself.

I was early the next morning, wearing my white shirt, which was almost spotless, and a pair of trousers. I only had one pair of trousers and couldn't believe that the person who invented the concept for women had done us any favours whatsoever, but they were black and smartish and looked quite a lot like what Chalitha had been wearing in the interview, so I was going along with that. I got a bit of a shock taking off on my bicycle, as the traffic was rather different at 8.30 a.m. than it was at 9 p.m., so I managed to get nearly killed three or four times and be hollering a gypsy curse on all white van drivers by the time I screeched to a halt beside That Special Someone. Mrs Bigelow was unlocking the door, and looked up with a faintly shocked expression on her face.

'Ah, Miss Livingstone.'

I dismounted in an ungainly fashion, which I think included flashing my pants at her.

'It's Holly. Hello again. Ehm, is there anywhere I can put the bike?'

She stared at me as if I was a Martian.

'No.'

We stood there, facing each other.

'OK then . . .' I checked around, and, for want of anything better, connected the bike to the nearest lamppost, in prime person-tripping and vandalism position. Mrs Bigelow watched me all the while, her several chins seeming to wobble reproachfully at me.

Finally, she opened the door and let me back into the shop I had seen only briefly the previous week.

It was small, with a floor covered in black rubber and the familiar heavy scent of flowers. Buckets of bouquets and posies sloshed around near the door, ready to be put outside for schoolchildren to pinch from. On the wall were several prominently displayed certificates from the Chelmsford School of Horticulture, made out to a Marilyn Gloria Bigelow.

She bustled through officiously.

'Now, here is the telephone,' she announced, pointing to the telephone. 'Incoming calls *only*, if you don't mind, unless you have to speak to suppliers, or me, or Mr Haffillton.'

'When might I need to speak to Mr Haffillton?'

She fixed me with a glare.

'Never! I am the only person who communicates with Mr Haffillton!'

I nodded my head as if this made sense.

The phone rang suddenly.

'Ah. Now, Holly, listen carefully: this is how we answer the telephone. Good *morning*, That Special Someone, how can I *help* you?'

Her helpful expression changed quickly, however, and she shot into the phone: 'You'd better make it quick, you procrastinating minx, or I'll be letting Mr Haffillton know, do you understand?'

Then she slammed the phone down and resumed her beatific smile.

'That was Chalitha. She's been a trifle . . . held up, but she oughtn't to be long. Now, through here, this is our staff room.'

There was a tiny chair behind a curtain, with a kettle on a shelf and a sink. There was no window, only a fluorescent bulb.

'We each bring our own tea, coffee, milk, cups and sugar; that makes life a lot easier, don't you find?'

I nodded in a way that indicated that in fact I found this the apotheosis of efficient tea-making.

'Ten minutes break in the morning and the afternoon, and forty-five minutes at lunchtime – quite generous, don't you think? Mr Haffillton always was most . . . generous.'

I tried to work out why she was talking in the past tense. Maybe he really was dead, and they just propped him up for formal occasions.

'The vans deliver at ten from the markets – *do* check the merchandise, they're never above trying to pass off those rancid African daisies, and it makes me *most* upset, do you understand? Then the orders for the day will be HERE –' she stabbed a long, deadly pink nail at the wall – 'and you start making them up immediately. Then you phone the collection boys . . .'

It seemed rude to enquire who the collection boys were –

'. . . They're positively indolent, *and* they get the tips, but we can't do it without them, unfortunately. Don't let them get away with anything, and keep an eye on them when they're in the shop. Now, have you got your NVQ in wedding floral artistry?'

I confessed that I hadn't. She let out a large sigh.

'Ohhh well. Perhaps we'll wait until we're on the job for that, shall we? Right, must be off, Chalitha will be in soon, one *supposes*. You *do* understand that I can't open the till until she gets here – you don't *seem* like a thief, dear, but they're everywhere, you know?'

'Where are you going?' I asked, worried that she was going to leave me.

'Oh, you don't think this is the only project Mr Haffillton has up his sleeve, do you? Oh no, I am the Executive Sales Director, and my days are most busy. But remember, be polite on the phone. And we do check all outgoing calls, you know, so don't think about trying anything – not that you would, I'm sure, but you never know, people have relatives all over the world these days. I'm sure that girl will be in shortly; normally we run an extremely tight ship, but she's officially been delayed, hopefully not in an accident or anything like that . . .' She appeared to fantasize about the possibility for an instant. 'No, I'm sure it wasn't. Now, you have got everything straight, haven't you? Orders off the phone, orders on to the nail, orders off the nail, orders through to the boys. I'm afraid you won't be able to take a break until Chalitha turns up, but then you don't appear to have any tea with you, so that won't be a problem anyway, will it? Bye!!!'

And she disappeared in a flash of polyester. I stared after her as she sped down the road, then slowly looked round the small shop. I remembered vaguely a TV show where people would be set up with new jobs, left on their own, and then gunge would be thrown at them, or someone pretending to be the President of the United States would phone up or something, and sighed. Also, suddenly, I was gasping for a cup of tea.

I wandered around the shop, picking at stray bits of ribbon, examining the stock – mostly dusty house plants – before the day's delivery turned up, and praying that the phone wouldn't ring.

Worse happened, though. The bell at the door of the shop went off as an enormous greasy hulk stooped his head to come in. He was wearing a filthy old leather jacket and jeans holed and stained with oil, and his hair was long. In fact, he resembled a Status

Quo fan from the eighties, and, as such, made me shudder. He popped his motorcycle helmet on the counter about a foot away from me and rubbed his stubble contemplatively with the heel of his hand.

''Oo are you?'

'I'm Holly Catherine Livingstone,' I replied, trying to sound insouciant. 'Who are you?'

He grunted by way of response. 'Where's Charlie, then?'

I had no idea whom he meant.

'Are you in the right flower shop?'

'What? Course I am. Are you?'

'Yes.'

We were at stalemate. He looked around cautiously, just in case he had, in fact, walked into the wrong flower shop.

'So 'as, Charlie, er, left, yeah?'

'He might have done . . . I'm new.'

He shook his head in disbelief. I noticed he was wearing one of those really visceral heavy-metal T-shirts – somebody's eyeball being punctured with a nail – and I tried not to concentrate on it.

'Yeah, all right then . . . sorry.'

'No problem!' I said, pleased with how well I'd dealt with my first customer.

'If you see 'er, right, tell 'er Gareth was looking for 'er.'

'Well, of course, I wouldn't know her if I did see her – but, as I said, no problem!' I replied jauntily.

He backed out of the shop, pausing at the doorway to look around it suspiciously one more time, as if I might have hidden her in one of the pot plants. Then he shook his head again, and the next thing I heard was a little hairdrier motorbike engine kicking into life. I patted my hands successfully, and started putting the flower buckets outside, using a black marker pen to strike out all the unnecessary apostrophes.

Eventually, whilst bending down by the kerb, I realized someone was watching me, and straightened up very slowly. The longhaired, dark-eyed girl from the interview was studying me appraisingly. I wiped my hands on my trousers and spluttered a bit.

'Hi . . . Chalitha . . .'

'Chali,' she said dismissively, marching into the shop, 'that's what most people call me.'

'Ah,' I said, then thought about it. 'Ah,' I said again.

I followed her into the back, where she slung off a black PVC mac and started touching up her already heavy eyeliner in a mirror the size of a cigarette packet.

'Ehm, I think someone was in here looking for you.'

'Really?'

'A big bloke. I didn't realize it was you and told him you didn't work here. I'm sorry . . .'

'Did you? Was he big and greasy with stupid long hair, and did he smell?'

'Ehm . . . well, yes, to all of the above.'

'Excellent!' Someone smiled at me for the first time that day. 'Where did you say I'd gone?'

'Nowhere in particular.'

'Good. But specifics are better – he might follow me there. Next time, could you tell him I'm in Bhutan?'

'Not a problem.'

She grinned again.

'Did the old witch get you started?'

'She . . . ehm, Mrs Bigelow was most helpful.'

'Really? Maybe she's had a brain transplant. Cup of tea?'

'Yes, please.'

I followed her through to the little kitchen. Chali was about nineteen years old, and today was wearing tight black leather trousers and a ripped top. Her silky black hair came down to her bum – something I had always longed for as a child – and she had matching gold hoops in her ears, nose and lip. She was gorgeous.

'OK, always use *Biggie's* tea,' she instructed, picking up the box of Earl Grey. 'And if she asks you, deny it. You have to get your fun where you can around here.'

'How long have you been working here?'

Chali snorted and raised her eyes.

'One hundred and forty-seven years. Milk and sugar?'

'Yes, please.'

We took our teas back into the main shop and sat down.

'God, I had a killer night last night. Do you go clubbing?'

There is nothing I despise more than being made

to dance in public in front of sulky teenagers in very little clothing whilst paying four pounds for a bottle of water.

'Yeah, you know . . . occasionally.'

'Right, where do you go?'

I searched my brains desperately, but all I could remember was the one down from my school where I grew up.

'Erm . . . Cinderella's Rockefellers?'

Seeing her disbelieving face, I hastily added, 'It's ironic.'

'Oh, cool. That sounds like a right laugh.'

'It is.'

'God, I got in at four this morning, E-ing off my head at Fabroche.'

I smiled politely.

'That's why this job isn't so bad in the long run – they don't care what you do, s'long as you turn up occasionally. Biggie gives you a bunch of shit, but you don't need to pay attention.'

She let out an elaborate yawn and went to open the door to the delivery men.

'Yo. Just dump them anywhere, as usual, boys.'

The two men brought in several boxes of flowers in different shapes and sizes and dumped them haphazardly on the floor. Chali ignored them, signed the chit without reading it and sighed theatrically at the pile. So far we hadn't had a single customer and the phone hadn't rung once.

I went over to start opening up the flowers. Sure enough, the African daisies *were* rancid.

'Who left the job before I came?' I asked, unwrapping the plastic carefully.

'Oh, no one,' she sighed. 'Really, you're here to keep an eye on me, because I was turning up later and later, and the shop wasn't opening at all.'

'Why don't they just sack you?' I said, before it had passed across my brain censor control. I cursed inwardly.

'They can't – Mr Haffillton's my uncle and thinks the sun shines out of my arse. *And* he only really runs it as a hobby – he's minted, and he likes flowers. You can't imagine how much that annoys Biggie.'

I started to feel a bit sorry for Biggie.

'So, do you feel up to babysitting duties?' She lit a cigarette.

I thought about it. Babysitting was definitely one up on where I'd just come from.

'Sure!'

'Excellent. Listen, do you know any singers?'

I thought about Josh singing in the bath and dismissed the image immediately.

'Not really.'

'Shame.' She tipped some cigarette ash into one of the flower buckets. 'That's what I *really* am, see? I'm just getting a band together.'

'What kind of band?'

'Kind of bhangra gangsta, do you know what I mean?'

I could see immediately why she thought I might know lots of people in those kinds of bands and nodded my head sagely. Finally the phone rang.

'Yeah? . . . Stodger. Yeah . . . No, I have left, yeah . . . No, I just came by to pick up some stuff, innit? I'm going to Bhutan . . . Yeah, it's in Peru, innit? . . . Maybe a year, maybe two . . . No, I don't think you can motorbike all the way there. There's an ocean or summink . . . No, I'll write to you. I will . . . Yeah. OK. Bye.'

She slammed the phone down, and reverted back to her normal voice.

'Where did you meet him?' I asked, genuinely curious.

'Oh, he said he was putting a band together,' she said dismissively. 'So I slept with him and everything, and next thing he's round here like effin' Hugh Grant every day of the week.'

I wasn't surprised. His gratitude must have been overwhelming.

The day passed in an easy round of selling the occasional bouquet, rearranging the occasional arrangement, cups of tea, and one and a half hour lunch breaks. I could tell I was going to like it here. Mrs Bigelow returned about four thirty.

'Hello, Biggie,' I said, quite innocently. She stared at me as if I'd just bitten her.

'It's Mrs Bigelow, as I thought you knew.'

'Erm, yes, sorry, Mrs Bigelow.'

'Did you have a busy day? You!' – indicating Chali – 'Cash up, please, madam, if it isn't too much trouble.'

''Ave you forgotten how to count again, Biggie? You ought to get out more.'

Biggie hissed at her and pretended to talk to me whilst watching Chali like a hawk. This didn't surprise me; Chali had already informed me that she used the float to supplement her meagre income, so I merely stared straight ahead in a neutral fashion until I was dismissed with a sniff from Biggie, suggesting that if I really, really behaved myself, one day I might get a set of keys.

It was bliss coming home when it was still light. I banged in the hall joyously shouting, 'Hi, honeys! I'm home!' and went straight through to the kitchen to start chopping onions for Josh.

I nearly threw up when I saw Kate was still there.

'*What*??? Are you OK? Did you take the day off work?'

'No,' she said quietly, 'I left early.'

'What happened – did the junior doctors form an action corps and get you released?'

'No . . . I just felt like an early night.'

Josh popped his head round the door. 'Holly, is that you? Can you take over suicide watch for me?'

'OK.' I nodded.

'Oh, and if you're chopping those onions, could you do them a bit finer this time?'

'OK, MR PRISSY.'

I sat down carefully. 'Ehm, Kate, you know, sometimes, bad things happen to good people.'

'Bugger off.'

'Okey-dokey. Read my lips. He – is – not – going –

to – phone – you. OK? You had a lovely night, he was clearly a dickhead and you will never hear from him again. But look on the bright side: at least you didn't take your knickers off, and that's what I'd have done, so reclaim your self-respect, girl. *Comprendez*? *Capisce*?'

Kate looked at me with pained eyes. 'Holly?' she said weakly.

'Yes?' Tough love. It always works.

'Would you mind watching the phone while I go to the toilet?'

'Argh. If he phones whilst you go to the toilet I am going to tell him you hate him and put the phone down on him, as it will save you the bother of doing it in two years time if you actually had a relationship with this man.'

'You don't know him!'

'Neither do you! You think he's Kevin Costner!'

She shrugged. I shrugged back at her and picked up the bag of onions, as she started manhandling her mobile and her pager into her dressing gown pockets and sidled backwards out of the room with the phone cord.

I hollered for Josh.

'*Do* something with her.'

'Sorry, darling – you know how much she listens to me. Why don't we all have a nice dinner and forget about it?'

'Huh.'

Kate marched back into the room.

'OK, that's enough,' she announced stridently, picking up the various bits of electric equipment.

'Oh no!' I whispered to Josh. 'She's reached breaking point! This is where she decides to start really beating up on herself for standing around waiting for a man to phone and then decides to get drunk, then phones up all her ex-boyfriends at four o'clock in the morning and berates them for treating her so badly, then falls asleep in a pool of her own vomit and wakes up overcome by self-disgust and remorse.'

'I give up,' said Kate. 'This is ridiculous. I am an adult, after all.'

Josh sniggered at me.

'Glass of wine, Holl?'

'And my old address book, please,' I replied glumly.

Four

Josh explained his party invitation strategies over dinner.

'OK, there's this girl in the office called Sophie, right? She's really gorgeous . . .'

'Is she blonde, posh and up herself?' said Kate, restored to near-normal service, and starving after her long vigil. How anyone could sit in a kitchen for forty-eight hours and forget there were one hundred and sixty-six Penguins in the cupboard was beyond me, but love does funny things. Kate was one of those people who complain that when they're depressed 'the weight just falls off me; I can't eat a thing; it's awful.'

'Ehm . . . well, she is blonde, and she did go to Cheltenham Ladies. Why?'

'No reason.'

'No, she is definitely not "up herself", as you so charmingly put it. In fact, she was in the top six of her year at the bar.'

'And she told you this, did she? You didn't find out from anyone else?'

'No, she told me.'

'Well, that proves it then,' said Kate, mopping up the remnants of her coq au vin. 'Definitely up herself.'

'She sounds nice,' I said comfortingly.

'Oh, she's brilliant. Normally she spends weekends in the country, but I've thought of a foolproof plan to get her to come to our party.'

'Oh no,' said Kate. She was obviously more used to Josh's seduction attempts than I was, but I did recall a few.

'It's not the one where you've got leukaemia, is it?'

'No!'

'Exchange student visiting?'

'No!'

'We're her possible half-sisters?'

'Oh, for goodness' sake!'

'Tell the truth, Josh.'

Josh hung his head.

'OK . . . um, well, I was going to tell her that you two were interested in reading for the bar, and could she come along and give you some tips.'

'What???!!!' we cried simultaneously.

'What's "the bar"?' I asked.

'And *that's* how you're planning on getting Sophie into bed?' asked Kate incredulously.

'Don't be disgusting.'

'Josh, you know, bed is not necessarily disgusting,' I said, refilling his wine glass. 'It's just been so long you can't remember.'

'I can't believe you think that that might get a girl to come to a party with you.' Kate was still amazed. 'Why don't you just ask her straight out if she'd like to come?'

'Ehm, well . . . because she might think I'm just trying to get her into bed.'

'But you *are*! You are, aren't you? Please say yes.'

'Yes, yes, of course. God, sometimes I think you lot would like to see me go and bugger Danny La Rue, but it's not going to happen.' He sighed. 'I hope. God, I don't know why it's all so damn complicated. I just want to, you know, meet someone nice to hold hands with, and talk about things.'

Kate and I stared at each other.

'Are you completely smooth in front, like an Action Man?' I asked him. He grimaced at me and went to fetch the rhubarb tart.

'Just ask her to the party,' said Kate. 'Look at you. You're cute. You're blond. You're posh. You're practically clones of each other . . .'

'Except you're not up yourself,' I added quickly, kicked myself under the table, then added: 'and I'm sure she isn't either.'

'. . . why wouldn't she come?'

Josh looked at us mournfully, holding the tart between his Heal's oven gloves.

Kate sighed. 'And yes, we will pretend that we are interested in the bar.'

Josh grinned and plonked the tart down with a flourish.

'Really, you won't regret it. You'll love her. Do you know, she stables her own ponies?'

'We love her already,' said Kate.

'And oh!' he said, as if he'd just remembered it. He got out of striking distance. 'She's a potential Conservative candidate.'

I snuck some coq au vin into Addison's room and didn't bother to tell him Josh had cooked it, in case he was into chicks that did that kind of thing. He waved a hand at me without turning round, which I'd learned meant he was in the middle of composing a particularly fluent line of code and was uninterruptible. I liked to think of him like Mozart, enraptured by his muse, except at the end of Mozart writing something he got lots of nice twiddly noises, and I had no idea what spilled out the end of Addison's frantic typing.

I sat down on the floor and started playing with a doll shaped like Jean-Luc Picard while he finished. I also picked at his chicken. Eventually, he turned round.

'How goes it?' I asked him, handing him a knife and fork. Addison stared at the food for a bit, then launched into it as if he hadn't eaten for a week, which would have surprised nobody.

'Hnfu bad,' he said, through a mouthful of pesto mash. 'It's boring really.'

'Not to me,' I said. I hoped he was designing something unbelievably hi-tech that would help disabled children and revolutionize the world.

'Well,' he sighed, 'I programme C++ and edit AVID.'

'Huh.'

'Would you mind not fiddling with that,' he said, indicating the doll. 'It's limited edition.'

'Sure,' I said, putting it down carefully. I forgive a lot in people whose eyelashes scratch their cheekbones.

'So . . . have you decided who to invite to the singles party yet?'

'Is that for real?' sighed Addison, putting down his forkful of carrot julienne. 'I hate parties.'

'Why?' I asked.

'Well,' he said, twisting himself nervously, 'I don't know if you've noticed, but . . . I'm actually quite shy.'

I choked, and tried to turn it into a cough.

'*Really*? No, actually, I hadn't noticed.'

'Yeah . . . I don't really like meeting people that much.'

I nodded sagely. 'Yes, I'm quite shy myself. In fact, you know, we could escape that night, go out somewhere else . . .'

'I don't really like going out much either,' he said apologetically. 'Do you think I'm weird?'

I shook my head. 'No. You know, really, it's not that great out there in the whole . . . big, world thing. You're not missing much.'

He smiled with relief.

'I'm really glad you moved in,' he said. A flame lit up in my heart like a pilot light. I gave him my patented doe-eyed sincere look.

'I'm glad too.'

He smiled shyly. 'Ehm, actually, there was someone I wanted to invite.'

'Yes?' I said coyly.

'Come here,' he said, and beckoned me over to his computer screen. I got up, trying not to trip over the extension wires in my excitement. He clicked his mouse on a corner icon and suddenly a face filled half the screen. A big, flat, potato-like face. With a moustache. On the other half was what appeared to be a continuing dialogue in two different colours of text.

'This is Claudia,' he said.

I peered more closely at the pixels, just to confirm that it was, in fact, a woman and not the lumpy builder I'd originally taken it for.

'Who's Claudia?' I asked petulantly.

'Ehm . . . she's kind of . . . like, my girlfriend,' said Addison, blushing.

I sat down heavily, then got up promptly when I realized I was sitting on the remnants of coq au vin.

'Oh!' I said, trying to make my voice sound not too hysterical. 'I didn't know you had a girlfriend! Where do you keep her? Under the bed? Ha ha!'

'Well, we've never met.'

'Ah, that famous imaginary girlfriend?'

'No, she's real all right,' he said proudly. 'I met her on the Internet.'

Yes, well, I'd gathered that.

'How do you know that's her picture?' I said, squinting at the troll-like image. 'She could . . . you know, be really ugly or something.'

Addison smiled. 'I know,' he said. 'But, even if that isn't her . . . well, I wouldn't care.'

'As long as she's a girl,' I said. 'And not twelve.'

'No, there –' he pointed to the picture again – 'she's holding up her driving licence.'

She looked like the Rosemary West mug shot.

'She looks nice,' I said.

'She is. She knows more about *Star Trek* than anyone I've ever met.'

I started fiddling with the Jean-Luc Picard doll again.

'That's very romantic,' I said. 'So . . . are you going to invite her to the party?'

'Well . . . she lives in Baltimore . . .'

Hurrah!

'. . . and she doesn't much like leaving the house either . . . But, you know, I will ask her!'

'What does she do?' I stumbled on, torturing myself.

'She does C++ too,' he said proudly. 'She works on government defence programmes. She's got security clearance and everything.'

Wow. A fat agoraphobic bomb-maker four thousand miles away was doing better with Addison than I was.

'If neither of you leaves the house, and you live on different continents,' I mused, 'do you think there's a lot of future in the relationship?'

Addison shrugged. 'Well, you know, science can do a lot these days.'

I struggled to work out what he was referring to, thought it might be sperm, decided it couldn't be, realized it had to be, and nearly threw up.

'I bet you wish they'd hurry up and invent the teleport, eh?' I said.

'Actually, it's not worth the trouble to invent the technology to evaporate and replicate an individual,' he said gravely. 'You're on much safer ground when you work at speeding up transportation as quickly as possible.'

Snap! I suddenly realized that I'd pulled Jean-Luc Picard's arm off. I held it behind my back.

'So, this is serious, then?'

He blinked at me, but I got distracted and yelled before I'd had the chance to think about it: 'Oh my God, the face is coming to life!!'

At first Addison's eyes darted to where my trembling finger was pointing like some harbinger of doom in an Edgar Allan Poe story, but he quickly relaxed.

'Don't worry – that's just a little computer thing we do. When Claudia's typing to me, her picture moves like it's speaking.'

And sure enough, Claudia was making like a ventriloquist's doll while words were coming up on the screen. It was reminiscent of the *Bride of Chucky*.

'What's she saying?'

Addison went coy.

'Oh, just, "Hi, how're you doing?" That kind of stuff.'

I leaned over to the computer screen.

'"I salute you, Captain?" Is that you?'

'Maybe.'

'Can I say hello?'

'Ehm, best let me.'

'Otherwise it'll be coming out of your mouth on her end?'

'Uh huh.'

'Actually, you know, Addison, I think maybe you are a bit weird.'

My panic had somewhat abated. I was still pissed off, but hey, she was there and I was here, standing and talking to him – and he was about to tell her about me. She might even get jealous. Low tactics, certainly, but necessary ones.

Addison started to type and I peered over his shoulder.

'Hello there,' he started. Seemingly unsure of how to proceed, he pressed return.

'Rn't I yr Uhuru tonight?' shot back.

'Addison!' I exclaimed.

'What?' he said, embarrassed. 'It's like a pet name.'

'What, a pet whore?' I said, then wished I hadn't. 'I didn't mean that.'

'Of course you are,' he typed back, ignoring me. 'I'm here with a friend.'

'???????????????' came up.

'Holly, my flatmate.'

Ha, that'll get you, I thought meanly.

'IS THAT A GIRL'S NAME?'

'I don't know, is that a girl's moustache?' I said to myself.

'Y.'

'DOES SHE LIKE STAR TREK?'

Addison looked at me and I nodded my head vehemently, still hanging on to the mutilated Jean-Luc.

'Y.'

'FAVOURITE CHARACTER?'

Oh God, I didn't care.

'Scotty?' I said hopefully to Addison, who dutifully typed it in.

'FAVOURITE NEXT GENERATION CHARACTER?'

Oh, I was in deep doo here.

'Ehm . . . still Scotty, definitely.'

'What, you mean from "Relics" where they step back in time and meet mirror images of themselves from the original crew?'

'Yes, that one.'

'Wow.'

There was a long pause whilst we waited for Claudia's answer. Finally, the strange mouth thing crept back to life.

'IS SHE YR GIRLFRIEND?'

Even I was surprised. Addison looked distraught.

'Oh no. What should I do?'

'Tell her, "no"?' I suggested. 'Point out the word "flatmate". Oh, they don't have that in America, do they? They call it "roommate". Maybe she thinks "flatmate" means "lover"!?'

He practically stumbled over the keys to type: 'No, of course not! Don't be silly!'

Thanks a lot.

'How could I possibly prefer anyone to you? Even if she does recognize Scotty's performance in "Relics".'

I sighed and hid the *Star Trek* doll under a full-size Darth Vader head.

'So, I'll see you at the party, then,' I said to Addison breezily.

'Yes, OK then, I'll see you at the party,' was what he clearly *meant* to say. Unfortunately, the words didn't come out of his mouth but were typed at high velocity on to the keyboard. Before he could think, he'd pressed 'return'.

He stared at me open-mouthed in horror at what he had done.

'Addison, you're a true cyborg,' I said. 'Did you get your navel removed and replaced with a three-way socket? Where's your bar code tattoo?'

'It's not funny,' he said. 'I'm so much more used to typing than . . . She'll think I'm making fun of her.'

'Or she might come,' I said, for him. The mouth on the screen was no longer gasping like a fish. He was studying it intently. He actually seemed slightly hopeful.

'Well, if she doesn't come, I'll dance with you,' I said. 'Maybe they'll play some Kraftwerk.'

'I love them,' he said, still staring angstily at the screen.

'I knew that,' I said. 'Now, compose your letter of apology. In Klingon.' He smiled, and I beat a retreat.

I heard 'Holly, have you seen my Jean-Luc Picard doll?' being yelled after me, but I pretended not to.

Chali wanted to know exactly what kind of music would be playing and what kinds of drugs would be available at the party before she even attempted to decide whether to consider acknowledging the invitation.

'Snoopy Dogg Dogg? Vodka jelly?'

She sneered at me, whilst sloppily tying up a princess bouquet – not the easiest of double acts to pull off. Mrs Bigelow had 'just popped in' to see how we were doing and Chali had accused her of spying, whereupon there'd been a bit of a yelling match, so she was now putting together the deliveries very, very slowly. I was supposed to be watching her and learning, but all I was learning was how I would put bouquets together if I were underwater. It was the week after I'd found out about Claudia. I was dealing with it, but slowly.

'Is it going to be full of old folk?'

I hadn't considered asking my mother – she could get down and frug with the best of them. Parents at parties stopped when you were of snoggable age – or at least, stayed upstairs praying – and started up again when you got engaged, there to continue for the rest of your life, I assumed. I explained this.

'No, I meant, lots of people, like, your age and that.'

I hit her with one of the thorny twigs.

'Mid twenties is NOT OLD.'

'Mid twenties, my bum. You're nearly thirty. And then, your life is over.'

'My life will *not* be over. Anyway, I won't be doing this when I'm thirty. Probably won't even be in the country.'

'Really? Why, what are you going to do?'

I had no idea.

'Oh, there's lots of possibilities. Lots of things.'

'Yeah, like climbing up on a shelf.'

'Shut up. Actually, you can't come to our party. It's only for mature, elegant individuals.'

'In smocks?'

Chali had on skinny little bootleg trousers and something chiffony. Her black hair curled in a long thick plait down to her waist. I was wearing a smock.

'Well, fine,' I said. 'If you want to miss out on all those City Porsche owners, that's up to you.' I hadn't forgotten the 'Gareth' incident. 'Or maybe you'd rather be going out with people who keep dogs on pieces of string.'

She didn't say anything for a bit. Then:

'You don't look like you've got lots of rich mates.'

'Well, you don't look like you jump up and down on the spot for ten hours a night and call it fun, but you do.'

'Hnn. Who's the DJ going to be then?'

There was a bit of controversy about this in the flat.

Josh obviously wanted to do it, but if we let him, he'd play Scritti Politti all night.

'He's called Fatboy Josh,' I said. 'He's great. He's got a real, ehm, vibe thing, etcetera.'

Chali glanced at me suspiciously.

'Can I bring a friend?'

'You have to, that's the rule of the party. You have to bring a single friend.'

'All my mates are single.'

'OK. You know, Chali, I KNOW you're nineteen. It won't last. Get over it.'

'I wonder if I'll get droopy upper arms when I'm old, like you?'

'Maybe you'll die of a poisoned ecstasy tablet first,' I said moodily.

'What a way to go, though,' she replied.

'Are you coming or not?'

'I suppose we can drop in on our way out for the evening. You'll probably be finished about two, won't you?'

Two seemed to me an OK time to finish a party.

'Well, we can go out properly after it. Flint!'

I had no idea what flint meant, and I wasn't about to demean myself by asking.

'Flint!' I said, cheerfully.

Four hours before the party was officially supposed to begin, three of us sat tensely around the kitchen table. The house was immaculate, and Kate wouldn't let any of us move, so we were just sitting and staring into space. We were also forbidden from opening any of the wine or touching any of the little nibbly things the caterers had dropped off, which was in itself a form of torture. There were flowers everywhere, as filched by me. Filching was not a problem; Chali took so much she'd get the blame anyway. And, morally, they were paying me just above minimum wage, so these were my contribution to the party. Kate and Josh had paid for everything else, hence the embargo on the mini pizzas. It felt a bit unfair to ask Addison for a contribution, given that a party was being imposed on his living space, but he had bought his own bolt for his door. I assumed it was for the party and not, e.g., to keep me out.

It had been a really beautiful May day, which should have gotten everyone in a party mood, but as we'd been inside cleaning all day and filling the bath with ice for the beer before remembering that we were all hot and sweaty and needed a bath, we were a bit cranky.

'OK,' Josh was saying, 'so, the champagne has been delivered.'

'What exactly are we celebrating, again?' asked Kate. 'Our communal loneliness?'

'We could have a competition,' I added. 'See who's got the most frozen lasagne boxes in their bin.'

'Once again,' said Josh, quite heavily for him, 'we are celebrating our youth and success and the beginning of summer.'

'Through the medium of canapés.'

'I wish we had a croquet lawn,' Josh sighed.

'We've got a fire escape,' I pointed out. It was rusty to the point of extreme danger and if you fell off you would arrive in downstairs' midden of a garden and be eaten by triffids, but it was outside, and it belonged to us.

'Great. That ought to compensate. We can take bets on who's going to be the first person to fall through it. OK, Kate, where are we with the guest list again?'

Kate sounded bored. 'Elton John, Elizabeth Taylor, the Beckhams, the Olivers, and an assortment of weather girls.'

'*Really*? Oh no, I mean, ha ha ha,' said Josh.

'The Jameses, who are bringing their other mates from the office; Sophie and all your poncey lawyer friends; Holly's florist mate; some of the old college crowd, who will sit in a corner and ignore everyone else all night. And us. Including Addison. Maybe.'

'How many's that?'

'About fourteen.'

'Oh God; we're catering for two hundred.'

'Well, I like sausage rolls,' I said, staring at the massive platters of food. 'But maybe not for the rest of my natural life.'

'All that houmous,' moaned Josh.

'Well, they're all bringing people,' said Kate. 'The Jameses have got me to deal with if they don't. So, I wouldn't worry.'

'Please can I have a beer?' I said.

'No,' said Kate. 'You'll have passed out by the time everyone arrives.'

'On one beer?'

'On the beer after the beer after the beer after the beer after the beer.'

We stared into space again.

'*What* time do you think they'll be here?' whined Josh, for about the billionth time.

'Either you stop asking or I'll slap you on the back of the legs,' said Kate.

'Don't have kids,' I said, with a shudder.

'Why would I need kids when I have you and Josh?'

'What about Addison?'

'And my autistic son, Addison.'

'Maybe he can just be your son-in-law,' I said.

'You know, interestingly enough, the odds of you and Addison getting married are almost *exactly the same* as you being my biological daughter.'

I ballooned my cheeks and blew the air out of them slowly to stop myself from biting her.

'Well, can we go to the pub then? That's what *most* people do when they're having a party. Relax, throw a couple of things together, then just let people turn up.'

'Do they?' asked Josh in alarm.

'Yes,' said Kate. 'That's why *most* parties are rubbish.'

The phone rang. It was one of the Jameses, phoning up to cancel. Just as well he didn't turn up to tell us in person; Kate might have eaten him.

'Well, either you turn up tonight or you don't bother turning up on Monday morning,' I heard her say menacingly down the telephone. Josh and I looked at each other with panicked expressions on our faces.

'You can't sack someone for not turning up to your party!' we chorused, as soon as she'd slammed down the phone.

'Why not?'

'Ehm, because it's wrong?'

'Why? It was wrong of him to lie about his grandmother being ill.'

'*If* he was lying,' said Josh.

'He was lying. He's a very good liar. That's why I hired him. He'll be here.'

The phone rang again.

'I'll get it!' yelled Josh, anxious to spare some other poor bastard.

'Ehm, yes, she is. Hold on a moment. Who's calling please?'

Josh slowly put his hand over the receiver and turned to face us with a dramatic expression on his face. He was clearly making the most of the moment.

'Ahem . . . Skates?'

'Uh huh?'

'It's someone called "John" for you. Or Kevin Costner, if you will.'

Kate's head shot up as if she'd just been goosed.

'Oh my God! But I haven't had a bath!'

'It's the *telephone*, not the smell-o-phone.'

'Tell him you're not here,' I hissed. 'Be dark and mysterious. And Josh: stop making camp remarks.'

'A month ago I could have been dark and mysterious,' Kate hissed back at me, beckoning for the receiver. 'But now I am *absolutely desperate*.'

'Fair enough.'

'Hello,' she purred down the telephone. Here was one man who wouldn't be getting a sacking. A sucking, maybe.

'Really? Oh, what a shame,' she purred on. 'Never mind: how *was* America?'

'The elder one was fine but the little one's had a bit of a cough,' I said to Josh under my breath.

'I'm terribly sorry, but we're rather in the middle of a party . . .'

Josh and I made huge 'no' motions in front of the phone, shaking our heads and waving our arms.

'You could come if you like . . .'

Josh mimed extreme despair as she gave our address. I stuck my fingers down my throat and made elaborate vomiting motions.

'OK, see you later!' And she made that weird giggling noise again.

'Yes!' she yelled as she put the phone down, bouncing her fist off the table.

'Here we go again,' said Josh quietly.

'Kate, by way of celebration, don't you think we should open a bottle of that wine?'

'No!'

Four hours later we were still sitting at the kitchen table, although we were a bit smarter. Josh, bless him, had his dinner jacket on. Huge amounts of hearty teasing hadn't persuaded him to dress otherwise, so we were contenting ourselves by calling him by his surname and ordering him to bring us drinks. As soon as nine o'clock came, Kate had sanctioned the opening of the wine, and we fell on it like ravenous beasts.

'What if nobody turns up?' I asked, cramming a handful of prawn thingies into my mouth.

'I'll kill myself,' said Josh. 'My life will be of no meaning.'

'I won't care,' said Kate. 'John will be here.'

'Aha – two such brilliantly well-balanced attitudes. I'm going to get Addison. The party's officially started, and he promised to be here.'

I went and knocked on his door. There was the heavy sound of bolts being drawn back that made me think unpleasantly of right-wing militia groups.

'Hey there . . . are you OK?'

'Unh huh.'

'It's the party now. Don't you want to come and have a glass of wine?'

'Are there other people in the house?'

'Nope, not yet. Come *on*.'

'You know, once I was in a house that burned down.'

I stopped in my tracks and stared at him. A voluntary phrase about his own life was almost completely unheard of.

'Oh my God! What happened?'

He ignored me.

'So, I was thinking, maybe I shouldn't have the bolts, in case there's a fire . . .'

'Did anyone die in the fire?'

He blinked.

'Yes. My father. So, do you think I should take the bolts down?'

I was utterly dumbfounded and simply stared at him, my heart aching.

'I'm so . . . I'm really, really sorry.'

'It was a long time ago. Do you think Kate will let me have a beer?'

If she knew this, she'd let him have her car.

'Ehm, I expect so,' I felt completely disconnected, and simply followed him through into the kitchen. I had two alive and rudely healthy parents, even if they did live at opposite ends of the country and hate each other's guts, and a sister who drove me crazy, and this was all way beyond me.

I wanted to grab him and sit on his lap and never let him go. So, I did the next best thing and got him a beer. He didn't mention it again.

Five

At ten thirty, Josh announced he was heading into the bathroom to slit his wrists, and would anyone like a beer while he was in there, since we had one hundred and fifty, and there were still only four of us.

I wasn't adding to the party mood at all – and neither was the music. We were letting Josh play 'Wood Beez' in an attempt to get it out of his system – post Addison's bombshell I was just staring into space. Oh my God, no wonder he was how he was. I was overflowing with love. I would make things OK for him. I would take care of him. I . . . well, I wouldn't light any open fires around him.

Kate was hyperventilating in case she'd given John Doe the wrong directions. Addison having collected his beer, dripping wet from the melted ice in the bath, had disappeared again. In honour of the occasion he was wearing shorts and a T-shirt with the cover of *The Wasp Factory* on it. Josh had loosened his bow tie in despair, and looked pleasingly *Brideshead*. I had debated with myself whether to tell them about Addison and decided no, there are better times to discuss enormous emotional trauma than right before a party. During a party, shouted out at high volume, whereby you'll completely forget about it the next day – that's fine.

Finally, at ten to eleven, the doorbell rang. Our collective sigh of relief was enormous, and Josh strode to the door manfully. There, attractive and composed, with a rather nice bottle of wine, was someone who couldn't have more been called Sophie if they'd had it tattooed on their forehead – not that a Sophie would ever entertain the possibility of getting a tattoo.

'Everyone, this is Sophie,' beamed Josh.

'No, really?' said Kate. I looked at her. She was usually beyond aggressive to women who crossed Josh's path. If the girls were nice, it was like watching *1984*. Fortunately they all tended to be blonde, posh and up themselves. Now I come to think of it, they were usually called Sophie as well.

'Nice to meet you. I'm Kate, and this is Holly.'

'Hellayerh!' she said, managing to use a quite extraordinary number of syllables. 'Naice to meet you! Nearw, which one of you is interested in joining the bar?'

Kate and I made Bugs Bunny-style simultaneous pointing motions at each other.

'Both of you? How farbulous!' She plonked down her pony-riding bottom. 'Gin and tonic, please, Joshua. I say, wasn't there supposed to be a party? Or was this just a ruse to get me to come along, hya hya hya.'

'No, actually, the ruse was . . .' I started, but Josh gave me an imploring look, so I shut up. Fortunately Sophie didn't appear to be the listening-to-people-when-they-talk type.

'The bar, yar? You know, I was in the top six of my year group there.'

'Were you *really*?' Kate said elaborately. 'Well, gosh, that makes you better than us.'

'Oh no, I'm sure it doesn't,' said Sophie, with a smile. 'First question though, is getting in. It's pretty tough. I mean, it's not quite "what does your father do . . . ?"'

'He works for social services,' I said promptly. Which was true.

'Oh. Well, you know, never mind. What about yours?'

'He's a GP,' said Kate, through gritted teeth.

'Oh, how very *mid*! That will do you no harm at all, ectually. Of course, my daddy's just a farmer, isn't he, Josh?'

'Eh?' said Josh, who was busy carving up lemons.

'I said, my daddy's just a farmer, *isn't* he?'

'Ehm, no, actually; Sophie's dad owns half of Cheshire! Ha!'

'Ha ha ha! Well, not *exactly* half.'

I glanced at Kate. Her face was a picture.

Josh brought over the drinks and sat next to Sophie, gazing at her adoringly.

'Next thing, you really have to grease up to any judges you know. Of course, I'm only doing it en route to a safe Tory seat – once we get rid of this bunch of charlatans, naturally.'

Thankfully, the doorbell rang. Kate and I both jumped up to get it, but I let her win. My heart sank when I heard an uncharacteristic yelp of delight. And, sure enough, she led in John, her face bright and glowing. He was definitely extremely suave, with a soft shirt on, which even though it *looked* just like an ordinary shirt in terms of buttons, collar, cuffs etc, was somehow also deeply, deeply tasteful and expensive. He was exceptionally handsome. He did resemble Kevin Costner, but in this light I realized it was Kevin Costner in his eighties baseball movies and not in his nineties post apocalyptic piss-drinking phase. He handed over a bottle of champagne and another of wine.

'You know Holly and Josh, of course . . .' We all nodded, although we didn't know him at all. 'And this is Sophie.'

I could hear from the faint tremor in her voice exactly what she was thinking: this is Sophie. She is blonde and she owns Cheshire. Do you prefer her to me? Well, do you?

John simply shook her hand, whilst Sophie giggled and blushed up at him.

'Oh, hello, John . . . Ooh, you're American. It's so lovely to meet an American.'

'Sophie was in the top six at her year in the bar,' I said helpfully. Kate and Josh both looked upset. 'But she's never met an American.'

'No, of course I have, Holly!' said Sophie earnestly. 'And I think they're really nice.'

'Well, thank you, ma'am.' John pretended to tip his cap at her. 'Any place a body can git a drink round here?'

'Listen to that lovely accent,' said Sophie.

Kate sidled up to me and grabbed the nearest thing that came to hand.

'Hit her with this and I'll throw her over the fire escape,' she hissed.

'It's a plastic colander.'

'So? Hit her a lot.'

The doorbell rang again, and I went to answer it. It was Chali and six complete strangers, most of whom were exceptionally scruffy, except Chali, of course, who was clearly their queen, and one other person who was unconscious and being carried. I was so pleased to see someone *I* knew that I went completely over the top, given that she was a work colleague and I'd known her for less than a month.

When I returned to the kitchen, the new age travellers in tow, Josh was still up fixing a drink for John, who was sitting between Kate and Sophie, who were both desperately trying to talk to him.

'So, here we are then!' I said stupidly. OK, so there were some people here, lots of booze, lots of food, music, candles and low lighting . . . yet, somehow, it didn't quite *feel* like an actual party. The temptation was to say, 'OK, everybody – start!'

'OK, everybody,' said Josh, popping open a bottle of champagne, 'start!' and he turned the volume up on 'Pray like Aretha Franklin'.

When the new age travellers saw all the canapés, their eyes lit up, they dropped the unconscious one in the doorway and leapt across the room, pockets ajar. Chali, however, stopped them with a raise of her hand. As we all turned to watch her, she felt in her minuscule handbag. I watched, fascinated to see what she would bring out – a home-made cheesecake? Crack cocaine? In fact, she brought out a CD with a pure white cover on it, cut off poor old Scritti, and inserted it.

Immediately the house started to bang as if it were about to fall apart, and the new age travellers all started to hop up and down. The doorbell rang again. The first person tripped over the guy in the doorway and spilt some of their booze. Prawn wingwangs were suddenly being crammed into faces and jammed into the carpet. Fags were lit.

'OK, everyone!' announced Chali. 'Start!'

Amazingly, after that, the place began to fill up. OK, I didn't actually know that many people who were there, but still, it was pleasingly noisy. I decided to get seriously drunk, to compensate for not knowing many people at my own party. I talked confusingly for a bit to some of the Jameses, who had all turned up from the pub in suits and ties, and seemed nervous.

One had even brought Kate another present, in case it was a continuation of her birthday party. I told him it was mine and took the present, but disappointingly it was a gizmo-gadget for her hand-held computer that told you share prices on the moon or something. I tucked it away anyway, in case I ever had to give Kate something.

Then I bounced through to the kitchen, carefully avoiding old friends from college who would doubtless be very happy to ask me how my career was going whilst talking about their new cars and that endlessly fascinating topic, London house prices. And, in fact, if I wasn't very much mistaken, one of them was checking their watch, worrying about the babysitter. Argh.

Back in the kitchen, Josh was sitting at the table desperately trying to pretend that he was in a party of four when he clearly wasn't – Kate and Sophie were both facing directly away from him. I sat down next to him and poured us both another glass of champagne.

'How's it going?'

'Oh, fine, fine,' he said, in his usual enthusiastic tones.

'No, I mean with Sophie.'

Sophie was currently telling John why she was going to be the new Margaret Thatcher, but without the wishy-washy social policies. John appeared to be listening. Kate was wearing a very tight-lipped smile.

'Oh, yes, yes, coming along quite nicely.'

'Josh, she's completely ignoring you.'

'Well, that's nice and normal, isn't it?'

I realized how hurt he was.

'No it's not! Either you should be in there fighting for her, or give her up as someone who's too up themselves. Look at that guy too! He's like a pig in shit.'

'I think they call them pigs in a blanket in America.'

'Really? Well, that's what he is.'

'So, you think I should win her back?' he asked, perking up.

'Well, I'm not sure you had her,' I said tactfully. His face fell. 'But, you know – yeah! Courtly love and all that.'

'Yes, right. That's exactly what I'm going to do. Sophie?'

'. . . that's why I love America: it's so classless,' Sophie was saying to a polite-looking John. 'Yes, Joshua? Oh, Joshua, *please* could you mix John and I another jug of Pimms?'

'Sure,' said Josh. I nudged him. 'And . . . I'll be wanting to talk to you when I get back!'

'Ooh, do you think I'm in trouble?' She nudged John flirtatiously.

Kate jumped out of her seat and came over to join me.

'Complete bitch!' she said loudly.

'What's that . . . you've got a terrible itch?' I said, conscious of our proximity to the other two at the table.

'No, didn't you hear me? I said, "What a COMPLETE BITCH!"'

'OK, OK, calm down. It shows he's not up to much either, doesn't it? And there are lots of other people here.'

'He didn't have much of a choice, with her sticking her BIG FAT BOVINE TORY TITS in his face.'

'OK, do you know what? I think we should perhaps go next door . . . Let's go dancing, shall we?'

I pushed a spluttering Kate out of the room. Josh's room was being used as a pot-smoking den, but the living room was full of people waving their arms in the air like they just didn't care, so we headed there. Chali was doing elegant Indian dancing to house music and looked fabulous. The crusties were all dancing round her like gnome servants. I collared one of them and shoved him and Kate together.

'OK! Dance,' I instructed them. The crusty immediately began to hop up and down in Kate's direction. Kate made a couple of sulky movements.

'Oh, you know, I can't be bothered. I think I might go to bed.'

'I think one of the Jameses and some young lovely have already thought of that,' I told her.

'Oh, for Christ's sake! What is this, a party for fourteen-year-olds? Did you see which one it was? I'll be having a word with him on Monday.'

'I'm afraid not,' I said, making a mental note to clear them out of there as soon as was humanly possible.

'This is turning into the worst . . .' started Kate

glumly. Then her face lit up and I followed her line of gaze.

'There you are,' said the tall American. 'You just disappeared and left me with that pony-riding politician girl.'

He smoothly bypassed the crusty.

'In America we call that cruel and unusual punishment,' he said, and moved very close to Kate.

'Can I cut in?'

Kate could only nod mutely, and he put his arms round her, in that half-necking/half-dancing thing. And they were away.

Balls! He was nice! Noticing the crusty starting to bounce in my direction I hit a hasty retreat.

Back in the kitchen, hotbed of action, Sophie was still carrying on exactly as before. In his place, of course, Josh was listening to her with a dreamy expression on his face. Oh no. And, worse than that, the party was now swinging with a life of its own – the dancers were dancing, the snoggers were snogging – and, given the amount of that going on, I would say our singles theme was definitely a success – the potters were potting away . . . and I hadn't found my own group in time. Now I would have to be horrible puppy-like party hostess, bounding from group to group to try and gain acceptance. Arse! And I couldn't go home, as home now had three hundred coats in it! And Addison hadn't bloody joined the party after all. I didn't feel up to going and getting him, not after what I now knew. So, I pretended to be coolly surveying the atmosphere by the fridge, helping people get their beers, that kind of thing.

How annoying – after all, this was supposed to be a singles party, and everyone was just hanging around, talking to their friends! That wasn't how things should be progressing at all. I scanned the room, a tad crossly. In the corner was a tall person who was clearly a friend of Kate or Josh's, judging by the absence of acne scars and slouching. He was wearing a leather jacket and a dark top and, if a bit smooth for my taste, had a nice crinkliness around the eyes. Also, the bloke he was talking to had just disappeared.

OK, I decided. Kate had pulled. Josh was at least being shouted at by the object of his desire. Addison was nowhere to be seen. I had to at least *try*.

I ran my tongue over my teeth and walked up to him brightly.

'Hi there,' I said, as insouciantly as I could, which isn't very. 'Are you having a nice time?'

He looked around slowly and gave me a bit of a once-over. I can't bear that, but it was a singles party.

'It's OK, thanks.'

'Great, well, hi, I'm Holly and I live here.' I gave him a big beaming smile, then, as a nervous tic, ran my tongue over my teeth again. Then I realized I'd just done that, and shut my mouth abruptly. It made an audible noise, like a fish. He glanced at me for another couple of seconds, then seemed to make up his mind about something.

'Well, very nice to meet you, Holly. I'm Geoffrey – I work with Kate. I've been trying to find her, but I couldn't see her, so please tell her I did look in, and it all seemed very nice, and now I must go.'

He started to pull his jacket on. I could feel other people looking at us, and I started improvising desperately.

'Oh, right, Kate made you come, did she? Oh, you can't go – have you had some punch? Why don't you stay for a little bit? I'm sure she'll be right in.'

'I really can't,' he said. His eyes took on a wary, hunted expression. 'I – ehm – I'm double-parked.'

'Oh, did you drive here? What kind of car do you have?'

'Ehm, a Porsche, actually. Right, OK, James,' he yelled to someone I couldn't make out, 'see you Monday! Lovely to meet you!' and he disappeared stage left.

Fuck. I wandered my lonely way back across the room. My only thought was at least no one had seen me, but I looked up and Sophie was staring at me with a malicious look on her face. Fuck, fuck, fuck. I was so glad that, because he had been a bit of a wanker, I was managing to hate myself.

I poured another glass of wine and felt extremely sorry for myself. Then I went and checked in the mirror. Sure enough, I had a bit of prawn vol-au-vent stuck to my chin. Well, *I* knew it was prawn vol-au-vent. To the uninitiated, it could well have been herpes.

I limped back into the party a broken soul. Suddenly, however, out of the corner of my eye I caught a flash of movement by the fire escape . . . It couldn't be. Oh, thank God. There was Addison, sitting outside – outside! I wondered how his eyes were adjusting to the light. Then I noticed that not only was he outside, but he was most definitely talking to someone!

This was all I needed. I was pissed off. It was a well-known fact that Addison spoke only to me and, well, Claudia, I supposed, if you counted that as speaking, and I didn't. A horrid thought struck me – maybe it *was* Claudia. Maybe she'd taken Addison up on his invitation, after all. Oh God. That had to be it. All this time while I was pratting around and worrying about my bloody flatmates, he'd been pinched from under my nose! Cock! I might as well kill myself now.

I leaned over to try and get a better view from the fridge without being seen to actually stomp up and demand to know what she was doing here. Addison's thick black hair was in the way, though, so I leaned over a little bit further and, with a little help from the white wine and, I told myself later, deep despair, found myself falling straight on to the floor with an enormous crash.

The entire party stopped immediately – in fact, I could have sworn there was a record player somewhere, because it was like that noise you hear when someone skites a needle off a disc. A couple of the Jameses laughed, and I cursed them. Josh hopped up worriedly, whilst Sophie appeared faintly amused at Josh's poor old drunken flatmate. And the two heads on the balcony whipped round simultaneously, and annoyingly enough, the one who wasn't Addison was Finn.

'I'm fine! I'm fine! I could only conceivably have hurt my pride and I have none of that anyway!' I shouted immediately, to stop people cooing round me and making concerned noises.

'We once had a parlour maid who drank,' I heard Sophie say.

Addison loomed over me.

'You hurt yourself a lot,' he said carefully.

'It was the floor,' I muttered. 'It attacked me by surprise.'

He extended his hand to me. 'Are you all right?'

'Yes, yes yes.' His large hand took hold of mine and I luxuriated in it as I stood up, accidentally on purpose falling against him. Casually – or, under the circumstances, as casually as I could make it whilst dusting myself down – I looked around the room and pretended to notice Finn for the first time.

'Oh, hello there . . . I'm so sorry, I can't remember your name.'

'Oh, really, are you very drunk?' he asked solemnly. I'd forgotten how annoying he was.

'No!' I spluttered. 'I just, you know, meet so many people it's hard to remember them all.'

'I see. Well, hello there, I'm Finn.'

'Well, yes, ehmm, I'm Holly,' I said, feeling increasingly stupid.

'Err, yes . . . I knew that.'

'So, how do you know Addy?' I said, in a way that might conceivably make it sound like Addison was my live-in boyfriend.

'Addy? Oh, Addison . . . ehm, I don't actually. I just met him – turns out we both went to see the eclipse. Fascinating man. Really, posited some very interesting theories . . . Why, is he your live-in boyfriend?'

'No,' I said crossly, but Addison was only three feet away. 'He's my flatmate.'

'Oh, right . . . nice bloke. Ehm, I know last time we met . . . I'm sorry about the misunderstanding.'

'What misunder – oh, that thing! Don't be silly, I didn't give it a second thought.'

I turned to Addison, in an attempt to convey how close we were. 'Thank you, darling . . . I'm quite fine now.'

'What?' said Addison. 'Oh, you were talking to me.'

'Shall we go back outside? Are you enjoying the outdoors, or do you find it a bit weird; you know, because sometimes the ceiling is blue and sometimes it's dark with little lights?'

'I'm not sure that fire escape of yours is too safe,' said Finn.

I turned round. 'Oh really? How do you know that: string theory?'

'Ehm, no, it's just completely over at an angle . . . Can I get you a drink?'

'No thank you . . . you might chemically alter it, or it might disappear into hyperspace.'

'God, you really stay pissed off at people for a long time, don't you? And also, hyperspace is only theoretical, so it couldn't really turn into the depository for your –'

'Of *course* I'm not pissed off with you,' I sniffed.

I was about to be sultry and elegant for once and wander off with Addison, leaving him there burbling, but suddenly a horrific sight caught the corner of my eye. It was Carol, hatchet-faced harridan of Harlesden, from whom I'd done a runner less than two months before. Fuck knows *what* she was doing here. Must have been a very distant single friend of a single friend. Dressed in a tight TIGHT pink dress which emphasized her orangey tan and carefully applied body make-up (blusher between the breasts, I noticed), she was running a long fingernail along the top of the units, checking for dust, and heading towards the fridge – where we were!

'Argh!' I said in a low voice to Finn. 'Quick, show me what's the matter with the fire escape.'

'What? Sorry, I didn't catch that –'

'Now!' I pushed him towards the kitchen door, practically hiding my face in his jacket. We collapsed down on the rickety brown metal.

'Ehm . . . OK, you see, here, when you sit down on it, it bounces?' said Finn.

'Huh? Oh, yes.' I stole a look back.

'So, I think the tension is probably unsafe . . .'

'I'm sorry, Finn . . . I just had to get away from someone over there.'

He craned his neck around to see.

'Who, her?'

'DON'T LOOK! Yes, her. I used to share a flat with her and she was mean to me. I'm trying to minimize the opportunities during which she can be mean to me again.'

'Oh, is she the one who punched you?'

'Ehm, no, that was somebody else.'

'Oh. Are a lot of people mean to you?'

'Yes. And none of it is ever my fault.'

'I see.'

I craned my neck round just a little to see if I could see her. She was about to open the fridge door when she spotted Addison, that well-known site of great natural beauty. I motioned to Finn to shush and leaned forward to try and hear what she was saying to him.

'Don't you think this kitchen is filthy?' she was saying. 'All this cookware, it simply gathers dust.'

Addison was facing us, and staring straight ahead, bright with embarrassment. She lifted up one ridiculously fingernailed hand. The claws grew bent over the top of her fingers and were painted bright pink, to match her dress. She was wearing three or four rings.

'Carol,' she said. 'Carol Patterson.'

Addison stared at us with a beseeching look in his eye.

'And this is my friend, Farah.'

He started staring at the floor.

'There are two of them?' asked Finn.

'Ehm, yes . . . Farah's on the short side.'

'I see. Oh my God, isn't that a monkey over there?'

'No, that's her.'

'Oh. Whoops.'

'Fine scientist you turn out to be.'

'So, one of the strong silent types, then?' Carol was saying, prodding Addison in the chest with her lethal fingernails. I winced.

'You could say that,' I whispered to Finn. He nodded.

'Ehm, as one of the hostesses, don't you think you ought to be circulating amongst your guests thereby saving Addison, rather than cowering behind the kitchen door spying on them? Just a suggestion,' added Finn hurriedly when he saw my cross face.

'She'll kill me! I never paid the phone bill.'

'You didn't pay the phone bill?' He looked shocked, then tried to retrieve himself. 'Oh well, I mean, right on, sister. Smash the state.'

'You are incredibly self-righteous, do you know that?'

'What? What did I say??'

But he was right in one respect. I would have to go and rescue Addison. Everyone else was ignoring them and he was a drowning man. And, as I knew, here was a man who'd been through enough in his life already.

I stood up shakily.

'OK, I'm going in. Do I look all right?'

'You look fine. Apart from that small piece of cheese attached to your head from when you fell over.'

I rubbed at my face. There was as well.

'Shit. OK, de-cheesed?'

'De-cheesed.'

'You stay here and guard the exits. This is going to be a lightning manoeuvre, so look sharp.'

Finn crouched in the doorway. I put my chin up, tried to pretend I knew what I was doing, and sashayed up to him. Well, I think it was a sashay. It might have looked like I had piles.

'Addy, there you are! I've been searching for you *everywhere*.' I put my hand territorially on his arm for the second time this evening. This time, however, he welcomed it.

'You *must* come and meet Finn.'

'But I've already –'

'Shut up,' I whispered *sotto voce*.

'Ohhh, I get it . . . YES PLEASE, I'D LOVE TO MEET FINN.'

Carol was staring at me. Her glitter eye-shadow had gone all crinkly as she tried to find a place for me in her mental card index.

'Look who it is!' yelped a voice from down below.

'Oh, hello, Farah,' I said, resisting the urge to punt her like a football.

'You!' hissed Carol dramatically. 'You owe us £57.20 for the council tax!'

'Ah, Carol, how lovely to see you again. I really missed you. You're looking fantastic. Really, I'd never thought of gold lipstick before, but it's certainly working for you – that "cheap" thing is so in, isn't it? Now, please excuse me whilst I take my boy-friend over here, and then why don't you get the fuck out of my house and take your monkey with you?'

Is what I *so*, *so* wanted to say. In fact, I did say it, next morning in the shower, to Kate's Clarins bottles. And they trembled, let me tell you.

'Ehm, yes, sorry about that. I'm putting the cheque in, ahem . . . Excuse us; I'm really, *really* sorry,' I said.

'Why don't you just write me a cheque now?'

'Ehm, Holly, I don't . . . do you think we should leave Finn on his own?' said Addison bravely.

'No, Addison, you're absolutely right, we should . . .'

'Do you live here? Great, because I'll know where to come to get the rest of the money. I'm doing a course round here actually, so I can pop in most days, see if you're home.'

'No,' I said. 'Actually I'm only here visiting from Bhutan. That's Bhutan, Peru.'

This was turning into a complete nightmare. Addison was tugging on my sleeve like a three-year-old who needed the toilet.

'I mean, really! Talk about irresponsible. Do you know what she did?' Carol asked him. I wanted to scratch her, hard.

Addison shook his head, he seemed more and more agitated.

'Well . . .'

'Hello, everyone!' boomed a voice behind us. 'I'm Finn!'

Christ. The cavalry had arrived.

'And you must be Holly.'

It felt like we'd now been introduced four billion times.

'Yes, hi, hi. And this is Addison.'

Addison and Finn mutely shook hands.

'Wonderful. Now, as hostess, can you take me to the punch?'

And with one hand round my arm, and Addison tagging along on my sleeve, we speedily fumbled our way over the dead body in the doorway and quickly away from the punch, which was sitting on top of the refrigerator in plain view.

Outside the kitchen door, I rested against the wall.

'God, that was close.'

'Don't worry; I saved you.'

'I know. My hero. Oh my God – here she comes!'

'Quick!'

And we all tumbled into the front room, where the dancers were subsiding into dreamy swaying moves. Chali had her arms round the grubbiest of the crusties and they were half dancing, half smooching across the room. She jabbed me in the arm.

'He's in a band!' she yelled.

'Oh, brilliant! Are you going to shag him?'

''spect so!'

Over in the corner, looking, frankly, sickening, Kate and John were dancing as though they'd been welded together. She was staring into his eyes with an intensity half blissful, half rather frightening. I didn't catch her eye in case I broke her spell. And anyway, we did have a rather pressing problem on our hands.

'OK,' said Finn to himself, kneeling down beside the pile of CDs and running his finger along the spines rapidly. 'Think, Finn, *think*.' His face creased in concentration.

'Aha!' he whipped one out and jammed it in the CD player, shoving up the volume knob.

'What . . . ?' I started, but I could get no further, because the speakers suddenly boomed –

'ONE STEP BEYOND . . .' and WHOP, high-decibel Madness came crashing out of the speakers.

The drowsy dancers jumped as if they'd been slapped, and stared menacingly at the infidel who'd dared to contaminate the mood, but Finn was protecting the CD player with a fierce look on his face. Sure enough, within two seconds, the entire crowd of Jameses and, in fact, every single boy of *un certain âge* at the party (Josh excluded, natch) rushed into the sitting room and started bouncing up and down, doing leg kicks, putting on sunglasses, pretending to walk downstairs, playing imaginary saxophones and generally having a fabulous time.

'Dance!' shouted Finn at us. I'd been staring, open-mouthed, at the scene, but on his command, Addison and I began bobbing up and down gamely, and I started to laugh. The room was absolutely heaving with aftershave and testosterone, and the noise was frightful as lots of people in Paul Smith started yelling about how baggy their trousers were. Kate was looking daggers at me, until John leaned over and said something in her ear and she lowered her head and smiled, and hand in hand they threaded their way out of the sitting room. I doubted we'd be seeing her again tonight, and possibly never again if she played her cards right. Finn bared his teeth at anyone approaching the stereo until it became clear that anyone trying to change it now would either get pounded en masse, or die from aftershave inhalation before they got there. Then he came and hopped up and down with us. Addison was hopelessly uncoordinated and danced like a three-legged dog running. I tried to dance ironically, as it was music from the eighties, but dancing ironically can't really be done, and you just expend a lot of effort and get sweaty and, anyway, no one was watching, so I gave up and went back to hopping along with Finn. The three of us were right at the far corner and there was no way Carol was going to get through the line of crazy boys – stockbrokers by day, phantom flying saxophonists by night. And, sure enough, halfway through 'House of Fun', we saw her slamming the gate and storming off down the road, Farah galloping along beside her to keep up.

'Woo,' I said, when the three of us had finally made our escape and landed up, as tradition dictated, back in the kitchen. We were red-faced, and I kept giggling when I thought of the mayhem still taking place next door.

'Those City boys sure know how to party,' I said, opening beers for the three of us.

'You could have fooled me,' said Finn. 'They were

talking about how they nearly got killed on their years off and whether or not they'd shag Sophie Rhys-Jones an hour ago.'

'Like I said; they *clearly* know how to have fun.'

Out of the corner of my eye, I suddenly caught sight of Kate's colleague again, enthusiastically chatting up one of those tiny Natalie Imbruglia types – those girls you could keep in your handbag. The lying bastard! He looked up when he sensed my eyes on him and mock shrugged whilst I turned away and felt absolutely horrible.

Josh and Sophie were *still* on the other side of the table, and from what I could make out she was still talking.

'So, of course, Daddy didn't really want me to get a job – you know what these ancient families are like, just want to carry on the line, don't they? But I said, "No, Daddy, I feel a higher calling – I think the country needs me, and it's my duty. And I'll do it with or without your help." And of course he realized he was beaten then, and that's when he bought the little run-around and the mews, and got me into chambers.'

'You really showed him,' said Josh admiringly.

'I know. So, anyway, what was your family doing pre 1700?'

Josh told her.

'Mine were picking potatoes,' I said.

'Mine were being purged from somewhere,' said Finn.

'You always have to go one better, don't you?'

I turned to Addison.

'How are you doing? Did Claudia decide not to come after all?'

He shrugged. 'She was a bit pissed off at me.'

'Why? Not for talking to me?'

'A bit that . . . and a bit for asking her. She really can't get out of the house.'

'Is this your girlfriend?' Finn asked with concern.

'No!' I felt like saying. 'She's a big fat girl with a warty chin whom Addison has never met. Really, I'm his girlfriend. Practically.'

'Uh huh,' said Addison. 'She's . . . she's agoraphobic.'

'Oh, that's nasty. You know, I saw this study in the SA . . .'

And that was it. They were away again. Amazing. It was like they were talking some bizarre language of their own.

Suddenly, I became aware of an absolutely disgusting smell. I turned round and, sure enough, there was Chali snogging her record producer. I nudged her in the back.

'Chali . . . he really smells.'

'I know,' she winced at me. 'Feel this – I've been running my fingers through his hair.'

She held out her hand. It was distinctly sticky.

'Are you sure about this?'

'Are you joking? How do you think Celine Dion got her career?'

'I don't know – kissing dirty people?'

'Exactly!'

'Exactly *not*!'

'Anyway, what do you think ecstasy is *for*?'

The crusty grunted crossly and she gave him a huge snog. I felt my stomach turn and sat back with a sigh, picking up an entire bowl of toffee popcorn and proceeding to listlessly chew my way through it whilst watching Addison and Finn. They had their heads together. Finn looked like a ten-year-old being told the facts of life by the coolest guy in the school.

Madness definitely marked some kind of high point to the evening, and people had started to drift around in gradual bags-goodbye-mini-cab rounds (except for the pot smokers, of course, who weren't technically allowed to leave until 5 a.m.). One of them was even now blearily attempting to make one hundred and forty-seven pieces of toast. On seeing the first people leave, Sophie leapt to her feet, Josh springing equally quickly up to pull out her chair.

'Well, thank you, Joshua, for a charming evening. And thank you *so* much for agreeing to take on those extra cases. Really, you're quite the sweetie. You remind me of my girlfriends. Now, call me a cab, will you?'

Josh moved as a man under hypnosis to do her bidding. I made a mental note to remember her address for Kate so she could order her one hundred takeaway pizzas and put her telephone number on one of those prostitute cards you get in telephone boxes.

The Jameses came traipsing in one by one to make sure Kate realized how late they had stayed. Their faces fell when I told them she'd left already, but they perked up again when they tried to competitively book limos home on their gold cards.

The people we didn't know melted away too, leaving no trace of themselves behind, although taking lots of our traces with them, mostly in the shape of CDs and small ornaments. And finally it was pretty much just Josh, Addison, Finn and me, huddling round the kitchen table surrounded by piled ashtrays, empty cans, crushed food, broken plates, the denful of pot smokers in Josh's room (we hadn't told him about them), and the collapsed person, who was still blocking the doorway, but we'd periodically checked on his breathing, and he seemed OK.

'Well, I thought that went pretty well,' said Josh.

'I don't know,' I said, pouring us all a whisky. 'Nobody vomited all over anybody's bed. Nobody got pregnant. The police didn't even come once. It hardly counts as a party at all.'

'There's a bloke passed out.'

'Yeah, but somebody brought him. Doesn't count.'

'Oh, yeah. And I spent the whole night talking to Sophie! I thought that went rather well too.'

'What? Josh, she's at home right now measuring you up for a gingerbread house.'

'Didn't you like her?'

'Well, she's very . . . posh.'

'She's not that posh. She went to school with one of my sisters.'

'Oh, right. Josh, your sisters went to Cheltenham Ladies.'

'I know . . . but, you know, she *went to school*.'

'Are you going to see her again?'

'Well, I'll see her on Monday,' he said brightly. 'I've offered to take on some of her extra work.'

'So you're going to be her fag?'

'Oh, for goodness sake, Holly – I will *not* be letting her . . .'

'What?' I constantly begged Josh to tell me what public school boys got up to, but usually he would have none of it. Had he just let his guard down?

'*Please* tell us what fags normally do,' I pleaded.

'Nothing,' he said crossly.

Finn looked around.

'Oh, I'm sorry – I guess it's time to go . . . ?'

'Yup.'

'I'd better . . .'

'Where do you live?' I asked him.

'Ehm . . . Lewisham.' Lewisham was right over the other side of London.

'God . . . are you going to try and book a cheap flight?'

He smiled weakly.

'I'll call a cab.'

'You can stay over if you like.'

'Mmm,' agreed Josh. 'You can kip on the sofa.'

Then, I said it practically before I'd opened my mouth. It was purely a product of a disappointing evening, that bloke running away, everyone else pairing up, the white wine, Kate being madly in love and the whole damn thing, but I said it anyway:

'Or you could stay in my room.'

There was a stunned silence. I could have chopped off my tongue with a cheese slice.

Addison was wearing a confused expression. Josh was grinning hugely with excitement. Finn's eyes flicked to the side, as if to check that he'd heard what he'd just heard.

'Ehm, sorry?'

'And I'll sleep on the sofa!!!' I immediately added, hoping that would sort it.

'Ha!' said Josh. 'Is that what you *really* meant?' Finn still appeared distinctly nonplussed.

'Yes it is!' I said immediately. 'I'm just being a good hostess, Josh.'

'Oh, in that case, why don't you and Finn take my room? I've got a double bed, at least, and I don't mind sleeping on the sofa.'

'Oh, shut up,' I said. 'Why don't *you* sleep with him then?'

That was even worse. In fact, that was up there with the rudest things I had ever said in my life, including calling Marion Annis a big fat cow and getting detention. I couldn't believe myself.

'No need to get bitchy about it,' Josh said, bitchily. 'I was only . . .'

'Oh, *there* you are!' said a small, precise voice.

We all looked round.

'Madeleine!' said Finn, leaping up. 'You came!'

I could not fucking believe it. It was the swotty girl from the Natural History Museum.

'Yes. Sorry I'm so late. Crisis in the gerbil wing.'

'That's OK – it's good to see you. I think things

are pretty much finished, but . . .'

'I'm just going off to shoot myself in the head,' I announced, getting up. 'Excuse me, everyone.'

After they'd gone, I slowly emerged back into the kitchen to apologize to Josh.

'Sorry about that, Holl,' said Josh. 'I didn't realize you were sweet on him.'

'I'm *not*,' I said in despair, giving Addison a wistful glance. 'It's just, he's the only other man I *know*. Who's not already going out with someone they met on the Internet.'

I gave Addison what I hoped was an appealing glance.

'Good night,' he said, horrified, and disappeared.

'Men find me DISGUSTING,' I hollered, with my head in my hands the next morning. 'I AM disgusting!'

'I too am DISGUSTING,' yelled Josh, who was sitting next to me. 'Everyone DESPISES me. Stop yelling!'

'How can I stop yelling? I HATE myself! AND my pathetic lifestyle. Is there anyone I DIDN'T try and get off with last night?'

'ME!' shouted Josh. 'Because I am SO DISGUSTING even YOU didn't want to get off with me!'

Suddenly, from the hallway, we heard the door open and somebody singing. We stared at each other, dumbfounded.

'Fuck off!' shouted Josh experimentally. He wasn't a swearer.

Kate put her head round the door, surprised. 'Hello, everyone! How are you? Anyone want some breakfast? I've got fresh croissants!'

'Oh, it's you,' Josh said wearily. 'Don't fuck off, then. Come in, in fact. We need cheering up immediately.'

Kate stepped over the comatose person who was still slumped in the doorway.

'Last night not go too well with Sophie then?' She didn't seem displeased. 'What's the matter? Aren't your parents related to each other?'

She hummed as she opened a carton of orange juice. I looked at her grumpily out of the corner of my eye and wondered what was wrong with the picture. Then it struck me.

'Ehm, Kate,' I said gingerly. She might seem in a good mood, but nothing was ever certain. 'Everything is clearly going fabulously well with, "John", yes?'

'Oooh, yes,' said Kate, switching on the coffee maker. 'Anyone want toast?'

'Me, please,' coughed the prostrate figure on the floor. We ignored him.

'Well, then . . . you know, shouldn't you still be there? Squeezing him orange juice and making him fresh coffee, given that we don't really give a toss what we drink, as long as it's got a side order of paracetamol?'

'Do you know, they should really make fizzy drinks

with paracetamol already in them,' mused Josh. 'It would save a lot of time in the morning.'

'Yes, Josh, that's a great idea – they could call it Suicide Juice,' said Kate dismissively. 'Well, actually, I am back here because after a *glorious* night in a hotel . . .'

'Ooh, the Ritz!?' I said.

'The Sheraton. Practically the Ritz.'

'But, by the same token, practically a Novotel. Go on.'

'He had to fly to Brussels.'

'At nine o'clock on a Sunday morning?'

'Four o'clock actually. He's very busy.'

'He's very married!' yelled Josh. 'Oh God, forget it. Why listen to me? I'm disgusting. At least you get to have sex.'

'Married!!!' yelled the guy on the floor, suddenly jumping to his feet and staring around him wildly. 'I'm meant to be getting married!!'

'We all were,' I said. 'But then, society lied to us.'

'No, no, I mean . . . what day is it?'

'Sunday.'

'Oh my God, I'm meant to be getting married – today!'

'OK,' I said.

'No, no – to Carrie.'

'Oh.'

'Shit, I must have been so pissed – where am I?'

We regarded him with some amusement.

'Pimlico. The seedy end, but it's not far from

the tube.'

'Where?'

'Pimlico.'

His face stubbornly refused to register.

'London?' Josh tried again.

The comatose guy turned ashen. 'London,' he said.

'Where did you think you were?'

His face twisted. 'Cardiff?' he said. 'Arrrggggghhhhh!' he said. Then he grabbed his shoes and vanished.

We rushed into the sitting room so we could see him scramble down the street.

'The tube's the other way!' yelled Josh.

'You've got a two in three chance it won't work anyway!' I shouted. 'You should cut your losses!'

'There's a cabbie who's going to get *extremely* rich today,' observed Kate.

'Oh, I'm sure he'll find his way back and have lots of wacky adventures on the way,' said Josh.

'No, Josh, you're thinking of all those TV programmes and films.'

'Ooh, so I am.'

We turned back to the kitchen to wearily start going round with the binbags.

'Oh God,' I groaned. 'I keep remembering other awful things I did.'

'Like what?' said Kate, perkily.

'Oh, some guy – actually, he said he works with you. Some oily chap. He was here . . .'

Kate went pale. 'Geoff? Geoff was here?'

'Yes, that was his name, the wanker. Anyway –'

'What did he say? Did he mention me?'

'He mentioned his Porsche. Wanker.'

'Oh God, it was him.'

Josh patted her gently on the shoulder as the penny finally dropped.

'The dog-dentist guy?'

'The married-with-children guy,' spat Kate.

'Well, you know, who cares?'

'Me! I wanted him to see me and John and how happy we were and then beg me to come back to him so I could say no!'

'Kate, has it ever crossed your mind that you might be the teensiest bit neurotic?'

'Are you joking? Why do you think I pay my therapist eighty pounds an hour?'

'To tell you you're neurotic?'

'Yes, and that it's OK.'

'Anyway. You didn't even let me finish the story of why I was so awful.'

'Huh! Thank God I'm only neurotic!'

'She asked Finn to go to bed with her,' said Josh.

'*Did* you?'

'God, Josh, that was *not* the way it happened, OK? It was a slip of the tongue and I didn't mean it.'

'No such thing as a slip of the tongue,' said Kate darkly.

'Oh, did your therapist tell you that as well? Was that before or after she explained why she wasn't a real doctor? Slip of the A-levels, maybe?'

'Do you think you might have an aggression problem?'

'My flatmates are accusing me of being a whore and

I'm the one with the problem.'

'Holly, calm down,' said Josh. 'We didn't mean it.'

'And you started the conversation,' pointed out Kate.

I sighed. 'I'm sorry. I'm just so completely fucked off with myself.'

'Well, do you like him?'

'No! Well, you know no! He's nerdy and he has dirty spectacles and I want a real man.'

'Rrrright. So, why did you ask him to go to bed with you?'

'I *didn't*. I offered him my bed while I slept on the sofa.'

'Really? That's remarkably generous.'

'Well, I suppose . . . I didn't . . . I mean, it would have been quite nice to have someone to sleep next to, you know? Other than Frank Sinatra the bear.'

Josh and Kate both nodded.

'I know what you mean,' said Kate. 'But would you shag him for a cuddle?'

'No!' I said shocked. Then, more shamefacedly, 'I might have . . . well, you know, let him have his tops or something.'

'I'd settle for just a snog with Sophie,' said Josh sadly, leading the way out with a bagful of rubbish. Kate smiled at me and followed on.

It was good to know they understood, I thought.

'Oh, but did she tell you she came on to Addison as well?' filtered along the corridor.

Bastards!

Six

Chali and I were in the shop, gassing away as usual, as I threw the roses together. I hated doing roses. One, they hurt, and two, they were only bought by teenagers and men who weren't very nice to their wives. Chali had decided to plait her hair with all the different-coloured ribbons in the shop and was intent on that, and chewing gum in the face of anyone who came in looking for service, so I was hovering near the front.

It was about a month since the party, although we were still finding bits of broken glass beside the washing machine. I had just about bitten down my embarrassment – i.e., whenever I thought about Finn, or Kate mentioned him, I didn't have to stuff my fingers in my mouth to stop myself from screeching out loud. Poor Kate, however, was on a huge anti-man mission, after John had failed to phone her *again*. She'd even shout at newsreaders on the TV, calling them 'lying bastards' apropos of nothing at all, and as for Americans, they were in serious trouble as a continent. Infuriatingly, Sophie had developed a habit of 'popping in' around dinner time, eating like Hector the Hungry Horse, dumping a pile of work on Josh, then disappearing. One night I thought I heard him cry. Kate accused him of being so emasculated his penis would disappear, 'which would be no bad thing, given the evilness of your entire gender.'

I had hardly seen Addison at all. After his momentary outburst of sociability, he seemed to have retreated again, and although I hovered late at night, the door was never open. I suspected I had frightened him – it was like *Badger Watch*. He might not reappear for months.

Chali had done better out of the party than anyone, though, as it turned out that the stinky guy really was connected to the music business, and had got her a gig doing backing vocals for a new band. So she was extremely excited and convinced her time had finally come.

'Loads of people start off being backing singers, you know.'

'Oh yes, I know,' I said. 'Alison Moyet did.'

'Who?'

'You know, "Alf" – Alison Moyet.'

'Nup. Was it pre-war?'

'Fuck off. Ehm, and that girl out of Fairground

Attraction. She was a backing singer for the Eurythmics.'

Chali looked blank. I swore she did this on purpose.

'You have heard of the Eurythmics?'

'Holl, right, don't take this the wrong way, right, but maybe you shouldn't come to this gig.'

'Of course I'm coming. We all are. You might get plucked out from the backing singers like . . . who were you thinking of?'

'Lauryn Hill, of course.'

'Oh, yeh, I knew that.'

'Do you have to bring that girly blond mate of yours?'

'Who, Sophie? No, she's not a friend of mine.'

'No, not her, the bloke.'

'Josh?'

'Yeh. He'll stand out like a prat.'

'Wow. You're almost as horrible as a *real* star already!'

'Do you think you'll *ever* find a boyfriend?'

I was giving her the V's when the door opened with a ting, and I glanced up without enthusiasm. Chali didn't bother looking up at all. That's pretty hard to do – you have to ignore your own basic physiological reflexes – and she had picked it up from snotty club entry policies and practised really hard.

The punter stood blinking as his eyes adjusted to the darkness of the shop after the brightness of the June day.

'Hello,' I yelled from the other end of the shop. 'Can I help you?'

He looked up, and with a shock I realized it was Finn. He realized at exactly the same time, and took a step backwards in surprise. He was wearing long khaki shorts over his skinny English legs, and a flowery shirt with two pens in the top pocket.

'Oh, er, gosh, hello!' he said, with the expression of a man who's just been told he's standing next to an unexploded bomb and if he moves he'll detonate it. 'I didn't know you worked here!'

'Why would you?'

'Ehm, no reason.'

Chali snapped up from her hair-plaiting, sniffing the air for gossip.

'I'd like some, er, flowers, please.'

'Oh, well, you've come to the right place,' I pointed out. 'Gerbils all recovered then?'

'What? Oh, no. Ehm, these are for my sister; she's just passed her exams.'

'Cute,' whispered Chali, nudging me hard in the ribs.

'Shut up,' I hissed violently, then turned back to him.

'Right, right – driving test, is it?'

'She's just taken a double first at Cambridge, actually.'

'Is that good or bad?' I said, putting on a concerned expression, purely to annoy him.

He looked bemused. 'Ehm, well, it's *quite* good,' he said. 'So, you know, not funeral flowers or anything like that.'

'OK,' I said briskly. 'Bouquet, or all one style? Or,

if she's a bit of a swot, she might prefer a house plant. It's got the Latin name on it.'

'I don't know . . . whatever you think. You know, I meant to ring and say thanks for the party.'

'Oh? Why didn't you? Maybe I could have embarrassed myself some more on the phone for you.'

'I don't know . . . I thought you might be . . .'

'Rude to you, like she's being now?' interjected Chali.

'What?' I said. 'I'm not being rude!'

Chali and Finn exchanged a glance.

'You are being a bit rude,' said Finn.

'Am I?'

'Darling, you're being a complete dog,' said Chali. 'Remember, you're not as young as you once were. You should take every opportunity that comes your way.'

I shot her a dirty look. 'OK, I'll stop being rude to him, but for that last remark I'm now going to be rude to you. Piss off.'

She shrugged. 'Like I care. You'll be sorry when I'm famous. Won't she?'

'I expect so,' said Finn.

'See?' She nudged me. 'A nice bloke comes in to ask you out, you can at least be civil.'

'I didn't . . .' he began, then he stopped and smiled suddenly. 'This seems to keep happening, doesn't it?' he said to me.

'What?' I asked nervously.

'We're mistaken for . . . you know.'

'No . . . normally what happens is that I think we

might be, then you gently point out that you don't like me.'

'I don't not like you!'

'Now, what a lovely thing to say.'

His brow furrowed in concentration. Then he obviously made some internal decision and put his hand on the counter.

'Ehm, Holl, maybe, I don't know – would you like to . . . sometime . . . you know?'

'What?'

'I don't know, maybe . . . you know . . . ?'

'Look, Finn, unless you absolutely spell it out for me, I'll probably take it the wrong way and it will all end up horribly, OK?'

'Absolutely, yes, I see your problem.'

He took a deep breath and his eyes darted around the shop. Chali had grabbed my elbow in a fit of excitement.

'Holly, would you like to . . . consider . . . coming out on a date with me?'

'Yes, she would,' yelled Chali. 'In fact, she would like to bring you as a guest to my gig.' And she thrust a badly photocopied leaflet into his face advertising her band, the Bhangpigs.

Finn considered it closely, until I realized he was actually waiting for me to say something.

'What kind of music are you into normally, like?' asked Chali.

'Ehmm . . . Vaughan Williams?'

'Oh God, you're not a poof, are you? That would be so embarrassing, if I'd got Holl a date with a poof.'

'Why, would it make any difference if I was?' said Finn, stiffly.

'If you were going out on a date with me, it would,' I said.

'Oh, yes . . . sorry. I'm so used to City people being awful homophobes all the time.'

'That's OK. They can't help it; it's all that buggering at school. They liked it, and now they're ashamed.'

'Right. Yes. Anyway – well?'

'What about that woman who handles the insides of dead animals?'

'What about her?' said Finn.

'Are you inserting your penis into her vagina on a regular basis?' I wanted to ask him, but couldn't.

'She's not my girlfriend, if that's what you mean,' he said.

What was she then? Casual shag? Bridge partner? Wife? But I decided to give him the benefit of the doubt. Finn was not, I reckoned, a typical Lothario.

'A proper date?' I asked.

'Well . . . what does that entail?'

'Snogging,' said Chali promptly.

'Dinner,' I said simultaneously.

'Dancing,' yelled Chali.

'Flowers and chocolates.'

'Multiple choice, then,' he said.

'Yes, but it can be, you know, "all of the above".'

'I'll remember that.'

I smiled. 'See you at the gig?'

'Then dinner afterwards?'

'That sounds nice.'

He smiled shyly, then retreated out the door.

'Oh God, Holl, I'm *so* sorry, yeh? I really didn't mean to call him a poof, right, it was just, with that flowery shirt and everything . . . I mean, not that I mind poofs, right, loads of my mates are. But, you know, if I'd asked him out for you . . . He's nice, though, inny?'

Chali harangued me as I ignored her and took out a nice bunch of daisies and started wrapping them up, so that I could put them in Finn's hand with minimum embarrassment when he reappeared two seconds later to collect what he'd come in for. Which, of course, he did, blushing like a demon.

Later, I wasn't quite sure how I felt about all this. I had to admit, though, that there was something about a person who had seemed so immune to my charms, however average they might be, then changed their mind. I definitely felt like I'd achieved something – made some kind of stand for every girl who has ever made a fool of herself in front of a bloke whilst a bit pissed. They didn't usually come back after that, but this one had.

Kate and Josh took it with less than ecstatic excitement. Josh barely tilted his head from the sofa, where he was frantically working on a case. I'd never seen him do that before, but, clearly, it was Sophie. She was in Barbados. With whom, I didn't dare ask.

'Is this the guy you already haven't got off with twice?'

'Uh huh. So, you know, playing hard to get is not the only way!'

'Holl, are you sure he didn't just ask you the time or something, and you misinterpreted?'

'Ha ha ha. He actually came in to see *me*, remember?'

Kate put her head up. She too was up to the eyeballs, having thrown herself into her work to try and forget thingummy. It was annoying for us, because in her quest for the annihilation of all things American we weren't allowed to watch *ER* or drink Diet Coke.

'How did he know where you worked? He didn't ask me.'

'Well, OK, he happened to walk into the shop . . .'

'Oh, so you were lying?'

'. . . *But* he couldn't bear to walk out again without a date from me.'

'Wow, he's lucky he didn't decide just to pick up a bunch of daffs at the petrol station. You get some right boilers working in there.'

'Thank you, Josh. How's your lifetime of servitude coming along?'

'I think I'm earning Sophie's love, thank you.'

'Love is a very close emotion to contempt, isn't it?' mused Kate. 'As in, "How contemptuous am I of John?"'

'Truly madly deeply?'

She sighed. 'Yes, dammit. Did I hear the phone ring just then?'

'No,' we chorused.

'I'm so glad we spent all that money on the singles party,' I said.

'Well, it gave me one wonderful night,' sighed Kate.

'And me,' said Josh.

'And it got me a date, I suppose.'

'So, there you go. Well worth four hundred quid.'

'And the weeks of anguish.'

'And all the cleaning up.'

'And the loss of *Pet Sounds*.'

'And . . .'

'OK, everyone, shut up now,' ordered Josh.

'Please come,' I said to Addison for the four hundredth time. This was my secret pact with myself. If Addison wouldn't come to the gig, I was going to get off with Finn. But if he came, I would save myself for him. If he *said* he was going to come and then didn't turn up, I would still save myself for him. But if he point-blank turned me down – well, he might as well just thrust me into Finn's arms. I couldn't say I wasn't giving him a chance.

'*Pleeeeese* come. They use a drum machine.'

'But I don't want to.'

'How do you know? They might be fantastic.'

'Then I'll download their album on MP3.'

'What?'

'Never mind. Look, I just don't feel like going out, OK?'

'Addison, you know, everyone goes out sometimes.'

'Not me.'

'Did you . . .' I couldn't bring myself to ask him directly. 'Did you always stay in a lot?'

He looked at me.

'No. I just like it now.'

He clammed up. I didn't feel I could pursue the matter, but I was burning – unfortunate phrase – to know what had happened. Also, if I'd been in a house fire I'd probably live out in the middle of an enormous field and never go indoors at all. I just didn't get it.

'How's Claudia?'

'I think she's forgiven me for the party thing.'

'But you didn't do anything wrong.'

'I frightened her, and I didn't mean to.'

'She's a mentalist!' I thought, but I kept it to myself.

'She sounds like, you know, she has a few problems.'

'No, she can be quite funny, really. The other day, she told this . . . OK, how does Captain Jean-Luc Picard change a lightbulb?'

'What?'

'"Make it glow!"' He laughed heartily.

'That is hilarious,' I said gravely. 'Addy, *pleeese* come to this gig. Otherwise, you know, I can't answer for the consequences.'

'What consequences?'

'Well, you know, I won't necessarily be your next-door flatmate forever. I might, you know, go to the gig, meet someone nice, get married, move away. And who would you talk to then?'

'Claudia?'

As if in reply to some sub-ether summons, the grotesque face suddenly appeared on screen. Addison had obviously done something to it, because now the head rotated in 3-D. It was like that scene from *The Exorcist*, only Claudia didn't need the Oscar-winning make-up job.

'Ahh!' I yelped.

'Oh, there she is.'

Words started appearing on screen in upper case. I couldn't help reading them.

'IS SHE THERE?' it said.

'Whoops,' I said. 'Guess someone's a bit jealous.'

'No,' typed Addison.

'No? Why don't you tell her the truth? That makes me feel like I'm invisible.'

He shrugged at me.

'It's OK! You can talk, you know – she can't hear you!'

'OK. Ehm, I'm sorry – she does get a bit jealous.'

'Ha! Better not go and visit her – have you ever seen the film *Misery*? You'll come back with no legs.'

He didn't respond, and started typing away heartily.

'Well, GOODBYE THEN!' I said loudly. 'I'm off to the gig ON MY OWN. DON'T WAIT UP! BYE, CLAUDIA!'

He turned round briefly.

'Have a good time.'

'THANK YOU. I will try and have a good time ALL BY MYSELF.'

'I hope you meet someone nice. I liked that person that was at the party. Someone like him would be all right.'

'SHUT UP.'

I stomped out, leaving him rather puzzled.

I wasn't going on by myself, of course. Josh and Kate were coming; (1) because they were interested in seeing Chali in a band and pretending they were hip young things, and (2) I needed the back-up in case it all went wrong with Finn.

I'd expected to be able to have a good laugh at Kate when she turned up for a gig in an Emporio Armani suit, but annoyingly she was wearing fashionably short jeans and a little top, and looked fantastic – there obviously was something in all this gym stuff after all. Josh wore a dark suit with a slightly louder tie than normal, but it wasn't as much fun to laugh at him.

It had suddenly turned cold, in typical English summer style, and the sky was grey and overcast. The gig was in a really nasty, scary pub in King's Cross, and didn't even start until ten. Lots of people who looked like they might have razors secreted about their person mooched about in front of us, and Scottish people yelled at us incoherently.

'Why are there so many drunk Scottish people here?' asked Josh loudly in his clipped accent.

'Shut up!' I pinched him hard, before we all got taken into a dark alley and duffed up. 'It's an exchange scheme. Edinburgh's full of pissed Cockneys asking people for ten pee for an eel pie.'

Chali had been nominally working today, but had spent the entire day in a fit of excitement, asking me whether I preferred the bolt or the hoop skewered through her eyebrow. She'd even tried to rope Mrs Bigelow into coming, who'd said she hadn't missed *Coronation Street* since Charles and Diana's wedding, and wasn't Chali a bit worried that people might mistake her for a professional, dressed like that?

At the door we were charged a revolting ten pounds to get in. Josh and Kate just handed it over as if it were nothing – which it was to them – so I tried not to grumble too much, but I did just have to try . . .

'Am I on the guest list?'

The bouncer, who was built like a brick factory for making shithouses, laughed in a way designed to show me how unfunny that was – like the Master does just after he's captured Dr Who and been offered a jelly baby.

'Are you from a record company, darlin'?'

'Yes!' I said immediately. Confidence is all. Josh stifled a giggle behind me.

'Which company is that then?'

'Ehm . . . Cross Scot's Records?'

He bent down and looked me straight in the eye. His one enormous eyebrow cast a shadow underneath his eyes. I tried to stare him out.

'Really?'

'Sure. Haven't you heard our latest number one –' I cast around for inspiration – "Piss in the Gutter"?'

He clasped an enormous paw on to my shoulder.

'No. Did you hear my last record, "Blood in the Gutter"?'

'No,' I gulped.

'No, sir,' I heard from Josh behind me.

'Well then, fuck off.'

I stared hard at the ground.

'Can I pay the ten pounds?'

'You can pay fifteen for cheek.'

'I'll get it,' said Josh rushing in. I squeezed his arm gratefully as he handed over twenty and waved away the change.

'Thank you for saving me, oh wimpy one,' I said, once we were safely inside.

'I only did it because I thought he was going to eat you.'

'So did I. This is going to be a great evening, I can tell.'

Inside it was boiling hot and absolutely heaving with people in weird trendy gear who looked much younger and immeasurably more self-confident than I did. I sighed. I was clearly missing the gene that made me want to hang about in places where the walls were wet with condensation. Right now I would kill to sit down.

Josh was fighting his way through the crowds to get to the bar, and the teenagers behind him were pointing and giggling at him as he went. After about six hours he returned with three slopping pints of watery lager in plastic glasses, and an extremely pained expression on his face.

'Well, it's not Harry's Bar,' was the only thing he said, sipping his pint with as much dignity as he could muster as we stood out like three banjos at a funeral.

‘God, here’s to not being students any more,’ said Kate. ‘They *have* to come here.’

‘I wouldn’t be too sure about that,’ said Josh. ‘That round cost me eight sixty.’

‘Yes, but they put on added tie tax for you,’ I said.

‘This had better be the Beatles at the Cavern Club,’ said Kate morosely.

‘More like The Roaring Boys at Guildford Town Hall,’ said Josh.

‘Who?’

‘Exactly. 1986. They were shit. And I tell you, it wasn’t three pounds a pint, either.’

I looked around faintly anxiously for Finn. I wasn’t going to get panicky quite yet, but I smoothed down my shirt and was vaguely conscious that my hands were sweaty.

‘I’m going to give it five minutes, then I’m going home,’ said Kate.

‘You can’t! You can’t leave me! You paid ten pounds!’

‘I’ll come with you,’ said Josh.

‘But you paid thirty!’

In front of us, a bald bloke with enormous Doc Martens and braces slipped up on a pool of beer and what might have been sick, and fell on his arse. Instead of leaping up, he sat there, howling with laughter, as all his mates pointed at him and screamed, as if he’d just pulled off a spectacular comic coup.

‘I’d pay a hundred to get out,’ said Josh.

I glanced nervously towards the door again. The

enormous bloke happened to be looking in at the same time. He caught my eye and sneered at me.

'You might have to,' I said.

Josh followed my gaze. 'I'm not scared of him.'

'Ehm . . . yes you are.'

'You didn't let me finish: I'm not scared of him more than I'm scared of everyone else in here.'

We huddled together for safety. The band were showing no sign of starting, and there were people wandering all over the stage and knocking into the drum kit. I hadn't seen Chali at all. I had a sudden premonition of a really terrible evening ahead and me being blamed for everything – whether we stayed or went.

Suddenly, stumbling slightly as he entered, Finn appeared. My overwhelming relief at seeing his handsome face was tempered with the fact that I wished he wasn't wearing a duffel coat and carrying a large satchel. It was like going on a date with Tucker Jenkins, without the raw sex appeal.

'Hello,' he said, forcing his way through the throng with the satchel. Then he was standing in front of me, pink-cheeked and messy-looking, his black curly hair all over the place.

'Hello,' I said, suddenly shy. It seemed for a second as though he was going to kiss me on the cheek, and he kind of leaned forward, and I jerked backwards at the wrong moment and hit my nose on his glasses.

Kate started to giggle.

'Hello, Finn.'

He turned to see her with her little tight trousers on.

'Oh, hello – you look, ehm, nice.'

'I don't sleep at the office you know.'

'Yes, well, OK,' I said quickly. I didn't want my date walking in and flirting with my flatmate, if that was all right with everyone.

'You look nice, too,' he said to me instantly. 'Here, I brought you these.'

He opened his satchel and brought out a box of chocolates. I stared at him in amazement.

'Well, if it's going to be a "proper" date,' he said, apologetically, and pushed them into my hands.

'Chocks! Top hole!' said Josh. 'I mean, ehm, wicked!'

I stood there in the crowded pub, holding the slightly battered box. 'Thank you. But, you know, where's my corsage?'

'Aha,' he said, and reached into his satchel again, fishing out a tiny sprig of heather wrapped in tinfoil. 'Some mad old Scottish woman outside wouldn't leave me alone.'

'Sounds like', whispered Josh to me, 'the mad old Scottish woman knew a good thing when she saw it.'

I slapped him away like a fly, and let Finn stick the heather in my buttonhole. Then we stared at each other again, grinning like idiots. I was ridiculously chuffed.

'Would you like a drink?' I finally asked him.

'Let the lady buy a drink on our first date? Of course not!'

'You know this is a "proper" date, not a "sexist" date, don't you?'

'Oh yes, I forgot. Let the woman buy a drink on the first date?'

'Let the man get kneed in the bollocks on the first date?'

'Pint of bitter?'

'You'll be lucky. Warm watery lager?'

'Mmm, yes, please.'

As I got back from the bar, there was an enormous roar from the other end of the pub, and masses of people swarmed across the room. We followed in their wake, ending up in the crush down one end, where the stage was set up – the stage being about the size of a bath, into which had somehow been crammed a frontman, two big stacks of keyboards, a DJ with turntables and, at the back, Chali – a vision in see-through scarlet (part of me thought 'I wonder if she knows it's see-through?' before mentally hitting myself on the forehead for being an idiot) – and an extremely tall black woman, also in scarlet. They looked fantastic. The two boys on the keyboard and the frontman, however, looked ridiculous. It was impossible to see the DJ, because he had a hat pulled down over his face, but the frontman was wearing a silver suit c/o Martin Fry 1984 and had hugely magnified pores. I glanced at the others, warily, but before anyone had a chance to say anything, the guy in the silver suit leaned over the front of the stage, propped one skinny shank on the speaker and yelled:

'AAAAAGH! FLAY ME! SLAY ME! DON'T FORGET TO PAY ME! SHOVE ME! LOVE ME! WITH A PLASTIC GLOVE – EE!'

'Cripes,' I heard Josh say behind me.

The DJ made some retro scratching noises.

'BITE ME! FIGHT ME! TRY AND EXTRADITE ME!'

Finn and I nodded in appreciation at his syllable count.

'USE ME! ABUSE ME! PUT MY FINGERS IN THE SOCKET AND FUSE ME . . .'

'Ooh, nasty scan.'

The noise was unbelievable. I could hear my eardrums rattle up and down. I kept an eye on Chali to see when she got to do her bit, but she was languidly dancing as if she was the most pissed-off person in the world – i.e., like a proper backing singer.

'PRICK ME! LICK ME! YOU CAN TRY AND DICK ME . . .'

'Here comes the catchy chorus,' I predicted to Finn.

''COS I HATE MYSELF AND I WANNA DIE/I CUT MYSELF AND I WANNA DIE/I HATE MYSELF AND I WANNA DIE/I'M ALL ALONE AND I WANNA DIE!'

The crashing keyboards rose to a great crescendo.

'WANNA DIE!' trilled Chali and the tall girl. 'WANNA DIE! WANNA DIE!'

Then everything cut off in a big wail of fake feedback. The singer took an elaborate bow.

'HELLO, KING'S CROSS!' he shouted 'IT'S GREAT TO BE HERE!'

The crowd went wild, except for us four, who just stared at him.

'I don't think that man wants to die at all,' said Kate eventually. 'Which is disappointing, as I, for one, would be very happy to see him dead.'

'It's kind of like Nirvana, isn't it?' said Finn. 'If they had never learned to play the guitar and, ehm, were, you know . . . shit.'

'Chali's good, though,' I said loyally.

'Yes, she is . . . I especially liked her "wanna dies".'

I nodded.

'Now!' The singer was still yelling. 'This is a song about how the state, right, it really tries to grind you down, right. So, just do your own thing, yeh?'

'I *thought* so,' said Josh.

'No, really, I'm sure those O-levels were quite handy,' I assured him.

'No, no, I mean, I *thought* I recognized him.'

'What?'

'He sounded different, of course, but, yes . . . it's Bladen-Start all right. I was in his house at school!'

'*Really*?'

'Yes, definitely. What was his first name again . . . ? Bladen-Start, Bladen-Start. Oh, yes – Tristram, that's it.'

'*Really*?' I said again. 'Fantastic!'

Onstage, Tristram was hollering over a drum and bass back beat:

'DON'T LISTEN TO WHAT THEY SAY/ IT'S ONLY BULLSHIT ANYWAY/SO GO GET PISSED AND HAVE SOME FUN/DON'T

MAKE YOUR BED OR PHONE YOUR MUM . . .'

The crowd was going crazy.

'Thick as two short planks,' yelled Josh. 'His dad had to practically build a new college to get him into Oxford.'

'SCHOOL'S FOR WIMPS AND THE CONFORMERS/FUCK ALL STUDENTS AND SIXTH FORMERS/LIVE YOUR OWN LIFE ON THE STREETS/ALL YOU NEED ARE DRUGS AND BEATS!'

'Yayy,' shouted the crowd.

'This sucks demon cock,' said Kate. I filled her in on what Josh had told me and her eyes gleamed.

'Go, Tristram!' she yelled, and burst out laughing.

'YOU DON'T HAVE TO! YOU DON'T HAVE TO! YOU DON'T HAVE TO! IF YOU DON'T FEEL LIKE IT!'

'Yeh!' yelled Chali, elegantly raising her arms.

'Shall we dance?' said Finn at my elbow.

'What??'

'You know . . . we're on a date . . . Isn't dancing the law?'

Tristram appeared to be trying to have sex with one of the speakers. The row at the front were hopping up and down trying to grab hold of his legs.

'OK?' I said tentatively.

Ceremoniously, Finn led me to the back of the crush. This end of the bar was comparatively quiet, away from all the spitting. Dumping the bags in a nasty pool of something, he bowed, then took me in a traditional dancing pose.

'What?' I said. 'What on earth are you doing?'

'Dancing,' he said, whirling me round.

'Finn!'

'You'll enjoy it more if you stop struggling.'

'Boys always say that though,' I yelled at him from the end of his arm, but he paid no notice and twirled me around again. Our pace was about a quarter of the beat that was lashing out from the stage, but fortunately everyone ignored us – they probably thought we were somebody's parents. I decided to give myself up to the moment and let myself be hurled about. Finn was an unexpectedly good dancer, and I enjoyed the experience of not being self-conscious and worrying about the music – (1) because what was playing wasn't music, and (2) we were so unhip that to this crowd we were invisible anyway.

'Where did you learn to dance?' I asked him breathlessly as he bent me back over his knee to the final chords of Tristram shouting:

'FUCK! FUCK! AND THEN SOME!'

Finn shrugged.

'Well, the boys on the football team stomped on my glasses, so my mum signed me up for dancing lessons instead.'

'And did that help your standing with the boys on the football team?'

He winced at the memory. 'I think I'm the reason why they took away free glasses on the NHS. I must have gone through five pairs that year alone.'

'Well, never mind – most of those boys are probably

in prison now.'

'Actually, I keep bumping into them in the City, hollering for bottles of Cristal and slapping waitresses on the arse.'

'Oh, did you go to private school?'

'Scholarship.' He grimaced. 'Little Jewish scholarship boy. Really, you do get used to it. I wash my hair in the toilet even now.'

'Were you a boarder?'

'Yep. Banged up at eight for a ten stretch.'

I squeezed his arm sympathetically.

'It's all over now, you're free to go.'

He smiled. 'I know. And at least I know how to do THIS!' Without warning, as Tristram crashed into another song, he flung me over his arms and into a dramatic bent-back pose, and held me there. I looked up at him – he was smiling at me, and his dark hair fell over his eyes. For a very short split second, everything around seemed to go very quiet, and I thought he was going to kiss me. And for a very short split second, even stranger, I found that I wanted him to.

'Yo ho!' yelled Josh. 'You two seem to be having fun. Shall we join in, Skates?'

We straightened up immediately.

'OK,' said Kate. 'Although I'm due in Antwerp at 10 a.m.'

'Oh, hang on,' said Josh, wandering off. 'I want to say hi to Tristram again.'

'I didn't want to dance really,' said Kate. 'Can I go home now, please?'

The band stopped playing peremptorily.

'WE'RE TAKING A SHORT BREAK NOW,' hollered Tristram. 'BUT I'LL BE OVER BY THE BAR IF ANYONE WANTS TO GIVE ME A BLOW JOB.' The crowd pissed themselves.

'UNLESS, OF COURSE, YOU'RE AN A&R MAN, WHEREUPON WE'LL SUCK YOURS.'

'Maybe I won't go and say hello after all,' said Josh.

Chali came dashing up to us, with her usual tribe of filthy supplicants in tow.

'Hey there! I'm so glad you came!'

'You were fantastic,' I said. 'And you look brilliant.' Which, at least, was true.

'Thanks,' she said. 'This is Stitches, Cockroach, Wayne and the Weed Boy.'

'Hey.' We nodded.

'These are the guys that had the party,' she explained to them. One raised his hand in an exhausted fashion.

'Hey.'

'Are you enjoying yourself?' Chali asked Finn mischievously.

'Very much so.' He smiled, looking at me. 'Thanks for asking us along. You're singing brilliantly.'

'I know,' she said. 'Oh, here, have you met Sha?'

Chali's singing partner had segued up beside her, sipping a tall drink through a straw. Sha raised her eyebrows fractionally at us, which is all you have to do when you look like Naomi Campbell. Then her eyes lingered on Josh, who had just let his floppy blond fringe drop into his beer, and was wiping it out of his eyes with his fingers. She whispered something to Chali, who shrugged her shoulders and beckoned me over.

I was prepared for the question.

'No, he's not . . . probably,' I whispered to Chali.

'Wow – how did you . . .'

Josh was thoughtfully licking his beery finger and holding it up to the wind.

'. . . Never mind.' She shook her head at Sha, who walked straight up to him.

'Are you hanging around after the gig?' she purred.

'What?' said Josh. 'Er, no, I don't think – Ow!'

I glanced away innocently.

'Ehm, possibly . . .'

'Good. Wait for me,' she said, then turned round and stalked off.

Josh's eyes were on stalks. 'Gosh – do you think . . . ? Why do you think she wants me to wait?'

'She's probably a lawyer in her spare time and wants you to help with the legwork,' said Kate snidely.

'You've pulled, mate,' said Chali.

'Have I? I mean, do you think . . . ? Gosh!' said Josh, and lapsed into a happy stupefaction.

'Oh God, I really *am* going home,' said Kate, right in front of Chali. 'I just can't take it any more. Sorry, no offence.'

Chali regarded her coolly.

'Sorry, who are you?'

Finn and I winced at each other, but Kate merely turned the chilly icemaidenometer up to eleven and announced, 'I'll just head out into a dangerous area and catch an unlicensed cab on my own then, shall I, Josh?'

Josh stared after her, blinking.

'What?'

But she was gone.

The second half passed in a blur. Tristram and his band crashed through 'THEY DESERVE TO DIE' (a long list, including fox hunters, religious fundamentalists and white people), 'IF DRUGS KILL, CAN WE FEED THEM TO THE PRIME MINISTER?' and 'I'M PROBABLY BISEXUAL, BUT I'LL KNOW FOR CERTAIN WHEN I GET ROUND TO GETTING OFF WITH A BLOKE'.

I barely noticed, however. I was standing close to Finn at the back, enjoying the closeness of us; the hairs on our arms were almost, but not quite, touching. Every so often, a lairy teenager would come crashing into us and send us hurtling into each other. I enjoyed this bit too; we would self-consciously apologize to each other, and hold each other's gaze a little longer than necessary. My insides were squirming, I could hear my own heart even above the condemned wailing of the band, and I was finding it quite difficult to understand why, after all, this geeky, annoyingly direct chap was having this effect on me. It couldn't just be because he was a good dancer, could it? I snuck a peek out of the corner of my eye. He was watching the band with an amused expression, but there was an aura of nervousness about him too. I assumed I was the cause of it, but I couldn't fathom which way – was he desperate to get rid of me, and had a prank instituted by Chali gone too far? Or did he feel the same way I did – nervous but, frankly, desperate for a kiss? And not just any old kiss – a proper, movie-star, blistering yet infinitely tender kiss, the type you reach your face up for so readily, and receive so rarely. I realized suddenly that I was fantasizing about him and had my tongue hanging out like a dog, and shook my head briskly to clear it.

The band rolled off eventually, Tristram head-banging in order to spread his circle of sweat as far as possible, and taking rather more encores than the audience had strictly demanded, including 'MY LOVE IS A FOETUS'. Finally, however, they were gone, and the audience started to drift away. Josh stayed rooted to the spot.

'Well?' I asked him.

'She said stay here,' he said rigidly.

'I'm not sure she meant the exact square centimetre.'

'You can't be too careful.' He thought for a second. 'I'm desperate for the loo, though.'

'Do you want Finn to stand there and pretend to be you for a minute while you get to have a wee?'

'No, thanks, I'll be fine.'

'Yes, until you go to kiss her and accidentally wet yourself.'

'That might happen anyway,' said Josh, suddenly

spotting her sashaying across the floor towards us with a purposeful expression on her face.

'Shall we go?' said Finn to me, subtly.

'Oh! Yes, of course. Bye, darling. We'll want a full report.'

'Probably, nothing,' said Josh, but he held up his fingers, which were tightly crossed.

I crossed mine back at him, and waved at Chali across the room, who was berating her crusty army for something.

'See you tomorrow!'

She looked over, then laughed.

'I will be extremely surprised,' she yelled, 'if *either* of us makes it into work tomorrow!'

I twinged with embarrassment.

'Yes, well, whatever.'

Finn opened the door for me, and the huge doorman recognized me and laughed.

'You know, I might have guessed you two would end up together when you came in.'

'Matchmaker, are you?' I was still cross with him for taking the twenty pounds.

'Neh – you're the only two wearing shoes.'

I glanced at my feet. Finn was wearing desert boots, and I had a pair of Startrite sandals for grown-ups on. Everyone else was in neon trainers.

'You're very good at your job,' I said.

He tipped his head to me.

'Thank you, ma'am. Have a good night now.'

* * *

Outside, it had started to rain. Finn shrugged back into his duffel coat, and immediately appeared more prosaic. Then he caught my eye and smiled warmly. My stomach started doing the samba again.

'Now – dinner!' he announced. I stared at him.

'You know it's quarter past midnight?'

'No – is it really? I don't wear a watch,' he said disappointedly. 'Time is just so completely irrelevant.'

'Unless you're trying to eat in London after midnight.'

'God, if only Einstein had thought of that. It could have changed *everything*.'

'It could have changed us getting food poisoning,' I said, looking around. There were places open around the railway station, but they were frankly terrifying – unidentifiable kebab shops next to watery hamburger joints, with little tin ashtrays full of an evening's worth of anxious cigarette butts from prostitutes, drug dealers and runaways – the standard clientele of the King's Cross cuisine trade. I had been hungry, but one look at these places would put a scabby dog off its dinner. Also, I could have been starving to death, but if there was a possibility of kissing on the agenda later on, then I wasn't going near the oral hygiene minefield that was a kebab. These things need careful planning.

This may also have occurred to Finn, because we wandered about for a while, unwilling to end the evening, uncertain of what our options were. Finally, thankfully, we stumbled across a late-night coffee shop, and Finn acquired two great mugs of soapy coffee and thin slabs of chocolate biscuit cake and sat down next to me on the tiny moulded plastic chairs.

'My ears are still ringing,' I complained.

'Well, it was worth it just to see the start of a new phenomenon, wasn't it?'

'A phenomenal pile of poo.'

'Oh – you didn't tell me you were reviewing it for *Time Out*.'

I sipped my coffee, looking closely at his hands. They were long and wiry, with long pale fingers. One was holding on to the cup so tightly the handle was in some danger, and the other was drumming nervously on the table top.

'So, what do you want to do when you grow up, then?' I asked him.

He shrugged his shoulders.

'After I win the Nobel Prize, I thought I'd become the new Dr Who, and then go into space.'

'Don't you get to go into space anyway, if you're Dr Who?'

'Whoops, yes, I keep forgetting it's a documentary.'

'You'd be a good Dr Who,' I said. He would; he was the right mix of bright, confused and severely dishevelled.

'And you can still win the Nobel Prize, can't you?'

He sighed, and rattled his coffee cup. 'Not at thirty, I don't think, unless I come up with something quick. Physicists tend to peak when they're about twenty.'

'Wow, just like . . .'

'Yes, yes, yes, I have heard it. And I was too

busy doing physics to pull . . . and, of course, I was doing physics, which rather limits your options in the first place.'

'Never mind,' I said.

'I'm sorry: do I sound like the most moany person in the world? I feel like I've just been moaning all night.'

'Well, it's closer to singing than Tristram was.'

'What about you? What are you going to be?'

'Hmm. Film star, I think.'

'Good choice.'

'Thank you. Although I'm not looking forward to all the porn I'll have to make before I get there.'

'Seriously. Are you a dedicated florist?'

I fiddled with a sugar packet.

'I don't know. It's OK. After my parents split up, neither of their flats had a garden, and I really missed it. This seems about the closest I can get at the moment. And I'd die if I had to work in an office. I couldn't handle . . . you know, the low-denier tights.'

He nodded. 'Why don't you go and work in gardens then? Or at least, you could go to an evening class.'

I stuck my hands in my ears. 'Not listening . . . la la la la . . . I know that . . . la la la la . . . I am completely pathetic . . . la la la!'

He smiled, and folded his arms, waiting for me to take my hands down.

'I'm sorry, but . . .'

'La! La la la la!'

'Or you could . . .'

'La la la! La la la la!'

'OK, OK. Ehm . . . do you want to go into space?'

'You asking?'

He smiled again. 'Well, I'm a bit busy this month.'

'Oh, yeah, me too. Well, you know how it is.'

'I think I've got a window about 2017, though.'

'Really? That's amazing. I'm free that decade too.'

'Maybe we could go then, then.'

'Only if I get the window seat.'

'OK. But no opening the duty-free space dust until we get in to land.'

'You're no fun.'

Suddenly, I found myself yawning. It was after one, and the coffee-shop owner was looking at us grumpily over the top of a mop which, judging from the floor, he had no intention of using.

Finn seemed a bit crestfallen. 'You're right, I am no fun and am in fact boring you senseless. Can I take you home?'

I waved him away. 'Don't be silly, of course you're not boring me. It's just late, that's all. I'll get a night bus, don't worry.'

'A night bus? On our date? I think not.'

He jumped up and stuck his head outside the door and, amazingly, hailed a cab almost immediately.

'Cab,' he said, sticking his head back round. There was rain dripping off the front of his glasses.

The mood changed as soon as we stepped into the cab. A man, a woman, in a cab, after a date. There must have been millions of us doing exactly the same thing all over the world at that very moment, with the same nerves and worries going through all of us.

All the way back we edged closer and closer together, but remained in almost complete silence. Occasionally, we'd smile nervously at one another. I wasn't really used to doing this without rather more alcohol in me than there was at the moment, so I was feeling terribly anxious. Finally, the cab pulled up, and Finn turned to me.

'Ehm . . . I'll just ask it to wait.'

Make your mind up time.

'You could . . . come in for coffee, if you like,' I said, staring hard at my hands.

'More coffee . . . ehm, great!' said Finn, paying the driver. I hopped out of the car, mentally checking what pants I had on. As we walked up the path, he reached out and gently took my hand, and I thought my heart was going to leap out of my mouth.

We went up the flight of stairs to the front door – underneath it there was a light on. We both saw it at the same time. And, just as I took out my key, Finn took me by the shoulders, and looked at me quizzically, as if checking everything would be all right. When I assured him with my eyes that it was, he leaned in very slowly and gently, and started to kiss me.

It was an international-standard kiss. Not desperately sexual, like one of those dog-humping-your-leg ones, and not coy either; strong, and sexy and very, very good indeed.

Eventually I pulled away.

'Your mother didn't put you in *that* class at school,' I said breathlessly.

'It was a very progressive school,' he said, adding, 'No, of *course* not!' when he saw my face.

I unlocked the door. 'Come in,' I said, taking him by both hands. 'Please.'

He followed me through the door. And we were gazing so intently at each other that I nearly fell over Addison, who was curled up in a ball by the telephone, silently crying his eyes out.

Seven

'What!?' I regained my balance, and let go of Finn's hands. 'Addison, what's the matter?'

He didn't look up. Finn crouched down beside him.

'Ehm, hello there . . . are you all right?' he asked, rather lamely.

I crouched down.

'Add? Addy?' I touched him lightly. With the desperation of a child, he grabbed me round the shoulders and clung to me as if his life depended on it. I glanced at Finn and grimaced.

'Would you mind making some tea?'

He nodded, and it was as if, on some level, we both knew that regardless of what was going on with Addison, making tea was not the same as having coffee.

I heard him clattering about unsteadily in the kitchen.

'What's the matter, Add? Speak to me.'

I took his chin in my hand. A sudden dash of fear ran through me like icy water.

'It's not Kate, is it? Kate came back, didn't she?'

He nodded miserably.

'She's asleep,' he sniffed.

'You mean she came in and didn't see you on the landing?'

'I pretended it was my contact lenses.'

Addison's glasses were as thick as beer bottles, and sitting on the telephone table.

'Wow. She must have been tired.'

'I'm tired,' said Addison quietly.

'Come on.' I hoisted him up. 'Come and sit in the kitchen and we can sort this out.'

I half hauled him into the kitchen and dumped his long frame into a chair.

Finn was still shuffling around the cupboards.

'Ehm . . . which tea should I use?'

I looked over my shoulder.

'The own-brand, obviously. The Earl Grey is Kate's, and she'd kill us.'

He nodded. 'And who is it lives off Penguin biscuits?'

'Ehmm . . . the penguin.' I turned back to Addison.

'Oh, right.'

I picked up Addison's hand, waiting for the last few tear drops to squeeze their way down his cheeks and for him to become composed enough to talk to us without snortling. Finally Finn put down the mugs of tea, and a plate of biscuits that everyone ignored.

'Do you mind me being here?' he said.

Fatally, I looked to Addison for the answer to that question. What I should have done was say, 'No, I don't mind – Addison, do you?' But I didn't. I didn't make any sign that Finn and I were in any way connected.

Addison lifted his head a fraction.

'I don't mind.'

'OK,' I said, grasping his hand more firmly. 'What's the matter?'

'Well,' he sniffed, 'the phone kept ringing and ringing and ringing . . .'

'You never answer the phone.'

'I know. But it wouldn't stop ringing.'

'It's not Claudia, is it?' I said, wondering before I could stop myself whether she'd met someone else.

'Oh no – Claudia! I haven't spoken to her all night. She'll be wondering where I am.'

'Well, let her wonder for just a little bit longer, tiger. Who was the phone call from?'

'My mum.'

'Your mum? She usually phones on a Sunday, doesn't she?'

He nodded.

'Well . . .'

'She phoned to wish me a happy birthday.'

'Oh, when's your birthday?'

His face crumpled.

'Today. And I forgot!!!'

He burst into noisy sobs again. Finn and I looked at each other, concerned.

I put my arm round his shoulder.

'You know, Add, that might be a little bit flakey, but I wouldn't get too upset about it.'

'You don't understand. The date of my birthday and the date of the fire . . . I get them mixed up, and I always remember the wrong one.'

It was the seventh of June.

'What was the date of the fire?' I asked quietly.

'The seventh of July.'

'How old were you?'

'Eleven years and – sniff – one month.'

'Ohh, Addison.'

He felt chilled and damp through from crying.

'Drink some tea.'

'When I know it's coming, it's not so bad . . . but this year I forgot.'

I wondered how he could forget his own birthday. As soon as November dawned, I was jumping about like a bumblebee in anticipation. Well, it used to be anticipation. These days, it was more like dread.

'I forget mine all the time,' said Finn. 'I'll be up to my eyes in the lab and someone will shout out the date and I'll remember.'

Addison nodded.

'I usually schedule some really difficult coding . . . just to take my mind off things.'

'I'm sorry, mate,' said Finn.

'I miss him, Holly,' said Addison.

I thought for a moment he meant Finn, then cottoned on.

'Your dad?'

'He bought me my first ZX81.'

'Err . . . did he? That was nice.'

'And he taught me C+. Rudimentary, obviously.'

'Obviously,' said Finn.

'OK, scientist boys . . .' I thought for a moment. 'You know, Add, I think maybe this year we need to celebrate your birthday.'

He looked up. 'I don't . . .'

'I know. But I think maybe you should. In fact, I think you have to. I think, maybe, it's been too long since you had a birthday party.'

Finn nodded in agreement.

'But . . .'

'We'll make it on another date. We'll crown you a new birthday.'

He sat, silent and worried.

'Don't worry, it will just be us in the flat.'

'Will you be there?' Addison asked Finn.

Finn looked at me. 'Yes, of course he will,' I said.

Addison appeared unconvinced.

'Now, come on. We'll talk about it more in the morning. Let's put you to bed. You don't sleep enough; you must be exhausted.'

There was a sense of tired relief on his face, as if just being able to tell someone had helped; was all he wanted. Addison let me lead him off to bed as dopily as a child. Finn looked up with a hopeful expression on his face just as I left the room.

I turned back.

'I'm going to . . . sit with him while he goes to sleep . . . just to make sure, OK?'

He seemed briefly disappointed, but quickly covered it up.

'Right, well, I'd better be . . . you know, it's pretty late.'

'It is,' I said.

'OK. I'll just . . . see you soon? You know, date two?'

'Yes – ehm, I'll ring you about Addison's birthday,' I said. 'Thank you for a lovely evening.'

'Thank you. Ehm . . .' He was standing by the door, with his satchel in his hand, and he appeared to be about to say something, but then changed his mind, and didn't. '. . . Bye.'

'Bye,' I said, and watched him turn round and walk down the steps. He didn't look back at me.

I tucked Addison in and he lay staring up at me while I gently stroked his high forehead.

'Thank you,' he said. 'Sometimes, I think I'm going mad.'

'If you think you're going mad, that means you aren't,' I said. 'I think. Unless it's the other way round, in which case we're all in trouble.'

'You know, they just found an ammonia ocean on one of Saturn's moons,' he said. 'It's deep down, buried under a hundred light years of gas. You could never see it with your eye, or touch it, or even get close to it, and it doesn't make a noise. But they still found it.'

'And?'

'I don't think you can hide,' he said, indistinctly as he closed his eyes, clearly wearied out from crying. 'I think you still get found.'

'I think you do too,' I said softly, and watched him as his breathing slowed and became more regular. I watched his face for a long time: peaceful, but with a little white line of salt encrusted round his eye. And finally, when I got very weary too, I lay down beside him on the narrow bed, and I slept as well, my right arm flung across him, as if it would give some sort of protection.

I woke up the next morning with a start, and not the faintest idea where I was. Blinking heavily, the still sleeping Addison came into focus. Oh my God! Beside me, the fine lines of his face were outlined against the pillow, his eyelashes casting a shadow, and he had a line of stubble along his chin. He was absolutely beautiful.

'Hey,' I whispered, and he twisted towards me. Slowly, his huge eyes opened, registering at first shock, then a certain amount of good manners.

'Ehm . . . hey!' he said, smiling gingerly. I started to register a slight embarrassment.

'How are you feeling?'

'Ehm . . . better, thank you.'

I realized my arm was trapped under his, but didn't

want to scare him by wiggling it away, so I gave it up to gangrene. We were in the extremely awkward position of waking up in bed together for the first time, and the fact that we hadn't done any naked stuff didn't seem to have any effect on how deeply embarrassing it was, which seemed unfair.

'Am I trapping your arm?'

'No! No, it's fine. Well, actually, yes.'

He moved and I was in the ridiculous contortion of lying on your side and having one arm too many getting in the way. I had an urge to slice it off, so we could lie facing each other in comfort.

'I . . . slept very well,' he said.

'Yes, me too.'

I hoped this was some sort of an invitation, but his body wasn't quite touching mine, and he seemed stiff. Well, his body language was stiff – I didn't know about the rest of him.

We regarded each other for a bit, until I absolutely had to say something.

'Add, you know . . . I'm absolutely desperate for the toilet.'

His face broke into a grin.

'Me too.'

'OK . . . I'll get up . . . Would you like some tea?'

'Yes please . . . Can I not have any sugar?'

'Not a problem.'

I crept to the door, preparing to sidle out of it like a jewel thief. I listened for any movement, and when I didn't hear anything, gently opened the door.

Kate was standing opposite me with the phone in

her hand and, as of precisely this moment, an extremely shocked expression on her face.

'What the fuck!??'

'Ssh.'

'Oh my God, I don't believe . . .'

'Shh! It's not what you think.'

'He obviously didn't find his contact lens,' she said, looking me up and down.

'I thought you were meant to be in Antwerp.'

'I was, you idiot. But instead I decided to have more fun by staying here and phoning the police. Where the fuck *were* you all?'

I shut the door behind me.

'What? I was . . .'

'In there, yes I'd gathered that. Josh isn't back – did you know? Or were you too busy shagging to check? How the hell was I to know you hadn't both been beaten up and left for dead? I mean, *Jesus* . . .'

'I'm sorry, you know, it's not the kind of situation you leave a note for.'

'Obviously not.'

'I *don't* mean that. Oh God, where is Josh?'

She raised her eyebrows. I remembered.

'Oh my God! Sha . . . Oh my God.' I grinned with delight. 'He must have gone home with her. Wow! You know, I can't get my head round that at all. Josh having sex – it completely changes my world view. Is water flowing upwards?'

'Well, you got off with Addison, so I wouldn't be relying on any magnets.'

I couldn't help grinning again. 'We didn't *get off*. We just slept together.'

Kate hit her hand on her forehead. 'I'm sorry, I keep forgetting you're *modern*.'

'Fuck off. No, I mean, really slept. In each other's arms.' I sighed with bliss.

'No monkeying?'

'No monkeying, I swear. Just good friends.'

'If you say so. God, I am *so* glad I have set back my entire career three years for this. Unlike some, I can't just take a day off when it suits me.'

She stomped into the kitchen. I followed her and put the kettle on.

'What do you mean, take a day off? It's only – shit!' It was after nine. Mrs Bigelow was going to have my arse for garters. I panicked, scrubbed my hands and face, pulled on a pair of jeans slightly too small for me and ran out of the house, only remembering halfway there that Addison would still be waiting for his tea. I closed my eyes again at the memory of him and nearly got run over by a white van. The driver had his windows shut, but I could lip-read the word he was using about me, and it wasn't a pretty one.

I swang round Edmonton Street, expecting to see the shop closed up, or Mrs Bigelow inside honking with disapproval, as Chali hadn't seemed as though she was on her way home for a cup of cocoa the night before, but everything seemed normal, and the gardenias out the front looked relatively healthy. I relaxed, and sauntered in.

'Woooooh!' greeted me when I entered. 'Late night

last night, had we?'

I shrugged. 'Might have done.'

Chali leapt off the counter where she'd been disdainfully painting her nails.

'Well? I want details. Width? Overcoat?'

'What on *earth* are you talking about?'

'Overcoat. You know, was he circumcised?'

The penny dropped.

'Chali, (1) you are a very dirty girl, and (2) nothing happened with Finn.'

She looked confused. 'But you had a late night.' Her eyes widened. 'Who with?'

'Well, you know my flatmate I've been telling you about . . .'

'You pulled him!?'

'Not exactly . . .'

I told her everything, but she wasn't quite as thrilled as I had hoped.

'So, let me get this straight: you blew off nice Finn for this completely fucked up wanker?'

'I didn't "blow off" Finn. Not everyone sleeps with their dates on the first night.'

'Yes, but you were about to.'

'No I wasn't.'

'You'd asked him in for coffee.'

'And that means "shag me", does it? Fine feminist you are.'

'How many times in your whole life have you asked a bloke in for a coffee, had a chat and not shagged him?'

'That's not the point! It's the principle!'

'How many times?'

'Well, you know . . . not many.'

'How many?'

'Nunce.'

'Exactly. But you threw him over for some complete weirdo.'

'Addison is not *weird*. He's damaged.'

'He's off his cake!'

'I know. But if you could see him . . .'

'I don't like handsome men. They make me feel insecure.'

'Is that why you hang out with all those disgusting crusties?'

'No, that's because I'm sleeping my way to the top of the music business.'

'Oh yes.'

'Speaking of which . . .'

She looked over my shoulder and I turned round.

A grotesquely fat, short man with slicked-back hair and sunglasses had just entered the shop.

'Hey . . . babyy! I was gonna bring you flowers, but I figured you already had some.'

His accent was mid-Atlantic via Birmingham. It made dogs whine and cover their ears with their paws.

'Bo!' Chali ran into his arms.

'Holly, this is Bo – he's a producer for the Shingles, and he's lined me up with an audition!'

'I'm very happy for you both.'

Bo put his arm round Chali and pinched her on the bum.

'C'mon, darling – I'm taking you out to brunch.'

'Is that all right, Holl?' asked Chali, snuggling up to him.

'Fine,' I said. 'I'll just sit here, planning how not to go out with, you know, *weirdoes*.'

She stuck her tongue out at me and danced out of the shop.

I spent the day fantasizing madly. By lunchtime I'd moved us to Tuscany, with four children – no, actually, make that two children, otherwise I'd have a body like a beanbag. By two thirty, he'd developed some computer thingy and we'd become as rich as Bill Gates but without the acne. I'd even mentally rehearsed what I was going to say when I got home. I wasn't going to rush up to him and fling my arms round him. I wasn't going to move my stuff into his room. I wasn't even going to pull down his trousers, strong as the urge might be. I would simply wait for Josh to cook us dinner, then invite him in. Then we would all sit together, and it would be lovely. We could hold hands. I might even let him feel me up under the table. No, nitch that – that would be disgusting. All four of us would, for once, partake in intelligent, grown-up debate without any name-calling or slanging matches. Hmm.

I knew something was wrong when I walked in the door, but I couldn't put my finger on it. Kate was in the sitting room, staring out of the window.

'What's going on?'

'He's not back,' she said flatly. 'Josh isn't back. His work called and asked if we'd seen him.'

That was it. There was no smell of cooking.

'Wow. Well, you know, he'll come back when he's ready, I suppose. Aren't you happy for him?'

'What if he never comes back? What if she keeps him in sex prison?'

'Well, that's still better than Sophie, isn't it?'

'I don't know.'

I looked at her. 'You're really upset, aren't you?'

'I'm not upset. I'm just pissed off that he couldn't even phone to tell us whether he'd been killed or not.'

'You are – you should see yourself! You're upset. You're jealous.'

'Of course I'm not jealous! He's one of my oldest friends, and I just think he could have had a little consideration, that's all.'

'Kate is jealous! Kate is jealous!'

'Piss off, would you? Oh, and if you're going to start having sex in the flat, can you try and keep it down? Oh God, if you two are together now it's going to be rut city around here. And Josh is in sex prison. What on earth is the matter with my life?'

'I don't know. Maybe you scare men,' I said.

'Thank you, that helps, that really helps. My therapist says I come over as too independent to cover up my essential neediness. Do you think that's true?'

'I think your therapist talks through his bottom. Can you pay me eighty quid a week? Then we'll sit for an hour and I'll say, "Don't go out with married men . . . Don't go out with married men . . . Don't go out with married men," and then you can completely ignore me.'

She grimaced at me.

'Actually, I'll be pleased when you start shagging Addison. Maybe it'll keep you quiet for a bit.'

'I wouldn't be too sure about that,' I said, and left her to it.

So much for my dinner plan. Addison's door was tightly shut, which was a bit ominous. I stood in the hall, suddenly wracked with indecision and what last night might have meant, if anything. Maybe he'd want to forget the whole thing?

I tapped lightly on his door, and heard no reply.

My absolute first urge was to forget the whole thing. This, I suddenly realized, is what makes boys with whom you have had a positively wonderful time decide in that utterly logical boy way of theirs not to call you afterwards for no reason whatsoever.

You know what it's like: boys you have met, had a brilliant time with, possibly even slept with – but not in a seedy way; in a fun, adult, getting-to-know-each-other way. You know how many siblings he has, how he gets on with his dad, what stupid things he did at college; you've spent all night exchanging information in an intense and fascinating manner. You laugh, you eat in bed, you have a bath together, it seems almost churlish to ask him if he's going to ring you as you clearly are such soul mates – and then he doesn't ring you! And, worse than that, it makes *you* feel bad about yourself.

I should/shouldn't have gone down on him, you think (delete as appropriate). *Why* did I tell him I used to go out with a policeman who accidentally broke my leg? Just mentioning 'I like dogs' isn't instant boy code for 'I'm desperate for a baby', is it? Is it? Maybe it is!

For years this amazed me. I decided that, like in *The Matrix*, boys were living in a completely different parallel universe and were attempting to 'enslave' us whilst waiting for 'the one', probably a short-haired girl who would astonish you with her dullness and all-round podginess when you ran into them both at a dinner party a year later, displaying their engagement rings and talking about Ikea. The great scientific minds of the age should be working on it. But of course they're mostly blokes, aren't they? I suspect conspiracy.

It isn't all one-way, though – sometimes, due to alcohol, boredom or a sheer sense of pity, one has been known to take men home on a 'mercy mission' basis. This type you will gladly hide from forevermore, including plastic surgery and moving to minor South American countries.

Addison, naturally, wasn't one of those. In fact, he was someone I'd been worrying about and thinking about for months. And here it was. Or, at least, here was the best opportunity I'd had so far. And I could suddenly understand why boys might think, 'Well, she's very nice, and I did have a brilliant time, but, you know, there's football on the telly and we've just ordered in a curry and – Oh, fuck it, I think I'll just wait around for someone a little dumpier. After all, I've got the whole of my thirties to get this sorted out.'

What I hadn't factored in was that if you live with someone it's slightly more difficult to avoid them for the rest of your life. Although, in Addison's case, not impossible. And I also hadn't factored in that the reason he hadn't opened his door might be that he didn't want to talk to me either.

Gulp.

I pushed open the door a little, my heart in my mouth. Addison wasn't there. His computer was switched off.

Oh no! He'd gone to South America!

Stunned and upset, I stomped into the kitchen to see where Kate had put the wine. Brilliantly, Addison was sitting at the kitchen table.

'Hey!' I said, more excitedly than I intended. 'You're not in your room!'

'No,' he said slowly.

'Why – did you think I was going to attack you?'

Aaargh! Why did I say that?

'Ehm . . . no. I just . . . thought I'd be here when you came home.'

Ooh! I loved him.

'Right – fine – ehm.'

I felt myself start to blush. He blushed in unison, until it felt like we were having a tomato competition.

'Josh isn't back then,' I observed, needlessly.

'No.'

'Looks like no dinner in that case.'

Addison shrugged. 'I don't usually care much about dinner.'

'Aren't you hungry?'

He thought about it.

'I suppose so.'

'Well then.'

I marched over to the cupboards and threw them open. I didn't seem to recognize anything inside them. What on earth was hoi sin sauce? Truffle oil?

'Ehm . . . what do you want to eat?'

He shrugged his shoulders.

'Whatever you're having?'

'What do you like?' I asked, as if he could name any of the world's major dishes and I'd whip it up for him then and there.

'I quite like cornflakes,' he said.

Perfect! (1) we had some, (2) I could make them, and (3) they are delicious. The man had taste.

'Coming right up,' I said. 'With sugar or *au naturel*?'

'What's the house style?'

'*À la maison* would be without sugar, using a luxurious amount of extremely creamy milk.'

'Can I have that, please?'

'Certainly, sir.'

I ceremoniously poured them out and we sat there, alternately scoffing and throwing shy glances at one another. It was bliss.

Kate stomped in in the middle of it.

'Oh my God. Is this your first romantic meal?'

We both nodded happily and looked a bit coy.

'Have you finished all the milk?'

We nodded again.

'Great great great great great.'

She seized the wine bottle and vanished. Addison and I grinned at each other.

'So . . . ehm.'

This was definitely a tad uncomfortable. Well, after all, I'd never actually officially 'lived with' anyone before, if you defined 'living with' as 'having the same door key as'. I'd always thought that one day I might, but those plans tended to include, you know, kissing them or something. We seemed to have gone straight from first meeting to end of year one. I mean, we might as well go out and get a Renault Espace. What if it was awful?

My old florist friend McKay had this theory. It's formally named after her, and it's called the McKay Button Mushroom Theory. And it goes like this: *always* sleep with someone as quickly as possible after you first meet them and decide they're a bit of all right. This can be within hours, although less than one isn't recommended.

Doing this saves you all the fuss and bother of finding out you have things in common, finding out you like them, realizing you're in love with them, and *then* deciding to seal the deal by bouncing the bishop and discovering that, after all this – the moonlight walks, the giggling dinners, the lingering glances – he has a penis the size and consistency of a button mushroom! But it's too late then! You're already in too deep! You've wasted all that time!

It's a good theory, and I had always tried to follow it as closely as possible. But it suddenly occurred to me that, actually, I had fallen hook, line and sinker for Addison before I'd so much as cocked a snook at his body, so to speak.

'Would you like to go for a walk?'

I was so wrapped up in my own thoughts I didn't hear him.

'Huh?'

'It's just that it's quite a nice night, so I thought when we'd finished dinner we could go for a walk.'

'Wow.' I pondered this. The ramifications of Addison actually suggesting to physically go outside were enormous.

'Are you sure?'

He swallowed. 'Why not? People go for walks all the time. Don't they?'

'Well, usually only when they need Rizlas, I think.'

'Oh, right well, we don't have to . . .'

'Don't be silly, I'd love to.'

He smiled shyly, and I felt something grabbing at my chest. I found I couldn't eat another cornflake in his presence. I immediately came over all self-conscious and had an almost overwhelming compulsion to put some lipstick on.

'Hang on . . .' I said, getting up.

'Where are you going?'

'Ehm . . .' I didn't want to tell him I was going to slather myself in overpriced animal fats in an attempt to make myself more alluring. 'Ehm, I'm going to the toilet.'

Yikes! Shit! Oh no! I might as well have added, 'And I'm going to do the most unbelievably smelly poo whilst I'm in there, as that's what you'll be expecting if I'm out of the room for more than twenty-five seconds.'

I had broken my golden rule, which was never to let a man know I had standard bodily functions – ever.

Flushed, I fled the room, feeling Addy looking after me. In desperate haste I stole Kate's Clarins lippy and got a bit of cornflake on it. When I tried to wipe it off, it looked as though I'd just cut off one of my fingers and was bleeding everywhere – Kate tended towards the thin scarlet slash in lipstick – and there was substantially less in the tube than there had been before. I swore hugely to myself and went to brush my teeth, trying not to make too much noise. I suspect there's something a tad off-putting about hearing someone brush their teeth just before you take a romantic walk with them, don't you? It takes away the spontaneity, and it's a bit like saying, you know, normally I have really awful halitosis but, seeing as it's you, I'll make an effort just this once . . .

Catching sight of myself in the mirror I remembered my mother's old maxim: 'Always brush your teeth *before* you put your lipstick on.' I swore once more for luck, ran my hands quickly through my tangled dark hair and sidled back into the kitchen, pleading that he wasn't going to say, 'Nice poo then?' Of course, Addison is not as other boys. He stood up when I came in, and I just stood staring at him. I had never felt so paralysingly shy in my entire life. Well, I'd never felt particularly shy – but I did now.

'Shall we go?' he asked, gently. I nodded, and he swept us out of the door, gracefully depositing the two cornflakes bowls in the sink. It felt like that tiny split second where a rollercoaster stops on the top of the rails.

It was truly a beautiful evening; the sun was setting, the clouds were tinged pink, and after a momentary tussle at the gate, as neither of us knew which way to go, we headed down to the river bank near the Tate Gallery.

Two minutes later, whilst I was trying to rack my brains to remember the difference between a Pentium and a Mac – or was it a PC and a Mac? – so I'd have something to talk to Addison about, a familiar figure came lurching up the road, tie askew, hair distinctly ruffled and wearing a broad smile.

'Josh!' I hollered at him.

He grinned, and actually broke into a run towards us.

'I had sex!!!' he yelled, as he drew nearer. 'I had sex!!'

'And I'm sure the whole of SW1 is very happy for you!' I said as he reached me and pounced like an over-eager puppy. 'Well done. And, please, don't cuddle me until you've had a shower.'

'I had sex! With a girl!'

'What was it like?' I asked mischievously.

'Oh, you know – brilliant!!' He leaned over, out of breath. 'Guess how many times we did it?'

I hadn't wanted to know anything quite so icky, but I knew how much Josh wanted to tell me.

'A squillion?'

'Ha ha. No, guess again.'

'Oh, I don't know. Seven.'

'Fifteen,' he said proudly.

I looked at him through new eyes.

'Bloody hell, Josh.'

'It hurt a bit at the end,' he said. 'And I nearly threw up once. But, you know, I had some ground to make up.'

I nodded sagely.

'She must be a bit weary.'

'Not really – ehm, the first few were pretty speedy.'

'Josh,' I said, 'too much information.'

'Right, right, yes, of course.'

He took in Addison for the first time.

'Gosh – hello there, big fellow!'

Addison did his usual peculiar half-wince greeting and gradually Josh took in the scene around him.

'Oh . . . where are you two going?'

'It's such a beautiful night we're going for a walk,' I said firmly. No point in telling him the whole story – the neighbourhood had heard enough girly screaming for one night.

'It is wonderful, isn't it? Everything is wonderful. I think I'll come with you.'

'I think you won't,' I said, racking my brains to think up a quick rationale.

'I showered, I promise,' said Josh, wounded. 'Blood came out and everything.'

'Yeuch! Josh, for Christ's sake.'

'I think I might have ruptured something,' he went on, gloomily. 'Worth it, though.'

'No, that's not what I meant. I mean, you have to go home and see Kate. She nearly had the police out for you this morning. She was worried sick when you didn't come in.'

'Didn't you tell her where I was?'

'Ehm . . . you know, I forgot.'

'Oh,' he said, clearly puzzled. 'Well, yes, OK, I'd better be getting back then.'

'OK! See you later.'

He looked confusedly at Addison.

'You know, you seem a lot bigger standing up,' he said.

'Everyone does,' I said. 'Sex has addled your brain. OK, go home. But don't tell Kate too much – she'll go all neurotic and bitter.'

'I'd hate to see that happen,' said Josh. 'OK, good-bye.'

He leaned over and kissed me full on the mouth.

'Josh, *what* are you doing?'

'I've decided to be a bit more assertive in my relationships. Sha thinks I ought to be.'

'Hmm. Well, I'm sure Sha is right in many things, but just remember; there's a thin line between assertive and date rape.'

'Right,' he said. 'Good one. I'll try and remember that.'

And he scampered off towards the house, clicking his heels once in the air in the style of Morecambe and Wise.

I glanced at Addison and grinned and he grinned back.

'Well, things are going to be a little different round our house,' I said.

'It's the summer,' said Addison. 'It brings out the pheromones. It makes people do strange things.'

I took his hand. 'Is this a strange thing?'

He smiled. 'It is for me.'

'Bad strange or good strange?'

'I'd have to analyse it.'

'Maybe you could devise a computer programme to measure its effects.'

'Maybe.' He screwed up his eyes and stared into the middle distance.

'Well, on a probability of 97.2 per cent, I'd say I'd have to go with my intuition that it's good strange.'

We wandered hand in hand down to the river. The Thames, though positively filthy, was as smooth as glass and the lights of the bridges twinkled romantically in the distance. I hoisted myself inelegantly up on to the river wall and Addison plumped himself next to me with ease.

'Talk to me,' I said to him. 'We've spent months living in the same house and you know practically everything about me and all I know about you is that you have a computer girlfriend and you like Jean-Luc Picard.'

'Everyone likes Jean-Luc Picard,' he said.

'Exactly. So I can discount that piece of information as being on a par with "and you breathe in and out". So, come on, tell me.'

He shifted and looked uncomfortable.

'I don't really . . .'

'. . . like talking about yourself; no, I know that. But I'd really like to get to know you,' I said, as sincerely as I could manage. For some reason I suddenly reminded myself of the boys who tried to get into my knickers when I was eighteen. They were sweet talkers too. But this was different! I really cared! This wasn't just McKay BMS. I hoped. I wondered what boys called it. Fried-egg syndrome? Clyde Tunnel syndrome? Yuk. I shook myself, and a thought occurred to me.

'How about I ask you questions?'

He glanced up at me through his thick dark lashes.

'What do you mean?'

'We'll turn it into an interview. Like *Parkinson*. Then, if you don't want to talk about something, you can say, "You can read all about that in my forthcoming book," or attack me with an emu.'

'OK.' He nodded.

I gesticulated to some ducks on the river.

'Good evening, ladies and gentlemen and ducks. And tonight on *Parkinson*, as my very special star guest, with an entire programme devoted solely to him – Addison Farthing!!!!'

The ducks failed to go wild, but I clapped uproariously and Addison gracefully raised a modest hand in acknowledgement.

'Now, Mr Farthing, obviously we're feeling most privileged and excited to have you on the wall . . .'

'Call me Addison, please.'

'Well, yes, of course . . . *Addison*. So, *Addison*, the story in all the papers at the moment and what everyone wants to know is . . .'

He looked worried.

'What *exactly* do you do for a living? And, you know, I'm going to need that in phrases the ducks can understand.'

His face relaxed. 'Well, people want to know if you can join computer systems together to make the most out of them. So they get me to work out what's compatible and whether they can be combined for optimum effect.'

Half the ducks took off from the riverside.

'Well, there's a rude audience for you.'

'It is a bit boring.'

'No, no. Don't forget you're on the most popular show on the river.'

'Hmm.'

'OK.' I hit him with a slightly harder one. 'What were you like when you were small?'

His brow furrowed for a second, as if he couldn't remember.

'Don't you want to know – like, what's my favourite colour or something?'

'What's your favourite colour?'

'Light blue.'

'OK. What were you like when you were small?'

'Can I attack you with an emu now?'

'No. Tell me.'

And slowly, carefully, he did. In an odd way, I hardly listened to him at all. It was mesmerizing just to hear his gruff, low voice as a gentle wind blew across his dark hair and he stared out, straight past me. I kept thinking, 'I'm here! With Addison! We're here! Together!' After thinking about it for so long it was like going on a date with Brad Pitt – difficult to enjoy for itself, more for what it meant and how many people could see you while it was actually happening.

But I did hear him. His mother was Croatian, which accounted for those dark looks and high cheekbones, and his dad a lecturer. Only child, shy at school, good at science, chess club, played the piano, everything going fine . . . until, of course, they went on holiday to France just before he was due to start secondary school and everything went so terribly wrong. He started to stutter at this bit.

'What started the fire?' I asked gently, hoping against hope he wasn't going to say, 'Well, I set this firework off for a joke . . .'

'Wiring, they thought,' he said. 'It was all very confused, and the French authorities didn't really want to know . . . My mother's English has never been that great, and her French is worse,' he said, now staring hard at his toes. 'I don't even remember how it happened or how long it took. It was all a big mess, then finally we got home – someone dropped us off, I can't remember who – and I went in the house and all I wanted to do was play the piano, for some reason. To play the piano like normal. Then I thought I had to stop because it was late and Dad didn't like me playing the piano late at night, it kept him awake.'

He stopped and bit his lip hard.

'Oh God, Addison.' I slipped my arm through his and held it tight. My head was spinning. I mean, I had wanted him to talk to me, but I hadn't thought he really would. I mean, what was it about me that was making him talk? I wasn't anything special. I couldn't quite see where I deserved these confidences. Unless, of course, he was in love with me . . . I was the first person he could speak to about these things – Oh my God. Oh my God!

Realizing I should perhaps be thinking less selfish thoughts when someone was pouring out something massive and deeply personal, I clutched his arm and rubbed my hand ineffectually up and down his leg.

'It's OK,' I said, in my best Mother Teresa soothing voice. 'It's OK. It's good to get it out.'

That sounded like he was vomiting. But he wasn't even crying, just staring very, very hard.

'Then I had to go to school, but they left me alone, pretty much. Then I got really into computers – the teacher let me sit in the lab during breaks . . .'

'What, you mean you missed out all that good smoking and swearing practice?'

'. . . then I got a degree in computer science and here I am. And I have been miserable for longer than I ever thought possible.'

He stopped short.

'I don't think I've ever said that out loud before.'

I looked up at him. 'It's probably a good thing that you did.'

He smiled weakly, and he was so adorable, I fell against him and gave him a huge hug, which he reciprocated. His hand touched my hair and I thought I was going to faint. We stayed like that for a while, whilst I considered kissing him and decided that revelations hour wasn't really the right time to start getting carnal. So eventually we drew apart.

'Do you think the ducks approved?' said Addison, as I pushed my hair back behind my ears.

'Who cares about the ducks?' I said. 'Bloody punters.'

He gazed out over the water.

'Thanks for telling me,' I said. 'I feel . . . honoured.'

I did.

'Oh,' Addison laughed, slightly embarrassed.

'That was down to Claudia. She's forever getting on at me to start living again; move on. Tell people, and get it out.' He looked at me. 'I'm very glad I did.'

What! *Claudia*!

If I'd had a mouthful of something I'd have spat it out.

I stared miserably at the ducks, thinking how much easier they had it than us. Then one began to peck another one really hard on the head and I remembered how much I'd miss *EastEnders* . . . but *still*. They had it easy. I was just confused. I mean, this was a date, wasn't it?

Addison turned towards me, excited.

'And you,' he said. Ah. This was getting better.

'But mostly her.'

Poo.

'She told me to get out, enjoy life, get to know people. Start over again. Then, you know, I met you, and it really seemed as if things were getting better, that I could get to know people.'

'Of course you can,' I said, more kindly than I felt. Actually, I felt like having a big fat tantrum, but it wasn't really that appropriate under the circumstances.

He shrugged. 'Then last night . . . I'd thought I was doing OK, I really did. And all the time I was just . . . sitting on it.'

'That's OK,' I said. 'Good to get it out.'

'You sound like Claudia.' He smiled.

Great. I sound like a pig.

'Last night was . . .' he looked shy '. . . really special for me.'

'Me too,' I said.

'And now . . .' He stood up unsteadily. 'Hey – I'm outside! It's a wonderful sunset! Wonderful ducks! Everything is going to be OK!'

He waved his hands in the air.

'OK, OK.' I smiled. 'You're feeling better. That's great.'

The sun was shooting deeply sexy pink things across the sky.

'No!' he said, towering above me. 'You haven't been locked in a room for fifteen years! It's wonderful!'

His happiness was infectious. Sod it, I thought. She's in America and I adore him. Sod it.

'It is wonderful,' I said, standing up next to him.

'It's brilliant!' he said.

'Yes, it is!' I said, flinging my arms out too.

I stared up at him, trying to manoeuvre myself into the most kissable position. The ducks started squawking and leaping up and down.

'Look at the ducks,' he yelled. 'They're celebrating.'

He started jumping up and down.

'We should celebrate too!'

'We should!' I tried a couple of experimental hops, then tilted my head up to his, and moved in for the kill.

'Huh?' he said, mid hop, peering down at me as I held up my face to be kissed.

'We should celebrate,' I said, reaching for him. 'Kiss me.'

Part II

Eight

You know those dreams you have, whereby you have to sit your O-level maths again, only you're naked and the whole test is in a language you've never seen before and they're making you take it in a swimming pool?

That's what the next moment was like; and will probably be like for my whole life.

Addison jumped back, nonplussed, when I unleashed my assault on him. Unfortunately, there wasn't a place to jump back to. It was that simple. One minute he was there, the next minute he dropped from sight. He didn't scream, there was just a scrambled yell, then a smash and a terrible, terrible thump as he crashed into the shallow, filthy water twenty feet below.

At first, I kept staring straight ahead, stupidly, my

lips puckered, my brain trying to compute where the hell he was.

Then I screamed, then I realized that I wasn't the one with something to scream about, and leaned crazily far out over the wall. What I saw made my heart stop. Addison, his eyes closed, only his head above the water, was bobbing up and down on the waves. A bird had shat on his head. I'd killed him.

I was about to launch myself in when I heard shouts and footsteps behind me, and a strong hand grabbed the back of my dress, and a man hauled me off the wall. A group of people had gathered ridiculously quickly, and hailed a policeman, who, unusually, happened to be passing by, rather than taking part in the normal constabulary occupation of stopping disproportionate numbers of young black men.

The policeman ran over, then spoke brusquely into his radio, took off his hat and gingerly but quickly lowered himself over the wall.

I stumbled backwards.

'I've killed him! I've killed him!' I said over and over again, freezing hot and white cold at the same time. The man who had pulled me off the wall – and probably saved me – had disappeared back into the crowd. A woman came over from the spectators.

'Don't worry,' she said, putting a tentative, English arm around me. 'I'm sure you didn't mean to kill him.'

I started to hyperventilate.

Neither Addison nor the policeman reappeared over the wall. If I'd been thinking straight, I would have realized there was no way they could have shinned up the sheer drop, and the tide was low enough for them to wait there until the ambulance arrived. All I could think was that I'd killed the policeman too.

An ambulance and a police car drew up with a screech of brakes. In my blind panic I wondered whether or not they let you have books and magazines in prison. I tried to take a step forward, but my leg buckled from under me, and the woman kept hold.

'Do you need to phone anyone?' said a man with a dog.

I thought of a solicitor, but I don't have one. I phoned home, but all I could get out was 'Kaaaaa . . .' before launching into floods of tears when Kate picked up the phone.

'John?' she said hopefully.

'Kaaaaaa . . .'

'Holly? Is that you? What the hell's the matter?'

'Kaaa . . .'

The man with the dog grabbed the phone back off me.

'Hello . . .' He turned to me. 'Is this your friend?'

I nodded.

'What's her name?'

'K . . . K . . . Kate.'

'Kate, hello. Listen, I've got a friend of yours here . . . there's been a bit of an accident. Yes, she does have messy hair . . . No, somebody fell into the river.'

There was a very long pause. Then he mentioned the name of a hospital and hung up.

'Your friend will meet you there,' he said to me. I nodded mutely, shivering uncontrollably.

By the riverside, the ambulancemen were letting down a stretcher on a kind of mountain climbers' apparatus. The scene was now attracting more of a crowd and the atmosphere felt like that before a football match. In my hysterical state, I still noticed one man with his video camera out, and bitterly hoped he choked on the £250 he'd get from one of those morbid TV shows if they managed to tape Addison being dragged from the river with fish eating his eyes.

At that thought, I choked, stumbled forward, and thought I was going to faint. Everything went fuzzy round the edges, and a small child dressed up as an ambulanceman rushed towards me and put a white hospital blanket round my shoulders.

'Are you the other person involved?' he asked me, and I nodded.

'Come over here and we'll make sure you're all right.' He half led, half dragged me over to the back of the ambulance, and sat me down.

'Did you fall down? Did you hit yourself? Did he hurt you?'

I shook my head. A policeman who'd been hanging about trying to make himself look useful hurried over.

'Good evening, miss,' he said, taking out his notebook.

'Excuse me,' said the baby ambulanceman, 'but I'm the paramedic and I'm checking to see if she's all right.'

'I think you'll find I've got to establish what

exactly the situation is here first,' said the policeman pompously.

'As soon as I've ascertained the clinical priority,' said the paramedic, just as snootily. I got the impression these two knew each other.

The policeman held up his hands. 'Fine. But keep it quick.'

'It'll get the clinical time it deserves.'

'OK.' The policeman sighed and had a look at his watch. The paramedic turned his attention back to me.

'All right. Ehm . . . how are you feeling?'

'I'm fine. I didn't fall, or hurt myself or anything. I just . . . Where's Addison?'

I started crying again.

'OK, OK.' He paused, then glanced at the policeman again. 'Right – how many fingers am I holding up?'

'Four . . . where's Addison?' I sobbed.

'That's right. Now, does it hurt when I do this?'

He pinched me on the leg.

'Ow! Yes! Where's Addison?'

'Now can I have a word with her, please?' said the policeman.

The paramedic stood back a bit sulkily. 'I diagnose that she's suffering from severe shock,' he said. 'She ought to have some oxygen.'

'In a sec,' said the policeman, then he crouched down beside me.

'What's your name then?' he said, in a deeply patronizing way.

'Holly,' I stuttered. 'Where is he?'

'Hang on,' said the policeman, and went and checked over the wall, where three men were hauling up ropes.

'Well,' he said, returning. 'He's not dead.'

I collapsed into noisy sobs again.

'I thought I'd killed him.'

It's a measure of how very upset I was that I said this in front of a policeman.

'Oh yes?'

'No, no, I didn't . . . I went to kiss him and he fell over.'

The policeman and the paramedic looked at each other.

'You must be some kisser,' said the paramedic.

'Can I see him?' I sniffed.

'Ehm . . . actually, you should sit down for a bit,' said the paramedic. 'But we'll take you both in at the same time.'

'Yes, and give me your name and address,' said the policeman hurriedly, presumably in case I had deliberately thrown Addison in the river, forgotten to run off, and was just about to hijack the ambulance.

So I sat there for what can't have been more than five minutes but felt like hours and hours. Amazingly, a woman came out of one of the nearby houses with a flask of tea and gave me a cup. I snottered at her in gratitude, and she didn't even ask intrusive questions – in fact, she simply waited until I'd finished, took the cup and disappeared again. That just made me snotter even more as the last act of kindness anyone would ever extend to me after they found out how I'd ruined Addison's life forever.

Suddenly there was a huge clatter and lots of shouting. I glanced up to see the stretcher coming over the wall. On it, out cold, was a very pale, very unconscious Addison, with a white collar round his neck like he had fleas.

'Oh my God,' I said. The baby paramedic ran back to me, to open the doors wide and guide the stretcher in.

'Get in,' he said to me, and I staggered back, with my hands at my mouth.

They pushed the stretcher in feet first. One policeman and two paramedics were screaming at Addison. At first I thought they were angry with him and couldn't figure out why; then an iron fist grabbed at my stomach again as I realized they were desperately trying to wake him up.

'What's his name?' one of them barked at me.

'Addison,' I said quietly.

'MR ADDISON! MR ADDISON! CAN YOU HEAR US?'

'It's Addison, not Mr Addison,' I murmured, but they weren't listening to me.

One of the paramedics was shining a torch into his eyes, and the other banged twice on the partition of the ambulance – where I was sitting – then we took off. At the other end of the van, the three men continued shouting at him. One, my baby paramedic, was looking at his watch worriedly. He spoke into a radio hanging down from the side of the van.

'ETA eight minutes,' he said. 'I think it's a GCS three.'

'Is that bad?' I whimpered. He didn't reply. Pretty bad then. I hoped a three was out of, say, ten and not a hundred.

I ached to reach over and wipe the duck shit off Addy's forehead, but I didn't dare. As if reading my mind, the baby paramedic leaned over and wiped it off with a piece of blanket.

'Poor bastard,' he said, and I didn't like his tone of voice.

'WAKE UP,' the other paramedic was shouting very loudly, slapping Addison round the face.

'WAKE UP FOR US NOW, SIR.'

I put my head in my hands. 'Wake up,' I whispered to myself. 'Wake up, Addison, wake up.' Then I reached out and rubbed the bottom of his trainers. 'Wake up. Wake up.'

The ambulance screeched to a halt, and I realized we were there. I expected an *ER*-style assault on the back of the ambulance, but thought I detected a certain lack of urgency in the paramedics and the nurses when they opened the back of the van.

'They think it's over,' I thought to myself. 'They think he's braindead. And it's over.'

I felt numb now. It was too real with him beside me to cry.

They pulled him out, and a chunky, bossy-looking girl with greasy hair came out. She was wearing a white coat with various things – books, papers, pens and weirdy medical equipment – protruding from it and forming a trail behind her, underneath which was an unironed shirt and a very unprepossessing pair of trousers. She went up to Addison and did that torch-in-his-eyes thing again then hastened him inside. She motioned to me, and I followed them.

The hospital was new and shiny and noisy, with shops and cafés. It was like an airport. People in uniform were marching about with serious looks on their faces, to show they were serious people doing a serious job. Addison disappeared into a thicket of them, laden with tubes and beepy machines. People were shouting and children were crying. I felt extremely disorientated. The chunky girl came up to me.

'Name?' she barked, rudely.

'Holly Livingstone,' I choked.

'Not your name, *his* name.'

'Addison. Addison Farthing,' I said, glad that this woman was doing her best to make me feel even worse than I did already.

'Has he been drinking? Drugs?'

'No,' I said.

'It's better if you tell us, you know. It could make all the difference.'

I seriously wanted to hit her, but daren't, in case she authorized some kind of new experimental medicine and killed Addison with octopus radiation.

'He hasn't taken anything, I promise.'

She gave me a look, just in case I didn't know she thought I was lying, then asked me if I was his next of kin. When I told her I wasn't, and didn't have his mother's telephone number, she gave a loud and exaggerated sigh.

'Well, let's just hope he doesn't require an operation,' she said. I reflected that it was a good thing we were in a hospital casualty department, for when I hit her with a brick.

'HOLLY!'

Kate and Josh came hurtling up the corridor.

'Is he here? What *happened*?' They threw their arms around me, whilst the podgy doctor stood by, tapping her foot.

'Are any of you next of kin?'

Kate looked round.

'I've contacted his mother, and she's on her way, but she lives in Lewes.'

My insides shrivelled even further when I thought of trying to explain to his mother what I had done to the only person (I imagined) she had in the world.

'Do you know what blood group he is?' countered the doctor.

'A negative,' said Josh surprisingly.

We all stared at him. 'It's on a sheet he gave me when he moved in,' he said, shrugging his shoulders. 'I don't know why, do I? He's the same as me, and it's rare, that's why I remembered, OK? Oh . . .' His voice went quiet. '. . . And he's an organ donor.'

Jesus. This just got worse and worse. I glanced at the podgy doctor to see if she would say, 'Oh, that's not going to be necessary', but she simply raised her eyebrows and said grudgingly, 'If you want to wait you can sit over there –' indicating a row of uncomfortable plastic chairs. Behind us, they were taking Addison elsewhere.

'But what are you going to do?' I asked helplessly.

She looked at me. 'Well, do you want me to stand here and explain it to you, or do you want me to go and see what I can actually do for him?'

What I actually wanted was to kick her in the nuts, but I retreated, and the three of us sat down in the corner, huddled together, terrified.

They both stared at me when I told them how it had happened. I had hoped that they would say, 'Oh, that could happen to anyone – once, I tried to kiss so-and-so and they fell out of a third-storey window – but they didn't. They just stared at me.

'Well, don't worry, Holl,' said Josh eventually, squeezing my arm. 'It'll make a great story to tell your grandkids.'

'Yes, when they ask why Grandpa's dribbling and has to wear his pyjamas all the time and can't walk and has to be fed with a spoon,' I said, swallowing hard.

'He's young and healthy,' said Kate. 'I might go and phone my dad, see what the prognosis is. Do you know where he bumped himself?'

I shook my head. 'No. By the time I saw him he was on a stretcher. I didn't see a mark on his face though. Well, apart from some duck poo.'

'Are you sure it was duck poo and not coagulated blood?'

'Or brains,' said Josh. 'Sorry,' he said, when we both glared at him.

'No, it was poo,' I said. 'But I didn't see the back of his head.'

Kate nodded. 'I couldn't ask Dad without knowing, and Dr Hitler in there doesn't seem inclined to help us out.'

'She's a witch,' I said. 'I specifically asked for Dr Greene.'

'Yes, she wouldn't be allowed in *ER* with those rat-tails tied up in an elastic band, that's for sure,' said Josh comfortingly. 'And you'd think, being a doctor, she'd know how to get rid of blackheads.'

'It's not that easy when you're inside under electric lighting for one hundred hours a week saving lives, you know,' said Kate.

'You know what I say . . . you can always make time for grooming.'

'You know, Josh, I thought having sex would make you less like a girl, not more. Maybe you're a lesbian.'

'Stop it you two,' I said, and I must have looked completely downtrodden, because they did. We sat there in silence for an hour and a half, pausing only to choke down some revolting substance which might have been from a coffee machine or a nasty medicine dispenser they'd installed for handiness. Josh leafed through some ancient *Women's Weekly*s, while I just stared into space. The policeman hadn't been back to talk to me – maybe they were waiting to see whether Add woke up, to decide whether they pressed for GBH or murder. Oh God. How did I get myself into these things? *How*? Kate took my hand, and squeezed it every so often, and I was glad of it.

People came and went across the hall – lots of people with cuts, and things held to their eyes, and a lot of yelping children. Only one other ambulance came in, and they brought out a woman so old you could see right through her, breathing through an oxygen mask almost big enough to cover her whole head. She looked very frightened when they all started yelling at her. I shivered, feeling awful and fluey and morbid. Suddenly, to my amazement, Tash limped in with a huge bruise on her head and scratches all over her face, accompanied by one of the boys from the flower yard. I hid behind Kate.

'What is it?'

'Big bully,' I whispered, 'at eight o'clock.'

'I'll fuckin' kill 'er the next time!' Tash was saying. 'No one fuckin' punches me.'

'She might be top bitch now though, right, Tash,' said her gormless companion.

'No fuckin' way,' said Tash and started to cry. 'And you can fuck off as well,' she said to the young doctor who'd approached her. 'Being fuckin' top bitch – it's all I fuckin' have! I'm going to have to have a fuckin' baby now!'

My eyebrows were in my hairline.

'She seems all right,' said Kate. 'Kind of person we could do with on the dealing floor. Never say die. I wonder if she needs a job?'

After an hour and a half, a young male nurse came

and got Josh and asked him if he would donate some blood. He leapt up immediately. Kate asked them for information, but the nurse shrugged and said they would have to wait for the next of kin.

'That means they want to turn off the machines!' I yelled dramatically.

'Don't be ridiculous,' said Kate. 'They don't ask for blood then turn off the machines. It sounds like they might be operating.'

'Oh God.' I put my head in my hands. 'Oh my God. It's all my fault.'

Just then, a tall and fine-featured woman walked in through the sliding doors. She was so distracted she seemed to be sleepwalking, and her sallow features were pale.

'That's her. That's his mum,' I said immediately, grabbing Kate's sleeve. 'Oh God. Hide me again. Ehm . . . I'm going to have to go home.'

The woman at the reception desk was even now pointing us out and calling over a nurse. They both approached us. Kate stood up, and hauled me up with her.

'Mrs Farthing?' she said. 'We're so sorry. They aren't telling us anything.'

'Oh, that boy. Always trouble,' she said, with a heavy Eastern European accent. She attempted a weak smile. 'Under other circumstances, I would be happy to meet . . . Are you Kate?'

Kate nodded.

'Ah, see, we have spoken so often on the phone.'

Kate nodded again and smiled.

'Thank you for phoning me today. To think we worried so much about him getting out . . . and he goes out and – pfuh!'

I let out a strangled sob. She turned to me. 'And you are . . . Holly, yes?'

'I'm so sorry!' I let out. 'I didn't mean to!'

'What?'

'Holly was there when it happened, Mrs Farthing. She feels responsible.'

'Ach no – the clumsiest of boys. I'm glad he went out with you. Can I see him now, please?' she said to the nurse.

'Follow me. You two can come as well, if you like.'

We followed her in, me feeling acutely ashamed of my emotional incontinence in the face of Addison's mother's obvious dignity.

Addison was in bed, hooked up to all sorts of machines, in that way they always have people in soap operas. Except in soap operas they're usually up and about twenty minutes later and never even smudge their lip gloss. Addison had two black eyes and his neck was supported by some weird contraption. One of his legs was in plaster. Half his head was shaved, and across it were three great black stitches still wet with blood. I could see his heart beating – slowly – on a screen.

'Can I speak to a doctor please?' said Addison's mother. 'Or can you help me?'

The young male nurse seemed nice. 'I'll just get her.' I winced, thinking: surely that witchy girl couldn't be chief doctor, could she? Surely she'd just passed him on to the grown ups? But my worst fears were confirmed when she huffed in, looking as if to say how dare Mrs Farthing inconvenience her in this way when she had so much doctoring to do, goddammit.

'Do you want these two to stay?' she said, indicating us.

'Yes, of course,' said Addison's mother, and I felt like saying, 'Ah ha ha ha!' – if of course it hadn't been wildly inappropriate.

'Right then.' She marched over and stood by Addison's head.

'Mr Farthing fell backwards on to shallow rocky ground. He broke one leg in two places, but more worrying is that he appears to have sustained some level of head injury. A CT scan indicates that there may have been some bleeding in the brain . . .'

Addison's mum stiffened, but motioned her to go on.

'. . . and he hasn't yet regained consciousness. This means, really, we can't tell when he's going to wake up, or even if.'

Addison's mum drew a very long breath.

'It could be hours, it could be days . . . or longer.'

'I understand.'

Beside me, Kate stifled a very small sob.

'Until he wakes up, we'll be unable to assess the extent of his other injuries. And that's it, I'm afraid. Please ask the nurse if you need anything. We'll be moving him upstairs to a more suitable ward – naturally, we need all the space we can get down here.'

And with that she turned on her cheap wide-fitting pump and disappeared.

We all stared at each other in silence.

'What does she mean, "other injuries"?' said Addison's mother. Then she realized. 'Oh my God . . . she meant brain damage, didn't she?' Her hand went to her mouth. 'Oh my God.'

She sank down next to Addison on the bed, who of course didn't stir, and cupped his head in her hand.

'I can't . . . this can't . . .'

Kate was at her side.

'Don't worry, Mrs Farthing . . . people come out of these things all the time. Haven't you seen *While You Were Sleeping*? He'll come round and he'll be fine. I'm sure of it. Look at him.'

We did. He seemed incredibly peaceful and very beautiful on the crisp white bed. 'There's nothing wrong with his enormous brain, is there?'

Mrs Farthing shrugged. 'You are very kind. But, please, could you leave us alone for a time?'

'Of course,' Kate said, and pushed me out of the cubicle. I was still numb, and stumbled backwards into the male nurse, who saw my stricken face.

'Listen, don't worry too much,' he said. 'Loads of people come out of stuff like this absolutely fine, OK? Come in a lot – even though you think he's unconscious, sometimes they respond to voices and music – it helps. And don't worry about the demon doc.' He leaned in towards us. 'She never gets any, you know.'

We smiled wanly. 'OK, they'll probably move him

to Baker Ward, which is a high-dependency unit – not quite ICU, but he'll be cared for there. You can come and visit him at any time, so try and come as often as you can. Oh, and bring your blond friend too – he'd brighten up anyone's day.'

And with a camp wave he disappeared behind a curtain.

Josh was sitting in reception looking very wobbly and pale. We rushed over to him.

'Are you OK?' I asked. 'Did they take a lot of blood?'

Josh stared at us blankly. 'Oh, that?' he said. 'No, that was fine. But do you know what? That nurse just asked me out . . . and I said yes. I think I'm going to faint.'

I hadn't thought I'd be able to sleep that night – indeed, I felt almost guilty even going to bed, just because I was in a position to decide when to go to bed and Addison wasn't – but I was so worn out I fell asleep instantly.

When I woke up, however, that awful stone was back – you've just been chucked, and you have to explain this fact to all your friends without admitting you've been chucked or downright lying; or you've got to sit your driving test for the fourth time; or you got off with your best mate's bloke, or . . . God, there were a lot of bad mornings in my past, but this was definitely the worst. I lay on my back gazing at the ceiling. He was going to be all right. He had to be. I would turn Florence Nightingale and nurse him ceaselessly round the clock, and when he came to he would be so grateful we would . . . ehm, get married or something, I didn't know. Anyway, it would be deeply moving, and he would be fine, and everything would be all right. Yes. Fine. I leapt out of bed to start my ceaseless vigil, pausing only long enough to fuel up on Coco Pops. Of course, nothing ever quite goes to plan. Lying in bed, I heard Kate bang the saucepan up and down the hall.

'House meeting!' she yelled. 'Everyone up!' I groaned and pushed myself under the covers. If this was about that bloody toothpaste of hers again, there was going to be serious trouble, I told Frank Sinatra the bear. I was in the middle of an enormous traumatic dramatic crisis and thus deserved special treatment at all times.

'HOLLY? Get up for fuck's sake!' There came the sound of a saucepan being pounded against the door of my coffin. I swore mightily, and padded into the kitchen.

Kate was sitting there with an enormous cafetiere of coffee, which was cheering, and an expression on her face which was not. Josh emerged, eyes still full of sleep, with his hair sticking up in all directions.

'Gosh, I was having the oddest dream . . .' He saw our faces.

'Oh,' he said. 'Bloody hell!' he said, and sat down.

'Right,' announced Kate. 'We have a situation on our hands.'

'We know that,' I pointed out to her, pouring

myself a cup of coffee.

'I'm not sure that you do,' said Kate, holding up a sheaf of papers.

'What's that?'

'This is the most up-to-date information on comas available on the Internet. And it's not good news.'

Josh leaned across the table. 'Let's have a look.'

And we did have a look, but it was just lots and lots of meaningless charts and long words like 'cerebral venicular expansion' and 'collateral sprouting'.

'Hmm, yes, I see,' said Josh.

'What?' I said.

He shrugged. 'She's going to tell us anyway,' he said to me in an aside. 'So, you might as well pretend you already know.'

'Ah. Yes, Kate, I see too.'

'Do you think this is funny?'

'No.'

'I've been up all night, you know. I haven't slept. This is the second night in a row I haven't slept because of trouble you two have got us in.'

'I say, that's hardly fair,' said Josh. 'Trouble *Holly* has got us in.'

I tutted, but only out of habit.

'So leave my coffee alone and make yourself some of your usual instant sludge and let me show you our plan of attack.'

'Kate, what are you talking about?' I asked.

'Right –' she said, and brought out an enormous magnetic whiteboard and stuck it to the fridge – 'this is our plan of attack'.

Day One

Kate had written 'Day One' in big letters on the whiteboard on the fridge door.

'Here's the deal,' she said. 'Basically, if Addison's going to get out of this thing, he's going to have to do it pretty quickly. Any more than a week, and he's probably going to have brain damage. Any more than a month, and he's probably not going to make it.'

'What?' we both gasped at the same time.

'He's going to be OK,' I said. 'He is.'

'Calm down, Holl, that just means you're officially in denial,' said Kate. 'We'll deal with that too. Now, the following things have been shown to have some probable effect on wakening people from comas: (1) An aggressive course of physical treatment (2) Committed attempts at rehabilitation from family and friends. OK? Now, this has certain ramifications for us, but the most important is that time is absolutely of the essence. We have several things to do, and we need to do them quickly.'

'What kinds of things?'

'These kinds of things,' said Kate, wielding an impressively stolen-looking whiteboard pen.

'Talking, number one.'

'I can do that,' I said.

'For several hours a day, in rotation.'

'Still not a problem.'

'Holly, it's OK, I've got a rota.'

'I hate rotas,' I said sullenly.

'Two, Music. Josh, we'll be relying on you.'

'Uh huh.'

'Relying on Josh? What, you're going to raise Addison with *The Pirates of Penzance*?'

'Lots of people rate *The Pirates of Penzance*,' said Josh.

'Yes, if they want to *put* people into comas.'

'Holly! I have a schedule, OK?'

'I hate schedules.'

'Three: touching and massage.'

'Ooh, I'm there.'

'He'll need constant stimulation and feeling; it can aid recovery.'

'Not a problem.'

Kate turned over the whiteboard, and the back was divided up into hundreds of small sections with our names written in them in different colours to itemize the particular task we'd be undertaking.

'OK then,' she announced. 'Here it is.'

Josh and I examined it closely.

'You're not asking Chali in to do music?' I said.

'Why not?'

'You're right – she'll piss all over *The Pirates of Penzance*.'

'Hey,' said Josh. 'I don't see you volunteering to do your famous pissed karaoke version of "Back For Good".'

'Yes you do,' said Kate. 'There, in the yellow.'

My first shift was, in fact, that morning. Actually, I seemed to have all the daytime hours, apart from lunch-time shifts. I mean, not that Kate thought my job was unimportant or anything. Still, it *was* my fault. And more, I realized: I really did want to see him. I wanted to see him open his eyes. And it might happen any minute!

I remembered myself long enough to phone in to work. And of course, things started going wrong almost immediately.

'I can't come in. I'm sick.'

'How sick are you? Are you phoning from hospital?' said Mrs Bigelow.

'No,' I said, wearily. 'But I really can't come in.'

'When was the last time you vomited?'

'New Year.'

'Fine. Then you're going to have to come in, because there's no sign of Chali and I can't have two chronically unreliable staff.'

'But . . .'

'But nothing. I'll see you here, or you needn't bother coming in at all. Ever again.'

I considered taking her to an industrial tribunal, but depressedly picked up my bicycle instead. I could steal the biggest bouquet in the shop and take it to the hospital after work. Kate was livid about me messing up her schedule before we'd even got started, but realizing she didn't have a choice in the matter, grumpily started rubbing it out with a duster and humming over it.

'My God, I can't wait to come into work now to hear the latest instalment of your life,' said Chali, who'd turned up by the time I got there. 'It's like *Brookside*.'

'No, it's like *The World at War*,' I said grimly.

'What are you going to do? Will they send you to prison?'

'I don't think so. Unless they can make kissing a crime.'

'Ooh, that sounds like a good title for a song.'

'Yes, in 1985. And thank you for your sensitivity.'

'Well, what are you going to do? Now you've thrown him off a wall, I mean.'

I fixed my sights on the middle distance in an attempt to appear noble.

'I'm going to nurse him back to health,' I said. 'I am never going to leave his side. When ascribed by Kate.'

'Does she know you're missing the first day? He might have woken up this morning.'

'I know that. I hope he hasn't . . . I mean, NO, I hope he has, but, you know, once I get out of here I am never going to leave his side. I have to talk to him, comfort him, and massage him.'

'Massage him?'

'Uh huh. Physical contact is very important.'

'What, so you're going to, like, pull him off while he's unconscious?'

I narrowed my eyes at her.

'Of course not. Piss off.'

'I'm sorry. I thought maybe . . .'

'No you didn't. Chali, it was over the line.'

'The catheter line . . .'

I sighed.

'Look, is being completely sick your only way of dealing with this?'

'Ehm, yes, I think it is.'

'OK. But can you keep it for your gunge crew and not inflict it on me?'

'Yes, you're right. We're a flower shop, not a vegetable shop.'

I put my head in my hands.

'Oh, just fuck off and leave me alone.'

She tugged at my elbow.

'Why don't you go early?' she said. 'I'll cash up.'

'You're not allowed to cash up.'

'I promise I won't filch a thing. Just for you. And the weird guy in hospital.'

'Addison's *not* weird.'

'He's been asleep for twenty-four hours! That's pretty weird!'

'Chali!' I hit her with a daffodil, but it was her way of being kind, so I filled the basket of my bicycle up with gardenias and little blue forget-me-nots and paddled along the horrible busy road to the hospital at four o'clock.

Addison's mother was still there, looking white and strained. She clearly hadn't slept. Baker Ward had none of the frantic anxiety of accident and emergency; it was quiet and sombre. Machines beeped and hummed, and unconscious people lay around. These were mostly older people, whose big bellies bulged under the sheets, but there were a few younger ones – all men. I wondered why. Maybe they just had the habit of falling off things.

I resolved to ask Josh's cute young nurse friend if I saw him.

'Hello,' I said quietly to Addison's mum. I was more composed today, determined to cling to my dignity, show that, whatever may have happened, I was completely committed to her son and would prove myself worthy of his love. When he woke up. Which he would.

'Hello,' she said. 'You're Holly, aren't you?'

'Yes, I am.'

'Call me Magda.'

'Magda. Yes, all right.'

I felt completely stupid and at a loose end, especially after my waterworks of the previous day. It wasn't easy to come on as noble and dignified so soon after that. We looked at each other.

'Ehm . . . Magda. Can I get you anything? Aren't you absolutely exhausted?'

'No . . . but would you mind sitting with him for a bit? I've been here since six this morning, and I need to stretch my legs and get something to eat. Do you mind? I'll only be down the hall.'

'Of course not. Stay as long as you like.'

She stood up, her hand still on Addison's pale one. The family resemblance was very strong.

'He hasn't moved all day,' she said. 'I think it's the longest conversation we've ever had.' She smiled wryly. 'I'm used to one-sided conversations with my son.'

'I'm sure he knows you're here,' I said lamely, and took her place.

The bruises round Addison's eyes had faded, and he looked less ghastly and more asleep. I wanted to tickle him to wake him up.

'The nurse is over there,' she said, indicating the desk. 'But I wouldn't recommend talking to the doctor. She's not very helpful.'

'I know,' I said. 'Right. Thanks.'

And she was gone, and the two of us were alone.

I cleared my throat nervously. I was due to be talking today.

'Well!' I said, feeling completely idiotic. 'Hello, Addison. It's Holly here!'

Unsurprisingly, he didn't stir.

'And I just want you to know how very sorry I am about what happened down at the riverside. But we're going to have to put all that behind us and concentrate on getting you well again, then the next time we kiss it can be . . . down a coal mine or something. If you want to kiss me again. Which you probably won't. And of course you'd be quite within your rights to feel that way.'

Oh no. This was all going a bit downbeat. I tried desperately to think of some good news.

'So, anyway, Chali sends her love. You've never met, but I'm sure you'd get on. Well, OK, so not get on, as such, at all, but you know, she's a person I know and you're a person I know and, well, she sent her love. Though not, as such.'

This was proving harder than it looked. I remembered back to old documentaries about people in comas. Wasn't I supposed to put stereo headphones on him and play lots of Cliff Richard records? But hadn't I hurt the poor guy enough?

'Ehm . . . oooh, and the big news of the day is that Josh has been invited out by a bloke. And he said yes! Which, as you know, comes only two days after him sleeping with a woman. So that's pretty exciting for us – we might be able to categorize Josh once and for all. But he's a bit scared and stockpiling lots of Vaseline products –'

'Is that true?' said a bleached blond head sticking through the curtains. It was the male nurse.

'You can't be supposed to listen to people talking to coma victims!' I said, annoyed. 'Anyway, I thought you worked downstairs.'

'I do,' he said. 'I came to check on your friend here.'

'Uh huh?' I said suspiciously.

'And see if he had any visitors.'

'He does,' I said. 'Me.'

'So I see. Hi . . . I'm Stephen.'

'Hello, Stephen. I'm Holly.'

'Yes, I know all about you,' he said.

'Oh,' I said, feeling that horribly disconcerted way you do when you drank too much tequila at a party and spoke to someone for ages and they come up and say hello the next day and you can't remember who they are. 'Well . . .' I said.

'But never mind about that. Tell me more about that yummy flatmate of yours.'

He was the first person I'd met in the last twenty-four hours who didn't think I was evil, so I was perhaps more willing to confide in him than I might otherwise have been.

'Josh is very sweet and a bit undecided.'

'Really?' he pouted. 'I prefer it if they're straight.'

'Well, you know, he probably is. He slept with a girl just this week.'

'Huh.'

'But he did agree to go out with you, didn't he?'

Stephen smiled shyly.

'Don't take him anywhere scary,' I warned. 'He's very innocent. Don't take him anywhere he has to put on a harness, or dance around in his underpants.'

'I thought I'd take him to dinner,' said Stephen. 'Is that OK, or do you have to write him a note?'

I smiled. 'OK. How's Addison doing?'

'Is he your boyfriend?'

'Kind of.'

'He's cute.'

'Isn't he?' We looked at him for a bit.

'He's going to be OK, isn't he?'

'I'm sure of it,' said Stephen, getting up to go.

'IS HE HERE?' The curtain was pulled back with indecent haste, and the greasy doctor stormed in, rushing over to the bed and bending over Addison's head. 'STEPHEN, GET ME A SPATULA, STAT!'

'What? What is it?' I jumped up, horrified. The doc shot me a dirty look. 'Could you step outside for a second, please.'

'Why, what's the matter?'

Stephen returned, out of breath, with a small piece of plastic.

'I'm not leaving until you tell me what's the matter,' I shrieked.

'You can stay,' Stephen said, coming round behind the doctor, who shot him a dirty look too.

'OK,' she said, slapping on a pair of unsavoury plastic gloves. Slowly, she prised open one of Addison's eyes and shone a light into it.

'What's she doing?' I hissed to Stephen. He shrugged his shoulders. That did not instil a sense of confidence.

The doc turned to me. 'What's his refraction index?'

'Duh huh huh?' I dribbled. What was she talking about? What was going to happen if I didn't know?

'I can't see anything,' she said to Stephen, 'can you?' He leaned over.

'What are you looking for?'

'It says on his chart that he's extremely short-sighted. Dr Costello thinks he may still have his contact lenses in.'

She leaned back off the bed, slightly shame-facedly.

'I didn't . . . see them yesterday.'

I picked up Addison's glasses, which were lying by his bed.

'He wears these.'

'Right, right, of *course*, I knew that. Just checking. OK. Ehmm. All clear.'

She tore off the gloves dramatically, then disappeared.

'*What* was that?'

Stephen shrugged. 'If you forget to take out someone's contact lenses and they're unconscious for a long time, the eyes get oxygen starvation and they can, you know, rot.'

'*WHAT*?'

'But it's OK.'

'Dr Hitler tried to blind my boyfriend and you are telling me it's OK?'

'Hey, you know, she caught it.'

'He could have worms coming out of his eyes!'

'Ehm, don't forget he may be able to hear you.'

'Oh, for fuck's sake!'

I sat back down beside him.

'I have to go.'

'I know. I'll say hi to Josh for you.'

'Cheers.'

'Oh, Add,' I said, when he'd gone. I put my head on his shoulder. He smelled of starch, and hospital beds. 'It's not easy self-sacrificing myself for you, you know. What if they've forgotten something else? I'm not going to know what it is, am I?'

My fingers idly tapped out a rhythm on his.

'You know,' I said, 'this is worse than the time I went to meet that guy who I thought looked like Andrew Ridgeley and I tripped up at the railway station and nearly fell on the track and that guy caught me and I broke my big toe. Still, at least it was me that got hurt. And, you know, it's not fair if you have only just woken up to life and everything and you get it whisked from under you. And if that's the case and there is a God then he's a SKANKY OLD MAN.'

I said this last bit a little louder than I intended,

because all of a sudden this rasping voice came: 'No I'm not!'

I jumped five feet, yelled, 'Fucking hell!' and looked all around, in case it was God.

'Is that God?'

'Yes,' rasped the voice. It appeared to be coming from somewhere to my left. I peered out from behind the curtain. In the next bed along was an old, old man who looked very sick indeed. He was hooked up to a ventilator. I went over to him.

'You're not God.'

'Close enough,' he wheezed. 'He's on his way.'

'Huh.' I pondered for a bit. 'You are a skanky old man though.'

'That's true. But on the inside, I'm divine.'

'Cool. A man said that to me once.'

He laughed, and it wasn't a pleasant sound.

'So, can you help my friend Addison?' I said eagerly. Any port in a storm.

'Unfortunately, I move in mysterious ways.'

'Is that a maybe?'

'Harrumph. Yes. It's a maybe. Now, could you put some whisky down my feeding tube?'

'I don't think that sounds very safe.'

'I'm God, you idiot. I'll be fine.'

'Mr McClockerty! Are you talking again?' Dr Greaseball arrived out of nowhere. She eyed me with her standard look of suspicion tinted with hatred. 'Please don't speak to the other patients. It's not good for them.'

'She wasn't talking, nurse, she was praying.'

'I'm not a nurse, I'm a doctor. And it's time for your medicine. And you can have a big vein or a small vein – it's your choice.'

The old man sighed and lapsed into silence.

'I'll just get back to Addison,' I said, more crawlingly than I'd intended.

'You do that,' she said, in the same crawly tone of voice.

Inside the cubicle I sighed, and experimented to see whether I could actually sit on the bed, but there wasn't space and I was terrified of disrupting a tube, like in that *Airplane* film, so I settled for dragging over the low and uncomfortable hospital stool and leaning over it, resting my chin on the bed. And for want of anything better to talk about, I told Addison about the time I'd shared a flat with a so-called terrorist who'd decided to go on dirty protest.

Around seven thirty, Josh turned up, looking even more dapper than usual – I couldn't work out what it was until I realized he was wearing a cravat.

'Did I miss the waking up?' he said eagerly.

'No.'

'Great! I mean, oh.'

He came and stood by the bed and made as if to touch Addison, but didn't, of course, being English and male.

'No change then.'

'Not in him,' I said. 'You, however, appear to be wearing a cravat.'

'Ah. Yes. Well, you saw the schedule, didn't you?'

'Uh huh. I hate schedules.'

'Well, it's time for me to . . .'

It dawned on me . . .

'No.'

''Fraid so.'

'It might make him worse.'

He turned to me stiffly.

'Arthur Sullivan and the great W. S. Gilbert have never in the history of the world been known to make someone feel worse.'

'Now, Josh, you know that's not true. What about that production you were in of *HMS Pinafore* when that guy in the audience pretended to faint and got carried out on a stretcher and fell off the stretcher and twisted his knee?'

'He didn't pretend to faint.'

'He limped into Casualty screaming, "It was worth it to get me out of there!"'

'Well. Anyway. It was on the rota.'

I sighed. Josh cleared his throat.

'Sing it quietly at least,' I said. 'Dr Hitler will probably get your neck amputated if she hears you.'

'Well, music can soothe the savage brow.'

'Yes, *music* can,' I said, sitting down disgruntledly in the corner chair. 'Not whatever it is you do.'

In fact, Josh had an exceptionally pleasant baritone voice, but it didn't stop me sitting there making 'rumpety pumpety rumpety pumpety' noises in the background as he sang:

'I am the very model of a modern Major-General, / I've information vegetable, animal, and mineral, / I know the kings of England, and I quote the fights historical, / From Marathon to Waterloo, in order categorical; / I'm very well acquainted, too, with matters mathematical, / I understand equations, both the simple and quadratical, / About binomial theorem I'm teeming with a lot o' news, / With many cheerful facts about the square of the hypotenuse.'

'WITH MANY CHEERFUL FACTS ABOUT THE SQUARE OF THE HYPOTENUSE,' I groaned.

'Thank you,' said Josh. 'Do you think it's working?'

'I had hoped', I said, 'that he would have gotten up now, just to point out how many more facts he knows than you about the square of the hypotenuse.'

'This verse might help,' said Josh.

'I'm very good at integral and differential calculus; / I know the scientific names of beings animalculous: / In short, in matters vegetable, animal, and mineral, / I am the very model of a modern Major-General.'

'IN SHORT, IN MATTERS VEGETABLE, ANIMAL, AND MINERAL, HE IS THE VERY MODEL OF A MODERN MAJOR-GENERAL,' I hollered.

We both took a peek at Addison. It didn't seem to be working.

'That's God's music!' shouted a voice from the next bed. I stuck my head out of the curtains.

'That's not God's music! Hymns are God's music!'

'God's music is whatever I say it is,' hacked God. 'Which today means it's Gilbert & Sullivan. And Climie/Fisher.'

'You are truly a wrathful God,' I said.

'I know. Now, tell him to sing again before I turn you into a bush.'

Josh raised his eyebrows, but one of his uncles thinks he's the Duke of Wellington, so he's pretty used to it.

'Ehm . . .'

'I know our mythic history, King Arthur's and Sir Caradoc's; / I answer hard acrostics, I've a pretty taste for paradox, / I quote in elegiacs all the crimes of Heliogabalus, / In conics I can floor peculiarities parabolous; / I can tell undoubted Raphaels from Gerard Dows and Zoffanies, / I know the croaking chorus from the Frogs of Aristophanes! / Then I can hum a fugue of which I've heard the music's din afore, / And whistle all the airs from that infernal nonsense *Pinafore*.'

'This is all nonsense,' I grumbled. 'And how come you can remember this rubbish and not your pin number?'

'Look, Holl, I thought this would be the best thing for someone as brainy as Addison so I spent all day learning it, OK?' said Josh hotly.

'OK, OK, I'm sorry.' The nurses had come and joined us from the nurses' station and seemed to be enjoying it.

'I forgive you,' came the rasp from next door, joining me in,

'AND WHISTLE ALL THE AIRS FROM THAT INFERNAL NONSENSE *PINAFORE*.'

'Which is also good,' said God. 'I'm glad I made it.'

'Shh,' said one of the nurses. 'Let him finish.'

'Then I can write a washing bill in Babylonic cuneiform, / And tell you ev'ry detail of Caractacus's uniform: / In short, in matters vegetable, animal, and mineral, / I am the very model of a modern Major-General.'

'IN SHORT, IN MATTERS VEGETABLE, ANIMAL, AND MINERAL, HE IS THE VERY MODEL OF A MODERN MAJOR-GENERAL.'

Josh looked strained. 'I can't remember the final verse though.'

'OK, we'll do that last bit again.'

And Josh and I stood, and God raised an ageing hand, and the nurses joined in and we all chorused:

'IN SHORT, IN MATTERS VEGETABLE, ANIMAL AND MINERAL, HE IS THE VERY MODEL OF A MODERN MAJOR-GENERAL!!!!'

Josh gave a smart military bow.

'WHAT is going on in here?' screeched Dr Hitler, pounding up the ward. The nurses scattered like pigeons in the road, leaving us staring guiltily at the floor.

'Uhm . . . apparently music is good for helping . . . uhm . . . you know . . .' Josh was trying on his best Hugh Grant, but he didn't appear to be getting anywhere.

'Yes, through *headphones*. This is just plain disruptive. Was Mr McClockerty involved?'

'Ooh no . . . God – I mean, Mr McClockerty warned us against it.'

'She speaks the truth,' came the voice.

'But we did it anyway,' I concluded, shooting an evil glance next door, then concentrating on the floor.

'Oh, but, Doctor,' said Josh, gazing at her imploringly. He came up opposite her and took both her hands.

'Take a pair of sparkling eyes,' he started, very softly.

'Hidden, ever and anon, / In a merciful eclipse / Do not heed their mild surprise / Having passed this Rubicon, / Take a pair of rosy lips; / Take a figure trimly planned / Such as admiration whets / (Be particular in this); / Take a tender little hand, / Fringed with dainty fingerettes, / Press it – in parenthesis – /Ah! Take all these, you lucky man / Take and keep them, if you can!'

Amazingly, Dr Hitler started to giggle and blush. Maybe Josh was right about Gilbert and Sullivan after all. The nurses started to creep back out of their holes to watch the bizarre spectacle. Josh took a deep breath and went on:

'Take a pretty little cot / Quite a miniature affair / Hung about with trellised vine, / Furnish it upon the spot / With the treasures rich and rare / I've endeavoured to define. / Live to love and love to live / You will ripen at your ease, / Growing on the sunny side / Fate has nothing more to give. / You're a dainty man to please / If you are not satisfied. / Ah! Take my counsel, happy man; / Act upon it, if you can! / Act upon it, if you can!'

There was a round of applause. Dr Hitler coloured and looked away.

'That's as may be,' she said finally. 'But –'

'Doctor!' shouted one of the nurses at one of the far beds. 'Come over here! It's Grant! I think he's moving!'

Josh and I stared at each other as the entire ward staff threw itself to the other side of the room.

'Fucking hell!' we said in unison and raced over to have a look. A nineteen-year-old was lying on the bed, blinking in the daylight with an extremely confused expression.

'First motorbike,' said one of the nurses to us in a hushed voice. 'When they sell them to young guys they just put a long bit of elastic on the back so that when the boys fall off them five minutes later, they come right back to the garage.'

'Gosh, really?' said Josh, not concentrating. The curtain was swiftly drawn round, however, and we were forced back.

'I've done it again,' said God.

'Have you really?' I said. 'We reckon it was Josh's singing, and we just need to find the right song for Addison.'

'And anyway,' said Josh, 'why did you put him in here in the first place?'

'Mysterious –'

'– ways. Yes, we know.'

God stared at us wistfully.

'Do you know how you could best please God whilst the nurses aren't looking?'

'Sponge bath?' I said.

'The whisky's in the cabinet,' he said. 'Just pour it

down this tube here. Not this one, or I'll choke to death on the stuff. What a way to go though.' He hacked strenuously at the idea.

'Nuh huh,' I said. 'I am in enough trouble already just on bed number four.'

He nodded.

'I know.'

'Yes, well, you're omniscient, aren't you?'

Addison's mother came back into the ward.

'I am sorry,' she said. 'I fell asleep in the doctors' canteen. It was so full of doctors sleeping.'

'Don't worry about it at all. Really, you know, he was no trouble.'

She looked at her son.

'I always wish he were more trouble.'

'I know what you mean.'

She sat down and cupped his head. 'You can go now,' she said quietly.

'We'll be back tomorrow,' I said.

She nodded, and we crept away.

Kate met us at the door as we trooped in.

'Well done, chaps,' she said. 'Did you sing?'

Josh nodded.

'We're pretty much on schedule then. And I made dinner.'

Josh and I glanced at each other suspiciously. There wasn't any smell of food. I wasn't allowed near a stove, but Kate was pretty much an unknown quantity. I suspected sliced raw green things. Bugger it.

'Here we go.'

In the kitchen was an enormous pile of boxes from Marks & Spencer. There was chicken in port wine, squash, confit, bananas and gravy, and pork in mustard, cumin, champagne and figs, as well as a box with julienne carrots in it, and a box full of mashed potatoes which had cost a couple of quid. Josh was practically speechless.

'Choose away.'

'Kate, this isn't food.'

'It better be; it cost me more than dinner at Bank.'

Josh picked up the various boxes as if they were active jellyfish.

'I don't think I can eat this.'

'But I went to so much trouble!'

'You went to Marks & Spencer!'

'That's trouble! Have you ever seen it at six thirty in the evening? I could have been killed!'

'OK, calm down,' I said. 'At least we're not eating through tubes.'

'I'd rather have this through a tube,' said Josh sullenly. 'At least it could bypass my taste buds.'

'Kate, I don't mind. I'll eat anything. Thanks for getting it.'

'Don't bother yourself,' she said huffily, and stormed out.

'See?' I said to Josh. 'As if today hasn't been hard enough. Don't upset Kate. That's my job.'

'I didn't mean to upset her,' he said, putting his apron on. 'I was only teasing.'

'You *know* Kate doesn't take teasing very well

from you,' I scolded. He looked immediately penitent.

'Skates!' he hollered through the door. 'I need you to help me chop things. Come here immediately.'

Amazingly, she came back in, slightly red in the face.

Between them, they took all the pre-packaged rubbish, chopped it all up, liquidized it and turned it into a slightly odd but warming soup and pasta sauce, and we all sat down at the table at last.

'Sweetcorn in pasta sauce,' I said. 'Not been done enough.'

'Shh,' said Josh. 'Please don't remind Kate that this pasta sauce cost £30. But, hey, the boxes will come in handy.'

'What for?'

'I don't know . . . sledges for hamsters?'

'All right, you two,' said Kate. 'How was he? I assume no better or you'd have said, but we now have only six days, as far as I can see.'

We told her about the accidental waking of another patient, and her eyes lit up. 'So, it's obviously Josh's singing. We just need to find the right song.'

'Oh yes, well, that shouldn't be a problem. Six days to sing him every song in the world.'

'Oh, I know,' I said. 'Why don't we go in his room and dig up his record collection and sing that?'

'Nice one,' said Kate.

'Thank you.'

After dinner had been cleared away – and Kate overwhelmingly thanked to a nauseous degree – we crept into Addison's room. It was eerier than ever without him there. The computer seemed to be working away on its own, blinking and whirring. The screen was off.

'I don't know where he keeps his albums,' I said, looking around in dismay. If Kate hadn't been there I would have gone up to his bed and smelled it.

'Over there?' said Josh, pointing to a pile of CDs underneath his desk. He went over to pick them up, and stumbled slightly on a *Star Wars* figure. This made him grab on to Add's desk, where he accidentally touched the computer keyboard, causing the screensaver to go off.

Instantly, Josh and Kate screeched.

'Guys, guys . . . relax,' I said, as they backed away. 'Perhaps this would be a good time to introduce you to Addison's *other* girlfriend.'

Clutching each other, the two peered closer at the screen. As if in agitation, Claudia's huge head was spinning even faster today. Down the side she had typed 'WHERE ARE YOU?' in increasingly large and panicked fonts.

'CHRIST!' said Kate. 'I know he likes sci-fi, but that's ridiculous.'

Josh cottoned on slightly quicker.

'You were losing out to that?' he said, putting his arm round me.

'No!' I said. 'I was playing the long game.'

We stared at Claudia for a bit.

'Somebody's going to have to tell her,' observed Kate.

'Why?' I asked.

'I don't know . . . given that Addison is probably the only person she knows in the world and he's just deserted her . . . I mean, Holly, how much blood do you want on your hands?'

'For fuck's sake,' I said.

'Go on, Holl,' said Josh. 'You have to.'

Josh and Kate retreated – the yellow-bellied bastards – and tentatively, I sat down in front of the computer screen. The chair was far too high for me – my legs dangled off the floor. I felt Add's presence very strongly, and missed him even more.

'Hey,' I typed.

Instantly there was a flurry of text on the screen, mainly along the lines of where had I been, bastard? Oh, fantastic. So, not only was she horrible in my head, she might actually be horrible in person too.

'This isn't Addison,' I typed. The flurry stopped. Then, after a pause:

'Is this Holly?'

'Yes.'

'WHAT HAVE YOU DONE WITH ADDISON?'

Ah.

'Nothing,' I typed. 'He had an accident.'

'WHAT DID YOU DO TO HIM?'

'Nothing. He fell off a wall.'

'All by himself?'

'Not exactly.'

'You set about trying to steal my boyfriend then you throw him off a wall?'

I really wished people would stop saying that.

'Have you any idea what it is like to be me?' she typed.

Thankfully not. Being me was bad enough at the moment.

'I've been housebound for six years. I only eat what I can get delivered, which is why I'm the weight I am. I never look in a mirror, because I know what it's going to say. Both my parents are dead. I hate my job. Addison and *Star Trek* are the only friends I have. Did you know that?'

'No,' I typed, feeling hideously ashamed.

'No, you wouldn't even think about it, would you? I expect you thought Add would be pretty easy to steal away from me, didn't you? You didn't even think about his problems, about whether he was ready to go. You just thought: Horrible old Claudia, she'll be easy to . . .'

'Hey, one secnod,' I typed, too cross to spell. '(1) If you've never met someone they are NOT officially your boyfriend. OK? And (2) do you want to go on and on about yourself or do you want to know how he is?'

There was a long pause. I really wanted to find the button to stop the head spinning, but I couldn't.

Finally:

'How is he?'

'He's not good. He's in a coma, in fact.'

There was a long pause.

'I hate you.'

Strange as it may seem, no one had ever said that to my face before, not even my parents.

'You know, I didn't have to let you know, you know,' I typed anxiously. 'I could have completely ignored you.'

'I wish you had.'

'Well, at least you know that it's not because he didn't . . .' I didn't want to say it, but I supposed I owed her that much '. . . love you.'

The head stopped spinning, and she didn't type any more.

'How did it go?' asked Josh later.

'Oh, no problem at all. She was fine about it,' I replied.

Nine

I was making up a funeral wreath. This, at least, felt apt. I let out a sigh as a tear dribbled down my nostril.

'I hope you're not making up family wreaths in company time,' observed Mrs Bigelow in passing.

'What an unfeeling bitch,' said Chali loudly.

I was grateful to her for voicing my thoughts from the impunity of being the boss's niece.

'. . . that Lassie really was,' she finished abruptly, as Mrs Bigelow's eagle eye found her. 'Nice wreath for Mr Collins, by the way.'

'Thanks,' I said. 'I hope his family like it, although of course I have never met any of them.'

Mrs Bigelow gave her traditional sniff and went off on one of her mysterious expeditions. Chali and I kicked back immediately.

'Still not much change then?' said Chali, pouring tea. I told her about Josh's near miss with the Savoy song book. Her eyes lit up.

'Hey, you know, we could do that!'

'What?'

'I'll get the band in. We could come and play. Maybe get the local papers down – *London Tonight* something like that.'

'*London Tonight* aren't going to want to cover your band!'

'Are you joking? They'd cover the St Winifred's School Choir if it filled up some between space. Oh, this is a fantastic idea.'

'Chali, you know, I really appreciate the offer, but I just don't think the hospital is going to want long sessions of anti-establishment art wank – I mean, rock. I mean, what if you tried to plug the amp in and pulled out someone's life-support system?'

'Pleeeasse. And anyway, I'm not with that band any more. My new band is going to be much more acoustic.'

'Oh yes? Like what?'

'Like . . . the most acoustic thrash-metal band you've ever seen.'

'Chali, this is a terrible idea.'

'Gutters!'

From the tiny back room, a filthy little blond-dreadlocked chap appeared. I hadn't noticed him when I'd come in; only, it became obvious, because he was covered in so much soil.

'I need you to go and get Mr Spangle.'

'*Who's* Mr Spangle?'

'Oh, he's Mr Big for this new band.'

'Mr Big Spangle? What's the name of the band?'

'Mr Big and the Spangles.'

'Chali, thank you so much for your kind offer, but I don't think the hospital's going to . . .'

'Only trying to help.' She shrugged, and turned her back on me.

'Hugnerh hugnerheh?' said Gutters.

'No, she doesn't want to help her boyfriend.'

'Huignerf heg a *hay*?'

'No, I don't understand it either.'

Gutters shot me a look of disdain – which was rich, coming from someone who had a filthy half-smoked roach dangling in their hair at nine thirty in the morning. I sighed.

'OK. Fine. You speak to Mr Big and I'll get Josh to speak to Stephen.' Josh's date was coming up. He was looking paler every day, but seemed to have braced himself, so to speak.

'Hey!' yelled Chali. 'World domination at last.'

'Yes – so many bands get started in the high-dependency unit of St Hugh's.'

'Well, there was . . .'

We thought for a while.

'Dr Hook?' I asked.

'The Cardiacs,' said Chali decisively.

'You're right.'

'Well, book us then.'

* * *

There was a crowd of people around Addison's bed. I broke into a run immediately. Stephen grabbed my elbow before I got there.

'Don't worry,' he said.

'What are they doing, giving him the last rites?'

'No, nothing like that. Candice Piper is here.'

'Who?'

'You know – haven't you seen *Emergency Pets in Danger?*'

'No!'

'You must have – it's that game show where they take a pet who's been ill and put them in a situation that requires the attention of the emergency services. For every minute the pet stays out of trouble, the owners double their money. It's brilliant – *everyone* watches it.'

'Not me.'

'Huh. Anyway, she's the presenter.'

'What's she doing here? Addison hasn't got any pets. Well, he's got an American pot-bellied pig.'

'She's come to talk to coma patients. It's for their Christmas special.'

'But it's June!'

'Yes, it gives them time to film someone waking up after Candice has spoken to them.'

'Bleagh! Bleagh bleagh bleagh!'

'It's good publicity for the hospital.'

'Hospitals don't need publicity! If no one came, that would be a good thing!'

'Well, anyway, that's what's going on. I'm just up to report back to the girls downstairs. They want to know what Candice is wearing.'

'Is that her? The one in fuchsia?'

'I know – divine, isn't it? See ya, darling – oh, see if you can't get into the shot. And, if you can, ask her which moisturizer she uses.'

Candice was wearing skin-tight fuchsia just in case anyone within a forty-mile radius hadn't immediately recognized her. She had an enormous blonde head and a minuscule, stick-like body – in fact, it was lucky she wasn't wearing black and white, or you could have taken her for a Belisha beacon. She had so much make-up on she looked like she'd been airbrushed, and a low husky voice that sounded too big for her frame.

I wandered slowly up to the group. Magda, Addison's mother, was standing off to one side with a pale and worried expression. Kate was next to her – I'd forgotten it was Kate's night on the rota.

'What are you doing here?' she hissed at me when I sidled up.

'What do you mean, what am I doing here? I'm always here.'

'Well, tonight's your night for cooking and learning "Please Release Me" on the recorder.'

'But I always come to see Addison! What do you think I'm doing here – showing off?'

Kate stared pointedly at the TV cameras and shrugged.

'Oh, for fuck's sake!'

I was furious. Kate really did think I was showing off. Candice didn't seem too thrilled either. She was trying to have a conversation with Dr Hitler.

'Can't we just close his mouth? It would make him seem more asleep, more attractive.'

'As his breathing tube is currently keeping him alive, I'm going to have to say no. We're trying to make him better, not encourage anyone to adopt him,' said Dr Hitler.

'Just for a second or two, while we get the shots . . . ? You know, like in America, where they just have those two little tubes going up the nostrils? That doesn't look bad at all.'

'No!'

'Go, Doctor Hitler!' I muttered under my breath.

'Well, I'm going to have to phone the producer,' said Candice, bringing out her mobile phone.

'I'll have that, thank you,' said the doctor, and whipped it off her. 'It interferes with machines.'

Candice's face was a picture.

'God, you'd think you lot were doing us a favour, letting cameras in here. Roger, get me a tall skinny latte, *pronto*.'

She walked round to the side of the bed we were on.

'Who are you?' she demanded brusquely.

'We're his flatmates,' said Kate before I could say anything.

'And I'm his girlfriend,' I added quickly.

She looked me up and down. 'Really?'

I brushed a leaf off my dress. 'Yes,' I said defiantly. Kate was glaring at me.

'Hmm. Lacking a bit in the personality stakes, is he? You know – Superbore?'

Now it was Magda's turn to look furious.

'No!' I said. 'And what are you doing here anyway?'

'Well . . . the show's called *Coma Alone*, and it's going out at Christmas. The idea is that I go and visit coma patients, and we really impart to the viewer what a very . . .'

'Lonely?'

'Lonely, that's right. What a lonely position it is to be in. Especially at Christmas.'

'But Addison's not alone!'

'Of course he isn't.'

'And I don't think he'd notice if it were Christmas,' murmured Kate.

'Right. OK, I *see*. Now, would you mind just getting out of the way while we film?'

Without waiting for an answer, Candice started clipping on a microphone, and a woman ran forward and began patting at her immaculate, robot-like hairdo.

'Roger? Yes, OK, start it rolling, thank you.'

That, as we found out, meant: Roger, forcibly push everyone out of the way and tell them to be quiet in a very loud voice designed to show that working in TV is a VERY IMPORTANT THING.

We moved back and stood in the corner.

'I had no idea this was happening, you know,' I said to Kate. 'I just wanted to see him.'

'Here at St Hugh's,' Candice started, 'lie the near corpse-like bodies of the unloved, the nearly dead and the unwanted at Christmas time.'

'Well, why are you so pally with Stephen all of a sudden?'

'With who?'

'That nurse. Josh's boyfriend.'

Candice moved round, the camera still on her, and sat on the bed, picking up Addison's hand.

'Like beautiful statues they lie here, almost asleep, were it not for the many tubes coming out of their mouths.'

'I wasn't asked to be a beautiful statue,' grumbled a voice behind me. I peered backwards. It was God.

'Hey – you got Michelangelo and Leonardo da Vinci and he got Candice Piper – you're winning, OK?'

'OK.'

'He isn't Josh's boyfriend,' I said to Kate.

'Well, he's about to be.'

'So what?'

'So what? So why is Josh Mr Popular all of a sudden?'

'Don't you think he deserves it? He's had a long enough dry spell. You've been edgy ever since he met that backing singer.'

'Edgy, who's edgy?'

'Who cares for these, these modern-day zombies? Well, today here with us we have Doctor Flowers, who has dedicated her life to the relief of those who can't even say thank you.'

Dr *Flowers?*

Candice smiled tenderly at the camera. I growled under my breath. 'Cut!' said Roger. 'That was great, darling.'

She dropped Addison's hand like a snake and jumped down off the bed.

'You've just got to keep a professional attitude, that's what I say. Now, where's that bloody doctor? And for God's sake, Make-up, can't you at least get her to comb her hair?'

'I'm here,' said Dr Hitler – or Dr Flowers, as I supposed I should call her. She was flushed red. For the first time ever I felt sorry for her.

'And I happen to think that what I do for a living is a *little* bit more important than make-up, don't you?'

Maybe I didn't.

'Suit yourself, dear,' said Candice. 'For some of us it's professional pride, for others it's . . .'

'. . . being too busy saving lives?'

They stood round the side of Addison's bed glowering at each other. The big light went on again and Candice broke into an enormous glowing white grin.

'So, Dr Flowers, thank you *so* much for having us here.'

'Always a pleasure, Candice. Thanks for coming in. Anything you can do to help these kiddies will be great for St Hugh's.'

'Well, we'll certainly try, Doc! So, anyway, what can you tell me about . . .' She indicated Addison.

'This young man. Well. Yes. I'm afraid he's an object lesson to people planning on standing on high walls over hard things like stones – don't do it!'

'Right. And, you know, if there are kids watching

at home, what would be your advice to them if they're thinking about climbing on high walls?'

'Ehm . . . don't do it!'

'Right. Or you *could* end up like him.'

'Hey!' I said.

'Cut! Who the fuck was that?'

'Just . . . you know, don't treat my boyfriend like a piece of meat, OK?'

'That's how I treat all my boyfriends. Ha ha ha!' laughed Candice.

Roger came over and nudged her, and they had a quiet discussion for a second. Then Roger beckoned me over. I dragged my feet – if they were going to chuck me out, it wasn't happening without a sulk – but he sat me down with his best 'I may have an important job in TV but that doesn't mean I don't care' face on.

'You know, we're all terribly upset about your boyfriend.'

I glanced over. Candice was signing autographs for several of the nursing staff, and giggling.

'Yeh? What's his name?'

'Look, obviously you're upset. What Candice thought was that perhaps we could take you aside when we film the next bit and interview you about . . . how emotional it is for you, your long lonely vigil at the bedside of your beloved, that kind of thing.'

'We've only been here three days.'

'Yeh, well, whatever. We think it could really add something to the piece.'

A thought occurred to me.

'Well, there was something we were thinking of doing that could really help . . .'

And I told him about Chali's band.

'Hmm,' he said. 'Hmm, ya. Maybe we could have it as the finale . . . can they do something really sad? Do you think they know "O Little Town of Bethlehem"?'

'Probably not.'

He called Candice over and explained the idea. Candice looked me up and down again, as if unable to believe that a thought or fully formed sentence could have come out of my mouth.

'What are the band called?'

'Mr Big and the Spangles.'

'Oh yes, I've heard of them.'

I was surprised at this, but I found out later that Candice had to pretend to have heard of everyone, in case they were incredibly cool and she looked like she was missing out.

'So, they'll be all right then?'

'Yeh, sure, that'll be fine. Jazz up this piece of crap anyway. Oh, sorry.'

'Don't mention it.'

Really, it was going to be worth it just to see Dr Hitler's face.

'What was all that all about?' hissed Kate.

'Oh, yeh, we were talking about you and Josh.'

'*Really*?'

'No!'

Candice went through her piece to camera twice more, then the entourage moved off to paediatrics.

'Have you got any undersized children?' she was

saying as they left. 'Maybe we can poke them a little, get them to move about a bit.'

Dr Hitler stalked past us and slammed the ward door behind them.

'I hope I'm not going to have to ban *all* visitors,' she said, brusquely changing Addison's drip.

We stared at her in horror.

'You couldn't do that!'

'Really, am I the only one thinking of the *patient* around here?'

We left Magda crooning a Croatian lullaby to Addison. We figured he'd probably have had enough excitement for one night.

Josh was at home steaming vegetables.

'Are you trying to lose weight?' asked Kate accusingly.

He blinked at her.

'Maybe just a bit. Why?'

'No reason,' said Kate miserably, and went off on her own.

'She must really be missing that John guy,' mused Josh.

'Everyone's missing somebody,' I said pointedly, and toyed with a wet string bean. And ached for my own wet string bean.

'Who do I have to sleep with?' asked Chali excitedly.

'No one!'

'You asked for a gig and got it, just like that?'

'Yup. And they need me – I'm like, grieving widow.'

'You did tell them what kind of a band we are?'

'What kind of a band are you? They want you to do "O Little Town of Bethlehem".'

'We can do "Little Girls Dead in the Park".'

'Oh God. Maybe this wasn't a good idea after all.'

Chali grabbed me. 'And there's going to be TV people there and everything?'

'Lights, cameras, make-up people – it could be your big break!'

'And I don't even . . . I mean, surely somebody wants a blow job?'

'Somebody always wants a blow job,' I said, to the consternation of the man picking the largest, tackiest bunch of red roses we had out of their bucket. 'I mean, just look at him.'

'I think that's a "brown wings" bunch of roses,' said Chali. 'It's the biggest one in the shop.'

'I wouldn't like to be his girlfriend tonight.'

'Oh no. Sore.'

The man hastily paid for his purchase and scampered off.

'You're not really a filthy heavy metal band are you?'

'Oh yes we are. I don't suppose they'll want to hear "I Wish I Could Die Every Day"?'

'Ehmm . . . what about "I Wish It Could Be Christmas Every Day"?'

'This could be tricky.' Chali nodded her head. 'I'm going to have to give this some serious thought.'

'OK, well, they're shooting next Monday, so be ready.'

'Huh! Even the roadies know me as "ever ready".'

'Especially the roadies, surely?'

I was amazed by how quickly my life had fallen into a routine. I got up, I went to work, I slacked off, then I went and sat with Addison for as long as I could. That was it. Plus occasional refereeing between Kate and Josh. It terrified me to think that this could go on for years. At what point, say the worst came to the worst, would I feel obliged to pack it in? Would I end up like Miss Havisham, doing the same thing every day, waiting for a kiss that was never going to come? Watching his beautiful face grow sunken from lack of use? Or worse, even – I pictured myself looking stoic but noble, as, with trembling hand and swelling choir, the machines were slowly switched off . . .

Two days after the attractive television incident, after daily hours of reading, talking and humming occasionally, I went in one rainy afternoon, shaking my head like a dog as I stomped up the stairs, through the familiar antiseptic-and-poor-people hospital fug. Patients cluttered around the doors, still smoking cigarettes with their drips in. Everyone looked as grey and worn as an old bra strap, including, I supposed, me. My grooming standards, never tip-top at the best of times, were gradually deteriorating. Putting on make-up felt like a betrayal.

As I paused at the door, Stephen crept up behind

me and tapped me on the shoulder. In my reverie – I was standing at the graveside looking elegant, I think – I wasn't paying attention and jumped six feet in the air.

'WHAT?'

Stephen looked hurt.

'Nothing. I just wanted to ask you what you thought of my new streaks.'

The top of his hair had gone a tacky, eighties-style blond, which didn't fit in well with his black spiky style.

'Club Tropicana?' I asked. He nodded. 'Are you going in for the super-gay awards?'

He smiled modestly. 'Are they really that good?'

'You're hyped up about this date, aren't you?'

'No.'

'Go on, admit it.'

He shrugged. 'Well, it makes a change from preaching to the converted.'

'OK . . . good luck.'

'Do you think I'm going to need it?'

'Stephen, I have known Josh for ten years . . . and I have no idea.'

'Oh well, it'll be a shoo-in, then. It's the really hetty bastards you have to watch out for.'

'Oh,' he added almost as an afterthought, 'and there's a new visitor today.'

'No, that's me – I just forgot to wash my hair,' I said.

'Behind the curtain. Definitely a fully signed-up member of the dweeb-o-rama brigade.'

Oh my God. It dawned on me instantly who the visitor had to be – let's face it, Addison's wide circle of friends had already been more or less exhausted. I winced when I thought of the alacrity with which I'd chucked Finn out on his ear when confronted with Add in the hallway – it seemed so long ago.

I peeked tentatively round the curtain of Addison's bed.

Finn was sitting on the bed, his corduroy trousers hitched up, his satchel on the floor, facing Addison, who looked as dead as he usually did. Finn was concentrating hard on something balanced on the sheet between them.

'OK, right, knight to knight's rook four,' he was saying. I realized he'd set up a chessboard between them. He stared at it for a long time.

'Oh, good move, Add.'

I moved closer, and inadvertently tripped on a trolley containing various dodgy stainless steel things that extracted Addison's poo or something. At least they were clean.

'Shite!'

Finn jumped up, upending the chessboard and scattering pieces everywhere.

'Jesus!'

We stood staring at each other, surrounded by detritus. The curtain was whipped back by Dr Hitler.

'What the hell is going on in here?'

Finn and I looked shamefacedly at each other.

'Oh. You,' she said to me. 'Do you actually *want* him to get better?'

'I thought the loud noise might . . . wake him up?' I said pathetically.

'Been reading up on the clinical trials, have we?'

'No . . .'

'I'm sorry, Doctor . . . it won't happen again,' said Finn.

'Oh? Who the hell are you?'

'I'm Dr Feynman Levy,' he said, proffering a hand.

'Oh . . . right,' she said, clearly disconcerted. She pushed back her thick hair and grinned at him almost coyly. 'I'm sorry . . . I didn't realize there was work going on.'

What *was* this magic effect Finn had on weird scientist girlies?

'Is she bothering you?'

What? I shot her a dirty look. Finn laughed.

'Yes, actually, she bugs the hell out of me. But I'm sure it would be OK if she stayed.'

'Well, thank you very much, Mr Cat Doctor,' I said when she'd gone, casting Finn a backwards glance that implied she'd quite like to square the root on *his* hypotenuse.

'I'm not a cat doctor.'

'Cats . . . wool . . . whatever it is.'

'String.'

'Huh.'

'Well, I got rid of her, didn't I?'

'I suppose so.'

'Next time I'm sending locusts,' came the voice from the next bed. I popped my head out.

'Hello, God.'

Finn popped his head out too.

'Are you God?'

God did his best to appear modest.

'Well, you know . . .'

'Huh. I don't believe in you,' Finn said.

'Really? Most people, a place like this – they at least make an odds-on bet.'

Finn nodded. 'I see your point. Well, very nice to meet you. Ehm . . . would you mind telling me how the universe works?

'Worth a shot,' he said to me quietly.

'Anything's better than that spaghetti thing you believe in,' I said.

'*String.*'

'Hmm,' said God. 'Really, you wouldn't like it if you knew.'

'Trust me – I'm a physicist.'

God contemplated it for a bit.

'Well, you know, to demonstrate it properly I'll need a bottle of whisky.'

Finn glanced at me, and I shook my head fiercely.

'I don't think . . .'

'Ach, you physicists – all the same. You think you want to know, but you don't really – it'd put you out of a job.'

And He immediately fell asleep, snoring loudly.

Finn smiled at me.

'Well . . . hello again.'

'Hello,' I said shyly. 'Ehm, I'm sorry I didn't . . .'

He shushed me. 'Not at all. I didn't realize . . . until Kate told me.'

We looked at Addison.

'It's very sad,' said Finn.

'Kate thinks she's got it worked out,' I said. 'Lots of singing and stuff.'

'I hope so.'

I moved round to the other side of the bed and picked up one of Addison's hands, trying to warm it. Finn started crawling around, picking up chess pieces and metal implements.

'Can you give us a song?' I asked.

'Absolutely not. Really, I've got a note from my mother.'

'What were you doing when I came in?'

He held up the board. 'Well, there's this game, you see, which was invented in the Middle East . . .'

'No, I know that much, you pillock. I mean, why?'

He shrugged. 'Well, I can't sing, so . . .'

'Do you think it's helping?'

'I can't tell . . . Still, he was winning.'

I picked up one of the pieces. 'How do you play this anyway?'

'You don't know how to play *chess*?'

'No, and I didn't buy my teacher a Christmas present either. Or hang around the computer lab at break-time.'

He looked embarrassed. 'Yeah, like I really missed out on learning how to smoke cigarettes.'

'Oh my God – I know what you are! You're a Teacher Pleaser! Teacher Pleaser!'

He hit me with a castley thing. 'Thank you for

adding another five years on to my therapy bill. Now, do you want to learn or not?'

'OK,' I said, sitting down. 'Did it upset you that you were too well behaved to get detention, when it would have meant more school, which you would have loved?'

He ignored me. 'OK. This is a prawn. This is a bish. And these are horsies. Horsies can jump.'

I eyed him suspiciously.

'What do the bishes do then? Swing both ways?'

'Yes, in a manner of speaking.'

So I sat next to him on the bed, and he taught me to play chess. Despite desperately doing his best to lose, it was physically impossible. I blamed all my moves on Addison and said he was psychically guiding me, but unfortunately not quite enough to save my queen from suicide missions.

After the third game, when I had taken to making all my lost pieces have little biting fights with each other, he said, 'So . . .' in that way that means, 'OK, enough fun and games young lady.'

'So . . .' I said. He looked at me, imploring me in a boyish way to, you know, talk about things and that, being the girl and everything.

'So . . .' I said. He glanced at Addison lying in the bed.

'I suppose I should be glad that it was him and not me.'

'What?!!'

Finn cringed. 'I'm sorry. I was trying to . . . you know . . . introduce the . . . Forget it.'

'That was well out of order.'

He hung his head even lower.

'I can't believe I even . . .'

'I think at least a hundred, possibly two.'

He glanced up. 'What?'

'Lines.'

Finn looked relieved.

'You know, I really really do hope he gets better, and that it works out fine for you.'

'He will,' I said fiercely, grasping Addison's hand. 'He has to. Otherwise . . . I'm going to set fire to the Houses of Parliament or something.'

'I know,' said Finn, and smiled his shy scruffy smile at me.

'God! I mean, we would never have got together, would we?'

'I don't know what you mean,' I said, crossly.

'Well, we're just so . . . chalk and cheese.'

I shrugged. 'Why, because you're such a big swot?'

'Maybe.'

I smiled at him.

'Are you seeing Madeleine?'

He shrugged. 'Now and again. She's finishing her PhD in cellular mitosis.'

'Wow. I can see how attractive that might be.'

I held out my clenched fists.

'Pick a prawn.'

'You can't wear pink! Are you crazy? That'd be like, if it was me going on a first date, wearing stockings and suspenders that you could see and a big T-shirt saying "Take me now".'

Kate and Josh both stared at me.

'. . . And that only happened the once. Josh, put the shirt away and go and put your grey top on.'

Kate sighed. 'Look, do you think you two girlies could get ready next door? Some of us have got *work* to do.'

'Ooh, bitchy,' said Josh. Then, to me: 'Oh my God, it's started!'

I smacked Josh on the head and dragged him into the living room to put some eyeliner on him.

'What did you do that for?'

'I don't know . . . practice?'

'I mean, why be nasty to Kate?'

'What? She's been super-nasty to me all week!'

'And it never occurred to you why that might be the case?'

'What do you mean?'

'Well, don't you think she started being particularly nasty to you when a certain someone started going out on dates . . . ?'

I waited for the penny to drop. One, two, three . . . ooh, there it was.

Josh's face was stricken.

'Oh my God.'

'Uh huh,' I said smugly.

'No wonder she's . . .'

'Yup.'

'But Stephen is *never* going to want to go out with her.'

I squeezed his shoulder. 'Please,' I said, 'just go.'

'What? What did I say.'

'Nothing. Now. Off you go. Have a wonderful time. Worry not.'

He paused.

'I am a bit worried, you know.'

'That's a healthy response.'

'Tell Skates I didn't mean it.'

'I will.'

'And tell my parents I love them.'

'Josh, you are *not* going on a date with Dennis Nilsen.'

'I know. But if I come back different then I just wanted to be . . .'

'You will never be different, J.'

'Fine. Good. Right. OK, bye then.'

'I mean, you walk funny now.'

'Piss off!'

He wiggled out the door.

Kate was sitting at the kitchen table, disconsolately pushing her computer mouse around.

'Don't tell me . . . you're playing patience as a displacement activity?'

She smiled wanly.

'So my therapist tells me.'

I sat down next to her.

'What else does your therapist tell you?'

'Well . . .'

'Go on, tell me. I've always been fascinated.'

'Yeah, you know, nosiness isn't always a good thing.'

'You're pointing that out to me? Or is that a piece of therapist wisdom? Either way, it's far too late.'

Kate sighed. 'What does my therapist tell me . . . ? Well, basically, I pay her eighty pounds an hour and she tells me that everyone is a bastard except me. Or rather, she agrees with me that everyone is a bastard except me.'

'You're joking!'

'Not at all. That's pretty much it. I go in and tell her who's being horrid and she agrees and says it's not my fault I'm so sensitive. Everyone. In the world. A cunt. Except me.'

'Wow,' I said. 'Actually, I can see why that might be appealing.'

'It's not designed to be appealing. It's the world of big business.'

'Are you sure you haven't just been watching too many films from the eighties?'

'Did you come in for a reason?'

'Yes. Message from Josh.'

Kate glanced up, momentarily startled.

'He didn't mean what he said.'

'That's it? That's the message?'

'Yup.'

'Bastard.'

'He's not one, though, is he?'

She looked at me sharply.

'What do you mean?'

'That's where your therapist runs into trouble. Josh doesn't have a bastard bone in his body.'

'So?'

'So, well, you know . . .'

Kate grabbed hold of a wine bottle which seemed to have just materialized.

'So, he's gay. OK, so it doesn't matter. All right?'

'He's not gay,' I said. I checked my watch. 'Well, not yet.'

Kate poured herself a large glass of wine but neglected to ask me if I wanted one.

'All this time. All this time, you know? "Everyone's a bastard, Kate. They're all bastards except us. The bigger the bastard you can find, the better you're doing."'

She contemplated her wine glass and sniffed loudly.

'Then I meet . . . then I *realize* that there is one guy in my life who is not a bastard, and what happens?'

'He goes out to find out what it's like to have other men touch him on the bottom?'

'Well, *exactly*!!'

I annexed some of the wine.

'Whatever happened to John then?'

'Nothing happened. I just realized that he was yet another in a long line of penis heads and that, you know, the person I really liked was . . . on my own doorstep.'

I squinted at her.

'And?'

'OK, so, and, I ran into John – or should I say *Arnold* –'

'I knew it!'

'– and his poxy wife at a bankers' conference. But that's got nothing to do with it.'

'OK,' I said, holding my fingers up in the air. 'Hold on a second. Exhibit one: you have never moved out of this house, despite having more money than Stella McCartney makes in a year during which people want to eat food, listen to music and wear clothes all at the same time. Exhibit two: Josh has started having sex. Exhibit three: you have stopped having sex altogether. Exhibit four: when *do* you turn thirty, exactly?'

She looked at me crossly. 'In eleven months and eight days, although I don't see why that's got anything to do with it.'

'Ha! I'm a genius,' I said. 'QED. You'll probably be married in a year.'

Kate sat back in her chair, staring into space. 'But . . . even if, I mean . . . I mean, how do you know he even likes me?'

'Kate,' I said, trying not to sound patronizing and failing – I even patted her on the hand – 'what's not to like about you?'

Ten

'It's not that I *want* children necessarily . . .' Kate and I were sprawled across cushions on the sitting-room floor. It was later the same evening, and there was still no sign of Joshua. We were commiserating with each other. There were rather more empty wine bottles around than I remembered seeing earlier.

'I mean, I'm independent, have a good living, got everything . . .'

'You're desperate, aren't you?' I asked her.

'Well, I wouldn't want to say desperate exactly . . .'

'Pining? Fretful? Terrified of an empty life with cats and no meaning?'

'Well, something like that. Why, don't you want one?'

'I think I'm too clumsy for children. I'd drop it

down the stairs, like I did with that bottle of port Josh was given for his christening.'

Kate nodded. 'Yeh. Or like that time you left your shoes in the fridge.'

'I think I'd manage not to leave a baby in the fridge.'

'Yes, but probably best not to risk it, eh?'

'Prob'ly.'

Kate looked at her watch.

'You know all those girls called Sophie?'

'Those were different girls?'

'You know what I mean.'

'Uh huh.'

'Well, why don't I ever get a bit of that adoration from Josh?'

'Because you're a real person?'

'I mean, if he liked me, why didn't he walk around with a piece of toast stuck to his jacket, like he did with them?'

'Because he might have a chance with you?'

'Oh, thanks very much.'

'Hear me out, hear me out. The boy's terrified. It's taking him just that little bit longer to get over puberty than everyone else, OK?'

'But *why*??'

I settled back on the carpet. 'How the hell should I know? You're the one with the MBA. Maybe *no one* gets through puberty.'

'Shit,' said Kate. 'Still, at least I got to get off with a film star.'

'Exactly. That pretty much constitutes the perfect

puberty thing. Now all we have to do is get Josh through his rites of passage –'

'So to speak.'

'Yes, well. And make sure Addison gets to actually *hit* puberty. Then we'll all be there. Maturity Central.'

'It's a horrible word, puberty.' Kate was staring at the ceiling. She'd twisted the tin foil from the cork into the shape of a big heart.

'It is. As a word it practically smells. Too close to pus and pubic. I'll tell you what's a nice word, though.'

'What . . . Josh Junior?'

'Euch! Really, no, I was thinking of Penguin. As in Penguin biscuits. As in – there are some in the kitchen, do you feel like going and getting them and calling them dinner?'

'Just because we're lying on the floor having a discussion doesn't mean I've forgotten that little incident, you know.'

'I bet a mature person wouldn't mind a bit.'

She eyed me crossly. 'Mature people don't eat Penguins.'

'OK.' I pushed myself up off the floor. 'You go buy biscuit shares. I'm going to eat them.'

'Can I have a red one?' she called after me.

'I bet Josh is saying that right at this very second,' I said as I came back in, but I wished I hadn't when I saw her face.

* * *

We tried to stay up till Josh came back but it was impossible. Well, we could probably have managed it, had not Kate degenerated into passive-aggressive mode, alternately ignoring me, then suggesting I get a career in the City. Then we watched some American import Friday-night TV, designed to make anyone who was already miserably at home on a Friday night feel worse about themselves by watching what glamorous young Americans were getting up to.

As I was the only one who had to go to work the next morning, as soon as I started to feel sick from eating too many biscuits I sloped off to bed, and I heard Kate follow shortly afterwards. I tried to listen for the door opening, but I didn't hear Josh come home.

The next morning I was woken horribly early by the phone. I left it for a bit – Kate was usually conscientious enough about these things to sort it out – but no one was moving, so I opened the door with my hand – easy enough given the size of my room – wrapped myself up in a sheet and pulled myself into the hall like a caterpillar.

'Reghh?'

'Hellllaaayyyrr!'

I shook my head to clear it. What was Princess Anne doing phoning at seven o'clock on a Saturday morning?

'It's *Sophie.*'

Oh God! This could be interesting!

'Oh, *hello*, Sophie. This is Holly.'

'Yars, well. Joshua, please.'

'Ah, that might be a bit of a problem . . .'

'Where is he?'

I so longed to tell her the truth, just to set her little Alice band on end, but I didn't dare.

'He's . . . in the country this weekend.'

'Oh yars, ahem, so am I, *naturally* . . .'

That was odd, as I was sure I'd just heard an ambulance siren going past her flat.

'Can I take a message?'

'Maybe *you* could help.'

I curtsied and put the V's up at the phone.

'Maybe . . .'

'Well, I hear Joshua's tenant is ill.'

'Yes . . . ?'

'The thing is, my father thinks that it would help *considerably* with my nomination if I were to be seen to give money to a hospital . . .'

'What nomination?' I asked stupidly. 'Are you going in for the Eurovision Song Contest?'

'Oh, Holly, you can't waste qualifications like mine, you know! Everyone says so! No, for when I enter the *hais*.'

'Sophie, it's very early. What on earth are you talking about?'

She sighed.

'Look, are you *sure* Joshua isn't around?'

'Yes! Do you want me to tell him you called or not?'

She sighed again.

'I'm going to be an MP. Eventually. Once this disgusting government has been overthrown. So we need lots of nice pictures of me handing over cheques to those grateful, ghastly NHS types, yah? And we thought we'd do it where that dorky tenant of Josh's is – keep it all friendly. Yah?'

'But that's evil!'

'Yars, well, there's a natural class of government, Holly. So, don't worry yourself about it. Now, which hospital is your little friend in?'

'I'm not telling you!'

Sophie's sighs were becoming increasingly less world-weary and more irritated.

'Well, you can either ensure your friend gets the best treatment modern medicine can buy, or you can just ignore him . . . let him linger. Up to you, really.'

'It's St Hugh's,' I said, involuntarily.

'Well done. I'll bring the photographer. And tell Joshua I'll need him to help out – maybe I can let him pose as my boyfriend. Always politic to have an attractive partner. And that should please him, don't you think?' She laughed conspiratorially.

'You're pure evil!' I gasped again.

'Yars, welcome to the real world, darling. OK?' And she put the phone down.

It was not turning into a good day. At work, a bug bit me, then when I went in to see Addison he was upside down. Literally. Only the underside of the bed was visible. At first I thought they'd cleared him away altogether and not bothered to tell me. I simply stood and stared, my heart in my throat.

Then I noticed the straps on the bed and the fact that the beeping machine was still beeping in a vaguely reassuring manner.

Stephen wasn't anywhere to be seen either – I didn't even want to think about that – but one of the younger nurses told me they had turned Add upside down to stop him getting bed sores. I hadn't thought it was for fun, like a fairground ride, but it did make me worry about how long they thought he was going to be here for – like, did they really think he was going to be here long enough to make his skin fall off?

I approached the bed. I'd bought a *Scientific American* to read out to him, and there weren't many other visitors around. After saying hello to God, who told me that it was the sixth day and God was having a rest – I said wasn't that Sunday and he said no, he had just declared it was Saturday and the Jews had always been right about practically everything anyway – I couldn't quite find a good position where I could be sure Add could hear me, so eventually I simply scooted down under the bed where I could lie on the ground facing up at him.

OK. This was weird. This was definitely weird. Addison's pale skin flopped loosely around the straps – it struck me that Japanese comics and a certain class of Englishmen tended to find that kind of thing quite sexy. Our respective positions were definitely on the unusual side too, although there was about a foot between us. It reminded me of the old James Bond film where they have sex in space at the end, except the towel covering them goes down instead of up.

The first thing I noticed was that Addison no longer had a tube in his mouth. This could only mean one thing – he was breathing! This was wonderful news. Well, it would have been more wonderful had he been awake – and there was a definite pool of spit and crustiness around his mouth – but still. This had to be a good sign.

'Hey!' I said softly, reaching my arm up to tickle him. I don't think tickling is well known as a coma cure and, unsurprisingly, it didn't work.

'You look like Superman. I bet if you were awake, you'd love this. I should take a photograph, so you can see yourself flying.'

Always so thin, he seemed to have got even thinner in the last few days – his ribcage was a series of angles.

'OK,' I said. 'Here we go. *Scientific American*. The latest scientific news from the country that doesn't believe in evolution. What do you fancy – "How Broadband Internet Access May Influence Social Metamorphoses"? You know what . . . that's probably a bit late for you. Ooh, how about "The Theory Formerly Known as String" by Dr Michael Duff?'

Addison showed no objection, so I launched in:

'"At a time when certain pundits are predicting the End of Science on the grounds that all the important discoveries have already been made, it is worth emphasizing that the two main pillars of twentieth-century physics, quantum mechanics and Einstein's general theory of relativity, are mutually incompatible. General relativity fails to comply with the quantum rules that govern the behaviour of elementary particles, whereas on the opposite scale, black holes are challenging the very foundations of quantum mechanics. Something big has to give. This predicament augurs less the bleak future of diminishing returns predicted by the millennial Jeremiahs and more another scientific revolution . . ." Blah blah blah.'

I yawned. 'You love this, don't you? You big weirdo.

'"Until recently, the best hope for a theory that would unite gravity with quantum mechanics and describe all physical phenomena was based on strings: one-dimensional objects whose modes of vibration represent the elementary particles. In the past two years, however, strings have been subsumed by M-theory. In the words of the guru of string theory, Edward Witten of the Institute for Advanced Study in Princeton, N.J., 'M stands for Magic, Mystery or Membrane, according to taste'. New evidence in favour of this theory is appearing daily, representing the most exciting development since strings first swept on to the scene."

'Oh my God!' I sat upright, and accidentally hit Addison on the nose, but it didn't make him bleed or anything. 'I wonder if Finn knows about this? This could really cack his work up!'

I was genuinely worried for him. I mean, he'd spent years on this.

'What do you think? Should I phone Finn and tell him it's all a bunch of crap! Oh no! And, he'll think I'm just doing it to annoy him.'

There was a chuckle and suddenly a pair of brogues

appeared beside the bed. A familiar person crouched down beside me, clutching a chessboard.

'You would really ruin an entire theory of the universe just to annoy me?'

'Oh no!' I said. 'Have you read this? You're in serious shit!'

He smiled again. 'Well, sometimes the paradigm changes, and you have to go along with it and add new ideas to your thinking. Let's just say that my "spaghetti" is now looking more like "ravioli".'

'Phew,' I said. 'So, you really do make it up as you go along?'

'Pretty much.'

'All those years of hard sums were for nothing then?'

'Well, I can work out twenty-four hour clock times.'

He leaned in to take a look at Addison. 'How's he doing?'

'Do you want to come in and see? His breathing tube's out! Isn't that fantastic?'

Finn looked concerned. 'Not really. Can I come under and see?'

'Sure!' I budged up. OK, this was now treble weird. I was in a bizarre sex sandwich between Finn and Addison, who was strapped up and completely unconscious.

'Weird huh?' I said, trying to break the ice.

'Well, not weird exactly,' said Finn, obviously completely unaware of our physical proximity. I cursed myself for being a sex maniac. 'It's just, they were probably hoping that if they took the breathing apparatus away it would stimulate him to breathe for himself . . .'

'Which it did . . .'

'. . . which in turn would stimulate him to wake up. Which it doesn't appear to have done.'

'You mean, this is *bad*?'

'It certainly implies that he could conceivably be under for longer than they thought. If his physical problems sort themselves out but he's still not conscious . . . that's not good, Holl.'

'Jesus,' I said, blinking back tears. 'I didn't realize.'

'It's OK,' said Finn, taking my hand. 'It's not over.' Then we stiffened as an unmistakable pair of scuffed pumps bossily made their way across the ward to Addison's bed.

'This way,' said Dr Hitler bossily. A shuffling bunch of shoes followed her. Without even being able to see them, they sounded like students. The curtains were drawn back abruptly. Finn and I looked at each other and winced. It was too late to move – we were already surrounded. Finn tightened his grip on my hand and we tried to stay stock still. I could hear my heart beating like a hammer.

'Right. If you'd like to examine the charts, what we're seeing here is a state of unarousable neurobehavioural unresponsiveness, currently in progress for ninety-six hours.'

How many days did that make it again I wondered? Finn shot me an incredulous look.

'*Four*,' he whispered.

'We're going to have to start looking at an intensive physiotherapy programme to forestall the onset of heterotopic ossification, although of course that's not exactly a primary concern.'

'When they catch us, they're going to put us in the cooler!' I whispered to Finn.

'Just remember,' he whispered, 'whenever they ask you a question, answer in German.'

'Thank you.'

'No! That's what did for Richard Attenborough!'

'How are we going to escape?'

Above us, the medical students were pontificating on poor old Add, or having a competition to see who could shout the longest words the loudest – I couldn't tell.

'Maybe they won't notice us.'

'Don't say that, you'll immediately have to sneeze or something.'

Our eyes went wide as we both realized how dusty it was underneath the bed and how, indeed, we did both have to sneeze. We'd cursed ourselves completely. We held on to our noses as our eyes watered and blinked. Finn squished his nose up like a rabbit, which meant that if I wasn't about to sneeze, I was certainly about to laugh.

It came like something out of a cartoon, when the Acme Company delivers an enormous box of pepper to someone. We simultaneously 'ATCHOOED' all over the place.

'He's sneezing! That's a conscious sign!' said one of the students.

'It sounded like a double sneeze though,' said another.

I sighed as, slowly, the owners of the six pairs of legs came into view. I closed my eyes and squeezed Finn's hand tightly (not the hands we'd sneezed into). He squeezed back.

'WWWEELLLLLL!' said Dr Hitler, as if she'd just found out I was born in a handbag.

'And so . . .' said Finn quickly, 'this is what we mean by the word *down*, and where we were before was what we mean by the word *up*.'

'I've been confusing those for *years*,' I said, scrambling out from under the bed and dusting myself down.

'Thank you, Dr Levy! So, this is *up*, yes?'

'That's correct. No more falling down for you!'

'Wow! Shall we go *down*stairs?'

'Indeed. And perhaps we can practise *near* and *far* by first attempting *far*.'

We started walking quickly away from the bed.

'Remind me again of the distinctions between *fast* and *slow*?' I asked.

The medical students watched in disbelief as we made our exit.

'It is at times like these when you may find your belief in the Hippocratic oath severely tested,' said Dr Hitler loudly, so I could hear.

'It's at times like this when you may wish Anthony Edwards was actually QUALIFIED,' I said loudly, as Finn shooed me away.

* * *

Finn had to go off to some boring thing at the Royal Geographical Society. Well, it may or may not have been boring, but I certainly wasn't invited, and – guess what – Madeleine was. How charming for them both. I stomped off home by myself, picturing Finn surrounded by hordes of smarty pants bespectacled lovelies, then got cross with myself for picturing it, then felt horribly disloyal and nasty, like those men you see in the drink-driving ads who leave their girlfriends after they've been in disfiguring accidents. So finding an atmosphere at 44 Bisthmus Road that you could make into ice sculpture was hardly ideal.

'Hey!' I said tiredly, walking in the door, hoping against hope that just *once* my flatmates would leap up, remove my coat and coo with endless sympathy at my burden before presenting me with gin and tonics and home-baked cakes. There was no reply. I wished we had a dog – or, better still, one of those Japanese robot dogs that could make you a gin and tonic *and* be pleased to see you.

I leafed through the post – you never know, despite acres and years of evidence to the contrary, someone might decide to send a nice surprise out of the blue – then, empty-handed, slouched through to the kitchen, trying not to think about the fact that it was Saturday night and I had fuck all to do. I didn't even have a meeting of the bloody Royal Geographical Society to go to, for fuck's sake. Josh was sitting slumped at the kitchen table with his back to me.

I eyed him closely. It wasn't a 'having trouble coming to terms with my new sexuality' slouch. On the other hand, he wasn't wearing a Jean-Paul Gaultier sailor's outfit either.

'Yo?' I said, experimentally. Josh waved an exhausted hand.

'Hey.'

I stepped round the table and sat opposite him. '*Well?*'

He raised his arms Gallicly. 'Well???'

'Well, go on . . . you are going to tell me, aren't you?'

Josh heaved a sigh.

'I suppose so.'

'Hooray! Do you want to wait for Kate? Please say no. Tell me first.'

'I don't have to wait for Kate. She's already here. She's sulking in her room.'

'*Oh.*'

There was a pause whilst I debated with myself how much I wanted to talk about Kate. Not at all!

'Well, *tell* me then.'

Josh gave a sigh.

'OK. Well, we went to Snows . . .'

'*And?*'

'Do you want to hear this or not?'

'I want to hear whether you did it, not whether you both had starters.'

Josh sat up suddenly.

'Holl, do you think I'm homophobic?'

'Well, given that you openly date men, probably not.'

'No, I mean, really.'

'I don't know – try this multiple choice. Do you call homosexuals a) botty burglars, b) uphill gardeners or c) darling . . . *I* don't know, do I? I don't think so.'

'OK. Well, then, ehm . . . I don't think I'm gay.'

'Because why?'

'No reason.'

'Josh! You did it, didn't you?'

He squirmed. 'Well, maybe.'

'You did! You're a cheap date! Oh my God! What was it like?!'

'What do you mean, what was it like? It was like going to bed with a man.'

'Oh, yeah, right. But you know, I *like* doing that.'

'Well, I didn't like it. It was all . . . hard, and hairy.'

'Hard and hairy are usually seen as positive attributes – Robin Williams excepted.'

'Huh. Well, I definitely didn't like it. I think I like . . . soft, and kind of mushy.'

I nodded understandingly. 'Yup. That'll be girls.'

He nodded. 'So.'

'Well then, aren't you pleased?' I said. 'Now you've sorted all that out? You can get on with having lots of meaningless relationships that end up in degradation and heartache, just like the rest of us!'

'I know,' he said. 'And that does feel good. It's just . . . well, Stephen is so nice, you know. I hate to let him down like this.'

'Ooh no,' I said. 'Stephen's my friend, and I won't have you pretending to be gay out of politeness. It's not fair to drag someone on like that. What about

Sophie and you? God, the way she treated you, I could have told her where to go when she rang this morning . . .'

'Sophie rang?'

'No!'

'Oh my God! Why didn't you *tell* me?'

'I don't know . . . Because you were out being Big Gay Al?'

'I'm just going to ring her . . .' he said, diving out of the room.

'Oh, well done,' I said, and gave myself a sarcastic round of applause.

As soon as I could hear him buzzing excitedly on the line, his vowels elongating by the second, the door creaked, and Kate popped her head in, red-eyed.

'*Well?*'

'Well what?' I said to annoy her.

'Well, is he or isn't he? I haven't been able to sleep, you know.'

'You sounded asleep this morning when I had to get up to answer the phone,' I grumbled.

'How can you say that? I've . . . never felt like this before. Please don't scoff at me.'

'What about the dog dentist bloke?'

'HOLLY!' she said, exasperated.

'OK, OK. Do you want the good news or the bad news?'

Kate sidled in and sat down.

'Good news, please. Is he in love with me?'

'Ehm . . . well, he's not gay.'

'Good! OK, what's the bad news?'

'Guess who he's on the phone to . . .'

She looked at me for a second.

'It can't be.'

'It is.'

I explained Sophie's evil scheme. Kate was clearly furious. Then she gave me a pleading look.

'No!' I said immediately.

'Well, you know . . .'

'You want me to overthrow a chance of Addison getting some extra money to make him better so that you can try and get off with Josh without any competition.'

'And stop the world being overrun by over-privileged fascists in parliament!' said Kate, scandalized. 'Do you think I'm completely heartless?'

'I don't know. But I am taking Sophie's money, I'm afraid.'

'Class traitor.'

'Haaa!' I turned on Kate, just as Josh bounced back into the room like the Andrex puppy.

'Guess what, everyone! That was Sophie!'

'Oh, I thought someone was dragging their fingernails down a blackboard,' said Kate.

Josh ignored her.

'And she's presenting a cheque to the hospital wing where Addison is! AND I told her about the television cameras coming to film Holly, so she's going to do it on Monday afternoon!'

'No. No no no. Please, not on TV,' I said.

'But think,' said Josh sincerely, 'this money could change the lives of hundreds, if not thousands –'

'– of prospective Conservative candidates,' said Kate. 'Josh! Holly! Please don't let this happen!'

'But . . .'

'And *I* think . . .'

'No way!'

We were well on our way to a full-blown barney when the doorbell rang.

We stopped scrapping, and looked at each other.

'Well, it's not Sophie, because she's in the country,' said Josh. I sniffed.

'And it's not John because he's NOT JOHN,' said Kate sourly.

They both looked at me. Even though I knew it couldn't possibly be Addison, I felt a sudden thrill of anticipation as I tiptoed to the door and down the stairs.

'Hello?' I asked tentatively.

'Jhnghf?' came the noise from the other side of our admittedly heavy door. I opened it nervously, preparing my face.

'Hello,' said Addison's mother, smiling nervously at me.

I obviously didn't prepare my face enough because it must have looked a bit disappointed.

'I am sorry . . . this is a bad time?'

'No! No, this is absolutely the *best* time!' I said, ushering her in.

'I made a goulash . . .' I noticed she was carrying a heavy bowl.

'Why, that's brilliant. Kate, Josh . . .'

I brought Magda into the kitchen. Both appeared surprised then managed to make themselves look pleased. I kicked myself for not sorting my face out better downstairs.

'I hope I am not intruding . . .'

'No, of course not,' we all said, in a totally over-the-top way, so that even though it was true it sounded false.

'Sit down,' said Josh, springing into gentlemanly action. 'Why don't I open a bottle of wine?'

We all made appreciative noises as Magda handed over her goulash. It became clear that she was simply in search of a bit of companionship, and there was nothing mysterious at all about her visit. Except for the obvious, which Kate asked her as soon as we were all sat round the table eating.

'Ehm, Magda . . . how did you know we'd all be in on a Saturday night?'

Magda shrugged tactfully. 'I just . . . no, really, I did not know.'

'I think the thing that worries me most,' said Magda when we had moved on to the sitting room to finish the wine, 'I think . . . is when he wakes . . . he will be different.'

'What do you mean?' asked Josh.

'No, I know,' said Kate. The imposition of an external – and maternal – force on us had made us be civil, and that had gradually relaxed into actually being pleasant – maintaining huff status, as everybody knows, being simply too exhausting and bothersome. 'I read about it. Sometimes people wake from periods of unconsciousness with different personality habits. One guy woke up speaking French.'

'Oh, whereabouts in France?' I asked, then wished I hadn't.

'Yes, that is the kind of thing I mean,' said Magda. 'Or that he has amnesia.'

'Oh, that would be *great*,' I said. Then, after a pause, I decided to get up and make the coffee.

'Wow. Addison with a different personality,' mused Josh, voicing our thoughts.

'You'd never shut him up.'

'Yes, he'd be off climbing mountains all over the world then boasting about it,' said Kate.

'Or he'd become a hippy and go and live in a field and kiss rabbits.'

'Or write poetry with a quill pen.'

'Or become a Radio One DJ,' I chipped in from the kitchen.

'Or a consumer affairs television presenter!'

We mused on the amount of opposite personalities Addison could have.

'I think I'd like my son back the way he was,' said Magda.

'Me too,' said Kate.

'Me three,' I said in a small voice.

Eleven

Six forty-five on Sunday morning. I lay fuming, listening to the phone blare at me. Wasn't it enough that my bedroom was small enough to cause carbon dioxide poisoning if you didn't keep a window open without having to suffer assault by phone?

Nope. Definitely no one else was moving. It suddenly occurred to me that it might be the hospital and I swore and performed my patented duvet jam roly-poly manoeuvre into the hall.

'Rrgh?'

'Is that Holly Ferguson?'

'Ehmm . . . yes?' I jerked awake. I always snap to attention when somebody uses my full name, in case I'm not listening and get arrested for something I didn't do.

'Oh, yes, hi, this is Roger Montserrat? I'm the producer for Candice Piper's show?'

'Hello,' I said grumpily. 'Don't tell me – you're at a coke-fuelled TV party and haven't been to bed yet?'

He pretended to laugh loudly.

'Actually, we thought we'd find you at the hospital.'

'It's six forty-five in the MORNING.'

'I know . . . it's just, one of the male nurses said you were very dedicated.'

'I am FUCKING dedicated. Didn't you hear me? It's six forty-five in the . . .'

'Quite, yes, all right. Anyway, just wanted a little chinwag about tomorrow?' He had one of those annoying nasal voices that turns everything into a question.

'OK,' I said, leaning against the telephone table and preparing to give a faintly sanitized history of my relationship with Addison. 'Well, we met . . .'

'What colours were you planning on wearing?'

'What?'

'Candice is most particular that no one clashes. She was planning on pistachio, so we'd be most grateful . . .'

'Hang on,' I said, shaking my head to clear it. 'What colour is pistachio? Pale brown?'

'It's green.'

'Green? Like, rotting nuts?'

'Ha ha ha. So, if you just steer away from the primary palettes, I'm sure everything will go perfectly smoothly. We haven't heard from your band's agent yet, but we'll be expecting you all around two, OK?'

'Hang on!' I said, panic-stricken. 'What am I actually going to *do*?'

He seemed stupefied by the question.

'Just . . . you know, dear, you'll be on *TV*!'

'Doing *what*?'

He sighed. 'Just turn up in non-clashing pastels and prepare to try and make yourself cry, darling. OK? We'll handle the rest. Remember: it's all for the best and you'll be on TV! Brilliant, eh?'

I went back to sleep and had one of those horrible early-morning nightmares – I was being pursued by Addison tied upside down on a board whilst trying to find a non-green smock in my wardrobe, which was inexplicably turning into a bowl of spaghetti. I finally got up when I heard Josh banging about in the kitchen washing up. Not having to do the washing-up – well, I was taking my small bonuses where I could find them.

I had to phone Chali about the next day. It occurred to me that if I was going to be there and she was going to be there, there was a small shop opening problemo, and I needed her advice.

Of course, a big troll thing picked the phone up.

'Chali?'

'Ugh??'

'CH-ALEE, PLEASE,' I said, enunciating very slowly.

'Ugh, uhu.'

After half an hour, Chali came on the line.

'Yes? Buster, stop that.'

'What's he doing?'

'You don't want to know. There's snuffling involved.'

'You're right. I don't want to know. Do you want me to phone back?'

'No, don't be silly, we're only having sex. Is this about the band?'

'Are you still ready to go ahead?'

'Is it still on? Oh, that's brilliant! We've written a special song.'

'What's it called?'

'"The New Coma Suture".'

'Oh God.'

'No, it'll be cool. It's still thrash, but I add an air of eastern exoticism.'

'What are we going to do about the shop?'

She thought for a moment.

'God. I'd ask my uncle, but apparently he's down to absolutely no faculties or marbles whatsoever. Hmm . . . Buster, lower.'

I hung on the phone. After about a minute she said, 'I've got it!'

'What?'

'We go on strike! We've got rights, haven't we?'

'I don't know about the right to take a day off to be on TV.'

'No, no, we should. Form a protest.'

'What for – communal tea bags?'

'Come on, Holl – Christ, we barely make minimum wage.'

'Yes, but you steal.'

'Not the point. I'll phone old butterbum now. Terrorize her into accepting our demands.'

'Hadn't you better wait a bit, in case she does accept them and we still have to turn up?'

'Good point. Fear not. I'll see you tomorrow.'

'Two o'clock,' I said. 'And don't wear anything pistachio.'

She snorted. 'God, could you *be* any more middle-aged? Buster, *stop* that.'

'Urhgh.'

'Oh no, don't stop *that*.'

I put the phone down.

'I rather *like* pistachio,' said Josh, holding up two ties whilst doing his Sunday night ironing.

'Josh, you don't know what you like, so shut up,' said Kate.

'Also, nobody must come,' I said. 'If I have to humiliate myself in this way, I'd rather do it alone.'

'Sophie asked me to come, so there,' said Josh, selecting the mulberry tie and poking his tongue out at me.

Kate heaved a sigh and pushed her salad around her plate with a fork.

'Not coming, Skates? Don't you want to be part of the television extravaganza? It'll be a laugh.'

'It's not *meant* to be a laugh,' I said.

'And of course in a very good cause . . .'

'I've got work,' said Kate finally. 'Do you think the Stock Exchange stops because someone's in a coma?'

Josh and I looked at each other.

'Depends who it is,' he said. 'I mean, if it was the Governor of the Bank of England . . .'

'Or the Pope, maybe,' I chipped in.

'. . . or your flatmate and friend,' said Josh.

'Look, just can it, OK?' said Kate. 'You and *Sophie* go off and have a brilliant time. Why don't you get famous, like that woman who couldn't drive a car? Make a record? Go to parties with Keith Chegwin? I really couldn't give a fuck. But just leave me alone, OK, Josh?'

She got up and stormed out of the room.

'Wow, has Kate got problems with her love life or something?' said Josh, peering after her.

I couldn't sleep. Every time I closed my eyes my mind began whirring through an exhausting litany of things that might happen, including:

- I get fired (because I deserved to be)
- I wear the wrong colour and they make me wear an old man's pyjamas
- The band get us banned from TV
- Candice makes nasty personal remarks about me
- Josh and Sophie get engaged and I have to cook for myself
- It doesn't work for Addison. Because, as I don't need Kate's flow chart to remind me, he is running out of time.

* * *

When I say I couldn't sleep I . . . well, I managed to sleep pretty late into the morning, then scrambled up in a panic. The house was quiet. Outside, it was threatening to turn into the most beautiful day. I wandered over and confronted my wardrobe. I had no idea I had so many green things. Black wasn't going to work either, not sitting next to someone with pitch-black hair who was as pale as death. I'd look like the Crow of Doom, perched on his shoulder. Is there a Crow of Doom? It didn't matter, I discarded all black and grey items forthwith. And navy – I could never tell the difference. OK. There wasn't a lot left now, and rather a lot of that seemed to be pink. I sighed. If only Kate ate less salad and more sausage rolls, I could have borrowed something of hers. I picked up an old T-shirt that said 'Free Nelson Mandela'. Well, it would have been a good message to get out on TV, but perhaps a little unnecessary now. Finally I settled on a stripy top and a plain long skirt, in a vain attempt at 'willowy'.

Before I left the house, I crept into Addison's room.

'Don't worry, guys,' I said to his stacked computers, 'I'll bring him home.'

Someone had turned the monitor off, so there was no Claudia. I walked around slowly, patting things. Magda had taken lots of his *Star Trek* stuff and put it round his hospital bed, so Add's room wasn't as cramped as usual. I picked up a small Han Solo figure.

'You're coming with me,' I said. 'You're known for getting people out of sticky situations. We need you now, Han.' And I put him in my pocket.

'Look at you,' I addressed the computers again. 'Enough power to run the space shuttle and you can't do a damn thing for the person that loves you the most.'

The computers winked at me.

'And don't be cheeky.'

I shut the door behind me quietly.

From the moment I stepped inside the hospital, I could tell there was something going on. Staff who normally slouched about the corridors were bustling officiously up and down. Everyone was moving a bit quicker than normal and had suspiciously clean hair. Yup, the TV cameras must be in.

I was so used to weird goings on in the high-dependency unit that I almost didn't notice when I walked through the familiar swing doors. This, however, was something else altogether. For starters, there was an enormous Christmas tree in the middle of the ward. Big, cheap and nasty plastic wreaths had been randomly placed on the walls, with what were obviously large empty cardboard boxes hastily covered in cheap wrapping paper, so you could still see the flavour of crisps the boxes had held. I nearly retched when I saw Addison's bed. Somebody had dressed him in garish red pyjamas, but that wasn't the worst thing – they had also seen fit to hang some mistletoe above his bed.

'What?' I said out loud. There were about four times

as many people as there normally were on the ward, and about twice as many nursing staff. Stephen spotted me and came to my rescue.

'Excited?' he said.

'To the point of vomiting,' I replied. 'What are you doing here?'

'It's my day off,' he said. 'I came in anyway. Plus, there's this particular sound recordist . . .'

'You tart!' I said. 'I expected to find you crying your eyes out over your lost love.'

'Who, your friend?' He grinned wickedly. 'I don't think so. It was a lot of fun to watch, though.'

'You're an *evil* tart!'

'Sweet!'

'Still, at least you helped,' I said, hitting him with a bit of tinsel.

'Good. Now, do you want to come over and join the party?'

I looked around – Chali and her menagerie clearly hadn't arrived yet, but the television crew was bustling around. Several other families were also with their patients, hovering nervously. Not one person was wearing green. Candice – a vision in snot – and Dr Hitler were in front of the nurses' station, talking very intently to each other in the way that people do when they're trying to pretend to the outside world that they aren't having a row.

'All I'm saying,' Candice was whining as Stephen and I walked over, 'is that I don't see why we can't just change that little room into make-up. God, it's only for a day.'

'And all I'm saying is could you please stop talking nonsense about things you don't understand, like how much we use the disinfecting room and the importance of clean things to sick people,' Dr Hitler hissed back at her.

'Hi,' I said. They both straightened up.

'Yes?' said Candice snottily.

'Ehm . . . I'm meant to be in your show.'

'Oh, well done. Why don't you go and speak to Roger, and I'll sort out any autographs later on, OK? . . . Look, Doctor, surely you have an operating theatre or something we could use?'

I glanced at Stephen and he made the thumbs-up sign at me.

'She's *such* a bitch,' he said. 'I *love* her.'

Roger was nowhere to be found so I went over to Addison's bed to try and remove the mistletoe.

'What's going on?'

I leaned across to the next bed.

'God, if *you* don't know, what hope is there for the world?'

'None. You're all doomed and you're all going to hell, especially the Protestants. And the Liberal Democrats. And David Essex.'

'You're a very grumpy God today.'

'Well, I'm not feeling well and they keep shining lights in my eyes. It's like being back in Japan in '44.'

'Why don't you ask them to close the curtains?'

'Not Christmassy enough, apparently.'

'Oh. Well, they're making a TV show and they're

having a band play to try and wake up some of the coma patients. Then hopefully they'll piss off and leave us alone.'

'Huh,' said God. 'Well, at least I get to wear my best pyjamas.'

'It's still a beautiful world,' I said.

'HOLL!'

A vision in silver came clopping up the ward in enormously high-heeled shoes.

'Aha – one of my angels!' said God.

'Not exactly,' I said. 'Chali? What's the matter?'

'Nothing. Well, my shoes are killing me. But apart from that, everything's fine. Mrs Bigelow is FURIOUS.'

'That's not fine.'

'Oh, yes it is. She's opening the shop by herself! I almost wish we weren't here, so we could see how she's getting on, doing a day's work for a change.'

'I'm sure she's finding it tough,' I said. 'Probably won't even have time to paint all ten fingernails.'

Chali stopped suddenly in front of Addison's bed, and looked at me.

'Is this him?'

I nodded.

'Oh, God, Holl, you didn't tell me he was so gorgeous.'

'Ehm, I think you'll find that's pretty much *all* I told you.'

She gently stroked his face. 'God. Wow. Hey, is this mistletoe?'

'No!' I grabbed it off her. She pouted.

'Well, his pyjamas are horrible, anyway. Where can we set up?'

'How many of you are there?' I said with some concern as a line of grubby blokes filed through the ward door, each carrying a piece of sound equipment or an extension lead.

'Ah,' said Chali. 'Well, when I told Mr Big . . . lots of people wanted to get on TV. So, the band's a bit . . . larger than it was.'

'How much larger?'

'Well . . . there was five of us . . . ?'

'Uh huh.'

'Now there's about fourteen.'

'Fourteen?'

'I'm still the only vocalist. Mr Big is on lead guitar. Two bass players. A rhythm guitarist, four drummers and five backing singers.'

'Jesus, Chali, we're trying to wake these people, not punish them.'

'It's my big break, remember? And don't worry, I'll make sure they're OK,' said Chali pleadingly.

'Urhg! Chocolates!' At the other side of the ward, one of the Spangles was half-inching gifts from a critically ill person.

I let out a long sigh. 'Well, it's not me you have to convince. There's a guy called Roger who . . .' As I spoke, Roger himself appeared.

'Quick, come and meet Roger.'

Roger was walking around half in a daze carrying a tray of designer coffees.

'Hi.'

He looked at us both with a complete lack of recognition.

'It's Holly Livingstone,' I said. 'I'm not surprised you don't recognize me during daylight hours.'

'Oh, yes, hello.' He took me in for the first time.

'Oh my God. Stripes?'

'What?'

'You're wearing stripes. I'm sorry, that won't do at all, yeh?'

'Yeah, well, forget about that. This is Chali Sanghara, lead singer with Mr Big and the Spangles.'

'The carol singers, right?'

'Ehm, well . . .'

'Great . . . just set up anywhere, yeh?'

And he ran away from us towards Candice, brandishing the coffee.

Chali and I looked at each other, and she shrugged and went over to help the band set up in the far corner. One of the gnome army, his mouth covered in chocolate, leaned down to plug in his amplifier, eliciting a screech from Dr Hitler, who was getting increasingly puce and agitated at her ward being turned into a three-ring circus.

Last to arrive were Josh and Sophie, who entered the scene like some weird couple from a genetically perfect future. Their matching blond hair gleamed in the sunlight through the windows. Sophie was ostentatiously carrying a cheque the size of a playing field, bearing her name in huge letters, and a quite enormous number of noughts.

They'll never fit that under the banking counter, I thought mutinously. 'Hi, Josh. Hi, Sophie.'

'Hey,' said Josh. 'How's it going?'

Out of the corner of my eye, I'm sure I saw Dr Hitler smack one of the gnome army.

'Hmm. Not bad.'

'I must go and talk to Candice,' said Sophie. 'I'm hoping to bring her on board as one of my celebrity supporters.'

'I wouldn't bother,' I said. 'She's a bit of a bitch.'

Sophie, however, had already swanned her way over there. Josh and I waited a couple of minutes for the expected rebuff, but within seconds Candice and Sophie were blathering away like old friends.

'Sophie really does get on with *everyone*,' said Josh proudly.

'OK, everybody!' A loud voice rattled around the ward. I looked up. Roger was standing on someone's bed, hollering through a megaphone.

'Get *off* that!' shouted Dr Hitler.

'It's OK – they're asleep!' shouted Roger. 'Now, everyone, just a few ground rules. First, please stick to your own corners. We're only filming a short ten-minute segment, so this shouldn't take more than eight or nine hours. During that time please do not change clothes or your hair and make-up, for continuity reasons. Unless of course you cry and we want you to do it again, in which case you'll be taken off to make-up. We're going to film Candice, then the band, then the cheque, OK? Refreshments will be provided; once we've finished filming you, you will find a sandwich waiting for you at the door. Please don't take more than one. Oh, and please, on no account address Candice unless she speaks to you. In fact, we'd rather you didn't make eye contact with her. So, keep quiet, keep out of the way, and, who knows – you might be on TV and have a nice souvenir for your loved one, if and when he or she is returned to you. OK, do we have any questions?'

Someone asked what if they needed to go to the toilet, and Roger requested that they didn't for the duration of filming, prompting a mad dash for the bathroom. Then Sophie very loudly asked if she was expected to say a few words when handing over her fifty thousand pound cheque. Roger glanced at Candice, who nodded and, behind Sophie's back, managed to mime something that looked as if it meant they could chop it out later.

'Of course,' said Roger. 'You're a very important part of the show.'

Sophie preened herself.

'Anyone else?'

One of the drummers played a 'ba boom – cha!' Roger wasn't amused.

'OK then, everyone. Places, please.'

I started looking around for what might be my place, but a tiny girl with an enormous walkie-talkie came up and manhandled me on to Addison's bed.

'Candice will come and talk to you, probably!' she said, as if Candice was Santa Claus.

'So, good luck! I'm sure you'll get on.'

'I'd rather get off,' I mumbled, but she had whisked away to shove some other people about.

The whole ward went silent and the Christmas tree lights were turned on. Candice strolled over and sat two beds down from Addy's, alongside a young lad called Carl who'd nicked a car, smashed it up, and had been in here for a year. He was fifteen. It wasn't pleasant.

She turned towards the camera and lit up with an enormous beaming smile.

'So, I'm here with Carl Foster and his mother, who are spending another "coma alone" Christmas this year. Mrs Foster . . . how *did* you feel when you first heard Carl had been in an accident?'

'Well, I felt terrible, yes, really bad,' said Carl's mother, who was shrunken and nervy.

'Right. Right, that must have been awful. And how did you feel when they told you he was in a coma and might never regain consciousness?'

'Yes, well, that was really terrible. It was really bad, yes.'

'Do you feel sad that he might never have a chance to grow up, get married, have a family, have a career – that he's missing out on so much?'

'Yes. Yes, really, it's terrible . . . really, you know . . . really bad.'

Candice turned her attention to Dr Hitler.

'So, Doctor, in a case like Carl's – what's the likely outcome?'

'It's very difficult to say,' said Dr Hitler, who looked like she'd smeared her glasses especially for the occasion.

'What – don't you know?' said Candice.

'Well, there are a number of possible outcomes. He could wake at any time, or he could be in a vegetative state for many years.'

'And you don't have anything better to offer Mrs Foster?'

Dr Hitler coloured. 'As I say, comas are very unpredictable things.'

'Right. Well . . . *thank you*, Doctor.'

Candice turned to face the camera.

'So, remember, kids, if you're thinking about joyriding tonight, you'll probably end up like Carl. Don't do it!'

'Yes!' said Sophie, who was standing nearby. 'When I become PM, I'll make going into a coma the punishment for joyriding!'

Candice moved on.

'Many of our stories here are tragic. Some are uplifting. And some, like our next stopping point, are even . . . romantic!'

To my surprise she sat down next to me.

'So, Holly, you've got a funny story to tell of how Addison came to be in this state, haven't you?'

'No.'

'You know – leaning in for a kiss and then – whoops!' She chuckled. I sat there stony-faced, unable to believe she would bring this up on TV. I caught sight of Stephen out of the corner of my eye wearing a contrite expression and shot him a dirty look, the grasser.

'No,' I said again.

'Cut!' yelled Candice. Roger hurried over so they could both have a go at me. Candice started:

'Now listen, ehm . . .'

'Holly,' I said.

'Yes, Holly. We've all got a job to do here, you know. And we can either make it hard or make it difficult – it's up to you.'

'We've got all day,' said Roger. 'And tomorrow and, you know, the day after that . . . But all these dedicated nurses and doctors here, they really want to get back to work to help sick people – like your boyfriend, yeah?'

'I mean, Christmas is a time for unselfishness,' said Candice.

'It's June!' I said. She ignored me.

'. . . and I'm sure everyone in this room would like to see us make the best programme we can as a tribute to the amazing work of . . .'

'And I need to go to the toilet,' shouted one of the Spangles.

'OK, OK,' I said. 'I'll do it. It'll be like one of those hostage videos they send back from the Middle East.'

'*There* you go,' said Candice. 'That wasn't too difficult, was it?'

Roger pressed Candice's shoulder. 'You're so diplomatic,' he said to her. 'Ready to go in three . . .'

Ping! Candice lit up her amazing smile again.

'So, Holly – you've got a funny story to tell of how Addison, here, came to be in this state, haven't you?'

'Yes I have, Candice,' I said dutifully.

'Would you like to share it with the viewers?'

'Well, we were . . . I was trying to kiss him on the top of a wall, and he fell over and hit his head,' I muttered.

'Oh! That is just so heart-warming,' said Candice. 'Even in the midst of human wreckage, there is romance.'

She turned back to me. 'Well, here on Babbleon TV, we thought that, since this started with a kiss, perhaps another kiss could wake the Sleeping Beauty . . .'

This made no sense to me whatsoever.

'So, why don't we all wish for a little bit of that Christmas magic for Holly right now . . . Go on, Holly, give him a kiss – you never know!'

'What?' I said.

'I'm not sure that's a particularly helpful course of treatment,' said Dr Hitler, watching critically from the sidelines.

'For all our viewers . . . just to try and get a little bit of Christmas magic into all our hearts.'

'*Whaat?*'

The room was completely silent as everyone stared at me. Feeling like one of those poor deer who have the option of tearing off their own legs or dying in a trap, I slowly turned towards Addison.

Even in this, my darkest hour, I was still conscious of how my bottom might appear directly facing camera, and inched my way sideways towards his face. His stupidly immobile, beautiful face.

'What if . . .' I was thinking to myself. 'What if it did . . . ? Not that it could, but, what if . . . ?'

I whispered to the next bed: 'God, if you felt like

doing any miracling, this would be a very good time.'

God snored back at me. For some weird reason I heard Enya music in my head. I hate Enya.

The ward was holding its breath. Slowly I leaned over and kissed him gently on the lips for the very first time. It was almost as if there was nothing there at all. Actually, it was like kissing a fish.

The silence held. I drew back. Addison didn't move. Not a nerve, not a flicker. Goddammit. God*dammit*. Candice came up to the bed and sat beside me.

'Are you OK?' she asked. 'Are you crying?'

Witch. Of course, if you ever want to make somebody cry, those are the only two sentences you need to use. She laid a supposedly comforting arm on me and, with the other, indicated for the cameraman to rush over and stick his camera in my face, which he did.

'And we'll be back with more tragic and heart-warming stories from the ward that time forgot after this break,' she managed to say whilst still patting me on the arm. 'Cut!'

Josh and Stephen comforted me as Candice whisked round the beds of those patients who weren't too old or ugly to be on TV, and the band set up.

'But why did you think that would work?' said Sophie.

'Oh, shut up, Sophie,' I said, more vehemently than I intended.

'Ooh, temper! Better watch out, or no fifty thousand pounds for you.'

Even Josh looked a bit surprised at that one.

Chali was removing her silver top to reveal a minuscule silver bra underneath.

'Ah, appropriate,' I said, sniffing, when she rushed up to me.

'I think we're just about ready,' she said. 'Would you like to meet Mr Big?'

'Oh my God, I thought that was a Muppet,' I said, as a tiny skinny creature entirely covered in hair came bouncing up.

'Hey – touching scene, man,' squeaked Mr Big.

'Thank you,' I said. 'I do everything for my public.'

'I've given the list of songs to Roger,' Chali said. 'But I don't think he's read it.'

Roger was in fact lighting a cigarette for Candice. Really, we should have clubbed together to buy Dr Hitler a skateboard so she could speed from crisis to crisis even quicker. And a foghorn, so she wouldn't have to wear her voice out. Roger got up on the bed with his megaphone again.

'Right, everyone, well done. Little treat for you now; we've got some friends in who are going to do some lovely carol singing.'

The Spangles had lined themselves up against the back wall. Mr Big's guitar was larger than he was. The drummers seemed to have one very long eyebrow between the four of them. Chali was already contorting herself into deeply erotic poses. Anything less like a bunch of carol singers but still in human form was difficult to imagine.

'So, if you would like to clap as much as you can and perhaps sing along . . . who knows what miracles might happen here? Music is good for coma patients, so the louder you sing, the better their chances are!'

Everyone arranged themselves into optimum carol-singing position. Except Josh and I: we put our hands over our ears.

There was an expectant hush. Chali raised her lovely arms above her head and, as she brought them down, there was a huge crash of drums.

'O LITTLE TOWN OF BETHLEHEM!' she screeched. 'HOW ILL WE SEE YOU LIE! AMONG YOUR DEAD AND BLOOD-SOAKED STREETS, THE CORPSES PILING HIGH!'

People looked a bit stunned, then started to shuffle uneasily.

'Oh God,' said Josh. 'This is going to be even worse than I thought.'

'Good,' I said.

'YET IN THE DARK STREETS SHINING AN EVERLASTING LIGHT / THE POWER OF ROCK RULES ALL THE WORLD / AND ROCKS WITH YOU TONIGHT!!'

BOOM! Mr Big launched into a massive squealing guitar solo that threatened to break the windows. He thrust his pelvis forward and placed his foot on one of the amps. Some of his sweat broke free and dowsed the nurses. I saw Stephen lick a bit.

'OH MORNING STARS TOGETHER PROCLAIM THE LORDS OF SOUND! / THE KIDS ON THE STREET GIVE HAIL TO THE BEAT AND LET THIS ROCK GO WILD! / KNEEL AT THE ALTAR OF HEAVY NOISE AND GIVE THE LORD HIS PRAYERS! / THAT YOU WILL DIE WITH A GUITAR IN YOUR HAND AND THE BLOOD OF A VIRGIN SLAYER!'

Roger and Candice were looking stunned and whispering feverishly to each other. All the relatives were becoming distinctly upset and querulous. Interestingly, Dr Hitler was tapping her feet and nodding her head almost imperceptibly. Chali took a quick breath and launched back in:

'HOW NOISILY, HOW NOISILY . . .'

'OK, OK!' Roger started shouting through his megaphone. 'That is quite enough.'

Of course, nobody could hear him. The drummers went into a prolonged drumming competition. More and more hospital staff were poking their heads round the doors.

'THE LORDS OF ROCK KICK ARSE!'

'Stop this!' screamed Roger.

'WE HATE THE PIGS WHO STOP OUR GIGS / JUST FOR SAYING THE WORD "MOTHERFUCKER"!'

'Yay!' said some of the nurses.

'MOTHERFUCKER! MOTHERFUCKER! MOTHERFUCKER! MOTHERFUCKER! MOTHERFUCKER! MOTHERFU–'

The music suddenly came to an abrupt screeching halt. Roger stood there with the cables in his hand.

'I think that's quite enough of that, don't you?' he shouted, visibly trembling.

'No!' shouted the nurses and Dr Hitler.

'Cut! I said Cut!'

'More!' shouted Stephen, and the drummers started to play a low, insistent beat that was soon joined by slow handclaps and whistles from members of staff. The drummers played faster and louder and the stamping grew more pronounced.

'STOP IT!' Roger was shouting through his megaphone. 'STOP IT IMMEDIATELY! AND CUT THOSE BLOODY CAMERAS.'

'Get me out of the building,' hissed Candice from behind us. 'I *asked* those tight bastards for security. "I'm a target," I said. But did they believe me?'

'MR BIG! MR BIG! MR BIG!' the room was now chanting. Chali was wrestling with Roger to try and plug the amplifiers back in. The noise level was unbelievable. Then suddenly, cutting right across the top of it, there was an ungodly scream.

Twelve

Instantly, there was silence. My first thought was that a combination of Chali, her silver-foil bikini and her wrestling with Roger over the plug socket had caused some ghastly accident. But it soon became clear this wasn't the case; she was staring around as confusedly as we were. It wasn't Candice, because she was still screaming into her mobile phone about helicopters and riot gear. Dr Hitler had reached out when the scream came and managed to grab one of the gnome army. She hadn't let go. I looked slowly around the room. By the first bed, Carl's mother was gesticulating and shaking.

We moved towards her.

'He opened his eyes!' she said. 'He opened his eyes!'

A very perplexed-looking teenager was taking in

the world around him.

'Is it Christmas?' he was saying groggily. 'Have I been out until Christmas?'

'No, no, it's only June,' a nurse reassured him.

'Oh, thank God,' he said.

'Of course, you missed last Christmas . . .' the nurse added.

Candice raced towards the scene at the speed of light.

'Did you *get* that?' she screeched at the cameramen. They nodded. 'Right. Fine. We can dub some real carol music over it later.'

She sat down beside Carl and switched on her beaming smile like headlights.

'So, viewers, we have indeed witnessed a miracle here. Through the healing power of music – and who knows what little sprinkle of Babbleon TV magic – Carl here has been returned to us! So, Carl, how do you feel?'

'Ehm . . . Terrible . . . like, you know, really bad,' said Carl.

'Shit,' I said, slumping next to Addison. 'Shit shit shit shit shit.'

'Holly, don't worry,' soothed Josh.

'How can I not worry? That was our last hope.'

'Don't be silly. No hope is the last hope. And, anyway, Sophie hasn't handed over the money yet.'

I shrugged.

'I don't see what good that's going to do.'

'There might be new treatments, new ways . . .'

'We might as well just face facts, Josh. He was mine, and now he's gone. Could you leave me alone for a bit, please?'

'OK then.' He got up and started to walk away.

'Ehm . . . I didn't mean for you to actually go.'

'Oh, no, of course you didn't. Hang on.'

He sat back down beside me and put his arm around me in a comforting way. Sophie was remonstrating with Roger and Candice, who looked to be giving in.

'OK, everyone,' said Roger finally through his megaphone. He seemed to have aged about ten years. Of course, all the staff were still around Carl's bed, but he waited until they turned back to him. 'We will now have a short presentation of a cheque to the high-dependency unit of St Hugh's from Sophie Masterton-Willis LLB.'

'Do you want some background music?' shouted one of the Spangles, to some guffawing.

Smiling graciously, Sophie snatched Candice's microphone and walked dead centre into the middle of the ward. The cameraman trained his camera on her alone.

'Thank you all so much for coming,' she said. 'Under this government, hospitals have been sadly neglected. That is why the private sector, as well as the charity of good people like myself, is needed to bolster up the whole sorry structure – which, of course, we all hope will eventually lead to an entirely private system that can remove this wretched burden from humble taxpayers.'

Josh nudged me. There, hanging back at the entrance to the ward, was Kate, looking uncharacteristically shifty.

'She came!' said Josh. 'Shame she missed the best bit!'

Kate appeared to be beckoning some people up the stairs, putting a finger to her lips.

'And that is why I, Sophie Masterton-Willis LLB, have decided to donate to St Hugh's the sum of –' Sophie held up the enormous cheque – 'fifty thousand pounds!' She raised her arms triumphantly, waiting for the round of applause.

Quick as a flash Kate entered with, as I counted, one two three four five six Jameses. They lined up behind Sophie, in full view of the camera.

'Now!' shouted Kate.

Six Jameses lowered their expensive Savile Row trousers and Calvin Klein boxer shorts, revealing six skinny white British arses to the camera, and waggling them about vigorously.

Instantly, there was a storm of applause. Sophie smiled graciously and bowed towards the camera. The Jameses waggled their arses even more fervently.

'Excellent,' said Kate. 'You all keep your jobs.'

As the applause continued, Sophie's smile began to waver. When it sank in that the eyes of the crowd weren't exactly on her, the grin disappeared altogether and she slowly looked round.

She went dangerously pale.

'Can we stop now?' one of the Jameses was saying. 'All the blood is rushing to my head.'

'You . . . you . . .' Sophie said to Kate. Then her face twisted. 'But . . . but *why?*'

Kate stood up straight and trembled. The camera swivelled so it was trained on both of them. Kate took a deep breath, paused, and then opened her mouth.

'Well, Sophie, one reason . . .' she said in a wobbly voice, 'is because you're a big evil fascist.'

'Nothing wrong with that,' said Sophie.

'And the other is . . . that you're stealing the man I'm in love with and being horrible to him!' Kate's voice went very high at this and finished off in a bit of a squeak.

There was a gasp from the crowd. I glanced at Josh. His face was a picture of confusion as he tried to work out who she meant.

'What?' said Sophie. But it was too late. Kate was striding across the ward to Josh. He looked at her for a few seconds.

'What . . . what, *me?*' he asked in disbelief.

'Why do you think I live in your shitty, awful flat, you moron?' said Kate, biting her lip.

'I quite like it,' said Josh.

'Do you quite like me?' asked Kate quietly.

'Cor! Yeah!' said Josh.

'Oh for fuck's sake!' said Sophie. 'I was going to marry him, you idiot. Perfect constituency wife he'd have made. Scones for the village fair and everything.'

'Well you can't,' said Kate, kissing him.

'This is *definitely* my week,' said Josh, kissing her back.

Sophie paused and looked around her.

'Well, fuck you all very much,' she said. And she ripped up the enormous cheque, leaving it in pieces on the floor, then stomped out of the ward.

'Oh my God! The money!' shouted Josh. Everyone looked horrified. Then one of the Jameses picked up a piece of the cheque.

'Fifty thou? Was that all?' he chuckled. 'God, that wouldn't even make a dent in our bonuses, would it, boys?'

'Not likely!' They started pulling out their cheque books.

'Well, I'm giving ten.'

'You limpdick! I'm giving fifteen!'

'You utter homosexual! I'm giving twenty!'

'Just a thought,' said Dr Hitler, 'but does anyone mind if I give the patients their anti-dying medication now?'

An hour later, things were getting back to relative normality, although no one had taken the Christmas tree down.

The camera crew had left with Candice, utterly jubilant, clutching Roger's arm and whispering, 'BAFTA, darling, no doubt about it at all.'

I apologized to Chali that she didn't get to play more of her songs, but she brushed it off, saying that Dr Hitler had asked them to play the doctors' summer do, and that they were definitely on their way *this* time.

Kate and Josh had disappeared somewhere, so I didn't want to turn up at home too quickly.

There was lots of fuss at Carl's end of the hall, which meant that God and Addison and I were left to our own devices, but I didn't think I had many more devices to give. I simply sat there, staring out of the window, humming a made-up song to myself, trying to ignore my rising panic.

At about four o'clock, Finn popped his head round the curtain.

'Did I miss it all?' he said.

I nodded.

'Kate made me promise to come, but I really, honestly wanted to stay out of the way of the mooning.'

'Why? Have you got a mutant arse?'

'No! I think I've got quite a nice arse.'

'Turn around,' I ordered. He did so. He did, in fact, have a lovely arse.

'I just don't like shoving it in people's faces, if you know what I mean.'

'You mean, you don't like getting your arse out on national television?'

'Something like that.'

'You are weird.'

He looked at Addison.

'So, no change then.'

I shook my head. 'Oh, Finn. Why the hell couldn't you be a medical doctor? Why the hell couldn't you have trained to sort this out?'

'I don't know,' he said. 'I'd change it if I could, I promise you.'

I sniffed.

'Would you . . . I mean, would you like to go for a drink or something?'

'Of course not,' I sniffed.

'No, of course not. OK. Maybe I should go.'

'Maybe you should.'

'I'm sorry, Holl.'

'Everyone's sorry,' I said. 'Nobody helps.'

Home was empty. I made myself five jam sandwiches and sat by myself on the fire escape eating them slowly. I felt completely wrung out, and toyed with the idea of sleeping in – after all, I'd probably lost my job. But when it came to it, I couldn't.

The next morning Chali was waiting by the door of That Special Someone beaming broadly as I wheeled up.

'What are you doing here at this time?' I asked incredulously – it was only twenty-five minutes after the shop was due to open.

'Ding dong!' she shouted. 'The witch is dead!'

'Which witch?' I asked.

'The wicked witch! Ding! Dong! The wicked witch is dead!'

Chali took my bike off me and proudly led it into the shop.

'Wake up, you sleepyhead! Rub your eyes, get out of bed!'

'OK, *OK*,' I said. 'I get it!'

'Ding! Dong! . . .'

'I *get* it. What happened?'

'Well,' said Chali, measuring out two disgustingly large spoonsful of coffee from Mrs Bigelow's private stash and ripping open a forbidden packet of bourbons with her teeth, 'this little boy came in the shop yesterday, right, with Biggers in charge? Turned out one of his friends had been run over by a car. And he didn't have enough money to pay the delivery charge.'

'No way,' I said.

'Utterly way. So, anyhow, Biggie told him he couldn't have the flowers, and it turns out his father owns a whole chain of conferencing suites.'

I shook my head in disbelief.

'And?'

'And, the dad phones my uncle and . . . she's gone! Gone gone gone! See, I told you that strike was a good idea.'

'Yes, good meaning "lucky" rather than "moral" or anything,' I grumbled, hauling out the displays.

'But don't you see? My uncle's given me the shop! It's ours! You can run it when I'm off doing world tours!'

'Which will be never,' I said, straightening up. 'Still, that's really good, isn't it?'

Chali nodded enthusiastically.

'I mean, we could really make something of this place,' I said, warming to it. After all, if my love life was over for all time, I was going to have to throw myself into my career. 'We could start doing trendier events . . . try and get into, you know, *Hello*! magazine and stuff like that. Send free samplers off. Start a mailing list . . .'

'Ah,' said Chali, 'actually I was rather hoping that it would mean even more slacking off for us.'

'No, no. We could really go places with this place.'

'Do you think the band could play here? So it could be like a flower shop-cum-gig? Kind of a place for the kids to hang out.'

'That', I said, 'is just about the worst business idea I've ever heard.'

Her face fell.

'OK, what about we grow opium poppies here and pretend we're selling flowers?'

'Actually, now I think about it, maybe you were on to a winner with that gig/flowers thing.'

'Yeh?'

'Yeh. It'll be brilliant.'

'I know,' she said. 'And now, as a celebratory gesture, I'm going to shut the shop for a day.'

'You're going to shut the shop on our first day of business?'

'I'm a very positive employer.'

'You're a very optimistic employer.'

'Well, I'm an employer with a rehearsal to go to. It's my new band, made up of tramps playing cardboard percussion instruments. Apparently MTV think it's the new big thing.'

'And a homeless tramp told you this, did he?'

'Uh huh.'

'OK. Where are you rehearsing?'

'King's Cross . . .'

She got sight of the look on my face.

'Huh. Well you won't be grinning when we're

playing Wembley.'

'Not unless I'm doing the flowers.'

'Tramps don't like flowers. Unless there's nothing else to eat.'

It was only eleven o'clock in the morning. What exactly did I do with myself before all this, I wondered? Maybe I knew a lot about *Hollyoaks*. I slalomed wearily into the hospital, carrying a copy of *SFX*, the magazine for lonely boys.

The smell of disinfectant seemed to be weighing me down. After the uproar of yesterday, even the corridors seemed quiet. Sighing loudly, I flounced through the doors. Addison was sitting up on the end of the bed.

I turned round and walked straight back out to find the right ward.

I stopped, smacked my head then turned around and walked in again.

My heart and my throat started fighting each other.

My throat won.

'ADDISON!' I screamed at the top of my voice and threw myself pell-mell towards him.

He looked up with a confused expression on his face.

'Hey, Speedy Gonzales,' said Stephen, deftly catching the back of my dungarees. 'If you knock him over again I will have to kill you.'

'Bha baha baha haha . . .' I said, arms flailing. Addison continued to regard me steadily. I couldn't read the expression on his face. Stephen put a restraining hand on my arm.

'Go gently, OK?'

'Buh huh huh huh,' I spluttered.

'Cnif Yarh Bah F!!!' I shouted as, slowly, from behind the curtain, a large – very large – figure emerged, and put a mirror-image protective hand on Addison's arm.

'Clahf . . . Clahff.'

'Do you need a paper bag to breathe into?' asked Stephen.

I struggled to regain control of myself.

'That's . . . that's *Claudia*!' I announced, panting desperately.

'Claudia Finkelman; yes. Apparently so,' said Stephen. 'She arrived about three o'clock this morning, sat with him, and . . . well.'

'Oh *God*!' I said. 'That's . . . that is so *unfair*!'

'Do you want to hear how he is or not?'

'Oh God,' I said again. 'Yes. Of course. I hate myself.'

'Put a brave face on it,' said Stephen. 'The physio and the neurologist have both checked him over, and it's not too bad. He'll have a bit of short-term memory loss, and his muscles will need to get used to not being asleep, but, on the whole, it's looking pretty good.'

As we were talking, I was taking little baby steps closer to the bed. Now I was close enough to speak.

'So, be brave,' Stephen whispered in my ear.

'Hey,' I said bravely.

'Hello,' said Claudia. And not in a friendly way either. In real life she was, if anything, freakier than on the computer. She was that big way only Americans get: so heavy it's as if your legs are pointing in the wrong direction from the knees downwards. Her hair was pinned back with two kirby grips, and her spectacles were huge, Deirdre Barlow-style. She was wearing an outsized *Red Dwarf* T-shirt.

'Hey,' said Addison, turning his big brown eyes on me.

I took another step towards him. Claudia hovered protectively.

'How are you feeling?' I asked, trying to control my quavery voice.

'Sticky,' he said.

I nodded. 'Here – I brought you this.' And handed him *SFX*, not knowing quite what else to do.

'Oh, great – I love this. Look, Claudia, there's an article on number science.'

'Is it an imaginary one?' she replied, and they both sniggered for some reason. I held on to the back of a chair for support.

'So . . .' I said. 'I mean, what happened?'

'I couldn't . . . you know,' said Claudia, 'just stand by while no one did anything for Add.'

I nodded my head gravely.

'You know, this is my first time out of the house in six years. And I made it to a different country.'

'You were very brave,' I said, through gritted teeth.

'I know.'

'Then what happened?'

'Well, I flew over, and arrived last night, and they let me in.'

I wouldn't keep out a monster that arrived at three o'clock in the morning, would you? I tried to quell such uncharitable thoughts, but it was impossible. My whole body felt hollowed out by misery. I wanted to take Addison's place on the bed and lose consciousness for a few months or so. It would definitely be easier than dealing with this. Hook me up, and wake me in time for one of those lovely global-warming summers we're always being promised.

'And I sang you your favourite song, didn't I, sweetheart?'

Addison looked faintly bashful.

'Which is?' I asked politely.

'Oh, a wunnerful British band called Take That. They've got a little song called "Back for Good"? I don't know if you've heard of it.'

'No, I've never heard of it,' I said quietly.

'Well, it's our song, isn't it, sweet pea?'

Addison shrugged and nodded.

'When you were . . . asleep,' I said, taking a deep breath, 'did you . . . did you know anything that was going on around you?'

He shook his head. 'Sorry, no. They told me you came to see me a lot.'

'Oh well, I popped in now and again. It's just as well you didn't hear me, really. Usually I was telling you how big your nose was.'

'She was vicious,' said Stephen, backing me up.

'When's Magda getting back from the phone? Does she have to inform every single one of your relatives?' asked Claudia. 'We're moving,' she informed me.

'Where?' I said, my *Misery* fears resurfacing.

'I can't walk very well,' said Addison. 'Claudia's putting me in a private hospital to rehabilitate.'

'I figured the food in here was probably bad enough through a tube without having to stick it in your mouth for four weeks,' said Claudia. 'And they need the bed here.'

'That's good of you,' I said, because it was.

'Well, he's my problem now,' she said, trying to make a joke out of it. 'And it saves on hotel costs if they'll let me stay in the room.'

Had I been a better person, I would have offered her Addison's room. I'm not.

Stephen insisted he was taking me to the pub for a brandy when he came off shift at lunchtime, so I had to stand back and wait while they packed everything up, trying desperately to hold on to my tears until they had all gone. 'I have a flower shop,' I told myself fiercely.

Magda was a different person, laughing and crying simultaneously, covering Addison in kisses every time he blinked. She and Claudia went on ahead with the carefully packed *Star Wars* miniatures, whilst a porter loaded Add into a wheelchair and began to transfer him to what was presumably a luxury ambulance.

'Well, I guess we'll see you soon,' I muttered.

'We?' said Addison, turning round.

'Uhm . . . yeah, me and Han Solo.' I took the figure out of my bag. 'We've been working together on this one.'

Addison hesitated.

'I didn't want to say this in front of Claudia,' he began, slowly reversing his wheelchair until he was next to me, 'but sometimes, when I was . . . asleep . . . things swam in and out . . . It was like diving very deep down in the ocean, down further than the fish and the submarines.'

'Like in *The Abyss*?' I suggested.

'The director's cut?'

'But of course.'

He half smiled, then took a deep breath and went on:

'And occasionally, I surfaced. And when I surfaced, you were always there.' He paused and looked away. 'And I did call out to you.'

I leaned over him and stroked his hair.

'Not loudly enough,' I said, the tears welling up.

'You were too far away,' he said, his own eyes watering. He kept his face turned away and rubbed his forehead fiercely. 'You were swimming in a different sea.'

I hugged him and let my tears run through his hair.

'Oh, Add,' I said. 'I'm so sorry.'

'No, I am,' he said.

'No, I am.'

He shook his head, and for a time we couldn't speak.

'I think Moby Dick's waiting for you,' I said finally, swallowing hard and glancing towards the door.

He followed my gaze, then took my hand.

'It's . . . it's hard to explain,' he said.

'Same sea?'

He shrugged. 'Same universe, maybe.'

I handed him Han Solo. 'Well, better take him with you. He's very good for people in sticky spots.'

'I'll remember that,' he said.

'Ehm, sorry but, like, the meter's running,' said the porter.

'Sure,' I choked, and let Add go. Behind me, the nurses were already expertly stripping the bed, wheeling away the tubes and the wires. I waited till they'd finished, then sat on the bed to wait for Stephen, feeling the springs under my hands. I still wanted to curl up on it. It felt like all I had left.

'We're going to be needing that bed,' warned Dr Hitler, flitting past me.

'God?' I whispered.

There was no answer.

'God? Really, I could do with a bit of spiritual guidance right now.'

There was a snorty sound from the next bed.

'God?'

God was lying flat out on the bed with an oxygen mask on. He was very grey and shrunken.

'God?'

He feebly motioned for me to take his oxygen mask off. I checked around for Dr Hitler, then, when she was nowhere to be seen, did so.

'How are you?'

'God is dead,' he said, every syllable coming with a very nasty rattle.

'Don't be ridiculous! Come on, do a miracle.'

'I did one,' he said laboriously. 'Sorry it didn't make you happy.'

'Oh that,' I said. 'Never mind, eh? Just make yourself better.'

'Not a lot of point in that,' he said. 'The world's a pile of shit.'

'Well, that's true,' I reflected. 'But still . . .'

'Neh,' he said. 'I tell you what I'd love, though . . .'

Fuck it, I thought, and opened his locker. Sure enough, there was a half-bottle of old-looking Scotch inside.

'I'm not putting it down your feeding tube, though,' I warned him. 'I may be a disaster area, but I'm not a murderer.'

'No, that'll be fine. Just lift me up a little . . . that's it. Would you like some?'

'I wouldn't mind.'

So I took a swig, then very carefully held up his head and let God sip a few drops, which he did with a bit of coughing, but eventually he managed to get some down.

'Oh, better,' he said. 'Well, I think it's just about time I was popping off.'

'Don't you have any family you want me to contact?' I asked, stupefied.

'Every living thing is my family,' he said. 'Besides, they all fucked off to Australia.'

He snuffled a bit more and settled down in the

pillows. I sat with him and let him have sips of whisky as often as he could manage them.

'You should go now, lass,' he said. 'I think you've a life to be getting on with.'

'I'm not sure I feel like it at the moment.'

'No. But do you want a last bit of advice from the mouth of the creator himself?'

'Yes please.'

'Hmm.' He appeared to fall asleep for a second, then woke up with a grunt.

'Hmm . . . advice. Right. Ehm, wear sunscreen?'

'I think that's been done.'

'No, really? Hmm.' He launched into one of his deathly coughing fits. 'How about – love they neighbour?'

'I adored your neighbour,' I said sadly. 'Didn't help me much.'

'Yes, right, right, I see.'

He paused again.

'Goodbye,' he said quietly. And suddenly, the terrible wheezing stopped. An instant later, one of his machines let out an alarm.

'DOCTOR!' I yelled, leaping up.

'Are you *squatting* here?' asked Dr Hitler, throwing herself up the ward behind the crash cart.

'No . . .'

'Well, please, could you leave? I'm not sure you're a good influence. But if you see that fat girl again, could you send her back in?'

* * *

I ran out of the ward, blinded. Stephen wasn't around, but I had to get out. I stumbled through the corridors, realizing that people were looking after me with concern. I pushed past them all.

'Hey!' shouted a familiar voice. I ran on.

'Hey!'

'Leave me alone,' I shouted and ran on. It quickly became obvious that someone faster than me was chasing me. I made it as far as the bicycle but couldn't undo the lock in time.

'Physically chasing women,' said Finn, out of breath, leaning his hand on the wall in front of me, 'there's a new macho experience for me. Would you like me to go and wrestle a bear now?'

I straightened up slowly and shook my head.

'What's the matter? Magda phoned Kate at work . . . Oh.'

I welled up.

'It was that other girl, wasn't it?'

'It's fine,' I said chokingly. 'It's better than fine, actually. It's great. I mean, he's alive. He's OK. At least . . . well, at least I won't be going to prison for manslaughter.'

He nodded. 'Always something, I suppose.'

I bent down again to try and unlock my bike.

'Where are you going now?'

'I don't know,' I confessed.

'Huh,' he said. Then, after a pause: 'Would you like to come with me?'

'Where are you going?' I asked timidly.

'Well, it's a beautiful day, so how about staying

inside and reading improving captions?'

'That sounds all right,' I said.

'The Science Museum?'

I nodded.

He held out his hand and I took it.

The Science Museum was practically deserted, and eerily, stunningly beautiful. I wandered through the massive atrium, hitting knobs at random and fiddling with things. Finn regarded me calmly.

'Did Madeleine get you in cheap for this too?' I asked, in what I thought was a deeply casual manner.

He laughed. 'I don't really see her . . .'

I looked at him. 'Were you ever seeing her?'

He shrugged. 'Not . . . maybe not as much as I mentioned her in your company.'

I stared at him in consternation.

'Sorry . . . sorry, am I getting this straight? Were you using a cell mitosis biologist to try and make me *jealous*??'

'Did it work?' he asked.

'Well, you know . . . yeah.'

He twisted slightly nervously.

'Holl, I don't . . . I mean . . . if you're still in love with Addison, I wouldn't want to ask you out or anything . . .'

I pushed a big red button that made lots of lights twinkle on and off behind us.

'I think . . .' I said shyly – examining my reasons for

doing things was never one of my favourite jobs – 'I think, maybe I was just in love with an idea of him.'

'I think so too,' said Finn, doing something very clever to the machine, so the lights made pretty sparkling patterns.

'Sometimes,' I went on, 'maybe the things you really want are . . .'

'A bit boring and nerdy?' He brushed his gorgeous dark hair out of his gorgeous dark eyes.

'Closer than you think.' I seemed to remember saying that before. 'Oh wow!' I announced, struck suddenly. 'I don't need to pretend to know lots about *Star Trek* any more!'

'And you already know lots about spaghetti.'

'Well, I certainly eat a lot of it.'

'That's what I meant.'

'Wow. Do you think I could have a true scientific heart?'

'I think,' said Finn, 'you could have this true scientific heart.'

We wandered hand in hand, feeling as small as children, across the Perspex bridge over the massive vaulted Victorian hall, looking on all the great machines and massive works that filled the space.

'That reminds me,' I said, gazing out over it all, 'I meant to tell you before: God died this morning.'

'I don't think he did really,' said Finn, leaning out with me. 'He's probably just playing dice with the universe.'

Epilogue

The end of July was beautiful. To celebrate it, and us, we staged an Addison-napping from his plush private hospital and took him to Hyde Park for a picnic. He grumbled all the way, but we insisted: he hadn't had his long-promised birthday party.

Add was improving, slowly. He had a tendency to forget things, and couldn't walk very far, but we were being cautiously optimistic. And his personality didn't seem to have changed, if his antipathy to being out in the open air was any guide. We needed five rugs so that none of his exposed flesh touched the grass.

'I'm going to be sick,' I said, looking up at Finn from my vantage point of his lap.

'Well, you shouldn't have eaten four Penguins, should you?' he said mildly, and continued examining a disgusting caterpillar he'd just picked up.

Kate poured some more champagne for us. She and Josh had a proper hamper filled with goodies, we had a plastic bag full of tangerines, and Claudia was having a McDonalds.

'I want to propose a toast to us . . .' Kate began. Suddenly, I spotted two people walking towards us.

'Fuck! Fuck! Fuck fuck!' I yelled, sitting upright.

'Well, Holly's pretty much summed up what I was going to say,' said Kate, raising her glass.

'No, look! It's Carol and Farah!'

'We all have to hide!' I yelled. 'Up!'

'Great!' said Josh.

'Let's hide behind Claudia,' I said quietly to Finn, who batted me on the nose.

'Under the blankets!' said Josh.

'Umm I don't think . . .' said Addison.

Carol and Farah were definitely heading this way.

'Quick! Roll Addison!' I ordered, and with much sniggering, we did so, then dived under. Of course, trying to lie very quietly and flatly anywhere is a recipe for disaster, so we giggled helplessly whilst trying to tell each other to be quiet.

'I mean,' Carol was saying, as they drew near, 'this park is a disgrace. Look, somebody's left a wheelchair over there.'

'And a picnic!' said Farah, hopping along. 'Ooh, look, bananas!'

'It's disgusting.'

'You're disgusting!' I said, before Finn clapped a hand over my mouth.

'Did you hear something?' said Carol. 'Oh, let's go. Farah, do you think you could fit up our chimney with a long-handled broom?'

As they walked off, I crept out, grabbing Finn by the hand.

'Don't come out yet,' I hissed to the others. 'They're not quite gone.'

Finn put his arms around me, and we moved a little away.

'It is nice,' I said, putting my arms around him back, 'to get you alone.'

He grinned at me.

'In the open air of the busiest park of the busiest city in a rapidly overpopulating world . . .'

'. . . where, for me,' I said, stopping him with a kiss. 'There is no one else but you.'

Then I kissed him again.

'Holly! Are they gone yet?' yelled Josh.

'Yes – I've got grass up my nose and Claudia smells!' shouted Kate. 'Sorry, Claudia.'

There were loud kissing noises.

'Huh? I wasn't listening,' said Claudia.

We looked around to the four forms wriggling under the blanket. Suddenly Claudia yelped.

'Gosh, sorry,' said Josh. 'Thought you were Skates.'

'You did not!' said Kate crossly.

'Ow!' said Josh.

Amanda's Wedding

Acknowledgements

Thanks to: Robin Colgan, Ian Wylie and Dr Andrew Teverson for their helpful remarks at an early stage; the amazing Ali 'don't mess with the' Gunn, Nick Marston, Carol Jackson and all at Curtis Brown; Rachel Hore for her brilliant editing, Anne O'Brien, Jennifer Parr, Fiona McIntosh, Yolande Denny, Julie Cass, Yvette Cowles, Alex Young, Dan Moore, Claire Round, and the team at HarperCollins; Salty Sandra McKay, Susan Hoyer, Andy Kennedy, and the Westminster red-hand gang for their support; Davids Bewers and Knowles for the extra two months; Fiona Hastings, much missed, for suggesting it; my parents for not asking about it, and Jill Edwards.

For Andrew McConnell Stott

Amanda's Wedding

One

Most of the really messy things in life don't actually have a beginning – they kind of bear down on you over years, like the consequences of not cleaning your bathroom floor (stickiness, cholera, etcetera).

This one did, though. It definitely did, and I remember it extremely clearly. Well, in a fuzzy kind of way.

Thank God – it was my bed. So: (1) I was actually in a bed, and (2) it was mine. I was beating the odds already.

I prised open one very sticky eye and attempted to focus it, to try and work out where the smell was coming from. I appeared to be jammed between the wall and an extremely large and unidentifiable chunk of flesh.

The chunk of flesh was connected to lots of other chunks, all in the right order, but I didn't notice this until after I'd sat bolt upright in terror at a potential *Godfather*-type situation in my bed.

Everything seemed weirdly out of proportion. Maybe I was still drunk. I pawed at the sticky stuff at the corner of my eyes. No, something was very wrong.

An inappropriate hand was slung across me. It appeared to be about the size of my stomach, and my stomach is not renowned for its tiny-ness . . . A thought began to worm its way into my head.

I knew that thought and tried to avoid it for as long as possible, but alongside my hangover voice that was howling 'Fluid! Fluid!' the thought whispered, 'Oh my God . . . it's Nicholas . . . Again!'

I grimaced like I'd just swallowed something nasty – which, let's face it, I probably had.

Slowly creeping my way off the end of the futon, and feeling worse and worse, I crawled into the kitchen in search of aspirin and Diet Coke. Fran, of course, was lying in wait. She didn't live here, but she made herself more at home than I did. Her own place was a three-foot-square studio which induced immediate Colditz fever, so I'd got used to her wandering in and out.

'Good morning!' trilled Fran, bright and breezy. She must have been putting it on. Through a strange fog – which I supposed was the alcohol in my system filling me right up to the eyes – she actually looked quite good. I couldn't focus on her mass of fuzzy hair, but I did notice that she was wearing one of my T-shirts, not quite covering thighs that didn't even meet in the middle. I hated that.

I summoned all my energy to pipe, 'Hello!'

'Hungover?'

'No, no, absolutely fine. I've just suddenly developed a taste for a half-bottle of warm, flat Coke, OK?'

'Oh, *right*.' There was a pause. Then she said, 'I take it you'll be wanting two glasses?'

'Aaaaaaargh!' I put my head down on the kitchen unit.

'Mel. Mel Mel Mel Mel Mel!'

'Urgugh?'

'*Nicholas* . . . !'

'Uh-huh . . .'

'*Twice* . . . !'

'Aaaargh!'

Fran backed away.

'I know, I know, I know,' I admitted. 'Oh my God. Shit. SHIT! I think maybe I'll just move house, starting now.'

'In a towel?'

'You're right – all my clothes are in my bedroom, and I'm never going in there again! Why don't I start a fire?'

'Well, it's a bit risky, and I don't think Nicholas would fit in a fire engine.'

'That's OK! He could die! In fact, that would be good!'

Fran poured us both a cup of tea and looked sorrowfully at me. 'Come on, don't worry. Look on the bright side.'

'There's an eight foot tall accountant in my bed who smells like a polecat, whom I have now woken up with TWICE, thus ruining ANY potential excuses – and you're telling me to look on the *bright* side?'

'Ehmm, how about . . . if you spill any tea on the towel, it won't matter, because you'll have a towel handy? OK then . . . ehmm . . . it means you're not the type of girl who has one-night stands?'

'Oh God, WHAT am I going to do? Is Linda around?' Linda was my dumpy flatmate. I only saw her about once a fortnight. Possibly, she hid from me.

'She scuttled past about twenty minutes ago. She looked pretty tired. We might have been a bit noisy last night. Wasn't Nicholas trying to pretend he could play the trumpet?'

I grimaced. 'That wasn't a trumpet.'

Fran grimaced back at the memory. 'Bloody Amanda!' she said. I nodded vehemently. Whenever anything *really* bad happened, Amanda was *always* mixed up in it somewhere.

Fran, Amanda and I were at school together in Woking, one of those dreary endless London suburban towns, not city or country, just lots of people hanging round bus shelters wondering if they were missing something. I'd met Fran when she ran past our house, aged four, chasing my older brother with a cricket bat.

Amanda lived next to us, and the three of us walked to school together for years, Amanda usually in possession of the latest Barbie-doll outfits, and extra sweets from the man at the corner shop with slightly dubious tendencies. Despite her blue eyes, strawberry blonde ringlets and general air of pinkness, she was pure evil, and played Fran and me off against each other with the talent of a Borgia poisoner.

Our biggest wish as children was to grow up famous and be on *Celebrity Squares*. Twenty years on, we were all still following this wish: Fran in the time-honoured method of going to drama school then hanging about for years and years and years, usually round my flat. I'd decided to do it by marrying someone very handsome and famous. I kept a close eye on *Hello!* magazine to check out when celebrities got divorced. Amanda, however, trumped all of us totally while still at school, by getting her dad to invent a new way of opening milk cartons or something, and suddenly becoming utterly stinking rich.

We didn't really notice at first, just that all through the last year of secondary school she kept sighing and talking about how boring everything was – but then, we were teenage girls. Only when we saw the new house, with the pool and the built-in bar, did we realize something was seriously up. Her dad had left her mum by this stage and was too busy chasing totty our age to really care what we did, so we had big parties, shopped, and got tipsy in the new jacuzzi with the gold taps: it was a fabulous year.

Eventually, Fran went off to the Central School of Drama to pretend to be a lizard for three years. Amanda was heading for Durham University and, not having much imagination, and rather less sense, I applied there too.

I hardly recognized Amanda when we went up on the first day of freshers' week – mainly because her hair had changed colour and she talked differently. She gave me a lift up in the open-topped sports car her dad had given her for getting into university, and cut through the town like she owned it.

I knew when she dumped me in my seven-foot-square midden in the nasty students halls with damp running down the walls and shouted, 'There you are, darling! See you around, yah?' that somehow things had changed. Things had. She never spoke to me again, except once every six months when she'd condescend to take me out for a drink to remind me how wonderful everything was for her. I don't think her glittering success meant as much to her if she didn't have someone to look down on, and that was my job. I fell for it every time; the next day, she'd ignore me in the corridor.

If things were fair, I reckoned, it would all go wrong for her one day. As things were, she got a good degree and, as a result of her blondeness, qualified for a job in PR, and now was invited to lots of show-biz parties. I got a terrible degree, probably something to do with the bile marks on the paper, and ended up reading copy for a boring stationery company in Holborn.

But I still saw her. Every so often she'd phone, Fran and I would go see her, she'd gloat, and we'd get her to pay for all the drinks. And that's how it had started last night, when the phone rang.

'Melanie, *darling*.'

I've finally worked out that *darling* is PR code for *inferior acquaintance*.

'Hi, Mandy.'

She hated that.

'Listen, how about you and Francesca and I meet up for a drinkey tonight . . . ?'

Tonight? As if we had nothing better to do.

'I have news!' she trilled.

'Really? What?'

'Oh no, this is definitely drinkey kind of news.'

'OK. Fran!' Fran was lying on the sofa drawing a moustache on herself. 'Fancy a drink with Amanda tonight?'

Fran made a snarling noise, shook her head violently and contorted her face into that of a cougar, which apparently they teach you at drama school.

'Great,' I said down the phone. 'We'd love to. Where?'

'The Atlantic?' she simpered.

No chance. Cocktails and nob-ends. Plus, she lived in posh North London and we lived in Kennington, one of the nice but scruffy ends of South London, so it was like trying to arrange an inter-galactic alliance. I parried with the Ship and Shovel – both dirty and potentially dangerous.

'Oh, for goodness' sake, Melanie. All right, the Ozone then.'

'I'll raise you to the Pitcher and Piano and no further.'

There was a sigh on the end of the line. 'Well, if you

must . . .' She pouted audibly, which had zero effect on me as I don't have a penis.

'What did you do that for?' groaned Fran once I got off the phone. 'She'll only have been promoted or been asked out by some poof in a West End musical or something.'

'You never know,' I said. 'Maybe something's gone horribly wrong. Maybe she's up the duff by some sailors, and we, as her oldest friends, are the only ones who can truly comfort her. Heh heh heh.'

'Did she have an up-the-duff voice on? Or perhaps a twee gloaty voice?'

I thought for a minute. 'Ehmm, twee gloaty voice.'

'Well, that's it then. Sean Connery's son has asked her to lunch. And we're going to have to listen to two boring hours of how fantastic everything is for her, and we'll be so bored we'll get accidentally drunk, then she'll drive off somewhere much more exciting, completely sober, and we'll stay and get totally plastered out of bitterness and self-loathing, and hate ourselves for days.'

'Unh huh. So, what are we going to wear?'

Amanda flounced into the bar on time. She was a three Ps girl – pert, pretty and petite.

'Darlings, hi!' she crowed across the bar. I forgot: when she got posh, she also got *loud*.

'White wine OK?'

'Special Brew for us, Amanda,' shouted Fran. 'But in a glass.'

Amanda finally wandered over with the drinks, after checking to see if she knew anyone, perched down on her perfect arse and turned to us with a smile like a morning weathergirl.

'What's your news, then?' I asked helpfully.

'You'll never guess what, girls!'

'Ehm, you've won the lottery, for double world fairness? You're actually a man? You're pregnant by forty sailors?' Fran said the last bit under her breath.

'I'm ENGAGED!!!'

'Oh my God! Who to?' we yelled simultaneously.

'You know him, Mel. You remember – Fraser McConnald, from Durham.'

'Fraser who?' said Fran.

But I remembered. Sweet big gentle Fraser, with the scraggy hair and old clothes. I fancied him madly, he ignored it, so I followed him around pretending to be his mate instead. Not one of my proudest moments. God, did this girl have to win *all* the time?

'You and Fraser! Arse Bastards!' I said. 'And also, I mean, wow, you're getting married! Congratulations, that's wonderful! God, and *quick*!'

Fraser never did anything quickly, I seemed to remember. I had a flash of him mooching about the college, trying to find somewhere to sit down and stretch out his incredibly long legs.

'Oh, I know.' She displayed the ring on her perfectly manicured finger. 'He says I just swept him off his feet! Hee hee hee!'

Swept him off his feet? Or ran him over with a steamroller? Fraser didn't even *like* being swept off his feet, I thought mutinously. Fraser liked striding about in the hills and reading *Viz* magazine and failing his engineering exams.

'I remember him,' said Fran, '. . . a couple of times when I came up. Lanky bloke. Lank. He didn't seem like your type . . .'

'Yes, well,' simpered Amanda.

'How did you meet him? Chess club?'

'No, actually, it was the funniest thing . . . I was purring . . .'

'What?' I said.

'Oh, my job, darling, you know.'

Grrrrr.

'I was working for these clients from Edinburgh who are launching some ancient castles guide. Anyway, who should I see in the portfolio brochure but my old friend from university, Fraser.'

I didn't point out that she can't have said two words to him the whole time, as he blushed a lot, and wore the same pair of Converse trainers every day for three years.

'Anyway, so I thought I'd go see him for a drink –'

'Hang on,' interrupted Fran, 'what the hell was he doing in a brochure? Was it a brochure for Converse trainers?'

Amanda tinkled her tinkly laugh. 'No, actually – and you'll think this is just mad: me, little Amanda Phillips from Portmount Comprehensive . . .'

Uh-oh.

'What?' demanded Fran.

'Well, actually . . . he's a laird!'

'A what?!'

I knew, though.

'Oh, I know, isn't it cute? Well, it's like a lord – only Scotch!'

'Is this true?' Fran looked at me.

'Ehm, I knew his uncle was. Maybe if his dad died, I suppose . . .'

Amanda looked at me in shock. 'Melanie, you knew all that time and you didn't tell me!'

'Amanda, you met him once at a party, and you said he smelled funny.'

'No-o, that can't have been me.' She laughed again. '*Anyway* –'

'Did he smell funny?' Fran asked me.

'Only when it rained.'

'*Darlings*!' said Amanda, with an edge in her voice. 'This is my BIG NEWS!'

We settled down, and her coy smile came back.

'*Anyway*, by sheer coincidence I spoke to the castles people and they gave me his mother's number, and she had his home number and it was just across London, so we got together and we had so much in common; we laughed and laughed . . . Then we went off to look at his land deeds, then one thing led to another at the Caledonian Ball . . .'

'*What* a coincidence!' said Fran.

'. . . and now I am going to be Lairdess Amanda Phillips-McConnald!' finished Amanda, all in one breath.

There was a silence.

'Hey, his name's Phillips too?' said Fran.

'No, no! You see, I'm keeping my name *and* taking

his name. It's a feminist statement really. Didn't you see me in *Tatler*?'

Fran said later my eyes were like saucers. So she asked, 'Is he rich?'

'Don't be silly, darling. What's in Scotland?'

'History? Great natural beauty? Mel Gibson?'

'Sheep and alcoholics, darling. No, he hasn't a bean . . . and there's a "castle" to do up – he couldn't pay for that looking at bridges all day long.'

Then Amanda went completely off on one about her interior design plans for the castle. I'd been there. (Fraser had asked a bunch of us along, but I'd tried to pretend it was a private outing for me alone.) It was really just an impressive exterior, two habitable rooms, and a Calor Gas heater, but she clearly didn't know that yet, given the lengths she was prepared to go to to put metal walls in it.

'I thought we'd go for a cutting-edge, post-industrialist look,' she was saying.

I knew I had to say something – anything – at this point. So I followed my time-honoured rule of saying the first thing that comes into my head:

'Wow, so really it's like a class-weds-money type of thing! That's practically . . .'

I was going to say Hogarthian, but too late. I got a look that could peel an apple whole, and a very long pause. Eventually:

'Well, of course, us Phillips can trace our ancestry back pretty far.'

'What, to Woking?' said Fran.

'Ha ha, very funny.' She turned. 'Are you getting

married, Fran? Oh no, I forgot, you're not seeing anyone, are you? Because maybe, if you ever do, we could make fun of you for a change.'

Fran raised her eyes to heaven and headed back to the bar for more drinks.

Tantrum over, Amanda leaned in chummily. 'So, you and Fraser were quite close, weren't you?' She smiled, as if to show that this *didn't* mean *ENVY ME! ENVY ME!*

'Not really,' I said, meaning: *Well, I fancied him and he completely ignored me.*

'Oh, you *must* come to the wedding. It's going to be absolutely wonderful. Daddy simply *insists* on making a fuss.'

Amanda's dad had been married about four times since we were sixteen. He got a discount.

'I'd love to.' I would be generous. She was the first of my friends to get married, and to a lovely bloke. Why shouldn't I be happy? Without warning, a thought of Alex popped into my head, and I winced.

'Great! Oh, I'm sorry I can't make you a bridesmaid, but Larissa and Portia are *such* good friends from varsity, I just had to ask them.'

'Oh, *right* . . .'

'You will meet someone, Melanie, you know. Someone nice. Such a shame about Alex dashing off like that. He was a bit of a one, wasn't he? And of course so terribly well connected.'

Meaning what exactly? I put my drink down, rather too emphatically.

'Well, I don't care about that, and I don't care about Alex.'

'No, of *course* you don't,' she said, patting me on the hand in an infuriating manner.

I was constantly forgetting Amanda's true potential for sheer malice. Revising my earlier estimate, I hoped she'd have a poxy marriage and get divorced before we'd finished the cake.

Fran came back with the drinks, but Amanda immediately hopped up and said she had to be elsewhere. She shook back her blonde sheet of hair – rootless – and sashayed her pert little leather-trousered arse out the door to her latest-model convertible, mobile phone already clamped to her ear, waving merrily behind her, off to somewhere infinitely more glamorous and exciting than the pub on a Friday night.

Fran and I sat in silence for a bit, till Fran said, 'Sod that, then!' and we drank her white wine as well as ours. Then we had another one to cheer ourselves up, and then a couple more, and before long we didn't care that Amanda Phillips had found her handsome – if scruffy – prince and was going off to live in a castle. Much.

Much, much later we were yabbering nonsensically about the last bloke Fran metaphorically kicked in the bollocks and threw out the house – actually, when I came to think of it, she had *literally* kicked him in the bollocks, and he had limped out of the house of his own accord – when across the crowded pub I spied what looked like a familiar pair of knees. Following upwards, I deduced that it was in fact Nicholas, tallest accountant in the world. (How did I know him again?) Gosh, he was tall. I liked tall.

I tugged on Fran's sleeve. 'Look – 's Nicholas.'

Fran looked roughly over. 'Wanker,' she said.

Had Fran not said wanker about every bloke we'd mentioned for the last hour and a half I might have listened to her and saved myself some trauma. Instead, I waved at him in huge circular motions. 'Knickerless!' And I dissolved in giggles. He flew over and gave me a big kiss. Oh, we must have been old friends, then.

'Melanie, *fantastic* to see you. I've just been having another crazy night out with the accountants.'

I squinted to make out anyone else who'd been at the other end of the bar, but they all seemed to have mysteriously disappeared.

'God, we're mad. Can't see us getting home tonight without a police caution! Chaw chaw chaw!'

'Buy 's a drink, Nicklas! You're loaded!'

'Sure, babe.' And he did so with the fervour of a man who knew only too well just how much alcohol he usually had to get down a woman to get her to sleep with him.

In normal circumstances I would have run six miles from Nicholas, whom I had accidentally slept with at a party once because he was, er, very tall. He'd phoned me up constantly since and I'd realized that, tall though he might be, he was also the most boring bastard who'd ever lived. In fact, he was the most boring *accountant* who'd ever lived. After the inevitable grilling I'd caught from Fran when he turned up to pick me up in stonewashed jeans and pink cowboy boots, I'd made Linda answer the phone for a month. Now here he was again, and he was desperate, and I was desperate for attention – a deadly combination.

Ensconced in a corner next to Fran – who looked half-asleep, but with a drowsy look that said she could still bite you on the face if you thought about trying anything – Nicholas started telling me all the latest pranks him and his fantastic accounting mates had been up to. By the time they'd finally got on the coach they'd hired to go see Bryan Adams, I was about to gnaw off my own hands in despair. With impeccable drunk logic, I decided I'd better kiss him to get him to shut the fuck up. It wasn't the easiest of tasks; almost on a par with climbing a tree. While pissed out of your head. So, once I got to the top, I decided I'd better stay until the tree fell asleep. I'd crawled from under the wreckage the following morning.

'So now what am I going to do?' I complained to Fran. 'There's a big stinky man in my bedroom, whom I hate, and if I go in and wake him he'll start telling me hysterical stories about tax again.'

'So?'

'So, ehm, could you go . . . like, ask him to move?'

'Me! Why me? You're the one with all his saliva! Anyway, plus, what if he's naked?'

'Oh, right, you've never seen a naked man before?'

'Not one that's six foot seven. It'll put me right off my sausage sandwich.'

Suddenly my ultra-loud doorbell rang, which made us both jump. Fran and I looked at each other and I limped dourly towards the door to stop the infernal noise.

WHOP! Straight out of my bedroom, an absolutely starkers, very hungover, six foot seven man ran full into me in panic, and it didn't look like he had the faintest idea what galaxy he was in.

'IS THERE A FIRE?!'

We stood for a while, looking straight at each other like rabbits caught in headlights. Then my psyche made an independent decision to turn me into my mother for as long as necessary.

'No, Nicholas, of course there's not. Go get dressed immediately! Now! – before I open the door.'

He blinked and retreated without saying a word, headed for the bedroom, then did a quick U-turn and made a bolt for the loo, where I could soon hear him having a six foot seven pee. Well, it was either him or a passing horse had got in there. So I had solved one problem – getting him out of my bedroom – and discovered another. Maybe I could keep him locked in there for ever and the neighbours would let us use their shower.

Finally, I opened the door, putting on an ingratiating look – not that the fat postman on the doorstep gave a toss.

'Parcel.'

I signed for it, trying not to get too excited, but this

was one huge parcel. Perhaps I had a secret admirer who was sending me precious gifts because they were totally rich and also perhaps completely famous.

Fran wandered through to try and use the loo. The fat postman noticed *her* – every man noticed her.

'Hello, fat postman,' she said. Then, indicating the parcel: 'Hey, is that for you?'

I turned it over in anticipation. 'No, it's for Linda. Bum bum bum.'

'God, what is it – the latest in the Woodland Farm Princess Diana *Star Wars* plate collection?'

'No, too heavy.'

The postman wobbled off. As ever, we looked at each other, wondering how a man who walked ten miles a day could get that fat.

'Books?'

'Linda doesn't read books. She eats them.'

'Is that true, or is it just that you don't like her?'

I looked at my feet.

'It's just that I don't like her.'

'Well then, can we open it?'

'No, of course not.'

'Why not? She wouldn't mind.'

'Fran, I believe she might, in fact, mind.'

To be honest, I had no idea whether she'd mind or not. In fact, all I knew about Linda was that she worked in a bank – I couldn't remember which one – was an only child, and had inherited money from her grandmother to buy this lovely flat and cover it in pastel tat. And I had learnt all this from the flat interview, where I had tried to look unbelievably fascinated, thus moving in under false pretences – which was a huge relief, as at the time I'd been on the run from a cabal of physiotherapists who were terrorizing me out of my shared flat in Edmonton, a period of my life I normally only flashed back to at four o'clock in the morning, wide awake and sweating.

As if hearing our thoughts – or, more likely, she'd had her ear up against the door earwigging our entire conversation – Linda stomped out into the corridor from her big bedroom at the back of the house, managing not to look either of us in the eye, even while grabbing the parcel out of my hand. She was short and round, with a definite aura of moustache. As she stomped back to her room, Fran and I swapped our familiar 'Linda' look.

'Erm, guys . . . ha ha . . .' came a strangulated voice, 'can I, er, come out of the bathroom now?'

Fran raised her eyes to heaven. 'Any time you like, darling. We'll be right here.'

I started to giggle.

'Right, OK, right . . .' came the voice. Then there was a pause, during which we didn't move back to the kitchen.

Finally, the door started to open and Nicholas emerged, with a mass of tissue paper covering his genitals. And I mean a *mass*.

'Bwah hah! Corking night, eh, ladies!' he hollered, putting on a good front, I have to say. 'What's for breakfast?'

'For you, a number sixty-eight bus,' said Fran. 'They deliver.'

'Haw haw haw – I'll get my dancing trousers on and be right with you. And how are *you*, my darling?'

We both looked round, till I realized he was talking to me.

'Oh, you know, some variation of fantastic,' I said, hunched over, still in my towel. 'The negative one.' Suddenly I saw something on the floor which I hadn't seen previously. I picked it up. It was a postcard, and this time it was for me.

'Fra-an!' my voice quavered as I followed her into the living room. 'It's a postcard.'

'So I see. Oh, and look over there, Nicholas – it's a door!'

'Cwah cwah!' came the voice from the other room. 'Just wait till I tell the boys at work about this.'

I sighed. '*Look*,' I said urgently. 'Look who it's from.'

The postcard was of the Empire State Building, almost completely obscured by a close-up of a woman's breasts. On the other side it said simply: *Darling, I'm so sorry – big mistake. I'm coming home. Alex.*

There was a long dramatic pause. Or, well, there would have been a long dramatic pause, except that Nicholas chose that moment to launch into the room wearing purple trousers (I hadn't noticed they were purple; the effect was like a terrible plum-canning factory accident), shouting, 'Hey, I know what would be *hysterical* – let's make some French toast!!'

Fran gave him a Paddington Bear hard stare. 'Go look for some chocolate, Nicholas.'

I was in shock, and scarcely noticed when Nicholas disappeared, then returned obediently with a dozen chocolate mini rolls. I was too busy staring straight ahead without blinking and trying to work everything out: Alex, Alex, Alex – my 'one true love', according to me. Alex, Alex, Alex, that 'low-level rat bastard' according to Fran and pretty much everyone else in the world.

The first time I ever saw Alex I thought, 'Phwoar, I'd like to get into his pants!' And he looked at me and thought exactly the same thing: it was a true meeting of minds. Oh! That shitty West London party (well, I should have known better than to go to parties in West London and expect to have a good time, but just that once it paid off).

I was searching for the more expensive beer that hosts hide at the back of the fridge, when:

'Is it just me,' growled a tall voice, 'or does everyone here look like they've got something uncomfortable up their bums?'

'That's *trendy*,' I hissed. 'You're supposed to be *envying* them. They're only *pretending* not to be having a good time.'

'Ohhhhh, now I understand. Right. So I can either try and get out of West London . . .'

'Can't be done,' I pointed out.

'True . . . Or I could get absolutely wasted and do something awful which I could later abdicate any responsibility for.'

This was so pointed that I gulped and took a closer look at this six foot two, dark-haired, unruly-looking character with the most heavy-lidded, pointy-lashed brown eyes I'd ever seen.

'That,' I said, 'sounds like it would be *completely* out of character.'

Eighteen astonishing hours later, damp, grubby and absolutely starving, lying in an unfamiliar bedroom having my tummy tickled with a tea bag, I realized I was on to something.

A year later I was blissful, swanning around with Alex, who was trying to make it as something in the music industry. He knew everyone; we always ended up at a party and all his friends were louche, slightly dodgy but with terribly nice accents. I was with the band: it was great. He wasn't exactly the most romantic character on the planet, but I didn't care; here I was, Melanie Pepper, twenty-six and watching minor pop-stars throw up in the corner of filthy nightclubs. Life was cool.

More than that, though, I absolutely adored him. I loved his cool long floppy hair, and his sad brown puppy eyes, and was constantly trying to get him to notice me. I would jump up and down trying to reach him, and he would give me his big lazy grin and check out who else was in on the conversation. Occasionally he would indulge me with his attention, and I would be like one of those pathetically affectionate little dogs they're always rescuing on programmes about the RSPCA. Other times he'd flirt with women for ages and I would be distraught. In short, he was not that good a boyfriend, no doubt about it. But in his leather trousers . . . well, you know, a girl is a girl, and leather trousers and pop-star friends are leather trousers and pop-star friends, so of course I did what the cool girls should NEVER do, which is fall in love with the cool boys. It blows the whole thing.

Still, he'd been coming round. I'd notice the occasional look of tenderness on his face. Or he'd phone me, for no reason. Or come home early from a gig. He was coming round, I could sense it. He loved me. He even passed the 'Would you mind just picking me up some Tampax on the way over?' test. So I was just about to suggest that we . . . possibly . . . think about moving in together – not seriously or anything, just a casual moving-in thing because, after all, all that toothbrush expense just didn't seem worth it, ha ha – when he vanished. Off the face of the earth.

I waited for him to call one weekend and he never did. It was that simple. Assuming it was an *X-Files* type incident and could have nothing to do with me, I let twenty-four hours go by before I finally phoned his flatmate, Charlie, who lived in Fulham. Charlie wasn't best pleased to have to put up with Alex's shit, and too posh to be kind. He informed me wearily that Alex had gone to the States to find himself, and was sorry he hadn't told me but it seemed easier that way.

Not even a desultory note! Alex had dumped me by moving continents and leaving a message with a laconic friend!

For weeks I was too strung out even to cry. It felt like someone had scooped out my insides with a cold spoon.

Fran was wonderful then; I'd never known anyone with a fuller range of colourful epithets and hexes. She spat venom for me; I sat in corners and rocked myself. I felt embarrassed just walking down to the shops for more crisps, with the sheer humiliation I felt must be written all over my face. It was pain like I'd never known, worse even than when I got the Spangles papers stuck up my nose (I was four; I'm not weird or anything).

As the months passed, everything had settled to the occasional dull ache, which I had most recently attempted to assuage with the guest now smacking his lips over the chocolate mini rolls as if they were caviar.

'OK,' said Fran. 'I'm just going to take this little piece of junk mail and put it where it belongs . . .'

I snatched it out of her hand.

'Come *on*, Mel. This is low-life trash bastard post. In fact, if you like, I'll even give you the honour of setting fire to it.'

'Hey, guys, what's going on?' said Nicholas the Intuitive, through a mouthful of chocolate mush. Apparently, if he didn't get 15,000 calories a day he'd die.

I opened my eyes.

'Look, I really don't want to be rude, but would you just GO AWAY!' I burst out, but I couldn't hold the moment. 'Ehm, it's just that Fran and I have this REALLY IMPORTANT THING to do that we've been planning for ages . . .'

'Yeah, it's called the Getting Away From Nicholas Thing,' said Fran, not quite under her breath.

'Sure, hey, not a problem, babe. How about I pick you up tonight at seven and we go for a ludicrously expensive dinner at my client's expense? Chaw chaw chaw!'

'Unfortunately this THING that Mel and I have to do lasts for AGES,' said Fran. '*So* sorry. But you have to go. NOW.'

'Hey, cool your jets. No one ever said that Nicholas Snodley couldn't take a hint.'

I suddenly ran to the other side of the room and started de-alphabetizing Linda's CDs in case he tried to give me a kiss. Linda's CDs: *The Greatest Love Songs Ever – One*, *The Greatest Love Songs Ever – Two* and, for a bit of variety, *The Greatest Love Songs in the World – Ever!* And some dolphin noises.

'Mel, babe, I'll ring you soon, huh? About the Brian May Appreciation bash?'

'Absolutely,' I said. 'BYE.'

He went for playing it cool: 'Yeah, right. What's your number again?'

I meant to give him the wrong number, but in my confused emotional state got mixed up and accidentally gave him the right one.

'Ciao then, babes,' he sleazed, and, bending under the doorframe, he was gone. I swear I could hear the echoing 'chaw chaw chaw' down the corridor in his wake.

* * *

Out of the frying pan, I thought to myself, picking up the postcard again. I moved back and collapsed on the sofa next to Fran, leaning my head on her shoulder.

'Please, never do the Nicholas thing again,' she said.

'But it's so much fun for you.'

'Mel, you know I'd rather grate myself than see you go anywhere near that eight-foot pole of slime.'

I held up the postcard weakly. 'I missed him so much.'

'I know you did.'

'I still do.'

'I know you do. But what kind of man would do what he did to you without being a total bastard?'

'*I* don't know. Boys are weird.'

'Yes, they are. All of them. And they think we're weird. But some of them are nice-weird and some of them are not. Think of Alex as an Amanda of the boy world. He made you feel exactly the same way as that snotty cow did when she took up with all those nobs and dropped you like a stone.'

'And I still see her.'

Fran sighed. 'And she makes you miserable. Which means you probably won't listen to a word I say.'

'Probably not.'

'OK, well, fuck that for sisterly advice then. Any mini rolls left?'

We regarded the debris of tinfoil strewn across the floor.

'That boy frightens me,' murmured Fran.

I lay back on the sofa, groaning. 'Oh God. First

Fraser, then Nicholas, and now this. I hope karma isn't true.' A thought struck me: 'You don't think Amanda's marrying Fraser just to fuck me off, do you?'

'Probably,' said Fran, stretching lazily and putting the TV on. 'Don't worry. If Alex is coming back, maybe she'll marry him instead.'

Neither prospect filled me with glee.

Two

I trudged back into work on Monday feeling low. I always felt low at work anyway, so fortunately nobody noticed. Which they could only have done if I'd actually talked to anyone, and I never did. So, just a typical week, really.

I had a dingy grey office with a dead plant and big piles of crap all over it where I was supposed to check copy for a stationery company in Holborn. It was a shitty job going absolutely nowhere, but it demanded minimum brain power and paid more than McDonald's, so I sat it out. In front of the office the secretarial staff tended to hover, sniffing suspiciously. Given that all I did in my job was read, whereas they typed and answered the phone too, they were very cagey about my presence – I swear I could hear them sharpening their extra-long nails whenever I walked in. Mostly, they ignored me. But even they couldn't ignore me for three whole days, standing peering out over Holborn Viaduct through my tiny filthy window which didn't open, holding a postcard and looking painfully wistful.

'What's the matter, love?'

Shirley was queen secretary, in her late thirties, with two-tone hair and attitude. Since Fran had given up on me in disgust, and Amanda would have said, 'Oh, petal, are you going to take him back? . . . Well, you know best, dear, but he is a Charterhouse boy and they really do have a reputation for it . . .' I was desperate for someone to confide in.

'I, erm, well, it's my boyfriend. Ex-boyfriend. Ehm, well, he left a year ago without telling me and went to America, and now he's coming back and I don't know what to do.'

'Got any kids?'

'Gosh, no.' I was surprised, and felt horribly middle class and at the same time cross that she thought I looked old enough to have kids.

''As he got any money?'

'I . . . well, not much really.'

'Tell 'im to fuck off then. Simple, innit? What's the point of having 'im 'anging around, treating you like that?'

That made perfect sense.

'Is that really what you'd do?' I asked.

'Every time my Stan pisses off, that's exactly what I do. He knows he loves me, see. So he always comes crawling back. And I make him pay, believe me.'

'Oh.' I was confused. 'So I shouldn't tell Alex to fuck off, just make him pay?'

'Up to you, love.'

'Right. Right. Thanks.'

Oh God, I didn't know when I was going to get round to picking up my dry-cleaning, never mind considering making a sensible decision about the bastard who tore my heart from its aorta, stomped up and down on it, and gleefully reduced me to the sort of person who considered Nicholas a fantastic night on the town.

Preparing myself a cup of my delicious coffee made with three different sorts of powder scraped off the bottom of other people's catering tins, I switched on my voice mail, a wonderful invention which had saved me the trouble of ever having to pick up the phone and speak to anyone at work, thereby avoiding being asked to do any. I had five new messages. Gosh, that made me sound popular. I perked up a bit.

It occurred to me, as it had done every half-hour since Saturday, that Alex might have phoned. After all, I'd hardly been hurling myself up the career ladder since he left; he knew where to find me. I got excited all over again, and drank my coffee without tasting it (a vast improvement).

'Hello, Melanie darling, wonderful to see you two the other night – looked like you were on for a bit of a party after I left!'

Great. It was Amanda 'La la la, I'm marrying the man I love and we're having fifteen adorable NCT children and living in a whole house done in National Trust colours for ever and ever' Phillips.

I beeped over the rest of it. It was definitely too early in the day to deal with that.

'Mel.' Phew. It was Fran. She would tell me what to do.

'I've thought this over very thoroughly. If you take him back you will have to die. And ring me – we have to decide whether we're going to bitchtastic Phillips's engagement party . . . and then decide to go anyway, like we always do, and have a shitty time, like we always do.'

That must have been what Amanda's message was about. Could I handle her and all her posh friends – whom I would hate and therefore get drunk so as not to mind talking to them, and then get too drunk and possibly end up getting off with aforesaid posh friends, thus maintaining the cycle of shame? Still, a party was a party, no matter how humiliating.

BEEP

'Melanie, yes, good morning . . . um . . . you wouldn't still have that brochure proof I gave you six weeks ago? The marketing chappies swear they don't have it, but it couldn't possibly still be with you, could it? I'll speak to you later then. Goodbye.'

Bugger it. My boss, Barney, was terribly polite, ethical, and saw the best in everyone. Therefore everyone considered him washed up and constantly took the piss. I looked in despair at my desk. Anything six weeks old had probably mulched by now.

BEEP

'Melanie, this is Flavi in marketing. We've had your boss on to us, and I really don't think . . .'

BEEP. I think, Flavi, that I've got rather more important things on right now, don't you? Like major emotional crises and stuff?

One message left. Did I feel lucky?

BEEP

'Mel! Great, hey, well, what a wild weekend, huh?'

The speed with which my stomach hit the floor on hearing Nicholas's nasal whine made me realize how much I really, really wanted to hear from Alex. Only to tell him a thing or two, of course. Or listen to him grovel. Where the fuck had Nicholas got this number anyway? I thought of Linda. She paid me back for not doing the washing-up in a myriad of different little ways.

'Anyway, yeah, I'm pretty busy with all my friends, right. We're off on some accountants' night out. God, they're nutters! But, hey, I might have some time on Tuesday night . . .'

Nicholas, it's Monday now, you plank. Not that I had anything planned, but God, of course I'm not going to say yes at that kind of notice!

'. . . or Wednesday, maybe . . . We could go out somewhere nice. Hey, give me a ring, it's 555 8923 – just ask for Crazy Nick, they all know me here! Hyaw! Hyaw! Ciao!'

Ciao? Suddenly I felt as depressed as I've ever felt in my entire life – or at least, in a month or so. This was it then. I was going to get niggled at in a shitty job I didn't care about, go to my so-called friends' fabulous engagement parties, live with someone who thought hoovering was a positive life choice, drink sludge instead of espresso, and date men who said 'ciao' until I got too old and ugly to date anyone at all.

I slumped down on my desk – the enormous mounds of paper gave it a cushioning effect – and reached out to switch off the speaker mode.

'A new message has been added to your voice mail,' said the mechanical voice.

Immediately, I knew.

I pressed '2'. An annoying voice in my head was singing, 'He's coming home, he's coming, Alex is coming home, he's coming home . . .'

BEEP

'Mel, hey, it's me . . . like, how're you doing?' People in the background. I could feel that big lazy grin of his spreading over his face and therefore mine. 'It's four o'clock in the morning, we're just hanging out . . . where the fuck are we?' 'The Village' – American woman's voice. Dirty. 'Yeah, it's absolutely brilliant and I am cummminngg', he started to sing, 'hooommmee tooooo yewwwww.' There was laughter in the background, a couple of 'whoops', then a pause, then: 'Hey, babe – I'll be at Heathrow. Today.' And then he hung up.

Oh. Oh! Chuffing hell. Every cell in my body renegotiated itself, and I shivered all over. Oh God. How was I going to cope? I would have to clean my bedroom for a start. And buy new pants. And start cooking again, boohoo. Could I reduce the size of my arse by – when? When was his today? Was it today or was it tomorrow? Piss! I started panicking. Why couldn't he tell me when his stupid flight gets in? He obviously hadn't been promoted from the space cadet corps.

Of course I would have to go. It never occurred to me otherwise. The adrenaline was coursing through my body: I felt as if I'd won; like I'd beaten America, his wanderlust and, well, any other lusts he might have experienced in passing. He was coming home. I was practically jumping up and down on the spot and decided to walk out immediately. Who would notice? Hey, it wasn't like I walked out over emotional crises a lot! Well . . . maybe occasionally.

Alex was coming back! Alex was coming back! He loved me! He loved me! I looked pitifully at the beautiful handwritten note my boss had left me vis-à-vis the delicate diplomatic situation between us and the marketing department, and decided to leg it. I took a deep breath, strode out in front of the secretaries, and announced, rather too loudly, 'Oh God, meetings all day. Ha! You know what it's like!!!' – then bolted, leaving them behind, hissing slightly. Free!

All the way to Heathrow I bounced up and down in the carriage like a toddler. Terminal Four was mobbed and I wandered off to buy myself a load of make-up and some magazines – who knew, he may be some time. I was just considering buying some shampoo and washing my hair when it hit me.

He'd phoned at nine o'clock. From New York. At

4 a.m. his time. And now it was twenty past eleven. Half past six in the morning? He probably hadn't even gone to bed, never mind got up, packed, swallowed his hangover, got to the airport, checked in for two hours, got on the plane, watched a couple of films, got drunk again and got here. Yes, it appeared I might well have time to wash my hair.

I was back in the Land of Alex; the place that made me go completely out of my fucking head.

ARRRGGGH. I was the skeggiest creature in the universe. No one in the world could ever have been such a twat before. I counted it up on my fingers. The earliest he could possibly be here would be 6 p.m. I twisted about in an agony of indecision. A part of me wanted to wait, right here. A part of me wanted to get on a plane and jump out and meet him halfway. NONE of me wanted to go back to the office with my tail between my legs. What I really wanted was to turn back time and have none of this ever happen. Simultaneously clenching my buttocks and hopping up and down, I wondered what the hell to do.

Of course, when in doubt, one should always phone one's closest confidante for their deep love and support.

'I would say the best thing to do now is break into airport security where they keep all the confiscated firearms, confiscate one and hit him with a sniper bullet before he can make it to baggage control.'

'Frraaannn! I've got to wait all day and I don't know what to do!'

'Grow up? Sort your life out? Start making some conscious decisions about yourself?'

'I thought I'd read some women's magazines,' I mumbled.

'Oh, now there's a good idea for someone as sad as you. They're full of articles on "How to keep that pathetic cheating low-down pigdog in your life happy".'

I snuffled. As pathetic as I was, it made sense to play up to it.

'Don't try that snuffle bollocks on me. I refuse to be sympathetic because you're welcoming back into your life a man who is only going to cause you pain – and you are entirely to blame.'

I said 'bye' and wandered back into the terminal feeling utterly lonely and unloved. That was a feeling I found was helped by being surrounded by young couples fleeing into each other's arms and long-lost family members kissing, hugging and crying all around me.

But when he got off that plane . . .

I decided to take in the entire airport experience, make it a positive thing. I went and had my hair done – not cut, just done, which made me feel like a TV weathergirl. I quite liked pretending to be the kind of person who had their hair done, however it may have clashed with the ladder in the inside leg of my tights (you could hardly see it). There isn't that much you can do with a heavy scrunch of unshiny brown curly stuff, but they tried their best and made lots of interested-sounding noises when I mentioned I was here to pick up my boyfriend from the airport as he'd been in America.

I kept getting flashbacks. That time he walked into my office at eleven o'clock in the morning, straight past the vulture brigade, into the office, pulled down the blind, and gave me one right there. The time we got absolutely rollocksed and tried to break into St Paul's Cathedral. That time the central heating broke down and we both refused to get up and get any food and stayed in bed for fifteen hours and we both peed out of the window . . . That time he 'went to comfort an old friend' for three days and I never found out who, or where . . . That time I met his mum and dad – oh no, I never did.

I blocked out the bad thoughts from my head, and decided that this time there were definitely going to be ground rules. If he wanted to come back, it was going to be on my terms. This time, Fran would be proud of me.

OK: we'd have lots of togetherness. No more him vanishing with the lads . . . But then, what if I was just being all clingy and wouldn't leave him alone and he got really, really bored and I did too and we ended up just staying in and saying things like, 'Err, do you want to go to the cinema then?' 'Errr . . . don't mind . . .' 'What do you want to go and see?' 'Don't mind . . .' until we both killed ourselves! Maybe nitch that one then.

OK, we'd have lots of open public affection. Not snogging, necessarily, but a bit of hand-holding wouldn't go amiss, so he didn't look like my cousin from the attractive end of the family if I ever met anyone I knew.

And he could at least try and get on with my friends. Although they all hated him.

I phoned Fran again.

'Leave me alone. You are no longer my friend. You fraternize with the untouchable ones.'

'Fraaan.' My genuine panic was beginning to show through.

'OK. Here's one test. He's been away for ten months, right?'

'Yep. I've had my hair done.'

'Oh, that's pretty subtle . . . Anyway, he's been away for ten months. After vanishing completely and never contacting you again . . .'

'Apart from the postcard.'

'The postcard you got two days ago when he remembered he'd left Charlie in the shit and needed to find somewhere else to stay.'

'Mmm.'

'OK. Those are the facts. You are dumb enough to be there waiting for him. As a hypothetical test, one might think it would be the least little considerate thing he could do to buy you a present, right?'

'Oh, Alex doesn't really believe in giving presents. He thinks it's bourgeois.'

Now what was she sighing for?

'God, Mel, what are you doing? Tell me you're not putting him up.'

'Mmm.'

'Fantastic. Have you told Linda about the new addition to your jolly little Kennington family?'

'Oh, she'll be fine. She won't say anything.'

'That means the same thing, does it?'

I was getting too upset to talk. I mean, what did my best friend since age four know about my life anyway?

'Mel, you know I wouldn't say anything if I wasn't worried about you and if I didn't care about you, don't you?'

'Yes,' I mumbled ungratefully.

'Give me a ring when he gets in then. When's that going to be?'

'Ehmm, anywhere in the next fifteen hours.'

'OK. Cool. Bye.'

It was true. Alex did a horrid, horrid thing to me. It's just, oh, Alex's problems – where to start? Public school, weird distant parents who divorced early, that whole deal. I was psychologically-tastic when it came to Alex. When I'd met him he'd just emerged from his last finding-his-own-anus phase in Goa. Well, I wasn't going to be his doormat any more.

Oh good, only six hours to go.

Wanting to avoid another ear-bashing, but desperate for someone to talk to, I phoned Amanda. Some bloke picked up the phone.

'Hello, is Amanda there?'

'No, she's not. Can I take a message?'

I recognized that accent!

'Frase! Hi, it's Melanie!'

There was a pause.

'Melanie . . .'

'Melanie Pepper. You remember! Mel!'

Jesus.

'Oh, hi, hi there. Yes. What are you up to these days?'

Oh, I'm just sitting in Heathrow Airport, where I've turned up fifteen hours early by mistake, having my hair set and waiting for my selfish ex-boyfriend who left me in shit nearly a year ago, and whom I still haven't got over, to – possibly – return from America, having walked out of my job this morning with no explanation.

'Oh, you know . . . usual stuff.'

'Right, great.'

God! Could we be any more scintillating?

'So, congratulations!' I said heartily. 'You're marrying my old buddy!'

I tried to imagine him bending over to kiss Amanda, but I couldn't make it fit. His curly hair would fall in her eyes. She'd hate that.

He laughed nervously. 'So it seems.'

'And you're a laird!' I added, helpfully.

'Yes, right, yes. Anyway, can I give her a message?'

'Ooooh . . . no message, actually. Just phoned for a girlie chat.'

'Right. OK. Bye.'

I often had romantic dreams of what it would be like to bump into an old crush from the past, when their eyes would be opened and they would see me anew: suave, sophisticated and thrillingly desirable.

Although played out in a variety of exotic locales, the two things the fantasies had in common were that they normally included the crushee remembering who I was, and then giving a shit. Me, and my hair, were starting to flop.

Stuff it. I was going back to basics. I called my mum. I owed her a call. Well, about nine, actually. My mum was sweet – really sweet; I mean, she bakes – but definitely a traditionalist in every sense of the word. She had looked like Miriam Margolyes since even Miriam Margolyes hadn't looked like Miriam Margolyes. I was convinced that really she was only about forty and deeply frivolous but put an old mum costume on every day and got the rolling pin out. It was the only way to explain me, anyway.

'Hi, Mum. How are you?'

'Melanie, I've just this second been talking about you.'

Given that talking about me and Stephen, my elder brother, was my mother's favourite thing after baking, this wasn't surprising. Other non-surprising things she could have been doing: watching television, playing bridge, talking non-stop to my father, who could only grunt. I seldom spoke to him on the phone, as the grunts couldn't be accompanied by comprehensible gestures (macaroni cheese; beer; remote control – really, my dad's Homer Simpson without the deep self-awareness) and was therefore pointless.

'Is it true what I hear – that Amanda Phillips is getting married to that nice young man you brought home?'

'Yes. Oh, and Alex is coming back.'

'Well, he was a lovely boy. Scottish, wasn't he? Such a nice smile. And so well behaved.'

'He's not four,' I said crossly. 'He doesn't have to be well behaved. Anyway, Alex is coming back.'

'. . . it's sure to be a big wedding – that family never do things by halves. You should see the new swimming-pool extension Derek's put on the manor house. Of course, I haven't seen it, but apparently it's nearly as big as the house!'

'That sounds great. Anyway, Alex is coming back.'

'Are you going to be a bridesmaid? Maybe there'll be more polite Scottish boys there and you could meet a *nice one*.'

My mother didn't mince her words.

'I'm not going to be a bridesmaid. I might not even get invited. But I'm at the airport . . .'

'Of course you'll get invited. Great little friends at school, you three were. How is Fran? Met a nice man yet?'

'No. But . . .'

'Well, maybe the both of you can go to the wedding and *get lucky this time*. OK, darling, have to go, I've got bath buns on the go, and you know their temperementiality. Speak to you soon. Bye, darling.'

It drove me mad when my mum used the word *temperementiality*. It wasn't even nearly a real word. She did it to annoy me. Perhaps, I thought, musing on the conversation, she did everything to annoy me. That would explain a lot.

One of the cleaners, whom I'd noticed earlier for

some reason, came past and caught my eye. He stared at me, a tad suspiciously, I thought. I wanted to run up to him and explain that, yes, I did have a home; no, I wasn't a terrorist (though I'd be strangely flattered if he thought so), but really I was choosing to be here to make some friendly phone calls, shop for consumer goods and WAIT FOR SOMEONE WHO LOVED ME, DAMN IT! So I grinned ingratiatingly. I checked the ongoing ladder in my tights. Shit. Where on earth was I going to find a pair of tights in an airport shopping mall?

Another three hours and I'd thought 'stuff it' and done the whole credit-card thing. I was top-to-toe coiffed: hair, Clinique lipstick, new top, poncey pants, hold-ups (the nineties girl's compromise, as far as I was concerned) and, sadly, the same old flat shoes, as even I couldn't bring myself to go that far. Unfortunately, the perfume ladies didn't see the shoes in time, checked out the posh togs and did a mass ambush on me, so I smelled like a tarts' annual general meeting.

Another two hours and I had managed to spend more than the clothes' total on coffee and nasty Danishes, and I was sitting uncomfortably, staring out of the window and reading 'What your man really means when he shags all your mates and has started to look at the dog – is this how the new soft new lad has to express himself?' I was ready to a) kill myself; b) go play in the arcades; c) buy the damned shoes. I'd been tempted to try and make friends with the cleaner, but he'd wandered off shift, still staring at me and shaking his head.

So I bought the shoes. Then I went and played in the arcades.

Five hundred years later, it seemed a reasonable time to start going to meet planes. I bought a toothbrush and toothpaste, and prepared myself.

Four New York planes later, and my fixed smile was starting to look a bit desperate. How did travel reps do it? Must be the drugs.

I started to think that maybe I'd missed him. Maybe he'd disembarked already and was on his way somewhere – he'd phoned one of his mates and been whooshed off in a taxi to some expensive postcode. Maybe he'd walked past while I was looking at the girl carrying the enormous stuffed elephant. Maybe when all that bloody coffee made me go to the loo again. Oh Christ. More than a whole day in an airport for absolutely nothing.

My anxiety levels were reaching their peak and I was about to put a call out for him over the intercom so I could at least attempt to head him off, when, at last, at last, at last, he loped out of the by now extremely familiar automatic doors.

My stomach hit the floor. He looked gorgeous. I arranged my face into a suitably affectionate, wry look and pointed myself in his general direction. He didn't see me (it must have been the hairdo), so I ended up having to run after him in my new super-sexy high-heeled shoes and attack him from behind like a mugger.

He jumped round as if he was about to kung-fu me, then gradually took it in.

'Mel!'

I was out of breath from running and out of breath from seeing him.

'Heh . . . heh . . . Alex!'

He gathered me up in his strong arms and gave me a huge movie-star bear hug. I wished the cleaner was still around to see.

'You . . . you complete and utter fuckhead,' I choked.

He buried his face in my hair.

'God, I missed you.'

Three

All the way back on the tube we yabbered and yabbered, genuinely thrilled to see each other again. He told me about his trip across America: the larks he got up to in New York; the English pop-star he bumped into in a deserted part of Montana and what great mates they became; his awful jobs and the amazing characters he'd met. His voice had taken on a new American tinge. I didn't mention the fact that I hadn't changed jobs, or flats, or, despite appearances, got it together at all since he went away, instead embroidering wildly the love lives of several mutual acquaintances, some boring parties and a hilarious imaginary cat of Fran's (I was getting desperate by that stage). Neither of us mentioned the inauspicity of his leaving; it was as if he'd simply been away, perhaps on business, perhaps for a fortnight, perhaps in prison.

We turned up at home at half past midnight. The flat was ominously quiet, which meant that Linda was wide awake, listening to our every move. However, it was a special occasion, so I pinched her bottle of vodka anyway, called in sick with a midnight vomiting fit (unpleasant but effective), and fell into bed with my big – OK, slightly smelly – darling, who managed to make me buzz all over before passing out for fourteen hours.

The following day I watched him sleep, and the time just drifted by. Maybe they should put beautiful sleeping males in airport waiting rooms.

He woke up dazed, stared at the ceiling for a second, then rolled over and grabbed me with a grin.

'Oh, Mel, darling. I will be yours for ever . . .'

This was more like it.

'. . . if you'd make me a bacon sandwich. Two bacon sandwiches. And some fried eggs. I am *starving*.'

'That', he said twenty minutes later, after I'd emptied the fridge of Linda's food, 'was the best bacon sandwich I have ever had. Americans just cannot make a bacon sandwich. They put it in brown bread and cover it in crap.'

'What, like vegetables?'

'Yeah!'

'You're right – bloody Americans and their healthy eating! That's why they're all in such fantastic physical shape.'

He giggled, then took my face in his hands. Here it came.

'Gee, Mel, it's good to be back. Americans . . . they never mean what they say. I never feel I can talk bullshit with anyone as much as I can with you.'

'I think that's possibly the nicest thing anyone's ever said to me,' I said gravely.

He laughed, and ruffled my hair.

'I mean . . . I behaved like a complete dork, Mel. I'm sorry. I really am. What I did to you, it really bit. You know, I had no idea what I was doing. With all my parents and stuff . . . I can find it really hard to open up . . . and I got scared. I was so worried you were going to . . . just ignore me. Which I would probably have deserved.'

'Yes, you would.'

'You're special to me, you know.'

'I do know. And if you ever EVER do anything like that again, I'm going to impale a testicle on each arm of a pair of scissors and start snipping.'

He winced. 'Is that nice?'

'You'll see.'

And that was it. I was very happy.

The next week passed in a blur – a dirty-sheeted, stupid, giggling, New York-time blur. I finally got it together to go into work, but was so glowing and smiley that I got away with more murder than usual. Even the secretaries couldn't hurt me. No one in the world had ever been as happy as us, ever, and in fact could have no idea what it was like. I floated around, occasionally stopping to pity people for not being as happy as me.

At home, I stopped answering the phone and made Linda do it, which was mean of me as she hated doing it and my friends hated speaking to her. Fran eventually stomped round in a fury, having gleaned, accurately, that things weren't exactly going the way she'd planned. This surmise was confirmed when she came to the door and Alex opened it, clearly in possession of both kneecaps.

'Hey there, Fran,' he said winningly. 'Good to see you again.'

I wondered what she was going to do. For a moment she looked as if she would completely ignore him, then she shook her mane of hair and smiled.

'Hello! Great to see you – you complete bastard! How nice!' she said, walking straight past him to kiss me on the cheek.

Alex grimaced at me, but I shrugged. Even if I hadn't been able to give him a hard time for what he'd done, I had no objections to Fran doing it.

I put the kettle on. From the other room I could hear Fran's trained voice, devastatingly polite.

'So, did you stay in lots of interesting places . . . cocksucker?'

'Well, yeah,' Alex stammered. 'Yeah, I moved around a bit, saw a few states. Bumming around, mostly.'

'Really? How unusual . . . for such a rampant arsehole.'

'MEL!' shouted Alex, coming through to the kitchen. 'How long do I have to put up with this?'

'As long as it takes . . . buttcheeks.'

'Buttcheeks? That's complimentary, surely?'

I blushed. 'Shut up and take in this tea. And try and make it up to Fran.'

'I didn't do anything to Fran.'

'What, you want to get on her bad side? Be nice.'

He sighed, hung his head, and we carried in the tea.

'I like knobchop's new fake accent,' Fran said to me. 'Do you remember when he came back from Goa? He talked about his karma all the time and wanted to be a hippie. Gosh, wasn't it jolly funny! What a wankfox!' And she laughed a tinkly little Amanda laugh.

'Fran, give me a break!' said Alex. 'I'm sorry. I'm sorry, goddamnit.'

'Gimme a break! Ah'm sawry, gawdamnit.'

'Oh, for God's sake, stop it!'

'Stawp it!'

'OK, OK, OK.' He got up and made to leave the room.

Fran wasn't finished. 'So what are your plans now, worthless anal wart?'

He looked at me and then at the floor.

'To make it up to Melanie and never leave abruptly again and be a good human being and find a good job and become respectable, SUH!'

Fran nodded slowly, winked at me, and smiled at Alex, who gradually sat down again. Then she launched into filling us in on the gossip. It looked like things were going to be OK.

And they were. Alex and I swanned about London, doing all the things we normally couldn't be bothered with, like Art and Culture, for example. I cooked us fabulous meals, to which I politely asked Linda. However, she didn't seem to fancy them. She'd had another big parcel, anyway, and stayed in her room a lot, not really giving me a chance to thank her for doing the washing-up.

Alex did have some plans. This pop-star bloke was apparently lined up to get him some work here in the record business, so it was all going to be cool and he might even try and get a band together. I nodded supportively . . . For the moment, I was simply happy to keep playing Hide the Trousers and didn't really care.

Eventually, I phoned Amanda back about the party. OK, I was happy, but it didn't stop me feeling an urge to get a gloat in, given half a chance.

'Darling, hi. I've just got a call on the other line – give me a second.'

Crap. This meant she must already have heard and had gone into defensive mode, which meant I wouldn't have the satisfaction of relaying the news.

'There,' she said, 'now what's all this about Alex? I couldn't believe it when I heard. Really, Melanie, haven't you ever thought of playing hard to get?'

Every time.

'No, it's great,' I said. 'We're really . . . happy to be

back together, get everything sorted out, you know. We worked out we wanted to be together.'

'Oh!' she squealed. 'Tell me you're going to get married too! We could have a joint celebration.'

She knew damn well I wasn't.

'No, of course not. That's for grown-ups. Which reminds me, we're coming to your do on Saturday night.'

'OK . . . well, Alex will know everyone, I suppose. You know it's black tie?'

'Uh huh.'

'OK, darling. Well, improvise as best you can. Must dash! We've got a Teletubby stuck in a lift! Bye, darling!'

By the following Saturday, I knew for a fact that everything was all right with the world and I was ready to hit Amanda's engagement do. I had it all worked out. No doubt there'd be a lot of nudging. Someone might even say, 'Hey, it'll be you two next!' and I'd blush modestly and do a shy smile, and Alex would look at me tenderly and say, 'Well, you never know . . . maybe one day, if I'm lucky!' and that'd get all round the party and I'd be the queen! By the time my imagination had supplied a huge circular staircase down which we could descend to mass applause, I had to pretend to be Fran and tell myself not to be so silly. But, oh – look how wonderfully compatible we were! We hadn't fallen out once, all week. He'd grovelled, he'd done his bit. He was home again, he was beautiful, and he was mine. Everything was brilliant.

Amanda's party turned out to be a pretty swish affair. Fortunately, what with all the shagging and healthy gourmet meals, I could get into last year's grey silk frock. And if I kept my right-hand side to the wall, the wine stain scarcely showed. Alex had shoved on his usual T-shirt and jeans, but looked gorgeous anyway.

I'd begged Fran to come, but she'd absolutely declined, on the grounds that I would be snogging Alex all night and everyone else would be horrible.

The party was in an exclusive club on the Thames: all noisy gravel and ginormous bouquets of unnatural-looking yellow flowers clustered around a bunch of braying men and sharp-lipsticked women. Everyone was taller than me and knew everyone else, and before I was two steps through the door, my carefully groomed confidence started to plummet, until once again I was Melanie Pepper, unruly loudmouth of 2C, worrying about puppy fat and what would happen if George Michael didn't want to marry me after all. (Well, who knew?)

This was definitely not my race, this mob of anorexic, complacent, poshtastic freeloaders. I caught sight of myself in the enormous gold-tinted mirror opposite, surrounded by the glitterprati. I looked like I was wearing my mother's shoes, en route to the dentist.

I turned round for the consolation of having the handsomest man in the room on my arm. But my heart sank again. How could I forget? Alex's hair flopped! He went skiing! His parents couldn't remember his first name! He was One of Them! Even before I had grabbed my first free glass of champers (*Don't grab, Mel! You have a right to be here, remember?*), he was practically being mobbed.

'Al! Al, darling! Where *have* you been?'

'Alex! Sara said she bumped into you in LA – had a few fantastic days, I hear?'

'Oh, come over and see Benedict and Claire – we haven't seen you since the pool party!'

I too had been at the pool party, having a thoroughly miserable time. I too hadn't seen any of these poncey poseurs since then. I pretended to look politely interested and waited for Alex to re-introduce me.

'Guys, you remember Melanie, don't you?'

A blonde horse glanced at me cursorily, and I wished – for God's sake! – that my name was a little less common.

There was a short pause in the conversation as they gave me simpering nob smiles and enquiring looks, then they fell back into loud guffaws as Alex recounted his adventures yet again, cast me one apologetic glance, then hurled himself into dissecting the rugby season and knocking back the 'poo.

So much for the grey silk dress. The entire circle, defying the laws of physics, appeared to have its back to me, and I felt out in the cold. Deflated, I wondered what had happened to my fantasy big night at Amanda's party. I would have made my excuses and left, but there was no one to give my excuses to. So I wandered off, pretending to be in search of a toilet, and wondering whether or not to go and have a little cry by myself.

Weighing up my options, I spotted Amanda. After all, she was the hostess, she had to talk to me! I wandered up to her group in my best 'I'm not at all desperate to talk to anyone at this party, ha!' manner.

'Hello, darling!' air-kissed Amanda. For once, her shallowness was pitched at precisely the right level for me, and I was extremely grateful for it. She was wearing a Barbie doll-sized dress made of some pastel, girlie, lacy thing that was almost, but not quite, see-through. 'That's flaunting it a bit when you're meant to be celebrating your union with someone you'll love for the rest of your life,' I thought nastily as a waiter did a full body-swerve trying to make out her nipples – but I decided not to mention it.

'Ehmm . . . are you having a nice party?' A stunning social opener from me.

'Darling, it's fantastic! There's a *Hello!* photographer here.'

There was social success, and there was social success.

Amanda was looking even tinier and more cutesy than ever. Her sly little features glowed in the gold of the room as she checked her reflection again in the mirrors and – I swear to God – simpered at herself.

'Ho!' I said heartily. 'Maybe he'd like to photograph me and Alex, back from the grave!'

This was meant to be a weak joke, but as I would so patently never be *Hello*! magazine material, it just came out as a bit sad.

'So, tell me all about it!' pouted the minuscule radiant one, while doing a quick scan of the room to make sure no one could see her talking to me.

I did start to try and explain, but other people's happy love lives are so unbelievably boring – we shagged, we stared deep into one another's eyes and, hey, we had this really funny private joke whereby we turned the pillowcase into a singing animal – and Amanda hid her boredom less than most. It also didn't help that the other half of this indivisible team was guffawing his head off, miles away. I found my voice trailing off into a litany of hmm, so, it's great, yeah, fine. Then there was a bit of a pause. My shoulder was being looked over. I knew I should have paid my homage and left by now, but I could hear big roars of laughter from Alex's clique – laughter I simply could not share (I was tending towards the melodramatic by this stage) – and my options remained either clinging desperately to Amanda like a limpet or bursting into tears in the toilet.

'So,' I stalled, 'where's Fraser?'

'Hullo thair,' lilted the Scottish tones behind me. I turned round, with the only genuine smile of pleasure I'd felt all evening. He must have remembered me after all.

'Frase!'

Despite the kilt, however, this character wasn't Fraser. He wasn't even looking at me – he was looking at Amanda, who returned a rather icy stare. I felt a complete fool.

'Angus,' pronounced Amanda beautifully, 'have you

met my old schoolfriend, Melanie? Melanie, this is Fraser's baby brother.'

I looked at him like a surprised fish.

'Hullo there,' he said again.

A rather ruddy-faced boy stared back at me. He was as tall as Fraser, but didn't share any of his features. His hair was reddy-brown, and he had freckles. Hmm.

'Hello,' I said casually. 'Are you the best man?'

Whoops. Patently not the thing to ask. Ongas, or whatever his name was, blushed to the roots of his – almost ginger in this light, really – hair and mumbled, 'Ehm, well, I don't think so . . . erm, no.' Amanda looked cross. 'Well, we had to make all these decisions for the church and so on!' This was so meaningless I took the point and didn't enquire further. Amanda had, however, managed to say this in transit and had already made her exit, leaving us with 'Unpopular at Parties' syndrome. We both knew we were the leftovers, so we certainly didn't want to be speaking to each other, but we didn't have anyone else to talk to.

'So, what do you do, Angus?' Jesus, I sounded like the Queen.

'I'm a mechanical engineer.'

'Oh, like your brother?'

'Ehm, no, it's a bit more boring than that.'

As if in cruel mockery, this remark was punctuated by yet another enormous laugh from Alex's group, who were obviously having the best time any one group of people had ever had, in any place, ever. Someone had a napkin tied on as a blindfold, I noticed.

Another long pause. Every fibre of my being screeched for Fran to mince in, or for Alex to run up declaring, 'I'm so sorry to have been parted from you, my darling. God, these awful bores, they just won't leave me alone. Come, let me ravish you in the gazebo, you amazing raunch-puppet.' Maybe then I could find out what a gazebo was.

'So, did you come down from Scotland?' This remark was pointless before it came out of my mouth, judging from the kilt. Actually, I was dying to ask why he and the lovely Fraser clearly didn't get on, and why they had fallen out, but looking at his face as he failed to hide his disbelief at the idiocy of my remark, I decided against it.

'Yes. Yes, I did.'

We dabbled, excruciatingly, in the myriad available modes of transport from Scotland to London, before lapsing, once more, into an uncompanionable silence. Finally, I decided that Tears in Toilet beat this hands down and, preparing to make my exit, I laid down my last small-talk tool:

'So, what do you think about your big brother and little 'manda then?'

Suddenly he faced me full on and, for the first time, managed to look cold and cross without going red. His eyes were a very bright blue. Out of nowhere he said, 'I think he's being a twat. And I'm sorry, but I think your friend is a witch. Excuse me.'

I really looked at him then. So much for party chitchat.

'Care to elaborate?' I asked, in what I hoped was a

casually wry manner, and not the kind of thing middle-aged women said when their husbands announced they were having an affair.

'She treats our mother like a skivvy, she treats Fraser like dirt, she treats that bloody title like a cure for cancer, and she wants to re-do the old place like some fucking King's Road bam-pot house. So, I apologize, but I'm not quite in the mood to meet her pals. Excuse me.'

And with that he stomped off, deserting me! Bloody hell, what a pig.

Secretly, I was quite impressed. It was kind of true. Amanda was a witch. Fraser was being a twat. But even so! There was I, trying to be nice to the poor bloke, who obviously didn't know anyone. He'd hardly needed to be so rude as to march off at the first opportunity. He could have at least waited for me to do so first. I stared after him, then examined the chandelier very hard in case anyone thought I was staring at someone who'd just walked away from me as opposed to doing some hearty chandelier-spotting.

Well, at least there were deliciously expensive hors d'oeuvres. I stuffed my face and wished I'd brought a magazine – I could almost enjoy myself.

Alex's group were by now completely plastered and utterly hysterical over nothing – well, not nothing, something about a chap called Biffy and an imaginatively cruel PE teacher – but, to be honest, I couldn't follow the details. Alex slung a drunken arm round me and hollered, 'Totty!' I pretended to laugh and inadvertently caught Fraser's brother's eye. The look on his face plainly showed that he thought we were all a big bunch of wankers. Over in one corner I could see Joan, Amanda's distinctly tipsy mother, pawing Alex's old flatmate, Charlie, who was clearly drunk himself but doing his best to reciprocate. It was not a pretty sight.

The speeches came and went as a welcome distraction, because everyone had to be quiet, and not just me. Fraser was eloquent, Amanda fluttered and blushed attractively. Then Amanda's dad said something, but God knows what – it was lost in the car crash of his new-posh and Estuary vowels. And then they brought on an Irish samba band, which was apparently the latest thing on the snooty party circuit. There was a mass screeching noise as three hundred people who could all ride horses scrambled for the dance floor. I decided to feign illness.

I sat down and tried to look pale and a bit brave, hoping someone would come up and ask me what was wrong and I could complain of feeling faint and not wanting to ruin anyone's night, thus drawing lots of sympathetic attention to myself. I was sitting there for quite some time until – AT LAST! – Alex came up to me when the crowd had dispersed on to the dance floor, and grabbed me under the arms.

'Having a good time, pumpkin pie chicken thing?'

I struggled to escape. 'Mm hmm . . .'

He ignored this blatant message of despair and started to tickle me.

'Come on, come dance with me.'

Perhaps the evening could be salvaged after all.

However, my image of a romantic smoochy dance-floor show of togetherness in which I could show everyone (well, that poxy brother of Fraser's) what a successful character I was lasted about two seconds, till I remembered that Alex was one of the world's all-time worst dancers. He counted out the beat, wrongly, while bouncing from foot to foot. Not only this, but he was so pissed that he got distracted and forgot who he was dancing with, so that he was bouncing around the room like Tigger before he takes his medicine, while I was left bopping along on my own, like a girl in a Human League video. I checked the clock and it was only midnight.

Cursing the fact that I didn't go with the feeling ill thing twenty minutes ago when I could still have caught the tube, I leaned over and, gently but firmly, grabbed Alex's attention.

'I'm going home.' I smiled sweetly.

'What?'

It was impossible to hear a damn thing.

'I'M GOING HOME! I'M HAVING A SHIT TIME AND I'M GOING HOME!' I hollered, exactly as the music stopped, and everyone turned around to play 'Spot the Harpy'. I flinched, tried a half-hearted grin, and decided to scram.

'Thanks, Amanda, it was wonderful, lovely to chat, speak to you soon, bye!' For once, I was the one doing my socializing on the run.

Heading out the door, an extremely puzzled and drunk Alex staggering behind me, I practically bumped into Fraser, who'd been saying goodnight to guests.

He looked at me for a second, quizzically. Fuck it. I wasn't going to remind him yet again how insignificant I'd been in his life.

Alex scrunched warily ahead down the gravel drive. Of course, the pre-booked taxis wouldn't turn up for hours yet, so it was a mile-long walk down the drive, then out into fucking Fulham to try and catch a black cab on a wet Saturday night just after pub chucking-out time.

'Melanie?' I heard behind me as I stomped off.

I turned round. He was wearing the same kilt as Angus, but with a less porcine effect, and his curly hair had fallen over his eyes from dancing. I resisted the urge to run up and give him a huge hug and rub him painfully on the head to show him how pleased I was to see him again.

'Hi,' I said, coolly. 'Ehm . . . great party.'

'I suppose. Yes. Yes, it was. I'm sorry I didn't recognize you on the phone.'

So, bring it up again whydoncha?

'Oh, no, I didn't recognize you either,' I stuttered.

That's why I shouted out 'Frase!'

'Well, I suppose it's been a while.'

'Yes, it has.'

'So, I'll see you around then.'

The beautiful grounds were quiet. Silhouetted against the big house, taller but less of the long streak of piss he used to be, Fraser looked both extremely familiar and, now, extremely foreign to me.

'No doubt.' Scintillating.

'C'mon, darling!' hollered Alex, sounding a bit worried. I smiled weakly at Fraser and followed him down the path. After being hustled out of the building, he wasn't sure whether or not he'd done anything wrong – and neither was I. After all, who was I cross at? Him? His friends? My parents, for not being better off? My parents' distant ancestors, for not being friends with the king? I could see his fuddled brain trying to work it out. Fortunately, he plumped for the former, to be on the safe side.

'Are you OK?'

I had to work out my strategy quickly. What I wanted to say was:

'No, I hate your friends because they're all horrible to me. Well, they're not even horrible, they just ignore me because I didn't go to the right school and have a crap name, so actually I'm jealous more than actual dislike, but I don't like it, waaaaaaah.'

Being an independent nineties girl with her own opinions, though, what I actually said was:

'Yes, gorgeous, I just couldn't wait to get you home – I had to get you out of there somehow.' And I added a girlish giggle for effect.

As the blazing golden lights of the illuminated mansion dimmed behind the trees and I looked at my big, strong, placated, slightly wobbly man, I felt better again.

We spent a wonderful Sunday morning in bed the next day, 'nursing' his hangover. Then – after he saw

I wasn't too interested in dissecting what a fantastic night it had been, 'particularly the bit when Barfield stuck the napkin up his arse, ha ha ha!' – he went out to see his mates.

I lolled around with the papers all day.

Back late, he barged in loudly, waking Linda, probably, and certainly me. After bouncing around the kitchen looking for something to eat (I never seemed to have any food in the house after my first week of being a show-off chef, so God knows what he found, although Linda was looking, if anything, even more fucked off these days, so it might have been that. You'd think she'd like having a man around the house – God knows, I did), he came in, sat on the end of the bed, kissed me squarely on the nose and announced, 'Hey, guess what! I've found a flat! Or rather, I've found my old flat – Charlie's forgiven me and I'm moving back in with him!'

I sat up. I hadn't rationally thought about it, but now he'd told me, I realized that I had planned our future out, after all, in my head. We would go find a room together somewhere nice, and eventually get our own place, once he had this music company job. Or we would both stay where we were – Linda wouldn't mind. Perhaps she'd even move out – oh no, she couldn't, it was her flat. Either way, I hadn't seen us being apart so soon, nor the decision so gleefully made on his part. Despite it being only two weeks, waking up next to him every day already felt a necessity of my life, something I didn't want to do without.

'Ermm, great!' I said casually. 'So, is Charlie still

living in . . . ?' As if Charlie and I had had tons of in-depth chats about our personal lives.

'Fulham, yeah. It's a great flat.'

'But it's bloody miles away! And it's in West London . . . you hate West London!'

'Well, I can't stay here pestering you for ever, can I?'

Actually, that's exactly what I'd been planning on.

I pouted prettily, in what I hoped was an appealing manner. 'I wouldn't mind.'

He looked at me and ruffled my hair again. But not as enthusiastically as before.

'It'll be fine. You're still my favourite pumpkin, aren't you?' I was. We dived under the bedsheets. End of matter. Well, apart from when I got up to get a glass of water at three o'clock in the morning and found myself inexplicably staring at my reflection in the kitchen window and starting to cry. I went back to bed and tried to forget all about it, clinging on to him in the night.

Four

Fran popped by on Monday evening before we went to the pub.

'Enjoy the party then?'

'Ha ha. You were missed.'

'Yes, only by you and Alex's ghastly mate Charlie, who seems to think that because I didn't go to public school he has God-given leave to put his hand on my arse every time he's pissed.'

'Ah, well, there's good news about Charlie . . .'

I told her everything. All I needed her to say was, 'Mel, just because he's moving out doesn't mean he doesn't love you. He's getting his own space together, that's all, so that wherever you do end up, you'll have chosen it yourself and everything will be absolutely fine.'

'Oh God, Mel!' she yelled. 'He needed somewhere to crash, he was worried about coming home alone, he wanted a bit of shagging attention . . . America probably wasn't half as much fun as he's telling everyone it is – I mean, does he have a job from his great pop-star mate yet? Honestly, how can you let yourself be taken advantage of like this? Aren't you worth more than this? Aren't you?'

Linda walked into the sitting room. Her fat face fell.

'Ehmm, I didn't know you were having people over.'

'Yeah, you know Fran, don't you?'

'Hello! How are you?' perked Fran, taking a momentary break from her onerous shouting duties.

'Fine.' Linda retreated. I heard her head out of the door with some elderly voices.

'Shit! Do you think those were Linda's parents?'

The door slammed.

'God, I feel awful. And it's Monday today. Sunday is parental visit day. Everyone knows that!' I was grumbling to myself. 'Why doesn't she tell me these things?'

'Isn't it written up on the calendar?'

'Who the fuck keeps a calendar, for fuck's sake?'

Fran pointed out the large thing covered in kittens on the back of the kitchen door. I thought that was Linda's idea of changing artistic taste. In big pink letters, it said 'parents coming today' under the date. There wasn't another single thing in the whole month.

'What is the matter with that girl?' I cringed. 'Why can't she just go out with her friends and get rat-arsed like everyone else?'

'Does she have any friends?'

'No. Don't think so.'

'Do you ever think of asking her out with us?'

I couldn't stand Fran pulling this saint act.

'You ask her!'

'She's your flatmate!'

This was getting childish, so I just sighed and made a half-hearted flapping motion which was supposed to mean OK without actually committing myself to anything. Alex temporarily forgotten in the light of someone else's troubles, something else occurred to me.

'I wonder what's in those enormous parcels she keeps getting.'

'So, to make her life a complete misery, why don't we snoop amongst her stuff as well?'

'You started it!'

'Did not!'

'Did too! When Nicholas was here!'

'Oh.'

We looked at each other enquiringly.

'Well . . .'

'That would be extremely . . . naughty.' Fran giggled nervously.

'Well, I've already ruined her day . . .'

We looked at each other and both leapt out of the room.

* * *

Linda's sanctum was possibly the most spotless place I have ever seen. Even the teddy bear looked like he'd been through teddy grooming school. Everything in it was either pink or peach, and the wall managed to be both, with the help of the type of nasty border normally only seen in motorway hotels. There were frilly things everywhere – tie-backs, potpourri holders, ornamental pigs. It looked like the wet dream of a seven-year-old girl.

'Wow,' said Fran, picking up the matching brush set from the glass top of the dressing table, under which rested a doily. 'Miss Havisham's cleaning rota's certainly improved.'

I couldn't see the parcel I was looking for and headed towards the cupboard. Fran picked up one of the Laura Ashley pinafore numbers Linda favoured and flounced round the room singing, 'I'm Linda, and I couldn't be sorrier for breathing! Sorry, please pay some rent, how about five pence a month? I'm just going out now – oh, of course, I never do . . .' I grimaced.

Suddenly, the phone rang. We both jumped out of our skins, as if we'd been caught doing something very wrong. Which, of course, we had.

'You answer it!' I hissed, absurdly, to Fran, and snatched the dress off her. Wrong-footed, she did as she was told.

I went to hang the dress back up and, as I did, I noticed the box peeping out of the back of the cupboard. Feeling thoroughly low, I picked it up anyway.

Inside there was layer upon layer of chocolate:

everything from little Flyte bars to enormous, one-acre Galaxys, and those huge Toblerones you can only get in Duty Free. Some were just empty wrappers, strewn about in a most uncharacteristic manner.

'Chuffing hell!' I exclaimed, as Fran walked back in.

'How did you know that was Nicholas from all the way in here?'

'Look at all this!'

'Oh my God. Eating disorder city. Jesus!'

'I know. She just gets fatter and fatter. She must eat in secret all the time.'

'What are you going to do?'

'What am I going to do? Oh, take full responsibility for it, obviously. I don't know! We don't even say good morning!'

We looked at each other.

On the overwrought bedside table, beside the crocheted tissue-box cover, there was only one picture, of Linda – a chubby child – standing next to a vicious-looking pony.

Oh God, what was I going to do – mention it to her? D'oh! What did advice columns say? Leave some handy leaflets lying about. I didn't know if they did ones that said, 'We were snooping in your room and found something you're obviously desperately trying to hide.' Go down the pub? I tried to judge a tasteful length of time before suggesting this. Fran gave me a look that plainly told me it wasn't long enough.

'Huh? Sorry, I was just thinking about Linda.'

'So what do you think we should . . .'

'I have absolutely no idea.'

Pause.

'I suppose I could try and be nicer to her,' I offered.

'Well, you do live together.'

'So do you, practically, and you're not nice to anyone.'

'That's because most people are boring. But Linda's like, you know, *sick*.'

'OK, OK already.'

I hoisted myself up and went and tackled some of Alex's and my washing-up. Well, it was a start.

'So, ehm, that was Nicholas on the phone then?'

And not, say, Alex (who was out buying furniture), having had a big change of heart and begging me to move with him to Fulham.

'Yes. You appear to be in demand.'

Well, hooray!

'However, I told him you weren't available, so he asked me out instead.'

Boo! OK, I may have despised the guy, but I'd like to think he could tell me apart from other members of the same species.

'Huh. Did you say yes?'

'What do you think?'

'I think you said yes, you would smoochily love him forever and ever, and did he have any more of his hilarious accounting stories?'

'Oh, and also he said you may have to test for some disease or other.'

'WHAT!?'

Fran gave me the finger and laughed evilly.

'Melanie, given that you're probably the only person who's ever gone to bed with him, I wouldn't worry too much.'

The brief tension gone, I told her about how awful the party had been, which I knew would please her. She was particularly interested in Angus.

'Sounds intriguing. Was he handsome?'

On the sniff, as usual.

'Ehm, I don't know. Have you seen that film *Babe*?'

'He looks like a pig?'

'Hear me out . . .'

'Farmer Hoggett?'

'No! You know the dog in it who goes bad and bites people . . . ?'

'He looks like a dog?'

'Well, he has an air of wounded nobility.'

'In dog form.'

'Ehm . . .'

We both sighed.

'God, there really are no men left,' exclaimed Fran for like the billionth time.

I couldn't help it, but I must have involuntarily made an Amanda-type look, because she pretended to knee me in the tits. She didn't quite pretend properly and unfortunately did hit me in the tits. Fran's always played rough.

Linda came back eventually, on her own. We both stiffened. As usual she headed straight past the sitting room for her bedroom. I held my breath, terrified she was going to find something out of place. Maybe she had a hair taped over the doorframe and some talc or something, and now she was going to kill us . . .

Fran gave me a meaningful look, so I heaved myself up again.

'Erm, Linda, do you want a cup of coffee?'

There was silence from beyond. No doubt this was a terrifying and unprecedented advance on my part. I felt horribly embarrassed and ashamed. Finally:

'No, thanks.'

'I think you've only got half a pound of sugar left anyway,' whispered Fran meanly.

'OK!' I shouted. 'We're off to the pub. Do you want to come?'

Linda came out of her room and looked at me, her pale eyes suspicious.

'Why?'

'Ehm, no reason . . . you know, Monday night . . .' I trailed off weakly.

'No, thanks. I'm going to clean my wardrobe out.'

'Ohhh – I mean: Oh, right, have fun!'

Then Fran and I fled to the pub to meet Alex and Charlie. 'Amanda & Fraser Ltd' had generously deigned to join us: the presence of two good-looking West London boys had obviously upped our social desirability somewhat.

Walking into the pub, I shot a sidelong glance at Fran. It was not looking good. Amanda was sitting in the middle of the three men, showing off in her pertiest manner. Fraser was watching her dutifully – or staring at her adoringly, I couldn't make out what was true and what was bitchiness on my behalf – and Alex and Charlie were sniggering and nudging each other.

Alex gave me a kiss, and I went to get some beers, while Amanda said something and everybody laughed. I looked at the beautifully cut profile of the man I loved and suddenly felt empty, even when he yelled, 'Mel, gorgeous gorgeous thing, get over here and sit on my knee immediately.'

How could he be so sweet and still want to move to Fulham with Charlie? I sat on his knee and tried not to mope, but it wasn't easy.

'So, anyway,' Amanda was squawking, 'I spoke to the designer and she says she's never seen such a tiny waist! They're going to have to do it all by hand specially, and it's going to cost an extra two thousand pounds! Can you imagine!'

'Bloody hell!' said Alex dutifully.

The other boys nodded blankly. That infuriated me: they listened to her because she was pretty, but they wouldn't know what a wedding dress cost at gunpoint.

Then she gave Fraser a look and snapped her fingers. He immediately got up and fetched her another drink. Fran and I looked at each other in amazement.

Anyway, to make myself sound at least vaguely interesting, I spilled the beans about Linda. Fran looked disapproving, but only because she didn't think to tell it herself. Everyone was enthralled, so I tried not to embellish too much. Well, everyone except Fran, who was being disapproving, and Charlie, who was staring at Fran's breasts. And Amanda, who was attempting to tell a rival story about her suspected anorexia, which she was trying to make sound like a pretty cool disease.

Suddenly, Angus walked in, and it was like a chill hit the air. Fraser smiled anxiously in welcome, while Amanda gave him a very tight look out of the corner of her beautifully made-up eyes and deliberately smiled without smiling.

'Oh, hello, Angus,' she said. 'So glad you could make it.'

'Aye.'

Good God, what was he, an extra from *Cold Comfort Farm*? Angus sat down stolidly.

Fraser looked around. 'Does everyone know Angus?' Everyone hummed and pretended to – even if (like Fran) they'd never clapped eyes on him before – so we didn't all have to go round and introduce ourselves.

I'd gotten to that delicate part of sitting on somebody's knee when I'd forgotten to balance my toes on the floor and they now had an extremely dead leg which they were being too polite to tell me about.

'Hey, elephant baby, darling, obviously I adore you, but if you don't get off my knee now I'm going to collapse and die,' my beloved announced loudly.

Amanda brayed with laughter, as she was the dictionary antonym of an elephant, whereas clearly, I was the synonym.

There was nowhere to sit, so I edged to the end of the group, red-faced but pretending to take it as a joke, next to the naturally red-faced Angus who was staring surlily at a pint of English bitter. This was a bad ploy, because by the time I re-emerged from my mild and unnoticed strop to re-enter the conversation, the conversation was away from my nutsoid flatmate altogether and back on to bloody *weddings* again.

'So,' Amanda was saying, 'we're going to hire out the entire castle and have heather and haggis and tartan swathing and pipers . . .'

'. . . parading out of my arse,' a voice said quietly in my ear, in a not bad approximation of Amanda's posh squawk. I giggled before coming to my senses that it had in fact been uttered by Angus the Sulky. No one else had noticed.

'Hello there,' I said, warmer than I had intended.

'Hullo.'

'Good time on Saturday?'

'Hmm,' he said, with a pointed look at the intended duo.

Our fast becoming habitual embarrassed silence stole over us.

'So, are you older or younger than Frase . . .' As soon as I asked the question I remembered I already knew. God, my small-talk radar was getting worse all the time.

'Still younger.' He almost half smiled. I briefly wondered what he'd look like if he really did smile.

Someone set another drink in front of me, and I smelled Alex's aftershave and closed my eyes.

'Oh, have you two met?'

Alex and Angus shook hands in that wary fashion blokes do when the girl they're going out with introduces them to another bloke.

'Hi. Err, you're Fraser's little brother?'

Well, of course he was. D'oh!

'Yes. Yes, I am.'

'You were at the engagement party, weren't you? Brilliant night, wasn't it?'

Then quite an odd thing happened. Angus and I exchanged glances, and I almost smiled.

'Yes. Yes, it was quite something.'

'So, what are you doing down here then? Working?'

'Yes, I've got a short-term contract in Docklands. If I like it I might stay . . .'

'Bet you miss the sheep in hoochter-choochter land though, eh?'

I cringed.

'No. Actually, I've met plenty of woolly twats since I arrived.'

Double rude! Yikes! Fortunately, Alex had already turned back to Charlie to make some other sheep-related remark and had missed it. But I was shocked, and puzzled: why did this ginger bloke hate us all so much? And if he did, why was he here?

Nothing happened to change my opinion as the evening wore on. Angus seemed staggeringly unimpressed by Alex's American stories, which I still found funny, even though I'd heard them several times. More pints were consumed, more chatter went round, and he didn't feel the need to offer a single comment, make one remark, or laugh – not even when Alex got on to the time he decided he was going to become a rodeo star!

I looked around for Fran. She had managed to get herself completely cornered by Charlie, whose eyes were as round as Fran's nicely shaped baps. He'd got her up against the wall at the back side of the table, and everyone else was in that mildly blootered universe where they didn't notice much around them (except Amanda, who was drinking Aqua Libra, but never noticed anyone other than herself anyway).

'Darling,' he was slurring, 'you're absolutely top totty . . .'

'Fuck off, Charlie.' Fran sounded dangerous.

'Come, give Charlie a little kiss –'

He reached out to grab her. Fran put her arms up and, without meaning to, slapped him in the face. The atmosphere turned suddenly.

'I say, did you bloody slap me, you bitch?'

That posh charm was obviously spread pretty thin.

Fran drew herself up to her full height, looking like she was on fire with humiliation and rage.

'No, but I fucking should have done, you wanker!'

'You fucking little bitch!'

Then, and I mean it, he really looked as though he was going to go for her. Everyone watched like they were caught in a sci-fi time freeze, except for Fran, who seemed to be moving backwards in slow motion. Then suddenly there was a flash of ginger as Angus leapt up, grabbed Charlie's arms, and in one movement threw him against the wall with the full force of his body.

'STOP IT!'

There was a long pause. For some reason, rather a lot of people seemed to be panting. The landlord was heading ominously in our direction, and Angus and Charlie were staring at each other very intently.

Alex leaned in. 'Come on, Charles, leave it,' he said softly.

After an agonizing wait, Charlie lowered the eye contact, put his fangs away and stomped out of the pub. We were all looking at each other, half worried, half thrilled to bits with excitement.

'Well, what a cunt!' said Fran. And that was a word we never, ever used.

Outside, Charlie was obviously wanting to go, but Alex was hovering to see me.

'Ehm, I'd better take Charlie home. I'll stay there tonight.'

I didn't want him to go, especially not with that . . . git.

'Good night then,' said Alex, and he walked off supporting Charlie.

The rest of us stood around wondering what to do next. Fran thanked Angus, but it seemed almost distasteful to mention it; like he had seen her being raped or something. Fraser was wandering over in our direction, looking concerned and worried, when Amanda grabbed him firmly by the arm, turned round and cheerily said, 'Well we'd better go!' as if they'd just spent the afternoon touring the village fête. As she hustled him off to her car, Fraser looked over his shoulder at Angus, who was standing looking a bit embarrassed, and gave him an awkward grin meant to convey shame, apology, pride and general goodwill all at once. Angus gave him one back, and they suddenly looked very alike.

'Right! All back to mine then?' I said, as usual. Fran

and I were dying to discuss it, obviously, but it would be a lot easier if Angus didn't come . . .

However, he was already striding off in the opposite direction.

'Oh, look at him,' said Fran, as he headed off towards the tube. 'He's my pig in shining armour. My Lone Rasher. My ginger . . .'

'Shush, Fran. He bloody sorted that out, OK?'

'Oh, for God's sake! I've had enough hassle tonight already, don't you think?'

Now Fran was in a mood.

'Come on, Franster, don't bother about it. That revolting prat mauling you – bleurgh . . . Come on back, have a glass of wine, stop worrying.'

We piled back to the flat, managing for once not to cackle on the stairwell. Fran was still a bit shocked, so I sat her down, poured her a big glass of whisky (yes, it was the one Linda had won in a raffle, but it was medicinal) and let her tell me about it all over again as if I hadn't been there.

I couldn't stop thinking aloud.

'It is good news for me, though,' I added, after what I thought was a considerate length of time.

'What?!'

'Well, Alex is hardly going to move in with Charlie now, is he? Now he knows he's practically a rapist. Hmmm, maybe we'll get a place of our own . . . move in properly.'

'Oh, well, I'm glad my being nearly pawed to death

is going to help out your domestic arrangements.' There was a glint in her eye. 'Do you want me to go down to King's Cross and turn a few tricks? Then maybe you can get a joint mortgage.'

'No! I was just saying . . .'

'If he moves in with Charlie –' Fran was showing her teeth, always an ominous sign – 'if he moves in with Charlie, after all this, you'll chuck him, won't you?'

Fuck! Moral dilemma-tastic!

'He won't; that's what I'm saying.' I was pretty blithe about the whole thing.

'But say he did.'

'He won't.' For God's sake.

'In a hypothetical universe, you'd chuck a bloke who moved in with the person who molested your best friend.'

'Are you emotionally blackmailing me? And anyway, technically, he didn't molest you.'

The second I said that, I realized what a dreadful thing it was to say and that I was the worst feminist of all time. We were shocked for the second time that night, and now I was behaving worse than Charlie. Suddenly I felt drunk and tearful and terribly tired.

'Let's not talk about it any more,' said Fran after a long silence.

I pulled out the spare mattress and we went to sleep in silence. For once, Linda should have been proud of me.

Five

Next morning we staggered around pretending to be more hungover than we really were so that we wouldn't have to talk to one another.

Fran had an audition, and I wished her good luck with it then set off for work. My boss was waiting in my office. That could not possibly be a good sign. I couldn't remember him ever being in there before. I hoped he hadn't been pawing through my desk: it was full of 'I love Alex' doodles.

'Ah, yes, good morning, Melanie.' He smiled at me, even more politely than usual. He was about five foot tall, but perfectly in proportion: you always had to resist the urge to pat him on his bald head.

'Erm, mm, there's been the most terrible fuss with marketing about the new brochure. Apparently the word "Fabricon" has been misspelled throughout.'

I sighed. 'It's a made-up marketing word though, isn't it?' I pointed out. 'It doesn't matter how you spell it, it still means sod all. I can hardly check it in the *Oxford English*, can I?'

'Nonetheless –' oh no, he was sounding pompous – 'nonetheless, it was the brand name of our latest product and was already on £45,000 worth of marketing literature. Which should be £48,000 worth, if we hadn't missed the window in the production schedule due to your – and I'm sorry to have to say it – frankly substandard work.'

Suddenly I felt incredibly small. *Substandard work*? Yup, I was back in the lower fourth. But this time it wasn't my lack of comprehension of wave motion that was the problem, it was my own sheer laziness. I ran through all the possible options in my head, and chose the worst, nastiest, most pathetic one of all.

'God, I'm sorry. It's just . . . well, my flatmate has bulimia, and it's been a really difficult time.'

I looked like I might, possibly, burst into tears. I was scum. I was lower than scummy scum scum. Truly, that should be a sackable offence.

'Oh, gosh, that must be really difficult for you.' My boss looked so heartfelt and sensitive and upset I nearly started crying for real. 'My sister had that.'

Shit! That was it: hell, handbag, me, en route.

He put a hand on my shoulder. 'I think it's just as hard for those around the person, sometimes. It's so frustrating, isn't it?'

I nodded plaintively, and embellished it a little. We

revelled in our mutual caring personae for another ten minutes, and I reckoned I'd just about got off scot-free when he said:

'I'm really sorry, Mel, and I know this isn't going to help, but marketing have asked if you could move downstairs into their office – so you can all work a bit closer together, as it were. You're going to be in their department from now on.'

He looked genuinely regretful. It was all I could do to speak, so I just nodded woefully.

'We'll get your stuff moved down as soon as possible. My dear, it's been a pleasure working with you.'

It couldn't have been, but I accepted the outstretched hand numbly, a billion growing threads of horror spawning through my head. The marketing department! Oh God, they had orange walls down there! And they used the term 'conceptual'! And now I would have to get drunk at the Christmas party and make a fool of myself! Oh no – I did that already. Anyway, it was going to be work, work, work all day from now on, just like real people had to! I groaned heartily to myself. The phone rang.

'Well, I can see you're busy, so I'll leave you to get sorted out.' My boss got up gracefully and floated off on his little handmade shoes.

It was Fran, of course.

'Well? Have you spoken to him?'

'Fran! I'm being shifted! They're putting me in marketing!'

'Oh my God, is that good or bad?'

Fran had no concept of what goes on in the world of work. To her, corporate affairs meant copping off with City blokes.

'Well, I'm going to have to work all day and never talk to you again surrounded by a big bunch of people who think it's really cool to be in marketing, and sit in a cubicle, not in an office, and suffer the smell of other people's baked potatoes at lunch time and hear their constant boring chatter about focus groups, and have people watching what I'm doing all the time and making bitchy comments about how I never wear anything orange . . . But apart from that it should be fine.'

'Oh, OK. Anyway, have you spoken to Alex yet?'

'Fran! This is IMPORTANT!'

'More important than your boyfriend moving in with a rapist?'

'Yes, actually!'

There was a bit of a pause. Fran couldn't see anything in life more important than the vagaries of our personal lives, and normally I agreed with her. So finally she must have sensed this was pretty bad.

'I'm sorry. Have you been sacked?'

'No, I haven't been bloody sacked. Oh, forget it!'

'Are you going to make less money?'

'Fran, I'll speak to Alex now, OK?'

Damn. Still, at least she didn't get the audition, or she'd have told me. I lived in constant fear that she would get unbelievably famous and never hang around with me ever again, and I'd be the old sop in the bar telling strangers boring stories they didn't believe about how she used to be my best friend.

I was pretty upset and frustrated and tired and pissed off, and the last thing I wanted to do was phone Alex and ask difficult questions. I wished he'd phone to tell me how he'd seen the light about that creep Charlie last night and beg to come and live with me instead, as he loved me SO MUCH. Then I caught a glimpse of my unhealthy pallor and dribbling mascara in the window and realized that: (1) I was actually crying a bit, and (2) if I were Alex and saw me, I'd run ten miles.

Fortunately I'm not, because the phone rang, and it was him.

'Hey, sweet chops.'

'Hey, nasty friend-chops.'

'God, yes, Charlie was a bit pished, wasn't he?'

'He really upset Fran, you know.'

'Fran? That girl eats Charlies for breakfast. If ginger boy hadn't leapt in, she'd have gnawed his nads off.'

This was undeniable.

'Are you still going to live with that wanker?'

'Well, it's either that or trail through *Loot* for the next two months and end up in some Turkish bedsit in SE13.'

'But Fulham . . . it's Tosserama over there.'

'Oh, they're not too bad once you get to know them.'

'But I can't get to know them! They're all ice weasels!'

He sighed. 'Is this about the public school thing again? Are you getting all chippy?'

'Yeah, right, like I want a private income, a cushy job in publishing and long flicky blonde hair.'

'Oh, come on, Mel, stop being daft. Anyway, I need to live somewhere. I mean, it's not . . . it's not like we could live together or anything.'

I paused, that one instant too long.

'No, of course not.' Oh God, that didn't even sound like my voice.

There was a bit of a silence. Then he said, 'You know, I'm sorry I hurt you when I left. But it was because of things like this. You always want to push too fast, pumpkin. I mean, I've only been back a fortnight. Can't you, like, chill out?'

'Right. Right then. Ehrm, I'll phone you later.'

'No, Mel, don't be like this. You'll upset yourself. All I'm saying is that there's no rush . . .'

I hung up. Oh, bloody bloody hell! Maybe I should just get a T-shirt printed: 'Incredibly needy woman; gets very upset without constant attention and immediate commitment. Histrionic tendencies. Unable to live independent life without man. Disloyal to friends. Bursts into tears over nothing.'

I burst into tears.

I knew it had only been two weeks, but it hadn't really, if you counted the year before he disappeared which now appeared to be my fault, but anyway . . .

My boss floated past again.

'Oh, my dear girl, I'm so sorry. Marketing will be absolutely fine, you know – they'll love you. Don't think of this as a setback, think of it as an opportunity. There there.'

He actually had a spotless handkerchief.

'And don't worry too much about your flatmate either.'

I struggled to remember why I might worry about her, and fortunately did.

'You can't take all the responsibilities of the world on your shoulders, you know. I tell you what . . .' He looked mischievous. 'Go on, take the day off. I won't tell a soul.'

I faked shock, but with a wounded little half-smile to show my complicity.

'I know, normally something I'd never do. But go on. I reckon you need it.'

Truly, the sweetest man in the world. He even walked me to the door, talking loudly about some imaginary new project. I felt an odd sense of *déjà vu*, then escaped to the fresh air – hooray!

A free day in London when I was feeling totally depressed and my boyfriend was moving to Fulham. What to do? Well, I could go shopping, I supposed. Or perhaps I could go shopping. I decided I was absolutely depressed and therefore deserved shopping and should go at it with a clean conscience. Linda hadn't put the rent up for two years, so actually I was fairly solvent. Even though I hadn't shaved my armpits and didn't have my shopping underwear on, I headed for Regent Street.

They'd put the Christmas decorations up, which made me realize it was only November. Months and months and months of winter to go. Oh, and Alex was going to leave me because I was a needy cow. And my best friend hated him. And my rival was getting married and going to have a perfect life. And she had size three feet! I nearly started blubbing again in the middle of the street, but pulled myself together in the usual way (imagining our school bully walking past, having become really successful, seeing me, and laughing), and headed for Dickins and Jones. The smell of perfume was instantly reassuring.

I wandered around Hobbs, thinking that it really was time to change my image and become a classy girl. But it was no use wearing brown with my brown frizzy hair and brown mousy eyes and brown freckles: I'd just look like one long walking poo.

Over in the sale section I started picking up bits and pieces, including a ridiculous pair of pink mid calf-length trousers a size too small for me because they were £79.99 reduced to £14.99 and, who knew, they might just make me look instantly fantastic. I don't know quite why I thought I suddenly resembled Fran, who had wonderful elongated limbs that were angular and gawky when we were small but were now wildly desirable. Anyway, it was hot in the changing room, and I kept falling out of the curtain trying to wriggle those things up my leg. By the time I had wangled myself into them and examined my overstuffed posterior in the mirror, I was feeling about as thoroughly foul as a person can without actual physical illness.

'Look at you!' I was saying to myself. 'You're miserable, so you come here and dress your legs up like two big fat pink sausages! What is the matter with you?'

I stomped out to see if the full-length mirror was going to help – chuh huh – and gazed helplessly at my dishevelled hair, sweaty red face, lumpy hips and the way my eyes appeared to have disappeared, as if in protest at all the crying, leaving behind only black smudges of mascara.

'Oh well, at least Alex isn't likely to walk past,' I thought, to console myself.

Angus walked past.

Slouching in what could only be described as an anorak, at first I thought he was going to miss me. Then he looked up and saw me in the mirror. For a second he seemed almost jolly, but he soon remembered himself – and my status as friend-of-Amanda-lover-of-Alex – and walked over stiffly.

'Hullo again.'

'What the hell are you doing in women's pants?' I hollered, using the well-known 'aggressive' technique to try and cover my embarrassment.

'Trying to buy my mother a birthday present. What's the matter with you?'

'Nothing. I'm FINE.'

'I like those trousers.'

'Bog off. Oh God, I'm sorry.' I was suddenly tired of being mean. 'I didn't really mean that. I've had a shitty day, then I got the day off and I thought that would be cool, but it's pissy and I'm FED UP.'

'Oh.'

We stood there, me in ridiculous pink trousers so tight that I couldn't get the zip done up, him in his anorak.

'Would you like a cup of tea and a bun?' he offered politely.

I snuffled a little. 'Yes, please.'

We sat together in the café rather awkwardly, surrounded by rich shouty women. I wondered if people were looking at us and speculating on what kind of relationship we had: I always did. Or maybe it was obvious he was my non-friend's fiancé's bitter little brother.

I looked a bit more presentable after I managed to get rid of the worst of the mascara with a wrinkle-creating rub, brushed my hair upside down, and shrugged back into my navy blue trouser suit – the one that almost made me look like my arse didn't stick out, although it did make me look flat-chested, and if I buttoned it up it was a bit Pee-wee Herman.

'Do you usually buy your mother lingerie?'

'No, I was just pissing about. I never know what to get her, so I drift about hoping something fantastic will leap out at me – then end up getting her a bath mat or something.'

I knew that feeling. I didn't know how many Delia Smith books my mother could take, but she was bearing up manfully.

'Why don't you and Fraser club together; send her on a cruise, maybe?'

'I don't know . . . How much money do you spend on your mother?'

'Hmm, well, about thirty pounds, I suppose.'

'Oh.'

There was a long pause, during which I started to worry in case I'd insulted his mother: I knew what the Scots were like. And just what I needed, too: to upset someone else in the world. I was losing a popularity contest with the ebola virus.

He frowned. 'That would get her about halfway into the Camden canal then?'

'Well, she is a bit of an old boot.'

He laughed at my utterly shit joke, which made me realize that he was feeling as uncomfortable as I was.

'Yes, I don't spend thirty pounds lightly,' I went on.

'I know. I could tell by those pink trousers.'

I smiled for the first time all day.

'Oh, thanks for the fashion tip, Anorak Man.'

He half smiled.

'What?' I demanded.

'Oh, nothing.'

'What? Is it, like, a magic anorak?'

'No.' But he was grinning now.

'Yes, it is, isn't it? It's a magic anorak that gives you – oh, I don't know, a supernatural ability to notate trains.'

'Hff. Actually, my lovely anorak is North Sea standard issue. I had to go see the BP people today and they take you more seriously if they think you just got out of the helicopter.'

'Wow, you've been in a helicopter?' D'oh. Who was I – Amanda?

'Yes,' he said seriously, 'just like Noel Edmonds.'

'Well, I didn't know you got to go in helicopters. I thought you went down pipes and stuff.'

'I do. But I need a helicopter to get me to the pipes. And the pipes are underwater.'

I was impressed, but wouldn't show it.

'So what are you saying, that this is, like, your James Bond anorak?'

He stared me straight in the eye.

'Yesh, schweetheart, thish ish my James Bond anorak.'

And, weirdly, that was the moment I fell in like with Angus McConnald.

An hour and a half later we'd bought his mother some hideous golfing memorabilia from the Disney shop. (She golfed. I'd wondered if maybe this was an obligatory Scottish thing to do, but apparently it was a real hobby.) And I'd bought some comfortable size fourteen navy blue trousers from Racing Green, which proved I was getting old, but I had to buy something.

A boy who liked shopping? I'd cheered up considerably, as I must have appeared to the world like the kind of girl that boys liked enough to go shopping with, even if they were a bit ginga. And we chatted easily about everything under the sun –

except when we passed an enormous crystal display in one of the glassware departments. A young, smartly dressed couple were looking at it and checking things off on an enormous list.

'Marcus, you must hurry up and choose the place settings,' the girl was saying bossily. Marcus, who looked exactly as he must have done at the age of six, only larger, pouted and turned red.

Angus leaned over to me.

'Does everyone in London look up new minor peers five minutes after their fathers have died and move in on them like piranha fish?'

I turned to him in surprise. 'Do you know him?'

'I know the type,' he said darkly, looking at the girl. That pissed me off.

'Well, excuse me. I didn't realize it was international sexist day. And for your information, the answer is yes. I personally am killing time with you on my way to seduce Prince William.'

'Huh!' he said. Then, less grumpily: 'I didn't mean it like that.' Then he clammed up like a, umm, clam.

Still, it was time to go home anyway, and I really felt quite relaxed.

'It was good to bump into you,' I said lamely at the tube station.

'Serendipity.' He grinned through his anorak.

'Oh, a word with lots of syllables in it! Was that meant to turn me on?'

God, WHY did I say that? Angus turned red and neither of us knew what to say.

'Erm, no, no, it wasn't. I'll . . . see you later.' And he scuttled off into the crowd.

'Angus!' I yelled after him.

I caught a glimpse of his neon orange trim bobbing up and down towards the tube, then just in time he turned round.

'Thanks,' I shouted. 'Thanks for last night. Fran was really appreciative.'

He grinned again, infectiously. 'At your lady's service, ma'am,' he said, bowing low in the middle of Piccadilly Circus.

Alex had left a message saying he'd gone to the football, so I looked almost as mournful as Linda when we came face to face in the hall. Then I remembered my niceness campaign.

'Hey, Linda, how's it going? Off out?'

God, could I say nothing right?

'No, eh . . .' she hesitated, 'I was going to watch *The English Patient*.'

This girl was so weird. But, what the hey, there was more to life than drinking, uncommitted men and falling out with all your mates, so I joined her and slumped down with a large glass of white wine (it doesn't count as drinking if you're in watching TV).

I spent most of the film trying to figure out why Kristin Scott Thomas got to be Kristin Scott Thomas and I had to be me, until I happened to glance at Linda. Her whole face was overflowing – tears, snot, the works.

'Are you OK?'

'It's so saaad!' she snortled.

'But you've seen it like two hundred times. What, are you thinking, "Hey, maybe he's going to make it to the cave this time"?'

'Shut up. It's my film and you don't care. Nobody does.' She stared down at her toes, her face looking like it was melting. I had noticed a Kit Kat wrapper in the bin earlier, which didn't seem excessive, but who knew?

Oh God, situation. If Fran were here she'd say something smart and buck-upish, but it was only me. Someone once said that only the young can afford to be selfish, which gave me about two and a half more years. I didn't want to cope with this now.

'Are you OK?' I asked again. 'Do you do this every time you watch this film?'

She sniffed loudly. 'Maybe. Where's Alex?'

That put me off a bit. 'Ehm, he's at the football with the boys. He's moving in with Charlie, in Fulham.' That ought to cheer her up.

'Oh.' She looked at me through her thick spectacles, all steamed up from crying. 'Oh . . . you'll miss him.'

'Yes, yes, I will.'

Good Lord, we were bonding.

'We're still seeing each other . . . It's just till we find somewhere for both of us, know what I mean?'

She nodded her head vaguely. Oh no, I hoped she didn't find anyone else to move in, that would be rubbish. But when I looked at her I realized she wasn't listening at all; she had re-immersed herself in the drama. Which part was she playing in there, I wondered, behind the thick specs and the psoriasis. How much didn't I know about this totally rotund person whom I live with? Then I thought, sod it, and – having (correctly) ascertained that there was no possibility of further Ralph Fiennes butt shots – lost interest in direct proportion, made myself some tea and had an early night for once. Well, it had been a big day.

Six

The following morning I awoke with the realization that: (1) for once, I didn't have a hangover, which felt weird, and (2) bugger it, today I had to go to work in marketing. And (3) Fran was pissed off with me, and (4) I would have to pretend to Alex that everything was FINE, and I'd never pressure him again, and (5) Alex wasn't lying there beside me, begging me not to get up, holding me to him, smelling good. Where the hell was he?

Was it raining? Oh, good.

I trudged into the office, almost but not quite late, in an insolent fashion. There were already strange men around my desk fiddling with my dead pot plant. Barney, wisely, was nowhere to be seen.

'So I'm moving already, am I?' I remarked to the builders (wryly, I thought).

'Don't worry, love.' The bigger of the two chaps looked at me with pity, as if they cleared out people's desks every day, which they probably did. God, they must be human misery experts. I thought he was about to say, 'Worse things happen at sea,' but he didn't.

'We'll have you out of here in no time.'

If only. Suddenly I realized that his mate with the funny ears and what looked like Copydex stuck to his chin was reaching towards my emergency didn't-get-home-but-had-to-go-to-work-drawer, the contents of which included knickers, tampons and the numbers of several reputable clinics.

'Errm, I'll get that,' I screeched, in what was patently not a casually helpful tone of voice.

The first guy gave the ear guy a 'seen it all before' look.

'Actually, love, we don't need to open the drawers to move the cabinet.'

'Right, OK, right.' Bugger it. I looked around for something else I could pretend to be helping with, but decided to settle for the 'I've just remembered something incredibly important' look and dashed off.

On the way downstairs to the marketing department, I paused to say goodbye to all my friends in the publishing unit, then I remembered I didn't have any.

'Off so soon?' I heard from Shirley.

'I thought she was part-time anyway,' said someone else and I made a face at her (to myself, obviously; I had no intention of getting my eyes clawed out with long fake fingernails with jewellery in them), and disappeared down to the bowels of the building.

The marketing department had been painted again – mmm, lime green and turquoise, how wacky. Somebody here wanted you to think of your job as fun – or else. Already I was scared.

'Hi there – you must be Melanie!' gushed someone who sounded so pleased to see me I assumed she must be a long-lost relative who thought I was rich. 'I'm Flavi!'

This was Flavi, prize bitch, with whom I'd been having a voice mail argument for nearly a year? Well, there you go. She looked like an over-made-up perfume counter assistant.

'Brilliant to see you! Are Tony and Elvis bringing your things?'

How does she know their names? I wondered nastily.

'Yes, I think so. I saw them upstairs . . .'

'Great, great, we have a space for you over here.'

Stop being so nice to me! What was this, first day at Malory Towers?

I moved to the space and looked at it, not quite sure what to do. The bloke to my right in the cheap suit and chains gave me a cheery Cockney nod. I recognized his face from various indistinct but possibly naughty photographs that got pinned up on the noticeboard after the annual Christmas party. No doubt I would recognize other parts of him as well.

He was about twenty-one, skinny as a whippet, with plastered forward hair, shiny and heavy with gel.

On the other side, a sweet-faced chubby girl gave me a half-smile half-grimace, and I realized she was probably reflecting my own expression. Out of the corner of my eye I noticed a run in her tights and warmed to her.

'Hello there!' I said heartily, putting a brave face on it, like I did in the majorettes when they picked Amanda to lead the marching band. Cheery Cockney lad gave me a smirk.

'Alwight, dorlin? Wot you in for then?'

'Five to ten, unless I behave myself.'

'Roit,' he said, with an odd little sidelong glance. He was obviously wondering if I was trying to be a smart arse and, if so, what I was doing trying to usurp his position.

I turned to the left, but the girl with the ladder in her tights was obviously having a deeply personal conversation on the phone. Huh. I busied around tidying things up – like that was something I usually did – so Flavi wouldn't come over to see how I was doing. When lunch time came, *at last*, I went out to find a payphone. Well, I didn't want to look too bad on my first day.

As I walked out into the freezing afternoon, I didn't even want to think about where Alex had spent the night. Last time I'd phoned Charlie's house, he'd been six thousand miles away.

And he hadn't even called me, the bastard. I was ready to get deeply upset when I remembered that Elvis and Tony had had the phone disconnected all morning, so he couldn't have got in touch even if he had wanted to. *If* he'd tried, I thought grimly. But I decided to give him the benefit of the doubt, and tried my house first. Surprisingly, Linda answered the phone. I really didn't want to talk to her. After a quick mental battle with myself as to whether to just say 'Sorry . . . long number' in a dreadful Chinese accent and hang up, I asked for Alex, without identifying myself.

'No, he's moved his stuff out. Melanie, is that you?' she asked wonderingly.

'No! Sorry! Bye,' I said, and put the phone down, slumping against the wall. He'd moved his stuff out. Another fucking moonlight flit. Where had he gone this time? I wondered to myself. China? Tibet? He could stick that North Pole up his arse, see if he could find himself with that. Fuck! How could he?! Again?

I noticed a particularly virulent prostitute's card stuck up in the phonebox. A woman was bent over with her wrists tied to her ankles. Above a childishly written phone number it said: 'Melanie, new to the area, submissive – loves punishment. Will service your every need.' It was a sign. Definitely a sign. But what could it mean?

I had a disconsolate sandwich and wandered back to my new home, where the rat-faced man to my right was vigorously enjoying a ridiculously stinky hamburger. Small pieces of lettuce and indescribable goo were dripping on to my . . . what looked like my . . . well, anyway, an enormous bunch of flowers dumped straight on to my desk. My mind went through the options: David Duchovny; the cast of *ER*; Alex, from the North Pole . . .

Out of the corner of my eye I noticed the girl with the ladder in her tights trying to weep inconspicuously.

Very carefully, I picked up the bouquet. 'Hey, pumpkin,' it said on the card. Terse as ever. I relaxed.

'Sending flowers to yourself again?' coughed Ratto, mildly spewing me with burger phlegm.

'No, actually, they're for you. Oh, have you got a boyfriend called Alex as well? What a coincidence!'

'Think you're funny?' muttered Ratto, and returned to his mastication.

I turned to the girl.

'Are you OK?'

'Yes, I'm fine,' she whimpered, clearly not fine. 'It's my contact lenses.'

The man with Copydex stuck to his chin eventually came downstairs with my phone sorted out. The voice mail appeared to have been switched off, and when I looked up Charlie's number in the phone book it had been scrubbed out furiously – although whether by me or Fran I couldn't say – so I was stuck sitting there, still vainly tidying, till it rang.

'Hey there.' Alex spoke softly. The tone of his voice made me soften.

'You've moved your stuff,' I said.

'Well, there didn't seem to be any point in hanging about. That flatmate of yours was giving me the evil eye.'

'Really, she's cross-eyed. She was really giving me the evil eye.'

'Ah.'

There was a pause.

'Did you . . .'

'I got . . .'

We spoke simultaneously.

'I got the flowers. Thank you. They're gorgeous.'

'I wanted to apologize. I didn't mean to hurt your feelings, and I should have phoned you when I stayed at Charlie's last night. I just don't want to take anything too fast. But, you know, we've got so much time. To get back together. For everything.'

'I know.' I sighed. 'It would have been daft. Far too quick. Etcetera.'

There was a silence, then he spoke tentatively.

'Friends again?'

'Just friends?'

'Oh no. And will you come and visit me in Fulham?'

'Nope.'

'Not even if I beg?'

'No, but you can try a bit of begging if you like.'

'Please!' he yelled. 'My darling Melanie, pearl and pumpkin of my life, take the immortal trip on the District Line and enter my realm of joy.'

I giggled.

'Nope.'

'Tonight?'

'Nope.'

'So I'll see you around six?'

'Nope.'

'Excellent. See you later then. Bring wine.'

He put the phone down and I smiled to myself.

''Oo's that, your lesbian lover?' said Cockney Boy.

'Yeah. Actually, it's your mum.'

'Fuck off.'

There was still Fran to deal with. I caught her at her house, or rather her bedsit. She lived sparsely, not far away from me in Kennington.

'Franster?'

'You've got your ingratiating tone on. Let me see: you want me to sponsor you on a round-the-world bike ride for badgers? You need me to donate some bone marrow? Or has Alex moved in with that creep Charlie and you haven't done anything about it?'

'Ehmm . . . are those all the options?'

'Yup.'

'I'm sorry! I couldn't, not for that! He wouldn't understand! Oh, Fran, don't make me . . .'

'God, what is this, *Sophie's Choice*? OK, fine. You want to go out with a wanker that lives with another wanker, then fuck it, that's how it is, flowers or no flowers.'

'You know about the flowers?'

'What? Yeah, I got a big bunch, from Charlie. Odious little creep.'

'Ohhh. I got flowers from Alex.'

'How nice. They obviously bought them in a job lot.'

'Hmm. How big was your bouquet?'

'ENORMOUS. What about yours?'

'Average. Average to good.'

'Ha ha ha. Listen, bloody Amanda phoned me again.'

'Wow, now she's falling in love with you.'

'She just wanted the gossip on Charlie. And she wants to know if we'll help her pick out a tiara.'

'I'd rather eat my feet with a spoon.'

'Me too.'

Seven

We were sitting in an All Bar One, after spending six hours with Amanda trying to choose a fucking tiara because her mother was in the Priory, a drying-out clinic so exclusive that Amanda managed to make it sound like an absolute honour to end up there, and her bridesmaids were all in Barbados or somewhere. Not only had I been forced to make admiring noises in Amanda's direction as she tried on four thousand identical filigree things that cost more than I make in three months, I'd had to stop Fran from shoplifting out of delirious boredom. It had been a tiring day.

'So, 'manda, when's your hen night, then?' asked Fran.

Unusually, Amanda didn't immediately start talking. Instead, she blushed.

'Ehm . . . I'm not sure I'm going to . . . you know, nothing big.'

'But you just said you wanted to do everything properly!' I said, the implications not hitting home. 'You can't get married without a hen night!'

'Ehm, yes, I know . . .' Her voice trailed off. 'Ectually, ehm, I am having one, but with a few close friends from varsity.'

I was genuinely shocked.

'What?!' said Fran. 'When? Why didn't you invite us, you bitch?'

'Ehm, it's in a couple of weeks. Look, I'm sorry. I didn't want to hurt your feelings.'

Yeah, right . . .

'. . . I'm sorry. But, you know, I didn't invite you because you'd probably get drunk and cause a fight. You two are always getting into trouble. I mean, aren't you, darlings?'

She gave a little laugh.

'Fraser and I, well, in the position we're in now, we have certain friends and, anyway, we're going to Quagli's, and that's so expensive, and then Yanna's, and, well, it's just going to be my close friends really. You do understand, don't you?'

'Close friends! Amanda, you came crying to us when you had two periods three days apart in primary seven!' Fran was furious. 'And when Daryl Stobson said you'd gone up the bikes with him and everyone believed him, we convinced them all otherwise for you, even though it was true!'

That was true?

'Oh, for God's sake, Francesca! Can't you see that this is exactly why I'm not inviting you? What if you started coming out with that kind of . . . crap in front of all my friends? You'd completely show me up. We're just . . . Things are different now.'

'No, they're not,' snarled Fran. 'You're still the spoilt little cow you always were. God, I pity Fraser. Come on, Mel, we're off.'

She dragged me up by the sleeve.

'Are . . . are we . . . still invited to the wedding?' I couldn't help asking, pathetically, as we left.

'Yes. But then everyone is,' sneered Amanda, turning away from us.

Outside, I could see Fran's nostrils flare like a horse.

'That stupid cow,' I said companionably.

'Oh, who gives a fuck!' said Fran. 'It's not like I even want to go to that poxy wedding anyway. What do I give a toss for? Prats in cravats? Some chinless wonder whose life she's about to make a complete misery?'

'Fraser's not a chinless wonder.'

'Yeah, right, and Alex isn't a complete piss weasel.'

We walked along in grumpy silence for a while. Then a brilliant idea occurred to me. Really, a brilliant, brilliant idea.

'Of course,' I began subtly, 'we could always . . .'

Fran looked at me sideways. 'What?'

'No, no, you probably wouldn't like the idea.' Heh

heh heh. My reverse psychology skills were second to none.

'OK, cock that then.'

We marched on in silence.

I started again.

'We could always' – it came tumbling out – 'ask Angus if we could go to the stag night instead, and really piss her off.'

'My reverse psychology skills are second to none,' said Fran. 'But, you know what?'

'What?'

'Oh no, you wouldn't be interested . . .'

'What?' I said.

'That is not at all a bad idea.'

'Thank you,' I said proudly.

'We could annoy them big time. In fact, a few little words in Fraser's ear . . . Maybe we should let him know what little missie is really like before he gives her a castle and stuff.'

I looked at her, shocked.

'What, like, talk to him about Amanda?'

'Why not? You're his friend, right?'

'I suppose so.'

'And if you saw a friend about to be eaten by a crocodile, you'd warn them, right?'

'Hmm.' It sounded a bit dubious to me.

'A big, poisonous crocodile, Mel!'

'Do you get poisonous crocodiles?'

A look at Fran's face convinced me that you did.

'Well,' I concurred, 'then, yes, I suppose I would.'

'Jamesh Bond?'

'Hullo thair, Moneypenny.'

'You know the Evil One, whom that brother of yours insists on marrying?'

'The person of whom you speak is not unfamiliar to me.'

'Well, I have a secret mission for you that could piss her off mightily.'

'Tell me more.'

I explained her treacherous betrayal, and he instantly saw no trouble at all in inviting us to Fraser's stag night.

'Even though I'm not best man, I'm still doing all the organizing. McLachlan can't sort his way out of a paper bag, as you'll see when you meet him.'

'Are there going to be strippers?'

'Why, do youse two want to do it?'

'Do you think Fraser would approve?'

'Och, you know my brother. He'll be hiding under the table anyway. Yes, there might be a stripper, but nothing, you know . . .'

'What?' I asked innocently. I could sense his pink face getting even pinker over the phone.

'Now, stop being a naughty girrul. It'll be fine. Saturday night, starting at the Princess Louise. And tell that skinny pal of yours not to get into any more fights.'

'Ha! You tell her! Then I can watch her kick your head in.'

* * *

Alex was faintly perturbed that he hadn't been invited to the stag do and we had.

'You don't even know him,' I pointed out. 'You've met him about twice.'

'I know Amanda and her friends.'

'Well, go to her hen night then.'

'No thanks. Bunch of screaming Harpies. Why aren't you going?'

I rolled my eyes at him.

'Long story. OK, look, why don't you tag along with us? No one's going to mind.'

Except Angus, who inexplicably hates you, I thought. Oh yes, and Fran, who barely tolerates you.

'Well, OK then,' he said diffidently, as if we'd all been begging him to come for hours.

He stretched his legs out on the chaise longue. Charlie's place, while lovely and clearly very expensive, was done up in boy-meets-mother style. Soft furnishings – no doubt spares from the country – shared house room with mountain bikes; expensive and overwrought stereo equipment rested on expensive and overwrought occasional tables. Over it all was a faint aroma de rugby kit. Still, I was making the two-hour trip to West London more and more often, as Alex showed a marked reluctance to cross the river now he didn't absolutely have to. It was Sunday afternoon.

Charlie walked in and ignored me as usual.

'Splinters!' he hollered at Alex.

'Fishcake!' returned Alex, and they burst out into hearty guffaws.

'I've got tickets to Twickers on Saturday.'

Alex leapt up. 'Fantastic! How'd you manage that, you old bastard?'

Charlie tapped his Huguenot nose. 'It's who you know, innit?' he said in fake Cockney.

'That's Fraser's stag night,' I said.

Charlie's heavy half-shut eyes lit up. 'Stag party! Wo ho ho!'

'And you are NOT invited,' I added.

'How do you know? It's a stag party. Blokes, beer and birds, way hey!'

'Because I'm going, and Fran's going and – oh yes, a whole bunch of other people who actually know the groom.'

Charlie was obviously ruffled by the mention of Fran but merely swept through to the kitchen saying, 'Totty at a stag party? Shouldn't be allowed. Sounds like absolute crap, if you ask me.'

'Shall we go out for lunch?' I asked Alex pointedly.

Alex gave me a hangdog look and trailed out the door after me.

'Got you by the apron strings there, hasn't she, matey boy?' I heard as we left.

'I don't think,' I said, walking down the street, 'that I could dislike that boy any more than I do. He's such an . . . an oaf.'

'Charlie is not an oaf!' said Alex, looking cross. 'And he doesn't like you either.'

'Boohoohoo,' I said. 'The molester doesn't like me.'

'You get more like that friend Fran of yours every day,' he said.

We ate lunch reading the papers sullenly. Eventually, I kicked him under the table and gave him a grin. He grinned back and raised his eyebrows, and we returned to the papers in relative harmony, reading out our favourite small-time celebrity shagger-of-the-week stories, before Alex had to disappear for a tour in his friend Henry's new car – a two-seater, natch.

That friend Fran of mine was waiting outside my flat when I got back later that afternoon.

'I can't see why you won't just give me a key,' she huffed.

'I can't see why you think you actually live at my house.'

Fran slouched herself off the wall and deigned to mount the stairs to my flat. She still looked good being pouty, given that most of us had grown out of it at nineteen.

'Anyway . . .' she said, sitting down and lighting a cigarette. This was strictly *verboten* in Linda's house, but she didn't look in the mood to be trifled with. 'That molesting bastard friend of your very own personal bastard phoned me to ask me out for a drink.'

'What? Charlie? NO! When?'

'About two hours ago.'

'Jesus. So, this time he's going to buy you dinner before he attempts to rape you.'

'Looks like it,' said Fran, narrowing her eyes.

'God. That really takes the piss. No wonder you got the big flowers. What did you say?'

'I didn't say anything: he left a message asking me out. Well, I think he did. You know what posh boys are like. He said, "Maybe a drink sometime, right, yars, OK, right, yars, sorry, right, bye then, yars." So, statistically, it could have meant anything.'

'What are you going to do?'

'I'm not sure. I mean, I could tell him to take the phone, stick it up his arse and dial 999 with his prostrate now, or I could do it loudly in front of a lot of other people somewhere public.'

Now I came to think of it, this could be good. This could be very good indeed.

'Ooh, do the second one. Where's the most public place you could actually dump him?'

'Well . . .' She exhaled in an actory way and leaned forward. 'First I thought, what's the highest-rated TV show? Then I realized that what we'd have to do is qualify for *Stars in Their Eyes*.'

'Don't tell me . . . Sonny and Cher?'

'Keith Harris and Orville.'

'Yuk. Who'd be Orville?'

'Who d'you think?'

I winced. 'Well, I suppose he'd be used to it.'

'Quite.'

'So, you'd dump him on *Stars in Their Eyes*?'

'Oh no. We'd win that, bring out a cover record, get asked on to pull the National Lottery lever, and *then* I'd dump him.'

'Wow! An almost flawless plan.'

'What do you mean, "almost flawless"?'

I put my arm around her.

'I'm sorry, dear. But I don't think even the real Keith Harris could win that show.'

She sighed melodramatically. 'I know. Unless we were up against the fake Joe Dolce.'

'What's Plan B?'

She giggled maliciously. 'Plan B is the table next to Amanda's bunch of slavering Sloane witches at her hen night. I thought I'd do lots of shouting and maybe set things on fire.'

I loved that plan.

'Oh yes, please, please do that, please.'

'Unfortunately it's on a Friday night, and they're full up.'

'You checked?' I asked, full of admiration.

'Well, I'm not called . . .' she paused. 'What am I called?'

The man-chomping gonzo of South London, I didn't say.

'Ehm . . . no one calls you anything. Except Fran.'

'Huh. Well, anyway, so, plan C.'

'?'

'Keep reading the papers.'

'What?'

Fran lifted up her profile dramatically.

'I am going to shag him to death.'

Oh no. Fran had done this shag-to-death routine before. It was never pretty. It involved a man having a night he would probably never forget, with a woman he would never normally have a hope of scoring with – i.e. Fran – then having to follow her around in humiliation for weeks begging for a second chance. It had never failed so far, and was a punishment kept for the most flagrant transgressors.

'Are you sure?' I asked her. 'That's pretty serious.'

'It's poetic justice,' she announced sternly, reaching for the phone.

'Charlie! Hello there! How lovely to hear from you!'

I danced up and down furiously in front of her doing more and more elaborate vomit-miming. She reciprocated by making wanker motions in time with her talking.

'Yes, that would be super.'

I couldn't not laugh.

'Eight thirty? I'll see you there . . . OK, bye now.'

She put the phone down and I let out a suppressed snort of laughter.

'He's dead!' I said. 'You just killed a man stone dead!'

'I doubt he'll be able to even get it out of his pants,' said Fran. 'It's almost too easy.'

Next day I got in the lift by mistake before remembering my rightful place back in the lime green basement.

Cockney Boy was on fine form. 'Hey, snoots!' he yelled at me. I gave him my best contemptuous look.

I was a bit worried that I was taking all my career angst out on him. Then I looked at the rash of unbroken pus spots under his shaving line and thought, well, if needs must . . .

'Snoots,' he said again, 'I got off with this girl last night, right. She was all over me.'

'I know,' I said, smiling sweetly. 'She's left some dog make-up on you.'

'Ha,' he said, without humour. 'Bet you just stayed in watching *EastEnders*, then?'

'Yes, I did, actually. I didn't know you had a part-time acting job as Robbie Jackson.'

He sneered at me and left me alone. On my right, Janie was red-eyed again. We hadn't got past the everyday stage of my asking her if she was all right when she clearly wasn't, to which she would vehemently nod while being on the brink of tears. I got her a coffee, and didn't get Cockney Boy one, and her eyes brimmed over at such basic human kindness.

At lunch time I took a book and a ciabatta roll – the cool effect rather spoiled by a packet of beef Hula Hoops – into an alcove I'd discovered behind reception. I was rather cross to find it already occupied. Janie was there, snivelling away into a disgusting piece of green tissue. I sighed and mentally abandoned my peaceful lunch.

'OK, tell me: what's the matter?' As long as it wasn't a lifelong infatuation with *The English Patient*, surely I ought to be able to do something. Oh God, I hoped it wasn't cancer or anything really tough. Or her parents dying – oh no! That would be awful. I cringed in anticipation. I'd always thought of myself as a kind person, but now I realized that was in fact a complete fallacy. I was really a path-of-least-resistance person. Damn!

Gradually, the sobbing started to slow down. I patted her tentatively on the shoulder, and said 'Don't worry!' encouragingly. This brought on a fresh wave. My sandwich began to fade away into some dried-out afterlife in my mind.

Finally she stumbled: 'It's James . . . my boyfriend . . . It's – boohoohoo . . .'

Oh well, at least it was something I could deal with. Not-quite-up-to-scratch boyfriends were my speciality.

'Right, tell me all about it,' I said. 'Has he moved to Fulham to live with someone you absolutely hate?'

'No,' she looked up, momentarily surprised.

'Whoops, no, that's me,' I remembered. 'Well, what's he done?'

'He wasn't at home last night . . . and he didn't even phone me.' The last part of the sentence was drawn out in melodramatic sobs.

'Ehm, so what?' I said gaily. 'Who are you, Ally McBeal? It's not that much of a problem! He was probably just out for a pint or something.'

She sniffed loudly. 'Why didn't he ring me, then?'

'Why? Are you two married?'

'No.'

'Have you got kids? Pets? Lice?'

'No.'

'Well, why did he have to ring you then? You're

both independent.'

God, this was good advice. I was brilliant at this.

She sniffed again.

'Did you phone him?'

'Yes,' she said quietly.

'More than once?'

'Yes.'

'How many times?' I asked, not wanting to know the answer.

'Oh, well . . . I pretty much just –'

'– pressed the redial button all night?' I interrupted.

She nodded mutely.

'Pfff. Bad news. How long have you two been together.'

'Six weeks.'

I heard *Psycho* music in my head.

'Oh . . . OK.'

I settled back into the potted plant. This story was obviously a long one.

It was, but nothing original. After being dumped by her fiancé well into plate-planning stage, she had clung on to any passing flotsam ever since. James was a stockbroker and sounded perfectly dull and nice and nothing to worry about.

'Nothing to worry about,' I said. 'He sounds perfectly . . . nice. And at least he's rich.'

'I know.' She pouted a little. 'When we get married I think we could get one of those nice houses in Clapham . . . if he ever speaks to me again.'

Hang on there, schizo girl!

'He doesn't know you're getting married, does he?'

'No.'

'Then for God's sake, Janie, leave him alone. He's going to do what he's going to do anyway, whether you're crying about it or not.'

She looked as if she was about to cry again.

'Come on. Stop it. You know it's true. Leave him alone. He sounds nice and you're going to drive him away.'

She sniffed in a final kind of a way and looked up at me.

'I know. I'm sorry. I just get a bit daft.'

'Huh! Don't worry about that,' I said heartily, trying to get my hand round to where my sandwich was.

'What about you?' she said suddenly. 'How's your love life?'

'Oh . . .' I raised my eyebrows quizzically. 'It's good. It's fine. No, really, I mean, it's OK, most of the time . . . Well, ha ha, you know how it is.'

'Oh well,' she said. 'Any time you want to talk about it, just let me know.'

Hang on, I thought. Wasn't this . . . I mean . . .

'Righty-ho!' I said. (I never say 'Righty-ho.')

I looked out through the atrium into the rain.

'Hula Hoop?'

'Thanks,' said Janie, and took four.

Eight

Alex phoned that night.

'Hey, pumpkin.'

'Hey yourself.'

'What are you up to?'

'Oh, you know, just hanging around the house in my black, silky, lacy underwear – oh, it's so warm! I must unfasten my negligée.'

'Yeah yeah yeah.'

'Oh! Is that the door? Goodness me, hello, plumber. Have you come to . . . clean out my pipes?'

'Mel, shut up for just one second.'

'OK . . . big boy.'

'Listen, ehm, Charlie really wants to come to this do on Saturday night.'

'No he doesn't. He said it sounded complete crap.'

'Well, when I got back on Sunday he said he really wanted to come, and could I ask you.'

'God, what's the matter with the boy, is he a Johnny No-Mates? Is this the first party he's ever been invited to? Hang on, no, I mean, is this the latest party he hasn't been invited to?'

'No, I don't know what it is. He just keeps pestering me, and I said I'd ring you, that's all.'

'Ah ha ho – I think I know.'

'What? What is it?'

'I'm not telling you. And no, he can't. He's annoying.'

'Oh, go on, Mel – please. Please. For a mate.'

'A mate? Who, you?'

'Well, you know what I mean.'

'You're my mate?'

'Yes,' he said. 'Your soul mate. Now, please, please can you get Charlie an invite?'

'Alex, is he going to chuck you out if you don't wangle him into this party?'

'Ehmm . . . yes?'

'Good. No, he definitely can't come.'

'I'll . . . do the washing-up.'

'I . . . probably wouldn't notice.'

'Oh, go on, Mel. It'll be a laugh.'

I sighed. 'Fine, fine, if it means that much to you.'

'Fantastic.' His voice turned curious. 'Why does he want to come so much then?'

Ha! I don't think Alex really needed to know that. Fran had obviously commenced the process.

'Ah,' I said. 'Well . . .' I said. Then inspiration

struck. 'Apparently, Charlie's never seen a stripper before and there apparently . . . might . . . be one.'

'No, really? I've never seen one either.'

'Good God, what is the public school system coming to these days? Anyway, good. I'm glad you're happy. I'll see you on Saturday . . . unless you feel like popping round now . . . ?'

'Jeez, Mel, it's two hours away.'

'Oh! So it is. Saturday, then.'

'Bye, pumpkin.'

'Bye, sweetpea.'

I phoned Fraser to check the rapidly extending guest list was going to be all right. Angus had already OK'd our presence by threatening to withhold stripper privileges if we weren't granted entrance, so at least Fran and I were in the clear. Amanda answered.

'Oh, hi,' I said coolly. I was prepared for this. 'Is Fraser there?' Hee hee hee.

'Is that you, Mel, darling?'

Uh-oh: what was this, scary reverse psychology? Maybe she was planning on turning my legs into the legs of a chicken.

'I'm dreadfully sorry about the other day, darling. Pre-wedding tension and all that.'

I didn't know what to say. She seemed to have had pre-wedding tension for the last twenty-six years.

'Don't worry about it,' I mumbled.

'Darling, I'd love you to come to my hen party. Honestly.'

'But . . .'

'No, no "but"s, darling. Please, do come.'

'What about Fran?' I said loyally. Also I'd be too scared to go on my own.

She sighed. 'Yes, and Fran too. It's Quagli's at eight, a week on Friday. We'll squeeze you in somehow.'

'Have you been dropped on the floor and landed on your head?'

'No, darling, it's just . . . I thought . . . Oh, it would be so silly and embarrassing for you two to have to go to Frase's stag night. I mean, the humiliation . . .'

'Oh no. We're still going to that. It's going to be a right laugh,' I said.

'Darling, don't be a silly. It's for boys. They won't want you!'

I knew it! She couldn't bear not being the centre of attention for even one tiny microsecond.

'Can I speak to Fraser, please? And thanks for inviting us . . . eventually. It's a sweet thought.'

'Look, I'm only saying this to be kind . . .' she said nastily, 'but he doesn't really want you there. It's only because that retarded brother of his thought it'd be a laugh. Fraser thinks it'll be embarrassing too. You'll be the laughing stock.'

SHUT UP, WITCH! I badly wanted to say.

'Look, Amanda,' I said, as calmly as I could, 'it'll be fine. We'll all be fine. Don't worry about us. Can you put Fraser on the phone, please?'

There was a pause, and some frantic whispering.

I wanted to hang up, but forced myself to stay on the line.

'Urr, hullo,' came a familiar gravelly voice.

'Ehm, hi, Frase . . .'

There was a bit of a pause. I could picture Amanda in the background, drawing her finger across her throat . . . dramatically uplit like the queen in *Snow White*.

'Frase, do you really mind us coming on your stag night?'

Fraser was obviously weighing up his options of girls plus stripper or nothing.

'NO. DEFINITELY NOT.'

The stern tone surprised me.

'DO YOU UNDERSTAND? DEFINITELY NOT, OKAY!'

Then he put the phone down. I hugged myself with glee. We were going all right. Although I did find Fraser tricking his fiancée slightly worrying. I mean, I was allowed to hate her – I wasn't going to marry her.

I remembered I'd forgotten to ask him about Alex and Charlie. Oh well, surely they could blend into the background.

Finally, with the phone feeling welded to my ear, I managed to catch up with Fran, and told her what had happened. She was pleased.

'I'd have given anything to be a ghost and have crept into her room and seen her face when that happened.'

'Er, wouldn't you rather just be a fly on the wall?' I said.

'Would I rather be a fly than a ghost?'

'OK, can we have this conversation later? Because NOW you are going to tell me what happened with Charlie.'

She laughed evilly. 'Oh, my dear, I couldn't possibly tell you on the phone. Really, it was disgusting. Quite brilliant. Almost a shame to have to punish him, really.'

'But you're going to.'

'Sadly, rules are rules. And I'll see you on Saturday. Has he phoned up and begged to come?'

'Yup.'

'*Excellente*!'

Saturday was fast approaching, and I realized that I had no idea what to wear to a stag night. Cockney Boy was most surprised that we'd been invited to a stag, and even offered to teach me how to make a selection of suggestively named cocktails.

Janie was looking much better, apart from jumping six feet every time the phone rang and asking me whether I thought it was too early to introduce James to her parents.

I pondered this for a bit.

'Well, I've always found the will reading to be the only really safe time. That might just be the boys I know, though.'

She turned green, and I wished I'd kept my mouth shut.

* * *

I debated with myself whether to wear jeans, then decided against it, in case we ended up in one of those nightclubs that preferred cheap shiny Top Shop suits to real clothes. A good frock, however, was not the thing, as it would surely be raining beer at some stage. Anything tight or short was out, in case of stripper identity problems. And nothing too plain, or I might be mistaken for a dyke, which is why I had to come to the boys' night out. Yikes. That pretty much just left my bought-on-a-whim catsuit, so called because if I ever walked past any cats in it their fur went on end and they made a 'sssssssssssssssssuuuuuuuuuu' noise.

Fran turned up, looking glorious in something dainty and impossibly trendy. This was getting worse. I picked my kilt up from the back of the cupboard. Fran shook her head imperiously. Just as I was hopping about in my black tights gazing at some weird Japanese kimono thing which had somehow turned up in my clothes, the doorbell rang again.

'Can you get that?' I said. 'It'll be Alex and Charlie.'

'Ah, my two favourite men,' she purred languidly.

Fran swanned out of my bedroom and I could hear rowdy voices. Oh well, she sounded like she was being civil. Then Alex's voice drifted into my room:

'PLEASE – look, will you just stop calling me a cocksucker?'

I grinned to myself.

They did sound noisy, though. Oh God, I hoped

they weren't drunk already. That would be dreadful.

Finally settling on smart chinos and a flowery shirt, I shoved on some mascara and lippy and popped outside.

Alex and Charlie had hauled out one of Linda's bottles of wine and were debating in loud voices exactly which hilarious rugby song they were going to sing next. Uh oh. I looked at Fran, who nodded and raised her eyes. They were absolutely, gloriously, buggeringly drunk.

'BESTIALITY'S GREAT, MATE!' shouted Charlie.

To which Alex immediately responded:

'PUT YOUR LOG IN A FROG, MATE!'

'PUT YOUR GEAR IN A STEER, MATE!' hollered Charlie lustily.

'BESTIALITY'S GREAT!' they concluded together, holding each other up.

'Oh God,' I said to Fran. 'We can't take these two with us. They'll be awful.'

'You tell them.'

'Oh, why does it always have to be me?'

'Yeah, right, like I invited Charlie.'

At the sound of Fran speaking his name, Charlie fell to the ground and clasped her round the ankles. She kicked him.

I turned round to face the boys. They were both very red in the face, and the wine was sloshing around dangerously.

'Alex, you're completely pissed,' I said, trying not to sound too headmistressy.

'Jesus, gorgeous, you sound just like my old headmistress,' he slurred, wobbling backwards and forwards.

'You're not coming to this stag night like that!'

'STAG NIGHT! STAG NIGHT!' they started chanting. Charlie got up off the floor and looked around, puzzled. 'Are we there?'

'Oh, shut up!' My patience was gone, and I couldn't cope. 'You're not coming, so you might as well just fuck off.'

'PUT YOUR LOAD IN A TOAD, MATE,' started Alex inexorably.

'PUT YOUR GOO IN A ROO, MATE,' Charlie joined in.

'Oh God,' I said to Fran. 'What shall we do? Make a run for it?'

'Oh, good idea,' she said. 'Then when Linda gets back from Singles Night at Tescos she can find them prostrate in vomit and weeing on her carpet.'

'BESTIALITY'S GREAT, MATE! BESTIALITY'S GREAT!'

'Maybe we can take them outside, then lose them.'

'Good idea. Just as well you've already taken Alex's set of keys back.'

'Shit.'

'Look, let's go. They'll probably be all right.'

'SHE CAN SHOOT GREEN PEAS FROM HER FUNDAMENTAL ORIFICE!' shouted Charlie suddenly. Fran and I stopped talking and turned round.

'That's the wrong song, you twat,' said Alex.

'I KNOW!' hollered Charlie. 'Err . . . PUT YOUR POLE IN A FOAL, MATE!'

'THAT'S MORE LIKE IT!' yelled Alex. 'PUT YOUR STAFF IN A GIRAFFE, MATE!'

'Oh God.' I sat down, then stood up again when I realized I was sitting in the wine and spittle range of fire.

'This is great. This is just great. First, Amanda is never speaking to us again for going behind her back.'

'Yeah. One: who cares, and two: how is she going to find out?'

'Oh, probably shortly after these two get arrested and in the papers.'

'HAVE A SHAG WITH A STAG, MATE!'

'HAVE INTERCOURSE WITH A HORSE, MATE!'

'Then,' I went on, bravely, 'we turn up at this thing and get thrown out, and Angus and Fraser never talk to us again. So, in the space of a day I've managed to alienate about thirty-three per cent of all my friends. Not to mention Alex, when he wakes up tomorrow and I'm beating his face to a bloody pulp.'

'Why don't you do it now, when he won't notice?'

'What would be the point of that?'

'Come on.' Fran took me by the arm. 'Let's get this over with. Maybe they'll fall out of the taxi . . .'

'Yeah, and into another dimension. C'mon, you two, we're going.'

They started to sway towards the door.

'UP THE CRACK OF A YAK, MATE!'

'HAVE A FRIG WITH A PIG, MATE!'

And the four of us sang, going down the hall:

'BESTIALITY'S GREAT, MATE! BESTIALITY'S GREAT.'

We nearly got thrown out the cab, and it took all my conciliatory powers to get us to the Princess Louise pub, in Holborn. I shot a nervous look at Fran, but she appeared extremely cool, even though Charlie was trying to get on his knees in front of her to express his true and heartfelt devotion in loquacious terms. Every time he got too close she kneed him on the crest of his rugby shirt.

I took a deep breath at the door, squared my shoulders and headed in.

'Neh, it's a private party up there, mate,' said this extraordinary talking-monkey thing.

'Yes, that's right,' I said. 'Fraser McConnald's stag do.'

'That's Laird McConnald,' added Fran helpfully.

The monkey raised its eyebrows.

''Ere, are you the . . .'

'No, we're not. We're invited guests. Come on, Mel –' and Fran shrugged us through imperiously.

As in werewolf films, the inn fell quiet when we entered the room. Lots of young men were standing around having a perfectly nice comfortable drink, and here were two pairs of breasts all set to ruin it. A couple of the blokes even had cigars, if it could be any more Freudian. I wanted to turn on my heel, but, fortunately, Angus came to the rescue.

'Hey, hullose there!' He walked over, beaming. 'Glad youse could make it.'

His smile fell as he looked over his shoulder and cottoned on to the collapsing figures of Alex and Charlie.

'I'm sorry!' I said straight away. 'They were going to get thrown into the river in a sack and we didn't have the heart to leave them.'

Angus half smiled. 'Och well, they're here now, I suppose. Is he –' indicating Charlie – 'going to cause any trouble?'

Fran had somehow managed to conjure a cigar out of nowhere and was proceeding to look felinely wonderful with it.

'Oh no,' she purred. 'He won't be any trouble, will you, big boy?' And she winked at Charlie like some thirties vixen until his eyes popped.

Angus looked understandably confused then turned back to me.

'Can I get you a drink?' he said eagerly.

'Ehm . . . bottle of Budvar, please.'

'I'll have a long vodka please,' ordered Fran imperiously.

'A what?' I said, when Angus had gone to the bar. 'What are you playing at? Queen of all the Vamps?'

'Oh, go on, Mel,' she said. 'Look around. There's forty blokes here and two of us. When's the last time I got off with a bloke?'

'Thursday.'

'He doesn't count. That was duty. And tonight he's hopelessly drunk, while I'm in the mood. I'm a prowling lioness. So stay out of my way.' She took a draw on her cigar and blew smoke rings at me.

'Huh. Well, my boyfriend's here . . .' I looked over. Alex was slumped on a sofa, stupefied. 'So I have to behave myself.'

'Do you?'

'Yes!'

Angus arrived back with the drinks, and Fran downed hers in one. Eyes shining, she looked around the room. 'Who's . . . that?' she said to Angus, eyes trained on a sweet-faced, wan young man standing by himself next to the punch, and helping himself liberally to it.

'That's Johnny McLachlan – he's the best man. Why, do you want to meet him?'

'Yes. Have him washed and –'

'Fran!'

Angus clearly thought we had both gone mad, but he beckoned Johnny McLachlan over anyway. Johnny McLachlan did a huge 'Who, me?' double take, and eventually sidled up, slightly hunched over.

'Johnny, meet two friends of ours, Melanie and Fran.'

'Hi,' I said.

'Enchanted!' exclaimed Fran. 'Now, tell me all about yourself and how you came to be darling Fraser's best man.'

'Aye, well, hullo,' said Johnny, in an accent so thick he made Angus sound like Princess Anne. 'Well, actually, like, Ah'm a geography teacher, likesay.'

'How fascinating!' Fran leaned over intimately. A sweat broke out on Johnny's forehead.

Through mutual eye contact Angus and I moved to one side.

'What on earth is going on with your friend? Is she on heat?'

'I think so.'

'Is she serious?'

'Serious? Well, if I were Johnny, I'd take out some life insurance.'

'Eaten alive?'

'Sucked clean.'

'Woo.' There was a pause.

'Oh, I remember what I came for,' I said.

Angus looked at me quizzically.

'The bridegroom? That whole wedding thing? Horseshoes and stuff? You remember!'

'Oh yes. I'm being a terrible host. Let me –' and he bowed and proffered me his arm – 'escort you to his lairdship's table.'

'You are too kind.'

Fraser was sitting on a large leather banquette in the corner, surrounded by some rather technical-looking young men, whom I assumed were fellow engineers. They all looked rather doleful, and not as if they were having a primeval bonding experience at all.

'Hey,' I said, still on Angus's arm.

Fraser looked up and grinned.

'Hey, yourself. Glad you could come.'

'Me too. Is it going to get you into trouble?'

'Och, Fraser's always in trouble – aren't you, lad?'

said Angus, and the whole table burst out laughing. Fraser smiled ruefully.

'Of course not. Everyone is sworn to secrecy.'

There was a chorus of, 'Yeah, right!' and 'How much are you going to pay us?'

'Did you bring that terrifying friend of yours?'

'Yes. She's over there, being terrifying.'

Fraser looked over.

'Oh my God, poor wee Johnny. You haven't set her loose on him?'

'Nothing to do with me, I'm afraid. Apparently she's being a lioness tonight.'

Angus and he swapped a look.

'I was at primary school with Johnny. Haven't seen him much since then, but he qualified as oldest pal when I was looking for a best man. God, I hope she doesn't get her claws into him . . .'

In the corner, Fran was quaffing another martini, with one hand on Johnny's lapel. He was laboriously trying to explain something to her – oxbow lakes, probably, but I could tell she wasn't listening, just throwing her head back with raucous laughter.

'He's been married eight years and his wife never lets him out of the house. He only got to come here because I promised there wouldn't be any strippers.'

'Fraser, just how many lies did you have to tell to get this party together tonight?'

'I don't even want to think about it. Who's for another?'

'Way hey!' shouted the boys at the table, and bumped up to make room for me.

They turned out not to be doleful at all, just serious about deconstructing the *X-Files*, e e cummings, politics, stand-up comedy and the general state of the world today, at least in so far as it related to the world of engineering and *Dr Who*. Strangely, I found them fascinating and non-judgemental company; infinitely relaxing. Of course, not having to buy any drinks helped.

Every so often there would be a loud grunt or guffaw, as Alex and Charlie seemed to have descended to the level of bestial communications. But just as I was thinking how very, very fond of Fraser's friends I was, there was a muttering at the door. In walked a woman in a large coat, out of which was peeping a pair of open-toed stilettoes and fishnet tights.

All relevant political and cultural debate instantly went flying out the window. I suddenly had a lot less room on the bench as the testosterone level rose and the boys suddenly needed plenty of space to splay their legs wide open.

Behind the stripper was an enormous man who managed to make finding a plug point for the tape recorder seem imposing. Immediately, 'Hey, Big Spender' started up. Without removing her cigarette, the woman walked nonchalantly to the centre of the room and, showing no perceivable interest, slipped out of her coat.

The previously well-mannered and charming boys beside me turned into a host of baying beasts. The roaring was incredible, punctuated with wolf howls as the woman did a desultory shimmer to 'Spend . . . a little time with me.'

Eventually, she started to walk towards our table. An excited 'Way hey!' went up as she bent over to have her bra strap undone, with the bloke she approached only just able to restrain himself – after a sharp look from the bouncer – from pinging it. The bra went whirling through the air and landed near a surprised Fran and Johnny, who were snogging like they'd just invented it over in the corner.

The bra got a big round of applause, but all eyes quickly came back round to the main attraction. The boys' eyes were wide as saucers as the woman stifled a yawn, shot me a dirty look (I thought), and stuck her leg up on the table to undo her suspenders.

I stifled a yawn myself, and looked over to where I'd last left Charlie and Alex, muttering like two old alkies at a railway station. Alex was tottering uneasily to his feet, being egged on by Charlie. As I watched, hypnotized, ignoring the mounting hysteria behind me, Alex picked up the gold lamé-trimmed bra and put it on over his shirt, dancing along to Shirley Bassey. He approached Fran and Johnny, making lewder and lewder movements, while Charlie shouted encouragement. Finally, when all eyes had gone past her, the stripper turned round to see Alex rubbing her costume like a towel between his legs.

''Ere!' she shouted, which was enough for the bouncer to stop looking menacing and do some actual bouncing.

He walked over to Alex and put his hand on his shoulder. Incredibly drunk, Alex leered up at him uncomprehendingly. Charlie, however, was back on his feet again.

'Leave him alone!' he shouted petulantly.

The bouncer gave Charlie his best ominous look.

'Yeah?'

'Yeah! Or you can just . . . fuck off!'

There was an ominous silence, except for the inaudible noise of me attempting to disappear. Oh my God, he'd done it again. And I had brought him.

Very deliberately, the bouncer retrieved the bra from Alex's limp hand and laid it on the table. Then slowly, almost tenderly, he led both the boys outside. Nobody moved as some cartoon scuffle noises reached us from the other side of the door. After about three minutes the bouncer came back in, actually dusting his hands down.

'You coming, Leese?' he said.

Leese was already dressed – in her own terms. She stood in front of Angus while he paid her, then the pair left in a dignified silence.

I closed my eyes in horror. Nobody said anything. Then finally a lone Glaswegian voice from the back said plaintively:

'Well, I thought the bloke was a better dancer, ken.'

I opened half an eye. Fraser turned round, but there was a glint in his eye.

'You mean I brought a stripper to my stag night for a crowd of fucking poofs?'

The whole room guffawed with relieved tension, and new rounds were ordered in. I went up to Angus.

'Oh God, I'm so sorry. I mean . . . oh, they're just . . . I'm sorry.'

'I know what you mean,' he said kindly. 'Why don't you tell me all about it?'

'I will, I need to go see if Alex is OK.'

'Why? He deserved it.'

'No he didn't! It was just a prank.'

'Not to her it wasn't.'

'Oh well, you know what boys are like.'

'Huh. Not all of them.'

I could feel him watching me as I headed out the door. Fran and Johnny were now looking distinctly biological, and I averted my eyes.

Outside, everything was quiet. I couldn't see the boys anywhere, or even hear any muffled groaning. I pondered the situation for nearly half a second, heard a burst of boyish laughter from upstairs and decided to head back to where the warmth and beer were.

Inside, everyone's faces were looking redder. Fran and Johnny were nowhere to be seen, but the lads were presenting Fraser with a blonde blow-up doll, which happened to look extremely like Amanda.

Blushing, he stood up as Angus sidled alongside me and pressed a bottle of beer into my hand, which I swigged gratefully.

'I wanted to say . . .' Fraser started manfully.

'Get yer tits oot!' shouted the Glaswegian wag.

'Shut up, Nash.'

I turned round to see who Nash was. *Gosh, he doesn't sound black*, I found myself thinking, then immediately felt like the stupidest person in the world.

'I just wanted to say,' continued Fraser 'that it's good to see so many of you here.'

'Apart fae yer best man!' someone shouted, and there was a burst of obscene laughter.

'Yes, well, apart from – ahem – Mr McLachlan, who seems to be otherwise disposed.'

'Aye, up the bits of some tart.'

'Hey!' I said to Angus. 'That's my friend they're talking about.'

'What, not your friend that was behaving completely like a tart?'

'Huh. Well, maybe.'

'OK, calm down . . .' Fraser looked slightly unsteady. 'I just wanted to thank you all for coming, and I know some of you came down a long way. Getting married is a frightening thing, although not as frightening as seeing you shower all in the same room at the one time.'

There was a friendly muttering.

'No, really. It's great to see you all. I'd like to thank my brother for getting everything organized, Mr Flaherty for the loan of his pub, and . . . well, just the whole big bunch of you lads.'

'And girls!' I squeaked.

'And honorary lads,' said Fraser, bowing in my direction. I grinned.

'So, get some drink down you. Oh, and sorry about the stripper . . .' he petered out.

'To Fraser!' shouted Angus.

'To Fraser!' said the company. I think I was the only one who noticed that he'd missed out the bride from the toast.

'To the stripper!' shouted someone else.

'To the dirty bint that's taken Johnny up the close!'

'What?' I asked Angus. 'Is that rude?'

'Never mind.'

We wandered back over to Fraser's table and rejoined the company.

The evening wore on – the landlord was an old drinking buddy of the McConnalds' father, and wasn't too bothered about licensing restrictions. I lapsed into lovely drunk time, where things just floated past, and I jumped in and out of different conversations at will. After dissecting the genius of Billy Connolly on one side, I tuned in like a radio to the other, where Angus and one of the Scottish boys were deep in serious conversation.

'Just talk to him,' Angus was saying.

'Look, I only met her once. She seemed all right.'

'She's not all right. She's a complete cow and she'll make his life hell. This is why I got you all down here – to persuade him not to do it.'

'What are you two talking about?' I exclaimed brightly.

'Nothing,' said Angus shortly, turning back to his pint.

'Have you met this "Amanda" that Frase is marrying?' asked the other chap.

'Course I have. I've known her all my life.'

Angus looked up at me.

'What's she like then?' the bloke asked.

I paused, not quite sure what to say. Idiotically, I suddenly felt quite loyal. It was all right for me and Fran to talk about Amanda having her gizzards ripped out by vultures, but with anyone else it wasn't really on.

'Well, she's . . . really pretty, and dead rich. She's nice.'

'Fair enough,' said the bloke to Angus. 'I'm not saying anything. You should never get involved in these things. My sister married this right bastard and she wouldn't be told anything.'

'What happened?' I asked.

'Oh, yeah, he turned out to be a right bastard. Left her with the kids and everything.'

'Oh, for God's sake, Mel!' burst out Angus. 'She's a complete bitch and you know it.'

I sighed.

'Sorry, forgive me if I'm being slow here, but you talk about her non-stop. I mean, why do you hate her so much? And Alex, and Charlie – well, it's OK to hate Charlie . . . But, I mean, when I met you, I thought you were really awful, 'cause you hated us all so much. But now I know you're not, you're actually really nice, so I don't understand it at all. Are you a secret communist? Do you hate posh people? You're posh anyway. Well, your brother's a complete nob . . . I didn't mean that last bit the way it sounded.'

'Have you finished?' asked Angus.

I thought for a second. 'Ehm . . . yes.'

He rubbed his eyes with the heel of his hands.

'Look,' he said, 'if I tell you something, do you promise on your life that you won't tell Fraser?'

The third bloke was still with us, unwilling to draw attention to himself by getting up and moving away, but embarrassed to be listening to something personal. He was staring very hard at the ashtray.

'Maybe,' I said. 'Maybe on my dog's life.'

'Be serious. You don't have a dog.'

'OK, no, I promise.'

He looked away. 'I overheard her. On her stupid minuscule mobile phone. When she came up to visit our mum a few weeks ago and behave patronizingly towards her. She had to lean out of the window to get a signal, and I was in the next room.'

'With a glass up against the wall?'

'With the window open. Look, do you want me to tell you or not?'

'Yes please,' I said meekly.

'Anyway, she was talking to *Hello!* magazine.'

He paused dramatically. I looked at him like he was crazy.

'*Hello!* magazine? That's it? You're trying to wreck their marriage before it even starts because of *Hello!* and its . . . its inane pictures of unhappy celebrities??'

He ignored me and went on.

'She was offering them the rights for the wedding. I heard her. She promised them she could "get Tara". You know, they love all that minor aristocracy bullshit. "Aren't Posh People Lovely? Here's a picture of one standing next to a horse." That kind of thing. Bitch!'

He grumbled into his pint.

'I don't understand,' I said. 'She was just trying to get her picture in the paper.'

'No,' he said slowly, as if I was an idiot. 'She asked them for £15,000 to let them take photos and have an –' he imitated her shrill tones – '"in-depth interview with me about the new castle . . . not much point talking to the aristo, darling – you know what they've got between the ears, hee hee."'

'Jesus. Did she get the money?'

He looked at me grimly.

'I don't know. Fraser certainly hasn't heard anything about it if she did.'

'No. You don't think she half-inched it do you?'

'You're talking about . . .' he turned away. 'You're talking about the woman who turned up, entirely by coincidence, in my brother's life a month after our dad dies, we're all completely fucking shell-shocked – still are – and guess what? He's blinking in the daylight and they're engaged. So she can get on the cover of fucking *Hello!* magazine. She's probably been through every Right Hon in the country. I think she's capable of it, don't you?'

'I'm sure that's not true,' I said, not sure at all. 'I'm sure she loves him.'

'Why? What, honestly, do you think someone like her sees in someone like him, apart from that stupid falling down piece of medieval crap in Kirkudbrightshire?'

I looked over. Fraser looked sweaty and dishevelled, and his curly hair was falling in his eyes. One arm was round his big pal Nash, the other round Amanda the blow-up doll, and they were all (the doll was faking it) singing 'Danny Boy' very very badly and making up the words.

'I think losing one member of her family's enough for my mum this year, don't you? That fucking title. Just because you're all modern women who can do anything, you think that kind of thing doesn't happen any more. But it does.'

He reverted to staring at his drink. His face was red. I stared hard at the table.

'I think we need another drink,' I said.

'I'll get them!' shouted the bloke at our table, jumping up and rushing across the pub. We both looked after him, startled. As we turned round, Fraser and Nash made a bravura attempt at the high note at the end of 'Danny Boy' then immediately fell away as, silhouetted in the doorway, stood the very wan, very dirty Johnny McLachlan, looking for all the world as though he had, indeed, just been mauled by a lioness.

A roar went up, as Johnny dazedly walked back amongst the tables with his eyes wide open. There was no sign of Fran behind him. He sat down, heavily at the bar, his eyes red.

'A large one, please.'

There was a crash as Nash and the doll fell over laughing. Everyone in the room was guffawing and clapping Johnny on the shoulder. I suddenly felt very much the lone female.

I picked up my drink and headed off to the loo, and to look for Fran. It was like one of those Agatha

Christie books, where the party gets picked off one by one. Everyone was extremely drunk now, and the whole scene was becoming confusing. I sat in the bathroom for a long time, fully dressed and staring intently at the dirty floor tiles while trying not to fall off the toilet.

I had no idea how long I'd been there when I heard someone get into the cubicle next to me.

'Fran!' I whispered urgently.

There was a long pause.

'Err . . . no. It's me.'

It was one of the brothers, but I couldn't tell which one. It sounded like Angus.

'What are you doing in here, you twat?'

'Oh, the boys loos are looking . . . pretty revolting. There's blood in them. Mixed with –'

'Oh, OK, I don't want to think about that right at the moment.'

'Sorry.'

'It's all right. Is that Angus?'

There was another pause.

'Erm . . . yes.'

'Oh. Look, I'm sorry about what I said. I'm really sorry. I didn't realize . . .'

'That's OK. I get a bit grumpy sometimes. I suppose it's because everyone thinks my brother's so great.'

I heard what sounded like a strangulated giggle, but chose to ignore it.

'Look, really I agree with you,' I said. 'I think Amanda's a cow, and you think Amanda's a cow, but your mate's right: there's no point in interfering, is there? People simply do things, whether you want them to or not. Tough. Who knows: maybe she's different with him than she is with everyone else on the planet.'

Suddenly the toilet next door flushed and the door banged. I gradually sat upright and let the blood flow back down from my head. Shakily, I opened the cubicle door. Shit.

'You lying fucker!' I yelled at him. I was furious.

Fraser was bright red. 'I just wanted to hear what you were going to say. What were you sorry about?'

'It's none of your fucking business was what I was going to say! I was talking to Angus, not you! What a stupid thing to do.'

'Right, just because you're too pissed to tell one voice from another.'

I stared at him. 'Oh, so it's my fault. What? I don't know. I don't know why I'm even having this conversation. I do NOT give a toss.' I headed out the door. He caught me.

'Look, I'm sorry. Please don't go.' There was a note of urgency in his voice.

'Fine!' I was on my high horse now. 'I can stay, go . . . I do NOT give a toss, remember?'

'Shush a minute. Please. I'm sorry.'

We stood there for a bit in silence. Then he set his lanky frame on the hand basins, his long legs kicking out in front. He got his arse wet, but didn't seem to notice.

'Is it true . . . ?' he faltered. 'I mean, do you . . . does everyone . . . ? Oh, fuck it.'

He took a deep breath and started again.

'Look, with Amanda and everything . . . I thought her and Angus just didn't hit it off. She point-blank refused to let him be my best man after he asked her why she was inviting all these people she barely knew just because they were famous.'

'Not Sean Connery's son?'

'Yes, people like that. Well, it's her job, isn't it?'

That sounded familiar.

'Ah mean,' he said quietly, 'you're practically her best friend. Don't you like her, either?'

His voice was so soft and sad I couldn't bear to hurt him.

'Sweetheart, she's not my best friend. I hardly see her. I hardly know her these days . . .'

I could tell by his face that that tack wasn't working. 'I mean, she's fine. Really, I've known her for ever . . . Look, do you remember at college, when I wanted to go out with Flattypuss Malloy? And you couldn't bear him because he had a lump on his neck?'

'It was gross! Really – especially from where I was standing.'

There was at least a foot's difference in height between us.

'And he was really nice after all?' I pursued.

'He was a lumpy bastard.'

'Well, sometimes people dislike other people without us understanding the reasons for it.'

'What happened to him, anyway?'

'I heard he painted a second face on it and rents himself out at parties.'

'Wow.'

We pondered that for a second. I looked at my reflection in the mirror. Either a mouse had walked across my face or I was having a seriously bad mascara attack.

I decided to make one last attempt.

'Look, when Amanda wants something,' I said, truthfully, 'she goes for it. She's completely single-minded and nothing holds her back.'

Quite unlike myself. I touched him gently on the face. His eyelashes cast a shadow on his cheek.

'So, therefore, she must really, really want you.'

He looked down at me with a wounded look in his eye.

'Do you really think so?'

'Yes, I do.'

He sighed.

'Do you love her terribly much?' I asked, suddenly longing for a bit of highly dramatic romance in my life.

'She's . . . you know, pretty and confident and, well, she knows lots of people and . . . stuff . . .' Fraser looked down. 'And, you know, she really wanted to marry me!'

'Was that so difficult to believe?'

He grinned. 'I don't know.'

* * *

We got a few limp 'Woah hos!' when we emerged from the ladies toilets together, but the single-entendre brigade was getting pretty tired, and the room was definitely a bleary party ready to go home. Fran was still nowhere to be seen, so I decided to brave it home alone . . .

I waved cheerily to Nash and found Angus in a corner, finishing a whisky contemplatively.

'I'm off,' I announced.

'Bye then.'

'Look, I'm sorry,' I said, for the second time that evening.

'What for?' he smiled wearily. 'We just had a discussion, that's all.'

'Yes, I suppose so.' I wasn't going to tell him about what happened in the loo . . .

'You never told me about . . .'

'What?'

'You never told me about Alex.'

'It's a long story.'

'So you said before. I've got lots of time.'

'Some other time then. Umm, when there's lots of it. And not tonight, when I have twenty-eight minutes and counting before I pass out wherever I am.'

I leaned in to kiss him good night. Unexpectedly, he put his arms round me and gave me a hug.

'Do you want me to come and find you a cab?'

'I'll be fine,' I said gratefully. 'This is Holborn, for God's sake – what are they going to do, sue me to death?'

'Goodnight then.'

I grinned, turned and left, before I could do something clumsy and spoil the moment.

Outside I spotted a cab and was just putting up my arm when I heard my name being called, weakly, from an alley.

Discounting the obvious, I assumed it was an evil spirit coming to reclaim me for the night, and jumped six feet in the air. When I saw the arm coming out of the alley, I discerned it was at least semi-human . . . I hoped.

I wandered over and crouched down beside the sorry specimen.

'Woooooooah, Alex! I came looking for you earlier – I thought you'd gone.'

'I wasn't feeling too well.'

'What on earth happened to you?'

'Um, he hit me. Then I felt a bit tired and had a sleep. Then I woke up and didn't know what to do. And then you came.'

'That's because I am in fact an angel from God,' I said severely. 'Can you stand up?'

I wanted to work out how bad a state he was in. Still pissed, he had a gorgeous black eye coming up, but his nice patrician nose remained in a nice patrician state, and I didn't think he'd broken anything too major. I hoisted him to his feet.

'And also, I was sick.'

'Aha, so you were!' I said, noticing suddenly, but managing not to drop him like a stone.

'Charlie?'

'Dunno.'

'Fran?'

'Dunno.'

I sighed.

'Come on, you.'

I hailed the cab. The driver slowed down, saw me half-carrying a bloody, vomity war victim and speeded up again.

'Bastard!' I yelled after it. 'Poxy poxy bastard.'

One freezing November hour later, all my pleasant, muddled, drunken feelings had evaporated and I was cursing London, cursing parties, cursing cab drivers, and especially cursing the enormous stinky sack of potatoes I had been delegated to haul around just because I was in love with it.

Finally we found a minicab driver too hashed up to care about the vomit – actually, judging from the smell of the cab, it was his speciality – and made it back to Kennington for 3.30 a.m. The entire building was silent and completely black.

Alex only wanted to get to bed, but he wasn't going anywhere near me in that state, so I dumped him fully clothed in the shower and turned the water on.

Instantly, he started to make a noise like a howling dog. I made a flying tackle through the air, which successfully cut off the howling, but not without pulling the shower curtain down. It fell with a huge clatter as I stood there, hand over his mouth, tilted at a horrible angle and getting soaking wet, with the curtain over us both like a huge ghost outfit, waiting for the entire neighbourhood to descend and throw shoes at me. Alex looked up at me, wide-eyed and lost, as I closed my eyes and tried to think where on earth I could possibly move to when I got summarily ejected from the flat.

Nothing happened. I flopped out from under the curtain and tilted my head like a fox. Not a sound. I pulled Alex out, having wiped most of the dried blood off his face. He stood there dumbly while I tried to silently fix the shower curtain then decided to ignore it and hope it went away by the morning.

Sunday was half over by the time I limped through into the kitchen desperate for fluid. I drank half a pint of milk – YUCK – which was all there was, and steeled myself to go check out the bathroom. It was immaculate, as if we'd never been in. The curtain was back up, the blood was washed away. I wondered for a second if I'd dreamt it, then shook my head to clear it.

'Ehm, Linda?'

I timidly knocked at her door. She opened it the way women do on *The Bill* when their men are escaping over the back fence.

'Yes?' She peered at me through her thick spectacles.

'I'm . . . sorry about the shower curtain.'

'S'OK.'

'I mean it . . . I'll, buy you another one, or . . . ehm, I'll buy you another one.'

'S'OK.'

I didn't want to get into a staring match with her, so I gradually backed away, feeling creepy, and went back to the bedroom with another glass of milk. Alex was still completely unconscious, and his eye was turning fluorescent.

'Alex,' I hissed, flopping down beside him. 'Alex! Wake up! I'm frightened of my anti-social flatmate! I think she's going to chop me up with an axe! And leave me here, and no one will find me for three weeks!'

'Pfnat.' Alex tried to open his eyes and realized he couldn't, because they'd been punched. He focused on the glass of milk, and his eyes bulged and his skin turned green.

'NO! Don't vomit!' I pulled the glass away. 'Again!'

His eyes slowly closed and he passed out.

'Great,' I thought to myself. 'Caught between the silent psycho and the unconscious phlegm machine.'

I had to get out of the flat. And, of course, I had to find out what had happened to Fran. I thought I'd go round rather than phone; get some fresh air and hangover supplies. Pulling on a pair of jeans and a couple of random jumpers, I wandered out into the frosty afternoon.

Fran lived in a practically empty bedsit, about half a mile down the road. It was white, immaculate and had absolutely nothing in it. This wasn't really a design statement: she had no imagination, and hated the place, which was why she practically lived around my house – it may have been full of psychos, but at least they were company. I set off manfully, stopping for some emergency Diet Coke infusions before I too vomited from a milk overdose. And a beer overdose, I suppose. The main door of the block was lying open as usual, and I made my way upstairs.

'Yoo hoo!' I yelled outside the door, banging on it loudly.

'Rise and shine, sweetie pie. We have BIG time gossip to do, ESPECIALLY you, Ms Yo-Yo Knickers.'

There were sounds from inside, and I could hear someone moving about.

'Come on!' I yelled impatiently. 'I need to find out about you and that skinny little twerp, and tell you about Angus and Fraser and everything.'

There was more noise on the other side of the door – what sounded like someone trying to pull on a pair of trousers, losing their balance, hopping about a bit then crashing over on to the floor.

It suddenly occurred to me that she may not, in fact, be in there alone. I tried to remember what had happened to Johnny McLachlan when he'd returned to the bar. Shit! He must have left and come back here! Argh! I hoped he hadn't heard me call him a twerp. And she didn't even know he was married! Or – yikes! – we hadn't found out what had happened to Charlie. Maybe she'd gone back on her shag-to-death routine for once. Wow, she'd be annoyed. Oh no, the married man or the prick! *Too* many cocktails.

I leaned into the door.

'Erm . . . d'you want me to go away and come back later . . . ?'

It was too late: Fran had already swung the door open. She stood there, looking exhausted, with a man's shirt on and a towel round her waist. I grimaced.

'I can go away, you know. It's no problem.'

'Hello, Mel,' she said wearily. 'No, I suppose it's OK.'

She drew back her arm from the door, and I entered the fuggy, darkened room – to see, of all people, Angus, looking extremely sheepish indeed, checking the zip on his flies was done up properly.

'!' I expostulated.

We stared at each other. He flushed beetroot, and I tried to recover myself.

'Hi!' I said brightly, shooting a fierce look at Fran.

'Hullo,' said Angus, looking at the floor. He pretended to look at his watch. 'Ehmmm . . . I'd better go . . . I told Fraser I was going to . . . ehm, help him pick a cravat.'

I nodded slowly. We all stood stock-still, until Fran realized it was her cue to take his shirt off. He practically grabbed it, and buttoned it up at lightning speed.

Fran, refusing to look embarrassed, stood poised in her bra. For a moment, I thought she was going to shake him by the hand and thank him very much for coming, as it were.

Angus left, stuttering. I left it a full half-second and turned round.

'WHAT the FUCK was that?!!!??'

'Oh for goodness' sake, Melanie, no need to get so overexcited.'

'Overexcited?? Me?? I'm not the one who managed to shag two people in an eight-hour period.'

'Neither am I, darling. Shall I put the kettle on?'

'Huh? What on earth is up with you?'

Fran walked around the small room pulling up blinds and opening windows, before putting the coffee maker on. I was standing in the middle of the room, wringing my hands in frustration.

'Tell me!' I begged her. 'I thought it was my job to get drunk and misbehave!'

Fran looked dreamily out of the window until I wanted to kill her. She'd always been fairly mercenary in her dealings with the opposite sex, but this was just too bizarre – first Charlie, then Johnny and now Angus, of all people. My new friend Angus, who, I had to admit to myself, I thought had rather liked me, (1), and (2) I had thought was rather noble.

Finally the coffee was ready and she sat down beside me in her 'Frankie Says Relax' T-shirt, which still fitted her.

'Please, Fran,' I said, trying to sound calm, 'just tell me what's going on. Are you on a special mission from space to sleep with everyone we know?'

She patted me gently on the hand. 'It's not what you think.'

'What, there are animals involved as well?'

'No.'

'What then?'

'Well, you know I was being a lioness?'

'Oh yes. So in fact there *are* animals . . .'

'Johnny wasn't quite up to being a lion.'

'I'm not surprised. You practically ripped his head off.'

'That is not true.' She shot me a sharp look. 'We'd gone outside . . .'

'Yeah, to get arrested.'

'. . . for a breath of fresh air . . .'

I snorted.

'. . . and before we'd gone two yards, he burst into tears.'

'Honestly, Frannie, that does not surprise me.'

'Mel, does anyone ever tell you that you talk too fucking much?'

'Ehm, yes, actually. Quite a lot. Funny, Alex was saying just the other day that I always talk more when . . . I'm –' I saw her thunderstruck face – 'nervous,' I finished.

Fran harrumphed. 'Anyway. He burst into tears and said he hated his wife and his life and his job and I was the nicest thing that had ever happened to him and how depressing everything was and this was the only party he'd been to for eight years and how I had no idea what it was like teaching geography day in day out to a bunch of illiterate animals.'

She paused, waiting for me to comment, but I wasn't saying anything.

'We ended up in the bar downstairs, with me having

the most boring, sober three hours ever, listening to someone else's ghastly life.'

'Why didn't you escape, and come and find me? I was having a great time.'

'Every time I made the slightest move, he started weeping into his pint again and saying I was the best friend he'd ever had.'

'Oh no.'

'Honestly, Mel,' she looked at me haggardly, 'have you any idea how much I know about the amount of paperwork involved in the National Curriculum?'

'Well, it'll come in handy if you ever play Miss Jean Brodie,' I said encouragingly.

'So, finally, I decided I was going to have to leave before I started plunging a fork into my thigh. And then he tried to get off with me!'

'Well, you can understand it from his point of view.'

'Cheeky bastard! If he's going to be a pale and interesting stranger, that's fine. If he's going to bore the tits off me for three hours about his wife, then he can go piss up a rope, as far as I'm concerned.'

'You are possibly the kindest person I've ever known.'

She sighed. 'I *know*. So, I sent him off with a flea in his ear.'

'Did you hit him?'

'Not that hard. Whining little toad! Then I sat and had a drink or two. And then I came back upstairs again, looking for you.'

'I stayed to the end, so I must have just gone.'

'You had – I saw you from the window, dragging Alex up the road.'

'And you didn't come and help?'

'It was freezing out there.'

'Yes, it was, thanks.'

'And there was almost no one left in the bar except for Angus, who was propping himself up with some double whiskies.'

'I know, I saw him before I left.'

'He looked pretty miserable, so I started talking to him.'

'Did he mention me at all?'

'Ehm, no, not at all.'

'Oh. OK.'

'Why?'

'No reason.'

'Huh.' She gave me another sharp look. 'Anyway, he was pretty drunk, so I let him stay here. And that's the end of it.'

I was extremely relieved.

'So, you didn't sleep with him?'

'Oh well, yes, I slept with him.'

'You are dreadful!'

'I'm dreadful? Who's worse, Angus or Nicholas?'

'That's not the point.'

'That's exactly the point. Anyway, it's hardly serious.'

'You don't even fancy him. You think he looks like a dog.'

'It was you that thought that.'

'Was it?' I couldn't remember thinking that now.

Except in the sense of dogs being strong but kind, I suppose. Hang on, dogs didn't have those qualities. What on earth was I thinking about . . . ?

'How's Alex?' asked Fran, sipping her coffee.

'Who? Oh, I think he's OK.' I told her about the shower.

'I hope he's not concussed or anything,' I said suddenly. 'Oh my God! What if he's in a coma for years, all because I didn't take him to the hospital!'

'Then I could perform my special little happy dance,' said Fran. 'Now, drink your coffee and I'll tell you what Angus is like in bed.'

And she did.

I left Fran an hour or so later so she could get some much needed sleep, and walked home, my head spinning.

After buying bacon and eggs, I let myself into the flat quietly. I couldn't hear anything. I was about to tiptoe into the kitchen when there came a sorrowful groan.

'Mel . . . is that you?'

I peeped into my bedroom, which reeked of whisky.

'Alex?'

'Yes . . .' he said weakly.

I sat down next to him on the bed. His eye had gone red and purple and green, but wasn't swollen shut any more.

'How are you feeling?' I asked tenderly.

'Like I've been run over by the Death Star.'

'Oh, sweetheart. Can I get you anything?'

'No milk, please,' he said. Then he half smiled. 'Were we awful?'

'You were naughty, and your friend was evil.'

He laughed, and then winced.

'We didn't mean anything. We just went to the rugby and had a few pints . . .'

'And then chaos happened. Amazing that, isn't it?'

He forced a slow grin. 'How awful?'

'You didn't do anything you didn't pay for.'

'I could have had him, you know.'

'Course you could, sweetheart.'

'If I met him again, I'd take him . . .' He reached out for me sleepily, and I let myself be grabbed.

'I'm the most tolerant girlfriend in the world, you know.'

'I know,' he said, asleep. 'I know.'

Nine

I was absolutely desperate for somebody to talk to at work, but the prospects weren't good. Only Cockney Boy, whose name was, inevitably, Steve, bothered to ask me how the stag went.

'It was great,' I said. 'Turned out the stripper was gay and I copped off with her.'

'Yeah?' he grunted, his eyes wide as saucers.

'No.'

'Lezzie cow! Probably couldn't cop off with anyone,' he muttered under his breath.

'Not true, actually. Normally I let the boys watch. But only the ones I like . . . so, tough luck!'

He grimaced at me and went back to his work, which as far as I could tell was mostly colouring in.

'How are you doing, Janie?' I asked her, using

the soft, invalid voice I reserved for the troubled of heart.

'Well,' she said bravely, 'he had a ticket for the rugby on Saturday, but came to Ikea instead.'

'See? He loves you. Anyway, I was at this party on Saturday night, right . . .'

'But then he didn't want to go to the Homes and Houses Exhibition at Earls Court . . .' She started to sniffle a bit. 'And he didn't come round until the end of *Football Focus*! When it was too late to go!'

I stared at her. 'Are you bonkers? You can't take him to the Homes and Houses Exhibition after two months. You can't ever take him to the Homes and Houses Exhibition. Jesus! You're going to have to stop reading the bloody *Daily Mail*. Anyway, there was this bloke at the party who I thought quite liked me, right, but he went off with my best mate. And I can't fancy him anyway, because my boyfriend is terrific and I'm completely in love with him. But he's – the first boy, not my boyfriend – trying to sabotage his brother's wedding and he wants me to help him. Apart from which, he's really nice. But, obviously, I'm in love with my boyfriend. But I'm really pissed off that the first bloke slept with my mate. Almost like I was jealous – if I got jealous, which, really, I don't. So, what do you think I should do?'

She stared at me, mouth open.

'Apart from take them both to the Homes and Houses Exhibition and see which one can find the hardest-wearing carpet?'

Unbelievably, she had tears welling up again.

'I only wanted to look at cushions. Cushions aren't too committed, are they?'

Arrgh! This was it. I was going to have to phone the Samaritans and ask them. Although, knowing my luck, they'd only give me lip or be completely distracted. I put on my martyred expression and turned towards Janie in a saintly fashion.

'Ookaay. So, first of all, why wouldn't you let him go to the rugby? He's a boy. Boys need rugby. Believe me, I know.'

She blinked at me. 'Do you let your boyfriend go?'

'Sure!'

'And it's OK?'

I reflected on this for a bit. I didn't want to say: *Well, apart from the beating and being insulting to strippers and throwing up on yourself and sleeping rough* . . .

'Sure!' I said. God, if he would only hurry up and leave her, so I could talk about my problems for a change.

'You know what you should do, dolls,' said Cockney Boy, who had somehow been managing to colour in and listen to our conversation at the same time. 'You should both learn to play rugby, yeah? Then you birds can run around the pitch yourself, getting all covered in mud and stuff. That way everyone will be happy – the blokes can watch the rugby, and you'd be, roight, playin' . . .'

We both turned and stared at him.

'You spent an awful long time alone in your bedroom as a teenager, didn't you?' I asked him.

'No,' he pouted. 'No, I didn't.'

'Day after day, just staring at the wall, picking your spots and listening to your Phil Collins albums.'

'Oh, shut up.'

'Dreaming of the day Linda Lusardi comes past and accidentally breaks down in front of your little Cockney house.'

He held up his arms and walked off. 'I don't have to listen to this.'

'Oh, Steve, Steve, thank you for fixing my car . . . what can I, Linda Lusardi, possibly do for you in return?'

He turned at the door and flicked me a V-sign. But he was smiling a little bit. I hoped.

I had three messages. One was from Fran, wanting to know what to wear to Amanda's hen night. If she thought she was going to that, she had another think coming. In fact, neither was I, given that I liked both my eyes the way they were, thank you.

The second was Alex, who had 'just called to say good morning, pumpkin.' He'd been terribly soppy since Saturday. Which was a good thing, clearly, although slightly unusual. Previously, in fact, unheard of. He sounded practically wimpy!

The third one started oddly. There was a long pause, and it kind of went 'urrr'. Then a throat was cleared noisily, and then apologized for. I realized who it was.

'Angus,' I said into the phone, even though it was only a message. 'Don't worry. It's only me. Yes, I do think you're a plonker, but that's OK. I don't mind.'

'Erm, hullo there, ehm, this is Angus. Umm, Angus McConnald.'

Ah, *that* Angus.

'So, really, Ah just wondered how you were going after Saturday night, and, ehmm, whether you wanted to go to lunch or something to talk about, you know . . . just for a chat . . . I won't talk about the wedding or anything . . .' There was a pause on the answerphone. 'Well, maybe a bit about the wedding . . . They can't . . . Oh God. Well, anyway . . . give me a ring on 555 2127. Sorry, 0171 555 2127. Poncey sodding English codes. Right. Sorry. OK. Bye.'

He wasn't going to let this alone, I could tell. Neither would Fran. I kind of wished they'd leave me out of it, but I hated being left out of things. Also, something in me wanted to see him again. I didn't phone him back right away, but I wrote his number in my address book in ink.

'We've been invited,' went on Fran, 'so, you know, we turn up and do something. The Hensterminators.'

'That's not even funny.'

'Maybe we could get that stripper to turn up at Quagli's.'

We'd met for a council of war. Or rather, Fran had come over to try and get me to do stuff, and Alex was at the flat anyway. I'd told Fran what Angus had said at the stag night, and she was excited at the potential for devilment, and more convinced than ever that we were in the service of the right by trying to bugger things up, even a bit. I wasn't quite so sure. Alex was reading *The Sunday Times* and couldn't give a toss.

The phone rang. I picked it up, then put my hand over the receiver and popped my head round the living-room door.

'It's Angus!' I hissed to Fran. Two phone calls in two days, I was thinking. I internally hugged myself with glee. I knew I was right. I'd thought maybe he had a little crush on me. Would have to be pretty little, though, for him to have copped off with Fran so quickly. I hated the nineties. A bit of courtly love would not have gone amiss. He should have worshipped me for about ten or fifteen years and then been happy with a mere flower, or something.

Fran shrugged.

'Well,' I said, 'shall I ask him to come over?'

'Why on earth would I mind?'

'I don't know . . . ehm, he's seen you from the inside?'

Alex looked up from the sports pages with his eyebrows raised, but then he'd known Fran for a while.

'Honestly, it's not a big deal,' she said. 'I'd like to see him. He's nice. And he can join in our plan.'

'Hmm.' I wasn't sure how closely I wanted those two working together.

'Hey!' I rejoined the phone call with an alacrity which betrayed exactly what I'd been doing.

'Why don't you come over? We're only sitting about drinking wine and being small-minded about people we know.'

'Aye, OK.'

I gave him the address, expecting him to take hours to find it and arrive cursing our poncey southern road system, but he made it in about half an hour, armed with a couple of helpful bottles of wine. Him and Alex smiled fixedly at each other and shook hands, whereupon Alex said, 'I think I'll let you three get on with ripping everyone to shreds,' and returned to his paper.

'Wooo,' said Fran, 'Mr Perfect strikes again.'

'OK, stop nipping at each other, you two.'

Fran shot him a final dirty look then joined us on cushions on the floor.

'So!' said Angus through clenched teeth. He'd obviously been thinking about what to say.

'This isn't at all embarrassing, is it?'

'What isn't?' said Fran.

I kicked her on the ankle. 'No, it's not,' I added. Fran smiled sweetly, leaving Angus looking uncomfortable.

'How's Fraser?' I asked.

'He's fine. Recovered. She's' – there was no mistaking the intonation: it sounded like how people used to talk about Margaret Thatcher – 'making him choose dinner patterns. Then every time he chooses one she tells him it's wrong.'

'I love that game,' I said.

Fran stretched herself out on the floor and turned to face the ceiling, arms behind her head.

'Look, why don't you just tell him. Go up and say, "Fraser, don't marry her, she's a bitch. She's a skinny-rumped, dyed-haired bitch bitch bitch. She's a complete and utter utter utter bitch. If she was a president, she'd be Bitchaham Lincoln."'

'What's your point?'

'If she was a cowboy, she'd be Bitch Cassidy.'

'Fran, that's a pretty subtle idea. But I think Angus might have already tried it, somehow.'

Angus half tilted his head.

'Kind of. I didn't do the whole bitch song, though.'

'Well, what happened?'

'He looked at me like a mopey dog and said,' – sincere voice – '"Angus, you two just haven't hit it off. Believe me, she's sweet. It's going to be OK."'

'Argh!' said Fran. 'I can't believe there's anything I hate more in the world than women men think are sweet but who are actually complete BITCHES!'

Alex rustled his paper and peered over the top of it. 'Really? What about women who can't stop bitching and shouting all day?'

'Oh yeah? What about men who run off to America and fuck their girlfriends about?'

I froze.

The way I heard Fran – and she always said everything on purpose – well, I suppose I'd assumed, guessed that Alex had been up to all sorts of things when he was away, but, well, I'd never known for sure, and I'd thought . . . I looked at him, already knowing that my eyes were full of tears, the kind that I tried to swallow until it hurt. Fran leaned over, suddenly worried about what she'd said.

'Melanie . . .'

Alex threw down his paper and stormed off. I

thought he was just going to leave – forever, probably. My throat felt as if I was being strangled.

Obviously not quite knowing what to do, Alex stormed back in the room again and nodded for me to follow him, but I was paralysed.

'Come on,' he said sharply. I stood up and walked out with him to the hall. He grabbed me and put his arms tightly around me, then tilted his forehead against mine, trying to regain his cool.

'Your friend really, really hates me, doesn't she?'

'Yes,' I said, biting my lower lip. I almost couldn't ask.

'D-did you?' I quavered.

'Mel, you know I had to discover myself. Try new things. So I could work out where I belonged. Here. With you.'

I dropped his very close gaze and stared fiercely at the ground.

'America . . . it feels like a different life to me now. I did tons of things there I wouldn't do here. Daft, meaningless things. You've got to believe me, pumpkin.'

I wanted to, so much.

'You're so special – I keep telling you that, but you don't believe in yourself. Look, hey, I came all the way back for you, right? You know how messed up my head is. But here I am!'

I looked him in the eye again. He seemed so sincere, so desperate to make it all right. He was nearly in tears himself.

'Please, Mel.'

We stared at each other for a long time.

'It's all right,' I said finally. 'It's all right. It was a long time ago.'

'Do you mean that? Fantastic you?'

'Yes,' I said quietly.

'I thought about you all the time,' he said.

'Really? I didn't think about you at all.' I forced a laugh.

'All that crap is over now, I promise. From now on, it's just you and me. In fact, if you could only dump that Fran character, it would be absolutely perfect.'

'Lex, she's my best friend.'

'And I'm not?'

'You're my soul mate, remember?'

'Oh, yes.'

I had to ask.

'Do you love me, Alex?'

He smiled and kissed me full on the mouth.

'Ah shags you, don't Ah?' he said in exaggerated Cockney.

'Just tell me.'

'Pet, as much as I love anyone, I love you.'

He left after that. I stood by the door, not wanting to return to the sitting room quite yet. There was a stack of post on a ghastly occasional table. I never bother looking at it usually; bills I let Linda take care of, and everything else she usually flicks under my door. But I leafed through it listlessly, wondering how many animal charities there are in the world. Suddenly I drew out an envelope addressed to Alex, care of me. It was stiff, white card. How bizarre. Underneath, there was one for me too.

It occurred to me immediately what these were – the wedding invites! After all, how many stiff card envelopes did I normally get? (This was my first.) I could put it on the mantelpiece! Except Linda had already covered it with miniature glass kittens.

I walked back into the living room. Angus and Fran were watching me with obvious concern.

'I'm sorry!' Fran yelled immediately, to get it in.

'I'm fine,' I said, sitting down to pour another glass of wine.

'I was only guessing, Mel. I didn't even think . . .' Fran looked absolutely stricken. I patted her on the hand.

'Come on outside. I need to tell you something.'

She followed me.

'Fran, don't worry. If anything, it did more good than harm. He . . .' I felt a bit shy and crap. 'I didn't want to say this in front of Angus, but . . . he said he loves me. For the first time.'

'That weasel?' Fran was immediately scornful again. 'He doesn't love anyone but himself.'

I shot her a look that said she wasn't forgiven.

'OK, OK, I'll stop. I'm pleased for you. I really am.'

'Look, Fran, I mean it: are you going to stop being so horrid whenever he's around?'

Fran groaned.

'Are you? I mean, it's driving him crazy – and me.'

'OK. OK. If that's what you really want, I'll curb my natural instincts towards that creep.'

I gave her a friendly squeeze. 'Fran, I'd love your natural instincts – if only they weren't those of a cornered cougar.'

She snarled at me affectionately. We headed back in.

'Do you two always live in such pitched drama?' asked Angus, who was quietly toying with his wine.

'Hang on – which one of us is trying to sabotage an entire wedding again? Oh, it's you, isn't it?' I reminded him. 'Ooh, which reminds me – look!'

I drew out the envelopes.

'Invitations?' Fran made a grab for them. 'How come you got two separate ones?'

'They can afford it, I suppose,' I said airily, opening mine.

I gazed at the gold-rimmed card in shock.

'That bitch!'

'What?'

'Look!'

Fran took it from me.

'Twenty fucking years! That BITCH!'

Joan and Derek Phillips, the card said, *invite you to the post-reception of the wedding of their daughter Amanda Serena Phillips to Fraser Alasdair McConnald at Pyrford Manor on December 21st. A coach will be available to pick up guests from Central London at 4.30 p.m. Formal dress will not be required.*

Fran and I stared at each other. Then she tore into Alex's. Sure enough, it said: *Joan and Derek Phillips invite you to the wedding of their daughter Amanda Serena Phillips to Fraser Alasdair McConnald at Pyrford village church, noon on December 21st, after which lunch at Le Coq Fantastique, followed by dancing at Pyrford Manor. Morning Dress.*

Enclosed with both of them was a wedding list, placed at Heal's. The cheapest thing on it was three hundred quid.

Fran and I stared at each other.

'OK,' I said to Angus. 'What do we have to do to fuck this wedding up the bum?'

'It's only fair,' added Fran. 'For years and years of all that shit she used to pull at school.'

I winced in remembrance. 'For that time she got the boys to hold us still while she pulled our hair.'

'For that time she insisted on taking our dinner money and giving it to charity,' hissed Fran.

'For that time she wouldn't own up to stealing the teacher's ruler and I took the blame.'

'For that time she told Stacey Norton I wanted to fight with her.'

Angus was watching us, agape.

'For that time she told on you for stealing lipstick from Woolworths!'

'Oh yes!' Fran remembered. 'For that time we were meant to be going to the pictures and she didn't want to go and pretended to be sick until it was too late and we missed it.'

'Aargh!' I said. 'That time she got into that nightclub and I didn't, and she didn't come back for me!'

'That time she got off with Legsy Forters just because you liked him!'

I buried my head under the cushion. 'Legsy! Legsy!' We were getting hysterical.

'Let's do it!' shouted Fran. 'For every mean little thing that bitch has ever done, let's do it.'

I was fired up. 'Yeah!'

We turned to look at Angus, who was backing away with a scared look on his face.

'You know, girruls, we only have to reason with them, not blow them up or anything.'

I opened the third bottle of wine.

'OK, we need a plan.'

'Well, we're going to the hen night,' said Fran.

'No we are not.' I shot her a dangerous look.

'Fine. If you want to stay at home and smooch with the love of your life, so be it. I'm going there for reconnaissance. And I'm going in wired.'

Nobody said anything.

'You're what?'

'You heard. Wire me up. I'll tape what she talks about and, if it's suitably evil, we'll play it back to Fraser. Painful, but effective.'

There was a further pause.

'That is absolutely brilliant!' said Angus.

'Well, I'd better come too then,' I volunteered. 'Um . . . you'd never get in otherwise.'

'Bet I could.'

'Stoap it, youse two. I've already got one partnership headache on my hands. OK, Francesca, that's an excellent idea.'

I was watching them closely for some hint of sexual tension, but it was as if nothing had ever happened.

'You'll need to wear something baggy, so it doesn't show.'

'I haven't got anything baggy. How do those tarty TV babes do it?'

'Doesn't matter. We'll sort something out.'

'Hang on,' I said. 'What if they aren't sitting together? There's going to be hundreds of people at this bash.'

'Well, you're both just going to have to be really friendly.'

Fran sneered. 'Yeah, given that she didn't even ask us in the first place, that's going to be easy.'

I had a flash of inspiration. 'I know! You could pretend you're completely pished and pass out underneath the table at her feet! Then you'll catch everything.'

Both of them looked at me with surprised faces.

'Maybe you could do that bit,' said Fran. 'Then we wouldn't have to pretend.'

'Ha ha ha,' I said sulkily.

'OK, right, just try and stay close to her and make sure she does a speech,' said Angus excitedly. 'Then we'll play it to Frase and he'll come to his senses!'

'How will he know we haven't taped the Queen's Christmas message? That's what she sounds like,' I said.

'Doesn't matter. Doesn't matter.'

I was pretty excited all week after that. Well, we had a mission now. The following night, Alex and I went out for a very cosy romantic dinner. He thought the plan was on the childish side, but I didn't mind so much about that. And he had an interview for a job, at a record company, which meant things were looking up. He lived rent-free at Charlie's gaffe, though, and got regular influxes of guilt money from both parents, so he was never going to starve. I toyed with my mussels and gazed out the window of Café Rouge – OK, not exactly the Ritz, but it would do for now.

Late-night opening, Fran and I went to find a microphone, which was easier said than done, especially in the high street electrical outlets.

'Have you got a small mike?' I asked the glazed-eyed brat standing next to the door. He looked blankly at the CD shelves and nervously pretended to look for something that clearly wasn't there.

'Eh, um, naow.'

'What's this?' asked Fran, smiling sweetly and picking up a microphone.

'Yeah, it's a mike, yeah.' The boy scratched himself nervously. Where did they grow these morons?

'Have you got any small ones?' Fran continued to encourage him.

'That's, uh, as small as they go, like.' I noticed the damp patches under his arms.

'So . . . what's this, then?' said Fran, picking up a smaller mike. I grimaced at her to stop.

The boy stood there, staring straight ahead in a catatonic state to avoid answering the question. I wondered if he ever got punched.

'Look,' I said to the boy, 'it's simple: we just want

a tiny microphone, like they have on TV – you know, TV? – that we can attach to a Walkman to tape something with.'

He focused again, and came out of about-to-be-punched mode. 'I'll . . . I'll check out the back.'

And he disappeared. For ever. Finally, Fran growled at an assistant manager long enough for him to sell us one.

She tried it on in the nearest wine bar, slotting the tape machine inside her jeans and the mike tucked inside her shirt. Then we disappeared into a toilet cubicle together to check whether it was working or not.

'God, you've got noisy tits,' I told her, rather too loudly.

'Shh! For God's sake. Now, hang on.' She wound the tape back and switched it on. And sure enough, there it was, slightly muffled: the boring conversation between two old bankers who'd been sitting next to us. Every word of their interminable discussion about insurance rates was clearly distinguishable. We grinned at each other over the seedy loo.

'Partying again?' said Cockney Boy on Friday morning, clocking my little glittery bag and spare pair of tights. 'You'll be turning into a right alcoholic at this rate.'

'What, you mean I'll feel ill in the mornings? I thought that was just the effect of seeing you.'

'You think you're well funny, don't you?'

'Actually, no. But as long as I'm annoying you, I don't care.'

He went and got himself and Janie a cup of coffee and didn't get me one. Bastard.

I was very worried about the night ahead. What if Amanda hadn't booked for us? What if she wouldn't let us in? What if everything cost £100 and we couldn't afford it? – Fran was permanently skint anyway.

And what on earth did we think we were doing? I mean, she deserved it in principle, but surely our interference wasn't going to make much difference: people would do what they were always going to do, except they'd hate me into the bargain.

I sighed deeply over my copy. Really, I wanted to stop my life for a moment, get off and catch my breath, then start again, instead of dashing on headlong. I tried to do some deep breathing exercises, but after thirty seconds I realized I was bored rigid, and if I stopped to think about everything that was going on I'd probably end up in a catatonic state listening to people pity me as they loaded me into an ambulance. So I phoned Fran and arranged what time I'd meet her.

Ten

Despite the cold, there was a buzz about the West End at eight o'clock on a Friday night. People had a set look on their faces, as if Fun was in serious trouble if they didn't find it. Students on some ghastly rag week spectacular were irritating passers-by, running around with buckets and pints and their legs tied together.

Fran was uncharacteristically nervous. 'This is going to be a laugh, isn't it?'

I didn't want to share my own misgivings. Going into a roomful of strangers predisposed to hating you, trying to ingratiate yourself, then taping the conversation – not my idea of a great night out.

'Course it is,' I said. 'Think of it as a great acting role. Your début in the West End.'

She grinned. 'If anything goes wrong, we leg it, OK?'

'Let's go, Mulder.'

'OK, Scully.'

We pushed open the heavy doors of the restaurant. Stiff napery and mirrors stretched for miles. The light was expensively dim and golden.

'God, not McDonald's again!' I whispered to Fran. She smiled, tilted her head, and with cut-glass drama school English and an imperious gait, walked over to the maître d', and smiled.

'The Phillips party, please.'

'Certainly, madame. Follow me.'

He led us through tables of elegant women and corpulent old gents. Everything tinkled and glistened, and heads turned to look at Fran, who kept her head high and looked as if she owned the place.

Tucked in a banquette in the corner were several manes of straight blonde hair. I stiffened.

'Amanda, darling!' Fran went over and gave her a kiss, careful not to get too close in case Amanda felt the wire, while also trying to avoid Amanda's very elaborate lip gloss.

I studied the pert little face intently. If she was annoyed to see us, she certainly wasn't showing it.

'Hello there, darlings!' Actually, there were some signs of strain. Looking round, I soon realized why.

We were half an hour late – we couldn't bear to walk in on our own – and all along the banquette there were places laid. There must have been thirty, stretching a quarter of the way up the restaurant.

However, surrounding Amanda there were five people, all identikit blonde types.

'Where is everyone?' I asked, and immediately wished I hadn't.

Amanda smiled sharply. 'Oh, they'll be joining us later on – most people have so much on in London at the weekend!'

'Oh, well, yes, of course.' I sat down and bit into a breadstick to stop myself biting her.

Fran sat next to Amanda, her brown hair bobbing in a sea of blonde.

'Introduce us to everyone, then.' She was plainly making the effort.

'Well, this is Jacintha, Araminta, Veronica, Larissa, and Mookie.'

'Hello, everyone!' said Fran gracefully.

'Umm . . . hello, Mookie,' I said.

There was an embarrassed silence.

'Right,' said Amanda. 'Din-dins!'

Fran and I shot each other a nervous glance as we picked up the menu. Sure enough, everything inside looked exceptionally complicated and extremely expensive. I found something that looked just about do-able, then realized it was the side vegetables. I hated thinking of all the cool stuff I could have bought instead.

Amanda waved over the waiter professionally.

'Four bottles of Bollinger,' she said crisply. 'For starters. And a bottle of Perrier for me.'

Fran and I shot each other a glance of pure terror at this latest development. Amanda caught it. 'Don't worry, girls, it's all on me,' she announced. 'It's so good to see my real friends.'

Her tone was tinged with disappointment, and I almost felt sorry for her, especially if she was including Fran and I in that analysis. Plus, the other five were so bland and identical-looking they only really counted as one person. So, quite a sad state of affairs really. I looked at the menu with renewed vigour and sampled my newly poured glass of Bollinger. What the heck, I thought. Friends were friends wherever you found them. And champagne was champagne and posh nosh was posh nosh, so I was bloody well about to enjoy myself.

'To Amanda!' I proposed, almost despite myself. 'And her gorgeous hubby-to-be.'

'Lady Amanda Phillips-McConnald,' squawked one of the blondies – Jacintha, I think. 'How absolutely glamorous!'

'Shame about the hubby!' squealed another one, and they all burst out laughing, and tinkled their glasses.

I ordered expensive pâté for starters and some very complex beef thing for the main course. I could also see the pudding trolley and was looking forward to it. Fran went for some extremely rare fish – unique, by the price of it – and young lamb. The other six ordered plain salads with lemon juice.

'Come on, girls!' I said jovially. 'I thought we were celebrating! What are you having to eat?'

They looked at me and giggled like I'd just made the most enormous joke.

'God, you wouldn't believe the size of my thighs in the mirror last week!' said one of them.

'Jesus, I know. I thought I was going to break eight stone!'

They all gasped in unison.

'I'm not eating more than five milligrams of fat a week until the wedding,' insisted Amanda.

'Five milligrams? You'll die!' I said in horror. 'Or you'll look like you're about to. Between you and Frase, you're practically two-dimensional anyway.'

She smiled gracefully at this mention of her life partner and went back to the juicy details of who was and who wasn't throwing their guts up daily in the cause of national celebrity.

'Well, you know she's on TV every day; she has to look thin all the time. I've heard she lives on Diet Coke, Dexedrine and dipsomania!'

The blonde brigade laughed themselves stupid as the waiter put down our starters. Suddenly, I was extremely conscious of my thighs rubbing together, and didn't feel hungry at all. I drank some more champagne. Fran looked at me enquiringly, then plunged in. She had one cooking ring in her bedsit, so didn't get around to cordon bleu that often.

The girls were now looking expectantly at my foie gras; salivating, I was sure of it. Even the cold toast would have been enough for them. To distract myself, I turned to the nearest blonde.

'So, what do you do?'

'Oh, telly, you know.'

I didn't, actually.

'Really, who for?'

'Oh, documentary programming. Terribly dull, really.'

'It doesn't sound dull. What have you worked on?'

'Ectually, I . . . it's more research ectually.'

Amanda nudged me from the other side.

'Araminta finds guests for *Trisha*,' she said, in a stage whisper. 'She doesn't like to talk about it.'

'Ohh. OK.'

Araminta was dabbing at her mouth with a napkin, although she hadn't eaten anything. I think I'd upset her. Still, the distraction was enough to get stuck into my food, which was absolutely glorious.

I obviously had upset her, as she immediately lit up a Marlboro Light and drew on it deeply. As if on cue, the other five did the same. I saw my pâté disappear below a wreath of anxious smoke.

'So,' she shrugged, 'what about you?'

'Oh, I lead Arctic biochemical expeditions.'

'Rally?'

Conversation over, she turned back to the blonde on our other side, and I said 'Fuck!' several times under my breath.

'So, anyway, I was in Gucci,' started one, 'and I told him; I said, "If Meg Matthews is wearing it, I want nothing to do with it, OK?" That told him.'

'Yah!' nodded all the heads around the table. In amazement I noticed Fran nodding vigorously too. What on earth was she on about?

'I mean, she's like the Antichrist, yah? Just do the opposite of what she does and you'll be all right?'

'And Kate hates her, apparently,' joined in another.

'I think she's fat,' said one.

'Are you kidding? She looks like she's been flayed!' I said.

Silence reigned. However, they were well brought up girls, and tried to be deliberately polite to us shitkickers.

'Oh, you know, I am going to be in a film after all!' yelled one suddenly. Fran's ears pricked up. 'Yah, Daddy stumped up a major stake. He'll never see it again, of course, but the director's so hunky, and apparently Rufus is interested.'

'Put the fork down,' I tried to psychically send to Fran, 'just put it down and no one will get hurt.'

She was coping well, even if she did look a bit strained. I still hadn't had a chance to ask her if she was going to see Angus again. Not that I should care. But she normally told me everything, and she'd hardly talked about this at all. Maybe it was only a drunken fumble that had passed.

Amanda was talking about the floral arrangements for the service, and I could see the caged look in Fran's eyes. Fearing for Amanda's safety, I distracted her.

'So, what's Fraser wearing for the big day then?'

'Oh God, he can't dress himself at all.'

'I like Converse trainers,' Fran interjected.

'Yes, well, some people like lager and some people like champagne, Francesca.'

Fran made clawing motions behind her back.

'Daddy took him to his tailor, so at least he'll look semi-decent.'

'Is he excited?'

'About what? Going to a tailor?'

'About the wedding, stupid.'

Amanda looked contemplatively at her glass.

'I suppose so.'

I shot a completely overt look at Fran, who raised her eyes to heaven and nodded her head. Yes, the tape was on.

I gushed on: 'Gosh, you two are going to be so happy together.'

She fixed me with a stare.

'You know, I'm only telling you this for your own good, but you can be incredibly naïve, Melanie.'

Huh, tell me something I didn't know.

'This . . . I mean, hell, it's a great excuse to have a party, but it's also a bloody practical affair. That castle needs sorting out, and Daddy's happy to put up the loot to do it with.'

My eyes widened. That was proof all right – I assumed. Then something struck me; she was so matter-of-fact about it. Maybe Fraser felt the same way? Maybe this was how tons of people got married. After all, the aristocracy had been doing it for generations. I supposed this was how it all worked. Not helped by the copious champagne, I suddenly felt sad.

'Don't you love him?'

She sniffed. 'He's a nice chap. It's a good situation. It'll be a fabulous wedding.'

'Hyear hyear!' said one of the Sloane clones.

Amanda took a drink and continued: 'You don't

believe in all that Hollywood crap, do you? I mean, God, how many times do you have to find out, Melanie? Men are complete bastards. Look at what Alex did to you. That wasn't a terribly Tom Hanks way to behave, was it, darling? This way, everyone wins. We'll have a beautiful home and a beautiful life, and we'll be as happy as any marriage is these days, because we went into it with our eyes open. Fraser is a nice boy and he'll have no objection to us both living our lives.' She turned to the waiter. 'I'm sorry, but I don't know why you waste your time bringing us anything at all if you can't get the lemon juice right.'

I looked at Fran for support, but she was nodding in agreement – presumably to keep Amanda talking, but it didn't feel that way. Suddenly the situation felt dangerous. The blood rushed to my head a bit. I stood up, unsteadily.

'I don't care,' I announced in a trembly voice. The waiter thought I was talking to him and stepped forward, then hopped back again. 'I do believe in all that crap. Well, not all of it. But some of it. The actually being in love with someone stuff. Ehm, yeah. And . . . and I think you lose. Because you've got a lovely bloke like Fraser and you take the piss out of him and you just think of that bloody castle – which I have seen, by the way, and it's a complete heap of shit – and that bloody title and you've absolutely no idea what you've got and how happy he could make you. So, I think you lose.'

I turned and made to walk out of the restaurant.

Realizing I didn't have my bag, I made a dignified right turn into the toilets, then leaned over and looked at myself in the low-lit mirror, breathing heavily. My throat felt tight.

What on earth was I doing? If I wanted to start a fight with Amanda, I should have done it a long time ago. And who, exactly, was I defending? But then, if Fraser did have his eyes open – which I doubted – Angus certainly didn't. He had a blind spot for Fraser the size of the chip on his shoulder. Oh God.

Fran came crashing into the bathroom after me with two fresh glasses of champagne. She was absolutely delighted.

'Ohmigod, the look on her face! What on earth were you talking about?'

I sunk my head into my hands.

'Really, I don't know.'

'You went for her.'

'I know. And I don't even know why!'

'Well, she was asking for it,' Fran reflected.

'No she wasn't! She might even be right, for all we know. That probably is the best way to get married: find a nice bloke that you get on with all right and then ignore each other for the next fifty years.'

'Well, I've heard stupider reasons.'

'Like what?'

'Well, you know my brother Brendan?'

'Yeah.'

'He got married because he kept losing his socks.'

'Fuck off!' I looked up briefly.

'It's true. He kept losing his socks, and one day he said, "That's it, I'm fed up of losing all my fucking socks. The next woman I meet I'm going to marry, as long as she can count socks." And he did.'

'How are his socks now?'

'Dreadful. She divorced him for being a sexist pig who talked about socks all day long.'

I giggled. 'Complete socks maniac.'

'Completely.'

We both smiled and sipped our champagne, and I felt better. It helped that the toilets were nicer than my entire flat.

'So, ehm . . .' I toyed with my glass.

'What am I going to do about Angus?'

'Psychic, you!'

She smiled. 'I thought he might come up sooner or later.'

'I thought he already did.'

'Have you got a soft spot for him?'

'No.'

'Lying cow.'

'Fuck off!'

'Well, to set your mind at rest – although, if you will let me be so bold, if you would dump Mr Trevelyan and go out with the dumpy yet delightful Mr McConnald I would be the happiest best friend alive – he phoned me to apologize.'

'To apologize? Why?'

'Because he wasn't going to phone me. To which I said it was quite all right, I didn't mind a bit.'

'No, no, hang on. I don't understand. He phoned

you to say he wasn't going to phone you?'

'Yes. So if I was hanging around the phone, I could stop and get on with my life. Which of course I wasn't. So we had a nice little chat and said our goodbyes. An extremely civilized end to a one-night stand, I have to say.'

'That is too weird. I don't know whether it's extremely polite or a damning indictment of today's decadent society.'

Fran checked her make-up in the mirror and I joined her, still wondering.

'What are you going to do now?' she asked.

I winced. 'Oh God. Apologize to Amanda, I suppose. I must be off my head. They're probably all pissing themselves laughing at me.'

'The only way you could make those girls laugh would be to tell them Anthea Turner's put on three stone. Do you want to stay?'

I weighed it up.

'Did you get it on tape?'

'If it works, then yes.'

'Well, I suppose there's no reason to stay, then.'

'Not really.'

I thought longingly of the dessert trolley.

'There's always pudding,' said Fran.

I clapped her on the shoulder.

'Will there always be pudding, Fran?' I asked gravely.

'There will always be pudding, Mel. I promise.'

* * *

I took a deep breath and walked out there. All the girls were huddled together, obviously talking about us, ignoring their spiky-looking salads. Our main courses were being kept on a hot plate by our faithful waiter.

I walked over and grabbed the back of my chair for support.

'I'm sorry,' I said to Amanda, as sincerely as I could.

'Oof, don't worry about it for a second,' she said, waving me to sit down. I smiled gratefully.

'You've been a little naïve, haven't you, darling? I shouldn't expect it to stop now, just because we're supposed to be grown-up!' She tinkled the patented Amanda laugh. Beside her, I watched Fran bare her teeth.

'Now! More champers all round! I absolutely insist.'

'Rah rah rah!' shouted the other girls, all of one mind. A half-witted one.

The waiter brought main courses for Fran and I, and we tucked in, letting the girls get on with discussing their boyfriends' cars. Suddenly, there was a near hush in the restaurant. Looking up from my trough, I turned round to see what the matter was. Weaving between the tables was one of the most beautiful girls I'd ever seen in real life. Almost six foot tall, her shiny, pure blonde hair glimmered in the lights. She was dressed in pale, slim-fitting, elegant flowing things, and appeared to float rather than walk. The ratio of her legs to the rest of her body was about 2:1.

'That's who I'm going to look like when I'm

grown-up,' I whispered to Fran, who nodded violently. Behind her was a gorgeous, gorgeous bloke, wearing an expensive – but not showy – suit. He looked vaguely familiar.

Amanda stood up, wearing an eager expression I didn't often see her use.

'Lili! Darling!' she screeched in her ladylike fashion. It was the most emphatic 'darling' I'd ever heard from her. 'Over here!'

Lili's swan-like neck moved a fraction, and she swept her eyes over our measly group. The empty spaces had been taken up by latecomers, noisy City boys showing off. Her eyes passed over me without even looking; I had obviously fallen below some imaginary bar whereby one became actively invisible.

Her white teeth glistened for a second as she bestowed the merest hint of a radiant smile. Amanda, amazingly, was all nerves and practically pleading.

'You've met Jacintha, of course, from Freud's . . . Araminta from Carlton . . . Please, take a seat. I'll pour you a glass – I see you've brought a friend, ha ha.' I could almost hear her accent crack.

Lili bent down elegantly, her white hands long and tapered. 'Oh, we can't stay, we're off to Philippa's bash. We just popped in to see everyone' – her deep voice sounded pointed – 'and now we're off.' She bestowed fifteen alternate kisses on Amanda's cheeks then turned and floated off in a cloud of rare and precious perfume. The broad shoulders of the man disappeared as he gently guided her elbow across the floor.

I stifled a sudden terrible urge to giggle. Well, just when you thought you were pretty far down in the food chain, you discovered a whole new layer you'd never even dreamt of.

'Who the hell was that?' demanded Fran, chewing the last of her lamb.

'Oh, isn't she great?' said Amanda, her eyes wide.

'Well, from that in-depth and emotional meeting, I'd say she's a bit of a stuck-up cow, actually.'

Amazingly, one of the blondies – I think it was Mookie – giggled independently, then blushed bright red and stared at her carpaccio.

Amanda sniffed. 'Well, you would say that about one of the most important fashion people in London. And she came to my hen night.'

Fran and I looked at each other. 'She didn't come to your hen night!' said Fran in amazement. 'She did a Red Arrows fly-past of your hen night.'

I kicked her on the ankle. But Amanda seemed unperturbed.

'Darling, she *showed*. That's all that matters.'

Fran looked at me, but I simply shrugged. Nothing Amanda did made any sense to me.

As the main excitement of the evening was clearly over, I saw Amanda beckon the waiter. Fran and I eyed the dessert trolley eagerly.

'Nobody wants pudding –' Amanda's voice rang out clearly – 'so, just the bill, please.'

I let my shoulders sag and drank a little more champagne.

'Can we go now?' whispered Fran. I nodded.

'And can you order us a couple of limos?' said Amanda.

Good God, I didn't even know you could do that. And I'd never been in a limo . . .

My eyes cut to Fran. She sighed and looked upwards, then nodded her head.

'OK, everyone?' shouted Amanda brightly. 'Are we ready to party?'

The girls giggled and shrieked, 'Yars!'

'I know the limos are naff, but, hey, it's my hen night! We're gonna go crazy!'

Seven reserved posh girls did their best to look crazy as Amanda signed her name with a flourish and flashed her gold card. Then we manoeuvred through the chairs. Outside, as if by magic, were two absolutely ludicrous jet black limousines.

'Our carriages await! Yanna's, please!' Amanda ordered the drivers.

Yanna's was some desperately exclusive club in Mayfair. Shrugging her shoulders, Fran squeezed into the first of the cars, and I followed her. There was a slight pause outside as we realized that the girls all wanted to go in the second limo with Amanda and not us, but that got sorted out somehow, and the one I'd identified as Mookie slid in gracefully.

I looked around the limo. It was done up in high seventies style, with lots of burgundy leather, and there was a white fur rug on the floor, as well as a phone on a string, a TV, and a little fridge in which – hooray – nestled even more champagne.

'My God, this is a white trash fantasy dream,'

sighed Fran as I opened the champagne. 'I wonder how many revolting old men have shagged teenage blonde girls in the back here?'

'Shall we ask the driver?' I said mischievously, pointing to the button that raised the screen.

'Do you really want to know? Yuck!'

'What, if Mick Jagger had fifteen young virgins on the floor? Sure.'

'It probably does one hundred and fifty hen nights a year and two smart functions,' said Fran gloomily. 'Really, it's a bit of a wanker's mobile.'

As if in confirmation, as the car inched its way down Regent Street, some students came up to the blackened window, shook something at us and yelled, 'Rich bastards!'

I looked at Fran in disbelief. 'We're rich bastards!'

'Well, hooray!' said Fran.

'Gosh, how terribly amusing,' said Mookie, looking at the students, although she wasn't smiling. Up till now she'd been sitting silently, and I'd assumed she was disgruntled at not getting into the Princess's limo. 'Did you know those chaps?'

I looked at her. 'Ehm, no. Why, did you?'

She giggled at this. 'No! Me neither!'

This felt almost like a conversation, but not quite.

'OK. Are you having a good time?'

'Why, erm . . . yars, of course.' She looked a bit mystified by the question. 'I mean, the restaurant was in *Vogue* this month, it's almost impossible to get bookings.'

'Really?' said Fran. 'God, we were lucky.'

'How long have you known Amanda?' I was persevering with the small talk, while making my usual subtle nudges to Fran to put the tape on. She glowered at me.

'Well, Jacintha and I are cousins, and we were at school together with Philippa – she's having another party tonight; she doesn't like Amanda . . .' – my eyebrows raised – 'I think she had her eye on Fraser herself. Well, most of the Right Hons are spoken for, or will only go out with models, or are complete poofters, so there's not that many left, rally,' she finished sadly.

Oh.

'Anyway, the Vryker-Lyons are old neighbours of ours from the village, so when Araminta went up, she met Amanda, and that's how it all fits together, rally.'

'Right. I see.'

'So,' said Fran, 'are you and Amanda really good friends?'

'Well, I'm going to be one of the bridesmaids.' Mookie was blushing more and more at being bombarded with these questions. I wondered if, underneath it all, she might be rather nice.

'That's lovely,' I said, reassuringly. 'And . . . what do you think of Fraser?'

I expected her to get stroppy, remembering my little outburst earlier, or silent and defensive.

Instead she looked mildly uncomfortable, and blushed again.

'Well,' she said. Fran helpfully refilled her glass.

'Go on, you can tell us,' I said. 'We won't tell anyone.'

Except, you know, Fraser, I thought.

'Scout's honour,' said Fran. With one hand behind her back.

She smiled. 'You won't tell Amanda?'

'Oooh no.'

Slightly drunk, she burped and said, 'You know, rally, I kind of agreed with what you said earlier.'

I nodded encouragement.

'Well, when Fraser first came on the scene, he was rally innocent, you know? He kept getting invited to these parties, and he thought it was because some people he knew from university rally liked him, you know?'

'How stupid can you get?' I said, smiling through gritted teeth.

'Rally! So at first we took the piss a bit, especially with Amanda rally coming on to him like that . . . I mean, she was still seeing that guy from *Les Mis* at the time.'

'Oh yes?'

'Rally – I think she finished it, though. For the wedding and stuff.'

'Well, that was good of her.'

'Anyway, then I got to know him a bit more. And now I think he's rally nice.'

'Oh, he is.'

'And Amanda bosses him about rally horribly. I mean, I know she's dead lovey-dovey in public, but honestly' – she lowered her voice – 'I've heard her be rally nasty to him.'

'There's a surprise,' I said.

Fran tutted. 'For God's sake, let's just kill her,' she said.

Mookie looked down suddenly and giggled. 'Oh, it must be the champagne,' she groaned. 'Please, promise me you won't tell anybody.'

'Ehm . . . we promise.'

'Then, kind of, I agree with you. Rally, I don't think they should get married.'

I was touched.

We stepped out of the ridiculous car. There was a crowd of people queuing on the pavement, but Amanda knew where she was going, and she waved us ahead fiercely. Evidently a lot of people who hadn't quite been able to drag themselves out for dinner were there, and Amanda passed up the line kissing and squealing with laughter. Yet again everyone was about eight foot taller than me, with designer clothes and loud voices. Mookie disappeared into a crowd of flowing blonde hair. The night was full of peacocks and screeching, and more exotic birds than us, and out of the club came the ghastly thumping of mid-eighties rock. All this detective work had made me extremely tired. I looked for Amanda. She was at the front of the queue, and I just overheard her say, 'Well, of course, Lili came.'

'Shall we go?' I said to Fran.

'Thought you'd never ask,' she said, and we finally collapsed into a cab and made our way home.

Neither of us spoke until we were nearly at my house. One after another, we let out huge sighs, for quite different reasons.

'Are you coming in?' I said as I paid the driver. However, she was already halfway up the mildewed stairs.

Eleven

We sat in my sitting room giggling and trying to play the tape. I was terrified about noise, as Linda had put a big sign up on my door that said, 'Please don't make nois!!' [sic], so I felt a bit in the last-chance saloon.

The tape crackled and spat through a lot of rustling – and a fair bit of chewing on Fran's part – and eventually cut into the conversation:

'You know, I'm only telling you this for your own good, but you can be incredibly naïve, Melanie.'

The familiar tinkle. I cringed.

'Why do I let her say this stuff?'

'Because you have no self-esteem,' observed Fran. 'If she said anything nice, you'd think she wasn't good enough for you, and you'd never see her.'

I tried to work this out as the tape ran on, but

the tape took over. It was unbearable. By the time it got to my famous 'I do believe in all that crap' speech, I was rolling on the floor in embarrassment – first, at my Estuary tones, and second, at the whole ghastly situation of hearing yourself talk bollocks when pissed, which in most of life is fortunately never repeated.

I leaned over and switched the tape recorder off.

'Well, that's it then,' I said.

'What?' Fran grabbed the recorder back fiercely.

'You're not playing that to Angus. Or Fraser. Or anyone. I'm throwing it out right now.'

'But, Mel,' said Fran innocently, 'I believe!'

'Shut up!'

'No! No, I do now truly believe in the power of love, thanks to your moving words.'

'Fuck off!' I leapt at her to try and grab the tape. She grabbed my arms and we rolled about on the carpet, knocking over a frilly lamp with a paisley shade. It crashed off the coffee table.

'Oh God.' I sat up, while Fran held the tape out of my reach. 'SHH!' From next door there came the almost imperceptible sound of a long sigh. Come on, I beckoned Fran quietly, and we went into my bedroom, which was the other side of the flat at least, and you could shut the door properly.

'You definitely can't play that bit,' I hissed. 'It makes me sound like fucking Barbara Cartland. Fraser will think I'm in love with him.'

Fran wasn't listening, instead gently crooning 'The Power of Love' to herself. I kicked her.

'Wind it on. Wind it on to that bit with Mookie in the limousine.'

Unfortunately, Mookie in the limousine sounded exactly like Bagpuss, only with less distinctive vowel sounds.

'What's she saying?' I leaned close to it. '"I agwee?" What does she agwee with? Jesus, that's dreadful.' The tape filled up with traffic noises.

'This is pointless,' I said.

Fran looked at me. 'It's not pointless. You're only going to have to play the first bit to the boys. So what if they think you're an over-romanticized idiot?'

'I think there are enough people in the world already who think I'm an idiot,' I grumbled sulkily. 'I don't want you to play that stupid tape. Let them get married. I don't care.'

'Fine. I don't care either.'

'Fine.'

'Fine.'

'Oh God.'

Fran's lip curled.

'OK, play the damn thing. Can you tell them it's not me?'

'That's right, it could be almost anyone of a million friends I had at that hen night. With a Woking accent.'

'I've got it! Stop it immediately before that bit. Then you just hear the Amanda being a cow bit and nobody gets to hear my speech.'

Fran pulled the spare mattress from under my bed and put the tape recorder under the pillow.

'But that would be no fun,' she protested.

'Hey, nobody said a detective's life is easy, schweetheart.'

Alex and I met up the next day. He'd been out with some of his pseudo rock-star mates, and looked pretty wasted. I wanted to do some early Christmas shopping, but knew there wouldn't be much point in suggesting it, so we were lazing around in Charlie's house, nursing our hangovers.

I'd told him about the invites, and he'd offered to phone up and get me into the wedding if it meant that much to me, then I'd had to explain that that wasn't the point, then he'd said, well, what was the problem then, and I'd looked at him like he was a moron and he'd shrugged his shoulders and said what did I want him to do, go read *Men Are from Mars and Women Are from Venus*? and I said no, forget it, I was having my period.

But I couldn't stay in a strop, because I had to tell him about the night before – in a highly edited version of course, centring around the idea that I might have some ethical concerns about the whole business. He couldn't believe we'd actually gone so far as to wire ourselves up, and thought it was pretty cool.

'Shall we join the FBI when we grow up?' I asked him dreamily.

'Yes, I think so. Do you think they get a million morons a day asking to join their alien division?'

'I don't know. Let's phone them up, ask to join, and measure how pissed off the person's voice is. Those are the kind of forensic detective skills you need to join.'

Alex nodded sagely. 'So what are you going to do with the tape?'

'I don't know. Fran thinks we should play it to Fraser. I'm not so sure.'

'Why not?'

'Well . . . it's illegal, isn't it?'

'So, you think Fraser might report you to the police?'

'No . . . although I couldn't join the FBI with a record.'

'Or without American citizenship. Come on, do you really think it's criminal?'

'No-o-o . . . I just think it was a bit embarrassing and I kind of wish we hadn't done it now. I mean, what if Fraser just shrugs his shoulders and never talks to us again?'

'Well, you know me, I don't really give a shit about this wedding . . . or any wedding for that matter . . .'

Point taken.

'. . . but if you think it's such a horrendous idea, well, then don't you want to stop it? Like you won't let your friends drive drunk, will you?'

'Oh God, not that damn crocodile again.'

'What?'

'Never mind. I do want to stop it. I just didn't think I'd actually, you know, have to do hard things.'

'That's why people tell other people to mind their own business.'

'I know.'

'But if they insist on interfering, pumpkin . . . they should carry it through. Can I hear it?'

'No.'

'Why not? What does it say on it? Does Amanda renounce Fraser because she's desperate for my body?'

'You wish.'

Alex shrugged.

'Really? Would you really wish?'

'No, my darling, I prefer my women more . . . Rubenesque.'

'Fuck off! I can't believe it. If she walked in here naked right now and offered it to you, would you take it?'

'Are you still here at this point?'

'No. Say I don't even exist.'

'Well, maybe.'

'Maybe?'

He grinned. 'Well, you know . . .'

'But she's evil!'

'So you say.'

'You've seen her be evil!'

'When?'

He was right. I couldn't remember a single occasion. God, she hid it well in front of men.

'You have the morals of a lobster,' I grumbled.

'Oh, come on. You asked.'

'Yes, and you're supposed to say "no". Always. Even if it's like a whole Helena Christensen/Naomi Campbell lesbian-type thing. You're always supposed to say no, you'd prefer me.'

'But you don't exist.'

'Yes, well, apart from that.'

Charlie wandered in. When he saw me, he looked slightly embarrassed. I didn't say anything.

'Hey,' said Alex.

'Hey,' said Charlie. Then he took a deep breath. 'Urm . . . Melanie.'

I looked up, surprised.

'I'm terribly sorry about last week.'

'Oh, I'd forgotten all about it,' I lied.

'Huh. Right-oh. Erm, how's that friend of yours?'

'Which one?' I asked him deliberately.

'Yas, you know, erm . . . Fran.'

I smiled, and decided to embellish it a bit. 'Oh, she's doing absolutely great! Ever since she started seeing Angus . . .'

'She's seeing Angus?' cut in Alex abruptly. 'Since when?'

'Since that night, actually.'

Charlie looked utterly crestfallen. 'Gosh, I rather buggered that up then.'

'What?' said Alex. 'She had her tongue down that other guy's throat when we left.'

'Well, you know Fran. Always up for a bit of adventure.'

Charlie perked up a bit. 'Really?'

'Only with Scottish people though,' I said sympathetically. His crest fell again and he turned and left the room.

'Damn gorgeous totty,' he muttered as he went.

Ooh, it was working.

I studied Alex. 'You looked utterly dumbfounded that Fran might have a boyfriend.'

He made a hangdog face. 'Not really. It's just I'd never have put those two together. Mind you, they're both pretty fierce.'

'No they're not!' I said indignantly. 'OK, Fran is pretty fierce. But Angus is a big pet. He's really sweet.'

'So, it won't last long then. D'ya want tea?' Alex went through to put the kettle on.

Actually, it's already finished, I thought to myself, slightly embarrassed for having fibbed about something so pointless.

'You told them WHAT!?' said Fran.

'I thought it would be funny. Wind Charlie up a bit.'

'I decide when I want to wind Charlie up.'

'Oh yeah, NEW RULE!'

'Oh, forget it. You really have a big mouth, don't you?'

'Yeah, you mentioned that.'

Hurt and annoyed, I slumped back in my chair. We were in a greasy caff in North London waiting for Angus, who had been pestering us to know what had happened to the tape. I fiddled disconsolately with the grubby sauce bottle and drank my slightly suspect tea.

'Angus!' she said in a pleased tone as he popped into our booth, shaking the rain off like a dog.

'Angus!' I mimicked under my breath, then gave up and grinned at him. He grinned back and sat down opposite me and next to Fran, his heavy ribbed grey jumper taking up more than half his side. He pushed back his dark red hair.

'Well?' he said heartily.

I looked at Fran. 'Breakfast first!' she said, and we trooped up and ordered bacon, sausage, mushrooms, tomatoes, beans, eggs, and white bread and butter, with a cholesterol seizure to follow.

'I am honour bound to say,' began Fran, once we were all tucking in, 'Mel doesn't want me to play this tape.'

'Why not?' said Angus, looking at me intently.

'Well, you know, there was this big bunch of free champagne, and Amanda says lots of incriminating things, and I say, you know, lots of moronic things,' I said quickly.

He smiled and his eyes went all crinkly. 'Och, I never say anything stupid when I'm drunk.'

I smiled back. 'Actually, normally I make trenchant political speeches about the European monetary system. I do not know what came over me on Friday.'

'Must have been a bad pint . . . of champagne.'

'OK, you two, have you got a sec?'

'Yes,' said Angus. 'Bravery of the officer noted.'

Fran brought the recorder out. I cringed, and paid very close attention to my sausage. Angus watched me quizzically.

The mannered tones came across clearly:

'You know, I'm only telling you this for your own good, but you can be incredibly naïve, Melanie. This . . .

I mean, hell, it's a great excuse to have a party, but it's also a bloody practical affair. That castle needs sorting out, and Daddy's happy to put up the loot to do it with.'

Angus's face went red. 'Bloody cow,' he said vehemently.

'Don't you love him?' That was me, and I winced.

'He's a nice chap. It's a good situation. It'll be a fabulous wedding.'

She went on to talk about Fraser being all right, and someone who would have no objections to her living her life.

'Does Fraser think that?' I whispered to Angus.

'Of course he fucking doesn't.' His fried egg was all but forgotten.

Here came my big set speech.

'I don't care,' I heard myself howl petulantly. 'I do believe in all that crap.' On and on and on. 'So, I think you lose!' My voice cracked at this bit, as I got ready for stomping off. My entire body cringed.

Fran switched the tape off after that.

'Thanks,' I grimaced at her. 'You could have switched it off before.'

'Could I?'

Then we just sat there in silence for a bit. Angus looked cross. 'He's so stupid,' he said. 'I can't believe he's a year older than me but so completely stupid.' Then he looked at me across the grimy table.

'Do you really think all that stuff you said?' he asked suddenly.

I shrugged. 'Maybe. I'm sorry about the castle bit.'

'Well, I don't think it's embarrassing at all. And the castle is complete crap. I think you were quite right,' he said. 'And so does Fraser. That's why we've got to stop him getting into this mess.'

'Are you going to play it to him?' asked Fran.

Angus heaved a sigh.

'I don't know.'

'Gus!' I implored him. 'After what I went through?'

'Oh yes, I only did the taping and wore the wire and sorted it all out and switched it on and off inconspicuously,' huffed Fran.

Angus looked at the remains of his breakfast. 'Oh God, it's just so embarrassing. And so wrong.'

We nodded our heads.

'But I suppose I have to.'

We nodded our heads again.

Fran got up to refill her coffee cup.

'Mel,' Angus whispered urgently, 'would you . . . would you come with me when I play the tape?'

I was touched.

'Well, yeah . . . Why did you ask me?'

'Ehm . . . in case it gets a bit messy and he tries to punch me or something. And you and Fran are the only women I know down here.'

'Oh, right. Why don't you ask her?'

'I will if you like. But you know Fraser and . . . and, well, I'd rather have you.'

'Cool. OK.'

'OK what?' said Fran, rejoining us.

'OK, that is definitely the best way to lift scum off a cup of tea,' I said, picking up my cup.

'Fascinating,' said Fran. 'Do you know, I think you two are made for each other.'

We had to pick a night Amanda would be out. Fortunately, that was every night, so it wasn't too difficult. She'd moved Fraser into her little pied-à-terre, after complaining too vehemently about his shared boy-tip in Finsbury Park and the copies of *FHM* left wrinkled up by the toilet for use in emergencies. They were only there temporarily: her father was scouring London for a large townhouse suitable for his noble offspring.

Where they lived at the moment turned out to be a small but immaculate apartment in a mansion block in St John's Wood, next to Regent's Park. Angus and I met up beforehand, to plan, and for moral support. The November wind was freezing as we walked across the park. Angus betrayed his nerves by constantly kicking leaves out of the way.

'Right,' said Angus, 'how are we going to do this?'

'Have you got the tape?'

'OK, let's start a little later than that bit.'

'Ehm . . . really, I think we should just go in and not be nice at all. Just push past him with stern faces and say, "Look Fraser, there's something we have to tell you."'

'In a deep American voice?'

'Yeah.'

I wrapped my arms around me.

'Are you cold?'

'Nervous. And cold.'

He clapped his arm round me briefly, which did the trick, as I blushed incredibly red and got warm almost immediately.

'We're nearly there.'

'We have to be brutal about this, Gus. We've got to walk in, just tell him, put the tape on and get out of there. He'll forgive you in – oh, four or five years.'

Angus didn't say anything.

'What? Are you wishing you had brought Fran after all?'

'No . . . I was just thinking.'

'What?'

He looked around.

'That it's a nice night for a walk. It feels such a shame that we're going to, well, you know . . .'

'Do a nasty thing.'

'Yes.'

We walked on.

'Actually, it's a freezing cold and miserable night for a walk,' I said.

'Yes. I suppose it is.'

'Shall we go and do a nasty thing then?'

'Yeah, all right.'

My mysterious and stone-faced FBI persona lasted about ten seconds after Fraser answered the door.

'Hi! Come in, great to see you! Hello, Mel dear.' He kissed me on the cheek. Every time I saw him, I remembered how lovely he was.

This was not going to be easy.

'Did you survive the hen night all right? 'manda told me it was amazing.'

'Yeah, yeah, it was.'

'Hello, Gustard.' He playfully punched Angus on the stomach. Angus was doing better than me, and gave a quiet half-smile.

'Come in, come in. What do you want? Beer, wine . . . ?'

He split off into the kitchen and we trooped into the tiny but tasteful living room. The carpet and the sofas were white, which made me extremely nervous. There was a leopardskin bean bag in the corner and some expensive-looking candlesticks dotted around. Fraser had put out little bowls of peanuts and crisps, obviously in anticipation of our visit. They gazed at me pitifully, so I ate a few for luck.

'Amanda doesn't like people coming round usually – she worries about the carpet,' said Fraser, emerging from the kitchen with three glasses and an open bottle of red wine. I gulped.

'Really? Where is she tonight then?' I asked.

Angus shot me a dirty look and I realized this was not the time for small talk.

Fraser motioned for us to sit down and make ourselves comfortable. The sofa was squashier than it looked and, as I sank into it, a dribble from the wine glass made its way over the side. Fortunately, it dropped on to my trousers. Angus stayed standing up.

'Oh, God knows. She's always disappearing to some do or other.' He laughed. 'I can't keep up.'

'Don't you go?'

'No chance. Totally BORING.'

I nodded, and took some more crisps. 'Actually, the hen night . . .'

Angus cleared his throat overdramatically and we both looked up at him. He pulled the tape recorder out and sat down next to me. I covered my glass with my hand.

'Fraser,' he said seriously, 'Melanie and I . . .'

Fraser smiled at the sombreness of the tone, but leaned forward to hear.

'We have something to say to you about your wedding.'

We did? I didn't remember agreeing this.

'Well, really, I'm more here for moral support . . .' I said.

Angus ignored me, continuing: 'Fraser, Ah hate to have to tell you this, but . . . Ah don't think you should marry Amanda.'

Fraser sighed and gulped his wine. 'I don't believe it. I mean, you have actually told me that before. In fact, nearly every day since I met her. Please don't say that's what you came here for. God, and I thought you were coming round to visit me.'

'Aye, well. And Mel agrees with me.'

Fraser looked at me, wounded.

'But I thought . . .'

I gazed back at his stricken face, feeling horribly guilty and embarrassed.

Angus ploughed on regardless: 'And we've got some proof . . . I'm sorry.' He put the tape recorder down on the table. One of the wrought-iron candlesticks fell over.

'What's going on?' asked Fraser. 'Are you forming some Moonie-type cult which aims to outlaw marriage for brothers?'

'No.'

'Then why the fuck don't you just keep your nose out of it?'

'Because your ma brother, for fuck's sake.'

'What's on that tape?'

'Melanie talked to her. She doesn't love you, you idiot. She just wants to have some kind of title and swank about and get in *Hello!* magazine and have posh people for friends because she's actually a completely shallow cow.'

Fraser looked at the tape as if it was a snake.

'Is that what she says?' he asked me.

'Not exactly,' I whispered. My voice sounded shaky. I felt absolutely terrible.

He stalked to the other side of the room – which, given the size of it, took two seconds – grabbed the sill and stared out of the sash windows.

'Play the damn thing then.'

Angus was looking at me, but I couldn't look back. This was much much worse than I ever thought it would be. I'd had visions of him even thanking us. Angus leaned over and clicked the switch, and there it came again:

'You're so naïve, Melanie.'

It echoed in my brain like a special effect.

'You're so naïve, Melanie.'

Of course I was, otherwise what was I doing in this tiny, pristine, overheated room, betraying one friend and losing another?

'You're so naïve, Melanie.'

Who did I think I was, Mystic Meg? What had I done this for? Silently, I began to cry. This lovely, gorgeous bloke was still going to get married, and he was going to hate me into the bargain.

Fraser stood stock-still, looking out into the rain and the heavy traffic. Fortunately, Angus managed to stop the tape before my big speech, so at least we were spared that.

Nobody spoke for what seemed like a long time. I was trying to dry my tears without anyone noticing. Unfortunately, to maintain the silence, I had to let some snot drop out of my nose so I didn't have to sniff. It plopped quietly on to the white rug, and I rubbed it with my foot.

Finally, Fraser turned round.

'So, actually, she didn't say any of those things you mentioned, about the title and the magazines and all that shit.'

I could feel Angus looking at me, but I couldn't return his gaze. Fraser's voice was furious.

'In fact, she spoke for ten seconds about keeping her individuality after she gets married and having thought the damn thing through beforehand, and you take that as proof that she's some kind of social-climbing bitch. Like you know anything about my wedding, or about my girlfriend or my own fucking life. Not only that, you manage to draft some of my friends into this idiotic scheme . . . Melanie, are you crying?'

'Nooo,' I whimpered.

He came and stood beside me and patted me on the arm – which of course made it worse – without stopping talking.

'I mean, Gus, what the fuck do you want? What do you really want? Do you want the damn title? Because you're making so much bloody fuss about it, you might as well have it. It doesn't matter to me, but it looks like it matters to you.'

'Of course it doesn't matter to me,' growled Angus, who looked sullen and red.

'Well, what then? What the hell is it? Why won't you leave this damn thing alone? You're trying to sabotage this whole thing, and I don't even know why.'

His face was a mixture of anger and misery, and genuine miscomprehension.

Angus bowed his head low. 'I'm sorry we came.'

'I'm sorry you came. And why are you dragging Melanie into it, for God's sake?'

I snuffled.

'I'm sorry I did that too,' said Angus. 'I meant well. I'm sorry.'

'Please,' said Fraser. 'Please, just . . . leave it alone. You're like a dog with something between its teeth, Gus. Always have been. You won't let things fucking well alone.'

'I'd better be going.'

'You better had.'

I stood up awkwardly to follow him.

Fraser took my arm and looked at me with some concern.

'Are you going to be OK?'

'Do you hate me?' I choked.

He smiled sadly. 'No, of course not. Gus, are you going to take her home?'

Angus nodded. Fraser turned away from us.

'Bye then.' It was a dismissal.

We trooped through the corridor. As we got to the door, Angus turned round and went back to the sitting room. Blindly, I followed him.

'Do you . . .' he began, as he stepped through the door.

Fraser was sitting there, staring at the tape recorder in his hands. He looked up at his brother, his eyes damp.

'What?' he growled, caught off guard.

Angus blushed furiously. 'Nothin'. Just wondering about cabs. Bye.'

That time we left for good.

Angus strode fiercely through the park, the rain blowing back his hair and coat, all mention of a cab apparently forgotten. I trotted along beside him, ashamed of myself, and terrified of what he was going to say. I felt like such a stupid girl. He didn't speak for what seemed like miles. I was tempted to slip quietly behind him and go the other way, but I didn't dare. Suddenly, in the dark, I tripped over something or other and let out a strangled yell. Angus whipped back and immediately his stony face softened.

'Are you OK?' he yelled across the wind.

'I'm . . . fine,' I croaked, although I didn't feel fine at all. I tried to stand up, and it was agonizing. Angus caught me keeling over.

'What've you done?'

'I . . . I think I've twisted my ankle.' I leaned on him heavily, feeling a bit green.

'Are you going to be sick?'

'I wouldn't . . .' I tried to take a step forward, 'rule it out as a possibility.'

'Great,' he said gloomily, supporting my elbow. 'Is this the best evening out you've ever had?'

I managed another step, wincing. 'Well, it's the best freezing cold family feud twisted ankle evening out I've ever had.'

'That's something, I suppose.'

He indicated a park bench, but I could see the lights of Camden in the distance and pointed to them.

'Can you make it?'

'Can you carry me?'

'I could try.'

I giggled. 'Only kidding. I'd kill you. Just let me lean on you for a bit.'

The next ten minutes were agony, but finally we collapsed in the first pub we came to. It was so good to be out of the cold and the wet, I felt better already. The pub was quiet and old-fashioned. It actually had a fire lit in the grate, and we sat beside it to dry off.

Angus got up to fetch me a whisky. I'd rather have

had a glass of white wine, but I stuck to his judgement in situations like this.

Angus returned with two large glasses. 'Thank God for civilization,' he said.

'Can I have some ice in mine?'

'No, you bloody well can't.'

'That's not very civilized, telling people what to do.'

We both stared into the fire for a bit.

'What do you think will happen?' I ventured finally. Angus heaved a sigh.

'I wish I knew,' he said. 'I felt like such a bloody fool. Tell me it had to be done, Mel.'

I thought of Fraser's face – so pained and miserable.

'Ehm . . . I suppose so.'

Angus rubbed his eyes. 'It's the rest of his life. Every day, having to wake up next to someone who thinks he's an idiot. Oh God, I don't know. I just hate her so much. And, you know, I've only got one brother. Since Dad died . . . we've been really close. Well, I thought we were.'

'Have you fallen out before?'

'Not like this. Apart from the whole *Star Wars* figures thing. But that was a long time ago. Normally, when I speak to him about the wedding he treats it as a joke . . . but it's getting so close.'

'God, yes . . . it's soon, isn't it?'

'Three weeks' time. Pyrford village church. Good Protestant vicar and four hundred guests to a five-course meal.'

'Not for me.'

'Oh, I'm sorry . . .'

'Nope, I don't care.'

'You may not have to. Did you see the way he was holding that tape recorder?'

'Yes, because he was so pissed off with you.'

'Did you think so? I thought he was pissed off with her.'

I sipped my drink.

'Hmm,' he said. 'Mel, can I ask you a question?'

I hate it when someone says that. What they usually mean is: *Mel, can I insult you and get away with it, having warned you in advance?*

'Uh-huh?'

'Why did you start crying?'

'That's, umm, a very good question.'

'Sorry. I don't mean to intrude.'

'It's OK. I'm really sorry, actually. I got upset about things – it seemed so rotten. Why can't everyone just be nice and end up with nice people? . . . That sounds pathetic.'

'No, it doesn't,' he said gently. 'Do you include yourself in "everyone"?'

'That's the standard definition, isn't it? I'm sorry. About all of it.'

'Oh, it's my fault. Don't worry, I'm sure we'll recover. We are brothers, after all. Blood and stuff. I think I'll give him a wee ring in the morning, once it's all blown over a bit.'

Phew, at least I didn't have to do that. I finished my whisky and suddenly felt enormously sleepy.

'How are you going to get home?' asked Angus.

I realized to my surprise that, actually, I didn't want to go home; I wanted to curl up in front of this big fire and put my head on his shoulder. But I didn't say that.

'I can't get a cab; it'll cost a fortune,' I said. 'I think I'll phone Alex. He can drive Charlie's car and come and pick me up.'

Angus lent me his phone.

'Does this work in underwater pipes?' I asked, picking up the big thing with a huge fluorescent stripe down it.

'Maybe,' he grinned.

Charlie answered.

'Is Alex there?'

'Erhm – what?'

'Charlie, it's Mel.' Brain of dough. 'Is Alex there?'

'Ehrr, um, I've just got in . . . Ehm, I'll go and check.'

I shot Angus a look. 'That boy gets more moronic every day.'

'It's the inbreeding.'

I nodded. There was a lot of scuffling in the background, and some whispering going on.

'Hello?' asked Alex doubtfully.

'Alex? Hi, it's me.'

'Oh, hello, pumpkin. I, ehm, thought you were out tonight.'

'I am. Was. Look, I've twisted my ankle, pretty badly. Do you think you could come and pick me up?'

'Ehm . . . where are you?'

'Camden.'

'Camden. Jesus, that's miles away! Can't you get a cab?'

'If I made twice the salary I do now, I would get a cab. Look, I'd rather not, I don't feel well and I've really hurt myself.' I started to get upset again. 'Can't you come and get me?'

'Look, Mel, sweetheart, I'm kind of in the middle of something right now.'

'What? What the hell is it? Why do I have to plead with you to come and pick me up?'

'Ehm, some of the lads are round and I've really had too much to drink to drive.'

'I don't believe you. I think you just don't want to come and get me.'

'Pumpkin, I would if I could, honest. Trust me, it's just impossible. Why don't you just take a cab home and I'll see you tomorrow?'

There was a pause. I didn't know what to say, so I hung up the phone.

Angus looked away, embarrassed. I waited till the urge to cry had passed and swallowed hard.

'Bastard,' I said.

'Sounds like one,' said Angus. 'I'd carry you home.'

I looked at him. 'You would too.'

'Damsel in distress. My speciality.'

I laughed. 'I'm tempted.'

'Be tempted.' His voice suddenly turned serious. He looked at me face on, with that direct gaze of his, and my heart started beating extremely fast. We looked at each other for what seemed like a long time. Our faces began to come a little closer. Then I moved slightly, and jarred my ankle really, really hard against the chair.

'AAAYICK!' I yelled, bending over. The whole sleepy bar looked over to see who was being murdered. I put my hands on my ankle, trying to make it better, but it was agony. Shockwaves of pain careered up my legs.

'Ow! Ow! Ow ow ow ow ow.'

'Oh, you poor thing.' Angus got up with me, as I started hopping about on one leg.

'Ow ow ow. God, my fucking ankle! It really fucking hurts.'

'Do you want to lean on me? Go to Casualty?'

'No, no no. Jesus! This has happened before. Ehm, the best thing I could do really is just go home and take some aspirin. Arsing hell.'

A look passed between us. The moment when whatever might have happened was going to happen had gone.

Angus went to the bar and called a cab. I was escorted out by him and the barman, and an hour later I was safely tucked up in bed with four Nurofen and the comfort of a guaranteed sickie in the morning.

Twelve

Unfortunately, my ankle felt practically fine in the morning. Well, stiff, and it hurt if I really put my weight on it, but not quite enough to justify sickie status. And as I felt, overall, that my morality rating wasn't at its highest, I got ready to go in.

My mind felt like scrambled eggs, so I decided to make some for breakfast.

'Linda, do you want some scrambled eggs?'

She emerged, fully dressed but looking sleepy, from her bedroom. The look on her face plainly told me how amazed she was at this whole me-cooking thing. However, surprisingly, she took me up on it. Well, there was food involved, I supposed.

There would be no point, I surmised, in asking for her advice. So I asked her about the bank instead.

'What bank?'

'Ehm, don't you work in a bank?'

'No.'

Actually, I could pull my own teeth out just fine, thank you.

'So, where do you work, again?'

'Brimley's.'

'Brimley's . . . ?'

'Insurance.'

'Right! Right . . . So, how's it going?'

'Fine.'

I sipped my tea. It was going to be a long day.

'I need the weekend,' she said suddenly.

I thought she might be asking me to give back something I'd borrowed off her, and I racked my brains to remember, but couldn't.

'The what?'

'The weekend,' she said, enunciating very slowly as I was clearly such an idiot.

'Right . . . the weekend,' I said. This was turning into some sort of perpetual conversational nightmare.

'Before Christmas. I need the flat for the weekend.'

'Oh, right. You want me to get out?'

She nodded. There didn't seem to be much room for argument.

'Fine, OK,' I said without thinking. 'That shouldn't be a problem. Which one?'

'All of it.'

'Which weekend?'

'The one before Christmas,' she explained patiently.

Oh. Speak in sentences, you dozy cow.

'OK. OK, fine.'

That was the weekend of the wedding, so I supposed we'd be away anyway, somehow or other. But what on earth was Linda up to? Her actually doing something threatened the stability of my already fragile view of the universe.

'What are you up to?' I asked her.

She stared at me, stood up abruptly from the table and walked out. Great.

I couldn't face washing up the scrambled egg pan, so I left it and limped into work.

'Ey up, snoots.' I bumped into Steve coming in. 'You been in the wars, then?'

I groaned. 'You should see the other guy. And he was a Cockney.'

'Yeah, right. You'd be dead.'

'Actually, now I think about it, that's true. I'd rather kill myself than have physical contact with a Cockney.'

I walked into the office, and got a huge sense of *déjà vu*. Sitting on my desk was another cheap bouquet; and there was another crying jag from my next-door neighbour.

'What's the matter now?' I said brusquely, dumping the flowers in the bin.

'I thought they were for me.'

'Do you want them?' I looked at them in the bin, now covered in banana skin and old plastic coffee cups.

'No. Aren't you even going to read the card?'

'I can predict the card.' Nonetheless, I took a quick peek.

'Sorry about your ankle, pumpkin. Can I see you tonight? I'll pick you up,' it said.

'Fuck off,' I said sourly, and plumped myself down on the stool. The phone rang.

'Fuck off,' I said again, and picked up all the unopened post that was spilling over my in-tray.

The phone rang fourteen times that morning. Each time I swore at it and concentrated on what I was doing instead. Finally, Janie leaned over and said quietly, 'You know, you could put that on voice mail, then you wouldn't even have to hear it ring.'

It pissed me off that that was such an eminently reasonable suggestion, so I just said 'huh,' and went back to being in a big sulk.

At lunch time the receptionist put her head round the open-plan office door.

'Melanie Pepper!' she shrieked.

I tentatively put my hand up.

'You're not answering your phone!'

Stop shrieking at me! I stood up carefully.

'There's someone here to see you in reception.'

Jesus. 'Is it a man?'

'It sure is.'

'Can you . . . tell him I'm on a business trip?'

'You ain't on no business trip!'

'No, but could you tell him that?'

'You can come right upstairs and tell him yourself.'

'How can I . . . ? Oh, forget it, never mind.'

The receptionist had already retreated up the stairs. I followed slowly, trying to figure out a strategy. The bastard. He was going to pay, the selfish bastard.

Fraser stood nervously at the top of the stairs, pretending to admire our annual report. He looked tense. If it were an earlier age, he'd have been playing with his top hat and gloves.

I stood looking at him for a second, then crept up behind him.

'Don't tell me: you're a masochist,' I said suddenly. Startled, he turned round, then smiled shyly.

'Hullo.'

'What are you doing here?'

'Well, Angus gave me your work address . . .'

'You spoke to Angus? What did he say?'

'I'll tell you in a minute. Would you like to go to lunch? I work quite near here. Anyway, there's a little Italian around the corner . . .'

'I know it,' I said. 'Yes, please.'

Steve was crossing the reception area.

'Hey, Steve, can you tell Flavi I've gone out for lunch?'

'Blow it out your arse.'

'Thanks.'

Fraser looked quizzical. 'One of those informal offices?'

'Something like that.'

The Italian was busy and smelled wonderful. I remembered that I hadn't had any dinner the night before, and the scrambled eggs were a few hours away, so I ordered spaghetti carbonara. And some garlic bread. With cheese. And minestrone soup. And a glass of wine.

'How's the ankle? Angus told me.'

'Much better, thanks. So, what happened between you two? Tell me everything.'

Fraser eyed me munching my way through the garlic bread. 'Well, you seem in good shape.'

I grimaced. 'Did you come over to see if I was still a snivelling wretch or not?'

'Something like that. Angus asked me to pop in and see if you were OK. He was worried about you, and he knew I worked nearby – you know the Xyler building?'

'The big pinky-coloured one? Yes, I know it, that's just across the road. Huh! And I thought you'd flown in to whisk me off to some glamorous lunch.'

'This isn't glamorous?'

We heard two of the waiters having a loud disagreement in Italian through the multicoloured plastic strips of door covering.

'Well, you know, for those of us more used to the delights of Quagli's . . .'

'Ha ha.'

He took some bread and mopped up the remnants of my soup with it.

'So, tell me,' I said, agog to know how they'd managed to make it up.

'Really, it was nothing. The Gustard and I fight all the time.'

'That's not what he said.'

'Oh yes, sure, *Star Wars* figures and, you know, all the usual stuff.'

'Girls?' I asked him mischievously.

He grinned.

'You're feeling better, all right. No, we don't usually fight about girls.'

'Except this one.'

He misunderstood.

'Who, you?'

'Ehm, no . . . Amanda.'

'Oh, right, I see what you mean.'

Momentarily embarrassed, we looked around in a flurry for our waiter.

A steaming plate of pasta was put in front of me, and I inhaled greedily.

'So, what did you say?' I urged.

'We made up. You're never going to eat all that.'

'Watch me, skinny boy.'

'He came round late last night after you'd gone, and apologized. Actually, I think he was more worried about you than me.'

'That was just a cover. Boy thing.'

'Hmm. Anyway, he took it all back, blah blah blah, promised not to mention the wedding any more, etcetera, etcetera.'

'Right.' I felt perversely disappointed.

'You're pissed off with him, aren't you?'

'No.'

'It's OK, you know.' He smiled. 'I don't mind if you don't want me to get married.'

'It's not that,' I protested, lying. 'I just don't want

you to get married to her.'

'Ah, so you admit it.'

'Of course I admit it. I'm sorry. Please don't hate me.'

'I don't hate you. I told you already. And, anyway, I listened to the rest of the tape.'

'Oh shit, did you?'

'Don't worry, I forgive you for what you said about my castle.'

'Your big pile of rocks.'

'Whatever.'

I toyed with my pasta.

'Don't marry her, Frase. It's only money.'

I realized I'd said the wrong thing again, but he took it all right.

'God, if it's not one thing it's the other with you two. Now suddenly, I'm the bastard. She's fine and I'm a money-grabbing bastard, marrying for the wrong reasons.'

'I'm sorry! I always say the wrong thing.'

'Forget it. I'm boring myself to death with this damn wedding business. Mel, please, we've been friends for a long time. Can you promise to stop going on at me, like Angus did?'

I thought about it. 'What, just because it's none of my business?'

He nodded.

'OK. Seeing as it's you. And we've been friends for such a long time. Apart from the five years in the middle when we lost touch.'

He held out his hands. 'You vanished. One moment

you were being a bit pissed at Graduation, next thing you phone up out of the blue five years later.'

I never had been able to say goodbye.

'OK then. I promise.'

Having finished his lasagne, he launched into my spaghetti.

'Don't you get fed at home?'

'Not really. Less than five milligrams of fat a week until the wedding.'

'See, you started it! Less than two seconds that lasted! Wedding, wedding, wedding. Here, help yourself.'

He smiled sadly, and I felt awful. I mean, what did we think we were playing at, with tape recorders and all that shit? This was someone's life we were fucking around with.

Whenever I get into one of those arguments about nature over nurture – which isn't that often, to be honest, as I don't seem to see my genetical ethicist biology friends so much these days – I always bring up my overwhelming desire to feed people I feel a bit sorry for, despite my absolute lack of culinary ability, and think about my mother.

'Do you want to come round to dinner?' I asked him. Damn genes.

Fraser of course has known me for a while and looked up from my plate, where he was gulping down pasta.

'Are you feeling sorry for me?'

'No, definitely not. Definitely, definitely not. In fact, I've been planning it for ages.'

'Really? Who were you thinking of inviting?'

'Well . . .' – fuck! – 'you're guest of honour, you choose.'

'God. How amazing. You're having a big dinner party?'

'YES!'

'With all of us?'

'Who's us?'

'You, me, Amanda and Angus.'

'I'm not sure about that definition of "us". But yes, why not?'

'Oh, can I bring Nash? He'll be down. McLachlan . . . kind of resigned as my best man, so I'm asking him instead.'

'Wow. Yes, sure.'

'And Amanda will want to bring one of her bridesmaids.'

'Don't push it.'

'I'm sorry, I thought you were doing a big thing.'

'I am. Ehm, can you make it be Mookie then?'

'I cannot for the life of me tell them apart. Why that one?'

'No reason.'

'Is she the one on the end of the tape who sounds like Bagpuss?'

'Maybe.'

'I thought so.'

He looked at me and smiled.

'Are you sure you want to put yourself to all this trouble?'

'What, just shopping, cooking, serving and washing up for six? How hard can it be? I made scrambled eggs this morning.'

'Well – what a nice surprise! Thank you. It's really kind.'

I beamed.

'Ehm, can I ask you something?'

Uh oh. Not another one of those.

'Just out of interest . . .' he leaned over the table, 'what exactly is going on between you and my wee brother?'

I was genuinely shocked.

'Nothing!'

'That's what he says. Which means one of you must be lying.'

'Thank you, Socrates.'

'Aw, go on. Tell me.'

'There's precisely nothing going on. I'm seeing someone.'

'Angus says he's a bastard.'

'Angus seems to think he has the last word on everyone's relationships around here.'

Fraser smiled. 'Well, yes. But do you like him?'

'Your wee brother?'

'Yes.'

'Why, what's he said?'

'Nothing.'

'Fine. I'm not saying anything either.'

'So you do.'

'Piss off, piss off, piss off!'

'Oh my God. You really like him.'

'Look, shut up,' I said. 'Truthfully, I don't know who or what I like at the moment. Everything is so fucked up. Everyone goes out with the wrong people. Everything's so mixed up at the moment. Alex is driving me crazy, but what's the difference between that and your brother driving me crazy? So, maybe you were right just now when you said that maybe we should all keep our heads in our own affairs.'

I must have sounded more serious than I'd intended, because Fraser dipped his head and slowly nodded.

'Yikes. Yes, ma'am.'

'Yes ma'am, indeed. Can you buy me lunch, given that you're nearly loaded?'

'You should buy me lunch for trying to ruin my wedding.'

'You should buy me lunch for turning up unannounced.'

'You should buy me lunch for ambushing me in my own house.'

'You should buy me lunch for asking inappropriate personal questions about your brother.'

He laughed.

'Ha! You should buy me lunch for giving me inappropriate diktats about my fiancée, don't you think?'

The waiter returned, holding the bill.

'Actually,' I said quietly. 'You should buy me lunch because I left my wallet in the office.'

He laughed. 'Minx! But it would be a pleasure.'

'I'll get it next time. Also, I want to see whether you write "laird" on your Switch card.'

'What, in case anyone around here doesn't already think I'm a wanker?'

We headed back up the road, through the crowds of

people wandering their lunch times away aimlessly.

'Thanks for taking me out to lunch,' I said.

'Thank Angus – he suggested it. Angus and Mel, up a tree, K-I-S-S-I-N –'

'Shut it.'

'How much abuse can one man take?'

'You're about to find out for the next forty years of your life. Now, scram.'

And I waved him off, much lighter in my heart than I had been just an hour before.

I had a record-breaking twelve voice-mail messages, a mixture of fawning from Alex and offence from the receptionist. And one from Fran. Immediately I heard it I thought, 'Oh my God, Fran!' I'd completely forgotten her for my dinner plan. But now we had a six, plus Alex, I supposed. Plus I probably had to invite Linda as she wouldn't be out . . . and I only had five chairs as it was . . . maybe I'd just not tell her. That was an alien thought to me. Normally I couldn't put my socks on without phoning her up a couple of times. I wrestled with my conscience slightly – I was going to have to invite Linda, because she'd be there anyway, and wasn't known for her ability to enhance the ambience . . . maybe I could persuade Amanda not to bring Mookie . . .

Suddenly it dawned on me what I'd let myself in for. God, what had I got myself into? I didn't have a pot big enough to scramble eggs for eight people. I didn't mind fiddling about in the kitchen when I had hours and it was just me, and Alex who would eat tadpoles if there was nothing else available, but this was bad. I wished I wasn't such a show-off, and so desperate to make it up to Fraser.

I decided to phone Angus. What was he up to anyway, backing down like that? It wasn't very Braveheart of him. He was busy, unfortunately. He'd been asked to stay longer in London, so at least his job was going well.

I took the voice mail off in case he rang. Which it immediately did. My heart leapt – God, he'd got back to me quickly. However, it was Alex.

'I'm sorry,' he said. 'Please, for God's sake. We were a bit pissed round the flat, and it got out of hand. I should have sent a cab for you.'

'You creep. You completely embarrassed me in front of my friends.'

'Who?'

Suddenly, I wasn't sure I wanted him to know I'd been out with Angus on my own.

'Just Angus and Fran – we went over to Fraser's.'

'Fran?'

'Yes, why?'

'Ehm, no reason, I thought I saw her on the tube last night.'

Bugger it, what a stupid lie.

'Ehm, I didn't mean Fran, I meant Holly.' I named another friend I scarcely saw these days.

'Right.'

There was a pause, and I was sure he knew I was lying. But he obviously decided to ignore it.

'Do you forgive me, pumpkin?'

I sighed.

'Why do I feel like I spend the whole of my life forgiving you? I'm getting sick of this.'

'What do you mean?'

I became very conscious of Janie and Steve on either side of me, ears on poles.

'Well, you know, I'm just . . .' I heard myself saying it: 'I'm not sure I want to put up with this kind of behaviour any more.'

There was a silence. Suddenly I felt very, very cold inside. Where had this come from?

'Look, I . . .' I could hear Alex run his fingers through his hair, like he did when something irritated him. He took a deep breath. 'Can we talk about this?'

'Not now.'

'Fine. Any time. Can I meet you from work? We'll go for a drink, maybe. I think . . . we need to talk.'

My heart was in my throat. Was this it? I mean, it was all so sudden. One minute I'd been planning to give him a hard time about being so selfish, and the next I seemed to have inadvertently started the chain which would eventually lead to the break-up process. It always started with 'we need to talk', always. Unless of course they simply left the country. God, I wasn't sure about this at all.

'Sure, whatever,' I managed to say, casually. Stage two, agreeing to the need to talk.

He named a place, and trembling, I wrote it down, put the phone down and stared into space in disbelief.

Janie was agog. 'Oh my God, did he just dump you?'

'No,' I said crossly. 'I nearly dumped him, as a matter of fact. He's currently pleading for his life.'

Her eyes widened. 'Why would you dump him?'

'Because he's a selfish son of a bitch who only pleases himself?'

Her expression didn't change.

'Have you ever dumped anyone?' I asked. She shook her head mutely.

'What do you think might be grounds for dumping someone?'

Still silent, she shrugged. I managed a half-smile.

'Don't worry. I've got a substitute.'

Her eyebrows nearly reached her hairline.

Cockney Steve was deliberately ignoring all this girlie chat – or had been, from the moment he found out I wasn't on the receiving end.

'Have you ever been dumped, Steve?'

'Course not.' He flushed to the roots of his over-gelled hair.

'Have you ever had a girlfriend, Steve?'

'Fuck off!'

'Are you sure you're not gay? Lots of people who work in marketing are, you know. Look at the colour of the walls.'

He fingered his gold chains and muttered at me.

It made me feel better, but didn't solve the problem. What in the hell was going on? This was beginning to feel like a very fucked up time in my life.

God, I'd spent months drooling over Alex, waiting

for him to come back to me. Which he had. And now, well, I didn't know what I was doing at all, or even how I felt. I loved him, but he was driving me crazy. More than anything, I wanted someone to come along and point me in one direction and say, *This way. This is the way to go to be happy. Go this way.*

I didn't think that was going to happen. But I phoned Fran anyway.

'I'm thinking of finishing it with Alex,' I said to her as soon as she picked up.

She gasped. 'Why?'

'What do you mean, "why"? You think he's a good-for-nothing cocksucker. Isn't that a good enough reason?'

'No, I mean, why now?'

'Oh, like about a billion little things. Like last night, I really hurt my ankle and he wouldn't even come and get me. He said he was in with some mates, but I don't believe him. I think he was just being a lazy bastard. I mean, he really doesn't care about me at all.'

'I think he does, you know.'

'What the hell is this, the Alex Appreciation Society?'

'Well, OK then. You know what I think. Chuck him immediately and go out with one of those nice McConnald boys.'

'What do you mean, one of those nice McConnald boys? Only one of them's free, you know.'

'So you'll take whatever's available?'

'Shut up! You're not helping.'

'Yes I am. Chuck Alex immediately and go out

with someone nice. What better help could I give you than that?'

'But Fran . . . you know, it's Alex.'

'Alex who you were madly in love with. I know. But now he's behaving like a prat, you're not in love with him any more. So, who gives a bison's bum? Move on!'

'But I'm a great big yellow cowardy custard!'

'All the more reason to do it now, while you're cross at him.'

'I don't know what I'm going to do. I don't think I'll know until I see him. I'll phone you later. God, I feel sick.'

'Fine, good, be sick, whatever. But please make sure you DITCH that sucker once and for all.'

'Hnnn,' I said.

The day wore on for about thirty-four hours. I tried to concentrate, but it wasn't easy. My heart was beating fast and I couldn't sit still. All the time, the mantra ran through my head: Life without Alex. Life without Alex. It had been so long since I'd considered the possibility – in fact, I never had.

I remembered the look on his face the day we'd planned the taping, when he'd said he loved me, and my gut wrenched. But, if he loved me, why couldn't he behave like it? Not just do what he wanted, all the time, then send apologies afterwards.

I wished there was some space to pace up and down in. That might have helped.

'Cheer up, might never happen,' winked Steve.

'I know that. But if that is the case, should I move on now? Or should I stick at it and work on something that might have just started to build?'

'You've gone bonkers, you 'ave,' he said moodily.

At last I was free. I ran out of the building at top speed, even for me. I was meeting Alex in a trendy bar just down the road in Covent Garden, and when I reached it, I saw he was already there. Sitting with his back to me, the figure, in his leather jacket, looked sad and despairing, nursing a beer and staring into space. My heart sank. I wanted to run up to him and put my arms round him, pull him back to me.

He turned round to check the door and saw me standing in it, gazing at him. Without a word, he got up and ran to me, pulling me to him. I felt his strong body against me and closed my eyes. Tears ran out.

'Please don't break up with me,' he said.

'You have got to stop doing things like this!'

His face looked grey and haggard.

'I know, I know.'

'We can't go on having these bloody conversations! That's all we ever do! You behave like a prick and I forgive you!'

'Shh. Come on. Sit down.'

We sat down at the table.

'Can I get you a drink?'

I had a coffee. I stared into space while he fetched it, trying to figure out what to say.

He came back and sat facing me, and there was a silence.

Finally, I swallowed, and said it. I needed to hear him deny it. I needed to hear him tell me that he needed me.

'Alex, I think we should maybe stop seeing each other for a while.'

He sat very calmly. Finally, and to my intense relief, he said, 'I know. Please don't do this, Mel. Please.'

'Give me one good reason why not. Really, since you got back, it's . . . it's been one slap in the face after another for me.'

'You can't finish this because I was too drunk to pick you up.'

'I'm not finishing it because of that. I'm finishing it because you turn up pished, you insult my friends, you fight with my friends, you let me down, and you won't commit. Is that a long enough list?'

Still calm, he reached out and took my hand, then looked to the ceiling as if trying to collect his thoughts.

'Mel, there's something I have to tell you . . .' Then he reconsidered. 'I mean, I can't tell you. But honestly, if you knew, it would change everything.'

'Tell me. Or it's not going to.'

'OK. Look, Mel, I didn't get that job. The one at the record company. That bloke who was going to help me . . . he won't return my calls, or see me or anything.'

He looked wretched.

'I don't think I'm ever going to get into the business.

I mean, I'm twenty-nine now, and apparently they only want sixteen-year-olds these days.'

I waited for him to go on.

'I don't know what I'm going to do for a living; I've never done anything much. In fact, my life, really, is a complete piece of shit.'

'Thanks . . .'

'Except for you,' he shushed me. 'I've been thinking about this – trying to use some of the techniques I picked up, you know, when I was in India. Trying to figure everything out. And I think what's happening, subconsciously, is that I don't think I'm good enough for you. I'm trying to push you away, to make you prove you love me by misbehaving.'

'That's a big piece of crap! And the worst excuse I've ever heard.'

'I'm sorry you think it's crap,' he said calmly. 'I'm sorry that you think that the state my life is in is just a piece of crap.' He stared at his empty glass.

'I don't,' I said. 'I just don't see why your being miserable means you get to be nasty to me.'

'I know. It doesn't. It's inexcusable. That's why I'm trying to explain it, to work it out in my own head. You're the last person on earth I want to hurt. But I'm doing it, nearly every day. I think . . . I mean, you know, you're doing really well, you've got a good job.'

'I've got a pissy job!'

'And you're quite together.'

'I'm . . . scrambled eggs!'

He looked at me curiously. 'Anyway, you've got your

life going on one track, and you don't need me. I think I'm just trying to get your attention. And trying to warn you off from such a fuck-up as me. Which, really, I don't want to do.' He paused. 'I want you.'

'You never think about me. You didn't think about me last night when I was in Camden, and miles from home, and hurt.'

'Believe me, I did. I thought about you all night. That's when I really started to work out why our relationship is the way it is.'

'It's the way it is because you're a big selfish pig.'

'No, Mel. It's the way it is because I'm scared . . . scared of how much I feel for you.'

He shook his hair out of his eyes fiercely.

'Honestly. And I want to believe in myself enough to be with you.'

I narrowed my eyes.

'So, I'm not going to be frightened any more,' he continued.

'You're not.'

He fiddled intensely with his coffee cup.

'No. I'm going to stick to my guns for once in my life. Mel, I thought –' he looked up at me briefly, then back at the table. 'Well . . . if you'll still have me . . . still want me . . . well, if you don't absolutely hate me like I hate myself at the moment, I thought we might – if you could forgive me, if you were willing to give it one last shot, we could maybe, hem, try and move in together? For a bit. See if we could take it to the next stage. After Christmas, ehm, I thought maybe we could find a room or a flat somewhere?'

I was as surprised as Wile E. Coyote is when he chases Road Runner off a mountain and realizes he's running in mid-air.

'I don't think we've been communicating since I got back,' Alex went on. 'We're always busy, and we're so concerned with other people's business, I think we've neglected our own.'

He looked up at me hopefully.

'Since I moved to Fulham, I hardly get to see you.'

'You moved out,' I pointed out. 'Four hundred miles away.'

'Yes, but I was just back. Trying to establish myself. Get myself straightened out. I told you, I didn't want to rush anything. But now I've thought it through. And I reckon you were right all along. We *are* meant to be together.'

I'd forgotten this was my idea to begin with.

'We should set up shop. Give it a shot. What do you think?'

He stared at me, still calm, I thought. Then I glanced downwards, and noticed his foot jiggling like it was auditioning for *Riverdance*. Suddenly, I felt a big wave of affection towards him.

'I don't know what to say,' I said. 'Have I been going out with your evil twin all this time?'

He took my hand. 'Well, in a funny way, you have.'

I moved my hand away. 'OK, you're scaring me now.'

'Sorry. I was up late last night thinking about a lot of this stuff.'

‘Right.’ I stared at the tablecloth, ears burning. This wasn’t what I was used to at all. In my world, ‘let’s meet for a chat’ meant being told that something or other was not working out and therefore it was all over on the job/love/friendship front. I wondered gloomily how Lili, Amanda’s glamorous friend, coped with things like this. She probably got asked about fifteen times a day. She probably got them to buy her a flat first, then turned them down and kept the flat.

‘You don’t have to decide anything now,’ said Alex, caring sharing hippy king.

‘Don’t I?’

‘No, of course not, I don’t want to pressure you.’ He grinned an old-fashioned Alex grin. ‘Although, obviously, you are driving me absolutely crazy, pumpkin.’

This sounded more characteristic. ‘Am I driving you mental?’ I asked.

‘I am at one with despair, until I get your answer.’

‘Good. Serves you right, for a change.’ I sat back and folded my arms.

He stood up and, without a word, went and got us a couple more coffees. I watched his broad back at the bar in wonder.

Suddenly, a tiny spark of excitement lit up inside me. Living together! Long lazy Sundays in bed, proper cooking, shopping for things, talking all night, taking baths together. No more trekking home on my own, no more empty house. Well, it was never empty, but it might as well have been for all the sparks of warmth there were. Dinner parties and coupley invitations. God, it was bourgeois, and God, it was boring, but . . . oh, I liked the idea.

Alex was still at the bar, his fingers tapping the top with nerves. My heart softened. How much had it taken him to ask this? He must have agonized for hours. Oh, and he'd have to tell Charlie. Hooray! And I'd get to tell Amanda, who had always made it perfectly clear that she didn't think I was good enough for him. And, oh my God, I'd get to meet his parents. My imagination was filled with the image of couples in furniture adverts who are always having pillow fights for some reason. That would be us. And where would we go? Alex was sure to get a bunch of money from his parents at Christmas time, so we'd be able to lay down a deposit on something quite nice. They might even pay all the rent, if we got lucky . . .

I'd started choosing the curtain material by the time he came back with two more cappuccinos.

He sat down. 'Tell me you're mentally choosing curtain material.'

'Don't be daft. I'm trying to think this whole thing through sensibly.'

'What's there to think? It's not like we're getting married or anything.'

'No, I suppose not.'

'C'mon, pumpkin, say yes. It'll be a laugh. I promise I'll be good. No Charlie, no rugby, just twenty-four-hour devotion to you.'

'You're a lying hound,' I said.

'I'm just a soul whose intentions are good,' he

pointed out. 'Oh Lord, please don't let me be misunderstood.'

I looked at him.

'Oh my God, what am I letting myself in for this time?'

'You said yes! She said yes!' he called out to the entire bar. Being English and not American, they didn't immediately burst out into spontaneous applause but looked at us as if we were a pair of loud-mouthed idiots.

We spent the rest of the evening in excited chatter, planning where, how, when. We compromised on somewhere nice and up and coming in North London. There was a fair chance his parents would pay the rent, which would be fabulous. I'd give Linda two months' notice and we'd start flat-hunting after Christmas. Flat-hunting! I was so excited. Then we went home and made love all night, to commemorate the beginning of something new.

'You'd better stay this way,' I said to him fiercely, as we were lying with our arms round each other. 'This is absolutely and utterly your last chance.'

'I know,' he said sleepily. 'And thank God I got it.'

Thirteen

Fran was furious. Absolutely fucking doing-her-nut furious. She was almost unspeakably angry, and enquired why I didn't just sell myself off to white slave traders now, if that's what I wanted to do with my life. I knew her feelings on the matter, but it still hurt, and she was really overreacting.

'You know why,' she said, nastily, when she'd exhausted all other modes of persuasion.

'Charlie doesn't want him there any more.'

'How the hell would you know?'

'Charlie and I have an . . . understanding,' she said.

'Have you seen him?'

'Maybe.'

'But! But . . . you can't! It's the rule!'

'Well, maybe the rules changed.'

'Shit! So you've been round there? Did you see Alex the other night?'

'For God's sake, I do not give a flying fuck about Alex.'

'And do you know what? I don't give a flying fuck about Charlie. You could shag Stephen Hawking for all I care, and I wouldn't get all pissy about it. Why can't you just let me be happy for once?'

She sighed. 'Look, can we not talk about this? We're only going to fall out.'

'As opposed to what we're doing at the moment?'

'Look, let's leave it. I'll be around to pick up the pieces, as usual, in about six months' time.'

'You always have to have the last word, don't you, Fran?'

'No, only when you cock up your life with a big FREAK.'

I put the phone down.

Angus had rung and left a message, but I didn't respond. I didn't want to think too much about that night. We'd perhaps been getting too close for comfort, and I was going to stick to my new policy of non-interference. The decision was made: I had one relationship to concentrate on now, and I was going to stick to it. His voice on the answerphone over the next couple of days grew increasingly confused, then he stopped calling altogether.

I didn't have time to miss him. Alex and I lunched together, spent every night together, at the cinema, out with his mates or just lazing around, looking at apartments to rent, planning what kind of thing we'd go see. We always went to my house. Paranoically, I did ask him about Charlie, but he dismissed it out of hand as nothing – I was the one who had to get up for work in the morning, and he was on twenty-four-hour devotion watch.

And I handed in my notice to Linda. She received it with the biggest, broadest smile I had ever seen, and said that would be absolutely fine. The light positively glinted off her spectacles. I wasn't sure if that was good or bad.

So everything seemed to be – at last – settling into place. Life was, suddenly, a lot less hectic. Almost quiet. Until Amanda phoned again . . .

'Darling, so kind of you to be putting this dinner on for us.'

What dinner? Oh my God, I'd completely forgotten.

'It is this weekend, isn't it?'

Was it this weekend? Jesus, I hadn't the foggiest.

'Ehmm . . .'

'I've invited Mookie . . . I'm amazed you two got on so well. Although she's always been a little on the eccentric side . . . And of course Nash is coming down from Glasgow a week early just to make it. Let me see . . . do you know, Fraser hardly mentioned it! God, he can be slow, that boy, wasn't even sure we should . . . whoops! I'm sorry! Almost forgot – can't slag off the hubby in front of Melanie. Ha ha ha! Anyway, I've got the address somewhere. Are you sure you want Angus there? You know what a drag he can be, especially if he's in one of his moods, which he is all the time. Why not ask that nice Charlie instead? He's great fun. Did you know his father owns a racing stable? Anyway, are you sure you can cope with all of us, darling? I mean, forgive me, but cooking's never been quite your strong point, has it? Unless, of course, it's a cheese-on-toast dinner party! Ha ha ha! Now, listen, is it formal? I assumed not, obviously, but just let me know if you want us to make the effort . . .'

'Ehm, can you hang on for just one second?'

'Of course, darling, no problem at all, lots to do, yah? We'll see you on Saturday. I'll assume it's eight for eight thirty – that's how people normally do dinner parties, darling. Ciao!'

I sat back, stupefied. Oh, Jesus. I'd forgotten all about it; events had rather overtaken things.

I couldn't see how I could have seven people round, a fair proportion of whom hated each other, one who thought making voodoo dolls of me and sticking pins in them had succeeded in driving me out of her dwelling, one whom I'd considered . . . gulp, well, whatever, and now wasn't returning the phone calls of, and two I didn't actually know.

Alex thought it was a great idea. Get everyone together, announce the fact that we were moving in – not that it was an announcement as such, I just hadn't seen anyone apart from him – drink and relax with our friends. He even promised to help me cook, which made me stare hard at him and wonder if the *X Files* was true and he was being brainwashed by the government through his asthma inhaler. Of course I couldn't tell him why I didn't want Angus to come.

I even managed to ask Linda. She gave me that look she had, which always went on too long without blinking.

'On Saturday night?'

'Yes, just dinner, a few friends, a couple of drinks . . . nothing wild.'

'But next weekend you'll be away?'

'Yes, I promise, next weekend I'll be away.'

The following weekend was the wedding – at last, the great occasion – and we had decided to book a bed and breakfast. I would have stayed with my parents, but post-wedding didn't seem the most auspicious time to introduce my new living-in-sin partner to them, and the wedding was actually being held in a beautiful little village called Pyrford, the nearest place to rural English gorgeousness you got in the Woking area.

She pondered it pudgily.

'OK.'

'Fantastic! Great!' I said, trying to imply how much we would be enriched by her company. When I got in later, it was written in pink letters on her kittens diary. 'Dinner. Saturday – 8 for 8.30 p.m.' I wondered how she would possibly manage to slot it in.

Friday night Fran phoned. I hadn't spoken to her all week. I was avoiding her. She knew it.

'Hey,' she said cheerfully, and nervously which

meant she was worried. If she'd thought everything was normal, she'd have been grouchy.

'What are you up to this weekend?'

'Oh, ehm . . . seeing Alex, you know, usual boring old stuff.'

'Right, right. So you're not having a dinner party or anything?'

My heart sank. Of course I should have known it would get back to her. I tried to think of an exit strategy that wouldn't make me look bad, but there wasn't one.

'Do you want to come?' I said quietly, waiting for the cutting put-down.

There was a pause.

'Yes!' she said tremulously. There was another pause. Then we both started, stupidly, to laugh. We laughed at nothing, we laughed because we were friends, and I laughed because I managed to persuade her to come early to help me with the cooking.

'Now we're going to be nine,' I mused. 'Aren't these things supposed to be balanced?'

'You could always invite Charlie . . .' she started.

'No way!' I said. 'Not you as well. But you are coming to this on the sole grounds that (1) you talk to Angus, because he thinks I hate him; and (2) you tell me EVERYTHING about Charlie – and I mean everything.'

'OK,' she said. 'You can ignore Angus all night while I talk to him, and that will prove you don't hate him?'

'Yes.'

'And I will talk to you about someone I hardly know and rarely see.'

'I don't believe you.'

'Huh. I'll see you tomorrow.'

'What are you up to tonight?'

'It's a secret. Bye!'

There was no doubt about it. Alex and I had to go shopping. In our new-found status as full-time couple, shopping was going to be something we were going to be doing a lot of, so we might as well get it off with a test run.

We had to buy dinner and wine for nine, as well as candles and flowers and all that crap – although how that would distract from the fact that all the chairs were of various hues, some from next door, some with floral tie-backs and one nasty seventies high stool which would make whoever ended up with it have to watch over the proceedings like a judge, I didn't know. All plumped round two tables of different heights put together and covered with an old plastic tablecloth. We also had to get a wedding present for Amanda and Fraser, plus a hat for me, plus a new tie and some new pants for Alex, whose pants had suddenly decided to spontaneously revolt all at once and make a break for freedom. (We never saw them again.)

Neither of us could face the hell that is central London on a Saturday close to Christmas, so we headed to the nearest South London equivalent: the Elephant and Castle Shopping Centre, a fearsome bright pink monstrosity that looked like a robot vomiting a strawberry milkshake. It sold lots of cheap international phone calls, but very few things that you could truly classify as a wedding present.

We stared dolefully at mops for an hour, avoided the manic Santa Claus, and had a quick look at the everything-for-99-pence shop, all without inspiration. Alex was obviously crazed with boredom but trying his hardest not to show it, even inviting me to try on the kind of hats that give you a start if you see one lying on the ground accidentally, because you think it's a mutated insect.

By two o'clock (we'd had a long, lazy lie-in, which had been wonderful, but tightened the schedule somewhat, particularly since I was planning on making lasagne), I'd started to panic slightly.

'If only they had a shop called "Everything You Need for a Run-Down Castle",' I lamented, picking up some eight foot imitation sunflowers for the fourth time.

'Well, what do they need?'

'Nothing! Absolutely nothing! Amanda has a Dualit toaster, a Philippe Starck lemon squeezer and every other bit of tat that's ever turned up in a magazine ever, plus an account at Heal's and an interior designer. And I've seen the wedding list and, I'm sorry, but I am just not ready to start selling my internal organs to rich Americans.'

'OK, pumpkin, calm down. What would Fraser like, then?'

I thought for a moment. 'Ehm, a Gameboy, probably.'

Alex clapped his hands together. 'Perfect. We'll get him one of those.'

'A Gameboy?'

'How many Gameboys do you think they're going to get?'

'Hmm. Well, none, I suppose.'

'There you go, then. Perfect.'

Two minutes later in Woolworths, it was done. Carry bag, extra games, the works. I paid, but then they were my friends.

'Piece of cake,' said Alex airily. 'And look –' he pointed to a shop which on first sight sold lots of different sizes of basins, but on closer inspection also sold CDs, teapots, pants and various other random items. 'Eight pairs of boxers for a fiver!' he exclaimed triumphantly.

'Oh, feel their bristling electrical quality.'

'I don't care. Maybe my other pants will get jealous of their new, inferior replacements and come home.'

'Good point.'

We were two points up now. Plus Alex had decided to wear his old school tie, which pissed me off, but only slightly, and almost put us ahead of the game. I'd given up on the hat.

Tesco's was a different matter altogether. Alex said the squalor and the crowds reminded him of India, but I ignored him in my search for an unbroken packet of spinach lasagne. Meanwhile, he loaded the trolley up with cheap red wine and a bottle of gin.

'That's a lot of wine,' I pointed out dubiously.

'There's a lot of people coming.'

I sighed. 'We'd better get on. I don't know how I'm going to cope with nine.'

'Nine? I thought you said eight.'

'Yeah, I know. Fran phoned and I felt really guilty, so I invited her too. It won't matter if it's uneven.'

Alex looked cross.

'Yes it will. God, Mel, she'll ruin it. Can't you phone her up and tell her not to come?'

'No! For God's sake, you two are dreadful. I already had a word with her about not being so rude to you. She'll be fine. I'll put her beside Angus or someone.'

'I still think it's too many. You could phone her. She'll understand.'

'Alex, isn't this a little early for us to stand about bickering in supermarkets? She's coming, OK? She's making up for Linda, who doesn't have a personality, and Mookie, who only has half of one. And she'll shut Amanda up if she's getting too mouthy.'

'Yeah, right. Only Fran's allowed to be mouthy. For Britain.'

'Stop this.' We were in the queue, finally, but it was a humdinger. A baby in a backpack in front of me hit me on the head with a rattle covered in biscuit and scum.

'It's sorted, OK?'

Alex looked a bit sulky for a moment, then wandered off.

'Hey,' I said. 'Aren't you going to help me out with this?'

'I want to,' he said, 'but I'm a bit short . . . Can you get this one and I'll get the next one?'

'But you put a hundred bottles of wine in!'

'Oh, don't cause a scene. Do you want me to take some of them back?'

'No, forget it. Just leave them. We'll drink them some other time if we don't drink them tonight.'

'Right, pumpkin – we'll never finish them tonight.'

'Oh God! I wish I'd never volunteered to do this.'

He put his arm round me. 'Don't worry. It'll be fine. It'll be great. You'll be a sparkling hostess, and everyone will love you, and we'll all be friends again. Chill out.'

I tried to chill out while signing the enormous Visa bill, but it wasn't easy. We got all the boxes back home around four and I dumped them on the kitchen table gratefully. Immediately Alex tried to drag me towards the bedroom for a little bit of afternoon messing. This, however, was not the day for it.

'Alex, I have four hours to cook a bunch of stuff that I don't know how to. Make yourself useful and chop something.'

'OK.' He kissed me playfully on the neck. 'I'll just go check out the football results.'

'You will not!'

'Ten minutes, pumpkin!'

He vanished, then reappeared two seconds later, confiscating one of the bottles, a glass and a bottle opener.

'And don't you dare get pissed!' I yelled. I followed him in to where he was cosily resting his feet up on the sofa. Linda was mutely removing her tape of *The English Patient* from the machine. I noticed it had been joined by *Titanic*. Interesting.

'I'll take that,' I said, smiling, and swiped the bottle of wine back. 'You know what happened last time.'

'Actually, I remember very little of it.' He zapped the remote control to the footie.

'My point exactly. Linda, do you want a glass of wine?'

She looked shocked at the hour. 'No . . . but perhaps a sherry.'

'Sherry, huh?' Linda had a fully stocked drinks cabinet, which was odd, as she scarcely ever drank. Occasionally, I helped her out with it.

'Go on, be daring.' I handed it to her. She turned a dull red and rushed back to her bedroom.

To even things up I poured myself a glass before I recorked the bottle. There was a long enough night ahead. I picked up the chopping knife and sighed to myself.

Two hours later, a big pot of mince, which I hadn't even wanted to touch, stood bubbling on the stove in a faintly impressive way. I was stirring it casually, feeling pretty hot, as it had only taken this long, plus of course the four attempts at a non evil and lumpy white sauce. The kitchen looked like one of those nasty splatter films, all bits of meat and tomato red. When I'd gone in to fetch Alex for chopping the fruit salad, he'd been asleep – extremely asleep, actually, as he didn't wake up even when I deliberately sat on him. Linda was nowhere to be seen. I guessed she was eating lots of chocolate so she wouldn't embarrass herself by going completely feral at the meal and ripping into the garlic bread.

At six the doorbell screeched, startling me out of my wits as usual, and I panicked until I remembered that Fran was coming over to help.

She came in, dark eyes sparkling and flushed from the cold – it had finally turned frosty and bitter outside, and was threatening to snow, which I reckoned it would next week, just in time for the big day. Amanda's dad had probably ordered it wholesale. She was armed with two bottles of wine and a quarter bottle of gin.

'Why on earth have you brought so much booze?' I asked in disbelief. The kitchen was turning into a wine cellar, and I'd already poured half a bottle into the lasagne.

She looked at me like I was a moron.

'Oh, no reason. Can I have a glass, please?'

I poured us both one, reminding myself to pace it. Alex suddenly appeared, looking thoroughly refreshed. He and Fran nodded at each other distantly as I refilled his glass, then he disappeared again, saying something cheery along the lines of 'too many cooks'.

Fran raised her eyes to heaven, then leaned her long body on the kitchen unit and proceeded to chat to me while I tried to cut equal-sized slices out of a kiwi fruit without meditating too long on the pointlessness of it all.

'Why don't you tell me all about Charlie now?' I interrupted her diatribe against the snotty cow who'd served her in the off-licence, once I'd ascertained that the girl didn't actually have to attend Casualty.

She sighed. 'Do I have to?'

'If you want to eat tonight, you do.' I removed the expensive pistachio nuts she was working her way through.

She refilled her glass. It was nearly seven.

'Really, he's a complete twat.'

'Really.'

'Everything went as normal: he was completely miserable and followed me around like a lost dog. So, I kind of . . . saw him again.'

'What!? You never do that!'

'I know. I've no idea what was the matter with me.'

'You LIKE him.'

'I do not. He's a loud-mouth piss bism.'

'You like that kind of thing. Oh my God, Fran's in love, Fran's in love!'

'Can you hand me that chopping knife, please?'

I'd passed it over without thinking before I realized my fatal mistake.

'OK, OK, I'll stop!'

'Sure?'

'Yes!'

Fran slowly lowered the knife to the table and I risked taking it back to chop up the rest of the kiwi fruit in silence.

Alex wandered into the kitchen in search of the expensive nuts.

'It's suspiciously quiet in here . . . who have you two just been massacring – I mean, talking about?'

'No one,' I said stoutly.

'Ah. So, it was either me or –' he shot a look at Fran, so he must have known – 'Charlie.'

'It was Charlie,' I said, desperate for him not to think that I was discussing him with my friends all day long.

'Oh. Shame,' he said. He tried to pick up the nuts in passing. Fran, without thinking about it, slapped him on the back of the hand, which he ignored, retreating, with nuts, to the TV, which had reached *Blind Date* stage.

'How's Alex?' asked Fran ruefully. From the sitting room I could hear him howling and whooping like a dog as the less blessed single women came on.

'Oh, usual responsible grown-up old Alex,' I said.

'I'm sorry I was so pissed off.'

'That's OK.'

'Arf arf arf,' came from next door.

'Can you give me a hand to put these salmon roulades together?'

Fran looked doubtful, and removed her cardigan. Underneath, she was wearing some beautiful ethereal dark blue thirties-style dress which looked almost see-through but actually wasn't, if you looked closely.

'Oh my God! No, don't worry,' I said heartily. 'That's a gorgeous dress. You look fantastic.'

'Thanks very much: I half-inched it from Madam Elizabeth.'

'No!'

Fran had a couple of days' work as an extra in a high-budget thirties melodrama. No wonder the dress fitted her so well: it'd been made for her. She twirled round slowly. It was slim and diaphanous and beautiful. I wished with all my heart that I could wear a dress like that, in a way that wouldn't make me look like a chunky five-year-old ballerina, and rolled up the salmon and cream cheese mush in approximately attractive ways.

'Do you think we've got enough food?' I wondered gloomily.

'Tons! Amanda and Mookie don't eat, remember.'

'Oh, yes.' I breathed a sigh of relief. 'It's just the boys and us then, really, isn't it?'

Fran indicated Linda's bedroom.

'Bugger it. Listen, would you nip across the road and get me another French stick?'

'But I'll get mugged and killed,' she complained.

'I'll send Alex with you.'

'Why don't you send Alex by himself?'

'Because he'll come back in three days with a fish supper and a new fishing rod. Alex!'

He appeared. Even he looked taken aback by the sight of Fran in her beautiful dress.

'Can you walk Fran across the road to get some bread . . . coffee – real coffee – and . . .' I tried to work out what else I'd forgotten. 'Oh, and some more candles.' I was sticking them in old wine bottles, just like real students do.

'I can go by myself,' said Fran, disgruntledly.

'And if you got mugged and killed, I'd hate it. It'd be rubbish,' I said, pushing both of them out the door. It slammed behind them and I heard them walking off in silence. Oh God, if they'd only get on, everything would be fine. Here I was, part of a couple, hostessing and actually cooking things. I felt uniquely proud of myself. Alex and I would have dinner parties all the time. Hey – we'd get on a dinner party circuit. It would be fantastic. Humming, I went in to lay the tables.

Half an hour later, stepping back to admire my handiwork, I was quite proud of myself. With all the lights out and candles everywhere, the dining room looked less Laura Ashley and more a state of gothic horror – the bows and frills everywhere took on sinister undertones and it looked like a ghostly bride's boudoir. I artistically placed some bowls of nuts around the place. The kitchen might look like a nuclear explosion, but in here was pretty good, particularly after I'd used some of Linda's Celine Dion CDs (she didn't have any books) to prop up the table legs so they almost matched. I toyed with the idea of placecards, then realized two things: (1) I was turning into an idiot, and (2) where the hell were Alex and Fran? The shop was only five minutes up the road. Maybe it hadn't had any bread and they'd had to go elsewhere.

This practical explanation wasn't enough for me, however. What if one of them had been run down and had to go to hospital? What if they'd been mugged? I started to panic. What if they'd had another big fight and Fran had given him a kicking and he was in intensive care and she was being held by the police? Oh God, that would be awful. I was so fascinated by this idea that I almost didn't hear the doorbell ring, despite its closeness to a submarine honk.

Thank God. I dashed to the door to demand where they'd got to. But it wasn't them. It was Angus, with Nash. We stood on either side of the open door, looking at each other, as I became more and more aware of the fact that not only were they three-quarters of an hour early, but I was still dressed in my cooking gear – which, as I didn't have any cooking gear, was in fact my pyjamas covered by Linda's apron, which had some pussy cats on it. And I hadn't brushed my hair – because I was cooking – and I was covered in gruesome stains. And I hadn't had a bath. Or cut my toenails, and my feet were bare. Fucking hell. Both of them had suits on, and Nash was even taller than Angus, gangly and handsome, so they just looked far too good to be here.

Nash looked worriedly at Angus.

'Are you sure it's tonight?' he whispered.

With that, I regained my composure.

'Nash! Angus!' I yelled, in a carefree manner. 'You're VERY, VERY early!'

'Sorry about that,' said Angus, 'we misjudged it. Do you want us to go out to the pub and come back?'

'Man, it's freezing out there,' said Nash. He caught sight of my scary wide-eyed Harpy look. 'But, you know, no problem . . .'

'NO! No, come in, come in. Sorry, you've caught me off guard, you know.'

I didn't know what to do first, particularly when

they started taking off their coats and scarves and handing them to me. I held on to them.

'Come through, come through,' I said, and led them through to the sitting room, wondering if I'd remembered to put any pants on.

The two tables filled up every square inch of the space, I noticed.

'Do you want us to sit at the table?' said Angus.

'No! No!' I indicated the sofa, which had been pushed flat up against the variety of chairs.

'Sit here!'

The boys moved over carefully, and crammed themselves in.

'I just need to change, and, well, you know, get ready.'

'Actually,' said Angus, 'I really like that spoon in your hair.'

I clapped my hand to my head, and found a teaspoon covered in tomato puree peeping out of one of my more unruly curls. I made a grab for it, but dropped one of the coats instead. Nash stood up again.

'Would you like a hand?'

'No, no, I'm fine,' I screeched, trying to reach down to the floor without exposing my breasts over the top of my baggy pyjamas. Despite being practically hysterical by this time, I remembered what came next in the good hostess book of gracious living.

'Would you like a drink?'

The boys muttered that that would be lovely, and started to bring out bottles of wine they'd brought. Angus had also brought a bottle of whisky. They handed them to me, although I already had my arms full of coats. Not knowing what to do, I indicated that they should pile the bottles on top of the coats. As they didn't know what to do either, they did so, and I staggered into the kitchen. Or tried to; I didn't quite make it, and everything fell on the floor. The boys dashed in looking worried when they heard the noise, but fortunately nothing had smashed, so my luck was in.

'Are you OK?' Angus lent me a hand and I scrambled up, blushing fiercely.

'Calm down,' he said, gently, not letting go of my hand. 'It's only us. Me, remember, who's nice, and Nash, who's a bit mad.'

'Aye, right enough,' said Nash.

'I'm sure dinner will be lovely, no one else will be here for ages, so why don't you let us get ourselves a drink, then you can disappear and get changed and beautify yourself, then re-emerge like a butterfly.'

'Will you pretend I'm somebody else?'

'If you like. Just leave those coats there, we'll sort everything out. Now, off you go.'

I escaped to the shower, and was in and out in double quick time. I shoved the grey silk dress on again and bunged on some slap. Twenty-five minutes later, I was just about presentable. Still no Fran and Alex.

I walked back into the sitting room, where the boys

applauded sweetly. They were intrigued when I explained my dilemma.

'Do you think I should call the police?' I asked them.

'Naw, they dinnae file until forty-eight hoors,' said Nash.

'What?'

'He means they won't listen unless they've been away for a couple of days,' Angus explained. 'Up until then it's assumed they're out on the razz somewhere.'

That didn't make me feel any better.

'Do you think they're up to anything?' asked Nash, as if the thought had just occurred to him. Angus frowned.

'No, they hate each other,' I explained. 'That's why I'm so worried.'

I got up and pottered around the kitchen, bringing in a bottle of wine.

'They've probably just gone for a pint somewhere to get out of helping you,' said Angus.

Relief that this was obviously the case was tempered with annoyance.

'You're right. They're like a pair of spoilt twins sometimes, those two.' And I stopped stuffing my mouth with pistachio nuts like they were going out of fashion.

The doorbell rang again.

'Christ, what was that?' said Nash.

'I'll get it.' I hoped it was them and I could give them a bollocking. On the other side of the door, however, stood Mookie, looking skinny, blonde and absolutely freezing.

'Hello! Come in!' I said.

'Thank you. Rally! South London. Well, you know, I have some friends in Chelsea, but I never normally get down this far!'

'That is fascinating,' I said, taking her Barbour jacket.

She snorted with laughter. 'I'm more used to Kensington than Kennington!' she said hilariously.

I laughed along merrily. 'You know, Mookie, you are really funny,' I said.

She stopped immediately.

'Do you rally think so?'

'No!' I said, and she laughed herself silly, even though I was being honest. I beckoned her through to the dining room. Angus and Nash were out of sight behind the table.

'Oh God, am I first? That's *so* embarrassing. I'm so mortified. I thought quarter past eight would be fine, but I've obviously completely messed it up. Oh God. This was always happening in Switzerland.'

'Mookie,' I said gently, 'it's fine.'

The boys stuck their arms out from behind the table and waved vigorously.

'What would you like to drink?' I asked.

'Vodka martini, please.'

Ahh. Linda's drinks cabinet was pretty wide, but we'd drunk all the vodka, and it didn't stoop to martini.

'Aha! Look at your face, it's rally funny,' said Mookie.

I was regretting asking her already. She'd seemed quite nice in the taxi.

'Here you are, darling!' And she drew out an enormous bottle of Absolut Vodka, some brand of martini I'd never heard of, and a jar of olives.

'I came prepared. Have you got some lemonade, darling? And some ice?'

I nodded, stunned at such largesse. I began to like her again.

'Would anyone else like one?' The boys nodded their assent, and I headed back to the kitchen with the bottles. Mookie tapped in behind me. 'Oh, let me make them,' she cooed. 'I'm very particular.'

So I left her to it and went and rejoined the boys. I was chain-munching pistachios again, which obviously meant I was getting tense. And sure enough, when Mookie brought back the delicious martinis, we sat perched in between the table legs in a not entirely comfortable silence. I sensed Angus giving me faintly wounded looks for not returning his calls.

'So what do you do, Nash?' asked Mookie.

'I work on the rigs, ken.'

'The oil rigs?'

'No, the Runrigs,' he said, guffawing heartily to himself. I didn't have a clue what he was on about.

'The Runrigs? Rally?' asked Mookie. 'What does one do there?'

Nash took pity on her. 'Don't worry,' he said. 'I meant the oil rigs. Hey, Angus, did you hear Runrig are doing a Stones tribute cover?'

'No,' said Angus, smiling.

'Yes, it's called "Hey, McLeod, get off of my ewe"!'

They cracked up at this, although I didn't quite get it. Neither did Mookie, judging by the way she was staring into the middle distance.

'Gosh, my daddy owns one of those,' she beamed. 'But I thought you said . . .'

Fortunately then the doorbell rang again. The draught swirled in with Amanda and Fraser, filling the air with glamorous perfume and a sprinkling of snow from their heavy coats.

'It's snowing!' I exclaimed. 'Fantastic!'

'Revolting, more like. Hello, darling. How are you?' said Amanda, giving me an air kiss.

Traitorous, I wanted to say, but didn't.

Fraser gave me a hug. 'Sorry to put you to all this trouble,' he whispered.

'Oh no! My fault! My fault entirely,' I said cheerily, when of course I should have said, *Not at all.*

'Come in, come in.'

'Well, I've never been to your humble abode, darling.' Amanda had divested herself of her coat and was prowling around.

'Yes, because the last time you were invited you didn't come,' I said. 'For my birthday.'

Amanda pretended she hadn't heard and made an entrance. She was wearing a beautiful champagne-coloured dress, not too fancy and not too plain. It set off her golden hair wonderfully.

Nash and Angus stood up to greet her. She nodded regally at them, and kissed Mookie, who toddled off to make some more martinis, bless her.

'Is this everyone?' asked Amanda.

'Umm . . . no. We're missing Alex and Fran . . .'

She turned to face me. 'Where are they?'

'Well, they went out for a loaf of bread about two hours ago and haven't returned. I'm very worried about them.'

'Worried? God, they've probably gone to America, darling. Now, where is there to sit? Or are we at table already?'

'Umm, no,' I said, controlling the urge to slap her. 'I'm afraid there's not much room, so if you wouldn't mind sitting on the sofa . . .' Nash bunched up, leaving a very small space between him and Angus, which she regarded disdainfully '. . . as soon as we're all here, we can eat.'

'I think I'll stand, darling. This dress creases terribly, you know.'

She accepted a drink from Mookie without saying thank you. And of course, everyone else then had to stand up too. So we leaned on the table, Nash nearly knocked over a candle, and Amanda geared herself up for the latest round of 'What's going on with the wedding?' I noticed she cast very significant glances at Fraser as she prattled on about flower arrangements, and he was nodding politely a fraction of a second too late.

And where the hell were those two? I bet they were in some fucking pub. Slagging me off, most like. They were probably having a Why-Melanie-is-so-awful competition. I was furious.

I decided to start dishing up the first course, as

I'd eaten all the pistachio nuts, so I slipped surreptitiously away as Amanda lurched into a detailed hymnal repertoire.

Angus followed me into the kitchen.

'Look, Melanie . . . I . . . Have I done anything to upset you?'

'No!' I said. 'No, definitely not.'

'Well, you know, I thought we were friends, but you didn't return my phone calls or anything . . .'

'I'm sorry,' I said. 'It's been absolutely hectic.' And I explained to him about moving in with Alex. He was amazed.

'I thought . . . I mean, he's a right bastard, isn't he? Sorry.'

'No, that's OK. He's not really. He just gets . . . well, mixed up in things, and he's going through a really tough time at the moment.'

'And you're not,' he said gently.

I hadn't thought I was, but before I had the chance to ask him, he'd picked up a bottle of wine and was heading for the living-room door.

'I'm sorry to have bothered you,' he said.

'You never bother me.'

He smiled ruefully and sweetly. As he opened the door, I involuntarily said, 'Angus!'

He turned and faced me, but I hadn't a clue what to say.

'I . . . er . . .'

There was a long pause.

'You sound like you're waiting for the doorbell to ring, as a useful interruption,' he said, smiling.

I tilted my head towards the door for a second. Just as I was on the point of giving up, it actually did ring.

'Yes!' I said, punching the air.

He smiled one more time and headed back to the others. I felt ashamed of myself.

'Where the hell have you two been?'

Covered in snow, pink-cheeked and giggling, Alex and Fran stood at the door like a couple of children.

Alex leaned forward and kissed me on the nose.

'We've been making up!' he announced. 'We thought you'd be pleased.'

'I'd have been more pleased if you hadn't disappeared into the pitch-black freezing cold in the middle of the night when you were meant to be gone for five minutes!'

'It's only quarter to nine, pumpkin. It's hardly the middle of the night.'

It felt like it.

'What have you two been doing?' I asked again incredulously.

Fran smiled shyly. I had never seen her do this in my entire life.

'We've decided to stop fighting. For you, Mel.'

This smelled fishy.

'You don't fight, you snipe,' I protested.

'Well, now we're moving in together . . .' Alex stepped inside and put his arm round my shoulders,

'Fran and I had a talk and decided that we would try and get on.'

'So we can all be friends,' added Fran.

I stared at them. Moonie Cult! Moonie Cult!

'Are you sure you're not zombies?' I asked them. 'Or vampires, that you have to ask over the threshold before they can eat you?'

'Vampires don't eat you,' said Alex. 'They have metaphorical sex with you. In fact, in many ancient cultures . . .'

'BORING!' Fran and I shouted simultaneously. And I relaxed, took their coats, and went to see how everyone was getting on next door.

Everyone was getting on very poorly next door, and I immediately felt hollow, both as a hostess and as a person.

Amanda was resting delicately on the edge of the sofa, nose to nose with Mookie, whom she looked to be telling off in some way. Angus and Nash were muttering quietly next to them. And Fraser was sitting on his own, staring off into space.

'The fugitives have returned!' I announced loudly, in an effort to break the tension. Everyone looked up like they were exhausted, and said hello briefly without any great warmth. Oh God, this was awful.

'Mookie!' I squealed. This was all getting a bit *Abigail's Party*.

'Could you possibly make us another round of those delicious martinis? And if everyone wants to take a seat, we can start.'

There was a general rumbling from the boys, who

were clearly starving to death. As soon as I got them seated, they launched into the bread like ravenous kestrels.

'Did you get the extra bread?' I whispered to Fran.

'No.'

Amanda sat at the head of the table. Fraser was on her right, and Mookie was to his right. Amanda was leaning right across him in order to talk to her. He sat there stoically.

I put Alex on one side of me and Nash on the other, with Fran and Angus joining up to Mookie. And, finally, I brought out the salmon roulades, which almost looked like the snail shapes they were supposed to. Not quite though.

I poured some of the white wine, and we all sat down at last, although some of us were at different heights than others.

'To the chef!' Angus proposed, and everyone else joined in. Finally, the ice was starting to break and I could relax. Alex began gabbing to Nash and Angus about the music business, and they were listening politely. Fran was listening to Amanda with a glint in her eye and a glass in her hand, which could, I suspected, cause problems later.

'I'll just go check on the lasagne,' I announced as everyone tucked in, except Amanda and Mookie who had politely declined – well, not that politely, actually. Amanda had announced:

'It's quite clear you eat dairy products, Melanie, but

some of us want to keep our figures,' and rudely handed back the two plates. I wasn't sure Mookie didn't want hers, but she wasn't getting much of a chance.

'Are you going to eat that?' Amanda said sharply to Fraser.

Fraser nodded dully. There was silence as everyone waited to see what she was going to do. However she simply made a martyr face and returned to ignoring him.

Two shocks awaited me in the kitchen. Number one was the lasagne that I had made up ready to go in the oven but hadn't actually got round to putting in there. In fact, the oven wasn't actually on.

'Fucking hell,' I moaned, looking at it in all its dark red and freezing glory.

The second was Linda, who was unobtrusively attempting to pour herself a glass of sherry.

'Fucking hell!' I yelled again. 'Squared! Linda! Why aren't you next door?' I blamed her instantly.

She stared at the floor and shrugged.

'Come on! Let me make you a vodka martini, then I'll take you next door to meet everyone.'

'Maybe I shouldn't come.'

I felt like a complete heel as I jammed the lasagne into the cold oven, turned the heat up, made her a vodka martini and tried to smile ingratiatingly all at the same time.

'Of course you should,' I said. 'Come on, they're dying to meet you,' I lied.

Shuffling and looking at her feet, Linda followed me into the sitting room.

'Ehm, everyone, this is . . . Linda,' I announced. I'd even forgotten to set her a place, so I plonked her down in my seat, although I'd already taken a bite out of the roulade. Then I poured her a large glass of wine and made eye signals to Fran to talk to her, which she studiously ignored.

Back I trailed to the kitchen, to drag in the extra-high stool I had thought I wouldn't have to use. I checked the lasagne in the flaming oven, but it was still so cold as to be solid. This night was not going to be easy. Sighing heavily, I dragged myself back into the sitting room with another couple of bottles of red wine.

'That was lovely,' said Angus, and there were mutters of agreement and a sniff from Amanda. 'What's next?'

'Ah,' I said. 'Well, there's a funny story about that . . . While I was in the kitchen, the lasagne went through a mystery freezing process which reversed its cooked status and took it back to a rudimentary uncooked state. I'm not sure whether it's a time slip or a cryogenic disorder, but the FBI are on their way over. In the meantime' – I put the wine on the table – 'we're just going to have to get drunk.'

There was a pause, then Alex started to uncork the bottles.

'Those aliens are pesky things,' he said. 'We'd better fight them off with this magic elixir.'

'How long have we got, Captain?' asked Fraser, perking up momentarily.

'I've reversed the polarity of the neutron flow,' I

announced gravely. 'We can expect to see reconstituted lasagne in about forty-five minutes.'

'God, they're so childish,' I could hear Amanda whisper to Mookie. And I was at the other end of the room.

'Have you got any more bread?' asked Nash.

'Sorry. I've got some salad.'

He stared at his empty plate mournfully.

'Real Scots don't eat salad.'

Strangely, the lack of foodstuffs seemed to break the ice. No one was going anywhere for a while and eventually a beautiful, warming smell of lasagne began to seep through into the room, the candles burnt on, and we found Nash a tin of cold beans in the fridge. Everyone else made do with increasing quantities of red wine, and the chatter level grew commensurably.

Only Fraser sat quietly amongst the kerfuffle. And Linda, of course, but I was less worried about her. I stuck my tongue out at him. He stuck his back, so I felt that he wasn't suicidal quite yet. On the other side, Amanda was trying to make small talk about castle furnishings, and Fran was pretending to listen and making increasingly sarky comments that Amanda was oblivious to. Nash and Alex were having a conversation about rugby versus football (I wasn't sure who was on which side) which looked like it may degenerate into bodily harm, and on my other side Angus was chatting quietly to Linda behind Nash. Linda was staring terrified at her place, but occasionally nodding along. Suddenly Alex shouted out, 'Game! Game!'

Everyone stopped talking.

'What game?' said Fran.

'I don't know. Let's play a game. Something. Ehm, Truth or Forfeit.'

Everyone groaned.

'If only we were all fifteen,' said Fran, 'that would be a great idea.'

'No, come on, guys . . . just for a laugh.'

Fran passed him an empty bottle. 'Hey, maybe then we can spin this!'

'Fine, OK.' Alex hated losing his cool like that. 'I don't give a toss. Just thought it might add a bit of spark, given that we're sitting here starving to death.'

'Thanks very much,' I flared up from the top of my high chair. Then I remembered that they were my guests and I was starving them to death, so I shut up again.

'Rally, I don't mind, but why don't you ask the first question and we'll see if we want to play or not?' said Mookie quietly. The girl was a born compromiser.

Alex still looked a bit sulky. Then he took another drink of wine and sat back.

'OK then.' There was a general groaning around the table, but the wine was going down easy and we couldn't talk football for ever. I looked at Angus, and he seemed relieved that his nursemaiding duties would be over for a bit.

'Here we go,' said Alex. 'Who's –'

'Wait a wee minute,' said Nash. 'Whit's the forfeit?'

'You'll find out.' Alex showed his teeth.

'Och, that's no fair, ken. You cannae just make up the rules.'

'For God's sake, you two!' said Fran. 'Jesus, you can't let boys anywhere near each other when it comes to games.'

Nash sat back in his chair.

Alex decided to start with Mookie, across the table.

'OK, Mookie, who's the most embarrassing person you've ever fancied?'

'Hang on,' I said, 'famous or not famous?'

'Famous. Unless everyone else knows them.'

'Fine.'

Mookie thought for a minute.

'Well, we did have this very dishy stable hand, but I don't suppose that counts.'

'Boy or girl?' asked Alex curiously. I threw my napkin at him.

'Oh, rally,' said Mookie, blushing. 'No, I suppose it would have to be . . . Adam Ant.'

'Adam Ant's not embarrassing!' said Fran and I practically simultaneously. The boys howled with laughter.

'Oh God, what turned you on most?' asked Alex, laughing. 'The highwayman or the pirate?'

'Shut up! At the time, it was not embarrassing!'

'Erm, actually, I fancy him now,' said Mookie, going red.

'Ohhh.' That put a different slant on things.

'Who is he now?' I asked.

'I don't know. Still a highwayman, probably,' she said dreamily. My mouth dropped open as Fran and I looked at each other in horror.

'Definitely straight into the lead there,' said Alex.

'I thought this was Truth or Forfeit?' said Nash. 'How come there's points?'

'There's points for the most embarrassing truth,' said Alex.

'Oh, right. New rule,' said Nash. Everyone else yelled at him to shut up.

'OK, you next,' said Alex.

'I'm no going if Ah don't know what the forfeit is.'

Alex looked exasperated. 'Melanie,' he yelled at me unexpectedly, 'even though we're moving in together, we're never having kids in case they end up like him, OK?'

I nodded understandingly.

'The forfeit is, if you don't answer the question, I hang you out of the window by your ankles for two minutes.'

'That's no a forfeit for me, that's a forfeit for you.'

'Believe me, it's a forfeit for you.'

Nash thought about it for a moment.

'Aye, all right then.'

'So, who's the most embarrassing person you've ever fancied?'

Nash looked shyly at his hands for a moment, then smiled to himself.

'Gail Tilsley.'

It took us a moment to figure out who this character was, before remembering *Coronation Street*.

'No!'

'When?'

'How?'

'Well, ken, I just felt sorry for her, and it kind of went from that, really.'

'Felt sorry for her how?' asked Fran. 'Because she still uses curling tongs on only half her hair?'

Nash still couldn't help himself grinning with embarrassment.

'No, like, after Brian died and that.'

I laughed merrily to myself. This was working out well after all.

'That's pretty good,' said Alex.

'Do Ah get more points?'

'No, I'm afraid a twenty-year attachment to a man named after an insect is worth more than a passing sympathy fuck for a fictional character.'

Amanda was next.

'This is a stupid game,' she said.

'Oh my God – not the pony!' yelled Fran. Everyone burst out into guffaws. Definitely, there was a bit too much wine floating about for this early in the evening.

'Don't be ridiculous, Francesca.' Amanda's face resumed its habitual snotty look.

'Forfeit! Forfeit! Forfeit!' Angus and Nash took up the chanting.

'Oh, for goodness' sake!' she looked furious.

'Forfeit! Forfeit! Forfeit!' Alex had started banging his cutlery on the table.

'Oh, bloody hell. OK, then: bloody Gerry Adams. Now, fuck off.'

Instantly there was silence. Fran clapped a hand over her mouth.

'No!'

'Ha, so, now you don't believe me!'

'No, but just . . .'

'Don't say it. He's a politician, that's all.'

'He's not a politician! He's a . . .'

Amanda shot Fran a very dangerous look. Fran grinned and edged away slightly.

'You don't . . . know him, do you?'

'No, of course not. Right, can we move on now, please? I've done mine.'

Alex raised his eyebrows. 'I'm afraid dodgy Irish type beats dandy highwayman. Sorry, Mooks.'

Amanda looked cool as a cucumber, but as the attention moved to Fraser, I saw her take a huge swig of wine. Well, bloody hell. Maybe there were some depths to this woman, after all. Or maybe she just liked beards and a sense of danger. That must be it.

Fraser was pondering. 'I suppose I should say Amanda,' he said. Nobody laughed. 'Only kidding,' he said. Still, nobody laughed, although we did try to look encouraging.

'God, I don't know,' he sighed.

'I do,' said Angus, looking evil.

'Who?' said Fraser.

'You know.'

'No, I don't. Remind me.'

Immediately, Angus got up and started stroking and fondling imaginary long hair.

'Don't push too far . . .' he sang. 'Your dreams are/China in your hand . . .'

Fraser's smile widened. 'No way!'

'Don't wish too hard/Because they may come true.'

'That red-headed midget from T'pau . . . ?'

'. . . And you can't help them/Don't push too far . . .'

'Jesus, I can't even remember her name!'

'China in your hand . . .' finished Angus, managing to mime a huge pair of tits and look coy at the same time. 'I love you, Fraser McConnald.'

We gave him as much of a storm of applause as eight people could muster – seven, if you discounted Amanda, who was looking furious.

Fraser laughed heartily. 'So I did. I thought she was gorgeous, then I looked at her one day and thought she was absolutely awful.'

'She was awful,' I agreed, nodding my head vigorously.

'I know. Well, there you go. How do I do on the points-ometer, Alex?'

'Not too well, actually, old chap.'

'Why not?'

'Ha!' said Nash.

'Erm, no reason,' said Alex, blushing.

'Did you –' I started with delight. Fran coughed up her red wine until it came out her nose.

'Carol Decker!' she spluttered, getting red wine everywhere. 'That was her name!'

I was helpless with laughter watching Fran spit everywhere.

'But she was four foot one!' I yelled. 'She made Kylie Minogue look like a heifer!'

'Kylie Minogue only has the brains of a heifer,' said Fran.

'Ehm, Kylie was going to be mine, actually,' said Angus. 'I don't need to have a go now.'

'No!' I yelled. 'I can't believe what a THING you boys all have for fucking skinny midgets! Sorry, Amanda.'

I realized suddenly that I had put an apology in where there should never have been one.

Foot, mouth, and easy insertion instructions.

Amanda sniffed imperiously, and looked at her watch.

'Is this game finished? Because, Fraser, it's time we were going.'

'Amanda, it's only ten o'clock and we haven't eaten yet.'

'Well, I'm tired and I want to go home. Take me home, please.'

Fraser looked at her straightforwardly. 'I'm not ready to go yet. It would be rude, and I'm hungry and I want to stay here and chat to my friends.'

'Oh, for God's sake, Fraser! Do you want me to go by myself?'

'I don't mind.'

There was a silence.

'OK then, I will.' Her face went very tight. 'In fact, I think I'll just go out on my own.'

'I thought you were tired.'

'Shut the fuck up!'

Shakily, she stabbed at her mobile.

'Jacintha? Hi, darling, it's Amanda.'

'Yes . . . no, just at this really dull dinner party. Thought I might come over. Where are you? . . . Oh, Blinski's – great. I'll hop in a cab and see you there in half an hour. Ciao, darling.'

She hung up, then stalked imperiously out of the room.

'I'll get my own coat, thank you,' she shouted as she heard me get up.

'Mookie, are you coming?' we heard from the hallway.

Mookie looked at us, terrified. Fran shook her head vehemently. 'You don't have to go,' she whispered. Mookie took a deep breath.

'Ahem . . . no,' she said quietly. We could hear Amanda pausing outside.

'Say hello to Gerry for us!' hollered Fran.

Then the door slammed and she was gone.

Fourteen

Silence fell. Everyone gazed at their plates. Finally Fraser heaved a sigh.

'I'm sorry, everyone.'

'What, for your wife? Might as well get used to that,' Fran said.

'Shh,' I said to Fran. 'Don't worry about it, Frase. She must just be really tense.'

'Tense,' he said. We watched him with bated breath, but he didn't say any more.

'Rigid, more like,' said Alex, and Nash sniggered.

'Can we get on with the game, please?' Alex poured himself another glass of wine.

'Thanks, Mr Sensitivity,' I said snidely.

'God, it's the all-in couples fun match night tonight,' pointed out Fran. Alex grimaced at her and she shut up.

Out of the corner of my eye, I saw Nash risk a very small piece of salad.

'Oh my God! The lasagne!'

I dashed into the kitchen, followed closely by Angus. As I opened the oven and smoke poured out, he knelt down next to me with a serious look on his face.

'I think we should get Fraser NOW,' he whispered urgently.

'For God's sake, how many times do I have to tell you not to talk seriously to me while I'm holding burnt lasagne?'

He grinned. 'You know what I mean. I'll tell Mookie – she's on our side –'

'I don't have a side any more.'

'Och, come on. Yes, you do.'

'No, I don't.'

He ignored me.

'Then we'll get him pissed and talk him out of the wedding.'

I dumped the lasagne on the kitchen unit. It was black and hard round the edges. I started to file those bits away with a knife.

'What do you think this is, *Mission: Impossible?*'

'Come on. Look at the way she behaved. Bet you he's having second thoughts.'

'Gustard, no one ever has an idea of what's going on inside other people's relationships. We just don't know. I think we should leave them alone. He seems fine to me.'

'What seems fine to you?' said Alex, coming in to

get some more wine. He lost his grip on the doorway temporarily, but caught it again.

'Ehm, I always refer to my lasagnes as he's. Makes them, er, rise better.'

Alex stared hard at the blackened mass before him. 'Looks like fucking terminal cancer to me.'

'Yes, well, never mind about that. Go back in and sit down.'

Grabbing another bottle, he stumbled back into the living room, where I heard a whoop of laughter from Fran and Mookie. Must have been telling them about my lasagne, the bastard.

I stood back and prodded my handiwork with a knife.

'Maybe if I just feed Nash and get some pizza in for everyone else . . .'

'That would be great,' said Angus sweetly.

'I spent all day making this lasagne.'

'I know.'

'I put nutmeg in it and everything.'

'Don't worry.'

I walked back into the living room and cleared my throat. Fraser was still staring unhappily at his glass of wine, and downing it at an extraordinary rate, while Nash patted him companionably on the arm. Alex had moved to sit between Mookie and Fran, who were laughing around him like a couple of starlets, and he was interrogating Linda, whose face was a dreadful colour.

'Come on, pet,' he was insisting, 'just tell us who it is.'

Linda's face looked like it might explode.

'Yes, come on, do tell us,' encouraged Mookie. Everyone seemed to have forgotten Linda's name.

Finally, she gritted her teeth. 'Ralph Fiennes,' she said, almost inaudibly.

Fran waved her glass in the air. 'No, Linda, it's got to be someone embarrassing as opposed to someone rich and handsome and gorgeous and lovely and . . .'

'Four foot nine,' finished Alex snidely.

Linda looked up at him, eyes burning.

'You'd never understand!' she shouted. I'd never heard her shout. 'None of you could ever understand what he means to me!' And she stomped off to her bedroom, slamming the door behind her.

There was a silence.

'Two down,' said Alex, not very helpfully.

'Would you like me to go and see to her?' Mookie offered gravely.

'Thanks,' I said, 'but, well . . .'

'I'll go,' said Angus.

I turned round gratefully. 'Would you?'

He nodded. 'That means I'm not here when you tell them about the lasagne.'

'What about the lasagne?' said Nash, stricken.

'Ah.'

Half an hour later, everything was much improved. The pizzas had arrived and even Nash had had enough, although he insisted on picking every piece of vegetable matter off them first. Linda had gone to sleep, and

Angus assured us she was OK. Well, not suicidal. We'd cleared the stupid, mismatched tables out of the room and the seven of us sat bunched around the sofa or kicking our heels on the floor, trying not to knock over the candles, which had stayed with us. Van Morrison was playing, but very, very quietly.

'You haven't gone,' said Alex to Fran.

'Oh, go away, I don't want to go.'

He started poking her in the side.

'You've got to! Forfeit, remember?'

Fran rolled over and lay on her stomach.

'I'm refusing to answer. I'll take the forfeit.'

'Wooo,' we said. 'Forfeit! Forfeit!'

'What, though?'

Alex grinned. 'You could show us your tits.'

I kicked him. 'Don't be disgusting.'

Fran sighed. 'Yes, and everyone's seen them.'

'I haven't!' said Mookie.

Everyone looked at her.

'Later,' said Fran.

Angus was leaning against the sofa.

'I know what you could do, Francesca,' he said softly.

The room turned to listen to him.

'You're an actress. Why don't you do some acting for us? Do a piece. What are you auditioning for at the moment?'

There was a chorus of 'good idea'. Fran looked embarrassed but shrugged.

'I'm auditioning for *Much Ado*,' she said. 'To tour schools with. I'm trying out for Beatrice.'

'OK, give us a bit of that then.'

We shifted around to give her some room. For about a second she pretended not to be absolutely thrilled to be asked, then just got on with it.

'Beatrice has just been asked if she's going to get married,' she said, then began:

> 'Not till God make men of some other metal than earth. Would it not grieve a woman to be overmastered with a pierce of valiant dust?'

'Valiant dust?' whispered Alex loudly. 'Woo . . . scary.'

'Shhh,' I said.

> '. . . to make
> an account of her life to a clod of wayward marl?
> No, uncle, I'll none: Adam's sons are my brethren;
> and, truly, I hold it a sin to match in my kindred.'

She was extremely good; her voice was strong, and the words rang out with perfect clarity.

> 'The fault will be in the music, cousin, if you be not wooed in good time: if the prince be too important, tell him there is measure in every thing and so dance out the answer.'

'Not another man-hater,' said Alex. Truly he was

extremely drunk, and I pinched him hard on the thigh.

'. . . For, hear me, Hero:
wooing, wedding, and repenting, is as a Scotch jig,
a measure, and a cinque pace: the first suit is hot
and hasty, like a Scotch jig, and full as
fantastical; the wedding, mannerly-modest, as a
measure, full of state and ancientry; and then comes
repentance and, with his bad legs, falls into the
cinque pace faster and faster, till he sink into his
grave.'

Everyone clapped; then suddenly Fraser leaned forward and clasped his head.

'God!' he said. 'It's just so much! It's just such a huge thing to do!'

We fussed around him and told him not to worry.

'I'm not sure I want to dance the boring dances,' he sighed, holding his glass. 'Not yet.'

'You're right,' said Angus. 'Listen to your instinct. Don't do it. In fact, let's take a vote on it. Hands up all those who think Fraser shouldn't get married.'

'Please, don't do this, guys,' Fraser said, but too late. Angus's hand was already in the air, as was Fran's. Alex put his up, 'but only because all marriage is a bunch of crap.' As he was sitting on the floor, he lost his balance and tipped over backwards, then decided not to get up again. Once we'd ascertained he hadn't set his hair on fire, we left him there. 'I'll second that,' said Nash. Mookie, once she'd realized that everyone else had, put her own hand up tentatively.

Fraser looked straight at me. 'What about you, Mel? Are you conscientiously objecting? Has some doubt crept into your mind after my fiancée's delightful behaviour this evening?'

I realized I'd forgotten to put my own hand up.

'Oh, no, I, ehm, got momentarily distracted.'

'But you're still putting your hand up?'

I put my hand up and stared back at him resolutely.

'Yes. Definitely.'

'Just checking.'

'Are you putting yours up?' said Angus to Fraser.

Fraser laughed hollowly. 'What, you mean I'm allowed to have an opinion after you lot?'

'Yeah, go on, Fraser, what's your vote?' said Fran.

'Tell me what he does,' said Alex.

Fraser looked at his glass and laughed. 'I don't think I have a vote.'

'Of course you do,' said Angus. 'Make your own fucking decisions, man.'

Fraser got to his feet, wobbling. 'Against the might of the wedding industry, Pyrford Parish Church, Earthworks flower company, *Hello!* magazine, the PR industry, Charlotte Coleman Bridal Designs, Gieves & Hawkes the tailors, Sloane Caterers Inc, Asprey's, Moët & Chandon, Heal's furniture shops, the Phillipses, the McConnalds, and my great auntie Margaret, who is eighty-two and flying in from Australia,' he declaimed dramatically, 'I am afraid I have no vote,' he bowed from the waist. 'No vote at all.'

We all looked at him for a bit.

'That,' he said, 'would have been a great moment to depart. If I wanted to go, and not sit here and drink my little brother's whisky. As long as you promise to shut up about the fucking wedding.'

And so it was only once he'd gone to the loo that Mookie could come out with her idea about the bomb.

Alex sat bolt upright when he heard about the bomb.

'Whaaa . . .' he coughed. 'What bomb.'

Mookie was blushing, as usual, at being the centre of attention.

'Well, rally, I suppose, it was an awful prank at school.'

'What was?' Alex demanded.

'When we wanted to ride our ponies and not go to assembly.'

'Oh God, yes, we did that too, didn't we, Mel?' I shot Fran a Woking look.

'Anyway, we set off all these smoke bombs – oh, the mess of it, rally – and that set off the fire alarms, and by the time they'd sorted everything out it was far too late to do anything at all. And of course with weddings, they're one after another, rally, aren't they? It's like Heathrow. If you miss your slot, you're there for ever.'

We stared at each other, stunned by the criminal genius.

'Nash,' said Angus, taking command, 'go distract Fraser.'

'Hey, I'm the best man, ken. If I'm going to choke to death, I want to hear about it, OK?'

'Fair enough. Alex, could you do it?'

'Wha', walk into a toilet with your brother? He'll think I'm a fuggin' botty burglar.'

'Go on, Alex,' I said. 'You don't care anyway. Just distract him. Do a tap dance or something.'

'Tap dance. Yeah. Right. Tap dance.' He staggered to his feet. 'Fucking tap dance.'

Next thing we heard was the bathroom door opening and the sound of copious vomiting. Fraser's voice could be heard, enquiring as to whether he was all right.

'What a stroke of genius,' said Angus.

'What a fucking piss-head, more like,' I said, crossly.

'OK,' said Angus. 'This is a brilliant plan.'

'Like the last brilliant plan?' I added.

'But have we got the balls to carry it out?' Angus continued.

We looked at each other. Having come up with the idea, Mookie had retreated again and was staring at the floor.

Noticing our silence, Angus continued:

'Where do you get the bombs, Mookie?'

'Ehm, well, one of my cousins, he's pretty high up in the Met.'

'You're joking – we'd steal them off the police?'

'Not stealing, rally – he keeps a few around his house.'

Nash whistled through his teeth.

'Then we'd need a couple of people to check the fire

alarm – and a couple of people to make sure all the grannies get out and stuff.'

'Maybe we could keep the grannies out of the church all together?' someone said.

'Hang on!' I said. 'What if there's a mass stampede and hundreds of people are run over and killed? What if Amanda has a hysterical fit and commits suicide? What if Fraser never speaks to any of us again? What if you all get arrested?' God, I nearly wished I was going.

'It could be a sign,' said Angus. 'A beacon across the land to those in danger of wedlock.'

'Oh no! Dangerous David Koresh visionary thing!' I said, getting agitated. Off stage, the vomiting seemed to be quieting down. I hoped he wasn't going to use my toothbrush.

'For people to think more carefully about why they're getting married and who to. We'll only set off a little one. We'll make sure nobody panics. Then we'll run for it. Think of it in the slightly naughty rather than the deranged criminal stakes.'

'Well, I'm up for it,' said Fran.

'Of course you're up for it: it's got an element of chaos!' I said.

'Huh! Well, if that's what you think . . .'

'I know where to place the bombs for, you know . . . well, the best places for them to go off, rally,' said Mookie shyly.

'Great, great,' said Angus. 'And Nash, you'll be at the front, so you're on granny duty. Fraser will help you.'

'I doubt this will sound so good when we wake up in the morning,' I said sourly.

'And I'll do the fire alarms.'

'As well as being the criminal master mind,' I said. 'This is a terrible idea.'

'We don't really need you,' said Fran.

Great. My own house, and I didn't even get to feel needed. I mumbled something about putting the coffee on and wandered off.

Alex was drinking water at the sink in the kitchen.

'I feel great!' he said. 'Much better.'

'You look green.'

'But I feel . . . great!' He bounced back into the sitting room. 'More ale, mistresses.' There was laughter.

Fraser was still standing there beside the sink, trying to make himself useful. We smiled ruefully at each other.

'Thanks for doing all this, Mel,' he said sweetly. 'I did say you didn't have to.'

'I know. I never listen to sensible people.'

'Ah yes. Me, Fraser Sensible, Esq.'

'What will you say to Amanda?'

'I was planning on blaming it all on you . . . Is that all right?' His tone of voice was gentle, but quite serious.

'Don't you dare!'

'OK. Really, it has been lovely.'

'It's been ghastly.'

'All dinner parties are ghastly. This was better

than most.'

There was another gale of laughter from next door.

'See? They're having a great time.'

'You don't want to know what they're laughing about,' I said.

'Oh, I think I already do.'

He handed me a fresh glass of water. I took it.

'I'm sorry you've got mixed up in all this,' he said suddenly.

'That's OK,' I said cheerily. 'I'd never have met your brother otherwise.'

'Ah, yes . . . ehm, he's a nice chap.'

'Yes, he is – Oh, look!' I ran over to the window. 'The snow's lying!'

'So it is.' Fraser crossed over beside me to see. 'I love snow.'

'Me too. We should go out and make angels.'

He looked at me, smiling. 'OK, then.'

I looked at him. 'Is that a dare?'

'Might be. Are you up for it?'

I hesitated for only a second. 'Yes!' And we tiptoed to the door, shushing each other so as not to let people in on what we were up to. We crept outside, left the door on the latch, then bounded down the stairs, killing ourselves laughing.

The road outside was completely deserted, only the tall, crumbling Victorian buildings standing blankly all around. I launched myself first, then Fraser lay with his head touching my head, so we could make symmetrical angels. The snow wasn't very deep, and we were soon scraping gravel, lying there, soaking and freezing, laughing our heads off and looking at the cold, cold stars.

'It's all shit, isn't it, Mel?' yelled the voice from above my head.

'It's like the snow,' I yelled back, metaphysically. 'Looks gorgeous, but there's nothing but dog-poo and gravel underneath.'

He laughed. 'And once you're in it, it's cold and damp.'

'But if you weren't in it . . .'

'You wouldn't get any angels!' we chorused.

And we lay there for a while, till we knew we'd be missed, and realized we couldn't feel our extremities, and decided we'd better go in before we died in a tragic accident.

In one of my ludicrously small jumpers, Fraser helped me assemble the coffee cups and we took everything through. Only Angus bothered to look up; everyone else was far too pissed to notice the passage of time. The tone had changed completely, and people had started to espouse their personal theories of the world in drunk but desperately sincere tones, and finally I started to relax.

Drinking Angus's whisky, I let everything turn hazy and mused fitfully on things, occasionally dragged in to answer questions or provide opposition support when Alex finally did get round to suggesting a game of Spin the Bottle. Occasionally, I'd hear someone mention something to do with the wedding, or smoke, which would make everyone else go 'shhh!' and start to giggle. And finally, finally, Nash looked at his watch, and announced:

'Christ, I can't see what this watch says, ken. Which means it's time to go home.'

He heaved himself up to go phone a cab, and in a flurry of time I didn't notice swimming along, I waved, and kissed goodbye. Angus clapped his hands round me warmly. Fraser tried to refuse the piles of pizza which Alex insisted on passing him to take to his fiancée, as she hadn't eaten, but gave in in the end. The freezing cold air shot in briefly from outside as I touched his hand and said goodbye. His curly hair was still damp from the snow.

I wandered back into the living room and surveyed the carnage. Ashtrays and empty bottles littered the place; we seemed to have drunk everything in sight. Dreamily, I wandered into the kitchen to start hauling things away.

My first shock was this: I didn't walk into the kitchen, I walked into the airing cupboard.

Two: I must have been pissed, because I had no idea we had an airing cupboard.

Three: Alex and Fran were kissing in it.

Fifteen

I staggered backwards, grabbing for the wall. Alex didn't see me, but Fran did. Her dark eyes widened in horror, and she pushed at Alex's shoulder.

'Whaa?' he said, nuzzling her.

She indicated me, and he looked round.

Everyone looked at each other for a bit. I was frozen stiff; an icy waterfall seemed to be running through me, tightening up my throat and my heart, and chilling my stomach. I kept backing away. I knew I had to say something, but I couldn't get hold of what. All that went through my mind was the old cartoon strip of the husband coming home early and the lover hiding in the wardrobe. This wasn't funny though.

Finally, in a high-pitched squeak which didn't sound like me at all, I said, 'Go home!'

Alex lurched forward, jarred into sobriety.

'Yes, Fran, I think you should go. Melanie . . .' he hurtled towards me, arms outstretched.

'Melanie, what can I say? I'm . . . I can't believe . . . never happened before . . . too much wine . . .'

I couldn't even hear what he was saying.

'Go home!' came the terrible squeak again. 'Go away! Both of you! Go away! Go away!'

And I turned and ran from them into my room, and pitched forward on to the bed. I had intended to cry myself to sleep, or at least consider the situation, but the wine and the shock had a stronger hold than that, and I practically passed out on the bed.

I woke up at five o'clock in the morning, shivering uncontrollably. I was lying on top of the bed and, I dimly noticed, two coats. Instantly it came back to me, falling over me like a sheet of dark cloud. I crawled into bed and tried to get warm, but realized that my teeth were chattering for a different reason. I tried to think about it, but realized I didn't want to. All I could think of was them disappearing for two hours . . . they must have been laughing their heads off at me. I looked down on the bed. Still, I'd managed to make them leave without their coats. Thinking about this, I started to cry. And I didn't stop.

I cried all through the next day, while managing to forcibly prevent Linda from doing the washing-up. There appeared to be bits of burnt lasagne stuck to the ceiling. That would have made me laugh, if I hadn't been crying my heart out. I cried emptying the ashtrays, I cried taking the bottles to the bottle bank. Even pretending breaking the bottles was breaking their skulls didn't help. I cried every time the phone rang and I couldn't pick it up, and Linda took the thank you messages – none from Fran, though. I cried when I thought of the wedding, I cried when I thought of the flat we were going to have, I cried when I thought of the little bed and breakfast we'd booked for next week, I cried when I realized that I still had to get out of the flat for Linda's mystery reason and had nowhere to go, I cried when I thought of all the fucking money I'd spent so Alex could get pissed enough to make a pass at my best friend.

Alex showed up about noon. The bastard, couldn't even sleep outside my door all night. I threatened to call the police if he didn't stop ringing the ear-splitting doorbell.

'At least give me my coat,' he cried piteously.

'I've burnt it.'

'Please, Mel. Please.'

'Go round to Fran's. I'm sure she'll keep you warm.'

'Oh well, at least we're talking.'

I stomped off and ignored him. This bit, the bit where I got to shout at him, in some strange way, wasn't too bad. It was the bit that would come, the bit without him, which was going to be really difficult to bear.

He sat outside my door for four hours. He was

wearing two rugby shirts one over another, but he didn't have a flask with him.

Eventually, when it was clear that I wasn't coming anywhere near him, I heard him stand up to go.

'I'm going,' he yelled.

'That assumes I care.'

'If you don't want to talk about it like an adult . . .'

'You snog your girlfriend's friend – ex-friend – in an airing cupboard, then want to get into a maturity competition?'

'At least hear my side of it.'

'You have no side of it. You ask me to move in with you and six days later go after someone else. End of story. Change the fucking record, Alex.'

There was a big sigh on the other side of the door. Then he leaned down to the letter box and said gently, 'Just because I got pissed doesn't mean we can't move in together.'

'On the contrary; I think the European Court of Human Rights says that it does.'

'For God's sake, Melanie, have you no understanding at all? My way of behaving, it was all a reaction to the big step we're taking. It shows how much I love you – how scared I am; how much I'm willing to sacrifice. It was a spur-of-the-moment thing and, I swear to you, it will never ever happen again.'

'Yes, it will,' I yelled. 'But not to me. Now go fuck yourself.'

'Phone me,' he said. 'Phone me when you're ready to make the commitment. I think your over-reaction shows you're as scared as I am.'

I leaned over and slammed the letter box on his fingers. He yelped, and I felt better. He turned to go, paused for a second, then really did go.

I collapsed back into my bedroom. For all my bravado, I still felt hollowed out. The rain had come and driven away the snow and so everything outside nicely reflected my mood.

'What to do now?' I thought to myself. I really had no idea. There were no conscious thoughts in my head. I felt the urge to go somewhere, but I couldn't bring myself to move. I wanted to talk to someone, but there was no one on earth I wanted to talk to. I wanted to distract myself, but everything distracting would be full of images of happy, excited people, doing happy exciting things, and I wasn't. Wasn't wasn't wasn't. Single again. Single in December. At least I should have held on for a Christmas present. Although Alex thought they were bourgeois. Oh, God, what a twat.

I lay back, wishing I had a teddy bear or something equally crap to cling to in my hour of need. I wondered if I should phone the Samaritans. Although it wasn't like I was picking up the knives. I thought the Samaritans were only for really sad people. Not like me or anything. God, I missed him. No I didn't. Yes I did. No I didn't. Ticking like a mantra in my head, I started to cry again, even though I had absolutely nothing left to cry with and it came out dry. Finally, rocking myself back and forward, I sank right forward and finally got to sleep. And that was my weekend.

Having fallen asleep so early, I woke up on time the next day. My options being another day crying in bed or going to work, I decided to go to work. Big fat tears ran down my cheeks as I pulled my tights on. I looked in the mirror. I looked like one of those people they use to advertise the dangers of heroin. Gleh. Bleagh. Bleagh.

I walked into the office expecting everyone to instantly fall to their knees in sorrow as they caught a glimpse of me and my obviously huge tragedy, but, annoyingly enough, they all behaved exactly as usual.

'Hey, mate, another rough weekend for you, yeah? You look like a tart's backside,' said Steve as I dragged myself in, looking, I thought, like Mary Magdalene.

'I feel like one,' I replied despondently. 'Only less hairy.'

He eyed me strangely. 'What's the matter wiv you, like?'

'Oh, everything. I ditched my boyfriend.'

'Why? Don't tell me, he copped off with someone else and you had to save face by dumping him?'

'Jesus, Steve, when are you going to evolve frontal lobes? Piss off, I don't want to talk about it.'

Silently, Janie passed over her box of king-sized Kleenex. I took it gratefully, having decided just to let the tears drip down when they came rather than give myself a migraine pretending they weren't there.

'How's James?' I asked her, to relish the irony. They were probably getting married too.

'Oh God,' she began, grabbing the box of tissues back. 'We were at a party on Saturday and his ex-girlfriend was there.'

'That's legal.'

'So, of course I walked out immediately. Then he didn't want to come with me!'

'Where was the party?'

'Kent.'

'You came all the way back from Kent because his ex was at a party?'

'Well, for God's sake! It was so insensitive!'

'Did he know she was going to be there?'

'Well, he says no, but I don't know whether I believe him. It was at university, you see.' As if that explained everything.

'Ohh. What kind of party was it?'

'Oh, some college reunion . . .' Suddenly her face fell.

I looked at her. This woman was clearly bonkers.

'So, surely she might be expected to be there . . . ?'

'I didn't think,' she said, ashen.

'That's because you're a moron.'

'Oh my God, poor James. How could I?'

'Because you're a moron. Can I borrow the tissues again, please?'

'He's really going to dump me this time!' Her voice rose hysterically. She held on to the tissues for grim life.

'Jesus!' said Steve. 'That's it. I am putting in for a

transfer before my periods start to fall into synch with you two mad bitches.'

That lunch time, I ate my sandwich disconsolately, remembering the time Fraser had come and picked me up unexpectedly. I could do with that now. If I didn't get it out of my system soon, I was going to explode. Then I remembered that he had problems enough of his own in six days, and the last thing he wanted was to be poured upon by a dumb Harpy like me.

I thought of Angus too, but that was more difficult. Everything was so complicated.

I managed to raise my only smile that day by thinking about the smoke bombs. If they were going to carry it out . . . It was nuts, but, God, it might be funny. It might even work. Probably not though. I was sure the vicar could do the service anywhere these days. He could pop next door and do it in the pub.

I definitely wasn't going to go to the reception. There'd probably be armed guards on the door keeping me away, anyhow. And I couldn't feel less like a wedding. Fran would probably turn up. That girl had front enough for anything.

Fran. I hadn't even started to grieve for her yet. I was too busy splitting myself over Alex. Telling myself she was just a big slut didn't help. I'd known her all my life. And now . . . that was over, as if she'd died. She hadn't even phoned me. Too ashamed, I presumed. Maybe she didn't even care. That idea filled me with sadness. Maybe they were together even now. Alex was deciding he'd made a big mistake all along hanging out with me. Why would he want to – Fran was so gorgeous and skinny. She'd probably help him get a job with his pop-star mates, just by being thin and disdainful and glamorous. I had the horrible thought that he was trading up. And another equally horrible thought was on the bus right behind it: that I'd always known he would. I supposed I'd been waiting for it to happen. I didn't think I was good enough for that low-down piece of shit, which made me a gnat on the underside of the low-down piece of shit. I wept again. I just hadn't thought he'd go so close to home, that was all.

No flowers this time. He knew it wouldn't work any more. Probably too busy at home with Fran. They'd be laughing at something moronic I'd said. 'Oh God, it feels so good to be FREE!' Alex would be saying. 'Yeah, you nearly got trapped big time,' Fran would be saying. Maybe she didn't really hate him after all. Maybe all that time she'd been calling him a cocksucker because she was really in love with him, the way she used to push boys she liked off the wall at school. Maybe she'd just been getting his attention.

Well, she had it now, I thought grimly, and tried to concentrate on something, anything else.

Suddenly, as if summoned psychically by me, a conga-line of people threaded its way into the office, going: 'De-ner de der der deh deh . . . De-ner de der der deh deh,' with party hats on and streamers. A tape recorder was loudly playing Christmas hits. I was so surprised I nearly stopped crying for a second.

'What's going on?' I asked Steve, as one particularly

rotund woman knocked my stapler off my desk.

'Christmas party tonight, innit? Just getting in the mood. Gonna be dragging me under the mistletoe then, sweetheart?'

'I'd rather learn to kiss my own arse. Jeez, who has a party on a Monday night, anyway?'

'Every night's party night when I'm around,' leered Steve. 'You coming?'

And he grabbed my arm and forced me to join the conga line. It was then, prancing around trying to look dignified while doing a conga, devoid of friends, career and lover, that I realized I'd reached my nadir. Until ten seconds later, when the music changed to 'Do They Know it's Christmas?' and I realized I'd reached it again.

'This is sick,' I said to Steve. 'I'm not dancing to music about starving people! Let me out!'

Janie looked on impassively.

'Are you coming to the party tonight?' she asked.

'No way,' I said.

'Oh, go on. You have to stay for a bit. The drinks are free till seven.'

'They could buy me a house and I still wouldn't stay for this party. I am going home to eat crisps and feel sorry for myself. Is James coming? And don't cry, whatever the answer is.'

Her lip wobbled. 'He's got training.'

'Oh . . . brushing up on his running skills is he?'

She looked at me wonderingly. 'Yes . . . how did you know?'

'Lucky hunch.'

'Please stay for a bit,' she said. 'I . . . think I should stay for my career. Networking is very important.'

'Steve will look after you,' I said. Steve re-entered the room. His cheap silky tie was loosened and he was carrying an enormous balloon that was the shape of a penis. Janie looked at me.

'Please. Just stay for a bit.'

God knows why I agreed. To take my mind off things, I supposed. The day dragged on and on. Nobody even rang me to see if I was OK. Nobody cared. At five, Flavi clapped her hands together and made a little Christmas speech about what FUN the marketing department had been that year and how much FUN we were all going to have next year, working together as one big fluid copywriting machine. I stood at the back, making baa-ing noises when everyone else clapped.

Then cheap – very cheap, and my tastes weren't particularly rarefied – vino was passed round in plastic cups and we all stood self-consciously talking about work, like we would do anyway.

'Well, this is fun!' Flavi said to no one in particular. Her concept of fun was most peculiar. Steve tapped me on the shoulder.

'Come on,' he said, 'we're off to crash the accountants' party. It's always miles better.'

'I find that simultaneously easy and difficult to believe.'

Steve appropriated two bottles of the vino and the three of us set off to the other end of the building. You could hear the accountants' party a mile off. People were screaming and they already had the photocopier going. Inside, there were accountants jiving – always a sight to see – running around, leapfrogging each other; one chap was lying on the floor having wine poured into his mouth from a great height.

'Wow, who'd have thought being an accountant would be so much fun?' I remarked.

'Nah, it's only once a year,' said Steve. 'They spend the petty cash and they just go crraaazy.' An older businessman waltzed past, with a temp clinging on with her legs round his waist. 'They start at ten o'clock in the morning.'

'No kidding?' After the weekend, I was in no mood to get drunk, but I accepted a small glass of champagne and congratulated myself on my good distracting techniques. Every time I relaxed my grip, the howling precipice opened up beneath my feet, so I reminded myself yet again not to get drunk, and tried to focus on being a detached observer, even when someone pulled up my skirt accidentally and I whirled round ready to beat them to death.

Over in the corner, one of the accountants had just finished explaining why he wasn't really an accountant after all, he should really have been a drummer, and how he had once had an audition for Motorhead. He then proceeded to demonstrate this by taking two rulers and beating the hell out of everything, occasionally hitting the touch-tone phone keys for all-round percussionist setting. The cacophony churned round and round my head, and I suddenly realized I needed to get away. I dashed out of the room and opened the window in the empty corridor, taking deep breaths of the chilly air. The accountants' office was twelve storeys up, and I could see all the other buildings around. Over the rooftops, I identified Fraser's. I knew it was the funny old redbrick one with the carved birds around the eaves.

Suddenly, I just had to talk to him. I had to talk to someone, and it was him. Otherwise I was going to go bonkers, plain and simple. It wasn't that late, he wouldn't even have finished yet. I'd just pretend to be casually walking by and bump into him, then we could go for a quick coffee somewhere.

Although he probably had a million things to do. He probably had to go home and check out the fifteen bridesmaids dresses or something. Put the corsages together. Lick madam's boots.

I changed my mind half a dozen times in a second, then realized I was going to go anyway, so I might as well get a move on. Even to say hello would be enough.

Inside the accountants' party pit, things seemed to be getting wilder. I picked up my bag, then turned round to say goodbye to Steve and Janie. To my amazement, they were grappling with each other on the filing cabinet. Janie looked to have her dress down below her shoulders. Good Lord. Well, good for her. I was going to creep out without saying anything, but she caught sight of me over his shoulder, gave me a huge thumbs-up sign and threw her head back laughing. Well, well, well. I hope this cured her. She certainly looked happier than I'd ever seen her. Although why it had to be Steve . . .

Feeling slightly more optimistic, I bounced out of the building into the frosty night air.

I hovered outside Fraser's office for twenty minutes, trying to look casual and as if I was just walking past. I was absolutely freezing, and I'd lost any feeling in my nose. Finally, at about half-past six, he emerged, bent down against the wind. Oh God, this was a stupid idea. I didn't know how to walk past casually. I was going to look such a fool. I turned away to make a run for it.

'Were you waiting for me?' the Scottish tones said gently.

I looked round. 'No! Well, in fact, yes.'

He smiled. 'Is it serious?'

'Why, do you have to go somewhere? It's nothing really, I'm sorry, you know, I was just passing, but I have to be going . . .'

Fortunately for me, he pulled me into a nearby patisserie, the kind that sold overpriced coffee to lawyers and tourists.

'Come on. You look freezing.'

'No, not at all, just passing.' I calmed down.

'Etcetera,' I said.

'I phoned you on Sunday to say thanks, but you weren't in.'

'I was in. I just wasn't really in the mood to talk to anyone.'

'Not because of Amanda, surely?'

'No . . .'

And I told him everything. I told him about moving in, and I told him about the airing cupboard, and I told him about America, and I told him about Charlie, and I told him about Fran. With embarrassing pauses while the waitress brought us coffee and cakes – she could obviously tell we were having a big dramatic conversation and tried overly hard not to draw attention to herself, thus drawing lots of attention to herself – I let it all spill out, at last.

More tears – where on earth did they come from? – plopped on to my vanilla slice. I tried to smile and change the subject before I went to pieces completely.

'I see you're eating cakes again,' I said.

Fraser grinned. 'I decided that cakes were more important than looking two-dimensional at the wedding.'

'You're still going through with it, then?'

'I've come this far. Anyway, we're talking about you. What are you going to do?'

I sighed. 'I don't think I can do anything. I mean, I never want to see him again . . . It's almost like it's Fran I'm going to miss, really.'

He nodded his head sympathetically.

'I think you'll forgive her,' he said.

'Of course I can't forgive her! I can never forgive her!'

'You're being melodramatic. She got carried away. I mean, you've been best friends for years and she's always been a complete floozie, from what I can work out. I'm only surprised it hasn't happened before. You'll get over it.'

I thought about that for a bit.

'Ditch Alex,' he went on. 'He's a total loser. I could tell from the moment I met him. Total, utter, wanky loser. Run for it. But, you know, Fran just cocked up. She can't look at a bloke without mentally taking his pants off. She just chose the wrong one. I bet she's totally humiliated now, and can't even bring herself to ring you.'

'Or round at Alex's having a wonderful time.'

'Neh.' He loosened his tie. 'How's your cake?'

'Are you trying to distract me?'

'Yes.'

'Am I being boring?'

He sighed. 'No, don't be silly. I just think you should take your mind off it for a bit. Otherwise – I don't know, but I get into a loop of thinking about things and I just lie awake all night and worry about them. Don't do that.'

'What do you worry about?'

He thought for a moment.

'Ehm . . . what kind of cake is the best. What type are you eating?'

I gave up. 'Vanilla slice.'

'Is it the best?'

'Possibly . . . sometimes it runs a close thing with French cake. And birthday cake. And strawberry tarts.'

'See? It never ends.'

And gently, we drifted into normal talk – not emotional, not coy, just talking quietly – even giggling occasionally. The cake shop was empty and waiting to close up, but outside the darkness was all around and here, in this little pool of light, we were safe and comfortable and we didn't want to leave. There were enough things outside to make us cold.

I arrived home later, feeling more at peace. Linda was in the sitting room watching *Titanic*. Tears were dripping off her pudgy nose. Wordlessly, I went and sat beside her on the sofa. A complete first, she put out her hand. I took it, and moved closer. Finally, as the ship went down, I rested my head on her shoulder.

'But you still have to go away this weekend,' she said stiffly.

I'd forgotten that. Damn. Where the hell was I going to go? My parents, I supposed. I wasn't looking forward to answering the question, 'So, how's your love life, darling?'

'You don't need to go till Saturday morning.'

I thanked her for her magnanimity and sloped off to bed, where I lay for several hours plotting scenes of deadly revenge on Alex and Fran before finally sinking into an exhausted sleep.

No one was at work. Some people had left for early Christmas breaks, and quite a few more – mostly connected with financial services, I was unsurprised to hear – were recovering from the party.

Neither Janie nor Steve had made it in, but Steve

had left a message on my voice mail saying, 'Tell Flavi we're not coming in because we're too busy SHAGGING.' And I could hear Janie screaming with laughter in the background, shouting, 'And if James rings, tell him to FUCK OFF!'

Poor James has been through quite enough already, I thought. Mad pair of bastards! I did miss them, though, in an odd way. The less people around, the more time I had to dwell on the situation, and that was no fun.

Neither Fran nor Alex had rung me. Alex must have finally got the message it was over. He'd given up awfully quickly, though. Not, I sternly told myself, that that made any difference. I might never see the two of them again. Not too soon for me.

I'd phoned my mother, who of course knew that it was the big day on Saturday (the whole town did, this was the closest Woking got to society – unless you counted Paul Weller, who was born there and spent the rest of his life making disparaging remarks about the place), and couldn't understand why I wasn't going. I hadn't told her the whole truth, naturally. I told her we'd fallen out, in a kind of equal opportunities way.

'Oh, remember when you lost your purse and you all fell out about who had it? The three of you made that up in the blink of an eye.'

'Mum, Amanda took that purse and said if we didn't make friends with her again she'd have one of Year Seven beat us up.'

She ignored me. 'I'm sure you'll sort it out, whatever it is. Oh, Amanda's going to be such a lovely bride.

Always was so pretty, and so tiny.'

'And a witch.'

'What's that, darling? Oh, do come home, we're dying to see you. You can tell us all your news . . . How's your exciting new job going? Come and stay with us. But do go to the wedding – you'll regret it if you don't. Derek Phillips certainly knows how to splash out when he wants to!'

'Thanks, Mum. I'm not going to go, and that's that. But I'll see you about lunch time, Saturday?'

'Fine, fine, we'll see you then.'

And she tutted sorrowfully that I would dare to miss such a glorious occasion.

Sixteen

I woke up extremely early on Saturday with a sore head and a deep sense of foreboding. As consciousness returned, I realized what day it was, and my heart dropped like a stone. I hugged my duvet and told myself not to be so bloody silly. It was just a normal day, I would get up, go home and be nice to my mum for a change, instead of a bit sulky. Maybe do some shopping and watch a bit of TV. No problem.

Really, I wanted to lie face-down on the floor and kick and scream and have the mother of all tantrums. But no. I would get up, wash, and dress demurely, then go out and face the world with calm and ease. Alex and Fran might well turn up to the wedding together. Well, that would be lovely for them. I hoped they'd all have a lovely day. Even when the smoke alarms went off, I'm sure that would not stop things too much – and how they would all laugh about it in the years to come, one great big circle of friends. Perhaps Alex and Fran and Amanda and Fraser's children would all play together. They'd probably go on holiday too. How lovely lovely lovely.

Next door, I could hear the sound of shifting furniture. What on earth was Linda doing in there? I yawned, and shook my head to wake myself.

BRRRRRINNG! The doorbell went off with its usual soul-jerking intensity. BRRING! BRRIING! BRRING! That didn't sound like the fat postman. It better not be Alex. Grimly, I pulled on my pyjamas and got up to answer it. Linda poked her shiny face round the living-room door, obviously concerned that I might be disobeying her mandate. I waved at her and peered through the letter box. It was Angus.

'What is it?' I yelled.

'Can I come in?'

I pondered it for a bit.

'Why?'

'Let me in and I'll tell you!'

'What if it's a double-bluff?'

'What on earth are you talking about?'

I didn't know, so I opened the door and let him in. His mischievous smile left his face when he saw me.

'Jings, what's the matter with you? You look like you've been up a wall crying for a week.'

'How intuitive. What are you doing here? Haven't you got a wedding to attend?' I turned cold. 'Have they called it off?'

'Not as far as I know.'

'Oh.' I looked at him hazily.

'Have you just woken up?'

'Ehm, yes. Sorry. Nice kilt. Would you like a coffee?'

He looked at his watch. 'OK. Hi, Linda!'

Linda squeaked like a cross mouse and disappeared.

'I'm not supposed to be here,' I whispered. 'I told her I'd clear out today.'

'Because you're going to the wedding.'

'Of course I'm not going to the fucking wedding.'

He followed me into the kitchen. 'Oh, yes, hum, yes, in fact you are. Fraser told me everything. That's why I'm here. To pick you up. You have to come with me.'

I put the kettle on and turned to face him.

'Sorry. Much as I'd like to help you out on your bob-a-job week, (1) I'm definitely not coming, and (2) I'm not even invited.'

Angus ignored me, and got the cups down while I put the kettle on. In fact, he whistled a happy tune. Finally, we sat down. The kitchen table had disappeared. I ignored this fact, given that my world was already odd enough and I was having breakfast with a man in a skirt.

Angus sat down and continued whistling quietly until it became intensely irritating.

'Stop it,' I announced. 'I am *so* not coming to this wedding, it doesn't matter how much you whistle.'

He kept on whistling. 'I need to take a guest.'

'Take Kylie Minogue.'

He resumed whistling.

'I bet Alex won't be there,' he said between bars and contemplative sips of his coffee.

'I don't care.'

'Or Fran.' The melody had changed to 'Over the Sea to Skye'.

'I double don't care.'

'Come on. Get changed. I've hired a car, so it won't take that long to get down there.'

'No, it won't take you long at all. When you leave, now, and leave me alone.' I crossed my hands over my chest protectively. 'And stop whistling.'

He stopped obediently, and just sat there, waiting.

'Why do you want me to come, anyway? I'm not letting off any of your bloody smoke bombs.'

He shrugged. 'I want you to. And I think you should. So, you should come with me.'

My heart quickened a little. 'It'll be awful. Everyone there will know that my boyfriend's having it off with my best friend.'

'No they won't. And if they do, they won't care.'

'Amanda will be killing herself laughing.'

'I think Amanda's got enough on her mind, don't you?'

'S'pose . . . Oh, I can't, Angus. I can't go and watch two people pledge their troths or whatever the hell it is they're doing, and have the happiest fucking day of their lives while I'm in absolute hell. I'll just be sitting there weeping my head off. And I can do that on my own, thank you. I'd probably snort just when they got to their "I do"s and snotter all over the wedding cake.'

'That would fit in nicely,' said Angus.

'Don't tease me. I'm not coming and that's that. I am going to my mother's to talk about baking cakes and then eat some, hopefully.'

He nodded. 'You're coming.'

'What are you going to do, kidnap me?'

'You have to come. For two reasons. One, to hold your head high, and to say, fine, all this crap is finished with, look at me, I have survived, blah blah blah. You have to. You'll get a kick out of yourself. You'll be proud of it for years afterwards.'

Hmm. 'What's the other reason?'

He looked at me.

'I really, really want you to. And I really, really want you to come with me. Which you knew. But which you still asked. Which proves that you're teasing me. Which proves that you're not too depressed to leave the house. Which means you're coming.'

We stared at each other for a long time. I dropped my eyes first. His intense blue gaze didn't falter. My heart beat faster and faster.

'I . . . er . . .' I cleared my throat. 'I don't think I've anything to wear.'

He grinned broadly at my capitulation. 'Come in your pyjamas, I won't care.'

'Yes, but you're wearing a skirt.'

'Wear whatever you like. Doesn't matter to me. I think you're pretty anyway.'

He thinks I'm pretty! I thought to myself, suddenly jubilant. Then: *As if I'm little girl enough to fall for that one*. Then: *What the hell*?

'Ehm, OK, I'll . . . go and see what I can find.'

He nodded, as if he'd known all along, which he probably had.

'Fine. I'll put the kettle on again. Linda, would you like some tea? We'll be gone soon.'

'No thank you,' came the muffled reply, closely followed by some hammering. What was she doing in there?

In my room, I sat down on my futon and thought long and hard. I was incredibly excited. The urge . . . to do something, to have something happen . . . rose so strongly in me it was like a tidal wave. My stomach rumbled with anxiety.

I had been lying when I said I didn't have anything to wear. I had an old brocade dress in a deep mulberry colour, which I'd got cleaned the week before when Alex and I were busy preparing for things – ha. I slipped into it, and put on some twenties button-style shoes. No hat, but I had a matching ribbon to keep my curls out of the way. Dressing, I took a quick glance in the mirror. I did look pretty, for once. Good. My cheeks were flushed and my eyes sparkled. I was so excited I kept missing the buttons on the sleeve, but, finally, I was ready.

Angus was waiting for me. 'God, you look gorgeous,' he said.

'Thank you very much. So do you,' I replied, and he did cut a very handsome and sturdy figure in his kilt.

'Do you want me to phone your mother and tell her you're not coming?'

God, I'd nearly forgotten all about her.

'Ehm, unless you want the Spanish Inquisition as to who on earth you are and why are you kidnapping my youngest, then I'd say you probably shouldn't.'

I phoned her. She'd bought lots of baking materials, but sounded much happier that I was going to the wedding and that we'd all made up at last.

'Who knows – maybe you'll meet a nice man there,' she said.

I looked at Angus washing up the coffee cups.

'Who knows,' I said.

He turned as I got off the phone.

'Time to go?' he asked, proffering me his arm.

'Let's do it,' I said nervously, taking it.

'Bye, Linda!'

There was a snuffling noise, and we left her to it.

On the drive to the village, neither of us could say very much. There was too much going on. I was too nervous. My fingers tapped out a beat on my knee. Gently, Angus squeezed my hand in his. His hand was much larger than mine.

'Don't worry,' he said. 'Just keep your head up. We'll show 'em.'

Something occurred to me.

'You're not still going to do that smoke bomb thing, are you?'

'Ehm, I don't know. Mookie's not sure she can get them, and we've lost a foot soldier in that damned Francesca. So, it might not work.'

'But you still want to try?'

'If we have to.'

I nodded and stared straight ahead.

'You know it won't stop them?'

'No. But it'll annoy them.'

I turned to look at him. His eyes were crinkled up from smiling. I smiled too.

'Count me in.'

'Really?'

'Sure. If he's so stupid as to marry her after all this, a dose of smoke to the brain isn't going to hurt him anyway.'

'Exactly. You're on back granny watch.'

I laughed, and my nerves increased. I felt ready for anything; ready to do anything. Ready to break free, to leave everything behind. To have an adventure.

'I'm feeling very adventurous,' I announced.

'Really?' He looked intrigued.

'Just a warning.'

'OK.'

There was a watery sun in the air, which didn't look very committed. Small clouds were scudding around, as if they were scouting for the big clouds who were coming along later. The church, however, looked breathtaking. It was a picture-perfect little Victorian place. Holly was strewn everywhere, all round the kissing gate and over the church doors, with hawthorn and ivy and mistletoe. That all seemed a bit pagan to me, but it looked very pretty.

Scores of people were hovering about outside in that embarrassed way people do before weddings, looking off into the distance, or mentally preparing themselves for the long hours of small talk with strangers to come. There were couples who had driven long distances and obviously got lost, and who were now too cross with each other to speak, and an elderly relative contingent, who would grab anyone walking past and force them to reveal lots of personal details.

I noticed a real difference between what were clearly the two sides. Amanda's lot were loud and expensively dressed – lots of young women and rugby-playing men who were something in the City, or wanted you to think they were by their cufflinks. There were a fair number of open-topped sports cars dotted around – despite the fact that it was four degrees above freezing – and quite a few top hats and morning coats, which, despite myself, I rather liked.

Fraser's side, on the other hand, just looked . . . well, normal, apart from the predominance of skirts amongst the men. I saw their mother, and it was her that Angus took me over to meet first. She smiled at me in a slightly knowing fashion, but was charming and warm. Some of the lads from the stag night were hanging around too, and it was nice to say hello to them again. Then I caught sight of Nash, who was standing by himself under a tree. I waved him over.

'Hey there, how's it going?'

He looked green.

'Aye, no bad, ken.'

'Are you nervous?'

'Aye, you could . . . aye, yes, well, a bit, aye.'

'How's your best-man speech?'

He turned even more green and started patting himself up and down. 'Ehm, it's here somewhere, right enough . . .'

'Don't worry, you'll be fine. But, listen, I thought Fraser was supposed to be here with you? Surely that's your job, to get him to the church on time. Where is he?'

Nash looked positively nauseous. 'Aye, well, he said he'd see me there, like.'

Several other people had wandered over, enquiring over the whereabouts of the groom. People started to make crass jokes and asides. I looked at Angus, who shrugged his shoulders emphatically.

It was ten to twelve, and the ceremony was due to begin at twelve. This was cutting it pretty fine. I scanned the roads for a wedding car, but I didn't see one. More and more guests were arriving, and the news that the groom hadn't shown up yet was beginning to filter through the crowd. A photographer was clicking away furiously and approached us, consulting a list in his hand.

'So,' he said to Angus, 'you're the second laird?'

Angus looked at him, mystified, waving away the camera. 'Who are you?'

'Jof de Beauvoir. Photographer, *Hello!* magazine. And my mother's the daughter of the Earl of Suffolk.'

'Oh, in that case –' said Angus and strode past him rudely, grabbing me with him.

Over by the church gate stood a gaggle of bridesmaids – six full-sized blondes, two tiny. The little ones were tugging at their cream sashes, sticking their bottom lips out and kicking each other when they thought no one was looking. I felt a bit like that myself. None of the elder bridesmaids were paying the children any attention; they were too busy repeatedly asking each other if they looked all right and whisking away imaginary spots from each other's make-up.

Next to them stood an out-of-place man in a battered old Barbour. That would have made him stand out, if it were not for the fact that he was holding eight reins with white geese on the end of them. Not only this, but the geese appeared to be wearing cream bow-ties.

'Fuck me!' Angus and I exclaimed at the same time.

'I'm never getting married without geese,' I said.

'I hope they don't blow up in the explosion,' said Angus gloomily.

'Well, that would sort lunch out for me, given I don't have a place at the reception.'

Angus examined his watch, and I caught sight of it.

'God,' I said, retreating beside Angus. 'He's going to do a last-minute special on us and give everyone heart attacks.'

'Hmm,' said Angus thoughtfully.

Mookie slipped over to join us.

'Hello there!' I kissed her.

'I got them,' she whispered.

'It's OK, there's no one around – you don't have to whisper.'

She opened her Chanel bag to reveal two small cylindrical objects.

'Although I'm not sure you'll rally need them now, will you? Oh, and have you seen the geese?'

We all stood around until the vicar came out, and started hustling people inside. 'I'm terribly sorry, he'll be very embarrassed when he turns up, but I do have another service at two, so if you wouldn't mind awfully . . .'

I didn't mind. It was freezing outside. Angus grabbed hold of Nash and said something about 'sending the car round' which I didn't catch. Then we followed the crowd inside.

Inside, the church was just as beautiful as outside but faintly . . . well, über-wedding. Wreaths and ribbons decorated every area, and there were about five thousand candles. Rose petals covered the carpet and there was a floral tribute of their initials intertwined, a theme which was reproduced on every pew and on the elaborate Order of Service I was being handed. I was so taken aback, I couldn't answer the question 'Bride or groom?'

'What?'

'Are you a friend of the bride or the groom?'

I looked helplessly at Angus. 'I don't know,' I said.

'Groom,' said Angus. 'So you can sit beside me,' he added, when we got inside.

The organist was playing something extremely elaborate, and we sat down at the very front – Angus beside his mother, and me beside Angus. Being in the front pew felt odd and a bit wrong, but I didn't argue. I studied the Order of Service. From the looks of things, this was going to be a four-hour wedding.

'Kahil Gibran! How original!' I whispered to Angus. He raised his eyes.

'I think she planned the service.'

I looked at the fuchsia garlanding which obscured the altar. The large bible had a set of intertwined initials on it.

'You're kidding!'

From the other side of the church, Mookie waved and pointed out the fire alarm. We nodded back at her. The excitement was still there, in the pit of my stomach. The church filled up, and Jof the photographer, for want of something better to do, came and took pictures of the congregation, with reference to his little black book and the prettier of the blondes. People's heads kept turning, and the vicar wandered up and down the aisle in some trepidation. Nash was nowhere to be seen.

'What is going on?' I whispered to Angus. He shrugged again. I turned to look at his mum, but she didn't seem too perturbed; she was holding her hymnal quite calmly. I didn't know what to say to her, so I peered around the church again. Everyone was whispering and giggling. It was ten past, quarter past. I saw Amanda's mum. I don't know if the Priory did her much good, as she looked pissed to me. She was picking petals off her corsage and swaying.

I wondered if Fraser had had an extra stag night,

and was even now on a train from Aberdeen. 'Have you tied him up somewhere?' I whispered to Angus. 'You'd better not have.'

'I promise you, I have no idea where he is,' he whispered back. The entire congregation was shuffling and looking at their watches. It was twenty past, then twenty-five.

Suddenly, the doors at the back of the church burst open with a crash. As one, we turned round to see. Framed in the door stood Amanda.

She did look beautiful. The dress was white, but seemed to have been overlaid with gold. The cut-off sleeves emphasized her toned arms and delicate shoulders, and the skirt reflected her every move and clung to her like gossamer. She was wearing a pure white stole round her shoulders which looked like – surely not? – fur. God, it couldn't be polar bear, could it? But the effect was stunning.

Her face, on the other hand, was quite different. She was stone white and looked furious. Everyone was silent. She stalked slowly up the aisle – not quite as poised as usual. Several of the bridesmaids had shuffled in behind her, but had stopped short at the back of the pews. The organist started playing 'Here Comes the Bride', but someone obviously slapped him, as the keys stopped immediately with a dying hiss. Amanda advanced, pale and set. And stopped in front of us.

'Where the hell is he?' she hissed at Angus.

Angus looked straight back at her.

'I swear, I don't know.'

Her voice rose, and reverberated throughout the church:

'You fucking bastard, you've been fixing this from the start. You do fucking know. Where the fuck is he?'

His voice was gentle, not victorious. 'I'm sorry, Amanda. He didn't tell me anything about this. Honestly, if you think I knew, do you think I'd be here? He might just be late.'

'He's not fucking late,' she spat. 'You're all fucking morons, the whole fucking lot of you.'

She turned to me. 'Oh, the collaborator. You sad cow. I heard all about you. At least I made it this far.'

I was trembling from the attack, but in no position to say anything. Embarrassed, I looked around me.

Amanda turned back to Angus. As she did so, I caught sight of something and gasped: at the back of the church, behind the bridesmaids, silhouetted against the wintry churchyard, stood Fraser. He was wearing his hunting tartan, and a fresh baggy white shirt, and looked as if he'd just strode in from the moors. His mouth was set in a hard line, and he was listening intently. No one else had noticed him. Amanda was still in full flow and commanding everyone's attention.

'You can tell your idiotic, stupid, lanky, lousy brother that the next time he'll see me is in court, when I'm suing him for the cost of the wedding. If you can remember that, you stupid, provincial, sheep-shagging moron. God, to think I nearly got hitched into this repulsive family!'

The guests murmured in horror. Angus didn't say anything, but looked at her steadily. Infuriated, she took her huge themed bouquet and hurled it at him – and hit me by mistake . . . Well, I think it was by mistake.

A collective gasp went up from the congregation as I staggered backwards, then came upright again. I put my hand to my head, and it came away with blood on it, from the thorns. I suddenly felt giddy.

Amanda sneered and turned to go, like the wicked fairy at the feast. Then she faced the crowd.

'You bunch of bastards!' she yelled bitterly. Her Woking accent was back in all its glory. 'You're loving this . . . you're –'

Then two things happened. Her voice trailed off and her eyes became fixed as she focused on the back of the hall. Everyone followed her gaze and turned round. Except for me, because I knew who she was looking at.

The second thing that happened was that Amanda shrieked, and her shriek rapidly turned into a hefty coughing fit. The other side of the church from where we were suddenly started to choke, as a mass of dense smoke rose up . . .

I looked at Angus. His eyes were alight. 'Come on,' he whispered, 'get the grannies out . . .'

After that it was chaos. Everyone began piling for the door. There were hollers and yelps as loving couples trod over each other in their efforts to escape. One of the tall candles fell over, and it looked as if we might have a real fire on our hands when someone's over-priced synthetic Barbara Cartland hat caught the flame. A huge squawking went up as the geese took to the air to escape, and the man in the Barbour ran back into the church to rescue the birds.

I had already spotted the side entrance and fumbled my way towards it, pushing as many people as I could. The flowers – no doubt sprayed with terribly flammable perfume – were now ablaze, and as I herded people through the door, I caught sight of Angus doing his thing with a fire extinguisher. Amanda's mum stood in the middle of everything, wobbling as if she didn't know where she was, and I was relieved to see Mookie drag her away by the arm.

The vicar was dancing about outside in agony for his church.

'God, I wish I was a Catholic,' he said. 'Then I could drink the Communion wine.'

'It's fine . . . sir –' I didn't quite know what to call a vicar – 'I think it's under control.'

'You'd think this would be a nice change from all the normal boring weddings, ken,' said Nash, who was nearby doing a headcount.

It didn't look that way as worried, upset people hung about outside, coughing and fretting. I could hear a fire engine. Oh my God – what if we were liable for this and all got put in prison?

However, just as I was thinking this, a final belch of smoke came out of the church and Angus emerged, coughing violently.

'The fire's out,' he said. 'It's OK.' He looked like he was going to pass out, and I ran up to him.

Meanwhile, Amanda was striding past the whispering crowd, talking to no one. Jof, with the scoop of his life, snapped shots all the way, until she threatened to punch him, and he could tell she meant it. The eight bridesmaids – several with goose-poo on their frocks, I noticed – were huddling in a circle outside the church, having been unceremoniously informed by Amanda to 'Fuck off – you won't be fucking needed.'

Fraser was nowhere to be seen – you couldn't even see a car driving away. It was as if he'd vanished in the puff of smoke.

No one was daring to approach Amanda, who turned round, surveyed the war zone – smoke still drifting across the ground, and the small groups of hostile-looking people – and pushed herself into the gleaming limousine.

Her dad ran after her calling, 'Sweetheart, sweetheart, I'll make it all right, don't worry. I'll pay to have him killed – whatever you like.'

But she ignored him, slammed the door and indicated to the driver to get the hell out of there.

The big car purred past the arriving fire engine. I rubbed the rapidly forming scab on my forehead. This was turning out crazy.

'Glad you came?' muttered Angus, taking me by the arm.

'Well, it's different . . .' I said. My voice trailed off. Standing nervously at the other end of the churchyard, looking my way, were two very familiar figures.

* * *

They started to move towards me as soon as they realized I'd spotted them. I looked, petrified, at Angus.

'Don't worry,' he said. 'You should talk it out. You'd have to, sooner or later.'

He pushed me forward gently.

Fran looked tired and ravaged. She smiled at me reticently. I didn't return it. Alex had put on the fake swagger he always did when he was worried about something.

Eventually, we were facing each other. I stood with my arms folded.

'Hi,' said Fran.

'Hi,' I said back.

'We . . . well, I didn't think you'd talk to us on the phone.'

'Correct.'

'But we knew you'd be at the wedding.'

'Wasn't much of a wedding,' I said.

'So we saw.'

'Oh, so you're a "we". Well, that's good to know.'

Fran swallowed hard.

'Of course we're not, Mel . . . I mean, I'm not . . . and he's not . . . and it's all . . .'

I forced myself to ask.

'Since when? Before you went to America, or when?'

Alex spoke up: 'No, of course not.'

'Oh, so just at the party, was it?'

He hung his head.

Everything, horribly, fell into place. How could I have been such a fool?

'It was the night I twisted my ankle, wasn't it?'

Fran looked pained.

'Tell me.'

'I'd gone round to see Charlie and he wasn't back yet . . .' started Fran, but she didn't have to tell me any more. Charlie hadn't been there and Alex had, and he was never averse to anything on a plate.

I snorted and rubbed more dried blood from my forehead.

'God, the – How could you both? What the fuck were you up to at my dinner?'

'I'm sorry,' said Fran. 'I knew he was . . . moving in because of me. We had to talk . . . and then . . .'

I shook my head in disbelief.

'But you're . . . you were my best friend.'

'I know. I don't know . . .'

I took a step backwards and looked at Alex.

'Well, I suppose . . . he's all yours.'

Alex looked defensive and ashamed now. He knew the decision had been made for him. He wasn't in control here. He couldn't make the choices.

Fran looked no happier. She turned briefly to Alex, who was staring at the ground, and then to me.

'I think I'd rather have you,' she said to me. 'I'm so sorry.'

'It's a bit too late for that.'

'Think it over?'

Her face was so pleading, so miserable. I wasn't too happy either, but at least I knew. Fran shook her head sadly. Now she could have Alex to herself, it didn't look like she wanted him any more.

I shrugged, and moved backwards again. Angus was waiting for me on the other side of the churchyard. Amanda's dad had walked about the congregation, announcing loudly that as he'd paid for a slap-up meal, we might as well enjoy it – and, amazingly, people were getting into their cars and going on to the reception. I couldn't imagine why, although perhaps I just didn't need a good scandal when I was in the middle of my own.

I saw Alex go to take Fran's arm. She shook it off painfully. I couldn't imagine the two of them together. For the first time, I felt sorry for her.

Against the traffic leaving the churchyard, a sports car screeched to a halt right in front of us. I looked to see what this latest diversion was. A tousled figure leapt out of the car almost before it stopped, and dashed over to Fran. I moved for a closer look. Good God – it was Charlie.

'I knew you were coming,' he yelled. He went down on one knee. 'Please, don't torture me any more. You don't love this son of a bitch –' indicating Alex.

'No, I don't,' said Fran. Alex, amazingly, looked surprised at this announcement.

'I couldn't let you come here, with him! It's tearing me apart. Ever since that night . . . I adore you, Fran. You're meant for me!'

'But you're a violent, upper-class, drunken, moronic tosspot!'

'I know! And you're a violent, drunken, deceitful bitch! We're made for each other! Come on! Come away with me now . . . we are going to disappear somewhere to make violent, drunken, moronic love until we . . . burst!'

I looked over at Angus, who was shaking his head in disbelief. Fran looked at Charlie, looked at Alex, then looked straight at me.

'Ah,' she said, in those precise, trained tones. She turned back to Alex.

'I believe I'm off. Goodbye, darling . . . it's been interesting.'

'What!' said Alex. He looked devastated. 'Where the hell are you going?'

'I have precisely no idea. Goodbye, Melanie. I am sorry. I really am. Maybe one day we'll be able to be friends again.'

'Maybe,' I said. I couldn't help smiling.

'And remember what I told you about those nice McConnalds. Bye, Angus!'

She waved to him, and he waved back heartily.

Then Charlie and Fran leapt into the little sportster. Fran wrapped her scarf round her head like Audrey Hepburn and put on a big pair of sunglasses.

'Goodbye, everyone!' she waved regally. The car shot out of the churchyard and up the road, making a hell of a noise out of the back of the exhaust.

Those of us left behind just stared at each other. I couldn't help it. I suddenly started to half laugh, half cry all at the same time, making an unattractive snorting noise.

Instinctively, Alex moved forward to put his arm

around me. Before he had a chance, though, Angus was there too.

'Excuse me,' he said stiffly to Alex.

Alex looked embarrassed and stood back.

'Sorry.'

Angus put his warm coat round me and led me over to the car. Alex watched us, then turned and walked away.

'Are you OK?'

'Yes! – snort – I'm just . . . hysterical! I'm sorry! I'll be OK in a minute.'

He opened the car door and sat me sideways out in the passenger seat.

'Here,' he said, and reached for his sporran, bringing out a little hip-flask.

'I brought this along for Fraser, in case he needed it. Take a wee dram. You'll feel much better.'

I took it, snorting mightily, and took a sip. The warm liquid seemed to make its way through my whole body, bringing a glow and some calm. My breathing slowed down, and I returned to normal.

Angus came round to the driver's side, and we sat in the car together in silence for a bit.

'What should we do?' he said, eventually.

'Hm?'

'Well, what are you thinking about?'

'Fraser,' I replied truthfully. 'I mean, where is he? What's he doing? I suppose this probably means he's not getting married, doesn't it?'

My unpredictable heart started beating again.

Angus turned to face me.

'You're thinking about Fraser?'

'Ehm, yes.'

'Not . . . Alex, or, ahem, me?'

I looked at his sweet face. There was real worry in his eyes.

'Ehm, well, you know, Fraser's been through . . . God, it must have been awful, I don't know how he must be . . .'

Angus heaved a great sigh.

'I think about you all the time,' he said simply.

I stopped talking mid-babble and looked at him again. I didn't know what to say. I knew what I wanted to say – how he was the sweetest, most honourable, nicest, cutest man I knew, but that I was . . . I couldn't . . .

'But', he said, 'you're in love with my brother.'

'Don't be ridiculous,' I said immediately.

'Ah, yes, but unfortunately you are. I thought you liked me, but it's only because I remind you of him.'

'That's not true,' I said fiercely.

'Aye well, maybe.'

'Definitely. I like you for millions of reasons, and that's not one of them.'

'Only like?'

'No, I love you. Just, you know, not in that way.'

'The way that you love my brother.'

I didn't say anything. I couldn't think of anything.

'I knew, you know – probably before you did,' said Angus. 'You light up like a candle if he's within a ten-mile radius. But I'd always thought there'd be a chance . . . even a tiny chance. And I knew Frase was determined to go through with this whole ridiculous thing, so . . . God, selfish of me, really. But I had to give it a shot. Despite myself, I really liked you and I'd hoped . . .'

'What do you mean, you knew?' I interjected. 'There's nothing to know.'

But I was so intrigued.

'It was obvious. Remember that night we took him the tape? I think I know why you were sad that night.'

'That's not true . . .' It was true.

'You couldn't bring yourself to think about him, so you made friends with me.'

'That's not true, Gustard.'

'You even use his name for me.' His fingers fiddled on the dashboard. His ears were flushed.

'Angus, whatever else might be true, I made friends with you because I really like you. Because you're funny and smart and interesting and attractive and kind. And the rest of it . . . I never led you on, I don't think. I'm sorry . . . I mean, I don't think I did anything.'

'No, you didn't. I'm sorry. I should be a more graceful loser.'

'Oh God, it's me that's the loser. I've lost everyone, you know. And Fraser isn't going to want to see me. Look at all the shit he's got on his plate. The last thing he's going to want to do is pick up with one of Amanda's buddies. In fact, he's probably over at Amanda's right now, apologizing and planning the whole thing all over again.'

'I doubt it.'

'So, please, don't make me have to lose you as well, by saying that I used you. Because I promise I didn't. Or, if I did, I didn't mean to. I'm sorry.'

He looked at me suddenly. The twinkle was back, if a little dimmed.

'Did you . . .' he started. 'Did you ever even consider it?'

'Every day,' I said, almost truthfully.

He smiled.

'Come here,' he said, and pulled me to him. We hugged one another for a long time in the front of the car.

Seventeen

Eventually, we pulled apart.

'What are you going to do now?' he said.

'I really want to go home. Are you going back to London?'

'Actually, my mum's gone to the reception. So I'd better go and see everyone, especially as I'll be the only male McConnald around. It's a flak-taking exercise.'

'Do you think your mum was pleased?'

'Pleased? She'll be delighted. She'll be even more delighted to be over there drinking champagne and eating vol-au-vents at Mr Phillips' expense.'

'He can afford it. Ehm, could you give me a lift to the station?'

'It'd be my pleasure.'

* * *

Angus put me on the slow train back to London. He stood on the platform waving until the train pulled away, the sunlight glinting off his hair. I watched him until he grew tiny, then out of sight, then sat back in my chair with a sigh.

The woman opposite was staring at me strangely. Straining to see in the filthy train window, I realized I still had blood all over my head and mascara running down my face. Nice.

Suddenly, I realized I couldn't go back home; I was barred for Linda's big secret project. Jesus! Oh, fuck it. I didn't care if she was entertaining the Coldstream Guards in there, it was my home and that's where I had to go now. It wasn't my fault that I'd been to an imploding wedding. I'd stay in my room all day. Linda could cope.

I looked for a handkerchief in my pocket, before realizing that I was still wearing Angus's coat. God, the sweetie. It smelled reassuringly masculine, and there was indeed a handkerchief. It was embroidered in the corner with F.A.M. It was Fraser's, not Angus. I felt a bolt go through me. This was his. I clasped it like the most precious stone. I put it to my nose, but it only smelled of laundry, which I suppose in some ways was quite a relief. I dabbed a little at the blood and the mascara.

The woman opposite me leaned over. She was about fifty and a bit wholemeal-bread-looking – she was wearing lots of shawls, shoes that looked as though they'd been hewn from wood, and had thick wiry hair. She was attractive, in a fifty-ish kind of way.

'I'm psychic, you know.'

Oh God. Nutter on the train! Just when I needed it least. I looked around the carriage for help, but everyone was studiously ignoring us – of course! This was a British train, what could I have been thinking of?

I nodded dismissively to her and wished I had a newspaper to hide behind.

'I'm picking up very strong vibes from you.'

'What, vibes that I don't believe in psychics?' I said, trying to smile politely and get her to shut up.

She smiled. 'Well, that's OK. Lots of people don't. I have trouble myself, some days.'

I stared out of the window fixedly.

'There's trouble in your life.'

'Yes, well, that's probably a good average for everyone.'

'It's OK,' she said. 'Alexander loves you. Go to him.'

I sat bolt upright.

'What did you say?'

'I said, he loves you. Go to him.'

'No, no, no. You don't understand. Did you say Alex? He's a total pig. Are you by any chance a reverse psychic? Are you Australian?'

'No,' she said. 'Sometimes I get the message and I have to pass it on. I can tell it meant something to you. So, there it is.'

'It meant complete crap to me.'

'Well, sometimes that's what your head says when your heart says different.'

'No, sometimes that's what mad people say when you meet them on the train,' I muttered sullenly.

The psychic sat back, satisfied that her work was done, and I stared out the window, thinking furiously.

How on earth could she have known about Alex? I wouldn't put it past him to have set it up, the slimy little toad. But how could he have known I'd be on this train . . . this carriage? I shook my head fiercely to clear it and tried to concentrate on something else, anything else.

Like Fraser. As if the dam had burst, the lifting of the embargo let it all come flooding in. My angel in the snow. Striding like Mr Rochester from the church – I hadn't actually seen him do that, but I imagined it that way. His lopsided grin, his gentle eyes, his ready laugh . . . as London gradually came into view, through the suburbs and the railway stations. I couldn't possibly . . . well, I'd thought . . . but it was his wedding day, for Christ's sake. I couldn't hope to – I mean, he was probably trying to patch things up. After all, he'd turned up, hadn't he? Half an hour late, but he'd been ready and willing to get married.

Probably not the best time to ask him out.

At Waterloo, I moved through the crowds like I was swimming underwater. I knew I looked beyond ridiculous in my pretty dress and ruined face, but I didn't care. I just wanted to go home, pure and simple.

I caught a cab back to the flat. The street was quiet. It was bitterly cold, but inside Angus's coat I felt warm. I could, I supposed, go back to bed. Ignore the day altogether. It might be the sensible thing.

I crept up the stairwell and knocked quietly on the door before unlocking it with my key. Linda was there in an instant.

'I'm sorry!' I said through the door. 'I'm really sorry. The wedding went really wrong, and I didn't have anywhere else to go . . . Please, can I come in?'

Linda opened the door a crack and regarded me suspiciously.

'I might have known this would never work,' she said dolefully. But, reluctantly, she opened the door and let me in.

'Thank you!' I said gratefully. 'I'll keep out of your way, whatever you're doing, I promise. In fact, I'll go to bed straightaway and stay there until you say I can come out. In fact, probably longer.'

'It's OK,' she said. 'You might as well go join your friend in the kitchen. We've been having a nice chat.'

Friend? Chat? I had no idea who she meant. Suddenly very nervous, I walked towards the kitchen door. Maybe Fran had returned early from her little adventure. Despite everything, I wouldn't mind her around to talk to just now.

Slowly, I opened the door – and the sight that greeted me surprised me so much that I couldn't say a thing, for once.

It was freezing in the kitchen – the window was open, as were the fridge and the freezer doors, I noticed. All around the large room stood different model animals. There was a giraffe, a pelican, a wallaby – all large, and lovingly fashioned. They were brown, and so delicately made, that they appeared about to fly off, or gallop – as if they had been caught in filigree for an instant in mid-motion.

The kitchen table had been brought back in. Fraser was sitting at it. He looked tired and drawn, but he smiled at my amazement.

'Aren't they stunning?' he said. I nodded.

'I rather think your flatmate hides her light under a bushel.'

I turned to Linda.

'You did these?'

She blushed furiously and shrugged.

'What are they made of?'

'Chocolate.'

I span in amazement.

'All these are chocolate? Like Topics and Flyte and stuff?'

'I sculpt,' she said shyly. 'They're being picked up today for an exhibition. I practise small, but you have to put them together really quickly, otherwise it melts. And now it's hardening off. They're picking them up soon.'

'Jesus!' I looked around at the edible menagerie. 'They're absolutely gorgeous.'

Linda smiled. It was such a rare sight to see that I grinned right back. Then Fraser grinned at me. In an apologetic, lopsided kind of a way. It was like the reverse ending of *Reservoir Dogs*.

My heart plummeted to the bottom of my shoes. I moved closer to him. We were gazing at each other as if we'd been hypnotized.

I sat down opposite him at the table.

'You can eat the tortoise, if you like,' said Linda shyly. 'It came out wrong.'

'Thanks,' I said, 'but it's too beautiful to eat. Well, for a tortoise.'

And I kept gazing at Fraser. Realizing something was up – poor Linda, could I never let her be at home in her own house? – she retreated.

There was a silence.

'So?' I said flippantly.

He hung his head.

'So, you were right all along?' he said.

'No, that's not what I was asking . . . That was a "So, what happened?" so.'

He looked at me.

'You know, I never wanted to get married.'

I arched my eyebrows at him.

'Really, I didn't. It all happened so quickly . . . and after we got engaged, I started to realize . . . just how wrong it was. With a little help from you and my brother, of course.'

I looked down. 'Huh.'

'And the wedding was arranged before I'd had a chance to blink. I felt . . . well, we were betrothed. I'd made her a promise. It would have been wrong to break it off, just because I'd changed my mind.'

'No, it would have been kinder. In the long run.'

'Maybe. Anyway, every time I tried to bring it up,

she'd brush over it. Said we'd be fine.'

'I don't think that it was necessarily only you she wanted.'

'No, me neither.'

He sighed.

'I sat up all night last night. I don't even believe in God, but I nearly started to. Just for someone to give me guidance.'

'Medieval knights used to do that.'

'I know. It's very sore on the knees.'

'And? Didn't it help?'

'No. I sat there for ages, dozed off, woke up again – for hours. And then, by about eleven o'clock, I just thought: it's too late now. I'm a big cowardly bastard and I have to take what's coming to me. It was my punishment for not facing up to it earlier.'

'Huh.'

'And I didn't think she'd – well, do what she did. I thought she'd wait, and bollock me for being late.'

'She must have known deep down as well.'

'I suppose so. Ouch.'

'What?'

'Nothing. I just feel "ouch" every time I remember those things she said. Oh, and poor you!'

He touched my head and I suddenly became very conscious of what a fright I must look.

'Oh, no, it didn't really hurt. I just got scratched by the thorns.'

'She could have had your eye out.'

'Well, you know . . . anything to help.'

He smiled, and stroked the scar tenderly. I shivered.

'But, apart from that,' he said, 'I think she did me a favour. I got out of it, and it was nobody's fault.'

'Well, except for the fact that it was *your* fault.'

'Yes, God, you're right, aren't you? It was completely my fault. I suppose what I mean is, I'm glad I'm not the one who came across as a heartless bastard. Because I'm not one, really. Well, I don't think I am.'

'I don't think you are either.'

His hand still rested on my forehead.

'Why did you come round here?' I asked.

'To see you,' he said simply.

'Oh.'

He looked down and took his hand away.

'You and Angus . . . I'm sorry, I know it's completely none of my business, but is – was – well, anyway, there's not anything going on, is there? He said there wasn't, but I thought he might be trying to spare my feelings. He's like that.'

'I know,' I said. 'And no. There never was, really. I was . . . well, I hope I didn't hurt him. I think one of the reasons I liked him – not the only reason, because then I really, really liked him, you know, I think he's brilliant . . . But, well, I think, well, he kind of reminded me of you.'

His mild eyes blinked twice in surprise.

'Is that true?'

'Yes,' I said, swallowing the lump in my throat.

'You . . . well, me, well, you know . . . ?'

'Ehm, yes,' I said, trusting that that was the right answer.

His grip on my hand tightened and he brought his other hand down to cup my cheek. Outside the window, the snow was falling again.

'Eventually I realized . . .' he began. 'I realized that I was terrified you'd be with him, and make him happy and not me. I was so jealous.'

I gazed up at him.

'You were jealous? You were getting married!'

'I know. It just didn't seem fair to me that he got you because his timing was on and mine was as off as it could possibly be. As if I didn't have enough to worry about.'

I couldn't believe I was hearing this. I put my hand over his hand.

'I met a psychic on the train,' I said, smiling. 'I didn't believe it. Total nutcase. Do you know, she told me to go back to Alex.'

'You did,' said Fraser.

I looked at him enquiringly.

'Alasdair. It's my middle name. It's Gaelic for Alexander.'

I pulled out the handkerchief. D'oh! F.A.M. That mad woman had probably seen the 'A' when I was clutching it like a maniac, and gone for the educated guess. Unless, of course . . . I looked up at him, shiny-eyed.

Almost in slow motion, we began to touch each other on the arm and the face, discovering each other for the first time. I felt his strong shoulders through his white shirt. All the hairs on his forearm had raised themselves up from the cold air, and the closeness of us. I tentatively touched one of his buttons.

'If I cry any more, I think I'll go blind,' I muttered, trying to hold back.

'That would explain what you see in me then.'

'Ho ho ho.'

Suddenly I felt his strong arms clasp my waist, his grip tighten. The expression on his face was tentative, excited, nervous, unsure – well, actually, fairly sure.

I looked straight at this man.

'You know, if this was a book,' I said, 'it really should have ended with a wedding.'

'Not necessarily,' he said. 'It could just have ended with a kiss.'

And it did.

Epilogue

We wanted to sneak away immediately. We had a lot to discuss and a lot to do. Somewhere in the country, we thought, where we could walk, and talk and, well, the other thing. I was lit up like the Christmas lights outside. I grabbed together some warm things in a bag and we made our way to the door. On our way out, I heard the phone ring. Linda picked it up.

'Oh,' I heard her say. 'Mel!'

'I don't think I want to get that, do I?' I said to Fraser.

'Don't tell them I'm here either,' he said.

'Oh my God. I haven't even thought about trying to explain it to people.'

'Shh . . .' From behind, he put both arms around me

and leaned on my shoulder. 'There's plenty of time to worry about all that.'

'Mel!' Linda yelled. Linda yelling! What a day this was turning out to be. 'It's somebody called Nicholas! He wants to know if you're free this . . . hang on . . . tonight or the rest of the weekend?'

I raised my eyebrows at Fraser. He shook his head vehemently.

'I think that's going to be a "no", Linda,' I said.

There was a pause. Then she popped her head round the door.

'He's asked me out instead!' she said breathlessly.

'Oh . . .'

Well, how bad could it be? He was well off, he had a nice car, he was tall, he wasn't . . . well, he wasn't the heart of pure evil, and Linda needed to get out of the house.

'Why don't you go?' I said kindly. 'He's all right. It could be fun.'

Linda looked at me quizzically.

'That eight foot, wanky, dog-breath accountant? What the FUCK do you take me for?'